FINNEGANS WAKE

JAMES JOYCE

Finnegans Wake

THE VIKING PRESS · New York

FINNEGANS WAKE

riverrun, past Eve and Adam's, from swerve of shore to bend of
bay, brings us by a commodius vicus of recirculation back to Howth
Castle and Environs.

Sir Tristram, violer d'amores, fr'over the short sea, had passencore
rearrived from North Armorica on this side the scraggy isthmus of
Europe Minor to wielderfight his penisolate war: nor had topsawyer's
rocks by the stream Oconee exaggerated themselse to Laurens
County's gorgios while they went doublin their mumper all the time:
nor avoice from afire bellowsed mishe mishe to tauftauf thuartpea-
trick: not yet, though venissoon after, had a kidscad buttended a
bland old isaac: not yet, though all's fair in vanessy, were sosie
sesthers wroth with twone nathandjoe. Rot a peck of pa's malt had
Jhem or Shen brewed by arclight and rory end to the regginbrow
was to be seen ringsome on the aquaface.

The   fall   (bababadalgharaghtakamminarronnkonnbronntonner-
ronntuonnthunntrovarrhounawnskawntoohoohoordenenthurnuk!)
of a once wallstrait oldparr is retaled early in bed and later on life
down through all christian minstrelsy. The great fall of the offwall
entailed at such short notice the pftjschute of Finnegan, erse solid
man, that the humptyhillhead of humself prumptly sends an unquir-
ing one well to the west in quest of his tumptytumtoes: and their
upturnpikepointandplace is at the knock out in the park where
oranges have been laid to rust upon the green since devlinsfirst loved
livvy.

What clashes here of wills gen wonts, oystrygods gaggin fishy-
gods! Brékkek Kékkek Kékkek Kékkek! Kóax Kóax Kóax! Ualu Ualu
Ualu! Quaouauh! Where the Baddelaries partisans are still out to
mathmaster Malachus Micgranes and the Verdons catapelting the
camibalistics out of the Whoyteboyce of Hoodie Head. Assiegates
and boomeringstroms. Sod's brood, be me fear! Sanglorians, save!

Arms apeal with larms, appalling. Killykillkilly: a toll, a toll. What chance cuddleys, what cashels aired and ventilated! What bidimeto-loves sinduced by what tegotetabsolvers! What true feeling for their's hayair with what strawng voice of false jiccup! O here here how hoth sprowled met the duskt the father of fornicationists but, (O my shining stars and body!) how hath fanespanned most high heaven the skysign of soft advertisement! But was iz? Iseut? Ere were sewers? The oaks of ald now they lie in peat yet elms leap where askes lay. Phall if you but will, rise you must: and none so soon either shall the pharce for the nunce come to a setdown secular phoenish.

Bygmester Finnegan, of the Stuttering Hand, freemen's maurer, lived in the broadest way immarginable in his rushlit toofarback for messuages before joshuan judges had given us numbers or Hel-viticus committed deuteronomy (one yeastyday he sternely struxk his tete in a tub for to watsch the future of his fates but ere he swiftly stook it out again, by the might of moses, the very water was eviparated and all the guenneses had met their exodus so that ought to show you what a pentschanjeuchy chap he was!) and during mighty odd years this man of hod, cement and edifices in Toper's Thorp piled buildung supra buildung pon the banks for the livers by the Soangso. He addle liddle phifie Annie ugged the little craythur. Wither hayre in honds tuck up your part inher. Oftwhile balbulous, mithre ahead, with goodly trowel in grasp and ivoroiled overalls which he habitacularly fondseed, like Haroun Childeric Eggeberth he would caligulate by multiplicables the alltitude and malltitude until he seesaw by neatlight of the liquor wheretwin 'twas born, his roundhead staple of other days to rise in undress maisonry upstanded (joygrantit!), a waalworth of a skyerscape of most eyeful hoyth entowerly, erigenating from next to nothing and celescalating the himals and all, hierarchitectitiptitoploftical, with a burning bush abob off its baubletop and with larrons o'toolers clittering up and tombles a'buckets clottering down.

Of the first was he to bare arms and a name: Wassaily Boos-laeugh of Riesengeborg. His crest of huroldry, in vert with ancillars, troublant, argent, a hegoak, poursuivant, horrid, horned. His scut-schum fessed, with archers strung, helio, of the second. Hootch is for husbandman handling his hoe. Hohohoho, Mister Finn, you're going to be Mister Finnagain! Comeday morm and, O, you're vine! Sendday's eve and, ah, you're vinegar! Hahahaha, Mister Funn, you're going to be fined again!

What then agentlike brought about that tragoady thundersday

this municipal sin business? Our cubehouse still rocks as earwitness to the thunder of his arafatas but we hear also through successive ages that shebby choruysh of unkalified muzzlenimiissilehims that would blackguardise the whitestone ever hurtleturtled out of heaven. Stay us wherefore in our search for tighteousness, O Sustainer, what time we rise and when we take up to toothmick and before we lump down upown our leatherbed and in the night and at the fading of the stars! For a nod to the nabir is better than wink to the wabsanti. Otherways wesways like that provost scoffing bedoueen the jebel and the jpysian sea. Cropherb the crunchbracken shall decide. Then we'll know if the feast is a flyday. She has a gift of seek on site and she allcasually ansars helpers, the dreamydeary. Heed! Heed! It may half been a missfired brick, as some say, or it mought have been due to a collupsus of his back promises, as others looked at it. (There extand by now one thousand and one stories, all told, of the same). But so sore did abe ite ivvy's holired abbles, (what with the wallhall's horrors of rollsrights, carhacks, stonengens, kisstvanes, tramtrees, fargobawlers, autokinotons, hippohobbilies, streetfleets, tournintaxes, megaphoggs, circuses and wardsmoats and basilikerks and aeropagods and the hoyse and the jollybrool and the peeler in the coat and the mecklenburk bitch bite at his ear and the merlinburrow burrocks and his fore old porecourts, the bore the more, and his blightblack workingstacks at twelvepins a dozen and the noobibusses sleighding along Safetyfirst Street and the derry-jellybies snooping around Tell-No-Tailors' Corner and the fumes and the hopes and the strupithump of his ville's indigenous rome-keepers, homesweepers, domecreepers, thurum and thurum in fancy-mud murumd and all the uproor from all the aufroofs, a roof for may and a reef for hugh butt under his bridge suits tony) wan warning Phill filt tippling full. His howd feeled heavy, his hoddit did shake. (There was a wall of course in erection) Dimb! He stot-tered from the latter. Damb! he was dud. Dumb! Mastabatoom, mastabadtomm, when a mon merries his lute is all long. For whole the world to see.

Shize? I should shee! Macool, Macool, orra whyi deed ye diie? of a trying thirstay mournin? Sobs they sighdid at Fillagain's chrissor-miss wake, all the hoolivans of the nation, prostrated in their con-sternation and their duodisimally profusive plethora of ululation. There was plumbs and grumes and cheriffs and citherers and raiders and cinemen too. And the all gianed in with the shoutmost shoviality. Agog and magog and the round of them agrog. To the continuation

of that celebration until Hanandhunigan's extermination! Some in
kinkin corass, more, kankan keening. Belling him up and filling
him down. He's stiff but he's steady is Priam Olim! 'Twas he was
the dacent gaylabouring youth. Sharpen his pillowscone, tap up his
bier! E'erawhere in this whorl would ye hear sich a din again?
With their deepbrow fundigs and the dusty fidelios. They laid him
brawdawn alanglast bed. With a bockalips of finisky fore his feet.
And a barrowload of guenesis hoer his head. Tee the tootal of the
fluid hang the twoddle of the fuddled, O!

Hurrah, there is but young gleve for the owl globe wheels in
view which is tautaulogically the same thing. Well, Him a being
so on the flounder of his bulk like an overgrown babeling, let wee
peep, see, at Hom, well, see peegee ought he ought, platterplate.
ꟺ Hum! From Shopalist to Bailywick or from ashtun to baronoath
or from Buythebanks to Roundthehead or from the foot of the bill
to ireglint's eye he calmly extensolies. And all the way (a horn!)
from fjord to fjell his baywinds' oboboes shall wail him rockbound
(hoahoahoah!) in swimswamswum and all the livvylong night, the
delldale dalppling night, the night of bluerybells, her flittaflute in
tricky trochees (O carina! O carina!) wake him. With her issavan
essavans and her patterjackmartins about all them inns and ouses.
Tilling a teel of a tum, telling a toll of a teary turty Taubling.
Grace before Glutton. For what we are, gifs à gross if we are, about
to believe. So pool the begg and pass the kish for crawsake. Omen.
So sigh us. Grampupus is fallen down but grinny sprids the boord.
Whase on the joint of a desh? Finfoefom the Fush. Whase be his
baken head? A loaf of Singpantry's Kennedy bread. And whase
hitched to the hop in his tayle? A glass of Danu U'Dunnell's foamous olde Dobbelin ayle. But, lo, as you would quaffoff his fraudstuff
and sink teeth through that pyth of a flowerwhite bodey behold
of him as behemoth for he is noewhemoe. Finiche! Only a fadograph
of a yestern scene. Almost rubicund Salmosalar, ancient fromout
the ages of the Agapemonides, he is smolten in our mist, woebe-
canned and packt away. So that meal's dead off for summan, schlook,
schlice and goodridhirring.

Yet may we not see still the brontoichthyan form outlined aslum-
bered, even in our own nighttime by the sedge of the troutling
stream that Bronto loved and Brunto has a lean on. *Hic cubat edilis.*
Apud libertinam parvulam. Whatif she be in flags or flitters, reekie-
rags or sundyechosies, with a mint of mines or beggar a pinnyweight.
Arrah, sure, we all love little Anny Ruiny, or, we mean to say,

lovelittle Anna Rayiny, when unda her brella, mid piddle med pud-
dle, she ninnygoes nannygoes nancing by. Yoh! Brontolone slaaps,
yoh snoores. Upon Benn Heather, in Seeple Isout too. The cranic
head on him, caster of his reasons, peer yuthner in yondmist.
Whooth? His clay feet, swarded in verdigrass, stick up starck where
he last fellonem, by the mund of the magazine wall, where our
maggy seen all, with her sisterin shawl. While over against this belles'
alliance beyind Ill Sixty, ollollowed ill! bagsides of the fort, bom,
tarabom, tarabom, lurk the ombushes, the site of the lyffing-in-wait
of the upjock and hockums. Hence when the clouds roll by, jamey,
a proudseye view is enjoyable of our mounding's mass, now Wallin-
stone national museum, with, in some greenish distance, the charmful
waterloose country and the two quitewhite villagettes who hear show
of themselves so gigglesomes minxt the follyages, the prettilees! Pene-
trators are permitted into the museomound free. Welsh and the
Paddy Patkinses, one shelenk! Redismembers invalids of old guard
find poussepousse pousseypram to sate the sort of their butt. For
her passkey supply to the janitrix, the mistress Kathe. Tip.

This the way to the museyroom. Mind your hats goan in! Now
yiz are in the Willingdone Museyroom. This is a Prooshious gunn.
This is a ffrinch. Tip. This is the flag of the Prooshious, the Cap
and Soracer. This is the bullet that byng the flag of the Prooshious.
This is the ffrinch that fire on the Bull that bang the flag of the
Prooshious. Saloos the Crossgunn! Up with your pike and fork! Tip.
(Bullsfoot! Fine!) This is the triplewon hat of Lipoleum. Tip. Li-
poleumhat. This is the Willingdone on his same white harse, the
Cokenhape. This is the big Sraughter Willingdone, grand and
magentic in his goldtin spurs and his ironed dux and his quarterbrass
woodyshoes and his magnate's gharters and his bangkok's best and
goliar's goloshes and his pulluponeasyan wartrews. This is his big
wide harse. Tip. This is the three lipoleum boyne grouching down
in the living detch. This is an inimyskilling inglis, this is a scotcher
grey, this is a davy, stooping. This is the bog lipoleum mordering
the lipoleum beg. A Gallawghurs argaumunt. This is the petty
lipoleum boy that was nayther bag nor bug. Assaye, assaye! Touchole
Fitz Tuomush. Dirty MacDyke. And Hairy O'Hurry. All of them
arminus-varminus. This is Delian alps. This is Mont Tivel, this is
Mont Tipsey, this is the Grand Mons Injun. This is the crimealine
of the alps hooping to sheltershock the three lipoleums. This is the
jinnies with their legahorns feinting to read in their handmade's
book of stralegy while making their war undisides the Willingdone.

The jinnies is a cooin her hand and the jinnies is a ravin her hair and the Willingdone git the band up. This is big Willingdone mormorial tallowscoop Wounderworker obscides on the flanks of the jinnies. Sexcaliber hrosspower. Tip. This is me Belchum sneaking his phillippy out of his most Awful Grimmest Sunshat Cromwelly. Looted. This is the jinnies' hastings dispatch for to irrigate the Willingdone. Dispatch in thin red lines cross the shortfront of me Belchum. Yaw, yaw, yaw! Leaper Orthor. Fear siecken! Fieldgaze thy tiny frow. Hugacting. Nap. That was the tictacs of the jinnies for to fontannoy the Willingdone. Shee, shee, shee! The jinnies is jillous agincourting all the lipoleums. And the lipoleums is gonn boycottoncrezy onto the one Willingdone. And the Willingdone git the band up. This is bode Belchum, bonnet to busby, breaking his secred word with a ball up his ear to the Willingdone. This is the Willingdone's hurold dispitchback. Dispitch desployed on the regions rare of me Belchum. Salamangra! Ayi, ayi, ayi! Cherry jinnies. Figtreeyou! Damn fairy ann, Voutre. Willingdone. That was the first joke of Willingdone, tic for tac. Hee, hee, hee! This is me Belchum in his twelvemile cowchooks, weet, tweet and stampforth foremost, footing the camp for the jinnies. Drink a sip, drankasup, for he's as sooner buy a guinness than he'd stale store stout. This is Rooshious balls. This is a ttrinch. This is mistletropes. This is Canon Futter with the popynose. After his hundred days' indulgence. This is the blessed. Tarra's widdars! This is jinnies in the bonny bawn blooches. This is lipoleums in the rowdy howses. This is the Willingdone, by the splinters of Cork, order fire. Tonnerre! (Bullsear! Play!) This is camelry, this is floodens, this is the solphereens in action, this is their mobbily, this is panickburns. Almeidagad! Arthiz too loose! This is Willingdone cry. Brum! Brum! Cumbrum! This is jinnies cry. Underwetter! Goat strip Finnlambs! This is jinnies rinning away to their ousterlists dowan a bunkersheels. With a nip nippy nip and a trip trippy trip so airy. For their heart's right there. Tip. This is me Belchum's tinkyou tankyou silvoor plate for citchin the crapes in the cool of his canister. Poor the pay! This is the bissmark of the marathon merry of the jinnies they left behind them. This is the Willingdone branlish his same marmorial tallowscoop Sophy-Key-Po for his royal divorsion on the rinnaway jinnies. Gambariste della porca! Dalaveras fimmieras! This is the pettiest of the lipoleums, Toffeethief, that spy on the Willingdone from his big white harse, the Capeinhope. Stonewall Willingdone is an old maxy montrumeny. Lipoleums is nice hung bushellors. This is hiena

hinnessy laughing alout at the Willingdone. This is lipsyg dooley
krieging the funk from the hinnessy. This is the hinndoo Shimar
Shin between the dooley boy and the hinnessy. Tip. This is the
wixy old Willingdone picket up the half of the threefoiled hat of
lipoleums fromoud of the bluddle filth. This is the hinndoo waxing
ranjymad for a bombshoob. This is the Willingdone hanking the
half of the hat of lipoleums up the tail on the buckside of his big
white harse. Tip. That was the last joke of Willingdone. Hit, hit,
hit! This is the same white harse of the Willingdone, Culpenhelp,
waggling his tailoscrupp with the half of a hat of lipoleums to insoult
on the hinndoo seeboy. Hney, hney, hney! (Bullsrag! Foul!) This
is the seeboy, madrashattaras, upjump and pumpim, cry to the Willingdone: Ap Pukkaru! Pukka Yurap! This is the Willingdone, born-
stable ghentleman, tinders his maxbotch to the cursigan Shimar Shin.
Basucker youstead! This is the dooforhim seeboy blow the whole
of the half of the hat of lipoleums off of the top of the tail on
the back of his big wide harse. Tip (Bullseye! Game!) How Copen-
hagen ended. This way the museyroom. Mind your boots goan out.
  Phew!
  What a warm time we were in there but how keling is here
the airabouts! We nowhere she lives but you mussna tell annaone
for the lamp of Jig-a-Lanthern! It's a candlelittle houthse of a month
and one windies. Downadown, High Downadown. And nummered
quaintlymine. And such reasonable weather too! The wagrant wind's
awalt'zaround the piltdowns and on every blasted knollyrock (if
you can spot fifty I spy four more) there's that gnarlybird ygathering,
a runalittle, doalittle, preealittle, pouralittle, wipealittle, kicksalittle,
severalittle, eatalittle, whinealittle, kenalittle, helfalittle, pelfalittle
gnarlybird. A verytableland of bleakbardfields! Under his seven
wrothschields lies one, Lumproar. His glav toside him. Skud ontorsed.
Our pigeons pair are flewn for northcliffs. The three of crows have
flapped it southenly, kraaking of de baccle to the kvarters of that
sky whence triboos answer; Wail, 'tis well! She niver comes out
when Thon's on shower or when Thon's flash with his Nixy girls
or when Thon's blowing toomcracks down the gaels of Thon. No
nubo no! Neblas on you liv! Her would be too moochy afreet. Of
Burymeleg and Bindmerollingeyes and all the deed in the woe. Fe
fo fom! She jist does hopes till byes will be byes. Here, and it
goes on to appear now, she comes, a peacefugle, a parody's bird,
a peri potmother, a pringlpik in the ilandiskippy, with peewee and
powwows in beggybaggy on her bickybacky and a flick flask fleck-

flinging its pixylighting pacts' huemeramybows, picking here, pecking
there, pussypussy plunderpussy. But it's the armitides toonigh,
militopucos, and toomourn we wish for a muddy kissmans to the
minutia workers and there's to be a gorgeups truce for happinest
childher everwere. Come nebo me and suso sing the day we sally-
bright. She's burrowed the coacher's headlight the better to pry (who
goes cute goes siocur and shoos aroun) and all spoiled goods go
into her nabsack: curtrages and rattlin buttins, nappy spattees and
flasks of all nations, clavicures and scampulars, maps, keys and wood-
piles of haypennies and moonled brooches with bloodstaned breeks
in em, boaston nightgarters and masses of shoesets and nickelly nacks
and foder allmicheal and a lugly parson of cates and howitzer
muchears and midgers and maggets, ills and ells with loffs of toffs
and pleures of bells and the last sigh that come fro the hart (buck-
lied!) and the fairest sin the sunsaw (that's cearc!). With Kiss. Kiss
Criss. Cross Criss. Kiss Cross. Undo lives 'end. Slain.

How bootifull and how truetowife of her, when strengly fore-
bidden, to steal our historic presents from the past postpropheticals
so as to will make us all lordy heirs and ladymaidesses of a pretty
nice kettle of fruit. She is livving in our midst of debt and laffing
through all plores for us (her birth is uncontrollable), with a naperon
for her mask and her sabboes kickin arias (so sair! so solly!) if yous
ask me and I saack you. Hou! Hou! Gricks may rise and Troysirs
fall (there being two sights for ever a picture) for in the byways
of high improvidence that's what makes lifework leaving and the
world's a cell for citters to cit in. Let young wimman run away
with the story and let young min talk smooth behind the butteler's
back. She knows her knight's duty while Luntum sleeps. Did ye
save any tin? says he. Did I what? with a grin says she. And we
all like a marriedann because she is mercenary. Though the length
of the land lies under liquidation (floote!) and there's nare a hair-
brow nor an eyebush on this glaubrous phace of Herrschuft Whatar-
welter she'll loan a vesta and hire some peat and sarch the shores
her cockles to heat and she'll do all a turfwoman can to piff the
business on. Paff. To puff the blaziness on. Poffpoff. And even if
Humpty shell fall frumpty times as awkward again in the beards-
boosoloom of all our grand remonstrancers there'll be iggs for the
brekkers come to mournhim, sunny side up with care. So true is
it that therewhere's a turnover the tay is wet too and when you
think you ketch sight of a hind make sure but you're cocked by
a hin.

Then as she is on her behaviourite job of quainance bandy, fruting for firstlings and taking her tithe, we may take our review of the two mounds to see nothing of the himples here as at elsewhere, by sixes and sevens, like so many heegills and collines, sitton aroont, scentbreeched and somepotreek, in their swishawish satins and their taffetaffe tights, playing Wharton's Folly, at a treepurty on the planko in the purk. Stand up, mickos! Make strake for minnas! By order, Nicholas Proud. We may see and hear nothing if we choose of the shortlegged bergins off Corkhill or the bergamoors of Arbourhill or the bergagambols of Summerhill or the bergincellies of Miseryhill or the countrybossed bergones of Constitutionhill though every crowd has its several tones and every trade has its clever mechanics and each harmonical has a point of its own, Olaf's on the rise and Ivor's on the lift and Sitric's place's between them. But all they are all there scraping along to sneeze out a likelihood that will solve and salve life's robulous rebus, hopping round his middle like kippers on a griddle, O, as he lays dormont from the macroborg of Holdhard to the microbirg of Pied de Poudre. Behove this sound of Irish sense. Really? Here English might be seen. Royally? One sovereign punned to petery pence. Regally? The silence speaks the scene. Fake!

So This Is Dyoublong?

Hush! Caution! Echoland!

How charmingly exquisite! It reminds you of the outwashed engravure that we used to be blurring on the blotchwall of his innkempt house. Used they? (I am sure that tiring chabelshoveller with the mujikal chocolat box, Miry Mitchel, is listening) I say, the remains of the outworn gravemure where used to be blurried the Ptollmens of the Incabus. Used we? (He is only pretendant to be stugging at the jubalee harp from a second existed lishener, Fiery Farrelly.) It is well known. Lokk for himself and see the old butte new. Dbln. W. K. O. O. Hear? By the mausolime wall. Fimfim fimfim. With a grand funferall. Fumfum fumfum. 'Tis optophone which ontophanes. List! Wheatstone's magic lyer. They will be tuggling foriver. They will be lichening for allof. They will be pretumbling forover. The harpsdischord shall be theirs for ollaves.

Four things therefore, saith our herodotary Mammon Lujius in his grand old historiorum, wrote near Boriorum, bluest book in baile's annals, f.t. in Dyfflinarsky ne'er sall fail til heathersmoke and cloudweed Eire's ile sall pall. And here now they are, the fear of um. T. Totities! *Unum.* (Adar.) A bulbenboss surmounted upon an

alderman. Ay, ay! *Duum*. (Nizam.) A shoe on a puir old wobban.
Ah, ho! *Triom*. (Tamuz.) An auburn mayde, o'brine a'bride, to
be desarted. Adear, adear! *Quodlibus*. (Marchessvan.) A penn no
weightier nor a polepost. And so. And all. (Succoth.)

So, how idlers' wind turning pages on pages, as innocens with
anaclete play popeye antipop, the leaves of the living in the boke
of the deeds, annals of themselves timing the cycles of events grand
and national, bring fassilwise to pass how.

1132 A.D. Men like to ants or emmets wondern upon a groot hwide
Whallfisk which lay in a Runnel. Blubby wares upat Ublanium.

566 A.D. On Baalfire's night of this year after deluge a crone that
hadde a wickered Kish for to hale dead turves from the bog lookit
under the blay of her Kish as she ran for to sothisfeige her cow-
rieosity and be me sawl but she found hersell sackvulle of swart
goody quickenshoon and small illigant brogues, so rich in sweat.
Blurry works at Hurdlesford.

(Silent.)

566 A.D. At this time it fell out that a brazenlockt damsel grieved
(*sobralasolas!*) because that Puppette her minion was ravisht of her
by the ogre Puropeus Pious. Bloody wars in Ballyaughacleeaghbally.

1132 A.D. Two sons at an hour were born until a goodman and
his hag. These sons called themselves Caddy and Primas. Primas
was a santryman and drilled all decent people. Caddy went to Wine-
house and wrote o peace a farce. Blotty words for Dublin.

Somewhere, parently, in the ginnandgo gap between antediluvious
and annadominant the copyist must have fled with his scroll. The
billy flood rose or an elk charged him or the sultrup worldwright
from the excelsissimost empyrean (bolt, in sum) earthspake or the
Dannamen gallous banged pan the bliddy duran. A scribicide then
and there is led off under old's code with some fine covered by
six marks or ninepins in metalmen for the sake of his labour's dross
while it will be only now and again in our rear of o'er era, as
an upshoot of military and civil engagements, that a gynecure was
let on to the scuffold for taking that same fine sum covertly by
meddlement with the drawers of his neighbour's safe.

Now after all that farfatch'd and peragrine or dingnant or clere
lift we our ears, eyes of the darkness, from the tome of *Liber Li-
vidus* and, (toh!), how paisibly eirenical, all dimmering dunes and
gloamering glades, selfstretches afore us our fredeland's plain! Lean
neath stone pine the pastor lies with his crook; young pricket by
pricket's sister nibbleth on returned viridities; amaid her rocking

grasses the herb trinity shams lowliness; skyup is of evergrey. Thus, too, for donkey's years. Since the bouts of Hebear and Hairyman the cornflowers have been staying at Ballymun, the duskrose has choosed out Goatstown's hedges, twolips have pressed togatherthem by sweet Rush, townland of twinedlights, the whitethorn and the redthorn have fairygeyed the mayvalleys of Knockmaroon, and, though for rings round them, during a chiliad of perihelygangs, the Formoreans have brittled the tooath of the Danes and the Oxman has been pestered by the Firebugs and the Joynts have thrown up jerrybuilding to the Kevanses and Little on the Green is childsfather to the City (Year! Year! And laughtears!), these paxsealing button-holes have quadrilled across the centuries and whiff now whafft to us, fresh and made-of-all-smiles as, on the eve of Killallwho.

The babbelers with their thangas vain have been (confusium hold them!) they were and went; thigging thugs were and houhnhymn songtoms were and comely norgels were and pollyfool fiansees. Menn have thawed, clerks have surssurhummed, the blond has sought of the brune: Elsekiss thou may, mean Kerry piggy?: and the duncle-dames have countered with the hellish fellows: Who ails tongue coddeau, aspace of dumbillsilly? And they fell upong one another: and themselves they have fallen. And still nowanights and by nights of yore do all bold floras of the field to their shyfaun lovers say only: Cull me ere I wilt to thee!: and, but a little later: Pluck me whilst I blush! Well may they wilt, marry, and profusely blush, be troth! For that saying is as old as the howitts. Lave a whale a while in a whillbarrow (isn't it the truath I'm tallin ye?) to have fins and flippers that shimmy and shake. Tim Timmycan timped hir, tampting Tam. Fleppety! Flippety! Fleapow!

Hop!

In the name of Anem this carl on the kopje in pelted thongs a parth a lone who the joebiggar be he? Forshapen his pigmaid hoagshead, shroonk his plodsfoot. He hath locktoes, this shortshins, and, Obeold that's pectoral, his mammamuscles most mousterious. It is slaking nuncheon out of some thing's brain pan. Me seemeth a dragon man. He is almonthst on the kiep fief by here, is Come-stipple Sacksoun, be it junipery or febrewery, marracks or alebrill or the ramping riots of pouriose and froriose. What a quhare soort of a mahan. It is evident the michindaddy. Lets we overstep his fire defences and these kraals of slitsucked marrogbones. (Cave!) He can prapsposterus the pillory way to Hirculos pillar. Come on, fool porterfull, hosiered women blown monk sewer? Scuse us, chorley

guy! You tollerday donsk? N. You tolkatiff scowegian? Nn. You
spigotty anglease? Nnn. You phonio saxo? Nnnn. Clear all so! 'Tis
a Jute. Let us swop hats and excheck a few strong verbs weak oach
eather yapyazzard abast the blooty creeks.

Jute. — Yutah!

Mutt. — Mukk's pleasurad.

Jute. — Are you jeff?

Mutt. — Somehards.

Jute. — But you are not jeffmute?

Mutt. — Noho. Only an utterer.

Jute. — Whoa? Whoat is the mutter with you?

Mutt. — I became a stun a stummer.

Jute. — What a hauhauhauhaudibble thing, to be cause! How,
Mutt?

Mutt. — Aput the buttle, surd.

Jute. — Whose poddle? Wherein?

Mutt. — The Inns of Dungtarf where Used awe to be he.

Jute. — You that side your voise are almost inedible to me. Become a bitskin more wiseable, as if I were you.

Mutt. — Has? Has at? Hasatency? Urp, Boohooru! Booru Usurp!
I trumple from rath in mine mines when I rimimirim!

Jute. — One eyegonblack. Bisons is bisons. Let me fore all your
hasitancy cross your qualm with trink gilt. Here have
sylvan coyne, a piece of oak. Ghinees hies good for you.

Mutt. — Louee, louee! How wooden I not know it, the intellible
greytcloak of Cedric Silkyshag! Cead mealy faulty rices
for one dabblin bar. Old grilsy growlsy! He was poached
on in that eggtentical spot. Here where the liveries, Mono-
mark. There where the missers moony, Minnikin passe.

Jute. — Simply because as Taciturn pretells, our wrongstoryshort-
ener, he dumptied the wholeborrow of rubbages on to
soil here.

Mutt. — Just how a puddinstone inat the brookcells by a riverpool.

Jute. — Load Allmarshy! Wid wad for a norse like?

Mutt. — Somular with a bull on a clompturf. Rooks roarum rex
roome! I could snore to him of the spumy horn, with
his woolseley side in, by the neck I am sutton on, did
Brian d' of Linn.

Jute. — Boildoyle and rawhoney on me when I can beuraly
forsstand a weird from sturk to finnic in such a patwhat

as your rutterdamrotter. Onheard of and umscene! Gut
aftermeal! See you doomed.

Mutt. — Quite agreem. Bussave a sec. Walk a dun blink round-
ward this albutisle and you skull see how olde ye plaine
of my Elters, hunfree and ours, where wone to wail whim-
brel to peewee o'er the saltings, where wilby citie by law
of isthmon, where by a droit of signory, icefloe was from
his Inn the Byggning to whose Finishthere Punct. Let
erehim ruhmuhrmuhr. Mearmerge two races, swete and
brack. Morthering rue. Hither, craching eastuards, they
are in surgence: hence, cool at ebb, they requiesce. Count-
lessness of livestories have netherfallen by this plage, flick
as flowflakes, litters from aloft, like a waast wizzard all
of whirlworlds. Now are all tombed to the mound, isges
to isges, erde from erde. Pride, O pride, thy prize!

Jute. — 'Stench!

Mutt. — Fiatfuit! Hereinunder lyethey. Llarge by the smal an'
everynight life olso th'estrange, babylone the greatgrand-
hotelled with tit tit tittlehouse, alp on earwig, drukn on
ild, likeas equal to anequal in this sound seemetery which
iz leebez luv.

Jute. — 'Zmorde!

Mutt. — Meldundleize! By the fearse wave behoughted. Despond's
sung. And thanacestross mound have swollup them all.
This ourth of years is not save brickdust and being humus
the same roturns. He who runes may rede it on all fours.
O'c'stle, n'wc'stle, tr'c'stle, crumbling! Sell me sooth the
fare for Humblin! Humblady Fair. But speak it allsosiftly,
moulder! Be in your whisht!

Jute. — Whysht?

Mutt. — The gyant Forficules with Amni the fay.

Jute. — Howe?

Mutt. — Here is viceking's graab.

Jute. — Hwaad!

Mutt. — Ore you astoneaged, jute you?

Jute. — Oye am thonthorstrok, thing mud.

(Stoop) if you are abcedminded, to this claybook, what curios
of signs (please stoop), in this allaphbed! Can you rede (since We
and Thou had it out already) its world? It is the same told of all.
Many. Miscegenations on miscegenations. Tieckle. They lived und
laughed ant loved end left. Forsin. Thy thingdome is given to the

Meades and Porsons. The meandertale, aloss and again, of our old
Heidenburgh in the days when Head-in-Clouds walked the earth.
In the ignorance that implies impression that knits knowledge that
finds the nameform that whets the wits that convey contacts that
sweeten sensation that drives desire that adheres to attachment that
dogs death that bitches birth that entails the ensuance of existen-
tiality. But with a rush out of his navel reaching the reredos of
Ramasbatham. A terricolous vivelyonview this; queer and it continues
to be quaky. A hatch, a celt, an earshare the pourquose of which
was to cassay the earthcrust at all of hours, furrowards, bagawards,
like yoxen at the turnpaht. Here say figurines billycoose arming and
mounting. Mounting and arming bellicose figurines see here.
Futhorc, this liffle effingee is for a firefing called a flintforfall. Face
at the eased! O I fay! Face at the waist! Ho, you fie! Upwap and
dump em, ▶face to ◀ace! When a part so ptee does duty for the
holos we soon grow to use of an allforabit. Here (please to stoop)
are selveran cued peteet peas of quite a pecuniar interest inaslittle
as they are the pellets that make the tomtummy's pay roll. Right
rank ragnar rocks and with these rox orangotangos rangled rough
and rightgorong. Wisha, wisha, whydidtha? Thik is for thorn that's
thuck in its thoil like thumfool's thraitor thrust for vengeance. What
a mnice old mness it all mnakes! A middenhide hoard of objects!
Olives, beets, kimmells, dollies, alfrids, beatties, cormacks and daltons.
Owlets' eegs (O stoop to please!) are here, creakish from age and
all now quite epsilene, and oldwolldy wobblewers, haudworth a wipe
o grass. Sss! See the snake wurrums everyside! Our durlbin is sworm-
ing in sneaks. They came to our island from triangular Toucheaterre
beyond the wet prairie rared up in the midst of the cargon of prohibi-
tive pomefructs but along landed Paddy Wippingham and the his
garbagecans cotched the creeps of them pricker than our whosethere
outofman could quick up her whatsthats. Somedivide and sumthelot
but the tally turns round the same balifuson. Racketeers and
bottloggers.

Axe on thwacks on thracks, axenwise. One by one place one be
three dittoh and one before. Two nursus one make a plausible free
and idim behind. Starting off with a big boaboa and threelegged
calvers and ivargraine jadesses with a message in their mouths. And
a hundredfilled unleavenweight of liberorumqueue to con an we
can till allhorrors eve. What a meanderthalltale to unfurl and with
what an end in view of squattor and anntisquattor and postprone-
auntisquattor! To say too us to be every tim, nick and larry of us, sons

of the sod, sons, littlesons, yea and lealittlesons, when usses not to
be, every sue, siss and sally of us, dugters of Nan! Accusative ahnsire!
Damadam to infinities!

True there was in nillohs dieybos as yet no lumpend papeer in
the waste and mightmountain Penn still groaned for the micies to
let flee. All was of ancientry. You gave me a boot (signs on it!)
and I ate the wind. I quizzed you a quid (with for what?) and
you went to the quod. But the world, mind, is, was and will be
writing its own wrunes for ever, man, on all matters that fall under
the ban of our infrarational senses fore the last milchcamel, the
heartvein throbbing between his eyebrowns, has still to moor before
the tomb of his cousin charmian where his date is tethered by the
palm that's hers. But the horn, the drinking, the day of dread are
not now. A bone, a pebble, a ramskin; chip them, chap them, cut
them up allways; leave them to terracook in the muttheringpot: and
Gutenmorg with his cromagnom charter, tintingfast and great primer
must once for omniboss step rubrickredd out of the wordpress else
is there no virtue more in alcohoran. For that (the rapt one warns)
is what papyr is meed of, made of, hides and hints and misses in
prints. Till ye finally (though not yet endlike) meet with the acquaintance of Mister Typus, Mistress Tope and all the little typtop-
ies. Fillstup. So you need hardly spell me how every word will be
bound over to carry three score and ten toptypsical readings throughout the book of Doublends Jined (may his forehead be darkened
with mud who would sunder!) till Daleth, mahomahouma, who oped
it closeth thereof the. Dor.

Cry not yet! There's many a smile to Nondum, with sytty maids
per man, sir, and the park's so dark by kindlelight. But look what
you have in your handself! The movibles are scrawling in motions,
marching, all of them ago, in pitpat and zingzang for every busy
eerie whig's a bit of a torytale to tell. One's upon a thyme and
two's behind their lettice leap and three's among the strubbely beds.
And the chicks picked their teeths and the dombkey he begay began.
You can ask your ass if he believes it. And so cuddy me only wallops
have heels. That one of a wife with folty barnets. For then was
the age when hoops ran high. Of a noarch and a chopwife; of a
pomme full grave and a fammy of levity; or of golden youths that
wanted gelding; or of what the mischievmiss made a man do. Mal-
marriedad he was reversogassed by the frisque of her frasques and
her prytty pyrrhique. Maye faye, she's la gaye this snaky woman!
From that trippiery toe expectungpelick! Veil, volantine, valentine

eyes. She's the very besch Winnie blows Nay on good. Flou inn, flow ann. Hohore! So it's sure it was her not we! But lay it easy, gentle mien, we are in rearing of a norewhig. So weenybeenyveeny-teeny. Comsy see! Het wis if ee newt. Lissom! lissom! I am doing it. Hark, the corne entreats! And the larpnotes prittle.

It was of a night, late, lang time agone, in an auldstane eld, when Adam was delvin and his madameen spinning watersilts, when mulk mountynotty man was everybully and the first leal ribberrobber that ever had her ainway everybuddy to his lovesaking eyes and every-billy lived alove with everybiddy else, and Jarl van Hoother had his burnt head high up in his lamphouse, laying cold hands on him-self. And his two little jiminies, cousins of ourn, Tristopher and Hilary, were kickaheeling their dummy on the oil cloth flure of his homerigh, castle and earthenhouse. And, be dermot, who come to the keep of his inn only the niece-of-his-in-law, the prankquean. And the prankquean pulled a rosy one and made her wit foreninst the dour. And she lit up and fireland was ablaze. And spoke she to the dour in her petty perusienne: Mark the Wans, why do I am alook alike a poss of porterpease? And that was how the skirtmisshes began. But the dour handworded her grace in dootch nossow: Shut! So her grace o'malice kidsnapped up the jiminy Tristopher and into the shandy westerness she rain, rain, rain. And Jarl van Hoother warlessed after her with soft dovesgall: Stop deef stop come back to my earin stop. But she swaradid to him: Unlikelihud. And there was a brannewail that same sabboath night of falling angles some-where in Erio. And the prankquean went for her forty years' walk in Tourlemonde and she washed the blessings of the lovespots off the jiminy with soap sulliver suddles and she had her four owlers masters for to tauch him his tickles and she converted him to the onesure allgood and he became a luderman. So then she started to rain and to rain and, be redtom, she was back again at Jarl van Hoother's in a brace of samers and the jiminy with her in her pina-frond, lace at night, at another time. And where did she come but to the bar of his bristolry. And Jarl von Hoother had his baretholo-bruised heels drowned in his cellarmalt, shaking warm hands with himself and the jimminy Hilary and the dummy in their first in-fancy were below on the tearsheet, wringing and coughing, like brodar and histher. And the prankquean nipped a paly one and lit up again and redcocks flew flackering from the hillcombs. And she made her witter before the wicked, saying: Mark the Twy, why do I am alook alike two poss of porterpease? And: Shut! says the wicked,

handwording her madesty. So her madesty a forethought set down
a jiminy and took up a jiminy and all the lilipath ways to Woeman's
Land she rain, rain, rain. And Jarl von Hoother bleethered atter
her with a loud finegale: Stop domb stop come back with my earring
stop. But the prankquean swaradid: Am liking it. And there was a
wild old grannewwail that laurency night of starshootings somewhere in Erio. And the prankquean went for her forty years' walk
in Turnlemeem and she punched the curses of cromcruwell with
the nail of a top into the jiminy and she had her four larksical moni-
trix to touch him his tears and she provorted him to the onecertain
allsecure and he became a tristian. So then she started raining, raining, and in a pair of changers, be dom ter, she was back again at
Jarl von Hoother's and the Larryhill with her under her abromette.
And why would she halt at all if not by the ward of his mansion-
home of another nice lace for the third charm? And Jarl von
Hoother had his hurricane hips up to his pantrybox, ruminating in
his holdfour stomachs (Dare! O dare!), and the jiminy Tougher-
trees and the dummy were belove on the watercloth, kissing and
spitting, and roguing and poghuing, like knavepaltry and naive-
bride and in their second infancy. And the prankquean picked a
blank and lit out and the valleys lay twinkling. And she made her
wittest in front of the arkway of trihump, asking: Mark the Tris,
why do I am alook alike three poss of porter pease? But that was
how the skirmishes endupped. For like the campbells acoming with
a fork lance of lightning, Jarl von Hoother Boanerges himself, the
old terror of the dames, came hip hop handihap out through the
pikeopened arkway of his three shuttoned castles, in his broad-
ginger hat and his civic chollar and his allabuff hemmed and his
bullbraggin soxangloves and his ladbroke breeks and his cattegut
bandolair and his furframed panuncular cumbottes like a rudd yel-
lan gruebleen orangeman in his violet indigonation, to the whole
longth of the strength of his bowman's bill. And he clopped his
rude hand to his eacy hitch and he ordurd and his thick spch spck
for her to shut up shop, dappy. And the duppy shot the shutter
clup (Perkodhuskurunbarggruauyagokgorlayorgromgremmitghund-
hurthrumathunaradidillifaititillibumullunukkunun!) And they all
drank free. For one man in his armour was a fat match always for
any girls under shurts. And that was the first peace of illiterative
porthery in all the flamend floody flatuous world. How kirssy the
tiler made a sweet unclose to the Narwhealian captol. Saw fore shalt
thou sea. Betoun ye and be. The prankquean was to hold her dummy-

ship and the jimminies was to keep the peacewave and van Hoother was to git the wind up. Thus the hearsomeness of the burger felicitates the whole of the polis.

O foenix culprit! Ex nickylow malo comes mickelmassed bonum. Hill, rill, ones in company, billeted, less be proud of. Breast high and bestride! Only for that these will not breathe upon Norronesen or Irenean the secrest of their soorcelossness. Quarry silex, Homfrie Noanswa! Undy gentian festyknees, Livia Noanswa? Wolkencap is on him, frowned; audiurient, he would evesdrip, were it mous at hand, were it dinn of bottles in the far ear. Murk, his vales are darkling. With lipth she lithpeth to him all to time of thuch on thuch and thow on thow. She he she ho she ha to la. Hairfluke, if he could bad twig her! Impalpabunt, he abhears. The soundwaves are his buffeteers; they trompe him with their trompes; the wave of roary and the wave of hooshed and the wave of hawhawhawrd and the wave of neverheedthemhorseluggarsandlistletomine. Landloughed by his neaghboormistress and perpetrified in his offsprung, sabes and suckers, the moaning pipers could tell him to his faceback, the louthly one whose loab we are devorers of, how butt for his hold hallibutt, or her to her pudor puff, the lipalip one whose libe we drink at, how biff for her tiddywink of a windfall, our breed and washer givers, there would not be a holey spier on the town nor a vestal flouting in the dock, nay to make plein avowels, nor a yew nor an eye to play cash cash in Novo Nilbud by swamplight nor a' toole o' tall o' toll and noddy hint to the convaynience.

He dug in and dug out by the skill of his tilth for himself and all belonging to him and he sweated his crew beneath his auspice for the living and he urned his dread, that dragon volant, and he made louse for us and delivered us to boll weevils amain, that mighty liberator, Unfru-Chikda-Uru-Wukru and begad he did, our ancestor most worshipful, till he thought of a better one in his windower's house with that blushmantle upon him from earsend to earsend. And would again could whispring grassies wake him and may again when the fiery bird disembers. And will again if so be sooth by elder to his youngers shall be said. Have you whines for my wedding, did you bring bride and bedding, will you whoop for my deading is a? Wake? *Usqueadbaugham!*

Anam muck an dhoul! Did ye drink me doornail?

Now be aisy, good Mr Finnimore, sir. And take your laysure like a god on pension and don't be walking abroad. Sure you'd only lose yourself in Healiopolis now the way your roads in Kapelavaster are

that winding there after the calvary, the North Umbrian and the
Fivs Barrow and Waddlings Raid and the Bower Moore and wet
your feet maybe with the foggy dew's abroad. Meeting some sick
old bankrupt or the Cottericks' donkey with his shoe hanging, clank-
atachankata, or a slut snoring with an impure infant on a bench.
'Twould turn you against life, so 'twould. And the weather's that
mean too. To part from Devlin is hard as Nugent knew, to leave
the clean tanglesome one lushier than its neighbour enfranchisable
fields but let your ghost have no grievance. You're better off, sir,
where you are, primesigned in the full of your dress, bloodeagle
waistcoat and all, remembering your shapes and sizes on the pillow
of your babycurls under your sycamore by the keld water where
the Tory's clay will scare the varmints and have all you want, pouch,
gloves, flask, bricket, kerchief, ring and amberulla, the whole treasure of the pyre, in the land of souls with Homin and Broin Baroke
and pole ole Lonan and Nobucketnozzler and the Guinnghis Khan.
And we'll be coming here, the ombre players, to rake your gravel
and bringing you presents, won't we, fenians? And it isn't our spittle we'll stint you of, is it, druids? Not shabbty little imagettes,
pennydirts and dodgemyeyes you buy in the soottee stores. But of-
ferings of the field. Mieliodories, that Doctor Faherty, the madison
man, taught to gooden you. Poppypap's a passport out. And honey
is the holiest thing ever was, hive, comb and earwax, the food for
glory, (mind you keep the pot or your nectar cup may yield too
light!) and some goat's milk, sir, like the maid used to bring you.
Your fame is spreading like Basilico's ointment since the Fintan
Lalors piped you overborder and there's whole households beyond
the Bothnians and they calling names after you. The menhere's
always talking of you sitting around on the pig's cheeks under the
sacred rooftree, over the bowls of memory where every hollow holds
a hallow, with a pledge till the drengs, in the Salmon House. And
admiring to our supershillelagh where the palmsweat on high is the
mark of your manument. All the toethpicks ever Eirenesians chewed
on are chips chepped from that battery block. If you were bowed
and soild and letdown itself from the oner of the load it was that
paddyplanters might pack up plenty and when you were undone
in every point fore the laps of goddesses you showed our labour-
lasses how to free was easy. The game old Gunne, they do be saying,
(skull!) that was a planter for you, a spicer of them all. Begog but
he was, the G.O.G! He's duddandgunne now and we're apter finding the sores of his sedeq but peace to his great limbs, the buddhoch,

with the last league long rest of him, while the millioncandled eye
of Tuskar sweeps the Moylean Main! There was never a warlord in
Great Erinnes and Brettland, no, nor in all Pike County like you,
they say. No, nor a king nor an ardking, bung king, sung king or
hung king. That you could fell an elmstree twelve urchins couldn't
ring round and hoist high the stone that Liam failed. Who but a
Maccullaghmore the reise of our fortunes and the faunayman at
the funeral to compass our cause? If you was hogglebully itself and
most frifty like you was taken waters still what all where was your
like to lay the cable or who was the batter could better Your Grace?
Mick Mac Magnus MacCawley can take you off to the pure perfection and Leatherbags Reynolds tries your shuffle and cut. But
as Hopkins and Hopkins puts it, you were the pale eggynaggy and
a kis to tilly up. We calls him the journeyall Buggaloffs since he
went Jerusalemfaring in Arssia Manor. You had a gamier cock than
Pete, Jake or Martin and your archgoose of geese stubbled for All
Angels' Day. So may the priest of seven worms and scalding tayboil,
Papa Vestray, come never anear you as your hair grows wheater
beside the Liffey that's in Heaven! Hep, hep, hurrah there! Hero!
Seven times thereto we salute you! The whole bag of kits, falcon-
plumes and jackboots incloted, is where you flung them that time.
Your heart is in the system of the Shewolf and your crested head
is in the tropic of Copricapron. Your feet are in the cloister of Virgo.
Your olala is in the region of sahuls. And that's ashore as you were
born. Your shuck tick's swell. And that there texas is tow linen.
The loamsome roam to Laffayette is ended. Drop in your tracks,
babe! Be not unrested! The headboddylwatcher of the chempel of
Isid, Totumcalmum, saith: I know thee, metherjar, I know thee,
salvation boat. For we have performed upon thee, thou abramana-
tion, who comest ever without being invoked, whose coming is unknown, all the things which the company of the precentors and of
the grammarians of Christpatrick's ordered concerning thee in the
matter of the work of thy tombing. Howe of the shipmen, steep wall!

Everything's going on the same or so it appeals to all of us, in the
old holmsted here. Coughings all over the sanctuary, bad scrant to
me aunt Florenza. The horn for breakfast, one o'gong for lunch
and dinnerchime. As popular as when Belly the First was keng and
his members met in the Diet of Man. The same shop slop in the
window. Jacob's lettercrackers and Dr Tipple's Vi-Cocoa and the
Eswuards' desippated soup beside Mother Seagull's syrup. Meat
took a drop when Reilly-Parsons failed. Coal's short but we've plenty

of bog in the yard. And barley's up again, begrained to it. The lads
is attending school nessans regular, sir, spelling beesknees with hat-
hatansy and turning out tables by mudapplication. Allfor the books
and never pegging smashers after Tom Bowe Glassarse or Timmy the
Tosser. 'Tisraely the truth! No isn't it, roman pathoricks? You were
the doublejoynted janitor the morning they were delivered and you'll
be a grandfer yet entirely when the ritehand seizes what the love-
arm knows. Kevin's just a doat with his cherub cheek, chalking
oghres on walls, and his little lamp and schoolbelt and bag of knicks,
playing postman's knock round the diggings and if the seep were
milk you could lieve his olde by his ide but, laus sake, the devil does
be in that knirps of a Jerry sometimes, the tarandtan plaidboy, making encostive inkum out of the last of his lavings and writing a
blue streak over his bourseday shirt. Hetty Jane's a child of Mary.
She'll be coming (for they're sure to choose her) in her white of
gold with a tourch of ivy to rekindle the flame on Felix Day. But
Essie Shanahan has let down her skirts. You remember Essie in our
Luna's Convent? They called her Holly Merry her lips were so
ruddyberry and Pia de Purebelle when the redminers riots was on
about her. Were I a clerk designate to the Williamswoodsmenu-
factors I'd poster those pouters on every jamb in the town. She's
making her rep at Lanner's twicenightly. With the tabarine tam-
tammers of the whirligigmagees. Beats that cachucha flat. 'Twould
dilate your heart to go.

    Aisy now, you decent man, with your knees and lie quiet and
repose your honour's lordship! Hold him here, Ezekiel Irons, and
may God strengthen you! It's our warm spirits, boys, he's spooring.
Dimitrius O'Flagonan, cork that cure for the Clancartys! You
swamped enough since Portobello to float the Pomeroy. Fetch nea-
here, Pat Koy! And fetch nouyou, Pam Yates! Be nayther angst of
Wramawitch! Here's lumbos. Where misties swaddlum, where mis-
ches lodge none, where mystries pour kind on, O sleepy! So be yet!

    I've an eye on queer Behan and old Kate and the butter, trust me.
She'll do no jugglywuggly with her war souvenir postcards to help
to build me murial, tippers! I'll trip your traps! Assure a sure there!
And we put on your clock again, sir, for you. Did or didn't we,
sharestutterers? So you won't be up a stump entirely. Nor shed your
remnants. The sternwheel's crawling strong. I seen your missus in
the hall. Like the queenoveire. Arrah, it's herself that's fine, too,
don't be talking! Shirksends? You storyan Harry chap longa me
Harry chap storyan grass woman plethy good trout. Shakeshands.

Dibble a hayfork's wrong with her only her lex's salig. Boald Tib
does be yawning and smirking cat's hours on the Pollockses' woolly
round tabouretcushion watching her sewing a dream together, the
tailor's daughter, stitch to her last. Or while waiting for winter to
fire the enchantement, decoying more nesters to fall down the flue.
It's an allavalonche that blows nopussy food. If you only were there
to explain the meaning, best of men, and talk to her nice of gulden-
selver. The lips would moisten once again. As when you drove with
her to Findrinny Fair. What with reins here and ribbons there all
your hands were employed so she never knew was she on land or at
sea or swooped through the blue like Airwinger's bride. She was
flirtsome then and she's fluttersome yet. She can second a song and
adores a scandal when the last post's gone by. Fond of a concertina
and pairs passing when she's had her forty winks for supper after
kanekannan and abbely dimpling and is in her merlin chair as-
sotted, reading her Evening World. To see is it smarts, full lengths
or swaggers. News, news, all the news. Death, a leopard, kills fellah
in Fez. Angry scenes at Stormount. Stilla Star with her lucky in
goingaways. Opportunity fair with the China floods and we hear
these rosy rumours. Ding Tams he noise about all same Harry chap.
She's seeking her way, a chickle a chuckle, in and out of their serial
story, *Les Loves of Selskar et Pervenche*, freely adapted to *The Nov-
vergin's Viv*. There'll be bluebells blowing in salty sepulchres the
night she signs her final tear. Zee End. But that's a world of ways
away. Till track laws time. No silver ash or switches for that one!
While flattering candles flare. Anna Stacey's how are you! Worther
waist in the noblest, says Adams and Sons, the wouldpay action-
neers. Her hair's as brown as ever it was. And wivvy and wavy.
Repose you now! Finn no more!

For, be that samesake sibsubstitute of a hooky salmon, there's
already a big rody ram lad at random on the premises of his haunt
of the hungred bordles, as it is told me. Shop Illicit, flourishing like
a lordmajor or a buaboabaybohm, litting flop a deadlop (aloose!)
to lee but lifting a bennbranch a yardalong (ivoeh!) on the breezy
side (for showm!), the height of Brewster's chimpney and as broad
below as Phineas Barnum; humphing his share of the showthers is
senken on him he's such a grandfallar, with a pocked wife in pickle
that's a flyfire and three lice nittle clinkers, two twilling bugs and
one midgit pucelle. And aither he cursed and recursed and was
everseen doing what your fourfootlers saw or he was never done
seeing what you coolpigeons know, weep the clouds aboon for smile-

down witnesses, and that'll do now about the fairyhees and the frailyshees. Though Eset fibble it to the zephiroth and Artsa zoom it round her heavens for ever. Creator he has created for his creatured ones a creation. White monothoid? Red theatrocrat? And all the pinkprophets cohalething? Very much so! But however 'twas 'tis sure for one thing, what sherif Toragh voucherfors and Mapqiq makes put out, that the man, Humme the Cheapner, Esc, overseen as we thought him, yet a worthy of the naym, came at this time-coloured place where we live in our paroqial fermament one tide on another, with a bumrush in a hull of a wherry, the twin turbane dhow, *The Bey for Dybbling*, this archipelago's first visiting schooner, with a wicklowpattern waxenwench at her prow for a figurehead, the deadsea dugong updipdripping from his depths, and has been repreaching himself like a fishmummer these siktyten years ever since, his shebi by his shide, adi and aid, growing hoarish under his turban and changing cane sugar into sethulose starch (Tuttut's cess to him!) as also that, batin the bulkihood he bloats about when innebbiated, our old offender was humile, commune and ensectuous from his nature, which you may gauge after the bynames was put under him, in lashons of languages, (honnein suit and praisers be!) and, totalisating him, even hamissim of himashim that he, sober serious, he is ee and no counter he who will be ultimendly respunchable for the hubbub caused in Edenborough.

Now (to forebare for ever solittle of Iris Trees and Lili O'Ran-
gans), concerning the genesis of Harold or Humphrey Chimpden's
occupational agnomen (we are back in the presurnames prodro-
marith period, of course just when enos chalked halltraps) and
discarding once for all those theories from older sources which would
link him back with such pivotal ancestors as the Glues, the Gravys,
the Northeasts, the Ankers and the Earwickers of Sidlesham in the
Hundred of Manhood or proclaim him offsprout of vikings who
had founded wapentake and seddled hem in Herrick or Eric, the
best authenticated version, the Dumlat, read the Reading of Hofed-
ben-Edar, has it that it was this way. We are told how in the beginning it came to pass that like cabbaging Cincinnatus the grand
old gardener was saving daylight under his redwoodtree one sultry
sabbath afternoon, Hag Chivychas Eve, in prefall paradise peace
by following his plough for rootles in the rere garden of mobhouse,
ye olde marine hotel, when royalty was announced by runner to
have been pleased to have halted itself on the highroad along which
a leisureloving dogfox had cast followed, also at walking pace, by a
lady pack of cocker spaniels. Forgetful of all save his vassal's plain
fealty to the ethnarch Humphrey or Harold stayed not to yoke or
saddle but stumbled out hotface as he was (his sweatful bandanna
loose from his pocketcoat) hasting to the forecourts of his public
in topee, surcingle, solascarf and plaid, plus fours, puttees and bulldog boots ruddled cinnabar with flagrant marl, jingling his turnpike
keys and bearing aloft amid the fixed pikes of the hunting party a
high perch atop of which a flowerpot was fixed earthside hoist with
care. On his majesty, who was, or often feigned to be, noticeably
longsighted from green youth and had been meaning to inquire
what, in effect, had caused yon causeway to be thus potholed, asking
substitutionally to be put wise as to whether paternoster and silver

doctors were not now more fancied bait for lobstertrapping honest
blunt Haromphreyld answered in no uncertain tones very similarly with a fearless forehead: Naw, yer maggers, aw war jist a
cotchin on thon bluggy earwuggers. Our sailor king, who was drain-
ing a gugglet of obvious adamale, gift both and gorban, upon this,
ceasing to swallow, smiled most heartily beneath his walrus moustaches and indulging that none too genial humour which William
the Conk on the spindle side had inherited with the hereditary
whitelock and some shortfingeredness from his greataunt Sophy,
turned towards two of his retinue of gallowglasses, Michael, ethel-
ing lord of Leix and Offaly and the jubilee mayor of Drogheda,
Elcock, (the two scatterguns being Michael M. Manning, proto-
syndic of Waterford and an Italian excellency named Giubilei according to a later version cited by the learned scholarch Canavan of
Canmakenoise), in either case a triptychal religious family symbol-
ising puritas of doctrina, business per usuals and the purchypatch
of hamlock where the paddish preties grow and remarked dilsydul-
sily: Holybones of Saint Hubert how our red brother of Pourin-
grainia would audibly fume did he know that we have for surtrusty
bailiwick a turnpiker who is by turns a pikebailer no seldomer than
an earwigger! For he kinned Jom Pill with his court so gray and his
haunts in his house in the mourning. (One still hears that pebble
crusted laughta, japijap cheerycherrily, among the roadside tree the
lady Holmpatrick planted and still one feels the amossive silence of
the cladstone allegibelling: Ive mies outs ide Bourn.) Comes the
question are these the facts of his nominigentilisation as recorded
and accolated in both or either of the collateral andrewpaulmurphyc
narratives. Are those their fata which we read in sibylline between
the *fas* and its *nefas?* No dung on the road? And shall Nohomiah
be our place like? Yea, Mulachy our kingable khan? We shall perhaps not so soon see. Pinck poncks that bail for seeks alicence where
cumsceptres with scentaurs stay. Bear in mind, son of Hokmah, if
so be you have metheg in your midness, this man is mountain and
unto changeth doth one ascend. Heave we aside the fallacy, as puni-
cal as finikin, that it was not the king kingself but his inseparable
sisters, uncontrollable nighttalkers, Skertsiraizde with Donyahzade,
who afterwards, when the robberers shot up the socialights, came
down into the world as amusers and were staged by Madame Sudlow as Rosa and Lily Miskinguette in the pantalime that two pitts
paythronosed, Miliodorus and Galathee. The great fact emerges that
after that historic date all holographs so far exhumed initialled by

Haromphrey bear the sigla H.C.E. and while he was only and long
and always good Dook Umphrey for the hungerlean spalpeens of
Lucalizod and Chimbers to his cronies it was equally certainly a
pleasant turn of the populace which gave him as sense of those nor-
mative letters the nickname Here Comes Everybody. An imposing
everybody he always indeed looked, constantly the same as and
equal to himself and magnificently well worthy of any and all such
universalisation, every time he continually surveyed, amid vociferat-
ings from in front of *Accept these few nutties!* and *Take off that
white hat!,* relieved with *Stop his Grog* and *Put It in the Log* and
Loots in his (bassvoco) *Boots,* from good start to happy finish the
truly catholic assemblage gathered together in that king's treat house
of satin alustrelike above floats and footlights from their assbawl-
veldts and oxgangs unanimously to clapplaud (the inspiration of
his lifetime and the hits of their careers) Mr Wallenstein Washing-
ton Semperkelly's immergreen tourers in a command performance
by special request with the courteous permission for pious purposes
the homedromed and enliventh performance of the problem passion
play of the millentury, running strong since creation, *A Royal Divorce,* then near the approach towards the summit of its climax,
with ambitious interval band selections from *The Bo' Girl* and *The
Lily* on all horserie show command nights from his viceregal booth
(his bossaloner is ceilinged there a cuckoospit less eminent than
the redritualhoods of Maccabe and Cullen) where, a veritable
Napoleon the Nth, our worldstage's practical jokepiece and retired
cecelticocommediant in his own wise, this folksforefather all of the
time sat, having the entirety of his house about him, with the in-
variable broadstretched kerchief cooling his whole neck, nape and
shoulderblades and in a wardrobe panelled tuxedo completely
thrown back from a shirt well entitled a swallowall, on every point
far outstarching the laundered clawhammers and marbletopped
highboys of the pit stalls and early amphitheatre. The piece was
this: look at the lamps. The cast was thus: see under the clock.
Ladies circle: cloaks may be left. Pit, prommer and parterre, standing room only. Habituels conspicuously emergent.

A baser meaning has been read into these characters the literal
sense of which decency can safely scarcely hint. It has been blurt-
ingly bruited by certain wisecrackers (the stinks of Mohorat are
in the nightplots of the morning), that he suffered from a vile dis-
ease. Athma, unmanner them! To such a suggestion the one self-
respecting answer is to affirm that there are certain statements which

ought not to be, and one should like to hope to be able to add, ought not to be allowed to be made. Nor have his detractors, who, an imperfectly warmblooded race, apparently conceive him as a great white caterpillar capable of any and every enormity in the calendar recorded to the discredit of the Juke and Kellikek families, mended their case by insinuating that, alternately, he lay at one time under the ludicrous imputation of annoying Welsh fusiliers in the people's park. Hay, hay, hay! Hoq, hoq, hoq! Faun and Flora on the lea love that little old joq. To anyone who knew and loved the christlikeness of the big cleanminded giant H. C. Earwicker throughout his excellency long vicefreegal existence the mere suggestion of him as a lustsleuth nosing for trouble in a boobytrap rings particularly preposterous. Truth, beard on prophet, compels one to add that there is said to have been quondam (pfuit! pfuit!) some case of the kind implicating, it is interdum believed, a quidam (if he did not exist it would be necessary quoniam to invent him) abhout that time stambuling haround Dumbaling in leaky sneakers with his tarrk record who has remained topantically anonymos but (let us hue him Abdullah Gamellaxarksky) was, it is stated, posted at Mallon's at the instance of watch warriors of the vigilance committee and years afterwards, cries one even greater, Ibid, a commender of the frightful, seemingly, unto such as were sulhan sated, tropped head (pfiat! pfiat!) waiting his first of the month froods turn for thatt chopp pah kabbakks alicubi on the old house for the chargehard, Roche Haddocks off Hawkins Street. Lowe, you blondy liar, Gob scene you in the narked place and she what's edith ar home defileth these boyles! There's a cabful of bash indeed in the homeur of that meal. Slander, let it lie its flattest, has never been able to convict our good and great and no ordinary Southron Earwicker, that homogenius man, as a pious author called him, of any graver impropriety than that, advanced by some woodwards or regarders, who did not dare deny, the shomers, that they had, chin Ted, chin Tam, chinchin Taffyd, that day consumed their soul of the corn, of having behaved with ongentilmensky immodus opposite a pair of dainty maidservants in the swoolth of the rushy hollow whither, or so the two gown and pinners pleaded, dame nature in all innocency had spontaneously and about the same hour of the eventide sent them both but whose published combinations of silkinlaine testimonies are, where not dubiously pure, visibly divergent, as wapt from wept, on minor points touching the intimate nature of this, a first offence in vert or venison which was admittedly an incautious but, at its wildest, a partial exposure with such attenuating circumstances (garthen gaddeth green hwere sokeman brideth girling) as an abnormal Saint Swithin's summer and, (Jesses Rosasharon!) a ripe occasion to provoke it.

We can't do without them. Wives, rush to the restyours! Ofman will toman while led is the lol. Zessid's our kadem, villapleach, vollapluck. Fikup, for flesh nelly, el mundo nov, zole flen! If she's a lilyth, pull early! Pauline, allow! And malers abushed, keep black, keep black! Guiltless of much laid to him he was clearly for once at least he clearly expressed himself as being with still a trace of his erstwhile burr and hence it has been received of us that it is true. They tell the story (an amalgam as absorbing as calzium chloereydes and hydrophobe sponges could make it) how one happygogusty Ides-of-April morning (the anniversary, as it fell out, of his first assumption of his mirthday suit and rights in appurtenance to the confusioning of human races) ages and ages after the alleged misdemeanour when the tried friend of all creation, tigerwood roadstaff to his stay, was billowing across the wide expanse of our greatest park in his caoutchouc kepi and great belt and hideinsacks and his blaufunx fustian and ironsides jackboots and Bhagafat gaiters and his rubberised inverness, he met a cad with a pipe. The latter, the luciferant not the oriuolate (who, the odds are, is still berting dagabout in the same straw bamer, carryin his overgoat under his schulder, sheepside out, so as to look more like a coumfry gentleman and signing the pledge as gaily as you please) hardily accosted him with: Guinness thaw tool in jew me dinner ouzel fin? (a nice how-do-you-do in Poolblack at the time as some of our olddaisers may still tremblingly recall) to ask could he tell him how much a clock it was that the clock struck had he any idea by cock's luck as his watch was bradys. Hesitency was clearly to be evitated. Execration as cleverly to be honnisoid. The Earwicker of that spurring instant, realising on fundamental liberal principles the supreme importance, nexally and noxally, of physical life (the nearest help relay being pingping K. O. Sempatrick's Day and the fenian rising) and unwishful as he felt of being hurled into eternity right then, plugged by a softnosed bullet from the sap, halted, quick on the draw, and replyin that he was feelin tipstaff, cue, prodooced from his gunpocket his Jurgensen's shrapnel waterbury, ours by communionism, his by usucapture, but, on the same stroke, hearing above the skirling of harsh Mother East old Fox Goodman, the bellmaster, over the wastes to south, at work upon the ten ton tonuant thunderous

tenor toller in the speckled church (Couhounin's call!) told the
inquiring kidder, by Jehova, it was twelve of em sidereal and tankard
time, adding, buttall, as he bended deeply with smoked sardinish
breath to give more pondus to the copperstick he presented, (though
this seems in some cumfusium with the chapstuck ginger which, as
being of sours, acids, salts, sweets and bitters compompounded, we
know him to have used as chawchaw for bone, muscle, blood, flesh
and vimvital,) that whereas the hakusay accusation againstm had
been made, what was known in high quarters as was stood stated
in Morganspost, by a creature in youman form who was quite beneath parr and several degrees lower than yore triplehydrad snake.
In greater support of his word (it, quaint anticipation of a famous
phrase, has been reconstricted out of oral style into the verbal for
all time with ritual rhythmics, in quiritary quietude, and toosam-
menstucked from successive accounts by Noah Webster in the re-
daction known as the Sayings Attributive of H. C. Earwicker, prize
on schillings, postlots free), the flaxen Gygas tapped his chronome-
trum drumdrum and, now standing full erect, above the ambijacent
floodplain, scene of its happening, with one Berlin gauntlet chop-
stuck in the hough of his ellboge (by ancientest signlore his gesture meaning: Ⅎ!) pointed at an angle of thirty-two degrees towards
his *duc de Fer's* overgrown milestone as fellow to his gage and after
a rendypresent pause averred with solemn emotion's fire: Shsh shake,
co-comeraid! Me only, them five ones, he is equal combat. I have
won straight. Hence my nonation wide hotel and creamery estab-
lishments which for the honours of our mewmew mutual daughters,
credit me, I am woowoo willing to take my stand, sir, upon the monument, that sign of our ruru redemption, any hygienic day to this
hour and to make my hoath to my sinnfinners, even if I get life for
it, upon the Open Bible and before the Great Taskmaster's (I lift
my hat!) and in the presence of the Deity Itself andwell of Bishop
and Mrs Michan of High Church of England as of all such of said
my immediate withdwellers and of every living sohole in every corner wheresoever of this globe in general which useth of my British
to my backbone tongue and commutative justice that there is not
one tittle of truth, allow me to tell you, in that purest of fibfib
fabrications.

Gaping Gill, swift to mate errthors, stern to checkself, (diag-
nosing through eustacetube that it was to make with a markedly
postpuberal hypertituitary type of Heidelberg mannleich cavern
ethics) lufted his slopingforward, bad Sweatagore good mur-

rough and dublnotch on to it as he was greedly obliged, and like
a sensible ham, with infinite tact in the delicate situation seen
the touchy nature of its perilous theme, thanked um for guilders
received and time of day (not a little token abock all the same that
that was owl the God's clock it was) and, upon humble duty to greet
his Tyskminister and he shall gildthegap Gaper and thee his
a mouldy voids, went about his business, whoever it was, saluting
corpses, as a metter of corse (one could hound him out had one
hart to for the monticules of scalp and dandruff droppings blaze
his trail) accompanied by his trusty snorler and his permanent reflection, verbigracious; I have met with you, bird, too late, or if not,
too worm and early: and with tag for ildiot repeated in his second-
mouth language as many of the bigtimer's verbaten words which he
could balbly call to memory that same kveldeve, ere the hour of the
twattering of bards in the twitterlitter between Druidia and the
Deepsleep Sea, when suppertide and souvenir to Charlatan Mall
jointly kem gently and along the quiet darkenings of Grand and
Royal, ff, flitmansfluh, and, kk, 't crept i' hedge whenas to many a
softongue's pawkytalk mude unswer u sufter poghyogh, Arvanda always aquiassent, while, studying castelles in the blowne and studding cowshots over the noran, he spat in careful convertedness a
musaic dispensation about his *hearthstone,* if you please, (Irish sa-
liva, *mawshe dho hole,* but would a respectable prominently connected fellow of Iro-European ascendances with welldressed ideas
who knew the correct thing such as Mr Shallwesigh or Mr Shall-
welaugh expectorate after such a callous fashion, no thank yous!
when he had his belcher *spuckertuck* in his pucket, pthuck?) muse-
fed with his thockits after having supped of the dish sot and pottage
which he snobbishly dabbed Peach Bombay (it is rawly only
Lukanpukan pilzenpie which she knows which senaffed and pibered
him), a supreme of excelling peas, balled under minnshogue's milk
into whitemalt winesour, a proviant the little bilker hoarsely relished,
chaff it, in the snevel season, being as fain o't as your rat wi'fennel;
and on this celebrating occasion of the happy escape, for a crowning
of pot valiance, this regional platter, benjamin of bouillis, with a
spolish olive to middlepoint its zaynith, was marrying itself (porko-
graso!) erebusqued very deluxiously with a bottle of Phenice-Bruerie
'98, followed for second nuptials by a Piessporter, Grand Cur, of
both of which cherished tablelights (though humble the bounquet
'tis a leaman's farewell) he obdurately sniffed the cobwebcrusted
corks.

Our cad's bit of strife (knee Bareniece Maxwelton) with a quick
ear for spittoons (as the aftertale hath it) glaned up as usual with
dumbestic husbandry (no persicks and armelians for thee, Pome-
ranzia!) but, slipping the clav in her claw, broke of the matter
among a hundred and eleven others in her usual curtsey (how faint
these first vhespers womanly are, a secret pispigliando, amad
the lavurdy den of their manfolker!) the next night nudge one as
was Hegesippus over a hup a' chee, her eys dry and small and speech
thicklish because he appeared a funny colour like he couldn't stood
they old hens no longer, to her particular reverend, the director,
whom she had been meaning in her mind primarily to speak with
(hosch, intra! jist a timblespoon!) trusting, between cuppled lips
and annie lawrie promises (mighshe never have Esnekerry pudden
come Hunanov for her pecklapitschens!) that the gossiple so delivered in his epistolear, buried teatoastally in their Irish stew would
go no further than his jesuit's cloth, yet (in vinars venitas! volatiles
valetotum!) it was this overspoiled priest Mr Browne, disguised as a
vincentian, who, when seized of the facts, was overheard, in his
secondary personality as a Nolan and underreared, poul soul, by
accident—if, that is, the incident it was an accident for here
the ruah of Ecclectiastes of Hippo outpuffs the writress of Havvah-
ban-Annah—to pianissime a slightly varied version of Crookedribs
confidentials, (what Mère Aloyse said but for Jesuphine's sake!)
hands between hahands, in fealty sworn (my bravor best! my
fraur!) and, to the strains of *The Secret of Her Birth*, hushly pierce
the rubiend aurellum of one Philly Thurnston, a layteacher of rural
science and orthophonethics of a nearstout figure and about the
middle of his forties during a priestly flutter for safe and sane bets
at the hippic runfields of breezy Baldoyle on a date (W. W. goes
through the card) easily capable of rememberance by all pickersup
of events national and Dublin details, the doubles of Perkin and
Paullock, peer and prole, when the classic Encourage Hackney
Plate was captured by two noses in a stablecloth finish, ek and nek,
some and none, evelo nevelo, from the cream colt Bold Boy Cromwell after a clever getaway by Captain Chaplain Blount's roe hinny
Saint Dalough, Drummer Coxon, nondepict third, at breakneck
odds, thanks to you great little, bonny little, portey little, Winny
Widger! you're all their nappies! who in his neverrip mud and pur-
pular cap was surely leagues unlike any other phantomweight that
ever toppitt our timber maggies.

'Twas two pisononse Timcoves (the wetter is pest, the renns are

overt and come and the voax of the turfur is hurled on our lande)
of the name of Treacle Tom as was just out of pop following the
theft of a leg of Kehoe, Donnelly and Packenham's Finnish pork
and his own blood and milk brother Frisky Shorty, (he was, to be
exquisitely punctilious about them, both shorty and frisky) a tip-
ster, come off the hulks, both of them awful poor, what was out on
the bumaround for an oofbird game for a jimmy o'goblin or a small
thick un as chanced, while the Seaforths was making the colleen-
bawl, to ear the passon in the motor clobber make use of his law
language (Edzo, Edzo on), touchin the case of Mr Adams what was
in all the sundays about it which he was rubbing noses with and
having a gurgle off his own along of the butty bloke in the specs.

This Treacle Tom to whom reference has been made had been
absent from his usual wild and woolly haunts in the land of counties
capalleens for some time previous to that (he was, in fact, in the
habit of frequenting common lodginghouses where he slept in a
nude state, hailfellow with meth, in strange men's cots) but on
racenight, blotto after divers tots of hell fire, red biddy, bull dog,
blue ruin and creeping jenny, Eglandine's choicest herbage, supplied
by the Duck and Doggies, the Galopping Primrose, Brigid Brewster's, the Cock, the Postboy's Horn, the Little Old Man's and All
Swell That Aimswell, the Cup and the Stirrup, he sought his well-
warmed leababobed in a housingroom Abide With Oneanother at
Block W.W., (why didn't he back it?) Pump Court, The Liberties,
and, what with moltapuke on voltapuke, resnored alcoh alcoho al-
coherently to the burden of *I come, my horse delayed,* nom num,
the substance of the tale of the evangelical bussybozzy and the
rusinurbean (the 'girls' he would keep calling them for the collarette
and skirt, the sunbonnet and carnation) in parts (it seemed he was
before the eyots of martas or otherwales the thirds of fossilyears, he
having beham with katya when lavinias had her mens lease to sea
in a psumpship doodly show whereat he was looking for fight niggers
with whilde roarses) oft in the chilly night (the metagonistic! the
epickthalamorous!) during uneasy slumber in their hearings of a
small and stonybroke cashdraper's executive, Peter Cloran (discharged), O'Mara, an exprivate secretary of no fixed abode (locally
known as Mildew Lisa), who had passed several nights, funnish
enough, in a doorway under the blankets of homelessness on the
bunk of iceland, pillowed upon the stone of destiny colder than
man's knee or woman's breast, and Hosty, (no slouch of a name),
an illstarred beachbusker, who, sans rootie and sans scrapie, sus-

picioning as how he was setting on a twoodstool on the verge of
selfabyss, most starved, with melancholia over everything in general,
(night birman, you served him with natigal's nano!) had been tow-
head tossing on his shakedown, devising ways and manners of
means, of what he loved to ifidalicence somehow or other in the
nation getting a hold of some chap's parabellum in the hope of taking a wing sociable and lighting upon a sidewheel dive somewhere
off the Dullkey Downlairy and Bleakrooky tramaline where he could
throw true and go and blow the sibicidal napper off himself for two
bits to boldywell baltitude in the peace and quitybus of a one sure
shot bottle, he after having being trying all he knew with the lady's
help of Madam Gristle for upwards of eighteen calanders to get out
of Sir Patrick Dun's, through Sir Humphrey Jervis's and into the
Saint Kevin's bed in the Adelaide's hosspittles (from these incurable
welleslays among those uncarable wellasdays through Sant Iago by
his cocklehat, good Lazar, deliver us!) without after having been
able to jerrywangle it anysides. Lisa O'Deavis and Roche Mongan
(who had so much incommon, epipsychidically; if the phrase be
permitted *hostis et odor insuper petroperfractus*) as an understood
thing slept their sleep of the swimborne in the one sweet undulant
mother of tumblerbunks with Hosty just how the shavers in the
shaw the yokels in the yoats or, well, the wasters in the wilde, and the
bustling tweeny-dawn-of-all-works (meed of anthems here we pant!)
had not been many jiffies furbishing potlids, doorbrasses, scholars'
applecheeks and linkboy's metals when, ashhopperminded like no
fella he go make bakenbeggfuss longa white man, the rejuvenated
busker (for after a goodnight's rave and rumble and a shinkhams top-
morning with his coexes he was not the same man) and his broadawake bedroom suite (our boys, as our Byron called them) were up
and ashuffle from the hogshome they lovenaned The Barrel, cross
Ebblinn's chilled hamlet (thrie routes and restings on their then
superficies curiously correspondant with those linea and puncta
where our tubenny habenny metro maniplumbs below the ober-
flake underrails and stations at this time of riding) to the thrum-
mings of a crewth fiddle which, cremoaning and cronauning, levey
grevey, witty and wevey, appy, leppy and playable, caressed the
ears of the subjects of King Saint Finnerty the Festive who, in brick
homes of their own and in their flavory fraiseberry beds, heeding
hardly cry of honeyman, soed lavender or foyneboyne salmon alive,
with their priggish mouths all open for the larger appraisiation of
this longawaited Messiagh of roaratorios, were only halfpast

atsweeeep and after a brisk pause at a pawnbroking establishment
for the prothetic purpose of redeeming the songster's truly admirable
false teeth and a prolonged visit to a house of call at Cujas Place,
fizz, the Old Sots' Hole in the parish of Saint Cecily within the
liberty of Ceolmore not a thousand or one national leagues, that
was, by Griffith's valuation, from the site of the statue of Primewer
Glasstone setting a match to the march of a maker (last of the stew-
ards peut-être), where, the tale rambles along, the trio of whack-
folthediddlers was joined by a further—intentions—apply—tomorrow casual and a decent sort of the hadbeen variety who had just
been touching the weekly insult, phewit, and all figblabbers (who
saith of noun?) had stimulants in the shape of gee and gees stood
by the damn decent sort after which stag luncheon and a few ones
more just to celebrate yesterday, flushed with their firestuffostered
friendship, the rascals came out of the licensed premises, (Browne's
first, the small p.s. ex-ex-executive capahand in their sad rear like
a lady's postscript: I want money. Pleasend), wiping their laugh-
leaking lipes on their sleeves, how the bouckaleens shout their roscan
generally (seinn fion, seinn fion's araun.) and the rhymers' world
was with reason the richer for a wouldbe ballad, to the balledder
of which the world of cumannity singing owes a tribute for having
placed on the planet's melomap his lay of the vilest bogeyer but
most attractionable avatar the world has ever had to explain for.

This, more krectly lubeen or fellow — me — lieder was first poured
forth where Riau Liviau riots and col de Houdo humps, under
the shadow of the monument of the shouldhavebeen legis-
lator (Eleutheriodendron! Spare, woodmann, spare!) to an overflow
meeting of all the nations in Lenster fullyfilling the visional area
and, as a singleminded supercrowd, easily representative, what with
masks, whet with faces, of all sections and cross sections (wineshop
and cocoahouse poured out to brim up the broaching) of our liffey-
side people (to omit to mention of the mainland minority and such
as had wayfared *via* Watling, Ernin, Icknild and Stane, in chief
a halted cockney car with its quotal of Hardmuth's hacks, a northern
tory, a southern whig, an eastanglian chronicler and a landwester
guardian) ranging from slips of young dublinos from Cutpurse Row
having nothing better to do than walk about with their hands in
their kneepants, sucking airwhackers, weedulicet, jumbobricks,
side by side with truant officers, three woollen balls and poplin in
search of a croust of pawn to busy professional gentlemen, a brace

of palesmen with dundrearies, nooning toward Daly's, fresh from snipehitting and mallardmissing on Rutland heath, exchanging cold sneers, massgoing ladies from Hume Street in their chairs, the bearers baited, some wandering hamalags out of the adjacent cloverfields of Mosse's Gardens, an oblate father from Skinner's Alley, bricklayers, a fleming, in tabinet fumant, with spouse and dog, an aged hammersmith who had some chisellers by the hand, a bout of cudgel players, not a few sheep with the braxy, two bluecoat scholars, four broke gents out of Simpson's on the Rocks, a portly and a pert still tassing Turkey Coffee and orange shrub in tickeyes door, Peter Pim and Paul Fry and then Elliot and, O, Atkinson, suffering hell's delights from the blains of their annuitants' acorns not forgetting a deuce of dianas ridy for the hunt, a particularist prebendary pondering on the roman easter, the tonsure question and greek uniates, plunk em, a lace lappet head or two or three or four from a window, and so on down to a few good old souls, who, as they were juiced after taking their pledge over at the uncle's place, were evidently under the spell of liquor, from the wake of Tarry the Tailor a fair girl, a jolly postboy thinking off three flagons and one, a plumodrole, a half sir from the weaver's almshouse who clings and clings and chatchatchat clings to her, a wholedam's cloudhued pittycoat, as child, as curiolater, as Caoch O'Leary. The wararrow went round, so it did, (a nation wants a gaze) and the ballad, in the felibrine trancoped metre affectioned by Taiocebo in his *Casudas de Poulichinello Artahut,* stumpstampaded on to a slip of blancovide and headed by an excessively rough and red woodcut, privately printed at the rimepress of Delville, soon fluttered its secret on white highway and brown byway to the rose of the winds and the blew of the gaels, from archway to lattice and from black hand to pink ear, village crying to village, through the five pussyfours green of the united states of Scotia Picta—and he who denays it, may his hairs be rubbed in dirt! To the added strains (so peacifold) of his majesty the flute, that onecrooned king of inscrewments, Piggott's purest, *ciello alsoliuto,* which Mr Delaney (Mr Delacey?), horn, anticipating a perfect downpour of plaudits among the rapsods, piped out of his decentsoort hat, looking still more like his purseyful namesake as men of Gaul noted, but before of to sputabout, the snowy crested curl amoist the leader's wild and moulting hair, 'Ductor' Hitchcock hoisted his fezzy fuzz at bludgeon's height signum to his companions of the chalice for the Loud Fellow, boys' and *silen-*

tium in curia! (our maypole once more where he rose of old) and the canto was chantied there chorussed and christened where by the old tollgate, Saint Annona's Street and Church.

And around the lawn the rann it rann and this is the rann that Hosty made. Spoken. Boyles and Cahills, Skerretts and Pritchards, viersified and piersified may the treeth we tale of live in stoney. Here line the refrains of. Some vote him Vike, some mote him Mike, some dub him Llyn and Phin while others hail him Lug Bug Dan Lop, Lex, Lax, Gunne or Guinn. Some apt him Arth, some bapt him Barth, Coll, Noll, Soll, Will, Weel, Wall but I parse him Persse O'Reilly else he's called no name at all. Together. Arrah, leave it to Hosty, frosty Hosty, leave it to Hosty for he's the mann to rhyme the rann, the rann, the rann, the king of all ranns. Have you here? (Some ha) Have we where? (Some hant) Have you hered? (Others do) Have we whered? (Others dont) It's cumming, it's brumming! The clip, the clop! (All cla) Glass crash. The (klikkaklakkaklaskaklopatzklatschabattacreppycrottygraddaghsemmihsammihnouithappluddyappladdypkonpkot!).

{ *Ardite, arditi!*
{ Music cue.

"THE BALLAD OF PERSSE O'REILLY."

Have you heard of one Hump-ty Dump-ty how he
fell with a roll and a rum-ble and curled up like Lord O-la-fa
Crum-ple by the butt of the Mag-a-zine Wall of the
Mag-a-zine Wall Hump, hel-met and all Da Capo

Have you heard of one Humpty Dumpty
How he fell with a roll and a rumble
And curled up like Lord Olofa Crumple
By the butt of the Magazine Wall,
  (Chorus) Of the Magazine Wall,
    Hump, helmet and all?

He was one time our King of the Castle
Now he's kicked about like a rotten old parsnip.
And from Green street he'll be sent by order of His Worship
To the penal jail of Mountjoy
      (Chorus) To the jail of Mountjoy!
           Jail him and joy.

He was fafafather of all schemes for to bother us
Slow coaches and immaculate contraceptives for the populace,
Mare's milk for the sick, seven dry Sundays a week,
Openair love and religion's reform,
      (Chorus) And religious reform,
           Hideous in form.

Arrah, why, says you, couldn't he manage it?
I'll go bail, my fine dairyman darling,
Like the bumping bull of the Cassidys
All your butter is in your horns.
      (Chorus) His butter is in his horns.
           Butter his horns!

(Repeat) Hurrah there, Hosty, frosty Hosty, change that shirt on ye,
Rhyme the rann, the king of all ranns!

           Balbaccio, balbuccio!
We had chaw chaw chops, chairs, chewing gum, the chickenpox
                            [and china chambers
Universally provided by this soffsoaping salesman.
Small wonder He'll Cheat E'erawan our local lads nicknamed him
When Chimpden first took the floor
      (Chorus) With his bucketshop store
           Down Bargainweg, Lower.

So snug he was in his hotel premises sumptuous
But soon we'll bonfire all his trash, tricks and trumpery
And'tis short till sheriff Clancy'll be winding up his unlimited
                            [company
With the bailiff's bom at the door,
      (Chorus) Bimbam at the door.
           Then he'll bum no more.

Sweet bad luck on the waves washed to our island
The hooker of that hammerfast viking
And Gall's curse on the day when Eblana bay
Saw his black and tan man-o'-war.
    (Chorus) Saw his man-o'-war.
        On the harbour bar.

Where from? roars Poolbeg. Cookingha'pence, he bawls Donnez-
           [moi scampitle, wick an wipin'fampiny
Fingal Mac Oscar Onesine Bargearse Boniface
Thok's min gammelhole Norveegickers moniker
Og as ay are at gammelhore Norveegickers cod.
    (Chorus) A Norwegian camel old cod.
        He is, begod.

Lift it, Hosty, lift it, ye devil ye! up with the rann, the rhyming
           [rann!

It was during some fresh water garden pumping
Or, according to the *Nursing Mirror,* while admiring the monkeys
That our heavyweight heathen Humpharey
Made bold a maid to woo
    (Chorus) Woohoo, what'll she doo!
        The general lost her maidenloo!

He ought to blush for himself, the old hayheaded philosopher,
For to go and shove himself that way on top of her.
Begob, he's the crux of the catalogue
Of our antediluvial zoo,
    (Chorus) Messrs. Billing and Coo.
        Noah's larks, good as noo.

He was joulting by Wellinton's monument
Our rotorious hippopopotamuns
When some bugger let down the backtrap of the omnibus
And he caught his death of fusiliers,
    (Chorus) With his rent in his rears.
        Give him six years.

'Tis sore pity for his innocent poor children
But look out for his missus legitimate!

When that frew gets a grip of old Earwicker
Won't there be earwigs on the green?
    (Chorus) Big earwigs on the green,
           The largest ever you seen.

Suffoclose! Shikespower! Seudodanto! Anonymoses!

Then we'll have a free trade Gaels' band and mass meeting
For to sod the brave son of Scandiknavery.
And we'll bury him down in Oxmanstown
Along with the devil and Danes,
    (Chorus) With the deaf and dumb Danes,
           And all their remains.

And not all the king's men nor his horses
Will resurrect his corpus
For there's no true spell in Connacht or hell
    (bis) That's able to raise a Cain.

Chest Cee! 'Sdense! Corpo di barragio! you spoof of visibility in a freakfog, of mixed sex cases among goats, hill cat and plain mousey, Bigamy Bob and his old Shanvocht! The Blackfriars treacle plaster outrage be liddled! Therewith was released in that kingsrick of Humidia a poisoning volume of cloud barrage indeed. Yet all they who heard or redelivered are now with that family of bards and Vergobretas himself and the crowd of Caraculacticors as much no more as be they not yet now or had they then notever been. Canbe in some future we shall presently here amid those zouave players of Inkermann the mime mumming the mick and his nick miming their maggies, Hilton St Just (Mr Frank Smith), Ivanne Ste Austelle (Mr J. F. Jones), Coleman of Lucan taking four parts, a choir of the O'Daley O'Doyles doublesixing the chorus in *Fenn Mac Call and the Serven Feeries of Loch Neach, Galloper Troppler and Hurleyquinn* the zitherer of the past with his merrymen all, zimzim, zimzim. Of the persins sin this Eyrawyggla saga (which, thorough readable to int from and, is from tubb to buttom all falsetissues, antilibellous and nonactionable and this applies to its whole wholume) of poor Osti-Fosti, described as quite a musical genius in a small way and the owner of an exceedingly niced ear, with tenorist voice to match, not alone, but a very major poet of the poorly meritary order (he began Tuonisonian but worked his passage up as far as the we-all-hang-together Animandovites) no one end is known. If they whistled him before he had curtains up they are whistling him still after his curtain's doom's doom. *Ei fù*. His husband, poor old A'Hara (Okaroff?) crestfallen by things and down at heels at the time, they squeak, accepted the (Zassnoch!) ardree's shilling at the conclusion of the Crimean war and, having flown his wild geese, alohned in crowds to warnder on like Shuley Luney, enlisted in Tyrone's horse, the Irish whites, and soldiered a bit with Wolsey under the

assumed name of Blanco Fusilovna Bucklovitch (spurious) after
which the cawer and the marble halls of Pump Court Columbarium,
the home of the old seakings, looked upon each other and queth
their haven evermore for it transpires that on the other side of the
water it came about that on the field of Vasileff's Cornix inauspi-
ciously with his unit he perished, saying, this papal leafless to old
chap give, rawl chawclates for mouther-in-louth. *Booil.* Poor old dear
Paul Horan, to satisfy his literary as well as his criminal aspirations,
at the suggestion thrown out by the doomster in loquacity lunacy,
so says the Dublin Intelligence, was thrown into a Ridley's for in-
mates in the northern counties. Under the name of Orani he may
have been the utility man of the troupe capable of sustaining long
parts at short notice. He was. Sordid Sam, a dour decent deblancer,
the unwashed, haunted always by his ham, the unwished, at a word
from Israfel the Summoner, passed away painlessly after life's
upsomdowns one hallowe'en night, ebbrous and in the state of nature, propelled from Behind into the great Beyond by footblows
coulinclouted upon his oyster and atlas on behanged and behooved
and behicked and behulked of his last fishandblood bedscrappers, a
Northwegian and his mate of the Sheawolving class. Though the
last straw glimt his baring this stage thunkhard is said (the pitfallen
gagged him as 'Promptboxer') to have solemnly said — as had the
brief thot but fell in till his head like a bass dropt neck fust in till a
bung crate (cogged!): Me drames, O'Loughlins, has come through!
Now let the centuple celves of my egourge as Micholas de Cusack
calls them, — of all of whose I in my hereinafter of course by recourse demission me — by the coincidance of their contraries re-
amalgamerge in that indentity of undiscernibles where the Baxters
and the Fleshmans may they cease to bidivil uns and (but
at this poingt though the iron thrust of his cockspurt start might
have prepared us we are wellnigh stinkpotthered by the mustard-
punge in the tailend) this outandin brown candlestock melt Nolan's
into peese! *Han var.* Disliken as he was to druriodrama, her wife
Langley, the prophet, and the decentest dozendest short of a frusker
whoever stuck his spickle through his spoke, disappeared, (in which
toodooing he has taken all the French leaves unveilable out of
Calomnequiller's Pravities) from the sourface of this earth, that
austral plain he had transmaried himself to, so entirely spoorlessly
(the mother of the book with a dustwhisk tabularasing his obliteration done upon her involucrum) as to tickle the speculative to all
but opine (since the Levey who might have been Langley may have

really been a redivivus of paganinism or a volunteer Vousden) that
the hobo (who possessed a large amount of the humoresque) had
transtuled his funster's latitat to its finsterest interrimost. *Bhi she.*
Again, if Father San Browne, tea and toaster to that quaintesttest
of yarnspinners is Padre Don Bruno, treu and troster to the queen
of Iar-Spain, was the reverend, the sodality director, that eupeptic
viceflayer, a barefaced carmelite, to whose palpitating pulpit (which
of us but remembers the rarevalent and hornerable Fratomistor Naw-
lanmore and Brawne.) sinning society sirens (see the [Roman Cath-
olic] presspassim) fortunately became so enthusiastically attached
and was an objectionable ass who very occasionally cockaded a raf-
fles ticket on his hat which he wore all to one side like the hangle
of his pan (if Her Elegance saw him she'd have the canary!) and
was semiprivately convicted of malpractices with his hotwashed ta-
bleknife (glossing over the cark in his pocket) that same snob of
the Dunhill, fully several yearschaums riper, encountered by the
General on that redletter morning or maynoon jovesday and were
they? *Fuitfuit.*

When Phishlin Phil wants throws his lip 'tis pholly to be fortune
flonting and whoever's gone to mix Hotel by the salt say water there's
nix to nothing we can do for he's never again to sea. It is nebuless
an autodidact fact of the commonest that the shape of the average
human cloudyphiz, whereas sallow has long daze faded, frequently
altered its ego with the possing of the showers (Not original!).
Whence it is a slopperish matter, given the wet and low visibility
(since in this scherzarade of one's thousand one nightinesses that
sword of certainty which would indentifide the body never falls)
to idendifine the individuone in scratch wig, squarecuts, stock lava-
leer, regattable oxeter, baggy pants and shufflers (he is often alluded
to as Slypatrick, the llad in the llane) with already an incipience
(lust!) in the direction of area baldness (one is continually first-
meeting with odd sorts of others at all sorts of ages!) who was
asked by free boardschool shirkers in drenched coats overawall, Will,
Conn and Otto, to tell them overagait, Vol, Pov and Dev, that
fishabed ghoatstory of the haardly creditable edventyres of the Hab-
erdasher, the two Curchies and the three Enkelchums in their Bearskin ghoats! Girles and jongers, but he has changed alok syne
Thorkill's time! Ya, da, tra, gathery, pimp, shesses, shossafat, okode-
boko, nine! Those many warts, those slummy patches, halfsinster
wrinkles, (what has come over the face on wholebroader E?), and

(shrine of Mount Mu save us!) the large fungopark he has grown!
Drink!

Sport's a common thing. It was the Lord's own day for damp (to
wait for a postponed regatta's eventualising is not of Battlecock Shet-
tledore - Juxta - Mare only) and the request for a fully armed
explanation was put (in Loo of Pat) to the porty (a native of the sis-
terisle — Meathman or Meccan? — by his brogue, exrace eyes, lokil
calour and lucal odour which are said to have been average clown-
turkish (though the capelist's voiced nasal liquids and the way he
sneezed at zees haul us back to the craogs and bryns of the Silurian
Ordovices) who, the lesser pilgrimage accomplished, had made,
pats' and pigs' older inselt, the southeast bluffs of the stranger step-
shore, a *regifugium persecutorum*, hence hindquarters) as he paused
at even chime for some or so minutes (hit the pipe, dannyboy! Time
to won, barmon. I'll take ten to win.) amid the devil's one duldrum
(Apple by her blossom window and Charlotte at her toss panomancy
his sole admirers, his only tearts in store) for a fragrend culubosh
during his weekend pastime of executing with Anny Oakley dead-
liness (the consummatory pairs of provocatives, of which remained
provokingly but two, the ones he fell for, Lili and Tutu, cork em!)
empties which had not very long before contained Reid's family
(you ruad that before, soaky, but all the bottles in sodemd histry will
not soften your bloodathirst!) stout. Having reprimed his repeater
and resiteroomed his timespiece His Revenances, with still a life
or two to spare for the space of his occupancy of a world at a time,
rose to his feet and there, far from Tolkaheim, in a quiet English
garden (commonplace!), since known as Whiddington Wild, his
simple intensive curolent vocality, my dearbraithers, my most dear-
brathairs, as he, so is a supper as is a sipper, spake of the One and
told of the Compassionate, called up before the triad of precoxious
scaremakers (scoretaking: Spegulo ne helpas al malbellulo, Mi
Kredas ke vi estas prava, Via dote la vizago rispondas fraulino) the
now to ushere mythical habiliments of Our Farfar and Arthor of
our doyne.

Television kills telephony in brothers' broil. Our eyes demand their
turn. Let them be seen! And wolfbone balefires blaze the trailmost
if only that Mary Nothing may burst her bibby buckshee. When
they set fire then she's got to glow so we may stand some chances of
warming to what every soorkabatcha, tum or hum, would like to
know. The first Humphrey's latitudinous baver with puggaree behind, (calaboose belong bigboss belong Kang the Toll) his fourin-

hand bow, his elbaroom surtout, the refaced unmansionables of gin-
gerine hue, the state slate umbrella, his gruff woolselywellesly with
the finndrinn knopfs and the gauntlet upon the hand which in an
hour not for him solely evil had struck down the might he might-
havebeen d'Esterre of whom his nation seemed almost already to be
about to have need. Then, stealing his thunder, but in the befitting
legomena of the smaller country, (probable words, possibly said, of
field family gleaming) a bit duskish and flavoured with a smile, seein
as ow his thoughts consisted chiefly of the cheerio, he aptly sketched
for our soontobe second parents (sukand see whybe!) the touching
seene. The solence of that stilling! Here one might a fin fell. Boom-
ster rombombonant! It scenes like a landescape from Wildu Pic-
turescu or some seem on some dimb Arras, dumb as Mum's mutyness,
this mimage of the seventyseventh kusin of kristansen is odable to
os across the wineless Ere no œdor nor mere eerie nor liss potent of
suggestion than in the tales of the tingmount. (Prigged!)

And there oftafter, jauntyjogging, on an Irish visavis, insteadily
with shoulder to shoulder Jehu will tell to Christianier, saint to sage,
the humphriad of that fall and rise while daisy winks at her pinker
sister among the tussocks and the copoll between the shafts mocks
the couple on the car. And as your who may look like how on the
owther side of his big belttry your tyrs and cloes your noes and para-
digm maymay rererise in eren. Follow we up his whip vindicative.
Thurston's! Lo bebold! *La arboro, lo petrusu.* The augustan peace-
betothem oaks, the monolith rising stark from the moonlit pinebar-
ren. In all fortitudinous ajaxious rowdinoisy tenuacity. The angelus
hour with ditchers bent upon their farm usetensiles, the soft belling
of the fallow deers (*doerehmoose genuane!*) advertising their milky
approach as midnight was striking the hours (*letate!*), and how
brightly the great tribune outed the sharkskin smokewallet (imitation!) from his frock, kippers, and by Joshua, he tips un a topping
swank cheroot, none of your swellish soide, quoit the reverse, and
how manfally he says, pluk to pluk and lekan for lukan, he was to
just pluggy well suck that brown boyo, my son, and spend a whole
half hour in Havana. Sorer of the kreeksmen, would not thore be
old high gothsprogue! Wherefore he met Master, he mean to say,
he do, sire, bester of redpublicans, at Eagle Cock Hostel on Lorenzo
Tooley street and how he wished his Honour the bannocks of Gort
and Morya and Bri Head and Puddyrick, yore Loudship, and a
starchboxsitting in the pit of his St Tomach's, — a strange wish for
you, my friend, and it would poleaxe your sonson's grandson utterly

though your own old sweatandswear floruerunts heaved it hoch many as the times, when they were turrified by the hitz.

Chee chee cheers for Upkingbilly and crow cru cramwells Downaboo! Hup, boys, and hat him! See! Oilbeam they're lost we've found rerembrandtsers, their hours to date link these heirs to here but wowhere are those yours of Yestersdays? Farseeingetherich and Poolaulwoman Charachthercuss and his Ann van Vogt. D.e.e.d! Edned, ended or sleeping soundlessly? Favour with your tongues! *Intendite!*

Any dog's life you list you may still hear them at it, like sixes and seventies as eversure as Halley's comet, ulemamen, sobranjewomen, storthingboys and dumagirls, as they pass its bleak and bronze portal of your Casaconcordia: Huru more Nee, minny frickans? Hwoorledes har Dee det? Losdoor onleft mladies, cue. Millecientotrigintadue scudi. Tippoty, kyrie, tippoty. Cha kai rotty kai makkar, sahib? Despenseme Usted, senhor, en son succo, sabez. O thaw bron orm, A'Cothraige, thinkinthou gaily? Lick-Pa-flai-hai-pa-Pa-li-si-lang-lang. Epi alo, ecou, Batiste, tuvavnr dans Lptit boing going. Ismeme de bumbac e meias de portocallie. O.O. Os pipos mios es demasiada gruarso por O piccolo pocchino. Wee fee? Ung duro. Kocshis, szabad? Mercy, and you? Gomagh, thak.

And, Cod, says he with mugger's tears: Would you care to know the prise of a liard? Maggis, nick your nightynovel! Mass Travener's at the mike again! And that bag belly is the buck to goat it! Meggeg, m'gay chapjappy fellow, I call our univalse to witness, as sicker as moyliffey eggs is known by our good househalters from yorehunderts of mamooth to be which they commercially are in ahoy high British quarters (conventional!) my guesthouse and cowhaendel credits will immediately stand ohoh open as straight as that neighbouring monument's fabrication before the hygienic gllll (this was where the reverent sabboth and bottlebreaker with firbalk forthstretched touched upon his tricoloured boater, which he uplifted by its pickledhoopy (he gave Stetson one and a penny for it) whileas oleaginosity of ancestralolosis sgocciolated down the both pendencies of his mutsohito liptails (Sencapetulo, a more modestuous conciliabulite never curled a torn pocketmouth), cordially inwiting the adullescence who he was wising up to do in like manner what all did (so as he was able to add) lobe before the Great Schoolmaster's. (I tell you no story.) Smile!

The house of Atreox is fallen indeedust (Ilyam, Ilyum! Maeromor Mournomates!) averging on blight like the mundibanks of Fenny-

ana, but deeds bounds going arise again. Life, he himself said once,
(his biografiend, in fact, kills him verysoon, if yet not, after) is a
wake, livit or krikit, and on the bunk of our breadwinning lies the
cropse of our seedfather, a phrase which the establisher of the world
by law might pretinately write across the chestfront of all manor-
wombanborn. The scene, refreshed, reroused, was never to be forgotten, the hen and crusader everintermutuomergent, for later in
the century one of that puisne band of factferreters, (then an
excivily (out of the custom huts) (retired), (hurt), under the sixty-
fives act) in a dressy black modern style and wewere shiny tan bur-
lingtons, (tam, homd and dicky, quopriquos and peajagd) rehearsed
it, pippa pointing, with a dignified (copied) bow to a namecousin
of the late archdeacon F. X. Preserved Coppinger (a hot fellow in
his night, may the mouther of guard have mastic on him!) in a pull-
woman of our first transhibernian with one still sadder circumstance
which is a dirkandurk heartskewerer if ever to bring bouncing brim-
mers from marbled eyes. Cycloptically through the windowdisks
and with eddying awes the round eyes of the rundreisers, back
to back, buck to bucker, on their airish chaunting car, beheld with
intouristing anterestedness the clad pursue the bare, the bare the
green, the green the frore, the frore the cladagain, as their convoy
wheeled encirculingly abound the gigantig's lifetree, our fireleaved
loverlucky blomsterbohm, phoenix in our woodlessness, haughty,
cacuminal, erubescent (repetition!) whose roots they be asches
with lustres of peins. For as often as the Archicadenus, pleacing
aside his *Irish Field* and craving their auriculars to recepticle par-
ticulars before they got the bump at Castlebar (mat and far!) spoke
of it by request all, hearing in this new reading of the part whereby,
because of Dyas in his machina, the new garrickson's grimacing
grimaldism hypostasised by substintuation the axiomatic orerotundity
of that once grand old elrington bawl, the copycus's description of
that fellowcommuter's play upon countenants, could simply imagine
themselves in their bosom's inmost core, as *pro tem locums*, time-
sported acorss the yawning (abyss), as once they were seasiders,
listening to the cockshyshooter's evensong evocation of the doomed
but always ventriloquent Agitator, (nonot more plangorpound the
billows o'er Thounawahallya Reef!) silkhouatted, a whallrhos-
mightiadd, aginsst the dusk of skumring, (would that fane be Saint
Muezzin's calling—holy places!—and this fez brimless as brow of
faithful toucher of the ground, did wish it were—blessed be the
bones!—the ghazi, power of his sword.) his manslayer's gunwielder

protended towards that overgrown leadpencil which was soon, mon-
umentally at least, to rise as Molyvdokondylon to, to be, to be his
mausoleum (O'dan stod tillsteyne at meisies aye skould show pon)
while olover his exculpatory features, as Roland rung, a wee dropeen
of grief about to sillonise his jouejous, the ghost of resignation dif-
fused a spectral appealingness, as a young man's drown o'er the fate
of his waters may gloat, similar in origin and akkurat in effective to
a beam of sunshine upon a coffin plate.

Not olderwise Inn the days of the Bygning would our Traveller
remote, unfriended, from van Demon's land, some lazy skald or
maundering pote, lift wearywilly his slowcut snobsic eyes to the
semisigns of his zooteac and lengthily lingering along flaskneck,
cracket cup, downtrodden brogue, turfsod, wildbroom, cabbageblad,
stockfisch, longingly learn that there at the Angel were herberged
for him poteen and tea and praties and baccy and wine
width woman wordth warbling: and informally quasi-begin to
presquesm'ile to queasithin' (Nonsense! There was not very much
windy Nous blowing at the given moment through the hat of Mr
Melancholy Slow!)

But in the pragma what formal cause made a smile of *that* to-
think? Who was he to whom? (O'Breen's not his name nor the
brown one his maid.) Whose are the placewheres? Kiwasti, kisker,
kither, kitnabudja? Tal the tem of the tumulum. Giv the gav of the
grube. Be it cudgelplayers' country, or fishfellows' town or leek-
lickers' land or panbpanungopovengreskey. What regnans raised the
rains have levelled but we hear the pointers and can gauge their
compass for the melos yields the mode and the mode the manners
plicyman, plansiman, plousiman, plab. Tsin tsin tsin tsin! The fore-
farther folkers for a prize of two peaches with Ming, Ching and
Shunny on the lie low lea. We'll sit down on the hope of the ghouly
ghost for the titheman troubleth but his hantitat hies not here. They
answer from their Zoans; Hear the four of them! Hark torroar of
them! I, says Armagh, and a'm proud o'it. I, says Clonakilty, God
help us! I, says Deansgrange, and say nothing. I, says Barna, and
whatabout it? Hee haw! Before he fell hill he filled heaven: a stream,
alplapping streamlet, coyly coiled um, cool of her curls: We were
but thermites then, wee, wee. Our antheap we sensed as a Hill of
Allen, the Barrow for an People, one Jotnursfjaell: and it was a
grummelung amung the porktroop that wonderstruck us as a thunder, yunder.

Thus the unfacts, did we possess them, are too imprecisely few

to warrant our certitude, the evidencegivers by legpoll too untrust-
worthily irreperible where his adjugers are semmingly freak threes
but his judicandees plainly minus twos. Nevertheless Madam's
Toshowus waxes largely more lifeliked (entrance, one kudos; exits,
free) and our notional gullery is now completely complacent, an
exegious monument, aerily perennious. Oblige with your blackthorns;
gamps, degrace! And there many have paused before that exposure
of him by old Tom Quad, a flashback in which he sits sated, gownd-
about, in clericalease habit, watching bland sol slithe dodgsomely
into the nethermore, a globule of maugdleness about to corrugitate
his mild dewed cheek and the tata of a tiny victorienne, Alys, pressed
by his limper looser.

Yet certes one is. Eher the following winter had overed the pages
of nature's book and till ceadurbar-atta-Cleath became Dablena
Tertia, the shadow of the huge outlander, maladik, multvult, mag-
noperous, had bulked at the bar of a rota of tribunals in manor
hall as in thieves' kitchen, mid pillow talk and chithouse chat, on
Marlborough Green as through Molesworth Fields, here sentenced
pro tried with Jedburgh justice, there acquitted contestimony with
benefit of clergy. His Thing Mod have undone him: and his mad-
thing has done him man. His beneficiaries are legion in the part
he created: they number up his years. Greatwheel Dunlop was the
name was on him: behung, all we are his bisaacles. As hollyday
in his house so was he priest and king to that: ulvy came, envy
saw, ivy conquered. Lou! Lou! They have waved his green boughs
o'er him as they have torn him limb from lamb. For his muertifica-
tion and uxpiration and dumnation and annuhulation. With schreis
and grida, deprofound souspirs. Steady, sullivans! Mannequins pause!
Longtong's breach is fallen down but Graunya's spreed's abroad.
Ahdostay, feedailyones, and feel the Flucher's bawls for the total
of your flouts is not fit to fan his fettle, O! Have a ring and sing
wohl! Chin, chin! Chin, chin! And of course all chimed din width
the eatmost boviality. Swiping rums and beaunes and sherries and
ciders and negus and citronnades too. The strongers. Oho, oho,
Mester Begge, you're about to be bagged in the bog again. Bugge.
But softsies seufsighed: Eheu, for gassies! But, lo! lo! by the threnning
gods, human, erring and condonable, what the statues of our kuo,
who is the messchef be our kuang, ashu ashure there, the unfor-
gettable treeshade looms up behind the jostling judgements of those,
as all should owe, malrecapturable days.

Tap and pat and tapatagain, (fire firstshot, Missiers the Refusel-

eers! Peingpeong! For saxonlootie!) three tommix, soldiers free, cocka-
leak and cappapee, of the Coldstream. Guards were walking, in
(*pardonnez-leur, je vous en prie, eh?*) Montgomery Street. One
voiced an opinion in which on either wide (*pardonnez!*), nodding,
all the Finner Camps concurred (*je vous en prie, eh?*). It was the
first woman, they said, souped him, that fatal wellesday, Lili Coning-
hams, by suggesting him they go in a field. Wroth mod eldfar, ruth
redd stilstand, wrath wrackt wroth, confessed private Pat Marchison
retro. (Terse!) Thus contenters with santoys play. One of our coming
Vauxhall ontheboards who is resting for the moment (she has been
callit by a noted stagey elecutioner a wastepacket Sittons) was inter-
feud in a waistend pewty parlour. Looking perhaps even more pewty-
flushed in her cherryderry padouasoys, girdle and braces by the
Halfmoon and Seven Stars, russets from the Blackamoor's Head,
amongst the climbing boys at his Eagle and Child and over the
corn and hay emptors at their Black and All Black, Mrs F . . .
A . . . saidaside, half in stage of whisper to her confidante glass,
while recoopering her cartwheel chapot (ahat! — and we now know
what thimbles a baquets on lallance a talls mean), she hoped Sid
Arthar would git a Chrissman's portrout of orange and lemonsized
orchids with hollegs and ether, from the feeatre of the Innocident,
as the worryld had been uncained. Then, while it is odrous compari-
soning to the sprangflowers of his burstday which was a viridable
goddinpotty for the reinworms and the charlattinas and all branches
of climatitis, it has been such a wanderful noyth untirely, added
she, with many regards to Maha's pranjapansies. (Tart!) Prehistoric,
obitered to his dictaphone an entychologist: his propenomen is a
properismenon. A dustman nocknamed Sevenchurches in the employ
of Messrs Achburn, Soulpetre and Ashreborn, prairmakers, Glinta-
look, was asked by the sisterhood the vexed question during his
midday collation of leaver and buckrom alternatively with stenk and
kitteney phie in a hashhoush and, thankeaven, responsed impulsively:
We have just been propogandering his nullity suit and what they
took out of his ear among my own crush. All our fellows at O'Dea's
sages with Aratar Calaman he is a cemented brick, buck it all! A
more nor usually sober cardriver, who was jauntily hosing his
runabout, Ginger Jane, took a strong view. Lorry hosed her as he
talked and this is what he told rewritemen: Irewaker is just a plain
pink joint reformee in private life but folks all have it by brehemons
laws he has parliamentary honours. Eiskaffier said (Louigi's, you
know that man's, brillant Savourain): *Mon foie,* you wish to ave

some homelette, yes, lady! Good, mein leber! Your hegg he must break himself. See, I crack, so, he sit in the poele, umbedimbt! A perspirer (over sixty) who was keeping up his tennises panted he kne ho har twa to clect infamatios but a diffpair flannels climb wall and trespassing on doorbell. After fullblown Braddon hear this fresky troterella! A railways barmaid's view (they call her Spilltears Rue) was thus expressed: to sympathisers of the Dole Line, Death Avenue, anent those objects of her pity-prompted ministrance, to wet, man and his syphon. Ehim! It is ever too late to whissle when Phyllis floods her stable. It would be skarlot shame to jailahim in lockup, as was proposed to him by the Seddoms creature what matter what merrytricks went off with his revulverher in connections with ehim being a norphan and enjoining such wicked illth, ehim! Well done, Drumcollakill! Kitty Tyrrel is proud of you, was the reply of a B.O.T. official (O blame gnot the board!) while the Daughters Benkletter murmured in uniswoon: Golforgilhisjurylegs! Brian Lynsky, the cub curser, was questioned at his shouting box, Bawlonabraggat, and gave a snappy comeback, when saying: Paw! Once more I'll hellbowl! I am for caveman chase and sahara sex, burk you! Them two bitches ought to be leashed, canem! Up hog and hoar hunt! Paw! A wouldbe martyr, who is attending on sanit Asitas where he is being taught to wear bracelets, when grilled on the point, revealed the undoubted fact that the consequence would be that so long as Sankya Moondy played his mango tricks under the mysttetry, with shady apsaras sheltering in his leaves' licence and his shadowers torrifried by the potent bolts of indradiction, there would be fights all over Cuxhaven. (Tosh!) Missioner Ida Wombwell, the seventeenyearold revivalist, said concerning the coincident of interfizzing with grenadines and other respectable and disgusted peersons using the park: That perpendicular person is a brut! But a magnificent brut! 'Caligula' (Mr Danl Magrath, bookmaker, wellknown to Eastrailian poorusers of the Sydney Parade Ballotin) was, as usual, antipodal with his: striving todie, hopening tomellow, Ware Splash. Cobbler. We have meat two hourly, sang out El Caplan Buycout, with the famous padre's turridur's capecast, meet too ourly, matadear! Dan Meiklejohn, precentor, of S.S. Smack and Olley's was probiverbal with his upsiduxit: *mutatus mutandus*. Dauran's lord ('Sniffpox') and Moirgan's lady ('Flatterfun') took sides and crossed and bowed to each other's views and recrossed themselves. The dirty dubs upin their flies, went too free, echoed the dainly drabs downin their scenities, una mona. Sylvia Silence, the girl detective (*Meminerva,* but by now one hears turtlings all over Doveland!) when supplied with informations as to the several facets of the case in her cozydozy bachelure's flat, quite overlooking John a'Dream's mews, leaned back in her really truly easy chair to query restfully through her vowelthreaded syllabelles: Have you evew thought, wepowtew, that sheew gweatness was his twadgedy? Nevewtheless accowding to my considewed attitudes fow this act he should pay the full penalty, pending puwsuance, as pew Subsec. 32, section 11, of the C. L. A. act 1885, anything in this act to the contwawy notwithstanding. Jarley Jilke began to silke for he couldn't get home to Jelsey but ended with: He's got the sack that helped him moult instench of his gladsome rags. Meagher, a naval rating, seated on one of the granite cromlech setts of our new fishshambles for the usual aireating after the ever popular act, with whom were Questa and Puella, piquante and quoite, (this had a cold in her brain while that felt a sink in her summock, wit's wat, wot's wet) was encouraged, although nearvanashed himself, by one of his co-affianced to get your breath, Walt, and gobbit and when ther chidden by her fastra sastra to saddle up your pance, Naville, thus cor replied to her other's thankskissing: I lay my two fingerbuttons, fiancee Meagher, (he speaks!) he was to blame about your two velvetthighs up Horniman's Hill — as hook and eye blame him or any other piscman? — but I also think, Puellywally, by the siege of his trousers there was someone else behind it — you bet your boughtem blarneys — about their three drummers down Keysars Lane. (Trite!).

Be these meer marchant taylor's fablings of a race referend with oddman rex? Is now all seenheard then forgotten? Can it was, one is fain in this leaden age of letters now to wit, that so diversified outrages (they have still to come!) were planned and partly carried out against so staunch a covenanter if it be true than any of those recorded ever took place for many, we trow, beyessed to and denayed of, are given to us by some who use the truth but sparingly and we, on this side ought to sorrow for their pricking pens on that account. The seventh city, Urovivla, his citadear of refuge, whither (would we believe the laimen and their counts), beyond the outraved gales of Atreeatic, changing clues with a baggermalster, the hejirite had fled, silentioussuemeant under night's altosonority, shipalone, a raven of the wave, (be mercy, Mara! A he whence Rahoulas!) from the ostmen's dirtby on the old vic, to forget in expiating manslaughter and, reberthing in remarriment out of dead seekness to devine previdence, (if you are looking for the bilder deep your ear on the movietone!) to league his lot, palm and patte, with a papishee. For mine qvinne I thee giftake and bind my hosenband I thee halter. The wastobe land, a lottuse land, a luctuous land, Emeraldilluim, the peasant pastured, in which by the fourth commandment with promise his days apostolic were to be long by the abundant mercy of Him Which Thundereth From On High, murmured, would rise against him with all which in them were, franchisables and inhabitands, astea as agora, helotsphilots, do him hurt, poor jink, ghostly following bodily, as were he made a ourse for them, the corruptible lay quick, all saints of incorruption of an holy nation, the common or ere-in-garden castaway, in red resurrection to condemn so they might convince him, first pharoah, Humpheres Cheops Exarchas, of their proper sins. Business bred to speak with a stiff upper lip to all men and most occasions the Man we wot of took little short of fighting chances but for all that he or his or his care were subjected to the horrors of the premier terror of Errorland. (perorhaps!)

We seem to us (the real Us!) to be reading our Amenti in the sixth sealed chapter of the going forth by black. It was after the show at Wednesbury that one tall man, humping a suspicious parcel, when returning late amid a dense particular on his home way from the second house of the Boore and Burgess Christy Menestrels by the old spot, Roy's Corner, had a barkiss revolver placed to his faced with the words: you're shot, major: by an unknowable assailant (masked) against whom he had been jealous over, Lotta Crabtree or Pomona Evlyn. More than that Whenn the Waylayer (not a Lucalizod diocesan or even of the Glendalough see, but hailing fro' the prow of Little Britain), mentioning in a bytheway that he, the crawsopper, had, in edition to Reade's cutless centiblade, a loaded Hobson's which left only twin alternatives as, viceversa, either he would surely shoot her, the aunt, by pistol, (she could be okaysure of that!) or, failing of such, bash in Patch's blank face beyond recognition, pointedly asked with gaeilish gall wodkar blizzard's business Thornton had with that Kane's fender only to be answered by the aggravated assaulted that that that that was the snaps for him, Midweeks, to sultry well go and find out if he was showery well able. But how transparingly nontrue, gentlewriter! His feet one is not a tall man, not at all, man. No such parson. No such fender. No such lumber. No such race. Was it supposedly in connection with a girls, Myramy Huey or Colores Archer, under Flaggy Bridge (for ann there is but one liv and hir newbridge is her old) or to explode his twelvechamber and force a shrievalty entrance that the heavybuilt

Abelbody in a butcherblue blouse from One Life One Suit (a men's wear store), with a most decisive bottle of single in his possession, seized after dark by the town guard at Haveyoucaught-emerod's temperance gateway was there in a gate's way.

Fifthly, how parasoliloquisingly truetoned on his first time of hearing the wretch's statement that, muttering Irish, he had had had o'gloriously a'lot too much hanguest or hoshoe fine to drink in the House of Blazes, the Parrot in Hell, the Orange Tree, the Glibt, the Sun, the Holy Lamb and, lapse not leashed, in Ramitdown's ship hotel since the morning moment he could dixtinguish a white thread from a black till the engine of the laws declosed unto Murray and was only falling fillthefluthered up against the gatestone pier which, with the cow's bonnet a'top o'it, he falsetook for a cattle-pillar with purest peaceablest intentions. Yet how lamely hobbles the hoy of his then pseudojocax axplanation how, according to his own story, he was a process server and was merely trying to open zozimus a bottlop stoub by mortially hammering his *magnum bonum* (the curter the club the sorer the savage) against the bludgey gate for the boots about the swan, Maurice Behan, who hastily into his shoes with nothing his hald barra tinnteack and came down with homp, shtemp and jumphet to the tiltyard from the wastes a'sleep in his obi ohny overclothes or choker, attracted by the norse of guns playing Delandy is cartager on the raglar rock to Dulyn, said war' prised safe in bed as he dreamed that he'd wealthes in mormon halls when wokenp by a fourth loud snore out of his land of byelo while hickstrey's maws was grazing in the moonlight by hearing hammering on the pandywhank scale emanating from the blind pig and anything like it (oonagh! oonagh!) in the whole history of the Mullingcan Inn he never. This battering babel allower the door and sideposts, he always said, was not in the very remotest like the belzey babble of a bottle of boose which would not rouse him out o' slumber deep but reminded him loads more of the martiallawsey marses of foreign musikants' instrumongs or the overthrewer to the third last days of Pompery, if anything. And that after this most nooningless knockturn the young reine came down desperate and the old liffopotamus started ploring all over the plains, as mud as she cud be, ruinating all the bouchers' schurts and the backers' wischandtugs so that be the chandeleure of the Rejaneyjailey they were all night wasching the walters of, the weltering walters off. Whyte.

Just one moment. A pinch in time of the ideal, musketeers! Alphos,

Burkos and Caramis, leave Astrelea for the astrollajerries and for
the love of the saunces and the honour of Keavens pike puddywhack-
back to Pamintul. And roll away the reel world, the reel world,
the reel world! And call all your smokeblushes, Snowwhite and Rose-
red, if you will have the real cream! Now for a strawberry frolic!
Filons, filoosh! *Cherchons la flamme!* Fammfamm! Fammfamm!

Come on, ordinary man with that large big nonobli head, and
that blanko berbecked fischial ekksprezzion Machinsky Scapolo-
polos, Duzinascu or other. Your machelar's mutton leg's getting
musclebound from being too pulled. Noah Beery weighed stone thousand one when Hazel was a hen. Now her fat's falling fast. Therefore, chatbags, why not yours? There are 29 sweet reasons why
blossomtime's the best. Elders fall for green almonds when they're
raised on bruised stone root ginger though it winters on their heads
as if auctumned round their waistbands. If you'd had pains in your
hairs you wouldn't look so orgibald. You'd have Colley Macaires
on your lump of lead. Now listen, Mr Leer! And stow that sweaty-
funnyadams Simper! Take an old geeser who calls on his skirt. Note
his sleek hair, so elegant, *tableau vivant*. He vows her to be his
own honeylamb, swears they will be papa pals, by Sam, and share
good times way down west in a guaranteed happy lovenest when
May moon she shines and they twit twinkle all the night, combing
the comet's tail up right and shooting popguns at the stars. Cream-
puffs all to dime! Every nice, missymackenzies! For dear old grumpapar, he's gone on the razzledar, through gazing and crazing and
blazing at the stars. Compree! She wants her wardrobe to hear from
above by return with cash so as she can buy her Peter Robinson
trousseau and cut a dash with Arty, Bert or possibly Charley Chance
(who knows?) so tolloll Mr Hunker you're too dada for me to dance
(so off she goes!) and that's how half the gels in town has got
their bottom drars while grumpapar he's trying to hitch his braces
on to his trars. But old grum he's not so clean dippy between sweet
you and yum (not on your life, boy! not in those trousers! not by
a large jugful!) for someplace on the sly, where Furphy he isn't
by, old grum has his gel number two (bravevow, our Grum!) and
he would like to canoodle her too some part of the time for he
is downright fond of his number one but O he's fair mashed on
peaches number two so that if he could only canoodle the two,
chivee chivoo, all three would feel genuinely happy, it's as simple
as A. B. C., the two mixers, we mean, with their cherrybum chappy
(for he is simply shamming dippy) if they all were afloat in a dream-

lifeboat, hugging two by two in his zoo-doo-you-doo, a tofftoff for thee, missymissy for me and howcameyou-e'enso for Farber, in his tippy, upindown dippy, tiptoptippy canoodle, can you? Finny.

Ack, ack, ack. With which clap, trap and soddenment, three to a loaf, our mutual friends the fender and the bottle at the gate seem to be implicitly in the same bateau, so to singen, bearing also several of the earmarks of design, for there is in fact no use in putting a tooth in a snipery of that sort and the amount of all those sort of things which has been going on onceaday in and twiceaday out every other nachtistag among all kinds of promiscious individuals at all ages in private homes and reeboos publikiss and allover all and elsewhere throughout secular sequence the country over and overabroad has been particularly stupendous. To be continued. Federals' Uniteds' Transports' Unions' for Exultations' of Triumphants' Ecstasies.

But resuming inquiries. Will it ever be next morning the postal unionist's (officially called carrier's, Letters Scotch, Limited) strange fate (Fierceendgiddyex he's hight, d.e., the losel that hucks around missivemaids' gummibacks) to hand in a huge chain envelope, written in seven divers stages of ink, from blanchessance to lavandaiette, every pothook and pancrook bespaking the wisherwife, superscribed and subpencilled by yours A Laughable Party, with afterwite, S.A.G., to Hyde and Cheek, Edenberry, Dubblenn, WC? Will whatever will be written in lappish language with inbursts of Maggyer always seem semposed, black looking white and white guarding black, in that siamixed twoatalk used twist stern swift and jolly roger? Will it bright upon us, nightle, and we plunging to our plight? Well, it might now, mircle, so it light. Always and ever till Cox's wife, twice Mrs Hahn, pokes her beak into the matter with Owen K. after her, to see whawa smutter after, will this kiribis pouch filled with litterish fragments lurk dormant in the paunch of that halpbrother of a herm, a pillarbox?

The coffin, a triumph of the illusionist's art, at first blench naturally taken for a handharp (it is handwarp to tristinguish jubabe from jabule or either from tubote when all three have just been invened) had been removed from the hardware premises of Oetzmann and Nephew, a noted house of the gonemost west, which in the natural course of all things continues to supply funeral requisites of every needed description. Why needed, though? Indeed needed (wouldn't you feel like rattanfowl if you hadn't the oscar!) because the flash brides or bride in their lily boleros one games

with at the Nivynubies' finery ball and your upright grooms that
always come right up with you (and by jingo when they do!) what
else in this mortal world, now ours, when meet there night, mid
their nackt, me there naket, made their nought the hour strikes,
would bring them rightcame back in the flesh, thumbs down, to
their orses and their hashes.

To proceed. We might leave that nitrience of oxagiants to take
its free of the air and just analectralyse that very chymerical com-
bination, the gasbag where the warderworks. And try to pour somour
heiterscene up thealmostfere. In the bottled heliose case continuing,
Long Lally Tobkids, the special, sporting a fine breast of medals,
and a conscientious scripturereader to boot in the brick and tin
choorch round the coroner, swore like a Norewheezian tailliur on
the stand before the proper functionary that he was up against a
right querrshnorrt of a mand in the butcher of the blues who, he
guntinued, on last epening after delivering some carcasses matton-
chepps and meatjutes on behalf of Messrs Otto Sands and Eastman,
Limericked, Victuallers, went and, with his unmitigated astoniss-
ment, hickicked at the dun and dorass against all the runes and,
when challenged about the pretended hick (it was kickup and down
with him) on his solemn by the imputant imputed, said simply:
I appop pie oath, Phillyps Captain. You did, as I sostressed before.
You are deepknee in error, sir, Madam Tomkins, let me then tell
you, replied with a gentlewomanly salaam MackPartland, (the meat-
man's family, and the oldest in the world except nick, name.) And
Phelps was flayful with his peeler. But his phizz fell.

Now to the obverse. From velveteens to dimities is barely a five-
finger span and hence these camelback excesses are thought to have
been instigated by one or either of the causing causes of all, those
rushy hollow heroines in their skirtsleeves, be she magretta be she
the posque. Oh! Oh! Because it is a horrible thing to have to say
to say to day but one dilalah, Lupita Lorette, shortly after in a
fit of the unexpectednesses drank carbolic with all her dear placid
life before her and paled off while the other soiled dove that's her
sister-in-love, Luperca Latouche, finding one day while dodging
chores that she stripped teasily for binocular man and that her jambs
were jimpjoyed to see each other, the nautchy girly soon found her
fruitful hat too small for her and rapidly taking time, look, she rapidly took to necking, partying and selling her spare favours in the
haymow or in lumber closets or in the greenawn *ad huck* (there
are certain intimacies in all ladies' lavastories we just lease to imagina-

tion) or in the sweet churchyard close itself for a bit of soft coal
or an array of thin trunks, serving whom in fine that same hot
coney *a la Zingara* which our own little Graunya of the chilired
cheeks dished up to the greatsire of Oscar, that son of a Coole.
Houri of the coast of emerald, arrah of the lacessive poghue, Aslim-
all-Muslim, the resigned to her surrender, did not she, come leinster's
even, true dotter of a dearmud, (her pitch was Forty Steps and
his perch old Cromwell's Quarters) with so valkirry a licence as
sent many a poor pucker packing to perdition, again and again,
ay, and again sfidare him, tease fido, eh tease fido, eh eh tease fido,
toos topples topple, stop, dug of a dog of a dgiaour, ye! Angealous-
mei! And did not he, like Arcoforty, farfar off Bissavolo, missbrand
her behaveyous with iridescent huecry of down right mean false
sop lap sick dope? Tawfulsdreck! A reine of the shee, a shebeen
quean, a queen of pranks. A kingly man, of royal mien, regally
robed, exalted be his glory! So gave so take: Now not, not now!
He would just a min. Suffering trumpet! He thought he want.
Whath? Hear, O hear, living of the land! Hungreb, dead era, hark!
He hea, eyes ravenous on her lippling lills. He hear her voi of day
gon by. He hears! Zay, zay, zay! But, by the beer of his profit,
he cannot answer. Upterputty till rise and shine! Nor needs none
shaft ne stele from Phenicia or Little Asia to obelise on the spout,
neither pobalclock neither folksstone, nor sunkenness in Tomar's
Wood to bewray how erpressgangs score off the rued. The mouth
that tells not will ever attract the unthinking tongue and so long
as the obseen draws theirs which hear not so long till allearth's dumb-
nation shall the blind lead the deaf. Tatcho, tawney yeeklings! The
column of lumps lends the pattrin of the leaves behind us. If violence
to life, limb and chattels, often as not, has been the expression,
direct or through an agent male, of womanhid offended, (ah! ah!),
has not levy of black mail from the times the fairies were in it,
and fain for wilde erthe blothoms followed an impressive private
reputation for whispered sins?

Now by memory inspired, turn wheel again to the whole of the
wall. Where Gyant Blyant fronts Peannlueamoore There was once
upon a wall and a hooghoog wall a was and such a wallhole did
exist. Ere ore or ire in Aaarlund. Or you Dair's Hair or you Diggin
Mosses or your horde of orts and oriorts to garble a garthen of Odin
and the lost paladays when all the eddams ended with aves. Armen?
The doun is theirs and still to see for menags if he strikes a lousa-
foritch and we'll come to those baregazed shoeshines if you just

shoodov a second. And let oggs be good old gaggles and Isther Estarr play Yesther Asterr. In the drema of Sorestost Areas, Diseased. A stonehinged gate then was for another thing while the suroptimist had bought and enlarged that shack under fair rental of one yearlyng sheep, (prime) value of sixpence, and one small yearlyng goat (cadet) value of eightpence, to grow old and happy (hogg it and kidd him) for the reminants of his years; and when everything was got up for the purpose he put an applegate on the place by no means as some pretext a bedstead in loo thereof to keep out donkeys (the pigdirt hanging from the jags to this hour makes that clear) and just thenabouts the iron gape, by old custom left open to prevent the cats from getting at the gout, was triplepatlockt on him on purpose by his faithful poorters to keep him inside probably and possibly enaunter he felt like sticking out his chest too far and tempting gracious providence by a stroll on the peoplade's eggday, unused as he was yet to being freely clodded.

O, by the by, lets wee brag of praties, it ought to be always remembered in connection with what has gone before that there was a northroomer, Herr Betreffender, out for his zimmer holedigs, digging in number 32 at the Rum and Puncheon (Branch of Dirty Dick's free house) in Laxlip (where the Sockeye Sammons were stopping at the time orange fasting) prior to that, a Kommerzial (Gorbotipacco, he was wreaking like Zentral Oylrubber) from Osterich, the U.S.E. paying (Gaul save the mark!) 11/- in the week (Gosh, these wholly romads!) of conscience money in the first deal of Yuly wheil he was, swishing beesnest with blessure, and swobbing broguen eeriesh myth brockendootsch, making his reporterage on Der Fall Adams for the Frankofurto Siding, a Fastland payrodicule, and er, consstated that one had on him the Lynn O'Brien, a meltoned lammswolle, disturbed, and wider he might the same zurichschicken other he would, with tosend and obertosend tonnowatters, one monkey's damages become. Now you must know, franksman, to make a heart of glass, that the game of gaze and bandstand butchery was merely a Patsy O'Strap tissue of threats and obuses such as roebucks raugh at pinnacle's peak and after this sort. Humphrey's unsolicited visitor, Davy or Titus, on a burgley's clan march from the middle west, a hikely excellent crude man about road who knew his Bullfoost Mountains like a starling bierd, after doing a long dance untidled to Cloudy Green, deposend his bockstump on the waityoumaywantme, after having blew some quaker's (for you! Oates!) in through the houseking's keyhole to attract attention, bleated through the gale outside which the tairor of his clothes was hogcallering, first, be the hirsuiter, that he would break his bulshey-wigger's head for him, next, be the heeltapper, that he would break the gage over his lankyduckling head the same way he would crack a nut with a monkeywrench and, last of all, be the stirabouter, that he would give him his (or theumperom's or anybloody else's) thickerthanwater to drink and his bleday steppebrodhar's into the bucket. He demanded more wood alcohol to pitch in with, alleging that his granfather's was all taxis and that it was only after ten o'connell, and this his isbar was a public oven for the sake of irsk irskusky, and then, not easily discouraged, opened the wrathfloods of his atillarery and went on at a wicked rate, weathering against him in mooxed metaphores from eleven thirty to two in the after-noon without even a luncheonette interval for House, son of Clod, to come out, you jewbeggar, to be Executed Amen. Earwicker, that patternmind, that paradigmatic ear, receptoretentive as his of Dio-nysius, longsuffering although whitening under restraint in the sitit-out corner of his conservatory, behind faminebuilt walls, his thermos flask and ripidian flabel by his side and a walrus whiskerbristle for a tuskpick, compiled, while he mourned the flight of his wild guineese, a long list (now feared in part lost) to be kept on file of all abusive names he was called (we have been compelled for the rejoicement of foinne loidies ind the humours of Milltown et-cetera by Josephine Brewster in the collision known as Contrasta-tions with Inkermann and so on and sononward, lacies in loo water, flee, celestials, one clean turv): *Firstnighter, Informer, Old Fruit, Yellow Whigger, Wheatears, Goldy Geit, Bogside Beauty, Yass We've Had His Badannas, York's Porker, Funnyface, At Baggotty's Bend He Bumped, Grease with the Butter, Opendoor Ospices, Cain-andabler, Ireland's Eighth Wonderful Wonder, Beat My Price, God-soilman, Moonface the Murderer, Hoary Hairy Hoax, Midnight Sunburst, Remove that Bible, Hebdromadary Publocation, Tummer the Lame the Tyrannous, Blau Clay, Tight before Teatime, Read Your Pantojoke, Acoustic Disturbance, Thinks He's Gobblasst the Good Dook of Ourguile, W.D.'s Grace, Gibbering Bayamouth of Dublin, His Farther was a Mundzucker and She had him in a Growler, Burnham and Bailey, Artist, Unworthy of the Homely Protestant Religion, Terry Cotter, You're Welcome to Waterfood, signed the Ribbonmen, Lobsterpot Lardling, All for Arthur of this Town, Hooshed the Cat from the Bacon, Leathertogs Donald, The Ace and Deuce of Paupering, O'Reilly's Delights to Kiss the Man*

behind the Borrel, Magogagog, Swad Puddlefoot, Gouty Ghibeline,
Loose Luther, Hatches Cocks' Eggs, Muddle the Plan, Luck before
Wedlock, I Divorce Thee Husband, Tanner and a Make, Go to
Hellena or Come to Connies, Piobald Puffpuff His Bride, Purged
out of Burke's, He's None of Me Causin, Barebarean, Peculiar
Person, Grunt Owl's Facktotem, Twelve Months Aristocrat, Ly-
canthrope, Flunkey Beadle Vamps the Tune Letting on He's Loney,
Thunder and Turf Married into Clandorf, Left Boot Sent on Ap-
proval, Cumberer of Lord's Holy Ground, Stodge Arschmann, Awnt
Yuke, Tommy Furlong's Pet Plagues, Archdukon Cabbanger, Last
Past the Post, Kennealey Won't Tell Thee off Nancy's Gown, Scut-
tle to Cover, Salary Grab, Andy Mac Noon in Annie's Room, Awl
Out, Twitchbratschballs, Bombard Street Bester, Sublime Porter, A
Ban for Le King of the Burgaans and a Bom for Ye Sur of all
the Ruttledges, O'Phelim's Cutprice, And at Number Wan Wan
Wan, What He Done to Castlecostello, Sleeps with Feathers end
Ropes, It is Known who Sold Horace the Rattler, Enclosed find
the Sons of Fingal, Swayed in his Falling, Wants a Wife and Forty
of Them, Let Him Do the Fair, Apeegeequanee Chimmuck, Plowp
Goes his Whastle, Ruin of the Small Trader, He — — Milkinghoney-
beaverbrooker, Vee was a Vindner, Sower Rapes, Armenian Atrocity,
Sickfish Bellyup, Edomite, — ' Man Devoyd of the Commoner Char-
acteristics of an Irish Nature, Bad Humborg, Hraabhraab, Coo-
coohandler, Dirt, Miching Daddy, Born Burst Feet Foremost,
Woolworth's Worst, Easyathic Phallusaphist, Guilteypig's Bastard,
Fast in the Barrel, Boose in the Bed, Mister Fatmate, In Custody
of the Polis, Boawwll's Alocutionist, Deposed, but anarchistically re-
spectful of the liberties of the noninvasive individual, did not re-
spond a solitary wedgeword beyond such sedentarity, though it was
as easy as kissanywhere for the passive resistant in the booth he
was in to reach for the hello gripes and ring up Kimmage Outer
17.67, because, as the fundamentalist explained, when at last shocked
into speech, touchin his woundid feelins in the fuchsiar the dominican mission for the sowsealist potty was on at the time and he
thought the rowmish devowtion known as the howly rowsary might
reeform ihm, Gonn. That more than considerably unpleasant bullocky before he rang off drunkishly pegged a few glatt stones, all
of a size, by way of final mocks for his grapes, at the wicket in
support of his words that he was not guilphy but, after he had
so slaunga vollayed, reconnoitring through his semisubconscious the
seriousness of what he might have done had he really polished off

his terrible intentions finally caused him to change the bawling and leave downg the whole grumus of brookpebbles pangpung and, having sobered up a bit, paces his groundould diablen lionndub, the flay the flegm, the floedy fleshener, (purse, purse, pursyfurse, I'll splish the splume of them all!) this backblocks boor bruskly put out his langwedge and quite quit the paleologic scene, telling how by his selfdenying ordnance he had left Hyland on the dissenting table, after exhorting Earwicker or, in slightly modified phraseology, Messrs or Missrs Earwicker, Seir, his feminisible name of multitude, to cocoa come outside to Mockerloo out of that for the honour of Crumlin, with his broody old flishguds, Gog's curse to thim, so as he could brianslog and burst him all dizzy, you go bail, like Potts Fracture did with Keddle Flatnose and nobodyatall with Wholyphamous and build rocks over him, or if he didn't, for two and thirty straws, be Cacao Campbell, he didn't know what he wouldn't do for him nor nobody else nomore nor him after which, batell martell, a brisha a milla a stroka a boola, so the rage of Malbruk, playing on the least change of his manjester's voice, the first heroic couplet from the fuguall tropical, Opus Elf, Thortytoe: *My schemes into obeyance for This time has had to fall:* they bit goodbyte to their thumb and, his bandol eer his solgier, dripdropdrap on pool or poldier, wishing the loff a falladelfian in the morning, proceeded with a Hubbleforth slouch in his slips backwords (*Et Cur Heli!*) in the directions of the duff and demb institutions about ten or eleven hundred years lurch away in the moonshiny gorge of Patself on the Bach. Adyoe!

And thus, with this rochelly exetur of Bully Acre, came to close that last stage in the siegings round our architcitadel which we would like to recall, if old Nestor Alexis would wink the worth for us, as Bar-le-Duc and Dog-an-Doras and Bangen-op-Zoom.

Yed he med leave to many a door beside of Oxmanswold for so witness his chambered cairns a cloudletlitter silent that are at browse up hill and down coombe and on eolithostroton, at Howth or at Coolock or even at Enniskerry, a theory none too rectiline of the evoluation of human society and a testament of the rocks from all the dead unto some the living. Olivers lambs we do call them, skatterlings of a stone, and they shall be gathered unto him, their herd and paladin, as nubilettes to cumule, in that day hwen, same the lightning lancer of Azava Arthur-honoured (some Finn, some Finn avant!), he skall wake from earthsleep, haught crested elmer, in his valle of briers of Greenman's Rise O, (lost leaders

live! the heroes return!) and o'er dun and dale the Wulverulverlord
(protect us!) his mighty horn skall roll, orland, roll.

For in those deyes his Deyus shall ask of Allprohome and call
to himm: Allprohome! And he make answer: Add some. Nor wink
nor wunk. *Animadiabolum, mene credidisti mortuum?* Silence was
in thy faustive halls, O Truiga, when thy green woods went dry
but there will be sounds of manymirth on the night's ear ringing
when our pantriarch of Comestowntonobble gets the pullover on
his boots.

Liverpoor? Sot a bit of it! His braynes coolt parritch, his pelt
nassy, his heart's adrone, his bluidstreams acrawl, his puff but a
piff, his extremeties extremely so: Fengless, Pawmbroke, Chil-
blaimend and Baldowl. Humph is in his doge. Words weigh no
no more to him than raindrips to Rethfernhim. Which we all like.
Rain. When we sleep. Drops. But wait until our sleeping. Drain.
Sdops.

As the lion in our teargarten remembers the nenuphars of his Nile (shall Ariuz forget Arioun or Boghas the baregams of the Marmarazalles from Marmeniere?) it may be, tots wearsense full a naggin in twentyg have sigilposted what in our brievingbust, the besieged bedreamt him stil and solely of those lililiths undeveiled which had undone him, gone for age, and knew not the watchful treachers at his wake, and theirs to stay. Fooi, fooi, chamermissies! Zeepyzoepy, larcenlads! Zijnzijn Zijnzijn! It may be, we moest ons hasten selves te declareer it, that he reglimmed? presaw? the fields of heat and yields of wheat where corngold Ysit? shamed and shone. It may be, we habben to upseek a bitty door our good township's courants want we knew't, that with his deepseeing insight (had not wishing oftebeen but good time wasted), within his patriarchal shamanah, broadsteyne 'bove citie (Twillby! Twillby!) he conscious of enemies, a kingbilly whitehorsed in a Finglas mill, prayed, as he sat on anxious seat, (kunt ye neat gift mey toe bout a peer saft eyballds!) during that three and a hellof hours' agony of silence, *ex profundis malorum,* and bred with unfeigned charity that his wordwounder (an engles to the teeth who, nomened Nash of Girahash, would go anyold where in the weeping world on his mottled belly (the rab, the kreeponskneed!) for milk, music or married missusses) might, mercy to providential benevolence's who hates prudencies' astuteness, unfold into the first of a distinguished dynasty of his posteriors, blackfaced connemaras not of the fold but elder children of his household, his most besetting of ideas (*pace* his twolve predamanant passions) being the formation, as in more favoured climes, where the Meadow of Honey is guestfriendly and the Mountain of Joy receives, of a truly criminal stratum, Ham's cribcracking yeggs, thereby at last eliminating from all classes and masses with directly derivative decasualisation: *sigarius* (sic!) *vindicat urbes terrorum* (sicker!): and so, to mark a bank taal she arter, the obedience of the citizens elp the ealth of the ole.

Now gode. Let us leave theories there and return to here's here. Now here. 'Tis gode again. The teak coffin, Pughglasspanelfitted, feets to the east, was to turn in later, and pitly patly near the porpus, materially effecting the cause. And this, liever, is the thinghowe. Any number of conservative public bodies, through a number of select and other committees having power to add to their number, before voting themselves and himself, town, port and garrison, by a fit and proper resolution, following a koorts order of the groundwet, once for all out of plotty existence, as a forescut, so you maateskippey might to you cuttinrunner on a neuw pack of klerds, made him, while his body still persisted, their present of a protem grave in Moyelta of the best Lough Neagh pattern, then as much in demand among misonesans as the Isle of Man today among limniphobes. Wacht even! It was in a fairly fishy kettlekerry, after the Fianna's foreman had taken his handful, enriched with ancient woods and dear dutchy deeplinns mid which were an old knoll and a troutbeck, vainyvain of her osiery and a chatty sally with any Wilt or Walt who would ongle her as Izaak did to the tickle of his rod and watch her waters of her sillying waters of and there now brown peater arripple (may their quilt gild lightly over his somnolulutent form!) Whoforyou lies his last, by the wrath of Bog, like the erst curst Hun in the bed of his treubleu Donawhu.

Best. This wastohavebeen underground heaven, or mole's paradise which was probably also an inversion of a phallopharos, intended to foster wheat crops and to ginger up tourist trade (its architecht, Mgr Peurelachasse, having been obcaecated lest he should petrifake suchanevver while the contractors Messrs T. A. Birkett and L. O. Tuohalls were made invulnerably venerable) first in the west, our misterbilder, Castlevillainous, openly damned and blasted by means of a hydromine, system, Sowan and Belting, exploded from a reinvented T.N.T. bombingpost up ahoy of eleven and thirty wingrests (*circiter*) to sternbooard out of his aerial thorpeto, Auton Dynamon, contacted with the expectant minefield by tins of improved ammonia lashed to her shieldplated gunwale, and fused into tripupcables, slipping through tholse and playing down from the conning tower into the ground battery fuseboxes, all differing as clocks from keys since nobody appeared to have the same time of beard, some saying by their Oorlog it was Sygstryggs to nine, more holding with the Ryan vogt it was Dane to pfife. He afterwards whaanever his blaetther began to fail off him and his rough bark was wholly husky and, stoop by stoop, he neared it (would manspare!) carefully lined the ferroconcrete result with rotproof bricks and mortar, fassed to fossed, and retired beneath the heptarchy of his towerettes, the beauchamp, byward, bull and lion, the white, the wardrobe and bloodied, so encouraging (insteppen, alls als hats beliefd!) additional useful councils public with hoofd offdealings which were welholden of ladykants te huur out such as the Breeders' Union, the Guild of Merchants of the Staple *et,* a.u.c. to present unto him with funebral pomp, over and above that, a stone slab with the usual Mac Pelah address of velediction, a very fairworded instance of falsemeaning adamelegy: We have done ours gohellt with you, Heer Herewhippit, overgiven it, skidoo!

But t'house and allaboardshoops! Show coffins, winding sheets, goodbuy bierchepes, cinerary urns, liealoud blasses, snuffchests, poteentubbs, lacrimal vases, hoodendoses, reekwaterbeckers, breakmiddles, zootzaks for eatlust, including upyourhealthing rookworst and meathewersoftened forkenpootsies and for that matter, javel also, any kind of inhumationary bric au brac for the adornment of his glasstone honophreum, would, met these trein of konditiens, naturally follow, halas, in the ordinary course, enabling that roundtheworlder wandelingswight, did suches pass him, to live all safeathomely the presenile days of his life of opulence, ancient ere decrepitude, late lents last lenience, till stuffering stage, whaling away the whole of the while (*hypnos chilia eonion!*) lethelulled between explosion and reexplosion (Donnaurwatteur! Hunderthunder!) from grosskopp to megapod, embalmed, of grand age, rich in death anticipated.

But abide Zeit's sumonserving, rise afterfall. Blueblitzbolted from there, knowing the hingeworms of the hallmirks of habitationlesness, buried burrowing in Gehinnon, to proliferate through all his Unterwealth, seam by seam, sheol om sheol, and revisit our Uppercrust Sideria of Utilitarios, the divine one, the hoarder hidden propaguting his plutorpopular progeniem of pots and pans and pokers and puns from biddenland to boughtenland, the spearway fore the spoorway.

The other spring offensive on the heights of Abraham may have come about all quite by accidence, Foughtarundser (for Breedabrooda had at length presuaded him to have himself to be as septuply buried as the murdered Cian in Finntown), had not been three monads in his watery grave (what vigilantes and ridings then and

spuitwyne pledges with aardappel frittling!) when portrifaction,
dreyfussed as ever, began to ramp, ramp, ramp, the boys are parch-
ing. A hoodenwinkle gave the signal and a blessing paper freed the
flood. Why did the patrizien make him scares with his gruntens?
Because the druiven were muskating at the door. From both Celti-
berian camps (granting at the onset for the sake of argument that
men on the two sides in New South Ireland and Vetera Uladh,
bluemin and pillfaces, during the ferment With the Pope or On
the Pope, had, moors or letts, grant ideas, grunted) all conditions,
poor cons and dives mor, each, of course, on the purely doffensive
since the eternals were owlwise on their side every time, were drawn
toowards their Bellona's Black Bottom, once Woolwhite's Waltz
(Ohiboh, how becrimed, becursekissed and bedumbtoit!) some for
want of proper feeding in youth, others already caught in the honourable act of slicing careers for family and carvers in conjunction;
and, if emaciated nough, the person garrotted may have suggested
to whomever he took the ham of, the plain being involved in darkness, low cirque waggery, nay, even the first old wugger of himself
in the flesh, whiggissimus incarnadined, when falsesighted by the
ifsuchhewas bully on the hill for there had circulated freely fairly
among his opposition the feeling that in so hibernating Massa
Ewacka, who, previous to that demidetached life, had been known
of barmicidal days, cook said, between soups and savours, to get
outside his own length of rainbow trout and taerts atta tarn as no
man of woman born, nay could, like the great crested brebe, devour
his threescoreten of roach per lifeday, ay, and as many minnow a
minute (the big mix, may Gibbet choke him!) was, like the salmon
of his ladderleap all this time of totality secretly and by suckage
feeding on his own misplaced fat.

Ladies did not disdain those pagan ironed times of the first city
(called after the ugliest Danadune) when a frond was a friend inneed to carry, as earwigs do their dead, their soil to the earthball
where indeeth we shall calm decline, our legacy unknown. Venuses
were gigglibly temptarix, vulcans guffawably eruptious and the
whole wives' world frockful of fickles. Fact, any human inyon you
liked any erenoon or efter would take her bare godkin out, or an
even pair of hem, (lugod! lugodoo!) and prettily pray with him (or
with em even) everyhe to her taste, long for luck, tapette and tape
petter and take pettest of all. (Tip!) Wells she'd woo and wills she's
win but how the deer knowed where she'd marry! Arbour, bucket-
room, caravan, ditch? Coach, carriage, wheelbarrow, dungcart?

Kate Strong, a widow (Tiptip!) — she pulls a lane picture for us, in a dreariodreama setting, glowing and very vidual, of old dumplan as she nosed it, a homelike cottage of elvanstone with droppings of biddies, stinkend pusshies, moggies' duggies, rotten witchawubbles, festering rubbages and beggars' bullets, if not worse, sending salmofarious germs in gleefully through the smithereen panes — Widow Strong, then, as her weaker had turned him to the wall (Tiptiptip!), did most all the scavenging from good King Hamlaugh's gulden dayne though her lean besom cleaned but sparingly and her bare statement reads that, there being no macadamised sidetracks on those old nekropolitan nights in, barring a footbatter, Bryant's Causeway, bordered with speedwell, white clover and sorrel a wood knows, which left off, being beaten, where the plaintiff was struck, she left down, as scavengers, who will be scavengers must, her filthdump near the Serpentine in Phornix Park (at her time called Finewell's Keepsacre but later tautaubapptossed Pat's Purge), that dangerfield circling butcherswood where fireworker oh flaherty engaged a nutter of castlemallards and ah for archer stunned's turk, all over which fossil footprints, bootmarks, fingersigns, elbowdints, breechbowls, a. s. o. were all successively traced of a most envolving description. What subtler timeplace of the weald than such wolfsbelly castrament to will hide a leabhar from Thursmen's brandihands or a loveletter, lostfully hers, that would be lust on Ma, than then when ructions ended, than here where race began: and by four hands of forethought the first babe of reconcilement is laid in its last cradle of hume sweet hume. Give over it! And no more of it! So pass the pick for child sake! O men!

For hear Allhighest sprack for krischnians as for propagana fidies and his nuptial eagles sharped their beaks of prey: and every morphyl man of us, pome by pome, falls back into this terrine: as it was let it be, says he! And it is as though where Agni araflammed and Mithra monished and Shiva slew as mayamutras the obluvial waters of our noarchic memory withdrew, windingly goharksome, to some hastyswasty timberman torchpriest, flamenfan, the ward of the wind that lightened the fire that lay in the wood that Jove bolt, at his rude word. Posidonius O'Fluctuary! Lave that bloody stone as it is! What are you doing your dirty minx and his big treeblock way up your path? Slip around, you, by the rare of the ministers'! And, you, take that barrel back where you got it, Mac Shane's, and go the way your old one went, Hatchettsbury Road! And gish! how they gushed away, the pennyfares, a whole school for scamper, with their sashes

flying sish behind them, all the little pirlypettes! Issy-la-Chapelle!
Any Lucans, please?

Yes, the viability of vicinals if invisible is invincible. And we
are not trespassing on his corns either. Look at all the plotsch!
Fluminian! If this was Hannibal's walk it was Hercules' work. And
a hungried thousand of the unemancipated slaved the way. The
mausoleum lies behind us (O Adgigasta, *multipopulipater!*) and
there are milestones in their cheadmilias faultering along the trames-
track by Brahm and Anton Hermes! Per omnibus secular seekalarum.
Amain. But the past has made us this present of a rhedarhoad. So
more boher O'Connell! Though rainyhidden, you're rhinohide. And
if he's not a Romeo you may scallop your hat. Wereupunder in the
fane of Saint Fiacre! Halte!

It was hard by the howe's there, plainly on this disoluded and a
buchan cold spot, rupestric then, resurfaced that now is, that Lut-
trell sold if Lautrill bought, in the saddle of the Brennan's (now
Malpasplace?) pass, versts and versts from true civilisation, not
where his dreams top their traums halt (Beneathere! Benathere!)
but where livland yontide meared with the wilde, saltlea with flood,
that the attackler, a cropatkin, though under medium and between
colours with truly native pluck, engaged the Adversary who had
more in his eye than was less to his leg but whom for plunder sake,
he mistook in the heavy rain to be Oglethorpe or some other ginkus,
Parr aparrently, to whom the headandheelless chickenestegg bore
some Michelangiolesque resemblance, making use of sacrilegious
languages to the defect that he would challenge their hemosphores
to exterminate them but he would cannonise the b—y b—r's life
out of him and lay him out contritely as smart as the b—r had his
b—y nightprayers said, three patrecknocksters and a couplet of
hellmuirries (*tout est sacré pour un sacreur, femme à barbe ou
homme-nourrice*) at the same time, so as to plugg well let the blubby-
wail ghoats out of him, catching holst of an oblong bar he had and
with which he usually broke furnitures he rose the stick at him. The
boarder incident prerepeated itself. The pair (whethertheywere Nip-
poluono engaging Wei-Ling-Taou or de Razzkias trying to recon-
noistre the general Boukeleff, man may not say), struggled apairently
for some considerable time, (the cradle rocking equally to one
and oppositely from the other on its law of capture and recapture),
under the All In rules around the booksafe, fighting like purple top
and tipperuhry Swede, (Secremented Servious of the Divine Zeal!)
and in the course of their tussle the toller man, who had opened his

bully bowl to beg, said to the miner who was carrying the worm (a handy term for the portable distillery which consisted of three vats, two jars and several bottles though we purposely say nothing of the stiff, both parties having an interest in the spirits): Let me go, Pautheen! I hardly knew ye. Later on, after the solstitial pause for refleshmeant, the same man (or a different and younger him of the same ham) asked in the vermicular with a very oggly chew-chin-grin: Was six victolios fifteen pigeon takee offa you, tell he me, stlongfella, by picky-pocky ten to foul months behindaside? There were some further collidabanter and severe tries to convert for the best part of an hour and now a woden affair in the shape of a webley (we at once recognise our old friend Ned of so many illor-temporate letters) fell from the intruser who, as stuck as that cat to that mouse in that tube of that christchurch organ, (did the imnage of Girl Cloud Pensive flout above them light young charm, in rib-bons and pigtail?) whereupon became friendly and, saying not his shirt to tear, to know wanted, joking and knobkerries all aside laying, if his change companion who stuck still to the invention of his strongbox, with a tenacity corrobberating their mutual tenitorial rights, happened to have the loots change of a tenpound crickler about him at the moment, addling that hap so, he would pay him back the six vics odd, do you see, out of that for what was taken on the man of samples last Yuni or Yuly, do you follow me, Capn? To this the other, Billi with the Boule, who had mummed and mauled up to that (for he was hesitency carried to excelcism) rather amusedly replied: Woowoo would you be grossly surprised, Hill, to learn that, as it so happens, I honestly have not such a thing as the loo, as the least chance of a tinpanned crackler anywhere about me at the present mohomoment but I believe I can see my way, as you suggest, it being Yuletide or Yuddanfest and as it's mad nuts, son, for you when it's hatter's hares, mon, for me, to advance you some-thing like four and sevenpence between hopping and trapping which you might just as well have, boy baches, to buy J. J. and S. with. There was a minute silence before memory's fire's rekin-dling and then. Heart alive! Which at very first wind of gay gay and whiskwigs wick's ears pricked up, the starving gunman, strike him pink, became strangely calm and forthright sware by all his lards porsenal that the thorntree of sheol might ramify up his Sheofon to the lux apointlex but he would go good to him suntime marx my word fort, for a chip off the old Flint, (in the Nichtian glossery which purveys aprioric roots for aposteriorious tongues this is nat

language at any sinse of the world and one might as fairly go and
kish his sprogues as fail to certify whether the wartrophy eluded at
some lives earlier was that somethink like a jug, to what, a coctable)
and remarxing in languidoily, seemingly much more highly pleased
than tongue could tell at this opening of a lifetime and the foretaste
of the Dun Bank pearlmothers and the boy to wash down which he
would feed to himself in the Ruadh Cow at Tallaght and then into
the Good Woman at Ringsend and after her inat Conway's Inn at
Blackrock and, first to fall, cursed be all, where appetite would
keenest be, atte, funeral fare or fun fain real, Adam and Eve's in
Quantity Street by the grace of gamy queen Tailte, her will and
testament: You stunning little southdowner! I'd know you anywhere,
Declaney, let me truthfully tell you in or out of the lexinction of life
and who the hell else, be your blanche patch on the boney part!
Goalball I've struck this daylit dielate night of nights, by golly! My
hat, you have some bully German grit, sundowner! He spud in his
faust (axin); he toped the raw best (pardun); he poked his pick (a
tip is a tap): and he tucked his friend's leave. And, with French hen
or the portlifowlium of hastes and leisures, about to continue that,
the queer mixture exchanged the pax in embrace or poghue puxy as
practised between brothers of the same breast, hillelulia, killelulia,
allenalaw, and, having ratified before the god of the day their tor-
gantruce which belittlers have schmallkalled the treatyng to cognac,
turning his fez menialstrait in the direction of Moscas, he first got
rid of a few mitsmillers and hurooshoos and levanted off with tubular jurbulance at a bull's run over the assback bridge, spitting his
teeths on rooths, with the seven and four in danegeld and their
humoral hurlbat or other uncertain weapon of *lignum vitae*, but so
evermore rhumanasant of a toboggan poop, picked up to keep some
crowplucking appointment with some rival rialtos anywheres between Pearidge and the Littlehorn while this poor delaney, who they
left along with the confederate fender behind and who albeit balls-
bluffed, bore up wonderfully wunder all of it with a whole number
of plumsized contusiums, plus alasalah bruised coccyx, all over him,
reported the occurance in the best way he could, to the flabbergaze
of the whole lab, giving the Paddybanners the military salute as for
his exilicy's the O'Daffy, in justifiable hope that, in nobiloroman
review of the hugely sitisfactuary conclusium of their negotiations
and the jugglemonkysh agripment deinderivative, some lotion or
fomentation of poppyheads would be jennerously exhibited to the
parts, at the nearest watchhouse in Vicar Lane, the white ground

of his face all covered with diagonally redcrossed nonfatal mam-
malian blood as proofpositive of the seriousness of his character and
that he was bleeding in self defience (stanch it!) from the nostrils,
lips, pavilion and palate, while some of his hitter's hairs had been
pulled off his knut's head by Colt though otherwise his allround
health appeared to be middling along as it proved most fortunate
that not one of the two hundred and six bones and five hundred
and one muscles in his corso was a whit the whorse for her whack-
ing. Herwho?

Nowthen, leaving clashing ash, brawn and muscle and brass-
made to oust earthernborn and rockcrystal to wreck isinglass but
wurming along gradually for our savings backtowards motherwaters
so many miles from bank and Dublin stone (olympiading even till
the eleventh dynasty to reach that thuddysickend Hamlaugh) and
to the question of boney's unlawfully obtaining a pierced paraflamme
and claptrap fireguard there crops out the still more salient point of
the politish leanings and town pursuits of our forebeer, El Don De
Dunelli, (may his ship thicked stick in the bottol of the river and
all his crewsers stock locked in the burral of the seas!) who, when
within the black of your toenail, sir, of being mistakenly ambushed
by one of the uddahveddahs, and as close as made no matter, mam,
to being kayoed offhand when the hyougono heckler with the Peter
the Painter wanted to hole him, was consistently practising the first
of the primary and imprescriptible liberties of the pacific subject
by circulating (be British, boys to your bellybone and chuck a chum
a chance!) alongst one of our umphrohibited semitary thrufahrts,
open to buggy and bike, to walk, Wellington Park road, with the
curb or quaker's quacknostrum under his auxter and his alpenstuck
in his redhand, a highly commendable exercise, or, number two of
our *acta legitima plebeia,* on the brink (beware to baulk a man at
his will!) of taking place upon a public seat, to what, bare by Butt's,
most easterly (but all goes west!) of blackpool bridges, as a public
protest and naturlikevice, without intent to annoy either, being
praisegood thankfully for the wrathbereaved ringdove and the fear-
stung boaconstrictor and all the more right jollywell pleased, which
he was, at having other people's weather.

But to return to the atlantic and Phenitia Proper. As if that were
not to be enough for anyone but little headway, if any, was made
in solving the wasnottobe crime cunundrum when a child of Maam,
Festy King, of a family long and honourably associated with the tar
and feather industries, who gave an address in old plomansch Mayo

of the Saxons in the heart of a foulfamed potheen district, was subsequently haled up at the Old Bailey on the calends of Mars, under an incompatibly framed indictment of both the counts (from each equinoxious points of view, the one fellow's fetch being the other follow's person) that is to see, flying cushats out of his ouveralls and making fesses immodst his forces on the field. Oyeh! Oyeh! When the prisoner, soaked in methylated, appeared in dry dock, appatently ambrosiaurealised, like Kersse's Korduroy Karikature, wearing, besides stains, rents and patches, his fight shirt, straw braces, souwester and a policeman's corkscrew trowswers, all out of the true (as he had purposely torn up all his cymtrymanx bespokes in the mamertime), deposing for his exution with all the fluors of sparse in the royal Irish vocabulary how the whole padderjagmartin tripiezite suet and all the sulfeit of copperas had fallen off him quatz unaccountably like the chrystalisations of Alum on Even while he was trying for to stick fire to himcell, (in feacht he was dripping as he found upon stripping for a pipkin ofmalt as he feared the coold raine) it was attempted by the crown (P.C. Robort) to show that King, *elois* Crowbar, once known as Meleky, impersonating a climbing boy, rubbed some pixes of any luvial peatsmoor o'er his face, plucks and pussas, with a clanetourf as the best means of disguising himself and was to the middlewhite fair in Mudford of a Thoorsday, feishts of Peeler and Pole, under the illassumed names of Tykingfest and Rabworc picked by him and Anthony out of a tellafun book, ellegedly with a pedigree pig (unlicensed) and a hyacinth. They were on that sea by the plain of Ir nine hundred and ninety-nine years and they never cried crack or ceased from regular paddlewicking till that they landed their two and a trifling selves, amadst camel and ass, greybeard and suckling, priest and pauper, matrmatron and merrymeg, into the meddle of the mudstorm. The gathering, convened by the Irish Angricultural and Prepostoral Ouraganisations, to help the Irish muck to look his brother dane in the face and attended thanks to Larry by large numbers, of christies and jew's totems, tospite of the deluge, was distinctly of a scattery kind when the ballybricken he could get no good of, after cockofthewalking through a few fancyfought mains ate some of the doorweg, the pikey later selling the gentleman ratepayer because she, Francie's sister, that is to say, ate a whole side of his (the animal's) sty, on a struggle Street, *Qui Sta Troia*, in order to pay off, hiss or lick, six doubloons fifteen arrears of his, the villain's not the rumbler's rent.

Remarkable evidence was given, anon, by an eye, ear, nose and throat witness, whom Wesleyan chapelgoers suspected of being a plain clothes priest W.P., situate at Nullnull, Medical Square, who, upon letting down his rice and peacegreen coverdisk and having been sullenly cautioned against yawning while being grilled, smiled (he had had a onebumper at parting from Mrs Molroe in the morning) and stated to his eliciter under his morse mustaccents (gobbless!) that he slept with a bonafides and that he would be there to remember the filth of November, hatinaring, rowdy O, which, with the jiboulees of Juno and the dates of ould lanxiety, was going, please the Rainmaker, to decembs within the ephemerides of profane history, all one with Tournay, Yetstoslay and Temorah, and one thing which would pigstickularly strike a person of such sorely tried observational powers as Sam, him and Moffat, though theirs not to reason why, the striking thing about it was that he was patrified to see, hear, taste and smell, as his time of night, how Hyacinth O'Donnell, B.A., described in the calendar as a mixer and wordpainter, with part of a sivispacem (Gaeltact for dungfork) on the fair green at the hour of twenty-four o'clock sought (the bullycassidy of the friedhoffer!) to sack, sock, stab and slaughter singlehanded another two of the old kings, Gush Mac Gale and Roaring O'Crian, Jr., both changelings, unlucalised, of no address and in noncommunicables, between him and whom, ever since wallops before the Mise of Lewes, bad blood existed on the ground of the boer's trespass on the bull or because he firstparted his polarbeeber hair in twoways, or because they were creepfoxed andt grousuppers over a nippy in a noveletta, or because they could not say meace, (mute and daft) meathe. The litigants, he said, local congsmen and donalds, kings of the arans and the dalkeys, kings of mud and tory, even the goat king of Killorglin, were egged on by their supporters in the shape of betterwomen with bowstrung hair of Carrothagenuine ruddiness, waving crimson petties and screaming from Isod's towertop. There were cries from the thicksets in court and from the macdublins on the bohernabreen of: Mind the bank from Banagher, Mick, sir! Prodooce O'Donner. Ay! Exhibit his relics! Bu! Use the tongue mor! Give lip less! But it oozed out in Deadman's Dark Scenery Court through crossexanimation of the casehardened testis that when and where that knife of knifes the treepartied ambush was laid (roughly spouting around half hours 'twixt dusk in dawn, by Waterhose's Meddle Europeic Time, near Stop and Think, high chief evervirens and only abfalltree in auld the land) there

was not as much light from the widowed moon as would dim a
child's altar. The mixer, accordingly, was bluntly broached, and
in the best basel to boot, as to whether he was one of those lucky
cocks for whom the audible-visible-gnosible-edible world existed.
That he was only too cognitively conatively cogitabundantly sure
of it because, living, loving, breathing and sleeping morphomelo-
sophopancreates, as he most significantly did, whenever he thought
he heard he saw he felt he made a bell clipperclipperclipperclipper.
Whether he was practically sure too of his lugs and truies names
in this king and blouseman business? That he was pediculously so.
Certified? As cad could be. Be lying! Be the lonee I will. It was Morbus O' Somebody? A'Quite. Szerday's Son? A satyr in weddens.
And how did the greeneyed mister arrive at the B.A.? That it was
like his poll. A crossgrained trapper with murty odd oogs, awflorated
ares, inquiline nase and a twithcherous mouph? He would be.
Who could bit you att to a tenyerdfuul when aastalled? Ballera job-
bera. Some majar bore too? Iguines. And with tumblerous legs, redi-
pnominated Helmingham Erchenwyne Rutter Egbert Crumwall
Odin Maximus Esme Saxon Esa Vercingetorix Ethelwulf Rupprecht
Ydwalla Bentley Osmund Dysart Yggdrasselmann? Holy Saint
Eiffel, the very phoenix! It was Chudley Magnall once more between the deffodates and the dumb scene? The two childspies
waapreesing him auza de Vologue but the renting of his rock was
from the three wicked Vuncouverers Forests bent down awhits,
arthou sure? Yubeti, Cumbilum comes! One of the oxmen's thinga-
bossers, hvad? And had he been refresqued by the founts of bounty
playing there — is — a — pain — aleland in Long's gourgling barral?
A loss of Lordedward and a lack of sirphilip a surgeonet showera-
down could suck more gargling bubbles out of the five lamps in
Portterand's praise. Wirrgeling and maries? As whose wouldn't, lav-
ing his leaftime in Blackpool. But, of course, he could call himself
Tem, too, if he had time to? You butt he could anytom. When he
pleased? Win and place. A stoker temptated by evesdripping aginst
the driver who was a witness as well? Sacred avatar, how the devil
did they guess it! Two dreamyums in one dromium? Yes and no
error. And both as like as a duel of lentils? Peacisely. So he was
pelted out of the coram populo, was he? Be the powers that be he
was. The prince in principel should not expose his person? Mac-
chevuole! Rooskayman kamerad? Sooner Gallwegian he would say.
Not unintoxicated, fair witness? Drunk as a fishup. Askt to whether
she minded whither he smuked? Not if he barkst into phlegms.

Anent his ajaciulations to his Crosscann Lorne, cossa? It was corso
in cursu on coarser again. The gracious miss was we not doubt sensible how yellowatty on the forx was altered? That she esually was,
O'Dowd me not! As to his religion, if any? It was the see-you-Sunday
sort. Exactly what he meant by a pederast prig? Bejacob's, just a
gent who prayed his lent. And if middleclassed portavorous was a
usual beast? Bynight as useful as a vomit to a shorn man. If he had
rognarised dtheir gcourts marsheyls? Dthat nday in ndays he had.
Lindendelly, coke or skilllies spell me gart without a gate? Harlya-
drope. The grazing rights (Mrs Magistra Martinetta) expired with
the expiry of the goat's sire, if they were not mistaken? That he
exactly could not tell the worshipfuls but his mother-in-waders had
the recipis for the price of the coffin and that he was there to tell
them that herself was the velocipede that could tell them kitcat. A
maundarin tongue in a pounderin jowl? Father ourder about the
mathers of prenanciation. Distributary endings? And we recom-
mends. *Quare hircum?* No answer. *Unde gentium fe . . . ?* No ah.
Are you not danzzling on the age of a vulcano? Siar, I am deed.
And how olld of him? He was intendant to study pulu. Which was
meant in a shirt of two shifts macoghamade or up Finn, three-
hatted ladder? That a head in thighs under a bush at the sunface
would bait a serpent to a millrace through the heather. Arm bird
colour defdum ethnic fort perharps? Sure and glomsk handy jotal-
pheson as well. Hokey jasons, then, in a pigeegeeses? On a pontiff's
order as ture as there's an ital on atac. As a gololy bit to joss? Leally
and tululy. But, why this hankowchaff and whence this second
tone, son-yet-sun? He had the cowtaw in his buxers flay of face.
So this that Solasistras, setting odds evens at defiance, took the laud
from Labouriter? What displaced Tob, Dilke and Halley, not been
greatly in love with the game. And, changing the venders, from the
king's head to the republican's arms, as to the pugnaxities evinxed
from flagfall to antepost during the effrays round fatherthyme's
beckside and the regents in the plantsown raining, with the skiddy-
stars and the morkernwindup, how they appealed to him then?
That it was wildfires night on all the bettygallaghers. Mickmichael's
soords shrieking shrecks through the wilkinses and neckanicholas'
toastingforks pricking prongs up the tunnybladders. Let there be
fight? And there was. Foght. On the site of the Angel's, you said?
Guinney's Gap, he said, between what they said and the pussy-
kitties. In the middle of the garth, then? That they mushn't toucht
it. The devoted couple was or were only two disappainted solici-

tresses on the job of the unfortunate class on Saturn's mountain
fort? That was about it, jah! And Camellus then said to Gemellus:
I should know you? Parfaitly. And Gemellus then said to Camellus: Yes, your brother? Obsolutely. And if it was all about that,
egregious sir? About that and the other. If he was not alluding
to the whole in the wall? That he was when he was not eluding
from the whole of the woman. Briefly, how such beginall finally
struck him now? Like the crack that bruck the bank in Multifarn-
ham. Whether he fell in with what they meant? Cursed that he
suppoxed he did. Thos Thoris, Thomar's Thom? The rudacist rotter in Roebuckdom. Surtopical? And subhuman. If it was, in yap-
panoise language, ach bad clap? Oo! Ah! Augs and ohrs with Rhian
O'kehley to put it tertianly, we wrong? Shocking! Such as turly
pearced our really's that he might, that he might never, that he
might never that night? Treely and rurally. Bladyughfoulmoecklen-
burgwhurawhorascortastrumpapornanennykocksapastippatappatup-
perstrippuckputtanach, eh? You have it alright.

　　Meirdreach an Oincuish! But a new complexion was put upon
the matter when to the perplexedly uncondemnatory bench
(whereon punic judgeship strove with penal law) the senior king of
all, Pegger Festy, as soon as the outer layer of stucckomuck had
been removed at the request of a few live jurors, declared in a loud-
burst of poesy, through his Brythonic interpreter on his oath, mhuith
peisth mhuise as fearra bheura muirre hriosmas, whereas take notice be the relics of the bones of the story bouchal that was ate be
Cliopatrick (the sow) princess of parked porkers, afore God and
all their honours and king's commons that, what he would swear
to the Tierney of Dundalgan or any other Tierney, yif live thurkells
folloged him about sure that was no steal and that, nevertheless,
what was deposited from that eyebold earbig noseknaving gutthroat,
he did not fire a stone either before or after he was born down and
up to that time. And, incidentalising that they might talk about
Markarthy or they might walk to Baalastartey or they might join
the nabour party and come on to Porterfeud this the sockdologer
had the neck to endorse with the head bowed on him over his out-
turned noreaster by protesting to his lipreaders with a justbeen-
cleaned barefacedness, abeam of moonlight's hope, in the same
trelawney what he would impart, pleas bench, to the Llwyd Josus
and the gentlemen in Jury's and the four of Masterers who had
been all those yarns yearning for that good one about why he left
Dublin, that, amreeta beaker coddling doom, as an Inishman was

as good as any cantonnatal, if he was to parish by the market steak
before the dorming of the mawn, he skuld never ask to see sight or
light of this world or the other world or any either world, of Tyre-
nan-Og, as true as he was there in that jackabox that minute, or
wield or wind (no thanks t'yous!) the inexousthausthible wassail-
horn tot of iskybaush the hailth up the wailth of the endknown
abgod of the fire of the moving way of the hawks with his heroes
in Warhorror if ever in all his exchequered career he up or lave a
chancery hand to take or throw the sign of a mortal stick or stone
at man, yoelamb or salvation army either before or after being pup-
tised down to that most holy and every blessed hour. Here, upon
the halfkneed castleknocker's attempting kithoguishly to lilt his holy-
mess the paws and make the sign of the Roman Godhelic faix,
(Xaroshie, zdrst! — in his excitement the laddo had broken exthro
Castilian into which the whole audience perseguired and pursuited
him *olla podrida*) outbroke much yellachters from owners in the
heall (Ha!) in which, under the mollification of methaglin, the
testifighter reluctingly, but with ever so ladylike indecorum, joined.
(Ha! Ha!)

   The hilariohoot of Pegger's Windup cumjustled as neatly with
the tristitone of the Wet Pinter's as were they *isce et ille* equals of
opposites, evolved by a onesame power of nature or of spirit, *iste*,
as the sole condition and means of its himundher manifestation and
polarised for reunion by the symphysis of their antipathies. Distinctly different were their duasdestinies. Whereas the maidies of
the bar, (a pairless trentene, a lunarised score) when the eranthus
myrrmyrred: Show'm the Posed: fluttered and flattered around the
willingly pressed, nominating him for the swiney prize, compliment-
ing him, the captivating youth, on his having all his senses about
him, stincking thyacinths through his curls (O feen! O deur!) and
bringing busses to his cheeks, their masculine Oirisher Rose (his
neece cleur!), and legando round his nice new neck for him and
pizzicagnoling his woolywags, with their dindy dandy sugar de
candy mechree me postheen flowns courier to belive them of all his
untiring young dames and send treats in their times. Ymen. But
it was not unobserved of those presents, their worships, how, of one
among all, her deputised to defeme him by the Lunar Sisters' Celi-
bacy Club, a lovelooking leapgirl, all all alonely, Gentia Gemma of
the Makegiddyculling Reeks, he, wan and pale in his unmixed
admiration, seemed blindly, mutely, tastelessly, tactlessly, innamorate
with heruponhim in shining aminglement, the shaym of his hisu

shifting into the shimmering of her hers, (youthsy, beautsy, hee's
her chap and shey'll tell memmas when she gays whom) till the
wild wishwish of her sheeshea melted most musically mid the dark
deepdeep of his shayshaun.

And whereas distracted (for was not just this in effect which had
just caused that the effect of that which it had caused to occur?)
the four justicers laid their wigs together, Untius, Muncius, Pun-
chus and Pylax but could do no worse than promulgate their standing verdict of Nolans Brumans whereoneafter King, having
murdered all the English he knew, picked out his pockets and left the
tribunal scotfree, trailing his Tommeylommey's tunic in his hurry,
thereinunder proudly showing off the blink pitch to his britgits
to prove himself (an't plase yous!) a rael genteel. To the Switz
bobbyguard's curial but courtlike: Commodore valley O hairy,
Arthre Jennyrosy?: the firewaterloover returted with such a vine-
smelling fortytudor ages rawdownhams tanyouhide as would turn
the latten stomach even of a tumass equinous (we were prepared
for the chap's clap cap, the accent, but, took us as, by surprise and
now we're geshing it like gush gash from a burner!) so that all the
twofromthirty advocatesses within echo, pulling up their briefs at
the krigkry: Shun the Punman!: safely and soundly soccered that
fenemine Parish Poser, (how dare he!) umprumptu rightoway
hames, much to his thanks, gratiasagam, to all the wrong dona-
trices, biss Drinkbattle's Dingy Dwellings where (for like your true
venuson Esau he was dovetimid as the dears at Bottome) he shat
in (zoo), like the muddy goalbind who he was (dun), the chassetit-
ties belles conclaiming: You and your gift of your gaft of your garbage abaht our Farvver! and gaingridando: Hon! Verg! Nau! Putor!
Skam! Schams! Shames!

And so it all ended. Artha kama dharma moksa. Ask Kavya for
the kay. And so everybody heard their plaint and all listened to
their plause. The letter! The litter! And the soother the bitther! Of
eyebrow pencilled, by lipstipple penned. Borrowing a word and
begging the question and stealing tinder and slipping like soap. From
dark Rosa Lane a sigh and a weep, from Lesbia Looshe the beam in
her eye, from lone Coogan Barry his arrow of song, from Sean Kelly's
anagrim a blush at the name, from I am the Sullivan that trumpeting
tramp, from Suffering Dufferin the Sit of her Style, from Kathleen
May Vernon her Mebbe fair efforts, from Fillthepot Curran his
scotchlove machreether, from hymn Op. 2 Phil Adolphos the weary
O, the leery, O, from Samyouwill Leaver or Damyouwell Lover

thatjolly old molly bit or that bored saunter by, from Timm Finn
again's weak tribes loss of strenghth to his sowheel, from the wedding
on the greene, agirlies, the gretnass of joyboys, from Pat Mullen,
Tom Mallon, Dan Meldon, Don Maldon a slickstick picnic made
in Moate by Muldoons. The solid man saved by his sillied woman.
Crackajolking away like a hearse on fire. The elm that whimpers
at the top told the stone that moans when stricken. Wind broke
it. Wave bore it. Reed wrote of it. Syce ran with it. Hand tore it and
wild went war. Hen trieved it and plight pledged peace. It was
folded with cunning, sealed with crime, uptied by a harlot, undone
by a child. It was life but was it fair? It was free but was it art? The
old hunks on the hill read it to perlection. It made ma make merry
and sissy so shy and rubbed some shine off Shem and put some
shame into Shaun. Yet Una and Ita spill famine with drought and
Agrippa, the propastored, spells tripulations in his threne. Ah,
furchte fruchte, timid Danaides! Ena milo melomon, frai is frau
and swee is too, swee is two when swoo is free, ana mala woe is we!
A pair of sycopanties with amygdaleine eyes, one old obster lumpky
pumpkin and three meddlars on their slies. And that was how Framm
Sin fromm Son, acity arose, finfin funfun, a sitting arrows. Now
tell me, tell me, tell me then!

What was it?

A . . . . !

? . . . . O!

So there you are now there they were, when all was over again,
the four with them, setting around upin their judges' chambers,
in the muniment room, of their marshalsea, under the suspices of
Lally, around their old traditional tables of the law like Somany
Solans to talk it over rallthesameagain. Well and druly dry. Suffering
law the dring. Accourting to king's evelyns. So help her goat and
kiss the bouc. Festives and highajinks and jintyaun and her beety-
rossy bettydoaty and not to forget now a'duna o'darnel. The four
of them and thank court now there were no more of them. So pass
the push for port sake. Be it soon. Ah ho! And do you remember,
Singabob, the badfather, the same, the great Howdoyoucallem, and
his old nickname, Dirty Daddy Pantaloons, in his monopoleums,
behind the war of the two roses, with Michael Victory, the sheemen's
preester, before he caught his paper dispillsation from the poke, old
Minace and Minster York? Do I mind? I mind the gush off the
mon like Ballybock manure works on a tradewinds day. And the

O'Moyly gracies and the O'Briny rossies chaffing him bluchface and playing him pranks. How do you do, todo, North Mister? Get into my way! Ah dearome forsailoshe! Gone over the bays! When gina-bawdy meadabawdy! Yerra, why would he heed that old gasometer with his hooping coppin and his dyinboosycough and all the birds of the southside after her, Minxy Cunningham, their dear divorcee darling, jimmies and jonnies to be her jo? Hold hard. There's three other corners to our isle's cork float. Sure, 'tis well I can telesmell him H_2 C E_3 that would take a township's breath away! Gob and I nose him too well as I do meself, heaving up the Kay Wall by the 32 to 11 with his limelooking horsebags full of sesameseed, the Whiteside Kaffir, and his sayman's effluvium and his scentpainted voice, puffing out his thundering big brown cabbage! Pa! Thawt I'm glad a gull for his pawsdeen fiunn! Goborro, sez he, Lankyshied! Gobugga ye, sez I! O breezes! I sniffed that lad long before anyone. It was when I was in my farfather out at the west and she and myself, the redheaded girl, firstnighting down Sycomore Lane. Fine feelplay we had of it mid the kissabetts frisking in the kool kurkle dusk of the lushiness. My perfume of the pampas, says she (meaning me) putting out her netherlights, and I'd sooner one precious sip at your pure mountain dew than enrich my acquaintance with that big brewer's belch.

And so they went on, the fourbottle men, the analists, unguam and nunguam and lunguam again, their anschluss about her whose-before and his whereafters and how she was lost away away in the fern and how he was founded deap on deep in anear, and the rus-tlings and the twitterings and the raspings and the snappings and the sighings and the paintings and the ukukuings and the (hist!) the springapartings and the (hast!) the bybyscuttlings and all the scandalmunkers and the pure craigs that used to be (up) that time living and lying and rating and riding round Nunsbelly Square. And all the buds in the bush. And the laughing jackass. Harik! Harik! Harik! The rose is white in the darik! And Sunfella's nose has got rhinoceritis from haunting the roes in the parik! So all rogues lean to rhyme. And contradrinking themselves about Lillytrilly law pon hilly and Mrs Niall of the Nine Corsages and the old markiss their besterfar, and, arrah, sure there was never a marcus at all at all among the manlies and dear Sir Armoury, queer Sir Rumoury, and the old house by the churpelizod, and all the goings on so very wrong long before when they were going on retreat, in the

old gammeldags, the four of them, in Milton's Park under lovely
Father Whisperer and making her love with his stuffstuff in the
languish of flowers and feeling to find was she mushymushy, and
wasn't that very both of them, the saucicissters, *a drahereen o
machree!*, and (peep!) meeting waters most improper (peepette!)
ballround the garden, trickle trickle trickle triss, please, miman, may
I go flirting? farmers gone with a groom and how they used her,
mused her, licksed her and cuddled. I differ with ye! Are you sure
of yourself now? You're a liar, excuse me! I will not and you're
another! And Lully holding their breach of the peace for them. Pool
loll Lolly! To give and to take! And to forego the pasht! And all
will be forgotten! Ah ho! It was too too bad to be falling out about
her kindness pet and the shape of OOOOOOOO Ourang's time.
Well, all right, Lelly. And shakeahand. And schenkusmore. For Craig
sake. Be it suck.

Well?

Well, even should not the framing up of such figments in the
evidential order bring the true truth to light as fortuitously as a
dim seer's setting of a starchart might (heaven helping it!) uncover
the nakedness of an unknown body in the fields of blue or as fore-
hearingly as the sibspeeches of all mankind have foliated (earth
seizing them!) from the root of some funner's stotter all the soundest
sense to be found immense our special mentalists now holds (*securus
iudicat orbis terrarum*) that by such playing possum our hagious
curious encestor bestly saved his brush with his posterity, you, charming coparcenors, us, heirs of his tailsie. Gundogs of all breeds were
beagling with renounced urbiandorbic bugles, hot to run him, given
law, on a scent breasthigh, keen for the worry. View! From his
holt outratted across the Juletide's genial corsslands of Humfries
Chase from Mullinahob and Peacockstown, then bearing right upon
Tankardstown, the outlier, a white noelan which Mr Lœwensteil
Fitz Urse's basset beaters had first misbadgered for a bruin of some
swart, led bayers the run, then through Raystown and Horlockstown
and, louping the loup, to Tankardstown again. Ear canny hare for
doubling through Cheeverstown they raced him, through Loughlins-
town and Nutstown to wind him by the Boolies. But from the good
turn when he last was lost, check, upon Ye Hill of Rut in full
winter coat with ticker pads, pointing for his rooming house his
old nordest in his rolltoproyal hessians a deaf fuchser's volponism
hid him close in covert, miraculously ravenfed and buoyed up, in

rumer, reticule, onasum and abomasum, upon (may Allbrewham have his mead!) the creamclotted sherriness of cinnamon syllabub, Mikkelraved, Nikkelsaved. Hence hounds hied home. Preservative perseverance in the reeducation of his intestines was the rebuttal by whilk he sort of git the big bulge on the whole bunch of spasoakers, dieting against glues and gravies, in that sometime prestreet protown. Vainly violence, virulence and vituperation sought wellnigh utterly to attax and abridge, to derail and depontify, to enrate and inroad, to ongoad and unhume the great shipping mogul and underlinen overlord.

But the spoil of hesitants, the spell of hesitency. His atake is it ashe, tittery taw tatterytail, hasitense humponadimply, heyheyheyhey a winceywencky.

Assembly men murmured. Reynard is slow!

One feared for his days. Did there yawn? 'Twas his stommick. Eruct? The libber. A gush? From his visuals. Pung? Delivver him, orelode! He had laid violent hands on himself, it was brought in Fugger's Newsletter, lain down, all in, fagged out, with equally melancholy death. For the triduum of Saturnalia his goatservant had paraded hiz willingsons in the Forum while the jenny infanted the lass to be greeted raucously (the Yardstated) with houx and epheus and measured with missiles too from a hundred of manhood and a wimmering of weibes. Big went the bang: then wildewide was quiet: a report: silence: last Fama put it under ether. The noase or the loal had dreven him blem, blem, stun blem. Sparks flew. He had fled again (open shunshema!) this country of exile, sloughed off, sidleshomed *via* the subterranean shored with bedboards, stowed away and ankered in a dutch bottom tank the Arsa, *hod* S.S. Finlandia, and was even now occupying, under an islamitic newhame in his seventh generation, a physical body Cornelius Magrath's (badoldkarakter, commonorrong canbung) in Asia Major, where as Turk of the theater (first house all flatty: the king, eleven sharps) he had bepiastered the buikdanseuses from the opulence of his omnibox while as arab at the streetdoor he bepestered the bumbashaws for the alms of a para's pence. Wires hummed. Peacefully general astonishment assisted by regrettitude had put a term till his existence: he saw the family saggarth, resigned, put off his remainders, was recalled and scrapheaped by the Maker. Chirpings crossed. An infamous private ailment (vulgovarioveneral) had claimed endright, closed his vicious circle, snap. Jams jarred. He had walked towards the middle of an ornamental lilypond when innebriated up to the point where braced shirts meet knickerbockers, as wangfish daring the buoyant waters, when rodmen's firstaiding hands had rescued un from very possibly several feel of demifrish water. Mush spread. On Umbrella Street where he did drinks from a pumps a kind of workman, Mr Whitlock, gave him a piece of wood. What words of power were made fas between them, ekenames and auchnomes, *acnomina ecnumina?* That, O that, did Hansard tell us, would gar ganz Dub's ear wag in every pub of all the citta! Batty believes a baton while Hogan hears a hod yet Heer prefers a punsil shapner and Cope and Bull go cup and ball. And the Cassidy — Craddock rome and reme round e'er a wiege ne'er a waage is still immer and immor awagering over it, a cradle with a care in it or a casket with a kick behind. Toties testies quoties questies. The war is in words and the wood is the world. Maply me, willowy we, hickory he and yew yourselves. Howforhim chirrupeth evereachbird! From golddawn glory to glowworm gleam. We were lowquacks did we not tacit turn. Elsewere there here no concern of the Guinnesses. But only the ruining of the rain has heard. *Estout pourporteral!* Cracklings cricked. A human pest cycling (pist!) and recycling (past!) about the sledgy streets, here he was (pust!) again! Morse nuisance noised. He was loose at large and (Oh baby!) might be anywhere when a disguised exnun, of huge standbuild and masculine manners in her fairly fat forties, Carpulenta Gygasta, hattracted hattention by harbitrary conduct with a homnibus. Aerials buzzed to coastal listeners of an oertax bror collector's budget, fullybigs, sporran, tie, tuft, tabard and bloody antichill cloak, its tailor's (Baernfather's) tab reading V.P.H., found nigh Scaldbrothar's Hole, and divers shivered to think what kaind of beast, wolves, croppis's or fourpenny friars, had devoured him. C. W. cast wide. Hvidfinns lyk, drohneth svertgleam, Valkir lockt. On his pinksir's postern, the boys had it, at Whitweekend had been nailed an inkedup name and title, inscribed in the national cursives, accelerated, regressive, filiform, turreted and envenomoloped in piggotry: Move up. Mumpty! Mike room for Rumpty! By order, Nickekellous Plugg; and this go, no pentecostal jest about it, how gregarious his race soever or skilful learned wise cunning knowledgable clear profound his saying fortitudo fraught or prudentiaproven, were he chief, count, general, fieldmarshal, prince, king or Myles the Slasher in his person, with a moliamordhar mansion in the Breffnian empire and a place of inauguration on the hill of Tullymongan, there had been real murder, of the rayheallach royghal raxacraxian variety, the MacMahon chaps, it was, that had done him in. On the fidd of Verdor the rampart combatants had left him lion with his dexter handcoup wresterected in a pureede paumee bloody proper. Indeed not a few thick and thin wellwishers, mostly of the clontarfminded class, (Colonel John Bawle O'Roarke, fervxamplus), even ventured so far as to loan or beg copies of D. Blayncy's trilingual triweekly, Scatterbrains' Aftening Posht, so as to make certain sure onetime and be satisfied of their quasicontribusodalitarian's having become genuinely quite beetly dead whether by land whither by water. Transocean atalaclamoured him; The latter! The latter! Shall their hope then be silent or Macfarlane lack of lamentation? He lay under leagues of it in deep Bartholoman's Deep.

Achdung! Pozor! Attenshune! Vikeroy Besights Smucky Yung Pigeschoolies. Tri Paisdinernes Eventyr Med Lochlanner Fathach I Fiounnisgehaven. Bannalanna Bangs Ballyhooly Out Of Her Buddaree Of A Bullavogue.

But, their bright little contemporaries notwithstanding, on the morrowing morn of the suicidal murder of the unrescued expatriate, aslike as asnake comes sliduant down that oaktree onto the duke of beavers, (you may have seen some liquidamber exude exotic from a balsam poplar at Parteen-a-lax Limestone. Road and cried Abies Magnifica! not, noble fir?) a quarter of nine, imploring his resipiency, saw the infallible spike of smoke's jutstiff punctual from the seventh gable of our Quintus Centimachus' porphyroid buttertower and then thirsty p.m. with oaths upon his lastingness (*En caecos harauspices! Annos longos patimur!*) the lamps of maintenance, beaconsfarafield innerhalf the zuggurat, all brevetnamed, the wasting wyvern, the tawny of his mane, the swinglowswaying bluepaw, the outstanding man, the lolllike lady, being litten for the long (O land, how long!) lifesnight, with suffusion of fineglass transom and leadlight panes.

Wherefore let it hardly by any being thinking be said either or thought that the prisoner of that sacred edifice, were he an Ivor the Boneless or an Olaf the Hide, was at his best a onestone parable, a rude breathing on the void of to be, a venter hearing his own bauchspeech in backwords, or, more strictly, but tristurned initials, the cluekey to a worldroom beyond the roomwhorld, for scarce one, or pathetically few of his dode canal sammenlivers cared seriously or for long to doubt with Kurt Iuld van Dijke (the gravitational pull perceived by certain fixed residents and the capture of uncertain comets chancedrifting through our system suggesting an authenticitatem of his aliquitudinis) the canonicity of his existence as a tesseract. Be still, O quick! Speak him dumb! Hush ye fronds of Ulma!

Dispersal women wondered. Was she fast?

Do tell us all about. As we want to hear allabout. So tellus tellas allabouter. The why or whether she looked alottylike like ussies and whether he had his wimdop like themses shut? Notes and queries, tipbids and answers, the laugh and the shout, the ards and downs. Now listed to one aneither and liss them down and smoothen out your leaves of rose. The war is o'er. Wimwim wimwim! Was it Unity Moore or Estella Swifte or Varina Fay or Quarta Quaedam? Toemaas, mark oom for yor ounckel! Pigeys, hold op med yer leg! Who, but who (for second time of asking) was then the scourge of the parts about folkrich Lucalizod it was wont to be asked, as, in ages behind of the Homo Capite Erectus, what price Peabody's money, or, to put it bluntly, whence is the herringtons' white cravat, as, in epochs more cainozoic, who struck Buckley though nowadays as thentimes every schoolfilly of sevenscore moons or more who knows her intimologies and every colleen bawl aroof and every redflammelwaving warwife and widowpeace upon Dublin Wall for ever knows as yayas is yayas how it was Buckleyself (we need no blooding paper to tell it neither) who struck and the Russian generals, da! da!, instead of Buckley who was caddishly struck by him when be herselves. What fullpried paulpoison in the spy of three castles or which hatefilled smileyseller? And that such a vetriol of venom, that queen's head affranchisant, a quiet stinkingplaster zeal could cover, prepostered or postpaid! The loungelizards of the pumproom had their nine days' jeer, and pratschkats at their platschpails too and holenpolendom beside, Szpaszpas Szpissmas, the zhanyzhonies, when, still believing in her owenglass, when izarres were twinklins, that the upper reaches of her mouthless face and her impermanent waves were the better half of her, one nearer him, dearer than all, first warming creature of his early morn, bondwoman of the man of the house, and murrmurr of all the mackavicks, she who had given his eye for her bed and a tooth for a child till one one and one ten and one hundred again, O me and O ye! cadet and prim, the hungray and anngreen (and if she is older now than her teeth she has hair that is younger than thighne, my dear!) she who shuttered him after his fall and waked him widowt

sparing and gave him keen and made him able and held adazillahs
to each arche of his noes, she who will not rast her from her
running to seek him till, with the help of the okeamic, some such
time that she shall have been after hiding the crumbends of his
enormousness in the areyou lookingfor Pearlfar sea, (ur, uri, uria!)
stood forth, burnzburn the gorggony old danworld, in gogor's name,
for gagar's sake, dragging the countryside in her train, finickin here
and funickin there, with her louisequean's brogues and her culunder
buzzle and her little bolero boa and all and two times twenty curli-
cornies for her headdress, specks on her eyeux, and spudds on
horeilles and a circusfix riding her Parisienne's cockneze, a vaunt
her straddle from Equerry Egon, when Tinktink in the churchclose
clinked Steploajazzyma Sunday, *Sola*, with pawns, prelates and
pookas pelotting in her piecebag, for Handiman the Chomp, Esquoro,
biskbask, to crush the slander's head.

Wery weeny wight, plead for Morandmor! *Notre Dame de la
Ville*, mercy of thy balmheartzyheat! Ogrowdnyk's beyond herbata
tay, wort of the drogist. Bulk him no bulkis. And let him rest, thou
wayfarre, and take no gravespoil from him! Neither mar his mound!
The bane of Tut is on it. Ware! But there's a little lady waiting
and her name is A.L.P. And you'll agree. She must be she. For
her holden heirheaps hanging down her back. He spenth his strenth
amok haremscarems. Poppy Narancy, Giallia, Chlora, Marinka, Ani-
leen, Parme. And ilk a those dames had her rainbow huemoures
yet for whilko her whims but he coined a cure. Tifftiff today, kissy-
kissy tonay and agelong pine tomauranna. Then who but Crippled-
with-Children would speak up for Dropping-with-Sweat?

> *Sold him her lease of nineninenineteee,*
> *Tresses undresses so dyedyedaintee,*
> *Goo, the groot gudgeon, gulped it all.*
> *Hoo was the C. O. D.?*
> Bum!

> *At Island Bridge she met her tide.*
> *Attabom, attabom, attabombomboom!*
> *The Fin had a flux and his Ebba a ride.*
> *Attabom, attabom, attabombomboom!*
> *We're all up to the years in hues and cribies.*
> *That's what she's done for wee!*
> Woe!

Nomad may roam with Nabuch but let naaman laugh at Jordan! For we, we have taken our sheet upon her stones where we have hanged our hearts in her trees; and we list, as she bibs us, by the waters of babalong.

In the name of Annah the Allmaziful, the Everliving, the Bringer of Plurabilities, haloed be her eve, her singtime sung, her rill be run, unhemmed as it is uneven!

Her untitled mamafesta memorialising the Mosthighest has gone by many names at disjointed times. Thus we hear of, *The Augusta Angustissimost for Old Seabeastius' Salvation, Rockabill Booby in the Wave Trough, Here's to the Relicts of All Decencies, Anna Stessa's Rise to Notice, Knickle Down Duddy Gunne and Arishe Sir Cannon, My Golden One and My Selver Wedding, Amoury Treestam and Icy Siseule, Saith a Sawyer til a Strame, Ik dik dope-dope et tu mihimihi, Buy Birthplate for a Bite, Which of your Hesterdays Mean Ye to Morra? Hoebegunne the Hebrewer Hit Waterman the Brayned, Arcs in His Ceiling Flee Chinx on the Flur, Rebus de Hibernicis, The Crazier Letters, Groans of a Briton-ess, Peter Peopler Picked a Plot to Pitch his Poppolin, An Apology for a Big* (some such nonoun *as Husband* or *husboat* or *hosebound* is probably understood for we have also the plutherplethoric *My Hoonsbood Hansbaad's a Journey to Porthergill gone and He Never Has the Hour*), *Ought We To Visit Him? For Ark see Zoo, Cleo-pater's Nedlework Ficturing Aldborougham on the Sahara with the Coombing of the Cammmels and the Parlourmaids of Aegypt, Cock in the Pot for Father, Placeat Vestrae, A New Cure for an Old Clap, Where Portentos they'd Grow Gonder how I'd Wish I Woose a Geese; Gettle Nettie, Thrust him not, When the Myrtles of Venice Played to Bloccus's Line, To Plenge Me High He Waives Chiltern on Friends, Oremunds Queue Visits Amen Mart, E'en Tho' I Granny a-be He would Fain Me Cuddle, Twenty of Chambers, Weighty Ten Beds and a Wan Ceteroom, I Led the Life, Through the Boxer Coxer Rising in the House with the Golden Stairs, The Following Fork, He's my O'Jerusalem and I'm his Po, The Best in the West, By the Stream of Zemzem under Zigzag Hill, The Man That Made His Mother in the Marlborry Train, Try Our Taal on a Taub, The Log of Anny to the Base All, Nopper Tipped a Nappiwenk to his Notylytl Dantsigirls, Prszss Orel Orel the King of Orlbrdsz, Intimier Minnelisp of an Extorreor Monolothe, Drink to Him, My Juckey, and Dhoult Bemine Thy Winnowing Sheet, I Ask You to Believe I was his Mistress, He Can Explain, From Victrolia Nuancee to Allbart Noahnsy, Da's a Daisy so Guimea your Handsel too, What Barbaras Done to a Barrel Organ Before the Rank, Tank and Bonnbtail, Huskvy Admortal, What Jumbo made to Jalice and what Anisette to Him, Ophelia's Culpreints, Hear Hubty Hublin, My Old Dansh, I am Older northe Rogues among Whisht I Slips and He Calls Me his Dual of Ayessha, Suppotes a Ventriliquorst Merries a Corpse, Lapps for Finns This Funnycoon's Week, How the Buckling Shut at Rush in January, Look to the Lady, From the Rise of the Dudge Pupublick to the Fall of the Potstille, Of the Two Ways of Opening the Mouth, I have not Stopped Water Where It Should Flow and I Know the Twentynine Names of Attraente, The Tortor of Tory Island Traits Galasia like his Milchcow, From Abbeygate to Crowalley Through a Lift in the Lude, Smocks for Their Graces and Me Aunt for Them Clodshoppers, How to Pull a Good Horuscoup even when Oldsire is Dead to the World, Inn the Gleam of Waherlow, Fathe He's Sukceded to My Esperations, Thee Steps Forward, Two Stops Back, My Skin Appeals to Three Senses and My Curly Lips Demand Columbkisses; Gage Street on a Crany's Savings, Them Lads made a Trion of Battlewatschers and They Totties a Doeit of Deers, In My Lord's Bed by One Whore Went Through It, Mum It is All Over, Cowpoyride by Twelve Acre Terriss in the Unique Estates of Amessican, He Gave me a Thou so I serve Him with Thee, Of all the Wide Torsos in all the Wild Glen, O'Donogh, White Donogh, He's Hue to Me Cry, I'm the Stitch in his Baskside You'd be Nought Without Mom, To Keep the Huskies off the Hustings and Picture Pets from Lifting Shops, Norsker Torsker Find the Poddle, He Perssed Me Here with the Ardour of a Tonnoburkes, A Boob Was Weeping This Mower was Reaping, O'Loughlin, Up from the Pit of my Stomach I Swish you the White of the Mourning, Inglo-Andean Medoleys from Tommany Moohr, The Great Polynesional Entertrainer Exhibits Ballantine Brautchers with the Link of Natures, The Mimic of Meg Neg and the Mackeys, Entered as the Lastest Pigtarial and My Pooridiocal at Stitchioner's Hall,*

Siegfield Follies and or a Gentlehomme's Faut Pas, See the First Book of Jealesies Pessim, The Suspended Sentence, A Pretty Brick Story for Childsize Heroes, As Lo Our Sleep, I Knew I'd Got it in Me so Thit settles That, Thonderbalt Captain Smeth and La Belle Sauvage Pocahonteuse, Way for Wet Week Welikin's Douchka Marianne, The Last of the Fingallians, It Was Me Egged Him on to the Stork Exchange and Lent my Dutiful Face to His Customs, Chee Chee Cheels on their China Miction, Pickedmeup Peters, Lumptytumtumpty had a Big Fall, Pimpimp Pimpimp, Measly Ventures of Two Lice and the Fall of Fruit, The Fokes Family Interior, If my Spreadeagles Wasn't so Tight I'd Loosen my Cursits on that Bunch of Maggiestraps, Allolosha Popofetts and Howke Cotchme Eye, Seen Aples and Thin Dyed, i big U to Beleaves from Love and Mother, Fine's Fault was no Felon, Exat Delvin Renter Life, The Flash that Flies from Vuggy's Eyes has Set Me Hair On Fire, His is the House that Malt Made, Divine Views from Back to the Front, Abe to Sare Stood Icyk Neuter till Brahm Taulked Him Common Sex, A Nibble at Eve Will That Bowal Relieve, Allfor Guineas, Sounds and Compliments Libidous, Seven Wives Awake Aweek, Airy Ann and Berber Blut, Amy Licks Porter While Huffy Chops Eads, Abbrace of Umbellas or a Tripple of Caines, Buttbutterbust, From the Manorlord Hoved to the Misses O'Mollies and from the Dames to their Sames, Manyfestoons for the Colleagues on the Green, An Outstanding Back and an Excellent Halfcentre if Called on, As Tree is Quick and Stone is White So is My Washing Done by Night, First and Last Only True Account all about the Honorary Mirsu Earwicker, L.S.D., and the Snake (Nuggets!) by a Woman of the World who only can Tell Naked Truths about a Dear Man and all his Conspirators how they all Tried to Fall him Putting it all around Lucalizod about Privates Earwicker and a Pair of Sloppy Sluts plainly Showing all the Unmentionability falsely Accusing about the Raincoats.

The proteiform graph itself is a polyhedron of scripture. There was a time when naif alphabetters would have written it down the tracing of a purely deliquescent recidivist, possibly ambidextrous, snubnosed probably and presenting a strangely profound rainbowl in his (or her) occiput. To the hardily curiosing entomophilust then it has shown a very sexmosaic of nymphosis in which the eternal chimerahunter Oriolopos, now frond of sugars, then lief of saults, the sensory crowd in his belly coupled with an eye for the goods trooth bewilderblissed by their night effluvia with guns like

drums and fondlers like forceps persequestellates his vanessas from
flore to flore. Somehows this sounds like the purest kidooleyoon
wherein our madernacerution of lour lore is rich. All's so herou from
us him in a kitchernott darkness, by hasard and worn rolls arered,
we must grope on till Zerogh hour like pou owl giaours as we are
would we salve aught of moments for our aysore today. Amousin
though not but. Closer inspection of the *bordereau* would reveal
a multiplicity of personalities inflicted on the documents or document
and some prevision of virtual crime or crimes might be made by
anyone unwary enough before any suitable occasion for it or them
had so far managed to happen along. In fact, under the closed eyes
of the inspectors the traits featuring the *chiaroscuro* coalesce, their
contrarieties eliminated, in one stable somebody similarly as by the
providential warring of heartshaker with housebreaker and of dram-
drinker against freethinker our social something bowls along
bumpily, experiencing a jolting series of prearranged disappoint-
ments, down the long lane of (it's as semper as oxhousehumper!)
generations, more generations and still more generations.

Say, baroun lousadoor, who in hallhagal wrote the durn thing
anyhow? Erect, beseated, mountback, against a partywall, below
freezigrade, by the use of quill or style, with turbid or pellucid
mind, accompanied or the reverse by mastication, interrupted by
visit of seer to scribe or of scribe to site, atwixt two showers or
atosst of a trike, rained upon or blown around, by a rightdown
regular racer from the soil or by a too pained whittlewit laden with
the loot of learning?

Now, patience; and remember patience is the great thing, and
above all things else we must avoid anything like being or becoming out of patience. A good plan used by worried business folk
who may not have had many momentums to master Kung's doctrine
of the meang or the propriety codestruces of Carprimustimus is just
to think of all the sinking fund of patience possessed in their conjoint
names by both brothers Bruce with whom are incorporated their
Scotch spider and Elberfeld's Calculating Horses. If after years upon
years of delving in ditches dark one tubthumper more than others,
Kinihoun or Kahanan, giardarner or mear measenmanonger, has got
up for the darnall same purpose of reassuring us with all the barbar
of the Carrageehouse that our great ascendant was properly speaking
three syllables less than his own surname (yes, yes, less!), that
the ear of Fionn Earwicker aforetime was the trademark of a broad-
caster with wicker local jargon for an ace's patent (Hear! Calls!

Everywhair!) then as to this radiooscillating epiepistle to which, cotton, silk or samite, kohol, gall or brickdust, we must ceaselessly return, whereabouts exactly at present in Siam, Hell or Tophet under that glorisol which plays touraloup with us in this Aludin's Cove of our cagacity is that bright soandsuch to slip us the dinkum oil?

Naysayers we know. To conclude purely negatively from the positive absence of political odia and monetary requests that its page cannot ever have been a penproduct of a man or woman of that period or those parts is only one more unlookedfor conclusion leaped at, being tantamount to inferring from the nonpresence of inverted commas (sometimes called quotation marks) on any page that its author was always constitutionally incapable of misappropriating the spoken words of others.

Luckily there is another cant to the questy. Has any fellow, of the dime a dozen type, it might with some profit some dull evening quietly be hinted — has any usual sort of ornery josser, flatchested fortyish, faintly flatulent and given to ratiocination by syncopation in the elucidation of complications, of his greatest Fung Yang dynasdescendanced, only another the son of, in fact, ever looked sufficiently longly at a quite everydaylooking stamped addressed envelope? Admittedly it is an outer husk: its face, in all its featureful perfection of imperfection, is its fortune: it exhibits only the civil or military clothing of whatever passionpallid nudity or plaguepurple nakedness may happen to tuck itself under its flap. Yet to concentrate solely on the literal sense or even the psychological content of any document to the sore neglect of the enveloping facts themselves circumstantiating it is just as hurtful to sound sense (and let it be added to the truest taste) as were some fellow in the act of perhaps getting an intro from another fellow turning out to be a friend in need of his, say, to a lady of the latter's acquaintance, engaged in performing the elaborative antecistral ceremony of upstheres, straightaway to run off and vision her plump and plain in her natural altogether, preferring to close his blinkhard's eyes to the ethiquethical fact that she was, after all, wearing for the space of the time being some definite articles of evolutionary clothing, inharmonious creations, a captious critic might describe them as, or not strictly necessary or a trifle irritating here and there, but for all that suddenly full of local colour and personal perfume and suggestive, too, of so very much more and capable of being stretched, filled out, if need or wish were, of having their surprisingly like coincidental parts separated don't they now, for better survey by the deft hand of an expert, don't you know? Who in his heart doubts either that the facts of feminine clothiering are there all the time or that the feminine fiction, stranger than the facts, is there also at the same time, only a little to the rere? Or that one may be separated from the other? Or that both may then be contemplated simultaneously? Or that each may be taken up and considered in turn apart from the other?

Here let a few artifacts fend in their own favour. The river felt she wanted salt. That was just where Brien came in. The country asked for bearspaw for dindin! And boundin aboundin it got it surly. We who live under heaven, we of the clovery kingdom, we middlesins people have often watched the sky overreaching the land. We suddenly have. Our isle is Sainge. The place. That stern chuckler Mayhappy Mayhapnot, once said to repeation in that lutran conservatory way of his that Isitachapel-Asitalukin was the one place, *ult aut nult,* in this madh vaal of tares (whose verdhure's yellowed therever Phaiton parks his car while its tamelised tay is the drame of Drainophilias) where the possible was the improbable and the improbable the inevitable. If the proverbial bishop of our holy and undivided with this me ken or no me ken Zot is the Quiztune havvermashed had his twoe nails on the head we are in for a sequentiality of improbable possibles though possibly nobody after having grubbed up a lock of cwold cworn aboove his subject probably in Harrystotalies or the vivle will go out of his way to applaud him on the onboiassed back of his remark for utterly impossible as are all these events they are probably as like those which may have taken place as any others which never took person at all are ever likely to be. Ahahn!

About that original hen. Midwinter (fruur or kuur?) was in the offing and Premver a promise of a pril when, as kischabrigies sang life's old sahatsong, an iceclad shiverer, merest of bantlings observed a cold fowl behaviourising strangely on that fatal midden or chip factory or comicalbottomed copsjute (dump for short) afterwards changed into the orangery when in the course of deeper demolition unexpectedly one bushman's holiday its limon threw up a few spontaneous fragments of orangepeel, the last remains of an outdoor meal by some unknown sunseeker or placehider *illico* way back in his mistridden past. What child of a strandlooper but keepy little Kevin in the despondful surrounding of such sneezing cold would ever have trouved up on a strate that was called strete a motive for future saintity by euchring the finding of the Ardagh chalice

by another heily innocent and beachwalker whilst trying with pious
clamour to wheedle Tipperaw raw raw reeraw puteters out of Now
Sealand in spight of the patchpurple of the massacre, a dual a duel
to die to day, goddam and biggod, sticks and stanks, of most of
the Jacobiters.

The bird in the case was Belinda of the Dorans, a more than
quinquegintarian (Terziis prize with Serni medal, Cheepalizzy's
Hane Exposition) and what she was scratching at the hour of
klokking twelve looked for all this zogzag world like a goodishsized
sheet of letterpaper originating by transhipt from Boston (Mass.)
of the last of the first to Dear whom it proceded to mention
Maggy well & allathome's health well only the hate turned the mild
on *the van* Houtens and the general's elections with a *lovely* face
of some born gentleman with a beautiful present of wedding cakes
for dear thankyou Chriesty and with grand funferall of poor Father
Michael don't forget unto life's & Muggy well how are you Maggy
& hopes soon to hear well & must now close it with fondest to
the twoinns with four crosskisses for holy paul holey corner holipoli
whollyisland pee ess from (locust may eat all but this sign shall
they never) affectionate largelooking tache of tch. The stain, and
that a teastain (the overcautelousness of the masterbilker here, as
usual, signing the page away), marked it off on the spout of the
moment as a genuine relique of ancient Irish pleasant pottery of
that lydialike languishing class known as a hurry-me-o'er-the-hazy.

Why then how?

Well, almost any photoist worth his chemicots will tip anyone
asking him the teaser that if a negative of a horse happens to melt
enough while drying, well, what you do get is, well, a positively
grotesquely distorted macromass of all sorts of horsehappy values and
masses of meltwhile horse. Tip. Well, this freely is what must have
occurred to our missive (there's a sod of a turb for you! please wisp
off the grass!) unfilthed from the boucher by the sagacity of a lookme-
little likemelong hen. Heated residence in the heart of the orange-
flavoured mudmound had partly obliterated the negative to start with,
causing some features palpably nearer your pecker to be swollen
up most grossly while the farther back we manage to wiggle the
more we need the loan of a lens to see as much as the hen saw. Tip.

You is feeling like you was lost in the bush, boy? You says: It
is a puling sample jungle of woods. You most shouts out: Bethicket
me for a stump of a beech if I have the poultriest notions what
the farest he all means. Gee up, girly! The quad gospellers may

own the targum but any of the Zingari shoolerim may pick a peck of kindlings yet from the sack of auld hensyne.

Lead, kindly fowl! They always did: ask the ages. What bird has done yesterday man may do next year, be it fly, be it moult, be it hatch, be it agreement in the nest. For her socioscientific sense is sound as a bell, sir, her volucrine automutativeness right on normalcy: she knows, she just feels she was kind of born to lay and love eggs (trust her to propagate the species and hoosh her fluffballs safe through din and danger!); lastly but mostly, in her genesic field it is all game and no gammon; she is ladylike in everything she does and plays the gentleman's part every time. Let us auspice it! Yes, before all this has time to end the golden age must return with its vengeance. Man will become dirigible, Ague will be rejuvenated, woman with her ridiculous white burden will reach by one step sublime incubation, the manewanting human lioness with her dishorned discipular manram will lie down together publicly flank upon fleece. No, assuredly, they are not justified, those gloompourers who grouse that letters have never been quite their old selves again since that weird weekday in bleak Janiveer (yet how palmy date in a waste's oasis!) when to the shock of both, Biddy Doran looked at literature.

And. She may be a mere marcella, this midget madgetcy, Misthress of Arths. But. It is not a hear or say of some anomorous letter, signed Toga Girilis, (teasy dear). We have a cop of her fist right against our nosibos. We note the paper with her jotty young watermark: *Notre Dame du Bon Marché*. And she has a heart of Arin! What lumililts as she fols with her fallimineers and her nadianods. As a strow will shaw she does the wind blague, recting to show the rudess of a robur curling and shewing the fansaties of a frizette. But how many of her readers realise that she is not out to dizzledazzle with a graith uncouthrement of postmantuam glasseries from the lapins and the grigs. Nuttings on her wilelife! Grabar gooden grandy for old almeanium adamologists like Dariaumaurius and Zovotrimaserovmeravmerouvian; (dmzn!); she feel plain plate one flat fact thing and if, lastways firdstwise, a man alones sine anyon anyons utharas has no rates to done a kik at with anyon anakars about tutus milking fores and the rereres on the outerrand asikin the tutus to be forrarder. Thingcrooklyexineverypasturesixdixlikencehimaroundhersthemaggerbykinkinkankanwithdownmindlookingated. Mesdaims, Marmouselles, Mescerfs! Silvapais! All schwants (schwrites) ischt tell the cock's trootabout him. Kapak kapuk.

No minzies matter. He had to see life foully the plak and the smut, (schwrites). There were three men in him (schwrites). Dancings (schwrites) was his only ttoo feebles. With apple harlottes. And a little mollvogels. Spissially (schwrites) when they peaches. Honeys wore camelia paints. Yours very truthful. Add dapple inn. Yet is it but an old story, the tale of a Treestone with one Ysold, of a Mons held by tentpegs and his pal whatholoosed on the run, what Cadman could but Badman wouldn't, any Genoaman against any Venis, and why Kate takes charge of the waxworks.

Let us now, weather, health, dangers, public orders and other circumstances permitting, of perfectly convenient, if you police, after you, policepolice, pardoning mein, ich beam so fresch, bey? drop this jiggerypokery and talk straight turkey meet to mate, for while the ear, be we mikealls or nicholists, may sometimes be inclined to believe others the eye, whether browned or nolensed, find it devilish hard now and again even to believe itself. *Habes aures et num videbis? Habes oculos ac mannepalpabuat?* Tip! Drawing nearer to take our slant at it (since after all it has met with misfortune while all underground), let us see all there may remain to be seen.

I am a worker, a tombstone mason, anxious to pleace averyburies and jully glad when Christmas comes his once ayear. You are a poorjoist, unctuous to polise nopebobbies and tunnibelly soully when 'tis thime took o'er home, gin. We cannot say aye to aye. We cannot smile noes from noes. Still. One cannot help noticing that rather more than half of the lines run north-south in the Nemzes and Bukarahast directions while the others go west-east in search from Maliziies with Bulgarad for, tiny tot though it looks when schtschupnistling alongside other incunabula, it has its cardinal points for all that. These ruled barriers along which the traced words, run, march, halt, walk, stumble at doubtful points, stumble up again in comparative safety seem to have been drawn first of all in a pretty checker with lampblack and blackthorn. Such crossing is antechristian of course, but the use of the homeborn shillelagh as an aid to calligraphy shows a distinct advance from savagery to barbarism. It is seriously believed by some that the intention may have been geodetic, or, in the view of the cannier, domestic economical. But by writing thithaways end to end and turning, turning and end to end hithaways writing and with lines of litters slittering up and louds of latters slettering down, the old semetomyplace and jupetbackagain from tham Let Rise till Hum Lit. Sleep, where in the waste is the wisdom?

Another point, in addition to the original sand, pounce powder, drunkard paper or soft rag used (any vet or inhanger in ous sot's social can see the seen for seemself, a wee ftofty od room, the cheery spluttered on the one karrig, a darka disheen of voos from Dalbania, any gotsquantity of racky, a portogal and some buk setting out on the sofer, you remember the sort of softball sucker motru used to tell us when we were all biribiyas or nippies and messas) it has acquired accretions of terricious matter whilst loitering in the past. The teatimestained terminal (say not the tag, mummer, or our show's a failure!) is a cosy little brown study all to oneself and, whether it be thumbprint, mademark or just a poor trait of the art- less, its importance in establishing the identities in the writer com- plexus (for if the hand was one, the minds of active and agitated were more than so) will be best appreciated by never forgetting that both before and after the battle of the Boyne it was a habit not to sign letters always. Tip. And it is surely a lesser ignorance to write a word with every consonant too few than to add all too many. The end? Say it with missiles then and thus arabesque the page. You have your cup of scalding Souchong, your taper's waxen drop, your cat's paw, the clove or coffinnail you chewed or champed as you worded it, your lark in clear air. So why, pray, sign anything as long as every word, letter, penstroke, paperspace is a perfect signature of its own? A true friend is known much more easily, and better into the bargain, by his personal touch, habits of full or undress, movements, response to appeals for charity than by his foot- wear, say. And, speaking anent Tiberias and other incestuish salacities among gerontophils, a word of warning about the tender- loined passion hinted at. Some softnosed peruser might mayhem take it up erogenously as the usual case of spoons, *prostituta in herba* plus dinky pinks deliberatively summersaulting off her bisexycle, at the main entrance of curate's perpetual soutane suit with her one to see and awoh! who picks her up as gingerly as any balmbearer would to feel whereupon the virgin was most hurt and nicely asking: whyre have you been so grace a mauling and where were you chaste me child? Be who, farther potential? and so wider but we grisly old Sykos who have done our unsmiling bit on 'alices, when they were yung and easily freudened, in the penumbra of the procuring room and what oracular comepression we have had apply to them! could (did we care to sell our feebought silence *in camera*) tell our very moistnostrilled one that *father* in such virgated contexts is not always that undemonstrative relative (often held up to our contumacy) who

settles our hashbill for us and what an innocent allabroad's adverb
such as Michaelly looks like can be suggestive of under the puden-
dascope and, finally, what a neurasthene nympholept, endocrine-
pineal typus, of inverted parentage with a prepossessing drauma
present in her past and a priapic urge for congress with agnates
before cognates fundamentally is feeling for under her lubricitous
meiosis when she refers with liking to some feeler she fancie's face.
And Mm. We could. Yet what need to say? 'Tis as human a little
story as paper could well carry, in affect, as singsing so Salaman
susuing to swittvitles while as unbluffingly blurtubruskblunt as an
Esra, the cat, the cat's meeter, the meeter's cat's wife, the meeter's
cat's wife's half better, the meeter's cat's wife's half better's meeter,
and so back to our horses, for we also know, what we have perused
from the pages of *I Was A Gemral*, that Showting up of Bulsklivism
by 'Schottenboum', that Father Michael about this red time of the
white terror equals the old regime and Margaret is the social revolu-
tion while cakes mean the party funds and dear thank you signifies
national gratitude. In fine, we have heard, as it happened, of Spar-
tacus intercellular. We are not corknered yet, dead hand! We can
recall, with voluntears, the froggy jew, and sweeter far 'twere now
westhinks in Dumbil's fair city ere one more year is o'er. We tourned
our coasts to the good gay tunes. When from down swords the sea
merged the oldowth guns and answer made the bold O' Dwyer. But.
Est modest in verbos. Let a prostitute be whoso stands before a door
and winks or parks herself in the fornix near a makeussin wall
(sinsin! sinsin!) and the curate one who brings strong waters (gingin! gingin!), but also, and dinna forget, that there is many asleeps
between someathome's first and moreinausland's last and that the
beautiful presence of waiting kates will until life's (!) be more than
enough to make any milkmike in the language of sweet tarts punch
hell's hate into his twin nicky and that Maggy's tea, or your majesty, if heard as a boost from a born gentleman is (?). For if the
lingo gasped between kicksheets, however basically English, were
to be preached from the mouths of wickerchurchwardens and meta-
physicians in the row and advokaatoes, allvoyous, demivoyelles,
languoaths, lesbiels, dentelles, gutterhowls and furtz, where would
their practice be or where the human race itself were the Pythag-
orean sesquipedalia of the panepistemion, however apically Vola-
pucky, grunted and gromwelled, ichabod, habakuk, opanoff,
uggamyg, hapaxle, gomenon, ppppfff, over country stiles, behind

slated dwellinghouses, down blind lanes, or, when all fruit fails, under some sacking left on a coarse cart?

So hath been, love: tis tis: and will be: till wears and tears and ages. Thief us the night, steal we the air, shawl thiner liefest, mine! Here, Ohere, insult the fair! Traitor, bad hearer, brave! The lightning look, the birding cry, awe from the grave, everflowing on the times. Feueragusaria iordenwater; now godsun shine on menday's daughter; a good clap, a fore marriage, a bad wake, tell hell's well; such is manowife's lot of lose and win again, like he's gruen quhiskers on who's chin again, she plucketed them out but they grown in again. So what are you going to do about it? O dear!

If juness she saved! Ah ho! And if yulone he pouved! The olold stoliolum! From quiqui quinet to michemiche chelet and a jambebatiste to a brulobrulo! It is told in sounds in utter that, in signs so adds to, in universal, in polygluttural, in each auxiliary neutral idiom, sordomutics, florilingua, sheltafocal, flayflutter, a con's cubane, a pro's tute, strassarab, ereperse and anythongue athall. Since nozzy Nanette tripped palmyways with Highho Harry there's a spurtfire turf a'kind o'kindling when oft as the souffsouff blows her peaties up and a claypot wet for thee, my Sitys, and talkatalka tell Tibbs has eve: and whathough (revilous life proving aye the death of ronaldses when winpower wine has bucked the kick on poor won man) billiousness has been billiousness during milliums of millenions and our mixed racings have been giving two hoots or three jeers for the grape, vine and brew and Pieter's in Nieuw Amsteldam and Paoli's where the poules go and rum smelt his end for him and he dined off sooth american (it would give one the frier even were one a normal Kettlelicker) this oldworld epistola of their weatherings and their marryings and their buryings and their natural selections has combled tumbled down to us fersch and made-at-all-hours like an ould cup on tay. As I was hottin me souser. Haha! And as you was caldin your dutchy hovel. Hoho! She tole the tail or her toon. Huhu!

Now, kapnimancy and infusionism may both fit as tight as two trivets but while we in our wee free state, holding to that prestatute in our charter, may have our irremovable doubts as to the whole sense of the lot, the interpretation of any phrase in the whole, the meaning of every word of a phrase so far deciphered out of it, however unfettered our Irish daily independence, we must vaunt no idle dubiosity as to its genuine authorship and holusbolus authoritativeness. And let us bringtheecease to beakerings on that clink, olmond bottler! On the face of it, to volt back to our desultory horses, and for your roughshod mind, bafflelost bull, the affair is a thing once for all done and there you are somewhere and finished in a certain time, be it a day or a year or even supposing, it should eventually turn out to be a serial number of goodness gracious alone knows how many days or years. Anyhow, somehow and somewhere, before the bookflood or after her ebb, somebody mentioned by name in his telephone directory, Coccolanius or Gallotaurus, wrote it, wrote it all, wrote it all down, and there you are, full stop. O, undoubtedly yes, and very potably so, but one who deeper thinks will always bear in the baccbuccus of his mind that this downright there you are and there it is is only all in his eye. Why?

Because, Soferim Bebel, if it goes to that, (and dormerwindow gossip will cry it from the housetops no surelier than the writing on the wall will hue it to the mod of men that mote in the main street) every person, place and thing in the chaosmos of Alle anyway connected with the gobblydumped turkery was moving and changing every part of the time: the travelling inkhorn (possibly pot), the hare and turtle pen and paper, the continually more and less intermisunderstanding minds of the anticollaborators, the as time went on as it will variously inflected, differently pronounced, otherwise spelled, changeably meaning vocable scriptsigns. No, so holp me Petault, it is not a miseffectual whyacinthinous riot of blots and blurs and bars and balls and hoops and wriggles and juxtaposed jottings linked by spurts of speed: it only looks as like it as damn it; and, sure, we ought really to rest thankful that at this deleteful hour of dungflies dawning we have even a written on with dried ink scrap of paper at all to show for ourselves, tare it or leaf it, (and we are lufted to ourselves as the soulfisher when he led the cat out of the bout) after all that we lost and plundered of it even to the hidmost coignings of the earth and all it has gone through and by all means, after a good ground kiss to Terracussa and for wars luck our lefftoff's flung over our home homoplate, cling to it as with drowning hands, hoping against hope all the while that, by the light of philophosy, (and may she never folsage us!) things will begin to clear up a bit one way or another within the next quarrel of an hour and be hanged to them as ten to one they will too, please the pigs, as they ought to categorically, as, stricly between ourselves, there is a limit to all things so this will never do.

For, with that farmfrow's foul flair for that flayfell foxfetor, (the calamite's columitas calling for calamitous calamitance) who that

scrutinising marvels at those indignant whiplooplashes; those so
prudently bolted or blocked rounds; the touching reminiscence of
an incompletet trail or dropped final; a round thousand whirligig
glorioles, prefaced by (alas!) now illegible airy plumeflights, all
tiberiously ambiembellishing the initials majuscule of Earwicker:
the meant to be baffling chrismon trilithon sign ᚛, finally called after
some his hes hecitency Hec, which, moved contrawatchwise, repre-
sents his title in sigla as the smaller △, fontly called following a
certain change of state of grace of nature alp or delta, when single,
stands for or tautologically stands beside the consort: (though for
that matter, since we have heard from Cathay cyrcles how the hen
is not mirely a tick or two after the first fifth fourth of the second
eighth twelfth — siangchang hongkong sansheneul — but yirely the
other and thirtieth of the ninth from the twentieth, our own vulgar
432 and 1132 irrespectively, why not take the former for a village
inn, the latter for an upsideown bridge, a multiplication marking
for crossroads ahead, which you like pothook for the family gibbet,
their old fourwheedler for the bucker's field, a tea anyway for a
tryst someday, and his onesidemissing for an allblind alley leading
to an Irish plot in the Champ de Mors, not?) the steady monologuy
of the interiors; the pardonable confusion for which some blame
the cudgel and more blame the soot but unthanks to which the pees
with their caps awry are quite as often as not taken for kews with
their tails in their or are quite as often as not taken for pews with
their tails in their mouths, thence your pristopher polombos, hence
our Kat Kresbyterians; the curt witty wotty dashes never quite just
right at the trim trite truth letter; the sudden spluttered petulance
of some capItalIsed mIddle; a word as cunningly hidden in its maze
of confused drapery as a fieldmouse in a nest of coloured ribbons:
that absurdly bullsfooted bee declaring with an even plainer dummp-
show than does the mute commoner with us how hard a thing it
is to mpe mporn a gentlerman: and look at this prepronominal
funferal, engraved and retouched and edgewiped and pudden-
padded, very like a whale's egg farced with pemmican, as were it
sentenced to be nuzzled over a full trillion times for ever and a night
till his noddle sink or swim by that ideal reader suffering from an
ideal insomnia: all those red raddled obeli cayennepeppercast over
the text, calling unnecessary attention to errors, omissions, repeti-
tions and misalignments: that (probably local or personal) variant
maggers for the more generally accepted *majesty* which is but a trifle
and yet may quietly amuse: those superciliouslooking crisscrossed

Greek ees awkwardlike perched there and here out of date like sick
owls hawked back to Athens: and the geegees too, jesuistically formed
at first but afterwards genuflected aggrily toewards the occident:
the Ostrogothic kakography affected for certain phrases of Etruscan
stabletalk and, in short, the learning betrayed at almost every line's
end: the headstrength (at least eleven men of thirtytwo palfry-
craft) revealed by a constant labour to make a ghimel pass through
the eye of an iota: this, for instance, utterly unexpected sinistro-
gyric return to one peculiar sore point in the past; those throne
open doubleyous (of an early muddy terranean origin whether man
chooses to damn them agglutinatively loo — too — blue — face — ache
or illvoodawpeehole or, kants koorts, topplefouls) seated with such
floprightdown determination and reminding uus ineluctably of
nature at her naturalest while that fretful fidget eff, the hornful
digamma of your bornabarbar, rarely heard now save when falling
from the unfashionable lipsus of some hetarosexual (used always
in two boldfaced print types — one of them as wrongheaded as his
Claudian brother, is it worth while interrupting to say? — throughout the papyrus as the revise mark) stalks all over the page, broods
Ɉ sensationseeking an idea, amid the verbiage, gaunt, stands de-
jectedly in the diapered window margin, with its basque of bay-
leaves all aflutter about its forksfrogs, paces with a frown, jerking
to and fro, flinging phrases here, there, or returns inhibited, with
some half-halted suggestion, Ŀ, dragging its shoestring; the curious
warning sign before our protoparent's *ipsissima verba* (a very pure
nondescript, by the way, sometimes a palmtailed otter, more often
the arbutus fruitflowerleaf of the cainapple) which paleographers
call *a leak in the thatch* or *the Aranman ingperwhis through the
hole of his hat,* indicating that the words which follow may be taken
in any order desired, hole of Aran man the hat through the whispering his ho (here keen again and begin again to make soundsense
and sensesound kin again); those haughtypitched disdotted aiches
easily of the rariest inasdroll as most of the jaywalking eyes we do
plough into halve, unconnected, principial, medial or final, always
jims in the jam, sahib, as pipless as threadworms: the innocent exhi-
bitionism of those frank yet capricious underlinings: that strange exotic serpentine, since so properly banished from our scripture, about
as freakwing a wetterhand now as to see a rightheaded ladywhite
don a corkhorse, which, in its invincible insolence ever longer
more and of more morosity, seems to uncoil spirally and swell lacer-
tinelazily before our eyes under pressure of the writer's hand; the

ungainly musicianlessness so painted in sculpting selfsounder ah
ha as blackartful as a *podatus* and dumbfounder oh ho oaproariose
as ten canons in skelterfugue: the studious omission of year number
and era name from the date, the one and only time when our
copyist seems at least to have grasped the beauty of restraint; the lubricitous conjugation of the last with the first: the gipsy mating of
a grand stylish gravedigging with secondbest buns (an interpola-
tion: these munchables occur only in the Bootherbrowth family of
MSS., Bb — Cod IV, Pap II, Brek XI, Lun III, Dinn XVII, Sup
XXX, Fullup M D C X C: the scholiast has hungrily misheard a
deadman's toller as a muffinbell): the four shortened ampersands
under which we can glypse at and feel for ourselves across all those
rushyears the warm soft short pants of the quickscribbler: the voca-
tive lapse from which it begins and the accusative hole in which it
ends itself; the aphasia of that heroic agony of recalling a once
loved number leading slip by slipper to a general amnesia of mis-
nomering one's own: next those ars, rrrr! those ars all bellical, the
highpriest's hieroglyph of kettletom and oddsbones, wrasted red-
handedly from our hallowed rubric prayer for truce with booty,
O'Remus pro Romulo, and rudely from the fane's pinnacle tossed
down by porter to within an aim's ace of their quatrain of rubyjets
among Those Who arse without the Temple nor since Roe's Distillery burn'd have quaff'd Night's firefill'd Cup But jig jog jug as
Day the Dicebox Throws, whang, loyal six I lead, out wi'yer heart's
bluid, blast ye, and there she's for you, sir, whang her, the fine oo-
man, rouge to her lobster locks, the rossy, whang, God and O'Mara
has it with his ruddy old Villain Rufus, wait, whang, God and
you're another he hasn't for there's my spoil five of spuds's trumps,
whang, whack on his pigsking's Kisser for him, K.M. O'Mara where
are you?; then (coming over to the left aisle corner down) the
cruciform postscript from which three *basia* or shorter and smaller
oscula have been overcarefully scraped away, plainly inspiring the
tenebrous *Tunc* page of the Book of Kells (and then it need not be
lost sight of that there are exactly three squads of candidates for
the crucian rose awaiting their turn in the marginal panels of Colum-
killer, chugged in their three ballotboxes, then set apart for such
hanging committees, where two was enough for anyone, starting
with old Matthew himself, as he with great distinction said then
just as since then people speaking have fallen into the custom, when
speaking to a person, of saying two is company when the third person is the person darkly spoken of, and then that last labiolingual

basium might be read as a *suavium* if whoever the embracer then
was wrote with a tongue in his (or perhaps her) cheek as the case
may have been then); and the fatal droopadwindle slope of the
blamed scrawl, a sure sign of imperfectible moral blindness; the too-
muchness, the fartoomanyness of all those fourlegged ems: and why
spell dear god with a big thick dhee (why, O why, O why?): the
cut and dry aks and wise form of the semifinal; and, eighteenthly
or twentyfourthly, but at least, thank Maurice, lastly when all is
zed and done, the penelopean patience of its last paraphe, a colo-
phon of no fewer than seven hundred and thirtytwo strokes tailed
by a leaping lasso — who thus at all this marvelling but will press
on hotly to see the vaulting feminine libido of those interbranching
ogham sex upandinsweeps sternly controlled and easily repersuaded
by the uniform matteroffactness of a meandering male fist?

Duff-Muggli, who now may be quoted by very kind arrangement
(his dectroscophonious photosension under suprasonic light control may be logged for by our none too distant futures as soon astone
values can be turned out from Chromophilomos, Limited at a milli-
centime the microamp), first called this kind of paddygoeasy part-
nership the ulykkhean or tetrachiric or quadrumane or ducks and
drakes or debts and dishes perplex (v. *Some Forestallings over that
Studium of Sexophonologistic Schizophrenesis*, vol. xxiv, pp. 2-555)
after the wellinformed observation, made miles apart from the Master by Tung-Toyd (cf. *Later Frustrations amengst the Neomugglian
Teachings abaft the Semiunconscience, passim*) that in the case of
the littleknown periplic bestteller popularly associated with the
names of the wretched mariner (trianforan deffwedoff our plum-
sucked pattern shapekeeper) a Punic admiralty report, *From Mac-
Person's Oshean Round By the Tides of Jason's Cruise*, had been
cleverly capsized and saucily republished as a dodecanesian baedeker
of the every-tale-a-treat-in-itself variety which could hope satisfac-
torily to tickle me gander as game as your goose.

The unmistaken identity of the persons in the Tiberiast duplex
came to light in the most devious of ways. The original document
was in what is known as Hanno O'Nonhanno's unbrookable script,
that is to say, it showed no signs of punctuation of any sort. Yet on
holding the verso against a lit rush this new book of Morses responded most remarkably to the silent query of our world's oldest
light and its recto let out the piquant fact that it was but pierced
butnot punctured (in the university sense of the term) by numerous stabs and foliated gashes made by a pronged instrument. These

paper wounds, four in type, were gradually and correctly understood to mean stop, please stop, do please stop, and O do please stop
respectively, and following up their one true clue, the circumflexu-
ous wall of a singleminded men's asylum, accentuated by bi tso fb
rok engl a ssan dspl itch ina, — Yard inquiries pointed out → that
they ad bìn "provoked" ay ∧ fork, of à grave Brofèsor; àth é's
Brèak — fast — table; ; acùtely profèššionally *piquéd,* to = intro-
dùce a notion of time [ùpon à plane (?) sù'' fàç'e'] by pùnct! ingh
oles (sic) in iSpace?! Deeply religious by nature and position, and
warmly attached to Thee, and smearbread and better and Him and
newlaidills, it was rightly suspected that such ire could not have
been visited by him Brotfressor Prenderguest even underwittingly,
upon the ancestral pneuma of one whom, with rheuma, he venerated shamelessly at least once a week at Cockspur Common as his
apple in his eye and her first boys' best friend and, though plain
English for a married lady misled heaps by the way, yet when some
peerer or peeress detected that the fourleaved shamrock or quadri-
foil jab was more recurrent wherever the script was clear and the
term terse and that these two were the selfsame spots naturally se-
lected for her perforations by Dame Partlet on her dungheap, think-
ers all put grown in waterungspillfull Pratiland only and a
playful fowl and musical me and not you in any case, two and two
together, and, with a swarm of bisses honeyhunting after, a sigh for
shyme (O, the pettybonny rouge!) separated modest mouths. So be
it. And it was. The lettermaking of the explots of Fjorgn Cam-
helsson when he was in the Kvinnes country with Soldru's men.
With acknowledgment of our fervour of the first instant he remains
years most fainfully. For postscrapt see spoils. Though not yet had
the sailor sipped that sup nor the humphar foamed to the fill. And
fox and geese still kept the peace around *L'Auberge du Père Adam.*

Small need after that, old Jeromesolem, old Huffsnuff, old Andy-
cox, old Olecasandrum, for quizzing your weekenders come to the
R.Q. with: shoots off in a hiss, muddles up in a mussmass and his
whole's a dismantled noondrunkard's son. Howbeit we heard not a
son of sons to leave by him to oceanic society in his old man without a thing in his ignorance, Tulko MacHooley. And it was thus
he was at every time, that son, and the other time, the day was in it
and after the morrow Diremood is the name is on the writing chap
of the psalter, the juxtajunctor of a dearmate and he passing out
of one desire into its fellow. The daughters are after going and loo-
jing for him, Torba's nicelookers of the fair neck. Wanted for mil-

linary servance to olderly's person by the Totty Askinses. Formelly
confounded with amother. Maybe growing a moustache, did you
say, with an adorable look of amuzement? And uses noclass billiard-
halls with an upandown ladder? Not Hans the Curier though had
he had have only had some little laughings and some less of cheeks
and were he not so warried by his bulb of persecussion he could
have, ay, and would have, as true as Essex bridge. And not Gopheph
go gossip, I declare to man! Noe! To all's much relief one's half
hypothesis of that jabberjaw ape amok the showering jestnuts of
Bruisanose was hotly dropped and his room taken up by that odious
and still today insufficiently malestimated notesnatcher (kak, pfooi,
bosh and fiety, much earny, Gus, poteen? Sez you!) Shem the
Penman.

So?

Who do you no tonigh, lazy and gentleman?

The echo is where in the back of the wodes; callhim forth!

(Shaun Mac Irewick, briefdragger, for the concern of Messrs
Jhon Jhamieson and Song, rated one hundrick and thin per store-
hundred on this nightly quisquiquock of the twelve apostrophes,
set by Jockit Mic Ereweak. He misunderstruck and aim for am ollo
of number three of them and left his free natural ripostes to four
of them in their own fine artful disorder.)

1. What secondtonone myther rector and maximost bridgesmaker
was the first to rise taller through his beanstale than the bluegum
buaboababbaun or the giganteous Wellingtonia Sequoia; went nudi-
boots with trouters into a liffeyette when she was barely in her
tricklies; was well known to claud a conciliation cap onto the esker
of his hooth; sports a chainganger's albert solemnly over his hul-
lender's epulence; thought he weighed a new ton when there felled
his first lapapple; gave the heinousness of choice to everyknight
betwixt yesterdicks and twomaries; had sevenal successivecoloured
serebanmaids on the same big white drawringroam horthrug; is a
Willbeforce to this hour at house as he was in heather; pumped the
catholick wartrey and shocked the prodestung boyne; killed his
own hungery self in anger as a young man; found fodder for five
when allmarken rose goflooded; with Hirish tutores Cornish made
easy; voucher of rotables, toll of the road; bred manyheaded
stepsons for one leapyourown taughter; is too funny for a fish and
has too much outside for an insect; like a heptagon crystal empris-
oms trues and fauss for us; is infinite swell in unfitting induments;
once was he shovelled and once was he arsoned and once was he
inundered and she hung him out billbailey; has a quadrant in his
tile to tell Toler cad a'clog it is; offers chances to Long on but stands

up to Legge before; found coal at the end of his harrow and moss-roses behind the seams; made a fort out of his postern and wrote F.E.R.T. on his buckler; is escapemaster-in-chief from all sorts of houdingplaces; if he outharrods against barkers, to the shoolbred he acts whiteley; was evacuated at the mere appearance of three germhuns and twice besieged by a sweep; from zoomorphology to omnianimalism he is brooched by the spin of a coin; towers, an ed-distoon amid the lampless, casting swannbeams on the deep; threat-ens thunder upon malefactors and sends whispers up fraufrau's froufrous; when Dook Hookbackcrook upsits his ass booseworthies jeer and junket but they boos him oos and baas his aas when he lukes like Hunkett Plunkett; by sosannsos and search a party on a lady of this city; business, reading newspaper, smoking cigar, ar-ranging tumblers on table, eating meals, pleasure, etcetera, etcetera, pleasure, eating meals, arranging tumblers on table, smoking cigar, reading newspaper, business; minerals, wash and brush up, local views, juju toffee, comic and birthdays cards; those were the days and he was their hero; pink sunset shower, red clay cloud, sorrow or Sahara, oxhide or Iren; arraigned and attainted, listed and lited, pleaded and proved; catches his check at banck of Indgangd and endurses his doom at chapel exit; brain of the franks, hand of the christian, tongue of the north; commands to dinner and calls the bluff; has a block at Morgen's and a hatache all the afternunch; plays gehamerat when he's ernst but misses mausey when he's lustyg; walked as far as the Head where he sat in state as the Rump; shows Early English tracemarks and a marigold window with mani-gilt lights, a myrioscope, two remarkable piscines and three well-worthseeing ambries; arches all portcullised and his nave dates from dots; is a horologe unstoppable and the Benn of all bells; fuit, isst and herit and though he's mildewstaned he's mouldystoned; is a quercuss in the forest but plane member for Megalopolis; mountun-mighty, faunonfleetfoot; plank in our platform, blank in our scouturn; hidal, in carucates he is enumerated, hold as an earl, he counts; shipshaped phrase of buglooking words with a form like the easing moments of a graminivorous; to our dooms brought he law, our manoirs he made his vill of; was an overgrind to the under-ground and accqueduced for fierythroats; sends boys in socks acoughawhooping when he lets farth his carbonoxside and silk stockings show her shapings when he looses hose on hers; stocks dry puder for the Ill people and pinkun's pellets for all the Pale; gave his mundyfoot to Miserius, her pinch to Anna Livia, that super-

fine pigtail to Cerisia Cerosia and quid rides to Titius, Caius and
Sempronius; made the man who had no notion of shopkeepers feel
he'd rather play the duke than play the gentleman; shot two queans
and shook three caskles when he won his game of dwarfs; fumes
inwards like a strombolist till he smokes at both ends; manmote,
befier of him, womankind, pietad!; shows one white drift of snow
among the gorsegrowth of his crown and a chaperon of repentance
on that which shed gore; pause and quies, triple bill; went by metro
for the polis and then hoved by; to the finders, hail! woa, you that
seek!; whom fillth had plenished, dearth devoured; hock is leading,
cocoa comes next, emery tries for the flag; can dance the O'Bruin's
polerpasse at Noolahn to his own orchistruss accompaniment;
took place before the internatural convention of catholic midwives
and found stead before the congress for the study of endonational
calamities; makes a delictuous *entrée* and finishes off the course
between sweets and savouries; flouts for forecasts, flairs for finds
and the fun of the fray on the fairground; cleared out three
hundred sixty five idles to set up one all khalassal for henwives
hoping to have males; the flawhoolagh, the grasping one, the kindler
of paschal fire; forbids us our trespassers as we forgate him; the
phoenix be his pyre, the cineres his sire!; piles big pelium on little
ossas like the pilluls of hirculeads; has an eatupus complex and a
drinkthedregs kink; wurstmeats for chumps and cowcarlows for
scullions; when he plies for our favour is very trolly ours; two psychic
espousals and three desertions; may be matter of fact now but was
futter of magd then; Cattermole Hill, exmountain of flesh was
reared up by stress and sank under strain; tank it up, dank it up,
tells the tailor to his tout; entoutcas for a man, but bit a thimble for
a maid; blimp, blump; a dud letter, a sing a song a sylble; a byword,
a sentence with surcease; while stands his canyouseehim frails shall
fall; was hatched at Cellbridge but ejoculated abroad; as it gan in
the biguinnengs so wound up in a battle of Boss; Roderick, Roderick, Roderick, O, you've gone the way of the Danes; variously
catalogued, regularly regrouped; a bushboys holoday, a quacker's
mating, a wenches' sandbath; the same homoheatherous checkin-
lossegg as when sollyeye airly blew ye; real detonation but false report; spa mad but inn sane; half emillian via bogus census but a no
street hausmann when allphannd; is the handiest of all andies and
a most alleghant spot to dump your hump; hands his secession to
the new patricius but plumps plebmatically for the bloody old centuries; eats with doors open and ruts with gates closed; some dub

him Rotshield and more limn him Rockyfellow; shows he's fly
to both demisfairs but thries to cover up his tracers; seven dovecotes
cooclaim to have been pigeonheim to this homer, Smerrnion, Rhoe-
bok, Kolonsreagh, Seapoint, Quayhowth, Ashtown, Ratheny; independent of the lordship of chamberlain, acknowledging the rule
of Rome; we saw thy farm at Useful Prine, Domhnall, Domhnall;
reeks like Illbelpaese and looks like Iceland's ear; lodged at quot
places, lived through tot reigns; takes a szumbath for his weekend
and a wassarnap for his refreskment; after a good bout at stoolball
enjoys Giroflee Giroflaa; what Nevermore missed and Colombo
found; believes in everyman his own goadkeeper and in Africa for
the fullblacks; the arc of his drive was forty full and his stumps
were pulled at eighty; boasts him to the thick-in-thews the oldest
creater in Aryania and looks down on the Suiss family Collesons
whom he calls *les nouvelles roches;* though his heart, soul and spirit
turn to pharaoph times, his love, faith and hope stick to futuerism;
light leglifters cense him souriantes from afore while boor brow-
benders curse him grommelants to his hindmost; between youlasses
and yeladst glimse of Even; the Lug his peak has, the Luk his pile;
drinks tharr and wodhar for his asama and eats the unparish-
able sow to styve off reglar rack; the beggars cloak them reclined
about his paddystool, the whores winken him as they walk their
side; on Christienmas at Advent Lodge, New Yealand, after a lenty
illness the roeverand Mr Easterling of pentecostitis, no followers
by bequest, fanfare all private; Gone Where Glory Waits Him (Ball,
bulletist) but Not Here Yet (Maxwell, clark); comminxed under
articles but phoenished a borgiess; from the vat on the bier through
the burre in the dark to the buttle of the bawn; is A1 an the highest but Roh re his root; filled fanned of hackleberries whenas all
was tuck and toss up for him as a yangster to fall fou of hockin-
bechers wherein he had gauged the use of raisin; ads aliments, das
doles, raps rustics, tams turmoil; sas seed enough for a semination
but sues skivvies on the sly; learned to speak from hand to mouth
till he could talk earish with his eyes shut; hacked his way through
hickheckhocks but hanged hishelp from there hereafters; rialtos,
annesleyg, binn and balls to say nothing atolk of New Comyn; the
gleam of the glow of the shine of the sun through the dearth of the
dirth on the blush of the brick of the viled ville of Barnehulme has
dust turned to brown; these dyed to tartan him, rueroot, dulse,
bracken, teasel, fuller's ash, sundew and cress; long gunn but not
for cotton; stood his sharp assault of famine but grew girther,

girther and girther; he has twenty four or so cousins germinating
in the United States of America and a namesake with an initial
difference in the once kingdom of Poland; his first's a young rose
and his second's French-Egyptian and his whole means a slump at
Christie's; forth of his pierced part came the woman of his dreams,
blood thicker then water last trade overseas; buyshop of Glintylook,
eorl of Hoed; you and I are in him surrented by brwn bldns; Elin's
flee polt pelhaps but Hwang Chang evelytime; he one was your of
highbigpipey boys but fancy him as smoking fags his at time of life;
Mount of Mish, Mell of Moy; had two cardinal ventures and three
capitol sinks; has a peep in his pocketbook and a packetboat in his
keep; B.V.H., B.L.G., P.P.M., T.D.S., V.B.D., T.C.H., L.O.N.; is
Breakfates, Lunger, Diener and Souper; as the streets were paved
with cold he felt his topperairy; taught himself skating and learned
how to fall; distinctly dirty but rather a dear; hoveth chieftains evry-
wehr, with morder; Ostman Effendi, Serge Paddishaw; baases two
mmany, outpriams al' his parisites; first of the fenians, *roi des
fainéants*; his Tiara of scones was held unfillable till one Liam Fail
felled him in Westmunster; was struck out of his sittem when he
rowed saulely to demask us and to our appauling predicament
brought as plagues from Buddapest; put a matchhead on an aspen-
stalk and set the living a fire; speared the rod and spoiled the lightning; married with cakes and repunked with pleasure; till he was
buried howhappy was he and he made the welkins ring with *Up
Micawber!*; god at the top of the staircase, carrion on the mat of
straw; the false hood of a spindler web chokes the cavemouth of his
unsightliness but the nestlings that liven his leafscreen sing him
a lover of arbuties; we strike hands over his bloodied warsheet but
we are pledged entirely to his green mantle; our friend vikelegal,
our swaran foi; under the four stones by his streams who vanished
the wassailbowl at the joy of shells; Mora and Lora had a hill of a
high time looking down on his confusion till firm look in readiness,
forward spear and the windfoot of curach strewed the lakemist of
Lego over the last of his fields; we darkened for you, faulterer, in
the year of mourning but we'll fidhil to the dimtwinklers when the
streamy morvenlight calls up the sunbeam; his striped pantaloons,
his rather strange walk; *hereditatis columna erecta, hagion chiton
eraphon*; nods a nap for the nonce but crows cheerio when they
get ecunemical; is a simultaneous equator of elimbinated integras
when three upon one is by inspection improper; has the most conical
hodpiece of confusianist heronim and that chuchuffuous chinchin

of his is like a footsey kungoloo around Taishantyland; he's as globeful as a gasometer of lithium and luridity and he was thrice ten anular years before he wallowed round Raggiant Circos; the cabalstone at the coping of his cavin is a canine constant but only an amirican could apparoxemete the apeupresiosity of his atlast's alongement; sticklered rights and lefts at Baddersdown in his hunt for the boar trwth but made his end with the modareds that came at him in Camlenstrete; a hunnibal in exhaustive conflict, an otho to return; burning body to aiger air on melting mountain in wooing wave; we go into him sleepy children, we come out of him strucklers for life; he divested to save from the Mrs Drownings their rival queens while Grimshaw, Bragshaw and Renshaw made off with his storen clothes; taxed and rated, licensed and ranted; his threefaced stonehead was found on a whitehorse hill and the print of his costellous feet is seen in the goat's grasscircle; pull the blind, toll the deaf and call dumb, lame and halty; Miraculone, Monstrucceleen; led the upplaws at the Creation and hissed a snake charmer off her stays; hounded become haunter, hunter become fox; harrier, marrier, terrier, tav; Olaph the Oxman, Thorker the Tourable; you feel he is Vespasian yet you think of him as Aurelius; whugamore, tradertory, socianist, commoniser; made a summer assault on our shores and begiddy got his sands full; first he shot down Raglan Road and then he tore up Marlborough Place; Cromlechheight and Crommalhill were his farfamed feetrests when our lurch as lout let free into the Lubar heloved; mareschalled his wardmotes and delimited the main; netted before nibbling, can scarce turn a scale but, grossed after meals, weighs a town in himself; Banba prayed for his conversion, Beurla missed that grand old voice; a Colossus among cabbages, the Melarancitrone of fruits; larger than life, doughtier than death; Gran Turco, orege forment; lachsembulger, leperlean; the sparkle of his genial fancy, the depth of his calm sagacity, the clearness of his spotless honour, the flow of his boundless benevolence; our family furbear, our tribal tarnpike; quary was he invincibled and cur was he burked; partitioned Irskaholm, united Irishmen; he took a svig at his own methyr but she tested a bit gorky and as for the salmon he was coming up in him all life long; comm, eilerdich, hecklebury and sawyer thee, warden; silent as the bee in honey, stark as the breath on hauwck, Costello, Kinsella, Mahony, Moran, though you rope Amrique your home ruler is Dan; figure right, he is hoisted by the scurve of his shaggy neck, figure left, he is rationed in isobaric patties among the crew; one asks was he poisoned, one thinks how much did he leave; ex-gardener (Riesenge-birger), fitted up with planturous existencies would make Roseoo-greedy (mite's) little hose; taut sheets and scuppers awash but the oil silk mack Liebsterpet micks his aquascutum; the enjoyment he took in kay women, the employment he gave to gee men; sponsor to a squad of piercers, ally to a host of rawlies; against lightning, explosion, fire, earthquake, flood, whirlwind, burglary, third party, rot, loss of cash, loss of credit, impact of vehicles; can rant as grave as oxtail soup and chat as gay as a porto flippant; is unhesitent in his unionism and yet a pigotted nationalist; Sylviacola is shy of him, Matrosenhosens nose the joke; shows the sinews of peace in his chest-o-wars; fiefeofhome, ninehundred and thirtunine years of copyhold; is aldays open for polemypolity's sake when he's not sun-times closed for the love of Janus; sucks life's eleaxir from the petti-pickles of the Jewess and ruoulls in sulks if any popeling runs down the Huguenots; Boomaport, Walleslee, Ubermeerschall Blowcher and Supercharger, Monsieur Ducrow, Mister Mudson, master gardi-ner; to one he's just paunch and judex, to another full of beans and brehons; hallucination, cauchman, ectoplasm; passed for baabaa blacksheep till he grew white woo woo woolly; was drummatoysed by Mac Milligan's daughter and put to music by one shoebard; all fitzpatricks in his emirate remember him, the boys of wetford hail him babu; indanified himself with boro tribute and was schenkt publicly to brigstoll; was given the light in drey orchafts and en-tumuled in threeplexes; his likeness is in Terrecuite and he giveth rest to the rainbowed; lebriety, frothearnity and quality; his reverse makes a virtue of necessity while his obverse mars a mother by in-vention; beskilk his gunwale and he's the second imperial, untie points, unhook tenters and he's lath and plaster; calls upon All-thing when he fails to appeal to Eachovos; basidens, ardree, kong-semma, rexregulorum; stood into Dee mouth, then backed broad-side on Baulacleeva; either eldorado or ultimate thole; a kraal of fou feud fires, a crawl of five pubs; laid out lashings of laveries to hunt down his family ancestors and then pled double trouble or quick quits to hush the buckers up; threw pebblets for luck over one sodden shoulder and dragooned peoplades armed to their teeth; pept as Gaudio Gambrinus, grim as Potter the Grave; ace of arts, deuce of damimonds, trouble of clubs, fear of spates; cumbrum, cumbrum, twiniceynurseys fore a drum but tre to uno tips the scale; reeled the titleroll opposite a brace of girdles in Silver on the Screen but was sequenced from the set as Crookback by the even more titulars, Rick, Dave and Barry; he can get on as early as the twenty-second of Mars but occasionally he doesn't come off before Virgintiquinque Germinal; his Indian name is Hapapoosiesobjibway and his number in arithmosophy is the stars of the plough; took weapon in the province of the pike and let fling his line on Eelwick; moves in vicous cicles yet remews the same; the drain rats bless his offals while the park birds curse his floodlights; Portobello, Equadocta, Therecocta, Percorello; he pours into the softclad shellborn the hard cash earned in Watling Street; his birth proved accidental shows his death its grave mistake; brought us giant ivy from the land of younkers and bewitthered Apostolopolos with the gale of his gall; while satisfied that soft youthful bright matchless girls should bosom into fine silkclad joyous blooming young women is not so pleased that heavy swearsome strongsmelling irregularshaped men should blottout active handsome wellformed frankeyed boys; herald hairy-fair, alloaf the wheat; husband your aunt and endow your nepos; hearken but hush it, screen him and see; time is, an archbishopric, time was, a tradesmen's entrance; beckburn brooked with wath, scale scarred by scow; his rainfall is a couple of kneehighs while his meanst grass temperature marked three in the shade; is the melt-ingpoint of snow and the bubblingplace of alcohol; has a tussle with the trulls and then does himself justice; hinted at in the eschato-logical chapters of Humphrey's *Justesse of the Jaypees* and hunted for by Theban recensors who sniff there's something behind the *Bug of the Deaf*; the king was in his cornerwall melking mark so murry, the queen was steep in armbour feeling fain and furry, the mayds was midst the hawthorns shoeing up their hose, out pimps the back guards (pomp!) and pump gun they goes; to all his fore-tellers he reared a stone and for all his comethers he planted a tree; forty acres, sixty miles, white stripe, red stripe, washes his fleet in annacrwatter; whou missed a porter so whot shall he do for he wanted to sit for Pimploco but they've caught him to stand for Sue?; Dutchlord, Dutchlord, overawes us; Headmound, king and martyr, dunstung in the Yeast, Pitre-le-Pore-in Petrin, Barth-the-Grete-by-the-Exchange; he hestens towards dames troth and wedding hand like the prince of Orange and Nassau while he has trinity left be-hind him like Bowlbeggar Bill-the-Bustonly; brow of a hazelwood, pool in the dark; changes blowicks into bullocks and a well of Ar-tesia into a bird of Arabia; the handwriting on his facewall, the cryptoconchoidsiphonostomata in his exprussians; his birthspot lies beyond the herospont and his burialplot in the pleasant little field;

is the yldist kiosk on the pleninsula and the unguest hostel in Saint
Scholarland; walked many hundreds and many score miles of streets
and lit thousands in one nightlights in hectares of windows; his
great wide cloak lies on fifteen acres and his little white horse decks
by dozens our doors; O sorrow the sail and woe the rudder that were
set for Mairie Quai!; his suns the huns, his dartars the tartars, are
plenty here today; who repulsed from his burst the bombolts of Os-
tenton and falchioned each flash downsaduck in the deep; apersonal
problem, a locative enigma; upright one, vehicule of arcanisation
in the field, lying chap, floodsupplier of celiculation through ebb-
lanes; a part of the whole as a port for a whale; Dear Hewitt
Castello, Equerry, were daylighted with our outing and are looking
backwards to unearly summers, from Rhoda Dundrums; is above
the seedfruit level and outside the leguminiferous zone; when older
links lock older hearts then he'll resemble she; can be built with
glue and clippings, scrawled or voided on a buttress; the night express sings his story, the song of sparrownotes on his stave of wires;
he crawls with lice, he swarms with saggarts; is as quiet as a mursque
but can be as noisy as a sonogog; was Dilmun when his date was
palmy and Mudlin when his nut was cracked; suck up the sease,
lep laud at ease, one lip on his lap and one cushlin his crease; his
porter has a mighty grasp and his baxters the boon of broadwhite;
as far as wind dries and rain eats and sun turns and water bounds
he is exalted and depressed, assembled and asundered; go away, we
are deluded, come back, we are disghosted; bored the Ostrov, leapt
the Inferus, swam the Mabbul and flure the Moyle; like fat, like
fatlike tallow, of greasefulness, yea of dripping greasefulness; did
not say to the old, old, did not say to the scorbutic, scorbutic; he
has founded a house, Uru, a house he has founded to which he has
assigned its fate; bears a raaven geulant on a fjeld duiv; ruz the halo
off his varlet when he appeared to his shecook as Haycock, Emmet,
Boaro, Toaro, Osterich, Mangy and Skunk; pressed the beer of aled
age out of the nettles of rashness; put a roof on the lodge for Hymn
and a coq in his pot pro homo; was dapifer then pancircensor then
hortifex magnus; the topes that tippled on him, the types that toppled off him; still starts our hares yet gates our goat; pocketbook
packetboat, gapman gunrun; the light of other days, dire dreary
darkness; our awful dad, Timour of Tortur; puzzling, startling,
shocking, nay, perturbing; went puffing from king's brugh to new
customs, doffing the gibbous off him to every breach of all size; with
Pa's new heft and Papa's new helve he's Papapa's old cutlass

Papapapa left us; when youngheaded oldshouldered and middlish-neck aged about; caller herring everydaily, turgid tarpon overnight; see Loryon the comaleon that changed endocrine history by loeven his loaf with forty bannucks; she drove him dafe till he driv her blind up; the pigeons doves be perchin all over him one day on Baslesbridge and the ravens duv be pitchin their dark nets after him the next night behind Koenigstein's Arbour; tronf of the rep, comf of the priv, prosp of the pub; his headwood it's ideal if his feet are bally clay; he crashed in the hollow of the park, trees down, as he soared in the vaguum of the phoenix, stones up; looks like a moultain boultter and sounds like a rude word; the mountaen view, some lumin pale round a lamp of succar in boinyn water; three shots a puddy at up blup saddle; made up to Miss MacCormack Ni La-carthy who made off with Darly Dermod, swank and swarthy; once diamond cut garnet now dammat cuts groany; you might find him at the Florence but watch our for him in Wynn's Hotel; theer's his bow and wheer's his leaker and heer lays his bequiet hearse, deep; Swed Albiony, likeliest villain of the place; Hennery Canterel — Cockran, eggotisters, limitated; we take our tays and frees our fleas round sadurn's mounted foot; built the Lund's kirk and destroyed the church's land; who guesse his title grabs his deeds; fletch and prities, fash and chaps; artful Juke of Wilysly; Hugglebelly's Fun-niral; Kukkuk Kallikak; heard in camera and excruciated; boon when with benches billeted, bann if buckshotbackshattered; heav-engendered, chaosfoedted, earthborn; his father presumptively ploughed it deep on overtime and his mother as all evince must have travailled her fair share; a footprinse on the Megacene, hetman un-whorsed by Searingsand; honorary captain of the extemporised fire brigade, reported to be friendly with the police; the door is still open; the old stock collar is coming back; not forgetting the time you laughed at Elder Charterhouse's duckwhite pants and the way you said the whole township can see his hairy legs; by stealth of a kersse her aulburntress abaft his nape she hung; when his kettle became a hearthsculdus our thorstyites set their lymphyamphyre; his year-letter concocted by masterhands of assays, his hallmark imposed by the standard of wrought plate; a pair of pectorals and a triple-screen to get a wind up; lights his pipe with a rosin tree and hires a towhorse to haul his shoes; cures slavey's scurvy, breaks barons boils; called to sell polosh and was found later in a bedroom; has his seat of justice, his house of mercy, his corn o'copious and his stacks a'rye; prospector, he had a rooksacht, retrospector, he holds the holpenstake; won the freedom of new yoke for the minds of jugoslaves; acts active, peddles in passivism and is a gorgon of self-ridgeousness; pours a laughsworth of his illformation over a larmsworth of salt; half heard the single maiden speech La Belle spun to her Grand Mount and wholed a lifetime by his ain fireside, wondering was it hebrew set to himmeltones or the quicksilversong of qwaternions; his troubles may be over but his doubles have still to come; the lobster pot that crabbed our keel, the garden pet that spoiled our squeezed peas; he stands in a lovely park, sea is not far, importunate towns of X, Y and Z are easily over reached; is an excrescence to civilised humanity and but a wart on Europe; wanamade singsigns to soundsense and yit he wanna git all his flesch nuemaid motts truly prural and plusible; has excisively large rings and is uncustomarily perfumed; lusteth ath he listeth the cleah whithpeh of a themise; is a prince of the fingallian in a hiberniad of hoolies; has a hodge to wherry him and a frenchy to curry him and a brabanson for his beeter and a fritz at his switch; was waylaid of a parker and beschotten by a buckeley; kicks lintils when he's cuppy and casts Jacob's arroroots, dime after dime, to poor waifstrays on the perish; reads the charms of H. C. Endersen all the weaks of his evenin and the crimes of Ivaun the Taurrible every strongday morn; soaps you soft to your face and slaps himself when he's badend; owns the bulgiest bungbarrel that ever was tiptapped in the privace of the Mullingar Inn; was born with a nuasilver tongue in his mouth and went round the coast of Iron with his lift hand to the scene; raised but two fingers and yet smelt it would day; for whom it is easier to found a see in Ebblannah than for I or you to find a dubbeltye in Dampsterdamp; to live with whom is a lifemayor and to know whom a liberal education; was dipped in Hoily Olives and chrysmed in Scent Otooles; hears cricket on the earth but annoys the life out of predikants; still turns the durc's ear of Darius to the now thoroughly infurioted one of God; made Man with juts that jerk and minted money mong maney; likes a six acup pudding when he's come whome sweetwhome; has come through all the eras of livsadventure from moonshine and shampaying down to clouts and pottled porter; woollem the farsed, hahnreich the althe, charge the sackend, writchad the thord; if a mandrake shricked to convultures at last surviving his birth the weibduck will wail bitternly over the rotter's resurrection; loses weight in the moon night but girds girder by the sundawn; with one touch of nature set a veiled world agrin and went within a sheet of tissuepaper of the option of three gaols; who could see at one blick a saumon taken with a lance, hunters pursuing a doe, a swallowship in full sail, a whyterobe lifting a host; faced flappery like old King Cnut and turned his back like Cincinnatus; is a farfar and morefar and a hoar father Nakedbucker in villas old as new; squats aquart and cracks aquaint when it's flaggin in town and on haven; blows whiskery around his summit but stehts stout upon his footles; stutters fore he falls and goes mad entirely when he's waked; is Timb to the pearly morn and Tomb to the mourning night; and an he had the best bunbaked bricks in bould Babylon for his pitching plays he'd be lost for the want of his wan wubblin wall?

Answer: Finn MacCool!

2. Does your mutter know your mike?

Answer: When I turn meoptics, from suchurban prospects, 'tis my filial's bosom, doth behold with pride, that pontificator, and circumvallator, with his dam night garrulous, slipt by his side. Ann alive, the lisp of her, 'twould grig mountains whisper her, and the bergs of Iceland melt in waves of fire, and her spoon-me-spondees, and her dirckle-me-ondenees, make the Rageous Ossean, kneel and quaff a lyre! If Dann's dane, Ann's dirty, if he's plane she's purty, if he's fane, she's flirty, with her auburnt streams, and her coy cajoleries, and her dabblin drolleries, for to rouse his rudderup, or to drench his dreams. If hot Hammurabi, or cowld Clesiastes, could espy her pranklings, they'd burst bounds agin, and renounce their ruings, and denounce their doings, for river and iver, and a night. Amin!

3. Which title is the true-to-type motto-in-lieu for that Tick for Teac thatchment painted witt wheth one darkness, where asnake is under clover and birds aprowl are in the rookeries and a magda went to monkishouse and a riverpaard was spotted, which is not Whichcroft Whorort not Ousterholm Dreyschluss not Haraldsby, grocer, not Vatandcan, vintner, not Houseboat and Hive not Knox-atta-Belle not O'Faynix Coalprince not Wohn Squarr Roomyeck not Ebblawn Downes not Le Decer Le Mieux not Benjamin's Lea not Tholomew's Whaddingtun gnot Antwarp gnat Musca not Corry's not Weir's not the Arch not The Smug not The Dotch House not The Uval nothing Grand nothing Splendid (Grahot or Spletel) nayther *Erat Est Erit* noor *Non michi sed luciphro?*

Answer: Thine obesity, O civilian, hits the felicitude of our orb!

4. What Irish capitol city (a dea o dea!) of two syllables and six letters, with a deltic origin and a nuinous end, (ah dust oh dust!)

can boost of having *a*) the most extensive public park in the world, *b*) the most expensive brewing industry in the world, *c*) the most expansive peopling thoroughfare in the world, *d*) the most phillo-hippuc theobibbous paùpulation in the world: and harmonise your abecedeed responses?

Answer: *a*) Delfas. And when ye'll hear the gould hommers of my heart, my floxy loss, bingbanging again the ribs of yer resistance and the tenderbolts of my rivets working to your destraction ye'll be sheverin wi' all yer dinful sobs when *we'll* go riding acope-acurly, you with yer orange garland and me with my conny cordial, down the greaseways of rollicking into the waters of wetted life. *b*) Dorhqk. And sure where can you have such good old chimes anywhere, and *leave* you, as on the Mash and how'tis I would be engaging you with my plovery soft accents and descanting upover the scene beunder me of your loose vines in their hairafall with them two loving loofs braceleting the slims of your ankles and your mouth's flower rose and sinking ofter the soapstone of silvry speech. *c*) Nublid. Isha, why wouldn't we be happy, avourneen, on the mills'money he'll soon be leaving you as soon as I've my own owned brooklined Georgian mansion's lawn to recruit upon by Doctor Cheek's special orders and my copper's panful of soybeans and Irish in my east hand and a James's Gate in my west, after all the errears and erroriboose of combarative embottled history, and your goodself churning over the newleaved butter (*more* power to you), the choicest and the cheapest from Atlanta to Oconee, while I'll be drowsing in the gaarden. *d*) Dalway. I hooked my thoroughgoing trotty the first down Spanish Place, Mayo I make, Tuam I take, Sligo's sleek but Galway's grace. Holy eel and Sainted Salmon, chucking chub and ducking dace, Rodiron's not *your* aequal! says she, leppin half the lane. *abcd*) A bell a bell on Shalldoll Steepbell, ond be'll go massplon pristmoss speople, Shand praise gon ness our fayst moan *neople*, our prame *Shandeepen*, pay name muy *feepence*, moy nay non *Aequallllllll!*

5. Whad slags of a loughladd would retten smuttyflesks, empt-out old mans, melk vitious geit, scareoff jackinjills fra tiddle anding, smoothpick waste papish pastures, insides man outsiders angell, sprink dirted water around village, newses, tobaggon and sweeds, plain general kept, louden on the kirkpeal, foottreats given to malafides, outshriek hyelp hyelp nor his hair efter buggelawrs, might underhold three barnets, putzpolish crotty bottes, nightcoover all fireglims, serve's time till baass, grindstone his kniveses, fullest

boarded, lewd man of the method of godliness, perchance he nieows and thans sits in the spoorwaggen, X.W.C.A. on Z.W.C.U., Doorsteps, Limited, or Baywindaws Bros swobber preferred. Walther Clausetter's and Sons with the H. E. Chimneys' Company to not skreve, will, on advices, be bacon or stable hand, must begripe fullstandingly irers' langurge, jublander or northquain bigger prefurred, all duties, kine rights, family fewd, outings fived, may get earnst, no get combitsch, profusional drinklords to please obstain, he is fatherlow soundigged inmoodmined pershoon but aleconnerman, nay, *that* must he isn't?

Answer: Pore ole Joe!

6. What means the saloon slogan Summon In The Housesweep Dinah?

Answer: Tok. Galory bit of the sales of Cloth nowand I have to beeswax the bringing in all the claub of the porks to us how I thawght I knew his stain on the flower if me ask and can could speak and he called by me midden name Tik. I am your honey honeysugger phwhtphwht tha Bay and who bruk the dandleass and who seen the blackcullen jam for Tomorrha's big pickneck I hope it'll pour prais the Climate of all Ireland I heard the grackles and I skimming the crock on all your sangwidges fippence per leg per drake. Tuk. And who eight the last of the goosebellies that was mowlding from measlest years and who leff that there and who put that here and who let the kilkenny stale the chump. Tek. And whowasit youwasit propped the pot in the yard and whatinthe nameofsen lukeareyou rubbinthe sideofthe flureofthe lobbywith. *Shite!* will you have a plateful? Tak.

7. Who are those component partners of our societate, the doorboy, the cleaner, the sojer, the crook, the squeezer, the lounger, the curman, the tourabout, the mussroomsniffer, the bleakablue tramp, the funpowtherplother, the christymansboxer, from their prés salés and Donnybrook prater and Roebuck's campos and the Ager Arountown and Crumglen's grassy but Kimmage's champ and Ashtown fields and Cabra fields and Finglas fields and Santry fields and the feels of Raheny and their fails and Baldoygle to them who are latecomers all the year's round by anticipation, are the porters of the passions in virtue of retroratiocination, and, contributting their conflingent controversies of differentiation, unify their voxes in a vote of vaticination, who crunch the crusts of comfort due to depredation, drain the mead for misery to incur intoxication, condone every evil by practical justification and condam any good to its own gratifica-

tion, who are ruled, roped, duped and driven by those numen daimons, the feekeepers at their laws, nightly consternation, fortnightly fornication, monthly miserecordation and omniannual recreation, doyles when they deliberate but sullivans when they are swordsed, Matey, Teddy, Simon, Jorn, Pedher, Andy, Barty, Philly, Jamesy Mor and Tom, Matt and Jakes Mac Carty?

Answer: The Morphios!

8. And how war yore maggies?

Answer: They war loving, they love laughing, they laugh weeping, they weep smelling, they smell smiling, they smile hating, they hate thinking, they think feeling, they feel tempting, they tempt daring, they dare waiting, they wait taking, they take thanking, they thank seeking, as born for lorn in lore of love to live and wive by wile and rile by rule of ruse 'reathed rose and hose hol'd home, yeth cometh elope year, coach and four, Sweet Peck-at-my-Heart picks one man more.

9. Now, to be on anew and basking again in the panoroma of all flores of speech, if a human being duly fatigued by his dayety in the sooty, having plenxty off time on his gouty hands and vacants of space at his sleepish feet and as hapless behind the dreams of accuracy as any camelot prince of dinmurk, were at this auctual futule preteriting unstant, in the states of suspensive exanimation, accorded, throughout the eye of a noodle, with an earsighted view of old hopeinhaven with all the ingredient and egregiunt whights and ways to which in the curse of his persistence the course of his tory will had been having recourses, the reverberration of knotcracking awes, the reconjungation of nodebinding ayes, the redissolusingness of mindmouldered ease and the thereby hang of the Hoel of it, could such a none, whiles even led comesilencers to comeliewithhers and till intempestuous Nox should catch the gallicry and spot lucan's dawn, byhold at ones what is main and why tis twain, how one once meet melts in tother wants poignings, the sap rising, the foles falling, the nimb now nihilant round the girlyhead so becoming, the wrestless in the womb, all the rivals to allsea, shakeagain, O disaster! shakealose, Ah how starring! but Heng's got a bit of Horsa's nose and Jeff's got the signs of Ham round his mouth and the beau that spun beautiful pales as it palls, what roserude and oragious grows gelb and greem, blue out the ind of it! Violet's dyed! then *what* would that fargazer seem to seemself to seem seeming of, dimm it all?

Answer: A collideorscape!

10. What bitter's love but yurning, what' sour lovemutch but a bref burning till shee that drawes dothe smoake retourne?

Answer: I know, pepette, of course, dear, but listen, precious! Thanks, pette, those are lovely, pitounette, delicious! But mind the wind, sweet! What exquisite hands you have, you angiol, if you didn't gnaw your nails, isn't it a wonder you're not achamed of me, you pig, you perfect little pigaleen! I'll nudge you in a minute! I bet you use her best Perisian smear off her vanity table to make them look so rosetop glowstop nostop. I know her. Slight me, would she? For every got I care! Three creamings a day, the first during her shower and wipe off with tissue. Then after cleanup and of course before retiring. Beme shawl, when I think of that espos of a Clancarbry, the foodbrawler, of the sociationist party with hiss blackleaded chest, hello, Prendregast! that you, Innkipper, and all his fourteen other fullback maulers or hurling stars or whatever the dagos they are, baiting at my Lord Ornery's, just becups they won the egg and spoon there so ovally provencial at Balldole. My Eilish assent he seed makes his admiracion. He is seeking an opening and means to be first with me as his belle alliance. Andoo musnoo play zeloso! Soso do todas. Such is Spanish. Stoop alittle closer, fealse! Delightsome simply! Like Jolio and Romeune. I haven't fell so turkish for ages and ages! Mine's me of squisious, the chocolate with a soul. Extraordinary! Why, what are they all, the mucky lot of them only? Sht! I wouldn't pay three hairpins for them. Peppt! That's rights, hold it steady! Leg me pull. Pu! Come big to Iran. Poo! What are you nudging for? No, I just thought you were. Listen, loviest! Of course it was *too* kind of you, miser, to remember my sighs in shockings, my often expressed wish when you were wandering about my trousseaurs and before I forget it don't forget, in your extensions to my personality, when knotting my remembrancetie, shoeweek will be trotting back with red heels at the end of the moon but look what the fool bought cabbage head and, as I shall answer to gracious heaven, I'll always in always remind of snappy new girters, me being always the one for charms with my very best in proud and gloving even if he was to be vermillion miles my youth to live on, the rubberend Mr Polkingtone, the quonian fleshmonger who Mother Browne solicited me for unlawful converse with, with her mug of October (a pots on it!), creaking around on his old shanksaxle like a crosty old cornquake. Airman, waterwag, terrier, blazer! I'm fine, thanks ever! Ha! O mind you poo tickly. Sall I puhim in momou. Mummum. Funny spot to have

a fingey! I'm terribly sorry, I swear to you I am! May you never
see me in my birthday pelts seenso tutu and that her blanches
mainges may rot leprous off her whatever winking maggis I'll bet
by your cut you go fleurting after with all the glass on her and
the jumps in her stomewhere! Haha! I suspected she was! Sink her!
May they fire her for a barren ewe! So she says: Tay for
thee? Well, I saith: Angst so mush: and desired she might not take
it amiss if I esteemed her but an odd. If I did ate toughturf I'm
not a mishymissy. Of course I know, pettest, you're so learningful
and considerate in yourself, so friend of vegetables, you long
cold cat you! Please by acquiester to meek my acquointance! Codling,
snakelet, iciclist! My diaper has more life to it! Who drowned you
in drears, man, or are you pillale with ink? Did a weep get past
the gates of your pride? My tread on the clover, sweetness? Yes,
the buttercups told me, hug me, damn it all, and I'll kiss you back
to life, my peachest. I mean to make you suffer, meddlar, and I
don't care this fig for contempt of courting. That I chid you, sweet
sir? You know I'm tender by my eye. Can't you read by daz-
zling ones through me true? Bite my laughters, drink my tears. Pore
into me, volumes, spell me stark and spill me swooning. I just
don't care what my thwarters think. Transname me loveliness, now
and here me for all times! I'd risk a policeman passing by, Magrath
or even that beggar of a boots at the Post. The flame? O, pardone!
That was what? Ah, did you speak, stuffstuff? More poestries from
Chickspeer's with gleechoreal music or a jaculation from the garden
of the soul. Of I be leib in the immoralities? O, you mean the
strangle for love and the sowiveall of the prettiest? Yep, we open
hap coseries in the home. And once upon a week I improve on
myself I'm so keen on that New Free Woman with novel inside.
I'm always as tickled as can be over Man in a Surplus by the Lady
who Pays the Rates. But I'm as pie as is possible. Let's root
out Brimstoker and give him the thrall of our lives. It's Dracula's
nightout. For creepsake don't make a flush! Draw the shades, curfe
you, and I'll beat any sonnamonk to love. Holy bug, how my high-
ness would jump to make you flame your halve a bannan in two
when I'd run my burning torchlight through (to adore me there
and then cease to be? Whatever for, blossoms?) Your hairmejig if
you had one. If I am laughing with you? No, lovingest, I'm not
so dying to take my rise out of you, adored. Not in the very least.
True as God made my Mamaw hiplength modesty coatmawther!
It's only because the rison is I'm only any girl, you lovely fellow

of my dreams, and because old somebooby is not a roundabout,
my trysting of the tulipies, like that puff pape bucking Daveran
assoiling us behinds. What a nerve! He thinks that's what the
vesprey's for. How vain's that hope in cleric's heart Who still pursues
th'adult' rous art, Cocksure that rusty gown of his Will make fair
Sue forget his phiz! Tame Schwipps. Blessed Marguerite bosses, I
hope they threw away the mould or else we'll have Ballshossers and
Sourdamapplers with their medical assassinations all over the place.
But hold hard till I've got my latchkey vote and I'll teach him when
to wear what woman callours. On account of the gloss of the gleison
Hasaboobrawbees isabeaubel. And because, you pluckless lankaloot,
I hate the very thought of the thought of you and because, dearling,
of course, adorest, I was always meant for an engindear from
the French college, to be musband, *nomme d'engien,* when we do
and contract with encho tencho solver when you are married to
reading and writing which pleasebusiness now won't be long for
he's so loopy on me and I'm so leapy like since the day he carried
me from the boat, my saviored of eroes, to the beach and I
left on his shoulder one fair hair to guide hand and mind to its
softness. Ever so sorry! I beg your pardon, I was listening to every
treasuried word I said fell from my dear mot's tongue otherwise
how could I see what you were thinking of our granny? Only I
wondered if I threw out my shaving water. Anyway, here's my arm,
pulletneck. Gracefully yours. Move your mouth towards minth, more,
preciousest, more on more! To please me, treasure. Don't be a,
I'm not going to! Sh! nothing! A cricri somewhere! Buybuy! I'm
fly! Hear, pippy, under the limes. You know bigtree are all against
gravstone. They hisshistenency. Garnd ond mand! So chip chirp
chirrup, cigolo, for the lug of Migo! The little passdoor, I go you
before, so, and you're at my apron stage. Shy is him, dovey? Mus-
forget there's an audience. I have been lost, angel. Cuddle, ye divil
ye! It's our toot-a-toot. Hearhere! Sensation! Let them, their whole
four courtships! Let them, Bigbawl and his boosers' eleven makes
twelve territorials. The Old Sot's Hole that wants wide streets to
commission their noisense in, at the Mitchells *v.* Nicholls. *Aves
Selvae Acquae Valles!* And my waiting twenty classbirds, sitting on
their stiles! Let me finger their eurhythmytic. And you'll see if I'm
selfthought. They're all of them out to please. Wait! In the name
of. And all the holly. And some the mistle and it Saint Yves. Hoost!
Ahem! There's Ada, Bett, Celia, Delia, Ena, Fretta, Gilda, Hilda,
Ita, Jess, Katty, Lou, (they make me cough as sure as I read them)

Mina, Nippa, Opsy, Poll, Queeniee, Ruth, Saucy, Trix, Una, Vela, Wanda, Xenia, Yva, Zulma, Phoebe, Thelma. And Mee! The reformatory boys is goaling in for the church so we've all comefeast like the groupsuppers and caught lipsolution from Anty Pravidance under penancies for myrtle sins. When their bride was married all my belles began ti ting. A ring a ring a rosaring! Then everyone will hear of it. Whoses wishes is the farther to my thoughts. But I'll plant them a poser for their nomanclatter. When they're out with the daynurse doing Chaperon Mall. Bright pigeons all over the whirrld will fly with my mistletoe message round their loverib-boned necks and a crumb of my cake for each chasta dieva. We keeps all and sundry papers. In th' amourlight, O my darling! No, I swear to you by Fibsburrow churchdome and Sainte Andrée's Undershift, by all I hold secret from my world and in my underworld of nighties and naughties and all the other wonderwearlds! Close your, notmust look! Now open, pet, your lips, pepette, like I used my sweet parted lipsabuss with Dan Holohan of facetious memory taught me after the flannel dance, with the proof of love, up Smock Alley the first night he smelled pouder and I coloured beneath my fan, *pipetta mia*, when you learned me the linguo to melt. Whowham would have ears like ours, the blackhaired! Do you like that, *silenzioso*? Are you enjoying, this same little me, my life, my love? Why do you like my whisping? Is it not divinely deluscious? But in't it bafforyou? *Misi, misi!* Tell me till my thrillme comes! I will not break the seal. I am enjoying it still, I swear I am! Why do you prefer its in these dark nets, if why may ask, my sweetykins? Sh sh! Longears is flying. No, sweetissest, why would that ennoy me? But don't! You want to be slap well slapped for that. Your delighted lips, love, be careful! Mind my duvetyne dress above all! It's golded silvy, the newest sextones with princess effect. For Rutland blue's got out of passion. So, so, my precious! O, I can see the cost, chare! Don't tell me! Why, the boy in sheeps' lane knows that. If I sell whose, dears? Was I sold here' tears? You mean those conversation lozenges? How awful! The bold shame of me! I wouldn't, chickens, not for all the juliettes in the twinkly way! I could snap them when I see them winking at me in bed. I didn't did so, my intended, or was going to or thinking of. Shshsh! Don't start like that, you wretch! I thought ye knew all and more, ye aucthor, to explique to ones the significat of their exsystems with your nieu nivulon lead. It's only another queer fish or other in Brin-brou's damned old trouchorous river again, Gothewishegoths bless us and spare her! And gibos rest from the bosso! Excuse me for swearing, love, I swear to the sorrasims on their trons of Uian I didn't mean to by this alpin armlet! Did you really never in all our cantalang lives speak clothse to a girl's before? No! Not even to the charmermaid? How marfellows! Of course I believe you, my own dear doting liest, when you tell me. As I'd live to, O, I'd love to! Liss, liss! I muss whiss! Never that ever or I can remember dearstreaming faces, you may go through me! Never in all my whole white life of my matchless and pair. Or ever for bitter be the frucht of this hour! With my whiteness I thee woo and bind my silk breasths I thee bound! Always, Amory, amor andmore! Till always, thou lovest! Shshshsh! So long as the lucksmith. Laughs!

11. If you met on the binge a poor acheseyeld from Ailing, when the tune of his tremble shook shimmy on shin, while his countrary raged in the weak of his wailing, like a rugilant pugilant Lyon O'Lynn; if he maundered in misliness, plaining his plight or, played fox and lice, pricking and dropping hips teeth, or wringing his handcuffs for peace, the blind blighter, praying Dieuf and Domb Nostrums foh thomethinks to eath; if he weapt while he leapt and guffalled quith a quhimper, made cold blood a blue mundy and no bones without flech, taking kiss, kake or kick with a suck, sigh or simper, a diffle to larn and a dibble to lech; if the fain shinner pegged you to shave his immartial, wee skillmustered shoul with his ooh, hoodoodoo! broking wind that to wiles, woemaid sin he was partial, we don't think, Jones, we'd care to this evening, would you?

Answer: No, blank ye! So you think I have impulsivism? Did they tell you I am one of the fortysixths? And I suppose you heard I had a wag on my ears? And I suppose they told you too that my roll of life is not natural? But before proceeding to conclusively confute this begging question it would be far fitter for you, if you dare! to hasitate to consult with and consequentially attempt at my disposale of the same dime-cash problem elsewhere naturalistically of course, from the blinkpoint of so eminent a spatialist. From it you will here notice, Schott, upon my for the first remarking you that the sophology of Bitchson while driven as under by a purely dime-dime urge is not without his cashcash characktericksticks, borrowed for its nonce ends from the fiery goodmother Miss Fortune (who the lost time we had the pleasure we have had our little *recherché* brush with, what, Schott?) and as I further could have told you as brisk as your D.B.C. behaviouristically *pailleté* with a coat of homoid icing which is in reality only a done by chance ridiculisation of the whoo-whoo and where's hairs theorics of Wine-stain. To put it all the more plumbsily. The speechform is a mere sorrogate. Whilst the quality and tality (I shall explex what you ought to mean by this with its proper when and where and why and how in the subsequent sentence) are alternativomentally harro-gate and arrogate, as the gates may be.

Talis is a word often abused by many passims (I am working out a quantum theory about it for it is really most tantumising state of affairs). A pessim may frequent you to say: Have you been seeing much of Talis and Talis those times? optimately meaning: Will you put up at hree of irish? Or a ladyeater may perhaps have casualised as you temptoed her *à la sourdine:* Of your plates? Is Talis de Talis, the swordswallower, who is on at the Craterium the same Talis von Talis, the penscrusher, no funk you! who runs his duly mile? Or this is a perhaps cleaner example. At a recent postvortex piece infustigation of a determinised case of chronic spinosis an extension lecturer on The Ague who out of matter of form was trying his seesers, Dr's Het Ubeleeft, borrowed the question: Why's which Suchman's *talis qualis?* to whom, as a fatter of macht, Dr Gedankje of Stoutgirth, who was wiping his whistle, toarsely retoarted: While thou beast' one zoom of a whorl! (Talis and Talis originally mean the same thing, hit it's: Qualis.)

Professor Loewy-Brueller (though as I shall promptly prove his whole account of the Sennacherib as distinct from the Shalmanesir sanitational reforms and of the Mr Skekels and Dr Hydes problem in the same connection differs *toto coelo* from the fruit of my own investigations — though the reason I went to Jericho must remain for certain reasons a political secret — especially as I shall shortly be wanted in Cavantry, I congratulate myself, for the same and other reasons — as being again hopelessly vitiated by what I have now resolved to call the dime and cash diamond fallacy) in his talked off confession which recently met with such a leonine uproar on its escape after its confinement *Why am I not born like a Gentileman and why am I now so speakable about my own eatables* (Feigen-baumblatt and Father, Judapest, 5688, A.M.) whole-heartedly takes off his gabbercoat and wig, honest draughty fellow, in his public interest, to make us see how though, as he says: 'by Allswill' the inception and the descent and the endswell of Man is *temporarily* wrapped in obscenity, looking through at these accidents with the faroscope of television, (this nightlife instrument needs still some subtractional betterment in the readjustment of the more refrangible angles to the squeals of his hypothesis on the outer tin sides), I can easily believe heartily in my own most spacious immensity as my ownhouse and microbemost cosm when I am reassured by ratio that the cube of my volumes is to the surfaces of their subjects as the sphericity of these globes (I am very pressing for a parliamentary motion this term which, under my guidance, would establish the deleteriousness of decorousness in the morbidisation of the modern mandaboutwoman type) is to the feracity of Fairynelly's vacuum. I need not anthrapologise for any obintentional (I must here correct all that school of neoitalian or paleoparisien schola of tinkers and spanglers who say I'm wrong *parcequeue* out of revolscian from romanitis I want to be) downtrodding on my foes. Professor Levi-Brullo, F.D. of Sexe-Weiman-Eitelnaky finds, from experiments made by hinn with his Nuremberg eggs in the one hands and the watches cunldron apan the oven, though it is astensably a case of Ket's rebollions cooling the Popes back, because the number of squeer faiths in weekly circulation will not be appreciably augmented by the notherslogging of my cupolar clods. What the romantic in rags pines after like all tomtompions haunting crevices for a deadbeat escupement and what het importunes our *Mitleid* for in accornish with the Mortadarthella taradition is the poorest commononguardiant waste of time. *His* everpresent toes are always in retaliessian out throuth his overpast boots. Hear him squak! Teek heet to that looswallawer how he bolo the bat! Tyro a toray! *When* Mullocky won the couple of colds, *when* we were stripping in number three, I would like the neat drop that would malt in my mouth but I fail to see *when* (I am purposely refraining from expounding the obvious fallacy as to the specific gravitates of the two deglutables implied nor to the lapses lequou asousiated with the royal gorge through students of mixed hydrostatics and pneumodipsics will after some difficulties grapple away with my meinungs). Myrrdin aloer! as old Marsellas Cambriannus puts his. But, on Professor Llewellys ap Bryllars, F.D., Ph. Dr's showings, the plea, if he pleads, is all posh and robbage on a melodeontic scale since his man's *when* is no otherman's *quandour* (Mine, dank you?) while, for aught I care for the contrary, the all is *where* in love as war and the plane where me arts soar you'd aisy rouse a thunder from and where I cling true'tis there I climb tree and where Innocent looks best (pick!) there's holly in his ives.

As my explanations here are probably above your understandings, lattlebrattons, though as augmentatively uncomparisoned as Cadwan, Cadwallon and Cadwalloner, I shall revert to a more expletive method which I frequently use when I have to sermo with muddle-crass pupils. Imagine for my purpose that you are a squad of urchins, snifflynosed, goslingnecked, clothyheaded, tangled in your lacings, tingled in your pants, etsitaraw etcicero. And you, Bruno Nowlan, take your tongue out of your inkpot! As none of you knows javanese I will give all my easyfree translation of the old fabulist's parable. Allaboy Minor, take your head out of your satchel! *Audi,* Joe Peters! *Exaudi* facts!

The Mookse and The Gripes.

Gentes and laitymen, fullstoppers and semicolonials, hybreds and lubberds!

Eins within a space and a wearywide space it wast ere wohned a Mookse. The onesomeness wast alltolonely, archunsitslike, broady oval, and a Mookse he would a walking go (My hood! cries Antony Romeo), so one grandsumer evening, after a great morning and his good supper of gammon and spittish, having flabelled his eyes, pilleoled his nostrils, vaticanated his ears and palliumed his throats, he put on his impermeable, seized his impugnable, harped on his crown and stepped out of his immobile *De Rure Albo* (socolled becauld it was chalkfull of masterplasters and had borgeously letout gardens strown with cascadas, pintacostecas, horthoducts and curry-combs) and set off from Ludstown *a spasso* to see how badness was badness in the weirdest of all pensible ways.

As he set off with his father's sword, his *lancia spezzata,* he was girded on, and with that between his legs and his tarkeels, our once in only Bragspear, he clanked, to my clinking, from veetoes to three-top, every inch of an immortal.

He had not walked over a pentiadpair of parsecs from his azylium when at the turning of the Shinshone Lanteran near Saint Bowery's-without-his-Walls he came (secunding to the one one oneth of the propecies, *Amnis Limina Permanent*) upon the most unconsciously boggylooking stream he ever locked his eyes with. Out of the colliens it took a rise by daubing itself Ninon. It looked little and it smelt of brown and it thought in narrows and it talked showshallow. And as it rinn it dribbled like any lively purliteasy: *My, my, my! Me and me! Little down dream don't I love thee!*

And, I declare, what was there on the yonder bank of the stream that would be a river, parched on a limb of the olum, bolt downright, but the Gripes? And no doubt he was fit to be dried for why had he not been having the juice of his times?

His pips had been neatly all drowned on him; his polps were charging odours every older minute; he was quickly for getting the dresser's desdaign on the flyleaf of his frons; and he was quietly for giving the bailiff's distrain on to the bulkside of his *cul de Pompe.* In all his specious heavings, as be lived by Optimus Maximus, the Mookse had never seen his Dubville brooder-on-low so nigh to a pickle.

Adrian (that was the Mookse now's assumptinome) stuccstill phiz-à-phiz to the Gripes in an accessit of aurignacian. But Allmookse must to Moodend much as Allrouts, austereways or wastersways, in roaming run through Room. Hic sor a stone, singularly illud, and on hoc stone Seter satt huc sate which it filled quite poposter-ously and by acclammitation to its fullest justotoryum and where-opum with his unfallable encyclicling upom his alloilable, diupetriark of the wouest, and the athemystsprinkled pederect he always walked with, *Deusdedit,* cheek by jowel with his frisherman's blague, *Bellua Triumphanes,* his everyway addedto wallat's collectium, for yea longer he lieved yea broader he betaught of it, the fetter, the summe and the haul it cost, he looked the first and last micahlike laicness of Quartus the Fifth and Quintus the Sixth and Sixtus the Seventh giving allnight sitting to Lio the Faultyfindth.

— Good appetite us, sir Mookse! How do you do it? cheeped the Gripes in a wherry whiggy maudelenian woice and the jackasses all within bawl laughed and brayed for his intentions for they knew their sly toad lowry now. I am rarumominum blessed to see you, my dear mouster. Will you not perhopes tell me everything if you are pleased, sanity? All about aulne and lithial and allsall allinall about awn and liseias? Ney?

Think of it! O miserendissimest retempter! A Gripes!

— Rats! bullowed the Mookse most telesphorously, the concionator, and the sissymusses and the zozzymusses in their robenhauses quailed to hear his tardeynois at all for you cannot wake a silken nouse out of a hoarse oar. Blast yourself and your anathomy infairioriboos! No, hang you for an animal rurale! I am superbly in my supremest poncif! Abase you, baldyqueens! Gather behind me, satraps! Rots!

— I am till infinity obliged with you, bowed the Gripes, his whine having gone to his palpruy head. I am still always having a wish on all my extremities. By the watch, what is the time, pace?

Figure it! The pining peever! To a Mookse!

—Ask my index, mund my achilles, swell my obolum, woshup my nase serene, answered the Mookse, rapidly by turning clement, urban, eugenious and celestian in the formose of good grogory humours. Quote awhore? That is quite about what I came on *my* missions with *my* intentions *laudibiliter* to settle with *you*, barbarousse. Let thor be orlog. Let Pauline be Irene. Let you be Beeton. And let me be Los Angeles. Now measure your length. Now estimate my capacity. Well, sour? Is this space of our couple of hours too dimensional for you, temporiser? Will you give you up? *Como? Fuert it?*

Sancta Patientia! You should have heard the voice that answered him! *Culla vosellina.*

—I was just thinkling upon that, swees Mooksey, but, for all the rime on my raisins, if I connow make my submission, I cannos give you up, the Gripes whimpered from nethermost of his wanhope. Ishallassoboundbewilsothoutoosezit. My tumble, loudy bullocker, is my own. My velicity is too fit in one stockend. And my spetial inexshellsis the belowing things ab ove. But I will never be abler to tell Your Honoriousness (here he near lost his limb) though my corked father was bott a pseudowaiter, whose o'cloak you ware.

Incredible! Well, hear the inevitable.

—*Your* temple, *sus in cribro!* Semperexcommunicambiambisumers. Tugurios-in-Newrobe or Tukurias-in-Ashies. Novarome, my creature, blievend bleives. My building space in lyonine city is always to let to leonlike Men, the Mookse in a most consistorous allocution pompifically with immediate jurisdiction constantinently concludded (what a crammer for the shapewrucked Gripes!). And I regret to proclaim that it is out of my temporal to help you from being killed by inchies, (what a thrust!), as we first met each other newwhere so airly. (Poor little sowsieved subsquashed Gripes! I begin to feel contemption for him!). My side, thank decretals, is as safe as motherour's houses, he continued, and I can seen from my holeydome what it is to be wholly sane. Unionjok and be joined to yok! Parysis, *tu sais,* crucycrooks, belongs to him who parises himself. And there I must leave you subject for the pressing. I can prove that against you, weight a momentum, mein goot enemy! or Cospol's not our star. I bet you this dozen odd. This foluminous dozen odd. *Quas primas*—but 'tis bitter to compote my knowledge's fructos of. Tomes.

Elevating, to give peint to his blick, his jewelled pederect to

the allmysty cielung, he luckystruck blueild out of a few shouldbe
santillants, a cloister of starabouts over Maples, a lucciolys in Teresa
street and a stopsign before Sophy Barratt's, he gaddered togodder
the odds docence of his vellumes, gresk, letton and russicruxian,
onto the lapse of his prolegs, into umfullth onescuppered, and sat
about his widerproof. He proved it well whoonearth dry and drysick
times, and *vremiament, tu cesses,* to the extinction of Niklaus altogether (Niklaus Alopysius having been the once Gripes's popwilled
nimbum) by Neuclidius and Inexagoras and Mumfsen and Thump-
sem, by Orasmus and by Amenius, by Anacletus the Jew and by
Malachy the Augurer and by the Cappon's collection and after that,
with Cheekee's gelatine and Alldaybrandy's formolon, he reproved
it ehrltogether when not in that order sundering in some different
order, alter three thirty and a hundred times by the binomial dioram
and the penic walls and the ind, the Inklespill legends and the
rure, the rule of the hoop and the blessons of expedience and the
jus, the jugicants of Pontius Pilax and all the mummyscrips in Sick
Bokes' Juncroom and the Chapters for the Cunning of the Chapters
of the Conning Fox by Tail.

While that Mooksius with preprocession and with proprecession,
duplicitly and diplussedly, was promulgating ipsofacts and sadcontras
this raskolly Gripos he had allbust seceded in monophysicking his
illsobordunates. But asawfulas he had caught his base semenoyous
sarchnaktiers to combuccinate upon the silipses of his aspillouts and
the acheporeoozers of his haggyown pneumax to synerethetise with
the breadchestviousness of his sweeatovular ducose sofarfully the log-
gerthuds of his sakellaries were fond at variance with the synodals
of his somepooliom and his babskissed nepogreasymost got the hoof
from his philioquus.

— Efter thousand yaws, O Gripes con my sheepskins, yow will
be belined to the world, enscayed Mookse the pius.

— Ofter thousand yores, amsered Gripes the gregary, be the goat
of MacHammud's, yours may be still, O Mookse, more botheared.

— Us shall be chosen as the first of the last by the electress of
Vale Hollow, obselved the Mookse nobily, for par the unicum of
Elelijiacks, Us am in Our stabulary and that is what Ruby and
Roby fall for, blissim.

The Pills, the Nasal Wash (Yardly's), the Army Man Cut, as
british as bondstrict and as straightcut as when that brokenarched
traveller from Nuzuland . . .

— Wee, cumfused the Gripes limply, shall not even be the last of the first, wee hope, when oust are visitated by the Veiled Horror. And, he added: Mee are relying entirely, see the fortethurd of Elissabed, on the weightiness of mear's breath. Puffut!

Unsightbared embouscher, relentless foe to social and business succes! (Hourihaleine) It might have been a happy evening but . . .

And they viterberated each other, *cants et coluber* with the wildest ever wielded since Tarriestinus lashed Pissasphaltium.

— Unuchorn!

— Ungulant!

— Uvuloid!

— Uskybeak!

And bullfolly answered volleyball.

Nuvoletta in her lightdress, spunn of sisteen shimmers, was looking down on them, leaning over the bannistars and listening all she childishly could. How she was brightened when Shouldrups in his glaubering hochskied his welkinstuck and how she was overclused when Kneesknobs on his zwivvel was makeacting such a paulse of himshelp! She was alone. All her nubied companions were asleeping with the squirrels. Their mivver, Mrs Moonan, was off in the Fuerst quarter scrubbing the backsteps of Number 28. Fuvver, that Skand, he was up in Norwood's sokaparlour, eating oceans of Voking's Blemish. Nuvoletta listened as she reflected herself, though the heavenly one with his constellatria and his emanations stood between, and she tried all she tried to make the Mookse look up at her (but *he* was fore too adiaptotously farseeing) and to make the Gripes hear how coy she could be (though he was much too schystimatically auricular about *his ens* to heed her) but it was all mild's vapour moist. Not even her feignt reflection, Nuvoluccia, could they toke their gnoses off for their minds with intrepifide fate and bungless curiasity, were conclaved with Heliogobbleus and Commodus and Enobarbarus and whatever the coordinal dickens they did as their damprauch of papyrs and buchstubs said. As if that was their spiration! As if theirs could duiparate her queendim! As if she would be third perty to search on search proceedings! She tried all the winsome wonsome ways her four winds had taught her. She tossed her sfumastelliacinous hair like *la princesse de la Petite Bretagne* and she rounded her mignons arms like Mrs Cornwallis-West and she smiled over herself like the beauty of the image of the pose of the daughter of the queen of the Emperour of Irelande and she sighed after herself as were she born to bride

with Tristis Tristior Tristissimus. But, sweet madonine, she might
fair as well have carried her daisy's worth to Florida. For the Mookse,
a dogmad Accanite, were not amoosed and the Gripes, a dubliboused
Catalick, wis pinefully obliviscent.

—I see, she sighed. There are menner.

The siss of the whisp of the sigh of the softzing at the stir of
the ver grose O arundo of a long one in midias reeds: and shades
began to glidder along the banks, greepsing, greepsing, duusk unto
duusk, and it was as glooming as gloaming could be in the waste
of all peacable worlds. Metamnisia was allsoonome coloroform brune;
citherior spiane an eaulande, innemorous and unnumerose. The
Mookse had a sound eyes right but he could not all hear. The Gripes
had light ears left yet he could but ill see. He ceased. And he ceased,
tung and trit, and it was neversoever so dusk of both of them. But
still Moo thought on the deeps of the undths he would profoundth
come the morrokse and still Gri feeled of the scripes he would escipe
if by grice he had luck enoupes.

Oh, how it was duusk! From Vallee Maraia to Grasyaplaina,
dormimust echo! Ah dew! Ah dew! It was so duusk that the tears
of night began to fall, first by ones and twos, then by threes and
fours, at last by fives and sixes of sevens, for the tired ones were
wecking, as we weep now with them. *O! O! O! Par la pluie!*

Then there came down to the thither bank a woman of no appearance (I believe she was a Black with chills at her feet) and she
gathered up his hoariness the Mookse motamourfully where he was
spread and carried him away to her invisible dwelling, thats hights,
Aquila Rapax, for he was the holy sacred solem and poshup spit
of her boshop's apron. So you see the Mookse he had reason as
I knew and you knew and he knew all along. And there came
down to the hither bank a woman to all important (though they
say that she was comely, spite the cold in her heed) and, for he
was as like it as blow it to a hawker's hank, she plucked down
the Gripes, torn panicky autotone, in angeu from his limb and cariad
away its beotitubes with her to her unseen shieling, it is, *De Rore
Coeli*. And so the poor Gripes got wrong; for that is always how
a Gripes is, always was and always will be. And it was never so
thoughtful of either of them. And there were left now an only elmtree
and but a stone. Polled with pietrous, Sierre but saule. O! Yes! And
Nuvoletta, a lass.

Then Nuvoletta reflected for the last time in her little long life
and she made up all her myriads of drifting minds in one. She

cancelled all her engauzements. She climbed over the bannistars; she gave a childy cloudy cry: *Nuée! Nuée!* A lightdress fluttered. She was gone. And into the river that had been a stream (for a thousand of tears had gone eon her and come on her and she was stout and struck on dancing and her muddied name was Missisliffi) there fell a tear, a singult tear, the loveliest of all tears (I mean for those crylove fables fans who are 'keen' on the prettypretty commonface sort of thing you meet by hopeharrods) for it was a leaptear. But the river tripped on her by and by, lapping as though her heart was brook: *Why, why, why! Weh, O weh! I'se so silly to be flowing but I no canna stay!*

No applause, please! Bast! The romescot nattleshaker will go round your circulation in *diu dursus.*

Allaboy, Major, I'll take your reactions in another place after themes. Nolan Browne, you may now leave the classroom. Joe Peters, Fox.

As I have now successfully explained to you my own naturalborn rations which are even in excise of my vaultybrain insure me that I am a mouth's more deserving case by genius. I feel in symbathos for my ever devoted friend and halfaloafonwashed, Gnaccus Gnoccovitch. Darling gem! Darling smallfox! Horoseshoew! I could love that man like my own ambo for being so baileycliaver though he's a nawful curillass and I must slav to methodiousness. I want him to go and live like a theabild in charge of the night brigade on Tristan da Cunha, isle of manoverboard, where he'll make Number 106 and be near Inaccessible. (The meeting of mahoganies, be the waves, rementious me that this exposed sight though it pines for an umbrella of its own and needs a shelter belt of the true service sort to keep its boles clean, — the weeping beeches, Picea and Tillia, are in a wild state about it — ought to be classified, as Cricketbutt Willowm and his two nurserymen advisers suggested, under genus Inexhaustible when we refloat upon all the butternat, sweet gum and manna ash redcedera which is so purvulent there as if there was howthorns in Curraghchasa which ought to look as plane as a lodgepole to anybody until we are introduced to that pinetacotta of Verney Rubeus where the deodarty is pinctured for us in a pure stand, which we do not doubt ha has a habitat of doing, but without those selfsownseedlings which are a species of proof that the largest individual *can* occur at or in an olivetion such as East Conna Hillock where it mixes with foolth accacians and common sallies and *is* tender) *Vux Populus,* as we say in hickoryhockery and I wish we had some more glasses of *arbor vitae*. Why roat by the roadside or awn over alum pot? Alderman Whitebeaver is dakyo. He ought to go away for a change of ideas and he'd have a world of things to look back on. Do, sweet Daniel! If I weren't a jones in myself I'd elect myself to be his dolphin in the wildsbillow because he is such a barefooted rubber with my supersocks pulled over his face which I publicked in my bestback garden for the laetification of siderodromites and to the irony of the stars. You will say it is most unenglish and I shall hope to hear that you will not be wrong about it. But I further, feeling a bit husky in my truths.

Will you please come over and let us mooremoore murgessly to each's other down below our vices. I am underheerd by old billfaust. Wilsh is full of curks. The coolskittle is philip deblinite. Mr Wist is thereover beyeind the wantnot. Wilsh and wist are as thick of thins udder as faust on the deblinite. Sgunoshooto estas preter la tapizo malgranda. Lilegas al si en sia chambro. Kelkefoje funcktas, kelkefoje srumpas Shultroj. Houdian Kiel vi fartas, mia nigra sinjoro? And from the poignt of fun where I am crying to arrive you at they are on allfore as foibleminded as you can feel they are fablebodied.

My heeders will recoil with a great leisure how at the outbreak before trespassing on the space question where even michelangelines have fooled to dread I proved to mindself as to your sotisfiction how his abject all through (the *quickquid* of Professor Ciondolone's too frequently hypothecated *Bettlermensch*) is nothing so much more than a mere cashdime however genteel he may want ours, if we please (I am speaking to us in the second person), for to this graded intellecktuals dime *is* cash and the cash system (you must not be allowed to forget that this is all contained, I mean the system, in the dogmarks of origen on spurios) means that I cannot now have or nothave a piece of cheeps in your pocket at the same time and with the same manners as you can now nothalf or half the cheek apiece I've in mind unless Burrus and Caseous have not or not have seemaultaneously sysentangled themselves, selldear to soldthere, once in the dairy days of buy and buy.

Burrus, let us like to imagine, is a genuine prime, the real choice, full of natural greace, the mildest of milkstoffs yet unbeaten as a risicide and, of course, obsoletely unadulterous whereat Caseous is obversely the revise of him and in fact not an ideal choose by any meals, though the betterman of the two is meltingly addicted to the more casual side of the arrivaliste case and, let me say it at once, as zealous over him as is passably he. The seemsame home and histry seeks and hidepence which we used to be reading for our prepurgatory, hot, Schott? till Duddy shut the shopper op and Mutti, poor Mutti! brought us our poor suppy, (ah who! eh how!) in Acetius and Oleosus and Sellius Volatilis and Petrus Papricus! Our Old Party quite united round the Slatbowel at Commons: Pfarrer Salamoss himself and that sprog of a Pedersill and his Sprig of Thyme and a dozen of the Murphybuds and a score and more of the hot young Capels and Lettucia in her greensleeves and you too and me three, twinsome bibs but hansome ates, like shakespill and eggs! But there's many a split pretext bowl and jowl; and (snob screwing that cork, Schott!) to understand this as well as you can, feeling how backward you are in your down-to-the-ground benches, I have completed the following arrangement for the coarse use of stools and if I don't make away with you I'm beyond Caesar outnullused.

The older sisars (Tyrants, regicide is too good for you!) become unbeurrable from age, (the compositor of the farce of dustiny however makes a thunpledrum mistake by letting off this pienofarte effect as his furst act as that is where the juke comes in) having been sort-of-nineknived and chewly removed (this soldier-author-batman for all his commontoryism is just another of those souftsiezed bubbles who never quite got the sandhurst out of his eyes so that the champaign he draws for us is as flop as a plankrieg) the twinfreer types are billed to make their reupprearance as the knew kneck and knife knickknots on the deserted *champ de bouteilles*. (A most cursery reading into the Persic-Uraliens hostery shows us how Fonnumagula picked up that propper numen out of a colluction of prifixes though to the permienting cannasure the Coucousien oafsprung of this sun of a kuk is as sattin as there's a tub in Tobolosk) *Ostiak della Vogul Marina!* But that I dannoy the fact of wanton to weste point I could paint you to that butter (cheese it!) if you had some wash. Mordvealive! Oh me none onsens! Why the case is as inessive and impossive as kezom hands! Their interlocative is conprovocative just as every hazzy hates to having a hazbane in her noze. Caseous may bethink himself a thought of a caviller but Burrus has the reachly roundered head that goes best with thofthinking defensive fideism. He has the lac of wisdom under every dent in his lofter while the other follow's onni vesy milky indeedmymy. Laughing over the linnuts and weeping off the uniun. He hisn't the hey og he lisn't the lug, poohoo. And each night sim misses mand he winks he had the semagen. It was aptly and corrigidly stated (and, it is royally needless for one *ex ungue Leonem* to say by whom) that his seeingscraft was that clarety as were the whole-borough of Poutresbourg to be averlaunched over him pitchbatch he could still make out with his augstritch the green moat in Ireland's Eye. Let me sell you the fulltroth of Burrus when he wore a younker. Here it is, and chorming too, in six by sevens! A cleanly line, by the gods! A king off duty and a jaw for ever! And what a cheery ripe outlook, good help me Deus v Deus! If I were to speak my ohole mouthful to arinam about it you should call me the ormuzd aliment in your midst of faime. Eat ye up, heat ye up! sings the somun in the salm. *Butyrum et mel comedet ut sciat reprobare malum et eligere bonum.* This, of course, also explains why we were taught to play in the childhood: *Der Haensli ist ein Butterbrot, mein Butterbrot! Und Koebi iss dein Schtinkenkot! Ja! Ja! Ja!*

This in fact, just to show you, is Caseous, the brutherscutch or puir tyron: a hole or two, the highstinks aforefelt and anygo prigging wurms. Cheesugh! you complain. And Hi Hi High must say you are not Hoa Hoa Hoally in the wrong!

Thus we cannot escape our likes and mislikes, exiles or ambusheers, beggar and neighbour and—this is where the dimeshow advertisers advance the temporal relief plea—let us be tolerant of antipathies. *Nex quovis burro num fit mercaseus?* I am not hereby giving my final endorsement to the learned ignorants of the Cusanus philosophism in which old Nicholas pegs it down that the smarter the spin of the top the sounder the span of the buttum (what the worthy old auberginiste ought to have meant was: the more stolidly immobile *in space* appears to me the bottom which is presented to use in time by the top primomobilisk &c.). And I shall be misunderstord if understood to give an unconditional sinequam to the heroicised furibouts of the Nolanus theory, or, at any rate, of that substrate of apart from hissheory where the Theophil swoors that on principial he was the pointing start of his odiose by comparison and that whiles eggs will fall cheapened all over the walled the Bure will be dear on the Brie.

Now, while I am not out now to be taken up as unintentionally recommending the Silkebjorg tyrondynamon machine for the more economical helixtrolysis of these amboadipates until I can find space to look into it myself a little more closely first I shall go on with my decisions after having shown to you in good time how both products of our social stomach (the excellent Dr Burroman, I noticed by the way from his emended food theory, has been carefully digesting the very wholesome criticism I helped him to in my princeps edition which is all so munch to the cud) are mutuearly polarised the incompatabilily of any delusional acting as ambivalent to the fixation of his pivotism. Positing, as above, too males pooles, the one the pictor of the other and the omber the *Skotia* of the one, and looking wantingly around our undistributed middle between males we feel we must waistfully woent a female to focus and on this stage there pleasantly appears the cowrymaid M. whom we shall often meet below who introduces herself upon us at some precise hour which we shall again agree to call absolute zero or the babbling pumpt of platinism. And so like that former son of a kish who went up and out to found his farmer's ashes we come down home gently on our own turnedabout asses to meet Margareen.

We now romp through a period of pure lyricism of shamebred music (technologically, let me say, the appetising entry of this subject on a fool chest of vialds is plumply pudding the carp before doevre hors) evidenced by such words in distress as *I cream for thee, Sweet Margareen,* and the more hopeful *O Margareena! O Margareena! Still in the bowl is left a lump of gold!* (Correspondents, by the way, will keep on asking me what is the correct garnish to serve drisheens with. Tansy Sauce. Enough). The pawnbreaking pathos of the first of these shoddy pieces reveals it as a Caseous effort. Burrus's bit is often used for a toast. Criniculture can tell us very precisely indeed how and why this particular streak of yellow silver first appeared on (not in) the bowel, that is to see, the human head, bald, black, bronze, brown, brindled, betteraved or blanchemanged where it might be usefully compared with an earwig on a fullbottom. I am offering this to Signorina Cuticura and I intend to take it up and bring it under the nosetice of Herr Harlene by way of diverting his attentions. Of course the unskilled singer continues to pervert our wiser ears by subordinating the space-element, that is to sing, the *aria,* to the time-factor, which ought to be killed, *ill tempor.* I should advise any unborn singer who may still be among my heeders to forget her temporal diaphragm at home (the best thing that could happen to it!) and attack the roulade with a swift *colpo di glottide* to the lug (though Maace I will insist was reclined from overdoing this, his recovery often being slow) and then, O! on the third dead beat, O! to cluse her eyes and aiopen her oath and see what spice I may send her. How? Cease thee, cantatrickee! I fain would be solo. Arouse thee, my valour! And save for e'er my true Bdur!

I shall have a word to say in a few yards about the acoustic and orchidectural management of the tonehall but, as ours is a vivarious where one plant's breaf is a lunger planner's byscent and you may not care for argon, it will be very convenient for me for the emolument to pursue Burrus and Caseous for a rung or two up their isocelating biangle. Every admirer has seen my goulache of Marge (she is *so* like the sister, you don't know, and they both dress ALIKE!) which I titled *The Very Picture of a Needlesswoman* which in the presence ornates our national cruetstand. This genre of portraiture of changes of mind in order to be truly torse should evoke the bush soul of females so I am leaving it to the experienced victim to complete the general suggestion by the mental addition of a wallopy bound or, should the zulugical zealot prefer it, a congorool teal. The hatboxes which composed Rhomba, lady Trabezond (Marge in her *excelsis*), also comprised the climactogram up which B and C may fondly be imagined ascending and are suggestive of gentlemen's spring modes, these modes carrying us back to the superimposed claylayers of eocene and pleastoseen formation and the gradual morphological changes in our body politic which Professor Ebahi-Ahuri of Philadespoinis (Ill) — whose bluebutterbust I have just given his coupe de grass to — neatly names a *boîte à surprises*. The boxes, if I may break the subject gently, are worth about fourpence pourbox but I am inventing a more patent process, foolproof and pryperfect (I should like to ask that Shedlock Homes person who is out for removing the roofs of our criminal classics by what *deductio ad domunum* he hopes *de tacto* to detect anything unless he happens of himself, *movibile tectu*, to have a slade off) after which they can be reduced to a fragment of their true crust by even the youngest of Margees if she will take plase to be seated and smile if I please.

Now there can be no question about it either that I having done as much, have quite got the size of that demilitery young female (we will continue to call her Marge) whose types may be met with in any public garden, wearing a very "dressy" affair, known as an "ethel" of instep length and with a real fur, reduced to 3/9, and muffin cap to tone (they are "angelskin" this fall), ostentatiously hemming apologetically over the shirtness of some "sweet" garment, when she is not sitting on all the free benches avidously reading about "it" but ovidently on the look out for "him" or so "thrilled" about the best dressed dolly pram and beautiful elbow competition or at the movies swallowing sobs and blowing bixed miscuits over "childe" chaplain's "latest" or on the verge of the gutter with some bobbedhair brieffrocked babyma's toddler (the Smythe-Smythes now keep TWO domestics and aspire to THREE male ones, a shover, a butlegger and a sectary) held hostage at armslength, teaching His Infant Majesty how to make waters worse.

(I am closely watching Master Pules, as I have regions to suspect from my post that her "little man" is a secondary schoolteacher under the boards of education, a voted disciple of Infantulus who is being utilised thus publicly by the *seducente infanta* to conceal her own more mascular personality by flaunting frivolish finery over men's inside clothes, for the femininny of that totamulier will always lack the musculink of a verumvirum. My solotions for the proper parturience of matres and the education of micturious mites must stand over from the moment till I tackle this tickler hussy for occupying my uttentions.)

Margareena she's very fond of Burrus but, alick and alack! she velly fond of chee. (The important influence exercised on everything by this eastasian import has not been till now fully flavoured though we can comfortably taste it in this case. I shall come back for a little more say farther on.) A cleopatrician in her own right she at once complicates the position while Burrus and Caseous are contending for her misstery by implicating herself with an elusive Antonius, a wop who would appear to hug a personal interest in refined chees of all chades at the same time as he wags an antomine art of being rude like the boor. This Antonius-Burrus-Caseous grouptriad may be said to equate the *qualis* equivalent with the older socalled *talis* on *talis* one just as quantly as in the hyperchemical economantarchy the tantum ergons irruminate the quantum urge so that eggs is to whey as whay is to zeed like your golfchild's abe boob caddy. And this is why any simple philadolphus of a fool you like to dress, an athemisthued lowtownian, exlegged phatrisight, may be awfully green to one side of him and fruitfully blue on the other which will not screen him however from appealing to my gropesarching eyes, through the strongholes of my acropoll, as a boosted blasted bleating blatant bloaten blasphorus blesphorous idiot who kennot tail a bomb from a painapple when he steals one and wannot psing his psalmen with the cong in our gregational pompoms with the canting crew.

No! Topsman to your Tarpeia! This thing, Mister Abby, is

nefand. (And, taking off soutstuffs and alkalike matters, I hope we can kill time to reach the salt because there's some forceglass neutric assets bittering in the soldpewter for you to plump your pottage in). The thundering legion has stormed Olymp that it end. Twelve tabular times till now have I edicted it. Merus Genius to Careous Caseous! *Moriture, te salutat!* My phemous themis race is run, so let Demoncracy take the highmost! (Abraham Tripier. Those old diligences are quite out of date. Read next answer). I'll beat you so lon. (Bigtempered. Why not take direct action. See previous reply). My unchanging Word is sacred. The word is my Wife, to exponse and expound, to vend and to velnerate, and may the curlews crown our nuptias! Till Breath us depart! Wamen. Beware would you change with my years. Be as young as your grandmother! The ring man in the rong shop but the rite words by the rote order! *Ubi lingua nuncupassit, ibi fas! Adversus hostem semper sac!* She that will not feel my fulmoon let her peel to thee as the hoyden and the impudent! That mon that hoth no moses in his sole nor is not awed by conquists of word's law, who never with humself was fed and leaves his soil to lave his head, when his hope's in his highlows from whisking his woe, if he came to my preach, a proud pursebroken ranger, when the heavens were welling the spite of their spout, to beg for a bite in our bark *Noisdanger,* would meself and MacJeffet, four-in-hand, foot him out? — ay! — were he my own breastbrother, my doubled withd love and my singlebiassed hate, were we bread by the same fire and signed with the same salt, had we tapped from the same master and robbed the same till, were we tucked in the one bed and bit by the one flea, homogallant and hemycapnoise, bum and dingo, jack by churl, though it broke my heart to pray it, still I'd fear I'd hate to say!

12. *Sacer esto?*

Answer: *Semus sumus!*

Shem is as short for Shemus as Jem is joky for Jacob. A few tough-necks are still getatable who pretend that aboriginally he was of respectable stemming (he was an outlex between the lines of Ragonar Blaubarb and Horrild Hairwire and an inlaw to Capt. the Hon. and Rev. Mr Bbyrdwood de Trop Blogg was among his most distant connections) but every honest to goodness man in the land of the space of today knows that his back life will not stand being written about in black and white. Putting truth and untruth together a shot may be made at what this hybrid actually was like to look at.

Shem's bodily getup, it seems, included an adze of a skull, an eight of a larkseye, the whoel of a nose, one numb arm up a sleeve, forty-two hairs off his uncrown, eighteen to his mock lip, a trio of barbels from his megageg chin (sowman's son), the wrong shoulder higher than the right, all ears, an artificial tongue with a natural curl, not a foot to stand on, a handful of thumbs, a blind stomach, a deaf heart, a loose liver, two fifths of two buttocks, one gleetsteen avoirdupoider for him, a manroot of all evil, a salmonkelt's thinskin, eelsblood in his cold toes, a bladder tristended, so much so that young Master Shemmy on his very first debouch at the very dawn of protohistory seeing himself such and such, when playing with thistlewords in their garden nursery, Griefotrofio, at Phig Streat 111, Shuvlin, Old Hoeland, (would we go back there now for sounds, pillings and sense? would we now for annas and annas? would we for fullscore eight and a liretta? for twelve blocks one bob? for four testers one groat? not for a dinar! not for jo!) dictited to of all his little brothron and sweestureens the first riddle of the universe: asking, when is a man not a man?: telling them take their time, yungfries, and wait till the tide stops (for from the first his day was a fortnight) and offering the prize of a bittersweet crab, a little present from the past, for their copper age was yet unminted, to the winner. One said

when the heavens are quakers, a second said when Bohemeand lips,
a third said when he, no, when hold hard a jiffy, when he is a gnaw-
stick and detarmined to, the next one said when the angel of death
kicks the bucket of life, still another said when the wine's at wits-
ends, and still another when lovely wooman stoops to conk him,
one of the littliest said me, me, Sem, when pappa papared the harbour, one of the wittiest said, when he yeat ye abblokooken and he
zmear hezelf zo zhooken, still one said when you are old I'm grey
fall full wi sleep, and still another when wee deader walkner, and
another when he is just only after having being semisized, another
when yea, he hath no mananas, and one when dose pigs they begin
now that they will flies up intil the looft. All were wrong, so Shem
himself, the doctator, took the cake, the correct solution being — all
give it up? — ; when he is a — yours till the rending of the rocks, —
Sham.

Shem was a sham and a low sham and his lowness creeped out
first via foodstuffs. So low was he that he preferred Gibsen's teatime
salmon tinned, as inexpensive as pleasing, to the plumpest roeheavy
lax or the friskiest parr or smolt troutlet that ever was gaffed between Leixlip and Island Bridge and many was the time he repeated
in his botulism that no junglegrown pineapple ever smacked like
the whoppers you shook out of Ananias' cans, Findlater and Gladstone's, Corner House, Englend. None of your inchthick blue-
blooded Balaclava fried-at-belief-stakes or juicejelly legs of the Grex's
molten mutton or greasilygristly grunters' goupons or slice upon
slab of luscious goosebosom with lump after load of plumpudding
stuffing all aswim in a swamp of bogoakgravy for that greeken-
hearted yude! Rosbif of Old Zealand! he could not attouch it. See
what happens when your somatophage merman takes his fancy to
our virgitarian swan? He even ran away with hunself and became
a farsoonerite, saying he would far sooner muddle through the hash
of lentils in Europe than meddle with Irrland's split little pea. Once
when among those rebels in a state of hopelessly helpless intoxication the piscivore strove to lift a czitround peel to either nostril,
hiccupping, apparently impromptued by the hibat he had with his
glottal stop, that he kukkakould flowrish for ever by the smell, as
the czitr, as the kcedron, like a scedar, of the founts, on mountains,
with limon on, of Lebanon. O! the lowness of him was beneath all
up to that sunk to! No likedbylike firewater or firstserved firstshot
or gulletburn gin or honest brewbarrett beer either. O dear no!
Instead the tragic jester sobbed himself wheywhingingly sick of

life on some sort of a rhubarbarous maundarin yellagreen funkle-
blue windigut diodying applejack squeezed from sour grapefruice
and, to hear him twixt his sedimental cupslips when he had gulfed
down mmmmuch too mmmmany gourds of it retching off to almost
as low withswillers, who always knew notwithstanding when they
had had enough and were rightly indignant at the wretch's hos-
pitality when they found to their horror they could not carry
another drop, it came straight from the noble white fat, jo, open-
wide sat, jo, jo, her why hide that, jo jo jo, the winevat, of the most
serene magyansty az archdiochesse, if she is a duck, she's a douches,
and when she has a feherbour snot her fault, now is it? artstouchups,
funny you're grinning at, fancy you're in her yet, Fanny Urinia.

Aint that swell, hey? Peamengro! Talk about lowness! Any dog's
quantity of it visibly oozed out thickly from this dirty little blacking
beetle for the very fourth snap the Tulloch-Turnbull girl with her
coldblood kodak shotted the as yet unremuneranded national apos-
tate, who was cowardly gun and camera shy, taking what he fondly
thought was a short cut to Caer Fere, Soak Amerigas, vias the ship-
steam *Pridewin*, after having buried a hatchet not so long before,
by the wrong goods exeunt, nummer desh to tren, into Patatapapa-
veri's, fruiterers and musical florists, with his *Ciaho, chavi! Sar shin,
shillipen?* she knew the vice out of bridewell was a bad fast man
by his walk on the spot.

[Johns is a different butcher's. Next place you are up town pay
him a visit. Or better still, come tobuy. You will enjoy cattlemen's
spring meat. Johns is now quite divorced from baking. Fattens, kills,
flays, hangs, draws, quarters and pieces. Feel his lambs! Ex! Feel
how sheap! Exex! His liver too is great value, a spatiality! Exexex!
COMMUNICATED.]

Around that time, moravar, one generally, for luvvomony hoped
or at any rate suspected among morticians that he would early turn
out badly, develop hereditary pulmonary T.B., and do for himself
one dandy time, nay, of a pelting night blanketed creditors, hearing
a coarse song and splash off Eden Quay sighed and rolled over, sure
all was up, but, though he fell heavily and locally into debit, not
even then could such an antinomian be true to type. He would not
put fire to his cerebrum; he would not throw himself in Liffey; he
would not explaud himself with pneumantics; he refused to saffro-
cake himself with a sod. With the foreign devil's leave the fraid born
fraud diddled even death. *Anzi*, cabled (but shaking the worth out
of his maulth: Guardacosta leporello? Szasas Kraicz!) from his

Nearapoblican asylum to his jonathan for a brother: Here tokay, gone tomory, we're spluched, do something, Fireless. And had answer: Inconvenient, David.

You see, chaps, it will trickle out, freaksily of course, but the tom and the shorty of it is: he was in his bardic memory low. All the time he kept on treasuring with condign satisfaction each and every crumb of trektalk, covetous of his neighbour's word, and if ever, during a Munda conversazione commoted in the nation's interest, delicate tippits were thrown out to him touching his evil courses by some wellwishers, vainly pleading by scriptural arguments with the opprobrious papist about trying to brace up for the kidos of the thing, Scally wag, and be a men instead of a dem scrounger, dish it all, such as: Pray, what is the meaning, sousy, of that continental expression, if you ever came acrux it, we think it is a word transpiciously like *canaille?*: or: Did you anywhere, kennel, on your gullible's travels or during your rural troubadouring, happen to stumble upon a certain gay young nobleman whimpering to the name of Low Swine who always addresses women out of the one corner of his mouth, lives on loans and is furtivefree yours of age? without one sigh of haste like the supreme prig he was, and not a bit sorry, he would pull a vacant landlubber's face, root with earwaker's pensile in the outer of his lauscher and then, lisping, the prattlepate parnella, to kill time, and swatting his deadbest to think what under the canopies of Jansens Chrest would any decent son of an Albiogenselman who had bin to an university think, let a lent hit a hint and begin to tell all the intelligentsia admitted to that tamileasy samtalaisy conclamazzione (since, still and before physicians, lawyers merchant, belfry pollititians, agricolous manufraudurers, sacrestanes of the Pure River Society, philanthropicks lodging on as many boards round the panesthetic at the same time as possible) the whole lifelong swrine story of his entire low cornaille existence, abusing his deceased ancestors wherever the sods were and one moment tarabooming great blunderguns (poh!) about his farfamed fine Poppamore, Mr Humhum, whom history, climate and entertainment made the first of his sept and always up to debt, though Eavens ears ow many fines he faces, and another moment visanvrersssas, cruaching three jeers (pah!) for his rotten little ghost of a Peppybeg, Mr Himmyshimmy, a blighty, a reeky, a lighty, a scrapy, a babbly, a ninny, dirty seventh among thieves and always bottom sawyer, till nowan knowed how howmely howme could be, giving unsolicited testimony on behalf of the absent, as glib as eaveswater to those present (who meanwhile, with increasing lack of interest in his semantics, allowed various subconscious smickers to drivel slowly across their fichers), unconsciously explaining, for inkstands, with a meticulosity bordering on the insane, the various meanings of all the different foreign parts of speech he misused and cuttlefishing every lie unshrinkable about all the other people in the story, leaving out, of course, foreconsciously, the simple worf and plague and poison they had cornered him about until there was not a snoozer among them but was utterly undeceived in the heel of the reel by the recital of the rigmarole.

He went without saying that the cull disliked anything anyway approaching a plain straightforward standup or knockdown row and, as often as he was called in to umpire any octagonal argument among slangwhangers, the accomplished washout always used to rub shoulders with the last speaker and clasp shakers (the hand-touch which is speech without words) and agree to every word as soon as half uttered, command me!, your servant, good, I revere you, how, my seer? be drinking that! quite truth, gratias, I'm youish, see wha'm hearing?, also goods, please it, me sure?, be filling this!, quiso, you said it, apasafello, muchas grassyass, is there firing-on-me?, is their girlic-on-you?, to your good self, your sulphur, and then at once focuss his whole unbalanced attention upon the next octag-onist who managed to catch a listener's eye, asking and imploring him out of his piteous onewinker, (*hemoptysia diadumenos*) whether there was anything in the world he could do to please him and to overflow his tumbletantaliser for him yet once more.

One hailcannon night (for his departure was attended by a heavy downpour) as very recently as some thousand rains ago he was therefore treated with what closely resembled parsonal violence, being soggert all unsuspectingly through the deserted village of Tumblin-on-the-Leafy from Mr Vanhomrigh's house at 81 bis Mab-bot's Mall as far as Green Patch beyond the brickfields of Salmon Pool by rival teams of slowspiers counter quicklimers who finally, as rahilly they had been deteened out rawther laetich, thought, busnis hits busnis, they had better be streaking for home after their Auborne-to-Auborne, with thanks for the pleasant evening, one and all disgustedly, instead of ruggering him back, and awake, recon-ciled (though they were as jealous as could be cullions about all the truffles they had brought on him) to a friendship, fast and furious, which merely arose out of the noxious pervert's perfect lowness. Again there was a hope that people, looking on him with the con-temp of the contempibles, after first gaving him a roll in the dirt, might pity and forgive him, if properly deloused, but the pleb was born a Quicklow and sank alowing till he stank out of sight.

All Saints beat Belial! Mickil Goals to Nichil! Notpossible! Already?

In Nowhere has yet the Whole World taken part of himself for his Wife;

By Nowhere have Poorparents been sentenced to Worms, Blood and Thunder for Life

Not yet has the Emp from Corpsica forced the Arth out of Engleterre;

Not yet have the Sachsen and Judder on the Mound of a Word made Warre;

Not yet Witchywithcy of Wench struck Fire of his Heath from on Hoath;

Not yet his Arcobaleine forespoken Peacepeace upon Oath;

Cleftfoot from Hempal must tumpel, Blamefool Gardener's bound to fall;

Broken Eggs will poursuive bitten Apples for where theirs is Will there's his Wall;

But the Mountstill frowns on the Millstream while their Madsons leap his Bier

And her Rillstrill liffs to His Murkesty all her daft Daughters laff in her Ear.

Till the four Shores of deff Tory Island let the douze dumm Eirewhiggs raille!

Hirp! Hirp! for their Missed Understandings! chirps the Ballat of Perce-Oreille.

O fortunous casualitas! Lefty takes the cherubcake while Rights cloves his hoof. Darkies never done tug that coon out to play nonexcretory, anti-sexuous, misoxenetic, gaasy pure, flesh and blood games, written and composed and sung and danced by Niscemus Nemon, same as piccaninnies play all day, those old (none of your honeys and rubbers!) games for fun and element we used to play with Dina and old Joe kicking her behind and before and the yellow girl kicking him behind old Joe, games like *Thom Thom the Thonderman, Put the Wind up the Peeler, Hat in the Ring, Prisson your Pritchards and Play Withers Team, Mikel on the Luckypig, Nickel in the Slot, Sheila Harnett and her Cow, Adam and Ell, Humble Bumble, Moggie's on the Wall, Twos and Threes, American Jump, Fox Come out of your Den, Broken Bottles, Writing a*

Letter to Punch, Tiptop is a Sweetstore, Henressy Crump Expolled,
Postman's Knock, Are We Fairlys Represented?, Solomon Silent
reading, Appletree Bearstone, I know a Washerwoman, Hospitals,
As I was Walking, There is Oneyone's House in Dreamcolohour,
Battle of Waterloo, Colours, Eggs in the Bush, Habberdasherisher,
Telling your Dreams, What's the Time, Nap, Ducking Mammy,
Last Man Standing, Heali Baboon and the Forky Theagues, Fickl-
eyes and Futilears, Handmarried but once in my Life and I'll never
commit such a Sin agin, Zip Cooney Candy, Turkey in the Straw,
This is the Way we sow the Seed of a long and lusty Morning,
Hops of Fun at Miliken's Make, I seen the Toothbrush with Pat
Farrel, Here's the Fat to graze the Priest's Boots, When his Steam
was like a Raimbrandt round Mac Garvey.

Now it is notoriously known how on that surprisingly bludgeony
Unity Sunday when the grand germogall allstar bout was harrily
the rage between our weltingtoms extraordinary and our pettythicks
the marshalaisy and Irish eyes of welcome were smiling daggers
down their backs, when the roth, vice and blause met the noyr blank
and rogues and the grim white and cold bet the black fighting tans,
categorically unimperatived by the maxims, a rank funk getting the
better of him, the scut in a bad fit of pyjamas fled like a leveret for
his bare lives, to Talviland, ahone ahaza, pursued by the scented
curses of all the village belles and, without having struck one blow,
(pig stole on him was lust he lagging it was becaused dust he shook)
kuskykorked himself up tight in his inkbattle house, badly the worse
for boosegas, there to stay in afar for the life, where, as there was
not a moment to be lost, after he had boxed around with his forte-
piano till he was whole bach bamp him and bump him blues, he
collapsed carefully under a bedtick from Schwitzer's, his face enveloped into a dead warrior's telemac, with a lullobaw's somnbomnet
and a whotwaterwottle at his feet to stoke his energy of waiting,
moaning feebly, in monkmarian monotheme, but tarned long and
then a nation louder, while engaged in swallowing from a large
ampullar, that his pawdry's purgatory was more than a nigger bloke
could bear, hemiparalysed by the tong warfare and all the shemozzle,
(*Daily Maily, fullup Lace! Holy Maly, Mothelup Joss!*) his cheeks
and trousers changing colour every time a gat croaked.

How is that for low, laities and gentlenuns? Why, dog of the
Crostiguns, whole continents rang with this Kairokorran lowness!
Sheols of houris in chems upon divans, (revolted stellas vespertine

vesamong them) at a bare (O!) mention of the scaly rybald ex-
claimed: Poisse!

But would anyone, short of a madhouse, believe it? Neither of
those clean little cherubum, Nero or Nobookisonester himself, ever
nursed such a spoiled opinion of his monstrous marvellosity as did
this mental and moral defective (here perhaps at the vanessance of
his lownest) who was known to grognt rather than gunnard upon
one occasion, while drinking heavily of spirits to that interlocutor
a latere and private privysuckatary he used to pal around with, in
the kavehazs, one Davy Browne-Nowlan, his heavenlaid twin, (this
hambone dogpoet pseudoed himself under the hangname he gave
himself of Bethgelert) in the porchway of a gipsy's bar (Shem always blaspheming, so holy writ, Billy, he would try, old Belly, and
pay this one manjack congregant of his four soups every lass of nex-
mouth, Bolly, so sure as thair's a tail on a commet, as a taste for
storik's fortytooth, that is to stay, to listen out, ony twenny minnies
moe, Bully, his Ballade Imaginaire which was to be dubbed *Wine,
Woman and Waterclocks,* or *How a Guy Finks and Fawkes When
He Is Going Batty,* by Maistre Sheames de la Plume, some most
dreadful stuff in a murderous mirrorhand) that he was avoopf
(parn me!) aware of no other shaggspick, other Shakhisbeard,
either prexactly unlike his polar andthisishis or procisely the seem
as woops (parn!) as what he fancied or guessed the sames as he was
himself and that, greet scoot, duckings and thuggery, though he was
foxed fux to fux like a bunnyboy rodger with all the teashop lionses
of Lumdrum hivanhoesed up gagainst him, being a lapsis linquo
with a ruvidubb shortartempa, bad cad dad fad sad mad nad vanhaty
bear, the consciquenchers of casuality prepestered crusswords in
postposition, scruff, scruffer, scrufferumurraimost andallthatsortof-
thing, if reams stood to reason and his lankalivline lasted he would
wipe alley english spooker, multaphoniaksically spuking, off the face
of the erse.

After the thorough fright he got that bloody, Swithun's day,
though every doorpost in muchtried Lucalizod was smeared with
generous erstborn gore and every free for all cobbleway slippery
with the bloods of heroes, crying to Welkins for others, and noahs
and cul verts agush with tears of joy, our low waster never had the
common baalamb's pluck to stir out and about the compound while
everyone else of the torchlit throng, slashers and sliced alike, mobbu
on massa, waaded and baaded around, yampyam pampyam, chanting the Gillooly chorus, from the Monster Book of Paltryattic

Puetrie, *O pura e pia bella!* in junk et sampam or in secular sink-alarum, heads up, on his bonafide avocation (the little folk creeping on all fours to their natural school treat but childishly gleeful when a stray whizzer sang out intermediately) and happy belongers to the fairer sex on their usual quest for higher things, but vying with Lady Smythe to avenge MacJobber, went stonestepping with their bickerrstaffs on educated feet, plinkity plonk, across the sevenspan ponte *dei colori* set up over the slop after the war-to-end war by Messrs a cheritable government for the only once (dia dose Finnados!) he did take a tompip peepestrella throug a threedraw eighteen hawkspower durdicky telescope, luminous to larbourd only like the lamps in Nassaustrass, out of his westernmost keyhole, spitting at the impenetrablum wetter, (and it was porcoghastly that outumn) with an eachway hope in his shivering soul, as he prayed to the cloud Incertitude, of finding out for himself, on akkount of all the kules in Kroukaparka or oving to all the kodseoggs in Kalatavala, whether true conciliation was forging ahead or falling back after the celestious intemperance and, for Duvvelsache, why, with his see me see and his my see a corves and his frokerfoskerfuskar layen loves in meeingseeing, he got the charm of his optical life when he found himself (*hic sunt lennones!*) at pointblank range blinking down the barrel of an irregular revolver of the bulldog with a purpose pattern, handled by an unknown quarreler who, supposedly, had been told off to shade and shoot shy Shem should the shit show his shiny shnout out awhile to look facts in their face before being hosed and creased (uprip and jack him!) by six or a dozen of the gayboys.

What, para Saom Plaom, in the names of Deucalion and Pyrrha, and the incensed privy and the licensed pantry gods and Stator and Victor and Kutt and Runn and the whole mesa redonda of Lorencao Otulass in convocacaon, was this disinterestingly low human type, this Calumnious Column of Cloaxity, this Bengalese Beacon of Biloxity, this Annamite Aper of Atroxity, really at, it will be precise to quarify, for he seems in a badbad case?

The answer, to do all the diddies in one dedal, would sound: from pulling himself on his most flavoured canal the huge chesthouse of his elders (the *Popapreta,* and some navico, navvies!) he had flickered up and flinnered down into a drug and drunkery addict, growing megalomane of a loose past. This explains the litany of septuncial lettertrumpets honorific, highpitched, erudite, neoclassical, which he so loved as patricianly to manuscribe after his name.

It would have diverted, if ever seen, the shuddersome spectacle of
this semidemented zany amid the inspissated grime of his glaucous
den making believe to read his usylessly unreadable Blue Book of
Eccles, *édition de ténèbres,* (even yet sighs the Most Different, Dr.
Poindejenk, authorised bowdler and censor, it can't be repeated!)
turning over three sheets at a wind, telling himself delightedly, no
espellor mor so, that every splurge on the vellum he blundered over
was an aisling vision more gorgeous than the one before t.i.t.s.,a
roseschelle cottage by the sea for nothing for ever, a ladies tryon
hosiery raffle at liberty, a sewerful of guineagold wine with bran-
comongepadenopie and sickcylinder oysters worth a billion a bite,
an entire operahouse (there was to be stamping room only in the
prompter's box and everthemore his queque kept swelling) of en-
thusiastic noblewomen flinging every coronetcrimsoned stitch they
had off at his probscenium, one after the others, inamagoaded into
ajustilloosing themselves, in their gaiety pantheomime, when, egad,
sir, acordant to all acountstrick, he squealed the topsquall im *Deal
Lil Shemlockup Yellin* (geewhiz, jew ear that far! soap ewer! lout-
gout of sabaous! juice like a boyd!) for fully five minutes, infinitely
better than Baraton Mc Gluckin with a scrumptious cocked hat and
three green, cheese and tangerine trinity plumes on the right handle
side of his amarellous head, a coat macfarlane (the kerssest cut, you
understand?) a sponiard's digger at his ribs, (*Alfaiate punxit*) an
azulblu blowsheet for his blousebosom blossom and a dean's crozier
that he won from Cardinal Lindundarri and Cardinal Carchingarri
and Cardinal Loriotuli and Cardinal Occidentaccia (ah ho!) in the
dearby darby doubled for falling first over the hurdles, madam, in
the odder hand, a.a.t.s.o.t., but what with the murky light, the
botchy print, the tattered cover, the jigjagged page, the fumbling
fingers, the foxtrotting fleas, the lieabed lice, the scum on his
tongue, the drop in his eye, the lump in his throat, the drink in his
pottle, the itch in his palm, the wail of his wind, the grief from his
breath, the fog of his mindfag, the buzz in his braintree, the tic of
his conscience, the height up his rage, the gush down his fundament, the fire in his gorge, the tickle of his tail, the bane in
his bullugs, the squince in his suil, the rot in his eater, the ycho in
his earer, the totters of his toes, the tetters on his tumtytum, the rats
in his garret, the bats in his belfry, the budgerigars and bumbosolom
beaubirds, the hullabaloo and the dust in his ears since it took him
a month to steal a march he was hardset to mumorise more than
a word a week. Hake's haulin! Hook's fisk! Can you beat it?

Whawe! I say, can you bait it? Was there ever heard of such low-down blackguardism? Positively it woolies one to think over it.

Yet the bumpersprinkler used to boast aloud alone to himself with a haccent on it when Mynfadher was a boer constructor and Hoy was a lexical student, parole, and corrected with the blackboard (trying to copy the stage Englesemen he broughts their house down on, shouting: Bravure, surr Chorles! Letter purfect! Culossal, Loose Wallor! Spache!) how he had been toed out of all the schicker families of the klondykers from Pioupioureich, Swabspays, the land of Nod, Shruggers' Country, Pension Danubierhome and Barbaropolis, who had settled and stratified in the capital city after its hebdomo-dary metropoliarchialisation as sunblistered, moonplastered, gory, wheedling, joviale, litcherous and full, ordered off the gorgeous premises in most cases on account of his smell which all cookmaids eminently objected to as ressembling the bombinubble puzzo that welled out of the pozzo. Instead of chuthoring those model house-holds plain wholesome pothooks (a thing he never possessed of his Nigerian own) what do you think Vulgariano did but study with stolen fruit how cutely to copy all their various styles of signature so as one day to utter an epical forged cheque on the public for his own private profit until, as just related, the Dustbin's United Scul-lerymaid's and Househelp's Sorority, better known as Sluttery's Mowlted Futt, turned him down and assisted nature by unitedly shoeing the source of annoyance out of the place altogether and taytotally on the heat of the moment, holding one another's gonk (for no-one, hound or scrublady, not even the Turk, ungreekable in purscent of the armenable, dared whiff the polecat at close range) and making some pointopointing remarks as they done so at the perfects of the Sniffey, your honour, aboon the lyow why a stunk, mister.

[Jymes wishes to hear from wearers of abandoned female cos-tumes, gratefully received, wadmel jumper, rather full pair of cu-lottes and onthergarmenteries, to start city life together. His jymes is out of job, would sit and write. He has lately commited one of the then commandments but she will now assist. Superior built, domestic, regular layer. Also got the boot. He appreciates it. Copies. ABORTISEMENT.]

One cannot even begin to post figure out a statuesquo ante as to how slow in reality the excommunicated Drumcondriac, nate Hamis, really was. Who can say how many pseudostylic shamiana, how few or how many of the most venerated public impostures, how

very many piously forged palimpsests slipped in the first place by
this morbid process from his pelagiarist pen?

Be that as it may, but for that light phantastic of his gnose's glow
as it slid lucifericiously within an inch of its page (he would touch
at its from time to other, the red eye of his fear in saddishness, to
ensign the colours by the beerlitz in his mathness and his educandees
to outhue to themselves in the cries of girlglee: gember! inkware!
chonchambre! cinsero! zinnzabar! tincture and gin!) Nibs never
would have quilled a seriph to sheepskin. By that rosy lampoon's
effluvious burning and with help of the simulchronic flush in his
pann (a ghinee a ghirk he ghets there!) he scrabbled and scratched
and scriobbled and skrevened nameless shamelessness about everybody ever he met, even sharing a precipitation under the idlish tar-
riers' umbrella of a showerproof wall, while all over up and down
the four margins of this rancid Shem stuff the evilsmeller (who was
devoted to Uldfadar Sardanapalus) used to stipple endlessly inar-
tistic portraits of himself in the act of reciting old Nichiabelli's
monolook interyerear *Hanno, o Nonanno, acce'l brubblemm'*as, ser
Autore, q.e.d., a heartbreakingly handsome young paolo with love
lyrics for the goyls in his eyols, a plaintiff's tanner vuice, a jucal in-
kome of one hundred and thirtytwo dranchmas per yard from
Broken Hill stranded estate, Camebreech mannings, cutting a great
dash in a brandnew two guinea dress suit and a burled hogsford
hired for a Fursday evenin merry pawty, anna loavely long pair of
inky Italian moostarshes glistering with boric vaseline and frangi-
pani. Puh! How unwhisperably so!

The house O'Shea or O'Shame, *Quivapieno,* known as the
Haunted Inkbottle, no number Brimstone Walk, Asia in Ireland,
as it was infested with the raps, with his penname SHUT sepia-
scraped on the doorplate and a blind of black sailcloth over its wan
phwinshogue, in which the soulcontracted son of the secret cell
groped through life at the expense of the taxpayers, dejected into
day and night with jesuit bark and bitter bite, calicohydrants of
zolfor and scoppialamina by full and forty Queasisanos, every day
in everyone's way more exceeding in violent abuse of self and others,
was the worst, it is hoped, even in our western playboyish world for
pure mousefarm filth. You brag of your brass castle or your tyled
house in ballyfermont? Niggs, niggs and niggs again. For this was
a stinksome inkenstink, quite puzzonal to the wrottel. Smatterafact,
Angles aftanon browsing there thought not Edam reeked more rare.
My wud! The warped flooring of the lair and soundconducting

walls thereof, to say nothing of the uprights and imposts, were per-
sianly literatured with burst loveletters, telltale stories, stickyback
snaps, doubtful eggshells, bouchers, flints, borers, puffers, amygda-
loid almonds, rindless raisins, alphybettyformed verbage, vivlical
viasses, ompiter dictas, visus umbique, ahems and ahahs, imeffible
tries at speech unasyllabled, you owe mes, eyoldhyms, fluefoul smut,
fallen lucifers, vestas which had served, showered ornaments, borrowed brogues, reversibles jackets, blackeye lenses, family jars, false-
hair shirts, Godforsaken scapulars, neverworn breeches, cutthroat
ties, counterfeit franks, best intentions, curried notes, upset latten
tintacks, unused mill and stumpling stones, twisted quills, painful
digests, magnifying wineglasses, solid objects cast at goblins, once
current puns, quashed quotatoes, messes of mottage, unquestionable
issue papers, seedy ejaculations, limerick damns, crocodile tears, spilt
ink, blasphematory spits, stale shestnuts, schoolgirls', young ladies',
milkmaids', washerwomen's, shopkeepers' wives, merry widows', ex
nuns', vice abbess's, pro virgins', super whores', silent sisters', Char-
leys' aunts', grandmothers', mothers'-in-laws', fostermothers', god-
mothers' garters, tress clippings from right, lift and cintrum, worms
of snot, toothsome pickings, cans of Swiss condensed bilk, highbrow
lotions, kisses from the antipodes, presents from pickpockets, borrowed plumes, relaxable handgrips, princess promises, lees of whine,
deoxodised carbons, convertible collars, diviliouker doffers, broken
wafers, unloosed shoe latchets, crooked strait waistcoats, fresh horrors from Hades, globules of mercury, undeleted glete, glass eyes
for an eye, gloss teeth for a tooth, war moans, special sighs, long-
sufferings of longstanding, ahs ohs ouis sis jas jos gias neys thaws
sos, yeses and yeses and yeses, to which, if one has the stomach to
add the breakages, upheavals distortions, inversions of all this cham-
bermade music one stands, given a grain of goodwill, a fair chance
of actually seeing the whirling dervish, Tumult, son of Thunder,
self exiled in upon his ego, a nightlong a shaking betwixtween
white or reddr hawrors, noondayterrorised to skin and bone by an
ineluctable phantom (may the Shaper have mercery on him!) writing the mystery of himsel in furniture.

Of course our low hero was a self valeter by choice of need so
up he got up whatever is meant by a stourbridge clay kitchenette
and lithargogalenu fowlhouse for the sake of akes (the umpple does
not fall very far from the dumpertree) which the moromelodious
jigsmith, in defiance of the Uncontrollable Birth Preservativation
(Game and Poultry) Act, playing lallaryrook cookerynook, by the

dodginess of his lentern, brooled and cocked and potched in an athanor, whites and yolks and yilks and whotes to the frulling fredonnance of *Mas blanca que la blanca hermana* and *Amarilla, muy bien,* with cinnamon and locusts and wild beeswax and liquorice and Carrageen moss and blaster of Barry's and Asther's mess and Huster's micture and Yellownan's embrocation and Pinkingtone's patty and stardust and sinner's tears, acuredent to Sharadan's *Art of Panning,* chanting, for all regale to the like of the legs he left behind with Litty fun Letty fan Leven, his cantraps of fermented words, abracadabra calubra culorum, (his oewfs à la Madame Gabrielle de l'Eglise, his avgs à la Mistress B. de B. Meinfelde, his eiers Usquadmala à la pomme de ciel, his uoves, oves and uves à la Sulphate de Soude, his ochiuri sowtay sowmmonay à la Monseigneur, his soufflosion of oogs with somekat on toyast à la Mère Puard, his Poggadovies alla Fenella, his Frideggs à la Tricarême) in what was meant for a closet (Ah ho! If only he had listened better to the four masters that infanted him Father Mathew and Le Père Noble and Pastor Lucas and Padre Aguilar — not forgetting Layteacher Baudwin! Ah ho!) His costive Satan's antimonian manganese limolitmious nature never needed such an alcove so, when Robber and Mumsell, the pulpic dictators, on the nudgment of their legal advisers, Messrs Codex and Podex, and under his own benefiction of their pastor Father Flammeus Falconer, boycotted him of all muttonsuet candles and romeruled stationery for any purpose, he winged away on a wildgoup's chase across the kathartic ocean and made synthetic ink and sensitive paper for his own end out of his wit's waste. You ask, in Sam Hill, how? Let manner and matter of this for these our sporting times be cloaked up in the language of blushfed porporates that an Anglican ordinal, not reading his own rude dunsky tunga, may ever behold the brand of scarlet on the brow of her of Babylon and feel not the pink one in his own damned cheek.

Primum opifex, altus prosator, ad terram viviparam et cunctipotentem sine ullo pudore nec venia, suscepto pluviali atque discinctis perizomatis, natibus nudis uti nati fuissent, sese adpropinquans, flens et gemens, in manum suam evacuavit (highly prosy, crap in his hand, sorry!), *postea, animale nigro exoneratus, classicum pulsans, stercus proprium, quod appellavit deiectiones suas, in vas olim honorabile tristitiae posuit, eodem sub invocatione fratrorum geminorum Medardi et Godardi laete ac melliflue minxit, psalmum qui incipit: Lingua mea calamus scribae velociter scribentis: magna*

voce cantitans (did a piss, says he was dejected, asks to be exon-
erated), *demum ex stercore turpi cum divi Orionis iucunditate
mixto, cocto, frigorique exposito, encaustum sibi fecit indelibile*
(faked O'Ryan's, the indelible ink).

Then, pious Eneas, conformant to the fulminant firman which
enjoins on the tremylose terrian that, when the call comes, he shall
produce nichthemerically from his unheavenly body a no uncertain
quantity of obscene matter not protected by copriright in the United
Stars of Ourania or bedeed and bedood and bedang and bedung
to him, with this double dye, brought to blood heat, gallic acid on
iron ore, through the bowels of his misery, flashly, faithly, nastily,
appropriately, this Esuan Menschavik and the first till last alshemist
wrote over every square inch of the only foolscap available, his own
body, till by its corrosive sublimation one continuous present tense
integument slowly unfolded all marryvoising moodmoulded cycle-
wheeling history (thereby, he said, reflecting from his own individual person life unlivable, transaccidentated through the slow fires
of consciousness into a dividual chaos, perilous, potent, common to
allflesh, human only, mortal) but with each word that would not
pass away the squidself which he had squirtscreened from the
crystalline world waned chagreenold and doriangrayer in its dud-
hud. This exists that isits after having been said we know. And
dabal take dabnal! And the dal dabal dab aldanabal! So perhaps,
agglaggagglomeratively asaspenking, after all and arklast fore arklyst
on his last public misappearance, circling the square, for the death-
fête of Saint Ignaceous Poisonivy, of the Fickle Crowd (hopon the
sexth day of Hogsober, killim our king, layum low!) and brandish-
ing his bellbearing stylo, the shining keyman of the wilds of change,
if what is sauce for the zassy is souse for the zazimas, the blond cop
who thought it was ink was out of his depth but bright in the main.

Petty constable Sistersen of the Kruis-Kroon-Kraal it was, the
parochial watch, big the dog the dig the bog the bagger the dugger
the begadag degabug, who had been detailed from pollute stoties
to save him, this the quemquem, that the quum, from the ligature-
liablous effects of foul clay in little clots and mobmauling on looks,
that wrongcountered the tenderfoot an eveling near the livings-
meansuniumgetherum, Knockmaree, Comty Mea, reeling more to
the right than he lurched to the left, on his way from a protoprosti-
tute (he would always have a (stp!) little pigeoness somewhure with
his arch girl, Arcoiris, smockname of Mergyt) just as he was butting
in rand the coyner of bad times under a hideful between the rival

doors of warm bethels of worship through his boardelhouse fongster, greeting for grazious oras as usual: Where ladies have they that a dog meansort herring? Sergo, search me, the incapable reparteed with a selfevitant subtlety so obviously spurious and, raising his hair, after the grace, with the christmas under his clutcharm, for Portsymasser and Purtsymessus and Pertsymiss and Partsymasters, like a prance of findingos, with a shillto shallto slipny stripny, in he skittled. Swikey! The allwhite poors guardiant, pulpably of ball-tossic stummung, was literally astundished over the painful sake, how he burstteself, which he was gone to, where he intent to did he, whether you think will, wherend the whole current of the after-noon whats the souch of a surch hads of hits of hims, urged and staggered thereto in his countryports at the caledosian capacity for Lieutuvisky of the caftan's wineskin and even more so, during, look-ing his bigmost astonishments, it was said him, aschu, fun the con-cerned outgift of the dead med dirt, how that, arrahbejibbers, con-spuent to the dominical order and exking noblish permish, he was namely coon at bringer at home two gallonts, as per royal, full poul-try till his murder. Nip up and nab it!

Polthergeistkotzdondherhoploits! Kick? What mother? Whose porter? Which pair? Why namely coon? But our undilligence has been plutherotested so enough of such porterblack lowneess, too base for printink! Perpending that Putterick O'Purcell pulls the coald stoane out of Winterwater's and Silder Seas sing for Harreng our Keng, sept okt nov dez John Phibbs march! We cannot, in mercy or justice nor on the lovom for labaryntos, stay here for the residence of our existings, discussing Tamstar Ham of Tenman's thirst.

JUSTIUS (to himother): Brawn is my name and broad is my nature and I've breit on my brow and all's right with every feature and I'll brune this bird or Brown Bess's bung's gone bandy. I'm the boy to bruise and braise. Baus!

Stand forth, Nayman of Noland (for no longer will I follow you obliquelike through the inspired form of the third person singular and the moods and hesitensies of the deponent but address myself to you, with the empirative of my vendettative, provocative and out direct), stand forth, come boldly, jolly me, move me, zwilling though I am, to laughter in your true colours ere you be back for ever till I give you your talkingto! Shem Macadamson, you know me and I know you and all your shemeries. Where have you been in the uterim, enjoying yourself all the morning since your last wet-bed confession? I advise you to conceal yourself, my little friend,

as I have said a moment ago and put your hands in my hands and
have a nightslong homely little confiteor about things. Let me see.
It is looking pretty black against you, we suggest, Sheem avick. You
will need all the elements in the river to clean you over it all and a
fortifine popespriestpower bull of attender to booth.

Let us pry. We thought, would and did. *Cur, quicquid, ubi,
quando, quomodo, quoties, quibus auxiliis?* You were bred, fed,
fostered and fattened from holy childhood up in this two easter island on the piejaw of hilarious heaven and roaring the other place
(plunders to night of you, blunders what's left of you, flash as flash
can!) and now, forsooth, a nogger among the blankards of this
dastard century, you have become of twosome twiminds forenenst
gods, hidden and discovered, nay, condemned fool, anarch, egoarch,
hiresiarch, you have reared your disunited kingdom on the vacuum
of your own most intensely doubtful soul. Do you hold yourself then
for some god in the manger, Shehohem, that you will neither serve
not let serve, pray nor let pray? And here, pay the piety, must I too
nerve myself to pray for the loss of selfrespect to equip me for the
horrible necessity of scandalisang (my dear sisters, are you ready?)
by sloughing off my hope and tremors while we all swin together
in the pool of Sodom? I shall shiver for my purity while they will
weepbig for your sins. Away with covered words, new Solemonities
for old Badsheetbaths! That inharmonious detail, did you name it?
Cold caldor! Gee! Victory! Now, opprobro of underslung pipes,
johnjacobs, while yet an adolescent (what do I say?), while still
puerile in your tubsuit with buttonlegs, you got a handsome present
of a selfraising syringe and twin feeders (you know, Monsieur Ab-
gott, in your art of arts, to your cost as well as I do (and don't try
to hide it) the penals lots I am now poking at) and the wheeze sort
of was you should (if you were as bould a stroke now as the curate
that christened you, sonny douth-the-candle!) repopulate the land
of your birth and count up your progeny by the hungered head and
the angered thousand but you thwarted the wious pish of your co-
godparents, soph, among countless occasions of failing (for, said
you, I will elenchate), adding to the malice of your transgression,
yes, and changing its nature, (you see I have read your theology for
you) alternating the morosity of my delectations — a philtred love,
trysting by tantrums, small peace in ppenmark — with sensibility,
sponsibility, passibility and prostability, your lubbock's other fear
pleasures of a butler's life, even extruding your strabismal apologia,
when legibly depressed, upon defenceless paper and thereby adding

to the already unhappiness of this our popeyed world, scribblative!
— all that too with cantreds of countless catchaleens, the mannish
as many as the minneful, congested around and about you for acres
and roods and poles or perches, thick as the fluctuant sands of Chal-
wador, accomplished women, indeed fully educanded, far from being old and rich behind their dream of arrivisme, if they have only
their honour left, and not deterred by bad weather when consumed
by amorous passion, struggling to possess themselves of your boosh,
one son of Sorge for all daughters of Anguish, *solus cum sola sive
cuncties cum omnibobs* (I'd have been the best man for you, myself),
mutely aying for that natural knot, debituary vases or vessels preposterous, for what would not have cost you ten bolivars of collar-
work or the price of one ping pang, just a lilt, let us trillt, of the
oldest song in the wooed woodworld, (two-we! to-one!), accompanied
by a plain gold band! Hail! Hail! Highbosomheaving Missmisstress
Morna of the allsweetheartening bridemuredemeanour! Her eye's
so gladsome we'll all take shares in the —— groom!

   Sniffer of carrion, premature gravedigger, seeker of the nest of
evil in the bosom of a good word, you, who sleep at our vigil and
fast for our feast, you with your dislocated reason, have cutely foretold, a jophet in your own absence, by blind poring upon your many
scalds and burns and blisters, impetiginous sore and pustules, by
the auspices of that raven cloud, your shade, and by the auguries
of rooks in parlament, death with every disaster, the dynamitisation
of colleagues, the reducing of records to ashes, the levelling of all
customs by blazes, the return of a lot of sweetempered gunpowdered
didst unto dudst but it never stphruck your mudhead's obtundity
(O hell, here comes our funeral! O pest, I'll miss the post!) that the
more carrots you chop, the more turnips you slit, the more murphies
you peel, the more onions you cry over, the more bullbeef you butch,
the more mutton you crackerhack, the more potherbs you pound,
the fiercer the fire and the longer your spoon and the harder you
gruel with more grease to your elbow the merrier fumes your new
Irish stew.

   O, by the way, yes, another thing occurs to me. You let me tell
you, with the utmost politeness, were very ordinarily designed, your
birthwrong was, to fall in with Plan, as our nationals should, as all
nationists must, and do a certain office (what, I will not tell you)
in a certain holy office (nor will I say where) during certain
agonising office hours (a clerical party all to yourself) from such
a year to such an hour on such and such a date at so and so much

a week *pro anno* (Guinness's, may I remind, were just agulp for you, failing in which you might have taken the scales off boilers like any boskop of Yorek) and do your little thruppenny bit and thus earn from the nation true thanks, right here in our place of burden, your bourne of travail and ville of tares, where after a divine's prodigence you drew the first watergasp in your life, from the crib where you once was bit to the crypt you'll be twice as shy of, same as we, long of us, alone with the colt in the curner, where you were as popular as an armenial with the faithful, and you set fire to my tailcoat when I hold the paraffin smoker under yours (I hope that chimney's clear) but, slackly shirking both your bullet and your billet, you beat it backwards like Boulanger from Galway (but he combed the grass against his stride) to sing us a song of alibi, (the cuthone call over the greybounding slowrolling amplyheaving metamorphoseous that oozy rocks parapangle their preposters with) nomad, mooner by lamplight, antinos, shemming amid everyone's repressed laughter to conceal your scatchophily by mating, like a thoroughpaste prosodite, masculine monosyllables of the same numerical mus, an Irish emigrant the wrong way out, sitting on your crooked sixpenny stile, an unfrillfrocked quackfriar, you (will you for the laugh of Scheekspair just help mine with the epithet?) semisemitic serendipitist, you (thanks, I think that describes you) Europasianised Afferyank!

Shall we follow each others a steplonger, drowner of daggers, whiles our liege, tilyet a stranger in the frontyard of his happiness, is taking, (heal helper! one gob, one gap, one gulp and gorger of all!) his refreshment?

There grew up beside you, amid our orisons of the speediest in Novena Lodge, Novara Avenue, in Patripodium-am-Bummel, oaf, outofwork, one remove from an unwashed savage, on his keeping and in yours, (I pose you know why possum hides is cause he haint the nogumtreeumption) that other, Immaculatus, from head to foot, sir, that pure one, Altrues of other times, he who was well known to celestine circles before he sped aloft, our handsome young spiritual physician that was to be, seducing every sense to selfwilling celebesty, the most winning counterfeuille on our incomeshare lotetree, a chum of the angelets, a youth those reporters so pettitily wanted as gamefellow that they asked his mother for ittle earps brupper to let him tome to Tindertarten, pease, and bing his scooter 'long and 'tend they were all real brothers in the big justright home where Dodd lives, just to teddyfy the life out of him and pat and pass him one with other like musk from hand to hand, that mother-smothered model, that goodlooker with not a flaw whose spiritual toilettes were the talk of half the town, for sunset wear and night-fallen use and daybroken donning and nooncheon showing and the very thing for teasetime, but him you laid low with one hand one fine May morning in the Meddle of your Might, your bosom foe, because he mussed your speller on you or because he cut a pretty figure in the focus of your frontispecs (not one did you slay, no, but a continent!) to find out how his innards worked!

Ever read of that greatgrand landfather of our visionbuilders, Baaboo, the bourgeoismeister, who thought to touch both himmels at the punt of his risen stiffstaff and how wishywashy sank the waters of his thought? Ever thought of that hereticalist Marcon and the two scissymaidies and how bulkily he shat the Ructions gunorrhal? Ever hear of that foxy, that lupo and that monkax and the virgin heir of the Morrisons, eh, blethering ape?

Malingerer in luxury, collector general, what has Your Lowness done in the mealtime with all the hamilkcars of cooked vegetables, the hatfuls of stewed fruit, the suitcases of coddled ales, the Parish funds, me schamer, man, that you kittycoaxed so flexibly out of charitable butteries by yowling heavy with a hollow voice drop of your horrible awful poverty of mind so as you couldn't even pledge a crown of Thorne's to pawn a coat off Trevi's and as how you was bad no end, so you was, so whelp you Sinner Pitre and Sinner Poule, with the chicken's gape and *pas mal de siècle*, which, by the by, Reynaldo, is the ordinary emetic French for grenadier's drip. To let you have your plank and your bonewash (O the hastroubles you lost!), to give you your pound of platinum and a thousand thongs a year (O, you were excruciated, in honour bound to the cross of your own cruelfiction!) to let you have your Sarday spree and holinight sleep (fame would come to you twixt a sleep and a wake) and leave to lie till Paraskivee and the cockcock crows for Danmark. (O Jonathan, your estomach!) The simian has no sentiment secretions but weep cataracts for all me, Pain the Shamman! Oft in the smelly night will they wallow for a clutch of the famished hand, I say, them bearded jezabelles you hired to rob you, while on your sodden straw impolitely you encored (Airish and naw-boggaleesh!) those hornmade ivory dreams you reved of the Ruth you called your companionate, a beauty from the bible, of the flushpots of Euston and the hanging garments of Marylebone. But the dormer moonshee smiled selene and the lightthrowers knickered: who's whinging we? Comport yourself, you inconsistency! Where is that little alimony nestegg against our predictable rainy day? Is it not the fact (gainsay me, cakeeater!) that, while whistlewhirling your crazy elegies around Templetombmount joyntstone, (let him pass, pleasegoodjesusalem, in a bundle of straw, he was balbettised after haymaking) you squandered among underlings the overload of your extravagance and made a hottentot of dulpeners crawsick with your crumbs? Am I not right? Yes? Yes? Yes? Holy wax and holifer! Don't tell me, Leon of the fold, that you are not a loanshark! Look up, old sooty, be advised by mux and take your medicine. The Good Doctor mulled it. Mix it twice before repastures and powder three times a day. It does marvels for your gripins and it's fine for the solitary worm.

Let me finish! Just a little judas tonic, my ghem of all jokes, to make you go green in the gazer. Do you hear what I'm seeing, hammet? And remember that golden silence gives consent, Mr Anklegazer! Cease to be civil, learn to say nay! Whisht! Come here, Herr Studiosus, till I tell you a wig in your ear. We'll do a whisper drive, for if the barishnyas got a twitter of it they'd tell the housetops and then all Cadbury would go crackers. Look! Do you see your dial in the rockingglass? Look well! Bend down a stigmy till I! It's secret! Iggri, I say, the booseleers! I had it from Lamppost Shawe. And he had it from the Mullah. And Mull took it from a Bluecoat schooler. And Gay Socks jot it from Potapheu's wife. And Rantipoll tipped the wink from old Mrs Tinbullet. And as for she was confussed by pro-Brother Thacolicus. And the good brother feels he would need to defecate you. And the Flimsy Follettes are simply beside each other. And Kelly, Kenny and Keogh are up up and in arms. That a cross may crush me if I refuse to believe in it. That I may rock anchor through the ages if I hope it's not true. That the host may choke me if I beneighbour you without my charity! Sh! Shem, you are. Sh! You are mad!

He points the deathbone and the quick are still. *Insomnia, somnia somniorum. Awmawm.*

MERCIUS (of hisself): *Domine vopiscus!* My fault, his fault, a kingship through a fault! Pariah, cannibal Cain, I who oathily forswore the womb that bore you and the paps I sometimes sucked, you who ever since have been one black mass of jigs and jimjams, haunted by a convulsionary sense of not having been or being all that I might have been or you meant to becoming, bewailing like

a man that innocence which I could not defend like a woman, lo,
you there, Cathmon-Carbery, and thank Movies from the innermost depths of my still attrite heart, Wherein the days of youyouth
are evermixed mimine, now ere the compline hour of being alone
athands itself and a puff or so before we yield our spiritus to the
wind, for (though that royal one has not yet drunk a gouttelette
from his consummation and the flowerpot on the pole, the spaniel
pack and their quarry, retainers and the public house proprietor
have not budged a millimetre and all that has been done has yet
to be done and done again, when's day's woe, and lo, you're
doomed, joyday dawns and, la, you dominate) it is to you, firstborn
and firstfruit of woe, to me, branded sheep, pick of the wasterpaper-
baskel, by the tremours of Thundery and Ulerin's dogstar, you alone,
windblasted tree of the knowledge of beautiful andevil, ay, clothed
upon with the metuor and shimmering like the horescens, astro-
glodynamonologos, the child of Nilfit's father, blzb, to me unseen
blusher in an obscene coalhole, the cubilibum of your secret sigh,
dweller in the downandoutermost where voice only of the dead may
come, because ye left from me, because ye laughed on me, because,
O me lonly son, ye are forgetting me!, that our turfbrown mummy
is acoming, alpilla, beltilla, ciltilla, deltilla, running with her tidings,
old the news of the great big world, sonnies had a scrap, woewoe-
woe! bab's baby walks at seven months, waywayway! bride leaves
her raid at Punchestime, stud stoned before a racecourseful, two
belles that make the one appeal, dry yanks will visit old sod, and
fourtiered skirts are up, mesdames, while Parimiknie wears popular
short legs, and twelve hows to mix a tipsy wake, did ye hear, colt
Cooney? did ye ever, filly Fortescue? with a beck, with a spring, all
her rillringlets shaking, rocks drops in her tachie, tramtokens in
her hair, all waived to a point and then all inuendation, little old-
fashioned mummy, little wonderful mummy, ducking under bridges,
bellhopping the weirs, dodging by a bit of bog, rapidshooting round
the bends, by Tallaght's green hills and the pools of the phooka and
a place they call it Blessington and slipping sly by Sallynoggin, as
happy as the day is wet, babbling, bubbling, chattering to herself,
deloothering the fields on their elbows leaning with the sloothering
slide of her, giddygaddy, grannyma, gossipaceous Anna Livia.

He lifts the lifewand and the dumb speak.

— Quoiquoiquoiquoiquoiquoiquoiquoiq!

O

tell me all about
Anna Livia! I want to hear all
about Anna Livia. Well, you know Anna Livia? Yes, of course,
we all know Anna Livia. Tell me all. Tell me now. You'll die when
you hear. Well, you know, when the old cheb went futt and did
what you know. Yes, I know, go on. Wash quit and don't be dab-
bling. Tuck up your sleeves and loosen your talktapes. And don't
butt me — hike! — when you bend. Or whatever it was they threed
to make out he thried to two in the Fiendish park. He's an awful
old reppe. Look at the shirt of him! Look at the dirt of it! He
has all my water black on me. And it steeping and stuping since
this time last wik. How many goes is it I wonder I washed it? I
know by heart the places he likes to saale, duddurty devil! Scorching
my hand and starving my famine to make his private linen public.
Wallop it well with your battle and clean it. My wrists are wrusty
rubbing the mouldaw stains. And the dneepers of wet and the
gangres of sin in it! What was it he did a tail at all on Animal
Sendai? And how long was he under loch and neagh? It was put
in the newses what he did, nicies and priers, the King fierceas
Humphrey, with illysus distilling, exploits and all. But toms will
till. I know he well. Temp untamed will hist for no man. As you
spring so shall you neap. O, the roughty old rappe! Minxing marrage
and making loof. Reeve Gootch was right and Reeve Drughad was
sinistrous! And the cut of him! And the strut of him! How he used
to hold his head as high as a howeth, the famous eld duke alien,
with a hump of grandeur on him like a walking wiesel rat. And
his derry's own drawl and his corksown blather and his doubling
stutter and his gullaway swank. Ask Lictor Hackett or Lector Reade
of Garda Growley or the Boy with the Billyclub. How elster is he

a called at all? Qu'appelle? Huges Caput Earlyfouler. Or where
was he born or how was he found? Urgothland, Tvistown on the
Kattekat? New Hunshire, Concord on the Merrimake? Who block-
smitt her saft anvil or yelled lep to her pail? Was her banns never
loosened in Adam and Eve's or were him and her but captain
spliced? For mine ether duck I thee drake. And by my wildgaze
I thee gander. Flowey and Mount on the brink of time makes wishes
and fears for a happy isthmass. She can show all her lines, with
love, license to play. And if they don't remarry that hook and eye
may! O, passmore that and oxus another! Don Dom Dombdomb
and his wee follyo! Was his help inshored in the Stork and Pelican
against bungelars, flu and third risk parties? I heard he dug good
tin with his doll, delvan first and duvlin after, when he raped her
home, Sabrine asthore, in a parakeet's cage, by dredgerous lands
and devious delts, playing catched and mythed with the gleam of
her shadda, (if a flic had been there to pop up and pepper him!)
past auld min's manse and Maisons Allfou and the rest of incurables
and the last of immurables, the quaggy waag for stumbling. Who
sold you that jackalantern's tale? Pemmican's pasty pie! Not a grass-
hoop to ring her, not an antsgrain of ore. In a gabbard he barqued
it, the boat of life, from the harbourless Ivernikan Okean, till he
spied the loom of his landfall and he loosed two croakers from under
his tilt, the gran Phenician rover. By the smell of her kelp they
made the pigeonhouse. Like fun they did! But where was Himself,
the timoneer? That marchantman he suivied their scutties right over
the wash, his cameleer's burnous breezing up on him, till with his
runagate bowmpriss he roade and borst her bar. Pilcomayo! Such-
caughtawan! And the whale's away with the grayling! Tune your
pipes and fall ahumming, you born ijypt, and you're nothing short
of one! Well, ptellomey soon and curb your escumo. When they
saw him shoot swift up her sheba sheath, like any gay lord salomon,
her bulls they were ruhring, surfed with spree. Boyarka buah!
Boyana bueh! He erned his lille Bunbath hard, our staly bred, the
trader. He did. Look at here. In this wet of his prow. Don't you
know he was kaldt a bairn of the brine, Wasserbourne the water-
baby? Havemmarea, so he was! H.C.E. has a codfisck ee. Shyr she's
nearly as badher as him herself. Who? Anna Livia? Ay, Anna Livia.
Do you know she was calling bakvandets sals from all around,
nyumba noo, chamba choo, to go in till him, her erring cheef, and
tickle the pontiff aisy-oisy? She was? Gota pot! Yssel that the limmat?
As El Negro winced when he wonced in La Plate. O, tell me all

I want to hear, how loft she was lift a laddery dextro! A coney-
wink after the bunting fell. Letting on she didn't care, sina feza,
me absantee, him man in passession, the proxenete! Proxenete and
phwhat is phthat? Emme for your reussischer Honddu jarkon! Tell
us in franca langua. And call a spate a spate. Did they never sharee
you ebro at skol, you antiabecedarian? It's just the same as if I
was to go par examplum now in conservancy's cause out of tele-
kinesis and proxenete you. For coxyt sake and is that what she is?
Botlettle I thought she'd act that loa. Didn't you spot her in her
windaug, wubbling up on an osiery chair, with a meusic before
her all cunniform letters, pretending to ribble a reedy derg on a
fiddle she bogans without a band on? Sure she can't fiddan a dee,
with bow or abandon! Sure, she can't! Tista suck. Well, I never
now heard the like of that! Tell me moher. Tell me moatst. Well,
old Humber was as glommen as grampus, with the tares at his thor
and the buboes for ages and neither bowman nor shot abroad and
bales allbrant on the crests of rockies and nera lamp in kitchen
or church and giant's holes in Grafton's causeway and deathcap
mushrooms round Funglus grave and the great tribune's barrow all
darnels occumule, sittang sambre on his sett, drammen and drom-
men, usking queasy quizzers of his ruful continence, his childlinen
scarf to encourage his obsequies where he'd check their debths in
that mormon's thames, be questing and handsetl, hop, step and a
deepend, with his berths in their toiling moil, his swallower open
from swolf to fore and the snipes of the gutter pecking his crocs,
hungerstriking all alone and holding doomsdag over hunselv, dree-
ing his weird, with his dander up, and his fringe combed over his
eygs and droming on loft till the sight of the sternes, after zwarthy
kowse and weedy broeks and the tits of buddy and the loits of
pest and to peer was Parish worth thette mess. You'd think all was
dodo belonging to him how he durmed adranse in durance vaal.
He had been belching for severn years. And there she was, Anna
Livia, she darent catch a winkle of sleep, purling around like a
chit of a child, Wendawanda, a fingerthick, in a Lapsummer skirt
and damazon cheeks, for to ishim bonzour to her dear dubber Dan.
With neuphraties and sault from his maggias. And an odd time
she'd cook him up blooms of fisk and lay to his heartsfoot her
meddery eygs, yayis, and staynish beacons on toasc and a cupenhave
so weeshywashy of Greenland's tay or a dzoupgan of Kaffue mokau
an sable or Sikiang sukry or his ale of ferns in trueart pewter and
a shinkobread (hamjambo, bana?) for to plaise that man hog stay

his stomicker till her pyrraknees shrunk to nutmeg graters while
her togglejoints shuck with goyt and as rash as she'd russ with her
peakload of vivers up on her sieve (metauwero rage it swales and
rieses) my hardey Hek he'd kast them frome him, with a stour of
scorn, as much as to say you sow and you sozh, and if he didn't
peg the platteau on her tawe, believe you me, she was safe enough.
And then she'd esk to vistule a hymn, *The Heart Bowed Down*
or *The Rakes of Mallow* or Chelli Michele's *La Calumnia è un
Vermicelli* or a balfy bit ov *old Jo Robidson*. Sucho fuffing a fife-
ing 'twould cut you in two! She'd bate the hen that crowed on
the turrace of Babbel. What harm if she knew how to cockle her
mouth! And not a mag out of Hum no more than out of the mangle
weight. Is that a faith? That's the fact. Then riding the ricka and
roya romanche, Annona, gebroren aroostokrat Nivia, dochter of
Sense and Art, with Sparks' pirryphlickathims funkling her fan,
anner frostivying tresses dasht with virevlies,—while the prom beauties sreeked nith their bearers' skins! — in a period gown of changeable jade that would robe the wood of two cardinals' chairs and
crush poor Cullen and smother MacCabe. O blazerskate! Theirs
porpor patches! And brahming to him down the feedchute, with
her femtyfyx kinds of fondling endings, the poother rambling off
her nose: *Vuggybarney, Wickerymandy! Hello, ducky, please don't
die!* Do you know what she started cheeping after, with a choicey
voicey like waterglucks or Madame Delba to Romeoreszk? You'll
never guess. Tell me. Tell me. *Phoebe, dearest, tell, O tell me* and
I loved you better nor you knew. And letting on hoon var daft
about the warbly sangs from over holmen: *High hellskirt saw ladies
hensmoker lilyhung pigger:* and soay and soan and so firth and so
forth in a tone sonora and Oom Bothar below like Bheri-Bheri
in his sandy cloak, so umbolosy, as deaf as a yawn, the stult! Go
away! Poor deef old deary! Yare only teasing! Anna Liv? As chalk
is my judge! And didn't she up in sorgues and go and trot doon
and stand in her douro, puffing her old dudheen, and every shirvant
siligirl or wensum farmerette walking the pilend roads, Sawy,
Fundally, Daery or Maery, Milucre, Awny or Graw, usedn't she
make her a simp or sign to slip inside by the sullyport? You don't
say, the sillypost? Bedouix but I do! Calling them in, one by one
(To Blockbeddum here! Here the Shoebenacaddie!) and legging a
jig or so on the sihl to show them how to shake their benders and
the dainty how to bring to mind the gladdest garments out of sight
and all the way of a maid with a man and making a sort of a

cackling noise like two and a penny or half a crown and holding up a silliver shiner. Lordy, lordy, did she so? Well, of all the ones ever I heard! Throwing all the neiss little whores in the world at him! To inny captured wench you wish of no matter what sex of pleissful ways two adda tammar a lizzy a lossie to hug and hab haven in Humpy's apron!

And what was the wyerye rima she made! Odet! Odet! Tell me the trent of it while I'm lathering hail out of Denis Florence Mac-Carthy's combies. Rise it, flut ye, pian piena! I'm dying down off my iodine feet until I lerryn Anna Livia's cushingloo, that was writ by one and rede by two and trouved by a poule in the parco! I can see that, I see you are. How does it tummel? Listen now. Are you listening? Yes, yes! Idneed I am! Tarn your ore ouse! Essonne inne!

By earth and the cloudy but I badly want a brandnew bankside, bedamp and I do, and a plumper at that!

For the putty affair I have is wore out, so it is, sitting, yaping and waiting for my old Dane hodder dodderer, my life in death companion, my frugal key of our larder, my much-altered camel's hump, my jointspoiler, my maymoon's honey, my fool to the last Decemberer, to wake himself out of his winter's doze and bore me down like he used to.

Is there irwell a lord of the manor or a knight of the shire at strike, I wonder, that'd dip me a dace or two in cash for washing and darning his worshipful socks for him now we're run out of horsebrose and milk?

Only for my short Brittas bed made's as snug as it smells it's out I'd lep and off with me to the slobs della Tolka or the plage au Clontarf to feale the gay aire of my salt troublin bay and the race of the saywint up me ambushure.

Onon! Onon! tell me more. Tell me every tiny teign. I want to know every single ingul. Down to what made the potters fly into jagsthole. And why were the vesles vet. That homa fever's winning me wome. If a mahun of the horse but hard me! We'd be bundukiboi meet askarigal. Well, now comes the hazelhatchery part. After Clondalkin the Kings's Inns. We'll soon be there with the freshet. How many aleveens had she in tool? I can't rightly rede you that. Close only knows. Some say she had three figures to fill and confined herself to a hundred eleven, wan bywan bywan, making meanacuminamoyas. Olaph lamm et, all that pack? We won't have room in the kirkeyaard. She can't remember half of the cradlenames she smacked on them by the grace of her boxing bishop's infallible slipper, the cane for Kund and abbles for Eyolf and ayther nayther for Yakov Yea. A hundred and how? They did well to rechristien her Pluhurabelle. O loreley! What a loddeon lodes! Heigh ho! But it's quite on the cards she'll shed more and merrier, twills and trills, sparefours and spoilfives, nordsihkes and sudsevers and ayes and neins to a litter. Grandfarthring nap and Messamisery and the knave of all knaves and the joker. Heehaw! She must have been a gadabout in her day, so she must, more than most. Shoal she was, gidgad. She had a flewmen of her owen. Then a toss nare scared that lass, so aimai moe, that's agapo! Tell me, tell me, how cam she camlin through all her fellows, the neckar she was, the diveline? Casting her perils before our swains from Fonte-in-Monte to Tidingtown and from Tidingtown tilhavet. Linking one and knocking the next, tapting a flank and tipting a jutty and palling in and pietaring out and clyding by on her eastway. Waiwhou was the first thurever burst? Someone he was, whuebra they were, in a tactic attack or in single combat. Tinker, tilar, souldrer, salor, Pieman Peace or Polistaman. That's the thing I'm elwys on edge to esk. Push up and push vardar and come to uphill headquarters! Was it waterlows year, after Grattan or Flood, or when maids were in Arc or when three stood hosting? Fidaris will find where the Doubt arises like Nieman from Nirgends found the Nihil. Worry you sighin foh, Albern, O Anser? Untie the gemman's fistiknots, Qvic and Nuancee! She can't put her hand on him for the moment. Tez thelon langlo, walking weary! Such a loon waybashwards to row! She sid herself she hardly knows whuon the annals her graveller was, a dynast of Leinster, a wolf of the sea, or what he did or how blyth she played or how, when, why, where and who offon he jumpnad her and how it was gave her away. She was just a young thin pale soft shy slim slip of a thing then, sauntering, by silvamoonlake and he was a heavy trudging lurching lieabroad of a Curraghman, making his hay for whose sun to shine on, as tough as the oaktrees (peats be with them!) used to rustle that time down by the dykes of killing Kildare, for forstfellfoss with a plash across her. She thought she's sankh neathe the ground with nymphant shame when he gave her the tigris eye! O happy fault! Me wish it was he! You're wrong there, corribly wrong! Tisn't only tonight you're anacheronistic! It was ages behind that when nullahs were nowhere, in county Wickenlow, garden of Erin, before she ever dreamt she'd lave Kilbride and go foaming under Horsepass bridge, with the great

southwestern windstorming her traces and the midland's grainwaster
asarch for her track, to wend her ways byandby, robecca or worse,
to spin and to grind, to swab and to thrash, for all her golden lifey
in the barleyfields and pennylotts of Humphrey's fordofhurdlestown
and lie with a landleaper, wellingtonorseher. Alesse, the lagos of
girly days! For the dove of the dunas! Wasut? Izod? Are you sarthin
suir? Not where the Finn fits into the Mourne, not where the Nore
takes lieve of Blœm, not where the Braye divarts the Farer, not
where the Moy changez her minds twixt Cullin and Conn tween
Cunn and Collin? Or where Neptune sculled and Tritonville rowed
and leandros three bumped heroines two? Neya, narev, nen, nonni,
nos! Then whereabouts in Ow and Ovoca? Was it yst with wyst
or Lucan Yokan or where the hand of man has never set foot?
Dell me where, the fairy ferse time! I will if you listen. You know
the dinkel dale of Luggelaw? Well, there once dwelt a local
heremite, Michael Arklow was his riverend name, (with many a
sigh I aspersed his lavabibs!) and one venersderg in junojuly, oso
sweet and so cool and so limber she looked, Nance the Nixie, Nanon
L'Escaut, in the silence, of the sycomores, all listening, the kindling
curves you simply can't stop feeling, he plunged both of his newly
anointed hands, the core of his cushlas, in her singimari saffron
strumans of hair, parting them and soothing her and mingling it,
that was deepdark and ample like this red bog at sundown. By that
Vale Vowclose's lucydlac, the reignbeau's heavenarches arronged or-
ranged her. Afrothdizzying galbs, her enamelled eyes indergoading
him on to the vierge violetian. Wish a wish! Why a why? Mavro!
Letty Lerck's lafing light throw those laurals now on her daph-
daph teasesong petrock. Maass! But the majik wavus has elfun anon
meshes. And Sinba the Slayer of his Oga is slewd. He cuddle not
help himself, thurso that hot on him, he had to forget the monk
in the man so, rubbing her up and smoothing her down, he baised
his lippes in smiling mood, kiss akiss after kisokushk (as he warned
her niver to, niver to, nevar) on Anna-na-Poghue's of the freckled
forehead. While you'd parse secheressa she hielt her souff'. But she
ruz two feet hire in her aisne aestumation. And steppes on stilts
ever since. That was kissuahealing with bantur for balm! O, wasn't
he the bold priest? And wasn't she the naughty Livvy? Nautic
Naama's now her navn. Two lads in scoutsch breeches went through
her before that, Barefoot Burn and Wallowme Wade, Lugnaquillia's
noblesse pickts, before she had a hint of a hair at her fanny to
hide or a bossom to tempt a birch canoedler not to mention a bulgic

porterhouse barge. And ere that again, leada, laida, all unraidy, too
faint to buoy the fairiest rider, too frail to flirt with a cygnet's plume,
she was licked by a hound, Chirripa-Chirruta, while poing her pee,
pure and simple, on the spur of the hill in old Kippure, in birdsong
and shearingtime, but first of all, worst of all, the wiggly livvly,
she sideslipped out by a gap in the Devil's glen while Sally her
nurse was sound asleep in a sloot and, feefee fiefie, fell over a spillway
before she found her stride and lay and wriggled in all the stagnant
black pools of rainy under a fallow coo and she laughed innocefree
with her limbs aloft and a whole drove of maiden hawthorns blushing and looking askance upon her.

Drop me the sound of the findhorn's name, Mtu or Mti, som-
bogger was wisness. And drip me why in the flenders was she
frickled. And trickle me through was she marcellewaved or was it
weirdly a wig she wore. And whitside did they droop their glows
in their florry, aback to wist or affront to sea? In fear to hear the
dear so near or longing loth and loathing longing? Are you in the
swim or are you out? O go in, go on, go an! I mean about what
you know. I know right well what you mean. Rother! You'd like
the coifs and guimpes, snouty, and me to do the greasy jub on
old Veronica's wipers. What am I rancing now and I'll thank you?
Is it a pinny or is it a surplice? Arran, where's your nose? And
where's the starch? That's not the vesdre benediction smell. I can
tell from here by their *eau de Colo* and the scent of her oder they're
Mrs Magrath's. And you ought to have aird them. They've moist
come off her. Creases in silk they are, not crampton lawn. Baptiste
me, father, for she has sinned! Through her catchment ring she
freed them easy, with her hips' hurrahs for her knees'dontelleries.
The only parr with frills in old the plain. So they are, I declare!
Welland well! If tomorrow keeps fine who'll come tripping to sight-
see? How'll? Ask me next what I haven't got! The Belvedarean ex-
hibitioners. In their cruisery caps and oarsclub colours. What hoo,
they band! And what hoa, they buck! And here is her nubilee letters
too. Ellis on quay in scarlet thread. Linked for the world on a flush-
caloured field. Annan exe after to show they're not Laura Keown's.
O, may the diabolo twisk your seifety pin! You child of Mammon,
Kinsella's Lilith! Now who has been tearing the leg of her drawars
on her? Which leg is it? The one with the bells on it. Rinse them
out and aston along with you! Where did I stop? Never stop! Con-
tinuarration! You're not there yet. I amstel waiting. Garonne,
garonne!

Well, after it was put in the Mercy Cordial Mendicants' Sitter-
dag-Zindeh-Munaday Wakeschrift (for once they sullied their white
kidloves, chewing cuds after their dinners of cheeckin and beggin,
with their show us it here and their mind out of that and their
when you're quite finished with the reading matarial), even the
snee that snowdon his hoaring hair had a skunner against him.
Thaw, thaw, sava, savuto! Score Her Chuff Exsquire! Everywhere
erriff you went and every bung you arver dropped into, in cit or
suburb or in addled areas, the Rose and Bottle or Phoenix Tavern
or Power's Inn or Jude's Hotel or wherever you scoured the countryside from Nannywater to Vartryville or from Porta Lateen to the
lootin quarter you found his ikom etched tipside down or the cor-
nerboys cammocking his guy and Morris the Man, with the role
of a royss in his turgos the turrible, (Evropeahahn cheic house, un-
skimmed sooit and yahoort, hamman now cheekmee, Ahdahm this
way make, Fatima, half turn!) reeling and railing round the local
as the peihos piped und ubanjees twanged, with oddfellow's triple
tiara busby rotundarinking round his scalp. Like Pate-by-the-Neva
or Pete-over-Meer. This is the Hausman all paven and stoned, that
cribbed the Cabin that never was owned that cocked his leg and
hennad his Egg. And the mauldrin rabble around him in areopage,
fracassing a great bingkan cagnan with their timpan crowders. Mind
your Grimmfather! Think of your Ma! Hing the Hong is his jove's
hangnomen! Lilt a bolero, bulling a law! She swore on croststyx
nyne wyndabouts she's be level with all the snags of them yet. Par
the Vulnerable Virgin's Mary del Dame! So she said to herself she'd
frame a plan to fake a shine, the mischiefmaker, the like of it you
niever heard. What plan? Tell me quick and dongu so crould! What
the meurther did she mague? Well, she bergened a zakbag, a shammy
mailsack, with the lend of a loan of the light of his lampion, off
one of her swapsons, Shaun the Post, and then she went and con-
sulted her chapboucqs, old Mot Moore, Casey's Euclid and the
Fashion Display and made herself tidal to join in the mascarete.
O gig goggle of gigguels. I can't tell you how! It's too screaming
to rizo, rabbit it all! Minneha, minnehi minaaehe, minneho! O but
you must, you must really! Make my hear it gurgle gurgle, like
the farest gargle gargle in the dusky dirgle dargle! By the holy well
of Mulhuddart I swear I'd pledge my chanza getting to heaven
through Tirry and Killy's mount of impiety to hear it all, aviary
word! O, leave me my faculties, woman, a while! If you don't like
my story get out of the punt. Well, have it your own way, so. Here,

sit down and do as you're bid. Take my stroke and bend to your bow. Forward in and pull your overthepoise! Lisp it slaney and crisp it quiet. Deel me longsome. Tongue your time now. Breathe thet deep. Thouat's the fairway. Hurry slow and scheldt you go. Lynd us your blessed ashes here till I scrub the canon's underpants. Flow now. Ower more. And pooleypooley.

First she let her hair fal and down it flussed to her feet its teviots winding coils. Then, mothernaked, she sampood herself with gala-water and fraguant pistania mud, wupper and lauar, from crown to sole. Next she greesed the groove of her keel, warthes and wears and mole and itcher, with antifouling butterscatch and turfentide and serpenthyme and with leafmould she ushered round prunella isles and eslats dun, quincecunct, allover her little mary. Peeld gold of waxwork her jellybelly and her grains of incense anguille bronze. And after that she wove a garland for her hair. She pleated it. She plaited it. Of meadowgrass and riverflags, the bulrush and water-weed, and of fallen griefs of weeping willow. Then she made her bracelets and her anklets and her armlets and a jetty amulet for necklace of clicking cobbles and pattering pebbles and rumbledown rubble, richmond and rehr, of Irish rhunerhinerstones and shell-marble bangles. That done, a dawk of smut to her airy ey, Annushka Lutetiavitch Pufflovah, and the lellipos cream to her lippeleens and the pick of the paintbox for her pommettes, from strawbirry reds to extra violates, and she sendred her boudeloire maids to His Af-fluence, Ciliegia Grande and Kirschie Real, the two chirsines, with respecks from his missus, seepy and sewery, and a request might she passe of him for a minnikin. A call to pay and light a taper, in Brie-on-Arrosa, back in a sprizzling. The cock striking mine, the stalls bridely sign, there's Zambosy waiting for Me! She said she wouldn't be half her length away. Then, then, as soon as the lump his back was turned, with her mealiebag slang over her shulder, Anna Livia, oysterface, forth of her bassein came.

Describe her! Hustle along, why can't you? Spitz on the iern while it's hot. I wouldn't miss her for irthing on nerthe. Not for the lucre of lomba strait. Oceans of Gaud, I mosel hear that! Ogowe presta! Leste, before Julia sees her! Ishekarry and washemeskad, the carishy caratimaney? Whole lady fair? Duodecimoroon? Bon a ventura? Malagassy? What had she on, the liddel oud oddity? How much did she scallop, harness and weights? Here she is, Amnisty Ann! Call her calamity electrifies man.

No electress at all but old Moppa Necessity, angin mother of injons. I'll tell you a test. But you must sit still. Will you hold your peace and listen well to what I am going to say now? It might have been ten or twenty to one of the night of Allclose or the nexth of April when the flip of her hoogly igloo flappered and out toetippit a bushman woman, the dearest little moma ever you saw, nodding around her, all smiles, with ems of embarras and aues to awe, between two ages, a judyqueen, not up to your elb. Quick, look at her cute and saise her quirk for the bicker she lives the slicker she grows. Save us and tagus! No more? Werra where in ourthe did you ever pick a Lambay chop as big as a battering ram? Ay, you're right. I'm epte to forgetting, Like Liviam Liddle did Loveme Long. The linth of my hough, I say! She wore a ploughboy's nailstudded clogs, a pair of ploughfields in themselves: a sugarloaf hat with a gaudyquiviry peak and a band of gorse for an arnoment and a hundred streamers dancing off it and a guildered pin to pierce it: owlglassy bicycles boggled her eyes: and a fishnetzeveil for the sun not to spoil the wrinklings of her hydeaspects: potatorings boucled the loose laubes of her laudsnarers: her nude cuba stockings were salmospotspeckled: she sported a galligo shimmy of hazevaipar tinto that never was fast till it ran in the washing: stout stays, the rivals, lined her length: her bloodorange bockknickers, a two in one garment, showed natural nigger boggers, fancyfastened, free to undo: her blackstripe tan joseph was sequansewn and teddybearlined, with wavy rushgreen epaulettes and a leadown here and there of royal swansruff: a brace of gaspers stuck in her hayrope garters: her civvy codroy coat with alpheubett buttons was boundaried round with a twobar tunnel belt: a fourpenny bit in each pocketside weighed her safe from the blowaway windrush; she had a clothespeg tight astride on her joki's nose and she kep on grinding a sommething quaint in her fiumy mouth and the rrreke of the fluve of the tail of the gawan of her snuffdrab siouler's skirt trailed ffiffty odd Irish miles behind her lungarhodes.

Hellsbells, I'm sorry I missed her! Sweet gumptyum and nobody fainted! But in whelk of her mouths? Was her naze alight? Everyone that saw her said the dowce little delia looked a bit queer. Lotsy trotsy, mind the poddle! Missus, be good and don't fol in the say! Fenny poor hex she must have charred. Kickhams a frumpier ever you saw! Making mush mullet's eyes at her boys dobelon. And they crowned her their chariton queen, all the maids. Of the may? You don't say! Well for her she couldn't see herself. I recknitz wharfore the darling murrayed her mirror. She did? Mersey me! There was

a koros of drouthdropping surfacemen, boomslanging and plugchew-
ing, fruiteyeing and flowerfeeding, in contemplation of the fluctua-
tion and the undification of her filimentation, lolling and leasing
on North Lazers' Waal all eelfare week by the Jukar Yoick's and
as soon as they saw her meander by that marritime way in her
grasswinter's weeds and twigged who was under her archdeaconess
bonnet, Avondale's fish and Clarence's poison, sedges an to aneber,
Wit-upon-Crutches to Master Bates: *Between our two southsates and
the granite they're warming, or her face has been lifted or Alp has
doped!*

But what was the game in her mixed baggyrhatty? Just the tembo
in her tumbo or pilipili from her pepperpot? Saas and taas and specis
bizaas. And where in thunder did she plunder? Fore the battle or
efter the ball? I want to get it frisk from the soorce. I aubette my
bearb it's worth while poaching on! Shake it up, do, do! That's
a good old son of a ditch! I promise I'll make it worth your while.
And I don't mean maybe. Nor yet with a goodfor. Spey me pruth
and I'll tale you true.

Well, arundgirond in a waveney lyne aringarouma she pattered
and swung and sidled, dribbling her boulder through narrowa
mosses, the diliskydrear on our drier side and the vilde vetchvine
agin us, curara here, careero there, not knowing which medway or
weser to strike it, edereider, making chattahoochee all to her ain
chichiu, like Santa Claus at the cree of the pale and puny, nistling
to hear for their tiny hearties, her arms encircling Isolabella, then
running with reconciled Romas and Reims, on like a lech to be
off like a dart, then bathing Dirty Hans' spatters with spittle, with
a Christmas box apiece for aisch and iveryone of her childer, the
birthday gifts they dreamt they gabe her, the spoiled she fleetly
laid at our door! On the matt, by the pourch and inunder the cellar.
The rivulets ran aflod to see, the glashaboys, the pollynooties. Out
of the paunschaup on to the pyre. And they all about her, juvenile
leads and ingenuinas, from the slime of their slums and artesaned
wellings, rickets and riots, like the Smyly boys at their vicereine's
levee. Vivi vienne, little Annchen! Vielo Anna, high life! Sing us
a sula, O, susuria! Ausone sidulcis! Hasn't she tambre! Chipping her
and raising a bit of a chir or a jary every dive she'd neb in her
culdee sacco of wabbash she raabed and reach out her maundy
meerschaundize, poor souvenir as per ricorder and all for sore aring-
arung, stinkers and heelers, laggards and primelads, her furzeborn
sons and dribblederry daughters, a thousand and one of them, and

wickerpotluck for each of them. For evil and ever. And kiks the
buch. A tinker's bann and a barrow to boil his billy for Gipsy
Lee; a cartridge of cockaleekie soup for Chummy the Guardsman;
for sulky Pender's acid nephew deltoïd drops, curiously strong; a
cough and a rattle and wildrose cheeks for poor Piccolina Petite
MacFarlane; a jigsaw puzzle of needles and pins and blankets and
shins between them for Isabel, Jezebel and Llewelyn Mmarriage;
a brazen nose and pigiron mittens for Johnny Walker Beg; a papar
flag of the saints and stripes for Kevineen O'Dea; a puffpuff for
Pudge Craig and a nightmarching hare for Techertim Tombigby;
waterleg and gumboots each for Bully Hayes and Hurricane
Hartigan; a prodigal heart and fatted calves for Buck Jones, the
pride of Clonliffe; a loaf of bread and a father's early aim for Val
from Skibereen; a jauntingcar for Larry Doolin, the Ballyclee
jackeen; a seasick trip on a government ship for Teague O'Flanagan;
a louse and trap for Jerry Coyle; slushmincepies for Andy Mac-
kenzie; a hairclip and clackdish for Penceless Peter; that twelve
sounds look for G. V. Brooke; a drowned doll, to face downwards
for modest Sister Anne Mortimer; altar falls for Blanchisse's bed;
Wildairs' breechettes for Magpeg Woppington; to Sue Dot a big
eye; to Sam Dash a false step; snakes in clover, picked and scotched,
and a vaticanned viper catcher's visa for Patsy Presbys; a reiz every
morning for Standfast Dick and a drop every minute for Stumble-
stone Davy; scruboak beads for beatified Biddy; two appletweed stools
for Eva Mobbely; for Saara Philpot a jordan vale tearorne; a pretty
box of Pettyfib's Powder for Eileen Aruna to whiten her teeth and
outflash Helen Arhone; a whippingtop for Eddy Lawless; for Kitty
Coleraine of Butterman's Lane a penny wise for her foolish pitcher;
a putty shovel for Terry the Puckaun; an apotamus mask for Pro-
moter Dunne; a niester egg with a twicedated shell and a dynamight
right for Pavl the Curate; a collera morbous for Mann in the Cloack;
a starr and girton for Draper and Deane; for Will-of-the-Wisp and
Barny-the-Bark two mangolds noble to sweeden their bitters; for
Oliver Bound a way in his frey; for Seumas, thought little, a crown
he feels big; a tibertine's pile with a Congoswood cross on the back
for Sunny Twimjim; a praises be and spare me days for Brian the
Bravo; penteplenty of pity with lubilashings of lust for Olona Lena
Magdalena; for Camilla, Dromilla, Ludmilla, Mamilla, a bucket, a
packet, a book and a pillow; for Nancy Shannon a Tuami brooch;
for Dora Riparia Hopeandwater a cooling douche and a warming-
pan; a pair of Blarney braggs for Wally Meagher; a hairpin slate-

pencil for Elsie Oram to scratch her toby, doing her best with her volgar fractions; an old age pension for Betty Bellezza; a bag of the blues for Funny Fitz; a *Missa pro Messa* for Taff de Taff; Jill, the spoon of a girl, for Jack, the broth of a boy; a Rogerson Crusoe's Friday fast for Caducus Angelus Rubiconstein; three hundred and sixtysix poplin tyne for revery warp in the weaver's woof for Victor Hugonot; a stiff steaded rake and good varians muck for Kate the Cleaner; a hole in the ballad for Hosty; two dozen of cradles for J.F.X.P. Coppinger; tenpounten on the pop for the daulphins born with five spoiled squibs for Infanta; a letter to last a lifetime for Maggi beyond by the ashpit; the heftiest frozenmeat woman from Lusk to Livienbad for Felim the Ferry; spas and speranza and symposium's syrup for decayed and blind and gouty Gough; a change of naves and joys of ills for Armoricus Tristram Amoor Saint Lawrence; a guillotine shirt for Reuben Redbreast and hempen suspendeats for Brennan on the Moor; an oakanknee for Conditor Sawyer and musquodoboits for Great Tropical Scott; a C_3 peduncle for Karmalite Kane; a sunless map of the month, including the sword and stamps, for Shemus O'Shaun the Post; a jackal with hide for Browne but Nolan; a stonecold shoulder for Donn Joe Vance; all lock and no stable for Honorbright Merreytrickx; a big drum for Billy Dunboyne; a guilty goldeny bellows, below me blow me, for Ida Ida and a hushaby rocker, Elletrouvetout, for Who-is-silvier — Where-is-he?; whatever you like to swilly to swash, Yuinness or Yennessy, Laagen or Niger, for Festus King and Roaring Peter and Frisky Shorty and Treacle Tom and O. B. Behan and Sully the Thug and Master Magrath and Peter Cloran and O'Delawarr Rossa and Nerone MacPacem and whoever you chance to meet knocking around; and a pig's bladder balloon for Selina Susquehanna Stakelum. But what did she give to Pruda Ward and Katty Kanel and Peggy Quilty and Briery Brosna and Teasy Kieran and Ena Lappin and Muriel Maassy and Zusan Camac and Melissa Bradogue and Flora Ferns and Fauna Fox-Goodman and Grettna Greaney and Penelope Inglesante and Lezba Licking like Leytha Liane and Roxana Rohan with Simpatica Sohan and Una Bina Laterza and Trina La Mesme and Philomena O'Farrell and Irmak Elly and Josephine Foyle and Snakeshead Lily and Fountainoy Laura and Marie Xavier Agnes Daisy Frances de Sales Macleay? She gave them ilcka madre's daughter a moonflower and a bloodvein: but the grapes that ripe before reason to them that devide the vinedress.

So on Izzy, her shamemaid, love shone befond her tears as from Shem, her penmight, life past befoul his prime.

My colonial, wardha bagful! A bakereen's dusind with tithe tillies to boot. That's what you may call a tale of a tub! And Hibernonian market! All that and more under one crinoline envelope if you dare to break the porkbarrel seal. No wonder they'd run from her pison plague. Throw us your hudson soap for the honour of Clane! The wee taste the water left. I'll raft it back, first thing in the marne. Merced mulde! Ay, and don't forget the reckitts I lohaned you. You've all the swirls your side of the current. Well, am I to blame for that if I have? Who said you're to blame for that if you have? You're a bit on the sharp side. I'm on the wide. Only snuffers' cornets drifts my way that the cracka dvine chucks out of his cassock, with her estheryear's marsh narcissus to make him recant his vanitty fair. Foul strips of his chinook's bible I do be reading, dodwell disgustered but chickled with chuckles at the tittles is drawn on the tattlepage. *Senior ga dito: Faciasi Omo! E omo fu fò.* Ho! Ho! *Senior ga dito: Faciasi Hidamo! Hidamo se ga facessà.* Ha! Ha! And *Die Windermere Dichter* and Lefanu (Sheridan's) old *House by the Coachyard* and Mill (J.) *On Woman* with *Ditto on the Floss.* Ja, a swamp for Altmuehler and a stone for his flossies! I know how racy they move his wheel. My hands are blawcauld between isker and suda like that piece of pattern chayney there, lying below. Or where is it? Lying beside the sedge I saw it. Hoangho, my sorrow, I've lost it! Aimihi! With that turbary water who could see? So near and yet so far! But O, gihon! I lovat a gabber. I could listen to maure and moravar again. Regn onder river. Flies do your float. Thick is the life for mere.

Well, you know or don't you kennet or haven't I told you every telling has a taling and that's the he and the she of it. Look, look, the dusk is growing! My branches lofty are taking root. And my cold cher's gone ashley. Fieluhr? Filou! What age is at? It saon is late. 'Tis endless now senne eye or erewone last saw Waterhouse's clogh. They took it asunder, I hurd thum sigh. When will they re-assemble it? O, my back, my back, my bach! I'd want to go to Achesles-Pains. Pingpong! There's the Belle for Sexaloitez! And Concepta de Send-us-pray! Pang! Wring out the clothes! Wring in the dew! Godavari, vert the showers! And grant thaya grace! Aman. Will we spread them here now? Ay, we will. Flip! Spread on your bank and I'll spread mine on mine. Flep! It's what I'm doing. Spread! It's churning chill. Der went is rising. I'll lay a few stones on the hostel sheets. A man and his bride embraced between them. Else I'd have sprinkled and folded them only. And I'll tie my butcher's apron here. It's suety yet. The strollers will pass it by. Six shifts, ten kerchiefs, nine to hold to the fire and this for the code, the convent napkins, twelve, one baby's shawl. Good mother Jossiph knows, she said. Whose head? Mutter snores? Deataceas! Wharnow are alle her childer, say? In kingdome gone or power to come or gloria be to them farther? Allalivial, Allalluvial! Some here, more no more, more again lost alla stranger. I've heard tell that same brooch of the Shannons was married into a family in Spain. And all the Dunders de Dunnes in Markland's Vineland beyond Brendan's herring pool takes number nine in yangsee's hats. And one of Biddy's beads went bobbing till she rounded up lost histereve with a marigold and a cobbler's candle in a side strain of a main drain of a manzinahurries off Bachelor's Walk. But all that's left to the last of the Meaghers in the loup of the years prefixed and between is one kneebuckle and two hooks in the front. Do you tell me that now? I do in troth. Orara por Orbe and poor Las Animas! Ussa, Ulla, we're umbas all! Mezha, didn't you hear it a deluge of times, ufer and ufer, respund to spond? You deed, you deed! I need, I need! It's that irrawaddyng I've stoke in my aars. It all but husheth the lethest zswound. Oronoko! What's your trouble? Is that the great Finnleader himself in his joakimono on his statue riding the high horse there forehengist? Father of Otters, it is himself! Yonne there! Isset that? On Fallareen Common? You're thinking of Astley's Amphitheayter where the bobby restrained you making sugarstuck pouts to the ghostwhite horse of the Peppers. Throw the cobwebs from your eyes, woman, and spread your washing proper! It's well I know your sort of slop. Flap! Ireland sober is Ireland stiff. Lord help you, Maria, full of grease, the load is with me! Your prayers. I sonht zo! Madammangut! Were you lifting your elbow, tell us, glazy cheeks, in Conway's Carrigacurra canteen? Was I what, hobbledyhips? Flop! Your rere gait's creakorheuman bitts your butts disagrees. Amn't I up since the damp dawn, marthared mary allacook, with Corrigan's pulse and varicoarse veins, my pramaxle smashed, Alice Jane in decline and my oneeyed mongrel twice run over, soaking and bleaching boiler rags, and sweating cold, a widow like me, for to deck my tennis champion son, the laundryman with the lavandier flannels? You won your limpopo limp fron the husky hussars when Collars and Cuffs was heir to the town and your slur gave the stink to Carlow.

Holy Scamander, I sar it again! Near the golden falls. Icis on us!
Seints of light! Zezere! Subdue your noise, you hamble creature!
What is it but a blackburry growth or the dwyergray ass them four
old codgers owns. Are you meanam Tarpey and Lyons and Gregory?
I meyne now, thank all, the four of them, and the roar of them,
that draves that stray in the mist and old Johnny MacDougal along
with them. Is that the Poolbeg flasher beyant, pharphar, or a fire-
boat coasting nyar the Kishtna or a glow I behold within a hedge
or my Garry come back from the Indes? Wait till the honeying of
the lune, love! Die eve, little eve, die! We see that wonder in your
eye. We'll meet again, we'll part once more. The spot I'll seek if
the hour you'll find. My chart shines high where the blue milk's upset. Forgivemequick, I'm going! Bubye! And you, pluck your watch,
forgetmenot. Your evenlode. So save to jurna's end! My sights are
swimming thicker on me by the shadows to this place. I sow home
slowly now by own way, moyvalley way. Towy I too, rathmine.

Ah, but she was the queer old skeowsha anyhow, Anna Livia,
trinkettoes! And sure he was the quare old buntz too, Dear Dirty
Dumpling, foostherfather of fingalls and dotthergills. Gammer and
gaffer we're all their gangsters. Hadn't he seven dams to wive him?
And every dam had her seven crutches. And every crutch had its
seven hues. And each hue had a differing cry. Sudds for me and
supper for you and the doctor's bill for Joe John. Befor! Bifur! He
married his markets, cheap by foul, I know, like any Etrurian Catholic Heathen, in their pinky limony creamy birnies and their turkiss
indienne mauves. But at milkidmass who was the spouse? Then all
that was was fair. Tys Elvenland! Teems of times and happy returns.
The seim anew. Ordovico or viricordo. Anna was, Livia is, Plurabelle's to be. Northmen's thing made southfolk's place but howmulty
plurators made eachone in person? Latin me that, my trinity scholard,
out of eure sanscreed into oure eryan! *Hircus Civis Eblanensis!* He
had buckgoat paps on him, soft ones for orphans. Ho, Lord! Twins
of his bosom. Lord save us! And ho! Hey? What all men. Hot? His
tittering daughters of. Whawk?

Can't hear with the waters of. The chittering waters of. Flitter-
ing bats, fieldmice bawk talk. Ho! Are you not gone ahome? What
Thom Malone? Can't hear with bawk of bats, all thim liffeying
waters of. Ho, talk save us! My foos won't moos. I feel as old
as yonder elm. A tale told of Shaun or Shem? All Livia's daughter-
sons. Dark hawks hear us. Night! Night! My ho head halls. I

feel as heavy as yonder stone. Tell me of John or Shaun? Who were Shem and Shaun the living sons or daughters of? Night now! Tell me, tell me, tell me, elm! Night night! Telmetale of stem or stone. Beside the rivering waters of, hitherandthithering waters of. Night!

2

Every evening at lighting up o'clock sharp and until further notice in Feenichts Playhouse. (Bar and conveniences always open, Diddlem Club douncestears.) Entrancings: gads, a scrab; the quality, one large shilling. Newly billed for each wickeday perfumance. Somndoze massinees. By arraignment, childream's hours, expercatered. Jampots, rinsed porters, taken in token. With nightly redistribution of parts and players by the puppetry producer and daily dubbing of ghosters, with the benediction of the Holy Genesius Archimimus and under the distinguished patronage of their Elderships the Oldens from the four coroners of Findrias, Murias, Gorias and Falias, Messoirs the Coarbs, Clive Sollis, Galorius Kettle, Pobiedo Lancey and Pierre Dusort, while the Caesar-in-Chief looks. On. Sennet. As played to the Adelphi by the Brothers Bratislavoff (Hyrcan and Haristobulus), after humpteen dumpteen revivals. Before all the King's Hoarsers with all the Queen's Mum. And wordloosed over seven seas crowdblast in cellelleneteutoslavzendlatinsoundscript. In four tubbloids. While fern may cald us until firn make cold. *The Mime of Mick, Nick and the Maggies,* adopted from the Ballymooney Bloodriddon Murther by Bluechin Blackdillain (authorways 'Big Storey'), featuring:

GLUGG (Mr Seumas McQuillad, hear the riddles between the robot in his dress circular and the gagster in the rogues' gallery), the bold bad bleak boy of the storybooks, who, when the tabs go up, as we discover, because he knew to mutch, has been divorced into disgrace court by

THE FLORAS (Girl Scouts from St. Bride's Finishing Establishment, demand acidulateds), a month's bunch of pretty maidens who, while they pick on her, their pet peeve, form with valkyrienne licence the guard for

IZOD (Miss Butys Pott, ask the attendantess for a leaflet), a bewitching blonde who dimples delightfully and is approached in loveliness only by her grateful sister reflection in a mirror, the cloud of the opal, who, having jilted Glugg, is being fatally fascinated by

CHUFF (Mr Sean O'Mailey, see the chalk and sanguine pictograph on the safety drop), the fine frank fairhaired fellow of the fairytales, who wrestles for tophole with the bold bad bleak boy Glugg, geminally about caps or puds or tog bags or bog gats or chuting rudskin gunerally or something, until they adumbrace a pattern of somebody else or other, after which they are both carried off the set and brought home to be well soaped, sponged and scrubbed again by

ANN (Miss Corrie Corriendo, Grischun scoula, bring the babes, Pieder, Poder and Turtey, she mistributes mandamus monies, after perdunamento, hendrud aloven entrees, pulcinellis must not miss our national rooster's rag), their poor little old mother-in-lieu, who is woman of the house, playing opposite to

HUMP (Mr Makeall Gone, read the sayings from Laxdalesaga in the programme about King Ericus of Schweden and the spirit's whispers in his magical helmet), cap-a-pipe with watch and topper, coat, crest and supporters, the cause of all our grievances, the whirl, the flash and the trouble, who, having partially recovered from a recent impeachment due to egg everlasting, but throughandthoroughly proconverted, propounded for cyclological, is, studding sail once more, jibsheets and royals, in the semblance of the substance for the membrance of the umbrance with the remnance of the emblence reveiling a quemdam supercargo, of The Rockery, Poopinheavin, engaged in entertaining in his pilgrimst customhouse at Caherlehome-upon-Eskur those statutory persons

THE CUSTOMERS (Components of the Afterhour Courses at St. Patricius' Academy for Grownup Gentlemen, consult the annuary, coldporters sibsuction), a bundle of a dozen of representative locomotive civics, each inn quest of outings, who are still more sloppily served after every cup final by

SAUNDERSON (Mr Knut Oelsvinger, Tiffsdays off, wouldntstop in bad, imitation of flatfish, torchbearing supperaape, dud halfsovereign, no chee daily, rolly pollsies, Glen of the Downs, the Gugnir, his geyswerks, his earsequack, his lokistroki, o.s.v.), a scherinsheiner and spoilcurate, unconcerned in the mystery but under the inflounce of the milldieuw and butt of

KATE (Miss Rachel Lea Varian, she tells forkings for baschfellors, under purdah of card palmer teaput tosspot Madam d'Elta, during the pawses), kook-and-dishdrudge, whitch believes wanthingthats, whouse be the churchyard or whorts up the aasgaars, the show must go on.

Time: the pressant.

With futurist onehorse balletbattle pictures and the Pageant of Past History worked up with animal variations amid everglaning mangrovemazes and beorbtracktors by Messrs Thud and Blunder. Shadows by the film folk, masses by the good people. Promptings by Elanio Vitale. Longshots, upcloses, outblacks and stagetolets by Hexenschuss, Coachmaher, Incubone and Rocknarrag. Creations tastefully designed by Madame Berthe Delamode. Dances arranged by Harley Quinn and Coollimbeina. Jests, jokes, jigs and jorums for the Wake lent from the properties of the late cemented Mr T. M. Finnegan R.I.C. Lipmasks and hairwigs by Ouida Nooikke. Limes and Floods by Crooker and Toll. Kopay pibe by Kappa Pedersen. Hoed Pine hat with twentyfour ventholes by Morgen. Bosse and stringbag from Heteroditheroe's and All Ladies' presents. Tree taken for grafted. Rock rent. Phenecian blends and Sourdanian doofpoosts by Shauvesourishe and Wohntbedarft. The oakmulberryeke with silktrick twomesh from Shop-Sowry, seedsmanchap. Grabstone beg from General Orders Mailed. The crack (that's Cork!) by a smoker from the gods. The interjection (Buckley!) by the firement in the pit. Accidental music providentially arranged by L'Archet and Laccorde. Melodiotiosities in purefusion by the score. To start with in the beginning, we need hirtly bemark, a community prayer, everyone for himself, and to conclude with as an exodus, we think it well to add, a chorale in canon, good for us all for us all us all all. Songs betune the acts by the ambiamphions of Annapolis, Joan Mock-Comic, male soprano, and Jean Souslevin, bass noble, respectively: O, Mester Sogermon, ef thes es whot ye deux, then I'm not surpleased ye want that bottle of Sauvequipeu and Oh Off Nunch Der Rasche Ver Lasse Mitsch Nitscht. Till the summit scenes of climbacks castastrophear, *The Bearded Mountain* (Polymop Baretherootsch), and *The River Romps to Nursery* (Maidykins in Undiform). The whole thugogmagog, including the portions understood to be oddmitted as the results of the respective titulars neglecting to produce themselves, to be wound up for an afterenactment by a Magnificent Transformation Scene showing the Radium Wedding of Neid and Moorning and the Dawn of Peace, Pure, Perfect and Perpetual, Waking the Weary of the World.

An argument follows.

Chuffy was a nangel then and his soard fleshed light like likening. Fools top! Singty, sangty, meekly loose, defendy nous from prowlabouts. Make a shine on the curst. Emen.

But the duvlin sulph was in Glugger, that lost-to-lurning. Punct. He was sbuffing and sputing, tussing like anisine, whipping his eyesoult and gnatsching his teats over the brividies from existers and the outher liubbocks of life. He halth kelchy chosen a clayblade and makes prayses to his three of clubs. To part from these, my corsets, is into overlusting fear. Acts of feet, hoof and jarrety: athletes longfoot. Djowl, uphere!

Aminxt that nombre of evelings, but how pierceful in their sojestiveness were those first girly stirs, with zitterings of flight released and twinglings of twitchbells in rondel after, with waverings that made shimmershake rather naightily all the duskcended airs and shylit beaconings from shehind hims back. Sammy, call on. Mirrylamb, she was shuffering all the diseasinesses of the unherd of. Mary Louisan Shousapinas! If Arck could no more salve his agnols from the wiles of willy wooly woolf! If all the airish signics of her dipandump helpabit from an Father Hogam till the Mutther Masons could not that Glugg to catch her by the calour of her brideness! Not Rose, Sevilla nor Citronelle; not Esmeralde, Pervinca nor Indra; not Viola even nor all of them four themes over. But, the monthage stick in the melmelode jawr, I am (twintomine) all thees thing. Up tighty in the front, down again on the loose, drim and drumming on her back and a pop from her whistle. What is that, O holytroopers? Isot givin yoe?

Up he stulpled, glee you gees, with search a fling did die near sea, beamy owen and calmy hugh and if you what you my call for me I will wishyoumaycull for you.

And they are met, face a facing. They are set, force to force. And no such Copenhague-Marengo was less so fated for a fall since in Glenasmole of Smiling Thrushes Patch Whyte passed O'Sheen ascowl.

Arrest thee, scaldbrother! came the evangelion, sabre accusant, from all Saint Joan's Wood to kill or maim him, and be dumm but ill s'arrested. Et would proffer to his delected one the his trifle from the grass.

A space. Who are you? The cat's mother. A time. What do you lack? The look of a queen.

But what is that which is one going to prehend? Seeks, buzzling is brains, the feinder.

The howtosayto itiswhatis hemustwhomust worden schall. A dark-tongues, kunning. O theoperil! Ethiaop lore, the poor lie. He askit of the hoothed fireshield but it was untergone into the matthued heaven. He soughed it from the luft but that bore ne mark ne message. He luked upon the bloomingrund where ongly his corns were growning. At last he listed back to beckline how she pranked alone so johntily. The skand for schooling.

With nought a wired from the wordless either.

Item. He was hardset then. He wented to go (somewhere) while he was weeting. Utem. He wished to grieve on the good persons, that is the four gentlemen. Otem. And it was not a long time till he was feeling true forim he was goodda purssia and it was short after that he was fooling mehaunt to mehynte he was an injine ruber. Etem. He was at his thinker's aunts to give (the four gentlemen) the presence (of a curpse). And this is what he would be willing. He fould the fourd; they found the hurtled stones; they fell ill with the gravy duck: and he sod town with the roust of the meast. Atem.

Towhere byhangs ourtales.

Ah ho! This poor Glugg! It was so said of him about of his old fontmouther. Truly deplurabel! A dire, O dire! And all the freightfullness whom he inhebited after his colline born janitor. Sometime towerable! With that hehry antlets on him and the baublelight bulching out of his sockets whiling away she sprankled his allover with her noces of interregnation: How do you do that lack a lock and pass the poker, please? And bids him tend her, lute and airly. Sing, sweetharp, thing to me anone! So that Glugg, the poor one, in that limbopool which was his subnesciousness he could scares of all knotknow whither his morrder had bourst a blabber or if the vogalstones that hit his tynpan was that mearly his skoll missed her. Misty's trompe or midst his flooting? Ah, ho! Cicely, awe!

The youngly delightsome frilles-in-pleyurs are now showen drawen, if bud one, or, if in florileague, drawens up consociately at the hinder sight of their commoner guardian. Her boy fiend or theirs, if they are so plurielled, cometh up as a trapadour, sinking how he must fand for himself by gazework what their colours wear as they are all showen drawens up. Tireton, cacheton, tireton, ba! Doth that not satisfy youth, sir? Quanty purty bellas, here, Madama Lifay! And what are you going to charm them to, Madama, do say? Cinderynelly angled her slipper; it was cho chiny yet braught her a groom. He will angskt of them from their commoner guardian at next lineup (who is really the rapier of the two though thother brother can hold his own, especially for he bandished it with his hand the hold time, mamain, a simply gracious: Mi, O la!), and reloose that thong off his art: Hast thou feel liked carbunckley ones? Apun which his poohoor pricoxity theirs is a little tittertit of hilarity (Lad-o'-me-soul! Lad-o'-me-soul, see!) and the wordchary is atvoiced ringsoundinly by their toots ensembled, though not meaning to be clever, but just with a shrug of their hips to go to troy and harff a freak at himself by all that story to the ulstramarines. Otherwised, holding their noises, they insinuate quiet private, Ni, he make peace in his preaches and play with esteem.

Warewolff! Olff! Toboo!

So olff for his topheetuck the ruck made raid, aslick aslegs would run; and he ankered on his hunkers with the belly belly prest. Asking: What's my muffinstuffinaches for these times? To weat: Breath and bother and whatarcurss. Then breath more bother and more whatarcurss. Then no breath no bother but worrawarrawurms. And Shim shallave shome.

As Rigagnolina to Mountagnone, what she meaned he could not can. All she meaned was golten sylvup, all she meaned was some Knight's ploung jamn. It's driving her dafft like he's so dumnb. If he'd lonely talk instead of only gawk as thought yateman hat stuck hits stick althrough his spokes and if he woold nut wolly so! Hee. Speak, sweety bird! Mitzymitzy! Though I did ate tough turf I'm not the bogdoxy.

— Have you monbreamstone?

— No.

— Or Hellfeuersteyn?

— No.

— Or Van Diemen's coral pearl?

— No.

He has lost.

Off to clutch, Glugg! Forwhat! Shape your reres, Glugg! Foreweal! Ring we round, Chuff! Fairwell! Chuffchuff's inners even. All's rice with their whorl!

Yet, ah tears, who can her mater be? She's promised he'd eye her. To try up her pretti. But now it's so longed and so fared and so forth. Jerry for jauntings. Alabye! Fled.

The flossies all and mossies all they drooped upon her draped brimfall. The bowknots, the showlots, they wilted into woeblots.

The pearlagraph, the pearlagraph, knew whitchly whether to weep or laugh. For always down in Carolinas lovely Dinahs vaunt their view.

Poor Isa sits a glooming so gleaming in the gloaming; the tincelles a touch tarnished wind no lovelinoise awound her swan's. Hey, lass! Woefear gleam she so glooming, this pooripathete I solde? Her beauman's gone of a cool. Be good enough to symperise. If he's at anywhere she's therefor to join him. If it's to nowhere she's going to too. Buf if he'll go to be a son to France's she'll stay daughter of Clare. Bring tansy, throw myrtle, strew rue, rue, rue. She is fading out like Journee's clothes so you can't see her now. Still we know how Day the Dyer works, in dims and deeps and dusks and darks. And among the shades that Eve's now wearing she'll meet anew fiancy, tryst and trow. Mammy was, Mimmy is, Minuscoline's to be. In the Dee dips a dame and the dame desires a demselle but the demselle dresses dolly and the dolly does a dulcydamble. The same renew. For though she's unmerried she'll after truss up and help that hussyband how to hop. Hip it and trip it and chirrub and sing. Lord Chuffy's sky sheraph and Glugg's got to swing.

So and so, toe by toe, to and fro they go round, for they are the ingelles, scattering nods as girls who may, for they are an angel's garland.

Catchmire stockings, libertyed garters, shoddyshoes, quicked out with selver. Pennyfair caps on pinnyfore frocks and a ring on her fomefing finger. And they leap so looply, looply, as they link to light. And they look so loovely, loovelit, noosed in a nuptious night. Withasly glints in. Andecoy glants out. They ramp it a little, a lessle, a lissle. Then rompride round in rout.

Say them all but tell them apart, cadenzando coloratura! R is Rubretta and A is Arancia, Y is for Yilla and N for greeneriN. B is Boyblue with odalisque O while W waters the fleurettes of novembrance. Though they're all but merely a schoolgirl yet these way went they. I' th' view o' th'avignue dancing goes entrancing roundly. Miss Oodles of Anems before the Luvium doeslike. So. And then again doeslike. So. And miss Endles of Eons efter Dies of Eirae doeslike. So. And then again doeslike. So. The many wiles of Winsure.

The grocer's bawd she slips her hand in the haricot bag, the lady in waiting sips her sup from the paraffin can, Mrs Wildhare Quickdoctor helts her skelts up the casuaway the flasht instinct she herds if a tinkle of tunder, the widow Megrievy she knits cats' cradles, this bountiful actress leashes a harrier under her tongue, and here's the girl who she's kneeled in coldfashion and she's told her priest (spt!) she's pot on a chap (chp!) and this lass not least, this rickissime woman, who she writes foot fortunes money times over in the nursery dust with her capital thumb. Buzz. All runaway sheep bound back bopeep, trailing their teenes behind them. And these ways wend they. And those ways went they. Winnie, Olive and Beatrice, Nelly and Ida, Amy and Rue. Here they come back, all the gay pack, for they are the florals, from foncey and pansey to papavere's blush, foresake-me-nought, while there's leaf there's hope, with primtim's ruse and marrymay's blossom, all the flowers of the ancelles' garden.

But vicereversing thereout from those palms of perfection to anger arbour, treerack monatan, scroucely out of scout of ocean, virid with woad, what tornaments of complementary rages rocked the divlun from his punchpoll to his tummy's shentre as he displaid all the oathword science of his visible disgrace. He was feeling so funny and floored for the cue, all over which girls as he don't know whose hue. If gossseys gazious would but fain smile him a smile he would be fondling a praise he ate some nice bit of fluff. But no geste reveals the unconnouth. They're all odds against him, the beasties. Scratch. Start.

He dove his head into Wat Murrey, gave Stewart Ryall a puck on the plexus, wrestled a hurry-come-union with the Gillie Beg, wiped all his sinses, martial and menial, out of Shrove Sundy MacFearsome, excremuncted as freely as any frothblower into MacIsaac, had a belting bout, chaste to chaste, with McAdoo about nothing and, childhood's age being aye the shameleast, tel a Tartaran tastarin toothsome tarrascone tourtoun, vestimentivorous chlamydophagian, imbretellated himself for any time untellable with what hung over to the Machonochie Middle from the MacSiccaries of the Breeks. Home!

Allwhile, moush missuies from mungy monsie, preying in his mind, son of Everallin, within himself, he swure. Macnoon maggoty mag! Cross of a coppersmith bishop! He would split. He do big squeal like holy Trichepatte. Seek hells where from yank islanders the petriote's absolation. Mocknitza! Genik! He take skiff come first dagrene day overwide tumbler, rough and dark, till when bow of the shower show of the bower with three shirts and a wind, pagoda permettant, crookolevante, the bruce, the coriolano and the ignacio. From prudals to the secular but from the cumman to the nowter. Byebye, Brassolis, I'm breaving! Our war, Dully Gray! A conansdream of lodascircles, he here schlucefinis. Gelchasser no more!

Mischnary for the minestrary to all the sems of Aram. Shimach,
eon of Era. Mum's for's maxim, ban's for's book and Dodgesome
Dora for hedgehung sheolmastress. And Unkel Silanse coach in
diligence. Disconnection of the succeeding. He wholehog himself
for carberry banishment care of Pencylmania, Bretish Armerica,
to melt Mrs Gloria of the Bunkers' Trust, recorporated, (prunty!)
by meteoromancy and linguified heissrohgin, quit to hail a hurry
laracor and catch the Paname-Turricum and regain that absendee
tarry easty, his città immediata, by an alley and detour with farecard
awailable getrennty years. Right for Rovy the Roder. From the safe
side of distance! Libera, nostalgia! Beate Laurentie O'Tuli, Euro
pra nobis! Every monk his own cashel where every little ligger is
his own liogotenente with inclined jambs in full purview to his
pronaose and to the deretane at his reredoss. Fuisfinister, fuyer-
escaper! He would, with the greatest of ease, before of weighting
midhook, by dear home trashold on the raging canal, for othersites
of Jorden, (heave a hevy, waterboy!) make one of hissens with a
knockonacow and a chow collegions and fire off, gheol ghiornal,
foull subustioned mullmud, his farced epistol to the hibruws. From
Cernilius slomtime prepositus of Toumaria to the clutch in Anteach.
Salvo! Ladigs and jointuremen! No more turdenskaulds! Free leaves
for ebribadies! All tinsammon in the yord! With harm and aches till
farther alters! Wild primates not stop him frem at rearing a writing
in handy antics. *Nom de plume!* Gout strap Fenlanns! And send
Jarge for Mary Inklenders! And daunt you logh if his vineshanky's
schwemmy! For he is the general, make no mistake in he. He is General Jinglesome.

Go in for scribenery with the satiety of arthurs in S.P.Q.R.ish
and inform to the old sniggering publicking press and its nation
of sheepcopers about the whole plighty troth between them, malady
of milady made melodi of malodi, she, the lalage of lyonesses, and
him, her knave arrant. To Wildrose La Gilligan from Croppy
Crowhore. For all within crystal range.

Ukalepe. Loathers' leave. Had Days. Nemo in Patria. The
Luncher Out. Skilly and Carubdish. A Wondering Wreck. From
the Mermaids' Tavern. Bullyfamous. Naughtsycalves. Mother of
Misery. Walpurgas Nackt.

Maleesh! He would bare to untired world of Leimuncononnul-
stria (and what a strip poker globbtrottel they pairs would looks!)
how wholefallows, his guffer, the sabbatarian (might faction split
his beard!), he too had a great big oh in the megafundum of his

tomashunders and how her Lettyshape, his gummer, that congealed
sponsar, she had never cessed at waking malters among the jemas-
sons since the cluft that meataxe delt her made her microchasm as
gap as down low. So they fished in the kettle and fought free and
if she bit his tailibout all hat tiffin for thea. He would jused sit it
all write down just as he would jused set it up all writhefully rate
in blotch and void, yielding to no man in hymns ignorance, seeing
how heartsilly sorey he was, owning to the condrition of his bike-
stool. And, reading off his fleshskin and writing with his quillbone,
fillfull ninequires with it for his auditers, Caxton and Pollock, a most
moraculous jeeremyhead sindbook for all the peoples, under the
presidency of the suchess of sceaunonsceau, a hadtobe heldin, thoroughly enjoyed by many so meny on block at Boyrut season and
for their account ottorly admired by her husband in sole intimacy,
about whose told his innersense and the grusomehed's yoeureeke of
his spectrescope and why he was off colour and how he was am-
bothed upon by the very spit of himself, first on the cheekside by
Michelangelo and, besouns thats, over on the owld jowly side by
Bill C. Babby, and the suburb's formule why they provencials drollo
eggspilled him out of his homety dometry narrowedknee domum
(osco de basco de pesco de bisco!) because all his creature comfort
was an omulette finas erbas in an ark finis orbe and, no master how
mustered, mind never mend, he could neither swuck in nonneither
swimp in the flood of cecialism and the best and schortest way of
blacking out a caughtalock of all the sorrors of Sexton until he would
accoster her coume il fou in teto-dous as a wagoner would his mud-
heeldy wheesindonk at their trist in Parisise after tourments of tosend years, bread cast out on waters, making goods at mutuurity,
Mondamoiseau of Casanuova and Mademoisselle from Armentières.
Neblonovi's Nivonovio! Nobbio and Nuby in ennoviacion! Occi-
tantitempoli! He would si through severalls of sanctuaries maywhat-
may mightwhomight so as to meet somewhere, if produced, on a
demi panssion for his whole lofetime, payment in goo to slee music
and poisonal comfany, following which, like Ipsey Secumbe, when
he fingon to foil the fluter, she could have all the g. s. M. she moo-
hooed after fore and rickwards to herslF, including science of sonor-
ous silence, while he, being brung up on soul butter, have recourse
of course to poetry. With tears for his coronaichon, such as engines
weep. Was liffe worth leaving? Nej!

Tholedoth, treetrene! Zokrahsing, stone! Arty, reminiscensitive, at
bandstand finale on grand carriero, dreaming largesse of lifesighs

over early lived offs—all old Sators of the Sowsceptre highly nutri-
tius family histrionic, genitricksling with Avus and Avia, that simple
pair, and descendant down on veloutypads by a vuncular process to
Nurus and Noverca, those notorious nepotists, circumpictified in
their sobrine census, patriss all of them by the glos on their germane
faces and their socerine eyes like transparents of vitricus, patruuts to
a man, the archimade levirs of his ekonome world. Remember thee,
castle throwen? Ones propsperups treed, now stohong baroque. And
oil paint use a pumme if yell trace me there title to where was a hovel
not a havel (the first rattle of his juniverse) with a tingtumtingling
and a next, next and next (gin a paddy? got a petty? gussies, gif it
ope?), while itch ish shome.

— *My God, alas, that dear olt tumtum home*
Whereof in youthfood port I preyed
Amook the verdigrassy convict vallsall dazes.
And cloitered for amourmeant in thy boosome shede!

His mouthful of ecstasy (for Shing-Yung-Thing in Shina from
Yoruyume across the Timor Sea), herepong (maladventure!) shot
pinging up through the errorooth of his wisdom (who thought him
a Fonar all, feastking of shellies by googling Lovvey, regally frey-
therem, eagelly plumed, and wasbut gumboil owrithy prods wretched
some horsery megee plods coffin acid odarkery pluds dense floppens
mugurdy) as though it had been zawhen intwo. Wholly sanguish
blooded up disconvulsing the fixtures of his fizz. Apang which his
tempory chewer med him a crazy chump of a Haveajube Sillayass.
Joshua Croesus, son of Nunn! Though he shall live for millions of
years a life of billions of years, from their roseaced glows to their
violast lustres, he shall not forget that pucking Pugases. Holihowls-
balls and bloody acres! Like gnawthing unheardth!

But, by Jove Chronides, Seed of Summ, after at he had bate his
breastplates for, forforget, forforgetting his birdsplace, it was soon
that, that he, that he rehad himself. By a prayer? No, that comes
later. By contrite attrition? Nay, that we passed. Mid esercizism?
So is richt.

And it was so. And Malthos Moramor resumed his soul. With:
Go Ferchios off to Allad out of this! An oldsteinsong. He threwed
his fit up to his aers, rolled his poligone eyes, snivelled from his snose
and blew the guff out of his hornypipe. The hopjoimt jerk of a ladle
broom jig that he learned in locofoco when a redhot turnspite he.
Under reign of old Roastin the Bowl Ratskillers, readyos! Why was
that man for he's doin her wrong! Lookery looks, how he's knots in

his entrails! Mookery mooks, it's a grippe of his gripes. Seekeryseeks,
why his biting he's head off? Cokerycokes, it's his spurt of coal. And
may his tarpitch dilute not give him chromitis! For the mauwe that
blinks you blank is mostly Carbo. Where the inflammabilis might
pursuive his comburenda with a pure flame and a true flame and
a flame all toogasser, soot. The worst is over. Wait! And the dubuny
Mag may gang to preesses. With Dinny Finneen, me canty, ho! In
the lost of the gleamens. Sousymoust. For he would himself deal a
treatment as might be trusted in anticipation of his inculmination
unto fructification for the major operation. When (pip!) a message
interfering intermitting interskips from them (pet!) on herzian
waves, (call her venicey names! call her a stell!) a butterfly from
her zipclasped handbag, a wounded dove astarted from, escaping
out her forecotes. Isle wail for yews, O doherlynt! The poetesser.
And around its scorched cap she has twilled a twine of flame to let
the laitiest know she's marrid. And pim it goes backballed. Tot burns
it so leste. A claribel cumbeck to errind. Hers before his even, posted
ere penned. He's your change, thinkyou methim. Go daft noon,
madden, mind the step. Please stoop O to please. Stop. What saying?
I have soreunder from to him now, dearmate ashore, so, so com-
pleasely till I can get redressed, which means the end of my stays
in the languish of Tintangle. Is you zealous of mes, brother? Did
you boo moiety lowd? You suppoted to be the on conditiously re-
jected? Satanly, lade! Can that sobstuff, whingeywilly! Stop up, mavrone, and sit in my lap, Pepette, though I'd much rather not. Like
things are m. ds. is all in vincibles. Decoded.

Now a run for his money! Now a dash to her dot! Old cocker,
young crowy, sifadda, sosson. A bran new, speedhount, outstripper-
ous on the wind. Like a waft to wingweary one or a sos to a coast-
guard. For directly with his whoop, stop and an upalepsy didando a
tishy, in appreciable less time than it takes a glaciator to submerger
an Atlangthis, was he again, agob, before the trembly ones, a spark's
gap off, doubledasguesched, gotten orlop in a simplasailormade and
shaking the storm out of his hiccups. The smartest vessel you could
find would elazilee him on her knee as her lucky for the Rio Grande.
He's a pigtail tarr and if he hadn't got it toothick he'd a telltale tall
of his pitcher on a wall with his photure in the papers for cutting
moutonlegs and capers, letting on he'd jest be japers and his tail
cooked up.

Goal! It's one by its length.

Angelinas, hide from light those hues that your sin beau may

bring to light! Though down to your dowerstrip he's bent to knee
he maun't know ledgings here.

For a haunting way will go and you need not make your mow.
Find the frenge for frocks and translace it into shocks of such as
touch with show and show.

He is guessing at hers for all he is worse, the seagoer. Hark to
his wily geeses goosling by, and playfair, lady! And note that they
who will for exile say can for dog while them that won't leave ingle
end says now for know.

For he faulters how he hates to trouble them without.

But leaving codhead's mitre and the heron's plumes sinistrant to
the server of servants and rex of regums and making a bolderdash
for lubberty of speech he asks not have you seen a match being
struck nor is this powder mine but, letting punplays pass to ernest:

— Haps thee jaoneofergs?

— Nao.

— Haps thee mayjaunties?

— Naohao.

— Haps thee per causes nunsibellies?

— Naohaohao.

— Asky, asky, asky! Gau on! Micaco! Get!

Ping an ping nwan ping pwan pong.

And he did a get, their anayance, and slink his hook away, aleguere
come alaguerre, like a chimista inchamisas, whom the harricana
hurries and hots foots, zingo, zango, segur. To hoots of utskut,
urqurd, jamal, qum, yallah, yawash, yak! For he could ciappaciop-
pachew upon a skarp snakk of pure undefallen engelsk, melanmoon
or tartatortoise, tsukisaki or soppisuppon, as raskly and as baskly
as your cheesechalk cow cudd spanich. Makoto! Whagta kriowday!
Gelagala nausy is. Yet right divining do not was. Hovobovo hafogate
hokidimatzi in kamicha! He had his sperrits all foulen on him; to
vet, most griposly, he was bedizzled and debuzzled; he had his tristiest
cabaleer on; and looked like bruddy Hal. A shelling a cockshy and
be donkey shot at? Or a peso besant to join the armada?

But, Sin Showpanza, could anybroddy which walked this world
with eyes whiteopen have looked twinsomer than the kerl he left
behind him? Candidatus, viridosus, aurilucens, sinelab? Of all the
green heroes everwore coton breiches, the whitemost, the goldenest!
How he stud theirs with himselfs mookst kevinly, and that ante-
revolitionary, the churchman childfather from tonsor's tuft to
almonder's toes, a haggiography in duotrigesumy, son soptimost of

sire sixtusks, of Mayaqueenies sign osure, hevnly buddhy time, inwreathed of his near cissies, a mickly dazzly eely oily with looiscurrals, a soulnetzer by zvesdals priestessd, their trail the tractive, and dem dandypanies knows de play of de eyelids, with his gamecox spurts and his smile likequid glue (the suessiest sourir ever weanling wore), whiles his host of spritties, lusspillerindernees, they went pea-henning a ripidarapidarpad around him, pilgrim prinkips, kerilour kevinour, in neuchoristic congressulations, quite purringly excited, rpdrpd, allauding to him by all the licknames in the litany with the terms in which no little dulsy nayer ever thinks about implying except to her future's year and sending him perfume most praypuffs to setisfire more then to teasim (shllwe help, now you've massmuled, you t'rigolect a bit? yismik? yimissy?) that he, the finehued, the fairhailed, the farahead, might bouchesave unto each but everyone, asfar as safras durst assune, the havemercyonhurs of his kissier li-cence. Meanings: Andure the enjurious till imbetther rer. We know you like Latin with essies impures, (and your liber as they sea) we certney like gurgles love the nargleygargley so, arrahbeejee, tell that old frankay boyuk to bellows upthe tombucky in his tumtum argan and give us a gust of his gushy old. Goof!

Hymnumber twentynine. O, the singing! Happy little girlycums to have adolphted such an Adelphus! O, the swinginging hopops so goholden! They've come to chant en chor. They say their salat, the madiens' prayer to the messiager of His Nabis, prostitating their selfs eachwise and combinedly. Fateha, fold the hands. Be it hon-oured, bow the head. May thine evings e'en be blossful! Even of bliss! As we so hope for ablution. For the sake of the farbung and of the scent and of the holiodrops. Amems.

A pause. Their orison arises misquewhite as Osman glory, ebbing wasteward, leaves to the soul of light its fading silence (allahlah lahlah lah!), a turquewashed sky. Then:

— Xanthos! Xanthos! Xanthos! We thank to thine, mighty inno-cent, that diddest bring it off fuitefuite. Should in ofter years it became about you will after desk jobduty becoming a bank mid-land mansioner we and I shall reside with our obeisant servants among Burke's mobility at La Roseraie, Ailesbury Road. Red bricks are all hellishly good values if you trust to the roster of ads but we'll save up ourselves and nab what's nicest and boskiest of timber trees in the nebohood. Oncaill's plot. Luccombe oaks, Turkish hazels, Greek firs, incense palm edcedras. The hypsometers of Mount An-ville is held to be dying out of arthataxis but, praise send Larix

U'Thule, the wych elm of Manelagh is still flourishing in the open, because its native of our nature and the seeds was sent by Fortune. We'll have our private palypeachum pillarposterns for lovesick letterines fondly affianxed to our front railings and swings, hammocks, tighttaught balletlines, accomodationnooks and prismic bathboites, to make Envyeyes mouth water and wonder when they binocular us from their embrassured windows in our garden rare. Fyat-Fyat shall be our number on the autokinaton and Chubby in his Chuffs oursforownly chuffeur. T will be waiting for uns as I sold U at the first antries. Our cousin gourmand, Percy, the pup, will denounce the sniffnomers of all callers where among our Seemyease Sister, Tabitha, the ninelived, will extend to the full her hearthy welcome. While the turf and twigs they tattle. Tintin tintin. Lady Marmela Shortbred will walk in for supper with her marchpane switch on, her necklace of almonds and her poirette Sundae dress with bracelets of honey and her cochineal hose with the caramel dancings, the briskly best from Bootiestown, and her suckingstaff of ivory mint. You mustn't miss it or you'll be sorry. Charmeuses chloes, glycering juwells, lydialight fans and puffumed cynarettes. And the Prince Le Monade has been graciously pleased. His six chocolate pages will run bugling before him and Cococream toddle after with his sticksword in a pink cushion. We think His Sparkling Headiness ought to know Lady Marmela. Luisome his for lissome hers. He's not going to Cork till Cantalamesse or mayhope till Rose Easter or Saint Tibble's Day. So Niomon knows. The Fomor's in his Fin, the Momor's her and hin. A paaralone! A paaralone! And Dublin's all adin. We'll sing a song of Singlemonth and you'll too and you'll. Here are notes. There's the key. One two three. Chours! So come on, ye wealthy gentrymen wibfrufrocksfull of fun! Thin thin! Thin thin! Thej olly and thel ively, thou billy with thee coo, for to jog a jig of a crispness nice and sing a missal too. Hip champouree! Hiphip champouree! O you longtailed blackman, polk it up behind me! Hip champouree! Hiphip champouree! And, jessies, push the pumkik round. Anneliuia!

Since the days of Roamaloose and Rehmoose the pavanos have been strident through their struts of Chapelldiseut, the vaulsies have meed and youdled through the purly ooze of Ballybough, many a mismy cloudy has tripped taintily along that hercourt strayed reelway and the rigadoons have held ragtimed revels on the platauplain of Grangegorman; and, though since then sterlings and guineas have been replaced by brooks and lions and some progress has been made

on stilts and the races have come and gone and Thyme, that chef
of seasoners, has made his usual astewte use of endadjustables and
whatnot willbe isnor was, those danceadeils and cancanzanies have
come stimmering down for our begayment through the bedeafdom
of po's taeorns, the obcecity of pa's teapucs, as lithe and limbfree
limber as when momie mummed at ma.

Just so stylled with the nattes are their flowerheads now and each
of all has a lovestalk onto herself and the tot of all the tits of their
understamens is as open as he can posably she and is tournesoled
straightcut or sidewaist, accourdant to the coursets of things feminite,
towooerds him in heliolatry, so they may catchcup in their calyzettes,
alls they go troping, those parryshoots from his muscalone pistil,
for he can eyespy through them, to their selfcolours, nevertheleast
their tissue peepers, (meaning Mullabury mesh, the time of appling
flowers, a guarded figure of speech, a variety of perfume, a bridawl,
seamist inso one) as leichtly as see saw (O my goodmiss! O my
greatmess! O my prizelestly preshoes!) while, dewyfully as dimb dum-
belles, all alisten to his elixir. Lovelyt!

And they said to him:

— Enchainted, dear sweet Stainusless, young confessor, dearer dearest, we herehear, aboutobloss, O coelicola, thee salutamt. Pattern
of our unschoold, pageantmaster, deliverer of softmissives, round the
world in forty mails, bag, belt and balmybeam, our barnaboy, our
chepachap, with that pampipe in your putaway, gab borab, when
you will be after doing all your sightseeing and soundhearing and
smellsniffing and tastytasting and tenderumstouchings in all Daney-
gaul, send us, your adorables, thou overblaseed, a wise and letters
play of all you can ceive, chief celtech chappy, from your holy post
now you hast ascertained ceremonially our names. Unclean you art
not. Outcaste thou are not. Leperstower, the karman's loki, has not
blanched at our pollution and your intercourse at ninety legsplits
does not defile. Untouchable is not the scarecrown is on you. You
are pure. You are pure. You are in your puerity. You have not
brought stinking members into the house of Amanti. Elleb Inam,
Titep Notep, we name them to the Hall of Honour. Your head
has been touched by the god Enel-Rah and your face has been
brightened by the goddess Aruc-Ituc. Return, sainted youngling, and
walk once more among us! The rains of Demani are masikal as
of yere. And Baraza is all aflower. Siker of calmy days. As shiver
as shower can be. Our breed and better class is in brood and bitter pass. Labbeycliath longs. But we're counting on the cluck. The

Great Cackler comes again. Sweetstaker, Abel lord of all our haloease, we (to be slightly more femmiliar perhips than is slickly more then nacessory), toutes philomelas as well as magdelenes, were drawpairs with two pinmarks, BVD and BVD dot, so want lotteries of ticklets posthastem (you appreciate?) so as to be very dainty, if an isaspell, and so as to be verily dandydainty, if an ishibilley, of and on, to and for, by and with, from you. Let the hitback hurry his wayward ere the missive has time to take herself off, 'twill be o'erthemore willfully intomeet if the coming offence can send our shudders before. We feem to have being elfewhere as tho' th' had pafs'd in our fufpens. Next to our shrinking selves we love sensitivas best. For they are the Angèles. Brick, fauve, jonquil, sprig, fleet, nocturne, smiling bruise. For they are an Angèle's garment. We will be constant (what a word!) and bless the day, for whole hours too, yes, for sold long syne as we shall be heing in our created being of ours elvishness, the day you befell, you dreadful temptation! Now promisus as at our requisted you will remain ignorant of all what you hear and, though if whilst disrobing to the edge of risk, (the bisifings in idolhours that satinfines tootoo!) draw a veil till we next time! You don't want to peach but bejimboed if ye do! Perhelps. We ernst too may. How many months or how many years till the myriadth and first become! Bashfulness be tupped! May he colp, may he colp her, may he mixandmass colp her! Talk with a hare and you wake of a tartars. That's mus. Says the Law. List! Kicky Lacey, the pervergined, and Bianca Mutantini, her conversa, drew their fools longth finnishfurst, Herzog van Vellentam, but me and meother ravin, my coosine of mine, have mour good three chancers, weothers, after Bohnaparts. The mything smile of me, my wholesole assumption, shes nowt mewithout as weam twin herewithin, that I love like myselfish, like smithereens robinsongs, like juneses nutslost, like the blue of the sky if I stoop for to spy's between my whiteyoumightcallimbs. How their duel makes their triel! Eer's wax for Sur Soord, dongdong bollets for the iris riflers, queemswellth of coocome in their combs for the jennyjos. Caro caressimus! Honey swarns where mellisponds. Will bee all buzzy one another minnies for the mere effect that you are so fuld of pollen yourself. Teomeo! Daurdour! We feel unspeechably thoughtless over it all here in Gizzygazelle Tark's bimboowood so pleasekindly communicake with the original sinse we are only yearning as yet how to burgeon. It's meant milliems of centiments deadlost or mislaid on them but, master of snakes, we can sloughchange in the nip of a napple solongas we can allsee for deedsetton your quick. By the hook in your look we're eyed for aye were you begging the questuan with your lutean bowl round Monkmesserag. And whenever you're tingling in your trout we're sure to be tangled in our ticements. It's game, ma chère, be off with your shepherdress on! Upsome cauda! Behose our hand-mades for the lured! To these nunce we are but yours in ammatures yet well come that day we shall ope to be ores. Then shalt thou see, seeing, the sight. No more hoaxites! Nay more gifting in men-nage! A her's fancy for a his friend and then that fellow yours after this follow ours. Vania, Vania Vaniorum, Domne Vanias!

Hightime is ups be it down into outs according! When there shall be foods for vermin as full as feeds for the fett, eat on earth as there's hot in oven. When every Klitty of a scolderymeid shall hold every yardscullion's right to stimm her uprecht for whimsoever, whether on privates, whather in publics. And when all us romance catholeens shall have ones for all amanseprated. And the world is maidfree. Methanks. So much for His Meignysthy man! And all his bigyttens. So till Coquette to tell Cockotte to teach Connie Curley to touch Cattie Hayre and tip Carminia to tap La Chérie though where the diggings he dwellst amongst us here's nobody knows save Mary. Whyfor we go ringing hands in hands in gyrogyrorondo.

These bright elects, consentconsorted, they were waltzing up their willside with their princesome handsome angeline chiuff while in those wherebus there wont bears way (mearing unknown, a place where pigeons carry fire to seethe viands, a miry hill, belge end sore footh) oaths and screams and bawley groans with a belchy-bubhub and a hellabelow bedemmed and bediabbled the arimaining lucisphere. Helldsdend, whelldselse! Lonedom's breach lay foulend up uncouth not be broched by punns and reedles. Yet the ring gayed rund rorosily with a drat for a brat you. Yasha Yash ate sassage and mash. So he found he bash, poor Yasha Yash. And you wonna make one of our micknick party. No honaryhuest on our sposhialiste. For poor Glugger was dazed and late in his crave, ay he, laid in his grave.

But low, boys low, he rises, shrivering, with his spittyful eyes and his whoozebecome woice. Ephthah! Cisamis! Examen of con-science scruples now he to the best of his memory schemado. Nu mere for ever siden on the stolen. With his tumescinquinance in the thight of his tumstull. No more singing all the dags in his sengaggeng. Experssly at hand counterhand. Trinitatis kink had mudded his dome, peccat and pent fore, pree. Hymserf, munchaowl, maden, born of thug tribe into brood blackmail, dooly redecant allbigenesis henesies. He, by bletchendmacht of the golls, proforhim penance and come off enternatural. He, selfsufficiencer, eggscumuddher - in - chaff sporticolorissimo, what though the duthsthrows in his lavabad eyes, maketomake polentay rossum, (Good savours queen with the stem of swuith Aftreck! Fit for king of Zundas) out of bianconies, hiking ahake like any nudgemeroughgorude all over Terracuta. No more throw acids, face all lovabilities, appeal for the union and play for tirnitys. He, praise Saint Calembaurnus, make clean breastsack of goody girl now as ever drank milksoep from a spoen, weedhearted boy of potter and mudder, chip of old Flinn the Flinter, twig of the hider that tanned him. He go calaboosh all same he tell him out. Teufleuf man he strip him all mussymussy calico blong him all same he tell him all out how he make what name. He, through wolkenic connection, relation belong this remarklable moliman, Anaks Andrum, parleyglutton pure blood Jebusite, centy procent Erserum spoking. Drugmallt storehuse. Intrance on back. Most open on the laydays. He, A. A., in peachskin shantungs, possible, sooth to say, notwithstanding far former guiles and he gaining fish considerable, by saving grace after avalunch, to look most prophitable out of smily skibluh eye. He repeat of him as pious alios cos he ast for shave and haircut people said he'd shape of hegoat where he just was sheep of herrgott with his tile togged. Top. Not true what chronicles is bringing his portemanteau priamed full potatowards. Big dumm crumm digaditchies say short again akter, even while lossassinated by summan, he coaxyorum a pennysilvers offarings bloadonages with candid zuckers on Spinshesses Walk in presents to lilithe maidinettes for at bloo his noose for him with pruriest pollygameous inatentions, he having that pecuniarity ailmint spectacularly in heather cliff emurgency on gale days because souffrant chronic from a plentitude of house torts. Collosul rhodomantic not wert one bronze lie Scholarina say as he, greyed vike cuddlepuller, walk in her sleep his pig indicks weg femtyfem funts. Of so little is her timentrousnest great for greeting his immensesness. Sutt soonas sett they were, her uyes as his auroholes. Kaledvalch! How could one classically? One could naught critically. Ininest lightingshaft only for lovalit smugpipe, his Mistress Mereshame, of cupric tresses, the formwhite foaminine, the ambersandalled, after Aasdocktor Talop's onamuttony legture. A mish, holy balm of seinsed myrries, he is as good as a mountain and everybody what is found of his gients he knew Meistral Wikingson,

furframed Noordwogen's kampften, with complexion of blushing
dolomite fanned by ozeone brisees, what naver saw his bedshead
farrer and nuver met his swigamore, have his ignomen from prima
signation of being Master Milchku, queerest man in the benighted
queendom, and, adcraft aidant, how he found the kids. Other ac-
cuse him as lochkneeghed forsunkener, dope in stockknob, all amelt-
ingmoult after rhomatism, purely simply tammy ratkins. The kurds
of Copt on the berberutters and their bedaweens! Even was Shes
whole begeds off before all his nahars in the koldbethizzdryel. No
gudth! Not one zouz! They whiteliveried ragsups, two Whales of
the Sea of Deceit, they bloodiblabstard shooters, three Dromedaries
of the Sands of Calumdonia. As is note worthies to shock his hind!
Ur greeft on them! Such askors and their ruperts they are putting
in for more osghirs is alse false liarnels. The frockenhalted victims!
Whore affirm is agains sempry Lotta Karssens. They would lick their
lenses before they would negatise a jom petter from his sodalites. In
his contrary and on reality, which Bichop Babwith bares to his whit-
ness in his *Just a Fication of Villumses,* This Mr Heer Assassor Neel-
son, of sorestate hearing, diseased, formarly with Adenoiks, den
feed all lighty, laxtleap great change of retiring family buckler,
highly accurect in his everythinks, from tencents coupoll to bargain
basement, live with howthold of nummer seven, wideawake, wound-
about, wokinbetts, weeklings, in black velvet on geolgian mission
senest mangy years his rear in the lane pictures, blanking same with
autonaut and annexes and got a daarlingt babyboy bucktooth, the
thick of a gobstick, coming on ever so nerses nursely, gracies to good-
ess, at 81. That why all parks up excited about his gunnfodder. That
why ecrazyaztecs and the crime ministers preaching him mornings
and makes a power of spoon vittles out of his praverbs. That why
he, persona erecta, glycorawman arsenicful femorniser, for a trial
by julias, in celestial sunhat, with two purses agitating his theopot
with wokklebout shake, rather incoherend, from one 18 to one 18
biss, young shy gay youngs. Sympoly far infusing up pritty tipidities
to lock up their rhainodaisies and be nice and twainty in the shade.
Old grand tuttut toucher up of young poetographies and he turn
aroundabrupth red altfrumpishly like hear samhar tionnor falls some
make one noise. It's his last lap, Gigantic, fare him weal! Revelation!
A fact. True bill. By a jury of matrons. Hump for humbleness, dump
for dirts. And, to make a long stoney badder and a whorly show a
parfect sight, his Thing went the wholyway retup Suffrogate Strate.

Helpmeat too, contrasta toga, his fiery goosemother, laotsey taotsey, woman who did, he tell princes of the age about. You sound on me, judges! Suppose we brisken up. Kings! Meet the Mem, Avenlith, all viviparous out of couple of lizards. She just as fenny as he is fulgar. How laat soever her latest still her sawlogs come up all standing. Psing a psalm of psexpeans, apocryphul of rhyme! His cheekmole of allaph foriverever her allinall and his Kuran never teachit her the be the owner of thyself. So she not swop her eckcot hjem for Howarden's Castle, Englandwales. But be the alleance of iern on his flamen vestacoat, the fibule of broochbronze to his wintermantle of pointefox. Who not knows she, the Madame Cooley-Couley, spawife to laird of manna, when first come into the pictures more as hundreads elskerelks' yahrds of annams call away, factory fresh and fiuming at the mouth, wronged by Hwemwednoget (magrathmagreeth, he takable a rap for that early party) and whenceforward Ani Mama and her fiertey bustles terrified of gmere gnomes of gmountains and furibound to be back in her mytinbeddy? Schi schi, she feightened allsouls at pignpugn and gets a pan in her stummi from the pialabellars in their pur war. Yet jackticktating all around her about his poorliness due to pannellism and grime for that he harboured her when feme sole, her zoravarn lhorde and givnergenral, and led her in antient consort ruhm and bound her durant coverture so as she could not steal from him, oz her or damman, so as if ever she's beleaved by checkenbrooth death since both was parties to the feed it's Hetman MacCumhal foots the funeral. Mealwhile she nutre him jacent from her elmer's almsdish, giantar and tschaina as sieme as bibrondas with Foli Signur's tinner roumanschy to fishle the ladwigs out of his lugwags, like a skittering kitty skattering hayels, when his favourites were all beruffled on him and her own undesirables justickulating, it was such a blowick day. Winden wanden wild like wenchen wenden wanton. The why if he but would bite and plug his baccypipes and renownse the devlins in all their pumbs and kip the streelwarkers out of the plague and nettleses milk from sickling the honeycoombe and kop Ulo Bubo selling foulty treepes, she would make massa dinars with her savuneer dealinsh and delicate her nutbrown glory cloack to Mayde Berenice and hang herself in Ostmannstown Saint Megan's and make no more mulierage before mahatmas or moslemans, but would ondulate her shookerloft hat from Alpoleary with a viv baselgia and a clamast apotria like any purple cardinal's princess or woman of the grave word to the papal legate from the Vatucum, Monsaigneur Rabbinsohn Crucis, with an ass of milg to his cowmate and chilterlings on account of all he qua-

queduxed for the hnor of Hrom and the nations abhord him and
wop mezzo scudo to Sant Pursy Orelli that gave Luiz-Marios Josephs
their loyal devouces to be offered up missas for vowts for widders.

Hear, O worldwithout! Tiny tattling! Backwoods, be wary!
Daintytrees, go dutch!

But who comes yond with pire on poletop? He who relights our
spearing torch, the moon. Bring lolave branches to mud cabins and
peace to the tents of Ceder, Neomenie! The feast of Tubbournig-
glers is at hand. Shopshup. Inisfail! Timple temple tells the bells.
In syngagyng a sangasongue. For all in Ondslosby. And, the hag they
damename Coverfew hists from her lane. And haste, 'tis time for
bairns ta hame. Chickchilds, comeho to roo. Comehome to roo, wee
chickchilds doo, when the wildworewolf's abroad. Ah, let's away
and let's gay and let's stay chez where the log foyer's burning!

It darkles, (tinct, tint) all this our funnaminal world. Yon marsh-
pond by ruodmark verge is visited by the tide. Alvemmarea! We are
circumveiloped by obscuritads. Man and belves frieren. There is a
wish on them to be not doing or anything. Or just for rugs. Zoo koud!
Drr, deff, coal lay on and, pzz, call us pyrress! Ha. Where is our
highly honourworthy salutable spousefounderess? The foolish one
of the family is within. Haha! Huzoor, where's he? At house, to's
pitty. With Nancy Hands. Tcheetchee! Hound through the maize
has fled. What hou! Isegrim under lolling ears. Far wol! And
wheaten bells bide breathless. All. The trail of Gill not yet is to be
seen, rocksdrops, up benn, down dell, a craggy road for rambling.
Nor yet through starland that silver sash. What era's o'ering? Lang
gong late. Say long, scielo! Sillume, see lo! Selene, sail O! Amune!
Ark!? Noh?! Nought stirs in spinney. The swayful pathways of the
dragonfly spider stay still in reedery. Quiet takes back her folded
fields. Tranquille thanks. Adew. In deerhaven, imbraced, alleged,
injoynted and unlatched, the birds, tommelise too, quail silent. ii.
Luathan? Nuathan! Was avond ere a while. Now conticinium. As
Lord the Laohum is sheutseuyes. The time of lying together will
come and the wildering of the nicht till cockeedoodle aubens Aurore.
Panther monster. Send leabarrow loads amorrow. While loev-
dom shleeps. Elenfant has siang his triump, *Great is Eliphas Magis-
trodontos* and after kneeprayer pious for behemuth and mahamoth
will rest him from tusker toils. Salamsalaim! Rhinohorn isnoutso
pigfellow but him ist gonz wurst. Kikikuki. Hopopodorme. Sobeast!
No chare of beagles, frantling of peacocks, no muzzing of the camel,
smuttering of apes. Lights, pageboy, lights! Brights we'll be brights.

With help of Hanoukan's lamp. When otter leaps in outer parts then
Yul remembers Mei. Her hung maid mohns are bluming, look, to
greet those loes on coast of amethyst; arcglow's seafire siemens lure
and wextward warnerforth's hookercrookers. And now with robby
brerfox's fishy fable lissaned out, the threads simwhat toran and
knots in its antargumends, the pesciolines in Liffeyetta's bowl have
stopped squiggling about Junoh and the whalk and feriaquintaism
and pebble infinibility and the poissission of the hoghly course. And
if Lubbernabohore laid his horker to the ribber, save the giregargoh
and dabardin going on in his mount of knowledge (munt), he would
not hear a flip flap in all Finnyland. Witchman, watch of your
night? Es voes, ez noes, nott voes, ges, noun. It goes. It does not go.
Darkpark's acoo with sucking loves. Rosimund's by her wishing
well. Soon tempt-in-twos will stroll at venture and hunt-by-threes
strut musketeering. Brace of girdles, brasse of beauys. With the width
of the way for jogjoy. Hulker's cieclest elbownunsense. Hold hard!
And his dithering dathering waltzers of. Stright! But meetings
mate not as forsehn. Hesperons! And if you wand to Livmouth,
wenderer, while Jempson's weed decks Jacqueson's Island, here
lurks, bar hellpelhullpulthebell, none iron welcome. Bing. Bong.
Bangbong. Thunderation! You took with the mulligrubs and we
lack mulsum? No sirrebob! Great goodness, no! Were you Marely
quean of Scuts or but Chrestien the Last, (our duty to you, chris!
royalty, squat!) how matt your mark, though luked your johl, here's
dapplebellied mugs and troublebedded rooms and sawdust strown
in expectoration and for ratification by specification of your information, Mr Knight, tuntapster, buttles; his alefru's up to his hip. And
Watsy Lyke sees after all rinsings and don't omiss Kate, homeswab
homely, put in with the bricks. A's the sign and one's the number.
Where Chavvyout Chacer calls the cup and Pouropourim stands
astirrup. De oud huis bij de kerkegaard. So who over comes ever
for Whoopee Weeks must put up with the Jug and Chambers.

But heed! Our thirty minutes war's alull. All's quiet on the felled
of Gorey. Between the starfort and the thornwood brass castle flambs
with mutton candles. Hushkah, a horn! Gadolmagtog! God es El?
Housefather calls enthreateningly. From Brandenborgenthor. At
Asa's arthre. In thundercloud periwig. With lightning bug aflash
from afinger. My souls and by jings, should he work his jaw to give
down the banks and hark from the tomb! Ansighosa pokes in her
potstill to souse at the sop be sodden enow and to hear to all the
bubbles besaying: the coming man, the future woman, the food that

is to build, what he with fifteen years will do, the ring in her mouth
of joyous guard, stars astir and stirabout. A palashe for hirs, a
saucy for hers and ladlelike spoons for the wonner. But ein and
twee were never worth three. So they must have their final since he's
on parole. Et la pau' Leonie has the choice of her lives between Jo-
sephinus and Mario-Louis for who is to wear the lily of Bohemey,
Florestan, Thaddeus, Hardress or Myles. And lead raptivity captive.
Ready! Like a Finn at a fair. Now for la belle! Icy-la-Belle!

The campus calls them. Ninan ninan, the gattling gan! Childs
will be wilds. 'Twastold. And vamp, vamp, vamp, the girls are mer-
chand. The horseshow magnete draws his field and don't the fillyings
fly? Educande of Sorrento, they newknow knowwell their Vico's
road. Arranked in their array and flocking for the fray on that old
orangeray, Dolly Brae. For these are not on terms, they twain, bar-
trossers, since their baffle of Whatalose when Adam Leftus and the
devil took our hindmost, gegifting her with his painapple, nor will
not be atoned at all in fight to no finish, that dark deed doer, this
wellwilled wooer, Jerkoff and Eatsoup, Yem or Yan, while felixed
is who culpas does and harm's worth healing and Brune is bad
French for Jour d'Anno. Tiggers and Tuggers they're all for ten-
zones. Bettlimbraves. For she must walk out. And it must be with
who. Teaseforhim. Toesforhim. Tossforhim. Two. Else there is danger of. Solitude.

Postreintroducing Jeremy, the chastenot coulter, the flowing taal
that brooks no brooking runs on to say how, as it was mutualiter
foretold of him by a timekiller to his spacemaker, velos ambos and
arubyat knychts, with their tales within wheels and stucks between
spokes, on the hike from Elmstree to Stene and back, how, running
awage with the use of reason (sics) and ramming amok at the brake
of his voice (secs), his lasterhalft was set for getting the besterwhole
of his yougendtougend, for control number thrice was operating
the subliminal of his invaded personality. He nobit smorfi and go
poltri and let all the tondo gang bola del ruffo. Barto no know him
mor. Eat larto altruis with most perfect stranger.

Boo, you're through!

Hoo, I'm true!

Men, teacan a tea simmering, hamo mavrone kerry O?

Teapotty. Teapotty.

Kod knows. Anything ruind. Meetingless.

He wept indeiterum. With such a tooth he seemed to love his wee
tart when abuy. Highly momourning he see the before him. Me-

lained from nape to kneecap though vied from her girders up. Holy
Santalto, cursing saint, sight most deletious to ross up the spyballs
like exude of margary! And how him it heaviered that eyerim rust!
An they bare falls witless against thee how slight becomes a hidden
wound? Soldwoter he wash him all time bigfeller bruisy place blong
him. He no want missies blong all boy other look bruisy place blong
him. Hence. It will paineth the chastenot in that where of his
whence he had loseth his once for every, even though mode grow
moramor maenneritsch and the Tarara boom decay. Immaculacy,
give but to drink to his shirt and all skirtaskortas must change her
tunics. So warred he from first to last, forebanned and betweenly,
a smuggler for lifer. Lift the blank ve veered as heil! Split the hvide
and aye seize heaven! He knows for he's seen it in black and white
through his eyetrompit trained upon jenny's and all that sort of
thing which is dandymount to a clearobscure. Prettimaid tints may
try their taunts: apple, bacchante, custard, dove, eskimo, feldgrau,
hematite, isingglass, jet, kipper, lucile, mimosa, nut, oysterette,
prune, quasimodo, royal, sago, tango, umber, vanilla, wisteria, xray,
yesplease, zaza, philomel, theerose. What are they all by? Shee.

If you nude her in her prime, make sure you find her complementary or, on your very first occasion, by Angus Dagdasson and
all his piccions, she'll prick you where you're proudest with her un-
satt speagle eye. Look sharp, she's signalling from among the asters.
Turn again, wistfultone, lode mere of Doubtlynn! Arise, Land-
under-Wave! Clap your lingua to your pallet, drop your jowl with
a jolt, tambourine until your breath slides, pet a pout and it's out.
Have you got me, Allysloper?

My top it was brought Achill's low, my middle I ope before you,
my bottom's a vulser if ever there valsed and my whole the flower
that stars the day and is solly well worth your pilger's fahrt. Where
there's a hitch, a head of things, let henker's halter hang the halunk-
enend. For I see through your weapon. That cry's not Cucullus.
And his eyelids are painted. If my tutor here is cut out for an oldeborre I'm Flo, shy of peeps, you know. But when he beetles backwards, ain't I fly? Pull the boughpee to see how we sleep. Bee Peep!
Peepette! Would you like that lump of a tongue for lungeon or this
Turkey's delighter, hys hyphen mys? My bellyswain's a twalf whule-
russpower though he knows as much how to man a wife as Dunckle
Dalton of matching wools. Shake hands through the thicketloch!
Sweet swanwater! My other is mouthfilled. This kissing wold's full
of killing fellows kneeling voyantly to the cope of heaven. And

somebody's coming, I feel for a fect. I've a seeklet to sell thee if old Deanns won't be threaspanning. When you'll next have the mind to retire to be wicked this is as dainty a way as any. Underwoods spells bushment's business. So if you sprig poplar you're bound to twig this. 'Twas my lord of Glendalough benedixed the gape for me that time at Long Entry, commanding the approaches to my intimast innermost. Look how they're browthered! Six thirteens at Blanche de Blanche's of 3 Behind Street and 2 Turnagain Lane. Awabeg is my callby, Magnus here's my Max, Wonder One's my cipher and Seven Sisters is my nighbrood. Radouga, Rab will ye na pick them in their pink of panties. You can colour up till you're prawn while I go squirt with any cockle. When here who adolls me infuxes sleep. But if this could see with its backsight he'd be the grand old greeneyed lobster. He's my first viewmarc since Valentine. Wink's the winning word.

Luck!

In the house of breathings lies that word, all fairness. The walls are of rubinen and the glittergates of elfinbone. The roof herof is of massicious jasper and a canopy of Tyrian awning rises and still descends to it. A grape cluster of lights hangs therebeneath and all the house is filled with the breathings of her fairness, the fairness of fondance and the fairness of milk and rhubarb and the fairness of roasted meats and uniomargrits and the fairness of promise with consonantia and avowals. There lies her word, you reder! The height herup exalts it and the lowness her down abseth it. It vibroverberates upon the tegmen and prosplodes from pomoeria. A window, a hedge, a prong, a hand, an eye, a sign, a head and keep your other augur on her paypaypay. And you have it, old Sem, pat as ah be seated! And Sunny, my gander, he's coming to land her. The boy which she now adores. She dores. Oh backed von dem zug! Make weg for their tug!

With a ring ding dong, they raise clasped hands and advance more steps to retire to the saum. Curtsey one, curtsey two, with arms akimbo, devotees.

Irrelevance.

All sing:

— I rose up one maypole morning and saw in my glass how nobody loves me but you. Ugh. Ugh.

All point in the shem direction as if to shun.

— My name is Misha Misha but call me Toffey Tough. I mean

Mettenchough. It was her, boy the boy that was loft in the larch. Ogh! Ogh!

Her reverence.

All laugh.

They pretend to helf while they simply shauted at him sauce to make hims prich. And ith ith noth circquette, Sally Lums. Not by ever such a lot. Twentynines of bloomers gegging een man arose. Avis was there and trilled her about it. She's her sex, for certain. So to celebrate the occasion:

— Willest thou rossy banders havind?

He simules to be tight in ribbings round his rumpffkorpff.

— Are you Swarthants that's hit on a shorn stile?

He makes semblant to be swiping their chimbleys.

— Can you ajew ajew fro' Sheidam?

He finges to be cutting up with a pair of sissers and to be buytings of their maidens and spitting their heads into their facepails. Spickspuk! Spoken.

So now be hushy, little pukers! Side here roohish, cleany fuglers! Grandicellies, all stay zitty! Adultereux, rest as befour! For you've jollywelly dawdled all the day. When ye coif tantoncle's hat then'll be largely temts for that. Yet's the time for being now, now, now.

For a burning would is come to dance inane. Glamours hath moidered's lieb and herefore Coldours must leap no more. Lack breath must leap no more.

Lel lols for libelman libling his lore. Lolo Lolo liebermann you loved to be leaving Libnius. Lift your right to your Liber Lord. Link your left to your lass of liberty. Lala Lala, Leapermann, your lep's but a loop to lee.

A fork of hazel o'er the field in vox the verveine virgins ode. If you cross this rood as you roamed the rand I'm blessed but you'd feel him a blasting rod. Behind, me, frees from evil smells! Perdition stinks before us.

Aghatharept they fleurelly to Nebnos will and Rosocale. Twice is he gone to quest of her, thrice is she now to him. So see we so as seed we sow. And their prunktqueen kilt her kirtles up and set out. And her troup came heeling, O. And what do you think that pride was drest in! Voolykins' diamondinah's vestin. For ever they scent where air she went. While all the fauns' flares widens wild to see a floral's school.

Led by Lignifer, in four hops of the happiest, ach beth cac duff, a marrer of the sward incoronate, the few fly the farbetween! We haul minymony on that piebold nig. Will any dubble dabble on the bay? Nor far jocubus? Nic for jay? Attilad! Attattilad! Get up, Goth's scourge on you! There's a visitation in your impluvium. Hun! Hun!

He stanth theirs mun in his natural, oblious autamnesically of his very proprium, (such is stockpot leaden, so did sonsepun crake) the wont to be wanton maid a will to be wise. Thrust from the light, apophotorejected, he spoors loves from her heats. He blinkth. But's wrath's the higher where those wreathe charity. For all of these have been thisworlders, time liquescing into state, pitiless age grows angelhood. Though, as he stehs, most anysing may befallhim from a song of a witch to the totter of Blackarss, given a fammished devil, a young sourceress and (eternal conjunction) the permission of overalls with the cuperation of nightshirt. If he spice east he seethes in sooth and if he pierce north he wilts in the waist. And what wonder with the murkery viceheid in the shade? The specks on his lapspan are his foul deed thougths, wishmarks of mad imogenation. Take they off! Make the off! But Funnylegs are leanly. A bimbamb bum! They vain would convert the to be hers in the word. Gush, they wooed! Gash, they're fair ripecherry!

As for she could shake him. An oaf, no more. Still he'd be good tutor two in his big armschair lerningstoel and she be waxen in his hands. Turning up and fingering over the most dantellising peaches in the lingerous longerous book of the dark. Look at this passage about Galilleotto! I know it is difficult but when your goche I go dead. Turn now to this patch upon Smacchiavelluti! Soot allours, he's sure to spot it! 'Twas ever so in monitorology since Headmaster Adam became Eva Harte's toucher, *in omnibus moribus et temporibus*, with man's mischief in his mind whilst her pupils swimmed too heavenlies, let his be exaspirated, letters be blowed! I is a femaline person. O, of provocative gender. U unisingular case.

Which is why trumpers are mixed up in duels and here's B. Rohan meets N. Ohlan for the prize of a thou.

But listen to the mocking birde to micking barde making bared! We've heard it aye since songdom was gemurrmal. As he was queering his shoolthers. So was I. And as I was cleansing my fausties. So was he. And as way ware puffiing our blowbags. Souwouyou.

Come, thrust! Go, parry! Dvoinabrathran, dare! The mad long ramp of manchind's parlements, the learned lacklearning, merciless as wonderful.

— Now may Saint Mowy of the Pleasant Grin be your everglass and even prospect!

— Feeling dank.

Exchange, reverse.

— And may Saint Jerome of the Harlots' Curse make family three of you which is much abedder!

— Grassy ass ago.

And each was wrought with his other. And his continence fell. The bivitellines, Metellus and Ametallikos, her crown pretenders, obscindgemeinded biekerers, varying directly, uruseye each oxesother, superfetated (never cleaner of lamps frowned fiercelier on anointer of hinges), while their treegrown girls, king's game, if he deign so, are in such transfusion just to know twigst timidy twomeys, for gracious sake, who is artthoudux from whose heterotropic, the sleepy or the glouch, for, shyly bawn and showly nursured, exceedingly nice girls can strike exceedingly bad times unless so richtly chosen's by (what though of riches he have none and hope dashes hope on his heart's horizon) to gar their great moments greater. The thing is he must be put strait on the spot, no mere waterstichystuff in a selfmade world that you can't believe a word he's written in, not for pie, but one's only owned by naturel rejection. Charley, you're my darwing! So sing they sequent the assent of man. Till they go round if they go roundagain before breakparts and all dismissed. They keep. Step keep. Step. Stop. Who is Fleur? Where is Ange? Or Gardoun?

Creedless, croonless hangs his haughty. There end no moe red devil in the white of his eye. Braglodyte him do a katadupe! A condamn quondam jontom sick af a suckbut! He does not know how his grandson's grandson's grandson's grandson will stammer up in Peruvian for in the ersebest idiom I have done it equals I so shall do. He dares not think why the grandmother of the grandmother of his grandmother's grandmother coughed Russky with suchky husky accent since in the mouthart of the slove look at me now means I once was otherwise. Nor that the mappamund has been changing pattern as youth plays moves from street to street since time and races were and wise ants hoarded and sauterelles were spendthrifts, no thing making newthing wealthshowever for a silly old Sol, healthytobedder and latewiser. Nor that the turtling of a London's alderman is ladled out by the waggerful to the regionals of pigmyland. His part should say in honour bound: So help me symethew, sammarc, selluc and singin, I will stick to you, by gum, no matter what, bite simbum, and in case of the event coming off beforehand even so you was to release me for the sake of the other cheap girl's baby's name plaster me but I will pluckily well pull on the buckskin gloves! But Noodynaady's actual ingrate tootle is of come into the garner mauve and thy nice are stores of morning and buy me a bunch of iodines.

Evidentament he has failed as tiercely as the deuce before for she is wearing none of the three. And quite as patently there is a hole in the ballet trough which the rest fell out. Because to explain why the residue is, was, or will not be, according to the eighth axiom, proceeded with, namely, since ever apart that gossan duad, so sure as their's a patch on a pomelo, this yam ham in never live could, the shifting about of the lassies, the tug of love of their lads ending with a great deal of merriment, hoots, screams, scarf drill, cap fecking, ejaculations of aurinos, reechoable mirthpeals and general thumb-tonosery (Myama's a yaung yaung cauntry), one must recken with the sudden and gigantesquesque appearance unwithstandable as a general election in Barnado's bearskin amongst the brawlmiddle of this village childergarten of the largely longsuffering laird of Lucanhof.

But, vrayedevraye Blankdeblank, god of all machineries and tome-stone of Barnstaple, by mortisection or vivisuture, splitten up or re-compounded, an isaac jacquemin mauromormo milesian, how accountibus for him, moreblue?

Was he pitssched for an ensemple as certain have dognosed of him against our seawall by Rurie, Thoath and Cleaver, those three stout sweynhearts, Orion of the Orgiasts, Meereschal MacMuhun, the Ipse dadden, product of the extremes giving quotidients to our means, as might occur to anyone, your brutest layaman with the princest champion in our archdeaconry, or so yclept from Clio's clippings, which the chroncher of chivalries is sulpicious save he scan, for ancients link with presents as the human chain extends, have done, do and will again as John, Polycarp and Irenews eye-to-eye ayewitnessed and to Paddy Palmer, while monks sell yew to archers or the water of the livvying goes the way of all fish from Sara's drawhead, the corralsome, to Isaac's, the lauphed butt one, with her minnelisp extorreor to his moanolothe inturned? So Per-richon with Bastienne or heavy Humph with airy Nan, Ricqueracq-brimbillyjicqueyjocqjolicass? How sowesthow, *dullcisamica*? A and aa ab ad abu abiad. A babbel men dub gulch of tears.

The mar of murmury mermers to the mind's ear, uncharted rock,

evasive weed. Only the caul knows his thousandfirst name, Hocus
Crocus, Esquilocus, Finnfinn the Faineant, how feel full foes in
furrinarr! Doth it not all come aft to you, puritysnooper, in the way
television opes longtimes ofter when Potollomuck Sotyr or Sourda-
napplous the Lollapaloosa? The charges are, you will remember, the
chances are, you won't; bit it's old Joe, the Java Jane, older even
than Odam Costollo, and we are recurrently meeting em, par
Mahun Mesme, in cycloannalism, from space to space, time after
time, in various phases of scripture as in various poses of sepulture.
Greets Godd, Groceries! Merodach! Defend the King! Hoet of the
rough throat attack but whose say is soft but whose ee has a cute
angle, he whose hut is a hissarlik even as her hennin's aspire. And
insodaintily she's a quine of selm ashaker while as a murder of
corpse when his magot's up he's the best berrathon sanger in all the
aisles of Skaldignavia. As who shall hear. For now at last is Longa-
bed going to be gone to, that more than man, prince of Bunnicombe
of wide roadsterds, the herblord the gillyflowrets so fain fan to flatter
about. Artho is the name is on the hero, Capellisato, shoehanded
slaughterer of the shader of our leaves.

Attach him! Hold!

Yet stir thee, to clay, Tamor!

Why wilt thou erewaken him from his earth, O summonorother:
he is weatherbitten from the dusts of ages? The hour of his closing
hies to hand; the tocsin that shall claxonise his wareabouts. If one
who remembered his webgoods and tealofts were to ask of a hooper
for whose it was the storks were quitting Aquileyria, this trundler
would not wot; if other who joined faith when his depth charge
bombed our barrel spillway were to —!

Jehosophat, what doom is here! Rain ruth on them, sire! The wing
of Moykill cover him! The Bulljon Bossbrute quarantee him! Cala-
vera, caution! Slaves to Virtue, save his Veritotem! Bearara Tolearis,
procul abeat! The Ivorbonegorer of Danamaraca be, his Hector
Protector! Woldomar with Vasa, peel your peeps! And try to sav-
iourise the nights of labour to the order of our blooding worold!
While Pliny the Younger writes to Pliny the Elder his calamolumen
of contumellas, what Aulus Gellius picked on Micmacrobius and
what Vitruvius pocketed from Cassiodorus. Like we larnt from that
Buke of Lukan in Dublin's capital, Kongdam Coombe. Even if you
are the kooper of the winkel over measure never lost a licence. Nor
a duckindonche divulse from bath and breakfast. And for the honour of Alcohol drop that you-know-what-I've-come-about-I-saw-your-

act air! Punch may be pottleproud but his Judy's a wife's wit better.

For the producer (Mr John Baptister Vickar) caused a deep abuliousness to descend upon the Father of Truants and, at a side issue, pluterpromptly brought on the scene the cutletsized consort, foundling filly of fortyshilling fostertailor and shipman's shopahoyden, weighing ten pebble ten, scaling five footsy five and spanning thirtyseven inchettes round the good companions, twentynine ditties round the wishful waistress, thirtyseven alsos round the answer to everything, twentythree of the same round each of the quis separabits, fourteen round the beginning of happiness and nicely nine round her shoed for slender.

And eher you could pray mercy to goodness or help with your hokey or mehokeypoo, Gallus's hen has collared her pullets. That's where they have owreglias for. Their bone of contention, flesh to their thorns, prest as Prestissima, makes off in a thinkling (and not one hen only nor two hens neyther but every blessed brigid came aclucking and aclacking), while, a rum a rum, the ram of all harns, Bier, Wijn, Spirituosen for consumption on the premises, advokaat withouten pleaders, Mas marrit, Pas poulit, Ras ruddist of all, though flamifestouned from galantifloures, is hued and cried of each's colour.

Home all go. Halome. Blare no more ramsblares, oddmund barkes! And cease your fumings, kindalled bushies! And sherrigoldies yeassymgnays; your wildeshaweshowe moves swiftly sterneward! For here the holy language. Soons to come. To pausse.

'Tis goed. Het best.

For they are now tearing, that is, teartoretorning. Too soon are coming tasbooks and goody, hominy bread and bible bee, with jaggery-yo to juju-jaw, Fine's French phrases from the Grandmère des Grammaires and bothered parsenaps from the Four Massores, Mattatias, Marusias, Lucanias, Jokinias, and what happened to our eleven in thirtytwo antepostdating the Valgur Eire and why is limbo where is he and what are the sound waves saying ceased ere they all wayed wrong and Amnist anguished axes Collis and where fishngaman fetched the mongafesh from and whatfor paddybird notplease rancoon and why was Sindat sitthing on him sitbom like a saildior, with what the doc did in the doil, not to mention define the hydraulics of common salt and, its denier crid of old provaunce, where G.P.O. is zentrum and D.U.T.C. are radients write down by the frequency of the scores and crores of your refractions the valuations in the pice of dinggyings on N.C.R. and S.C.R.

That little cloud, a nibulissa, still hangs isky. Singabed sulks before slumber. Light at night has an alps on his druckhouse. Thick
head and thin butter or after you with me. Caspi, but gueroligue
stings the air. Gaylegs to riot of us! Gallocks to lafft! What is amaid
today todo? So angelland all weeping bin that Izzy most unhappy is.
Fain Essie fie onhapje? laughs her stella's vispirine.

   While, running about their ways, going and coming, now at
rhimba rhomba, now in trippiza trappaza, pleating a pattern Gran
Geamatron showed them of gracehoppers, auntskippers and coney-
farm leppers, they jeerilied along, durian gay and marian maidcap,
lou Dariou beside la Matieto, all boy more all girl singoutfeller longa
house blong store Huddy, whilest nin nin nin nin that Boorman's
clock, a winny on the tinny side, ninned nin nin nin nin, about
old Father Barley how he got up of a morning arley and he met with
a plattonem blondes named Hips and Haws and fell in with a fellows of Trinity some header Skowood Shaws like (You'll catch it,
don't fret, Mrs Tummy Lupton! Come indoor, Scoffynosey, and shed
your swank!) auld Daddy Deacon who could stow well his place
of beacon but he never could hold his kerosene's candle to (The
nurse'll give it you, stickypots! And you wait, my lasso, fecking the
twine!) bold Farmer Burleigh who wuck up in a hurlywurly where
he huddly could wuddle to wallow his weg tillbag of the baker's
booth to beg of (You're well held now, Missy Cheekspeer, and your
panto's off! Fie, for shame, Ruth Wheatacre, after all the booz said!)
illed Diddiddy Achin for the prize of a pease of bakin with a pinch
of the panch of the ponch in jurys for (Ah, crabeyes, I have you,
showing off to the world with that gape in your stocking!) Wold
Forrester Farley who, in deesperation of deisipiration at the diasporation of his diesparation, was found of the round of the sound of the
lound of the. Lukkedoerendunandurraskewdyloooshoofermoyporter-
tooryzooysphalnabortansporthaokansakroidverjkapakkapuk.
   Byfall.
   Upploud!
   The play thou schouwburgst, Game, here endeth. The curtain
drops by deep request.
   Uplouderamain!
   Gonn the gawds, Gunnar's gustspells. When the h, who the hu,
how the hue, where the huer? Orbiter onswers: lots lives lost. Fionia
is fed up with Fidge Fudgesons. Sealand snorres. Rendningrocks
roguesreckning reigns. Gwds with gurs are gttrdmmrng. Hlls vlls.
The timid hearts of words all exeomnosunt. Mannagad, lammale-

louh, how do that come? By Dad, youd not heed that fert? Fulgitudes ejist rowdownan tonuout. Quoq! And buncskleydoodle! Kidoosh! Of their fear they broke, they ate wind, they fled; where they ate there they fled; of their fear they fled, they broke away. Go to, let us extol Azrael with our harks, by our brews, on our jambses, in his gaits. To Mezouzalem with the Dephilim, didits dinkun's dud? Yip! Yup! Yarrah! And let Nek Nekulon extol Mak Makal and let him say unto him: Immi ammi Semmi. And shall not Babel be with Lebab? And he war. And he shall open his mouth and answer: I hear, O Ismael, how they laud is only as my loud is one. If Nekulon shall be havonfalled surely Makal havan hevens. Go to, let us extell Makal, yea, let us exceedingly extell. Though you have lien amung your posspots my excellency is over Ismael. Great is him whom is over Ismael and he shall mekanek of Mak Nakulon. And he deed.

Uplouderamainagain!

For the Clearer of the Air from on high has spoken in tumbuldum tambaldam to his tembledim tombaldoom worrild and, moguphonoised by that phonemanon, the unhappitents of the earth have terrerumbled from fimament unto fundament and from tweedledeedumms down to twiddledeedees.

Loud, hear us!

Loud, graciously hear us!

Now have thy children entered into their habitations. And nationglad, camp meeting over, to shin it, Gov be thanked! Thou hast closed the portals of the habitations of thy children and thou hast set thy guards thereby, even Garda Didymus and Garda Domas, that thy children may read in the book of the opening of the mind to light and err not in the darkness which is the afterthought of thy nomatter by the guardiance of those guards which are thy bodemen, the cheeryboyum chirryboth with the kerrybommers in their krubeems, Pray-your-Prayers Timothy and Back-to-Bunk Tom.

Till tree from tree, tree among trees, tree over tree become stone to stone, stone between stones, stone under stone for ever.

O Loud, hear the wee beseech of thees of each of these thy unlitten ones! Grant sleep in hour's time, O Loud!

That they take no chill. That they do ming no merder. That they shall not gomeet madhowiatrees.

Loud, heap miseries upon us yet entwine our arts with laughters low!

Ha he hi ho hu.

Mummum.

As we there are where are we are we there UNDE ET UBI.
from tomtittot to teetootomtotalitarian. Tea
tea too oo.

With his broad
and hairy face,
to Ireland a
disgrace.

Whom will comes over. Who to caps ever. SIC.
And howelse do we hook our hike to find that
pint of porter place? Am shot, says the big-
guard.[1]

Menly about
peebles.

Whence. Quick lunch by our left, wheel, IMAGINABLE
to where. Long Livius Lane, mid Mezzofanti ITINERARY
Mall, diagonising Lavatery Square, up Tycho THROUGH
Brache Crescent,[2] shouldering Berkeley Alley, THE
PARTICULAR

Dont retch meat
fat salt lard
sinks down (and
out).

querfixing Gainsborough Carfax, under Guido UNIVERSAL.
d'Arezzo's Gadeway, by New Livius Lane till
where we whiled while we whithered. Old
Vico Roundpoint. But fahr, be fear! And
natural, simple, slavish, filial. The marriage of
Montan wetting his moll we know, like any
enthewsyass cuckling a hoyden[3] in her rougey
gipsylike chinkaminx pulshandjupeyjade and
her petsybluse indecked o' voylets.[4] When who
was wist was ware. En elv, et fjaell. And
the whirr of the whins humming us howe.
His hume. Hencetaking tides we haply return,

[1] Rawmeash, quoshe with her girlic teangue. If old Herod with the Corm-
well's eczema was to go for me like he does Snuffler whatever about his blue
canaries I'd do nine months for his beaver beard.
[2] Mater Mary Mercerycordial of the Dripping Nipples, milk's a queer arrangement.
[3] Real life behind the floodlights as shown by the best exponents of a royal
divorce.
[4] When we play dress grownup at alla ludo poker you'll be happnessised
to feel how fetching I can look in clingarounds.

trumpeted by prawns and ensigned with sea-
kale, to befinding ourself when old is said in
one and maker mates with made (O my!),
having conned the cones and meditated the
mured and pondered the pensils and ogled the
olymp and delighted in her dianaphous and
cacchinated behind his culosses, before a

Swiney Tod, ye
Daimon Barbar!

mosoleum. Length Withought Breath, of him,
a chump of the evums, upshoot of picnic or
stupor out of sopor, Cave of Kids or Hyma-
nian Glattstoneburg, denary, danery, donnery,

Dig him in the
rubsh!
Ungodly old
Ardrey, Cron-
wall beeswaxing
the convulsion
box.

domm, who, entiringly as he continues highly-
fictional, tumulous under his chthonic exterior
but plain Mr Tumulty in muftilife,[5] in his an-
tisipiences as in his recognisances, is, (Dominic
Directus) a manyfeast munificent more mob
than man.

Ainsoph,[6] this upright one, with that
noughty besighed him zeroine. To see in his
horrorscup he is mehrkurios than saltz of
sulphur. Terror of the noonstruck by day,
cryptogam of each nightly bridable. But, to
speak broken heaventalk, is he? Who is he?
Whose is he? Why is he? Howmuch is he?
Which is he? When is he? Where is he?[7] How
is he? And what the decans is there about him
anyway, the decemt man? Easy, calm your haste!
Approach to lead our passage!

This bridge is upper.

Cross.

Thus come to castle.

Knock.[8]

A password, thanks.

Yes, pearse.

Well, all be dumbed!

CONSTITU-
TION OF THE
CONSTITU-
TIONABLE AS
CONSTITU-
TIONAL.

PROBA-
POSSIBLE
PROLEGO-
MENA TO
IDEAREAL
HISTORY.

[5] Kellywick, Longfellow's Lodgings, House of Comments III, Cake Walk,
Amusing Avenue, Salt Hill, Co. Mahogany, Izalond, Terra Firma.

[6] Groupname for grapejuice.

[7] Bhing, said her burglar's head, soto poce.

[8] Yussive smirte and ye mermon answerth from his beelyingplace below the
tightmark, Gotahelv!

O really?[9]

Swing the banjo, Hoo cavedin earthwight
bantams, bounce- At furscht kracht of thunder.[10]
the-baller's When shoo, his flutterby,
blown to fook. Was netted and named.[11]

Thsight near Erdnacrusha, requiestress, wake em!
left me eyes And let luck's puresplutterall lucy at ease![12]
when I seen her To house as wise foll ages builded.
put thounce Sow byg eat.[13]
otay ithpot.

Staplering to tether, to, steppingstone to GNOSIS OF
Quartandwds. mount by, as the Boote's at Pickardstown. PRECREATE
And that skimmelk steed still in the ground- DETERMINA-
loftfan. As over all. Or be these wingsets leaned TION.
to the outwalls, beastskin trophies of booth AGONOSIS OF
POSTCREATE
of Baws the balsamboards?[14] Burials be bally- DETER-
houraised! So let Bacchus e'en call! Inn inn! MINISM.

Tickets for the Inn inn! Where. The babbers ply the pen.
Tailwaggers The bibbers drang the den. The papplicom,
Terrierpuppy the pubblicam he's turning tin for ten. From
Raffle. seldomers that most frequent him. That same
erst crafty hakemouth which under the assumed
name of Ignotus Loquor, of foggy old,
harangued bellyhooting fishdrunks on their
favorite stamping ground, from a father theo-
balder brake.[15] And Egyptus, the incenstrobed,
Mars speaking. as Cyrus heard of him? And Major A. Shaw
after he got the miner smellpex? And old
Whiteman self, the blighty blotchy, beyond
the bays, hope of ostrogothic and ottomanic
faith converters, despair of Pandemia's post-
wartem plastic surgeons? But is was all so long
ago. Hispano-Cathayan-Euxine, Castillian-
Emeratic-Hebridian, Espanol-Cymric-Helleniky?

[9] O Evol, kool in the salg and ees how Dozi pits what a drows er.
[10] A goodrid croven in a tynwalled tub.
[11] Apis amat aram. Luna legit librum. Pulla petit pascua.
[12] And after dinn to shoot the shades.
[13] Says blistered Mary Achinhead to beautifed Tummy Tullbutt.
[14] Begge. To go to Begge. To go to Begge and to be sure to reminder Begge.
Goodbeg, buggey Begge.
[15] Huntler and Pumar's animal alphabites, the first in the world from aab
to zoo.

Smith, no home.   Rolf the Ganger, Rough the Gangster, not
a feature alike and the face the same.[16]
Pastimes are past times. Now let bygones be
bei Gunne's. Saaleddies er it in this warken
werden, mine boerne, and it vild need olderwise[17] since primal made alter in garden of
Idem. The tasks above are as the flasks below,
saith the emerald canticle of Hermes and all's
Non quod sed   loth and pleasestir, are we told, on excellent
quiat.   inkbottle authority, solarsystemised, seriol-
cosmically, in a more and more almightily
expanding universe under one, there is rhyme-
less reason to believe, original sun. Securely
judges orb terrestrial.[18] *Haud certo ergo.* But
Hearasay in   O felicitous culpability, sweet bad cess to you
paradox lust.   for an archetypt!

    Honour commercio's energy yet aid the   Archaic
linkless proud, the plurable with everybody   Zelotypia
and ech with pal, this ernst of Allsap's ale   and the
halliday of roaring month with its two lunar   odium tel-
eclipses and its three saturnine settings! Horn   eologicum.
of Heatthen, highbrowed! Brook of Life, back-
frish! Amnios amnium, fluminiculum flami-
nulinorum! We seek the Blessed One, the
Harbourer-cum-Enheritance. Even Canaan
the Hateful. Ever a-going, ever a-coming.
Between a stare and a sough. Fossilisation, all
branches.[19] Wherefore Petra sware unto Ulma:
Bags.   By the mortals' frost! And Ulma sware unto
Balls.   Petra: On my veiny life!

    In these places sojournemus, where Eblinn   the locali-
water, leased of carr and fen, leaving amont her   sation of
shoals and salmen browses, whom inshore   legend
breezes woo with freshets, windeth to her   leading to
broads. A phantom city, phaked of philim   the legali-
     sation of

[16] We dont hear the booming cursowarries, we wont fear the fletches of
fightning, we float the meditarenias and come bask to the isle we love in spice.
Punt.
[17] And this once golden bee a cimadoro.
[18] And he was a gay Lutharius anyway, Sinobiled. You can tell by their
extraordinary clothes.
[19] Startnaked and bonedstiff. We vivvy soddy. All be dood.

pholk, bowed and sould for a four of hundreds of manhood in their three and threescore

Move up,
Mackinerny!
Make room for
Muckinurney!

fylkers for a price partitional of twenty six and six. By this riverside, on our sunnybank,[20] how buona the vista, by Santa Rosa! A field of May, the very vale of Spring. Orchards here are lodged; sainted lawrels evremberried. You have a hoig view ashwald, a glen of marrons and of thorns. Gleannaulinn, Ardeevin: purty glint of plaising height. This Norman court at boundary of the ville, yon creepered tower of a church of Ereland, meet for true saints in worshipful assemblage,[21] with our king's house of stone, belgroved of mulbrey, the still that was mill and Kloster that was Yeomansland, the ghastcold tombshape of the quick foregone on, the loftleaved elm Lefanunian abovemansioned, each, every, all is for the retrospectioner. Skole! Agus skole igen![22] Sweetsome auburn, cometh up as a selfreizing flower, that fragolance of the fraisey beds: the phoenix, his pyre, is still flaming away with trueprattight spirit: the wren his nest is niedelig as the turrises of the sabines are televisible. Here are the cottage and the bungalow for the cobbeler and the brandnewburgher:[23]

In snowdrop,
trou-de-dentelle,
flesh and helio-
trope.

but Izolde, her chaplet gardens, an litlee plads af liefest pose, arride the winnerful wonders off, the winnerful wonnerful wanders off,[24] with hedges of ivy and hollywood and bower of mistletoe, are, tho if it theem tho and yeth if you pleathes,[25] for the blithehaired daughter of Angoisse. All out of two barreny old perishers,

[20] When you dreamt that you'd wealth in marble arch do you ever think of pool beg slowe.

[21] Porphyrious Olbion, redcoatliar, we were always wholly rose marines on our side every time.

[22] Now a muss wash the little face.

[23] A viking vernacular expression still used in the Summerhill district for a jerryhatted man of forty who puts two fingers into his boiling soupplate and licks them in turn to find out if there is enough mushroom catsup in the mutton broth.

[24] H' dk' fs' h'p'y.

[25] Googlaa pluplu.

Tytonyhands and Vlossyhair, a kilolitre in
metromyriams. Presepeprosapia, the parent bole.
Wone tabard, wine tap and warm tavern[26] and,
by ribbon development, from contact bridge to
lease lapse, only two millium two humbered and
eighty thausig nine humbered and sixty radio-
lumin lines to the wustworts of a Finntown's
generous poet's office. Distorted mirage, aloo-
fliest of the plain, wherein the boxomeness of
the bedelias[27] makes hobbyhodge happy in his
hole.[28] The store and charter, Treetown Castle
under Lynne. Rivapool? Hod a brieck on it! But
its piers eerie, its span spooky, its toll but a till,
its parapets all peripateting. D'Oblong's by his
by. Which we all pass. Tons. In our snoo. Znore.
While we hickerwards the thicker. Schein.
Schore. Which assoars us from the murk of the
mythelated in the barrabelowther, bedevere
butlered table round, past Morningtop's necessity and Harington's invention, to the clarience
of the childlight in the studiorium upsturts.
Here we'll dwell on homiest powers, love at the
latch with novices nig and nag. The chorus: the
principals. For the rifocillation of their inclina-
tion to the manifestation of irritation: doldor-
boys and doll.[29] After sound, light and heat,
memory, will and understanding.

Here (the memories framed from walls are
minding) till wranglers for wringwrowdy
wready are, F Ⅎ, (at gaze, respecting, four-
teenth baronet, meet, altrettanth bancorot,
chaff) and ere commence commencement cata-
launic when Aetius check chokewill Attil's
gambit, (that buxon bruzeup, give it a burl!)
lead us seek, O june of eves the jenniest, thou

---

[26] Tomley. The grown man. A butcher szewched him the bloughs and
braches. I'm chory to see P. Shuter.

[27] I believe in Dublin and the Sultan of Turkey.

[28] I have heard this word used by Martin Halpin, an old gardener from the
Glens of Antrim who used to do odd jobs for my godfather, the Rev. B. B.
Brophy of Swords.

[29] Ravens may rive so can dove deelish.

who fleeest flicklesome the fond fervid frondeur
to thickly thyself attach with thine efteased
ensuer,[30] ondrawer of our unconscionable, flick-
erflapper fore our unterdrugged,[31] lead us seek,
lote us see, light us find, let us missnot Maida-
date, Mimosa Multimimetica, the maymeaminn-
ing of maimoomeining! Elpis, thou fountain of
the greeces, all shall speer theeward,[32] from
kongen in his canteenhus to knivers hind the
knoll. Ausonius Audacior and gael, gillie, gall.[33]
Singalingalying. Storiella as she is syung.
Whence followeup with endspeaking nots for

*There was a
sweet hopeful
culled Cis.*

yestures, plutonically pursuant on briefest
glimpse from gladrags, pretty Proserpronette
whose slit satchel spilleth peas.

Belisha beacon, beckon bright! Usherette, URGES AND
unmesh us! That grene ray of earong it waves WIDERURGES
us to yonder as the red, blue and yellow flogs IN A PRIMI-
TIVE SEPT.
time on the domisole,[34] with a blewy blow and
a windigo. Where flash becomes word and silents selfloud. To brace congeners, trebly
bounden and asservaged twainly. Adamman,[35]
Emhe, Issossianusheen and sometypes Yggely
ogs Weib. Uwayoei![36] So mag this sybilette be
our shibboleth that we may syllable her well!
Vetus may be occluded behind the mou in

*The Big Bear
bit the Sailor's
Only. Trouble,
trouble, trouble.*

*Forening Unge
Kristlike Kvinne.*

Veto but Nova will be nearing as their radient
among the Nereids. A one of charmers, ay, Una
Unica, charmers, who, under the branches of
the elms, in shoes as yet unshent by stoniness,
wend, went, will wend a way of honey myrrh
and rambler roses mistmusk while still the
maybe mantles the meiblume or ever her if have

[30] A question of pull.
[31] For Rose Point see Inishmacsaint.
[32] Mannequins' Pose.
[33] Their holy presumption and hers sinfly desprit.
[34] Anama anamaba anamabapa.
[35] Only for he's fathering law I could skewer that old one and slosh her out
many's the time but I thinks more of my pottles and ketts.
[36] All abunk for Tarararat! Look slipper, soppyhat, we've a doss in the
manger.

faded from the fleur,[37] their arms enlocked,
(ringrang, the chimes of sex appealing as con-
chitas with sentas stray,[38] rung!), all thinking
all of it, the It with an itch in it, the All every
inch of it, the pleasure each will preen her for,
the business each was bred to breed by.[39]

*Telltale me all
of annaryllies.*

Soon jemmijohns will cudgel about some a
rhythmatick or other over Browne and Nolan's
divisional tables whereas she, of minions' no-
vence charily being cupid, for mug's wumping,
grooser's grubbiness, andt's avarice and grossop-
per's grandegaffe, with her tootpettypout of
jemenfichue will sit and knit on solfa sofa.[40]
Stew of the evening, booksyful stew. And a
bodikin a boss in the Thimble Theatre. But all
is her inbourne. Intend. From gramma's gram-
mar she has it that if there is a third person, mas-
carine, phelinine or nuder, being spoken abad
it moods prosodes from a person speaking to her
second which is the direct object that has been
spoken to, with and at. Take the dative with his
oblative[41] for, even if obsolete, it is always of interest, so spake gramma on the impetus of her
imperative, only mind your genderous towards
his reflexives such that I was to your grappa
(Bott's trousend, hore a man uff!) when him
was me hedon[42] and mine, what the lewdy saying, his analectual pygmyhop.[43] There is com-
fortism in the knowledge that often hate on first
hearing comes of love by second sight. Have
your little sintalks in the dunk of subjunctions,
dual in duel and prude with pruriel, but even
the aoriest chaparound whatever plaudered perfect anent prettydotes and *haec genua omnia*

*Will you carry
my can and
fight the fairies?*

*Allma Mathers,
Auctioneer.*

*Old Gavelkind
the Gamper and
he's as daff as
you're erse.*

EARLY
NOTIONS OF
ACQUIRED
RIGHTS AND
THE INFLU-
ENCE OF
COLLECTIVE
TRADITION
UPON THE
INDIVIDUAL.

---

[37] One must sell it to some one, the sacred name of love.
[38] Making it up as we goes along.
[39] The law of the jungerl.
[40] Let me blush to think of all those halfwayhoist pullovers.
[41] I'd like his pink's cheek.
[42] Frech devil in red hairing! So that's why you ran away to sea, Mrs Lappy.
Leap me, Locklaun, for you have sensed!
[43] A washable lovable floatable doll.

may perhaps chance to be about to be in the case
to be becoming a pale peterwright in spite of all
your tense accusatives whilstly you're wall-
floored[44] like your gerandiums for the better
half of a yearn or sob. It's a wild's kitten, my
dear, who can tell a wilkling from a warthog.
For you may be as practical as is predicable
but you must have the proper sort of accident to
meet that kind of a being with a difference.[45]
Flame at his fumbles but freeze on his fist.[46]
Every letter is a godsend, ardent Ares, brusque
Boreas and glib Ganymede like zealous Zeus, the
O'Meghisthest of all. To me or not to me.
Satis thy quest on. Werbungsap! Jeg suis, vos

*Undante
umoroso.
M. 50-50.
οὐκ ἔλαβον
πόλιν.*

wore a gentleman, thou arr, I am a quean. Is a
game over? The game goes on. Cookcook! Search
me. The beggar the maid the bigger the mauler.
And the greater the patrarc the griefer the
pinch. And that's what your doctor knows. O
love it is the commonknounest thing how it
pashes the plutous and the paupe.[47] Pop! And
egg she active or spoon she passive, all them fine
clauses in Lindley's and Murrey's never braught
the participle of a present to a desponent horta-
trixy, vindicatively I say it, from her postcondi-
tional future.[48] Lumpsome is who lumpsum
pays. Quantity counts though accents falter.
Yoking apart and oblique orations parsed to one

*I'll go for that
small polly if
you'll suck to
your lebbens-
quatsch.*

side, a brat, alanna, can choose from so many,
be he a sollicitor's appendix, a pipe clerk or free
functionist flyswatter, that perfect little cad,
from the languors and weakness of limberlimbed
lassihood till the head, back and heartaches of
waxedup womanage and heaps on heaps of other
things too. Note the Respectable Irish Distressed
Ladies and the Merry Mustard Frothblowers of

---

[44] With her poodle feinting to be let off and feeling dead in herself. Is love
worse living?
[45] If she can't follow suit Renée goes to the pack.
[46] Improper frictions is maledictions and mens uration makes me mad.
[47] Llong and Shortts Primer of Black and White Wenchcraft.
[48] The gaggles all out.

Humphreystown Associations. Atac first, queck-
queck quicks after. Beware how in that hist sub-
taile of schlangder[49] lies liaison to tease oreilles!
To vert embowed set proper penchant. But learn
from that ancient tongue to be middle old modern to the minute. A spitter that can be de-
pended on. Though Wonderlawn's lost us for
ever. Alis, alas, she broke the glass! Liddell
lokker through the leafery, ours is mistery of
pain.[50] You may spin on youthlit's bike and
multiplease your Mike and Nike with your kick-
shoes on the algebrars but, volve the virgil page
O'Mara Farrell. and view, the O of woman is long when burly
those two muters sequent her so from Nebob[51]
Verschwindibus. see you never stray who'll nimm you nice and
nehm the day.

One hath just been areading, hath not one, CONCOMI-
ya, ya, in their memoiries of Hireling's puny TANCE OF
Ulstria, wars, end so, und all, ga, ga, of The O'Brien, COURAGE,
Monastir, The O'Connor, the Mac Loughlin and The COUNSEL
Leninstar and Mac Namara with summed their appondage, da, AND CON-
Connecticut. da, of Sire Jeallyous Seizer, that gamely torsk- STANCY.
mester,[52] with his duo of druidesses in ready ORDINATION
Cliopatria, thy money rompers[53] and the tryonforit of Oxthie- OF OMEN,
hosies history. vious, Lapidous and Malthouse Anthemy. You ONUS AND
may fail to see the lie of that layout, Suetonia,[54] OBIT. DIS-
but the reflections which recur to me are that TRIBUTION
so long as beauty life is body love[55] and so bright OF DANGER,
as Mutua of your mirror holds her candle to your DUTY AND
caudle, lone lefthand likeless, sombring Autum DESTINY.
of your Spring, reck you not one spirt of anyseed POLAR PRIN-
whether trigemelimen cuddle his coddle or nope. CIPLES.

---

[49] He's just bug nuts on white mate he hasn't the teath nor the grits to choo
and that's what's wrong with Lang Wang Wurm, old worbbling goesbelly.

[50] Dear and I trust in all frivolity I may be pardoned for trespassing but I
think I may add hell.

[51] He is my all menkind of every desception.

[52] All his teeths back to the front, then the moon and then the moon with
a hole behind it.

[53] Skip one, flop fore, jennies in the cabbage store.

[54] None of your cumpohlstery English here!

[55] Understudy my understandings, Sostituda, and meek thine complinement,
gymnufleshed.

She'll confess it by her figure and she'll deny it to your face. If you're not ruined by that one she won't do you any whim. And then? What afters it? Gruff Gunne may blow, Gam Gonna flow, the gossans eye the jennings aye. From the butts of Heber and Heremon, *nolens volens,* brood our pansies, brune in brume. There's a split in the infinitive from to have to have been to will be. As they warred in their big innings ease now we never shall know. Eat early earthapples. Coax Cobra to chatters. Hail, Heva, we hear! This is the glider that gladdened the girl[56] that list to the wind that lifted the leaves that folded the fruit that hung on the tree that grew in the garden Gough gave. Wide hiss, we're wizening. Hoots fromm, we're globing. Why hidest thou hinder thy husband his name? Leda, Lada, aflutter-afraida, so does your girdle grow! Willed without witting, whorled without aimed. Pappapassos, Mammamanet, warwhetswut and whowitswhy.[57] But it's tails for toughs and titties for totties and come buckets come bats till deeleet.[58]

The Eroico Furioso makes the valet like smiling.

The hyperape the mink he groves the mole you see now for crush sake, chawley!

Pige pas.

Dark ages clasp the daisy roots, Stop, if you are a sally of the allies, hot off Minnowaurs and naval actiums, picked engagements and banks of rowers. Please stop if you're a B.C. minding missy, please do. But should you prefer A.D. stepplease. And if you miss with a venture it serves you girly well glad. But, holy Janus, I was forgetting the Blitzenkopfs! Here, Hengegst and Horsesauce, take your heads[59] out of that taletub! And leave your hinnyhennyhindyou! It's haunted. The chamber. Of errings. Whoan, tug, trace, stirrup! It is distinctly understouttered that, sense you threehandshighs put your two-footlarge timepates in that dead wash of Lough

PANOPTICAL PURVIEW OF POLITICAL PROGRESS AND THE FUTURE PRESENTATION OF THE PAST.

Seidlitz powther for slogan plumpers.

---

[56] Tho' I have one just like that to home, deadleaf brown with quicksilver appliques, would whollymost applissiate a nice shiny sleekysilk out of that slippering snake charmeuse.

[57] What's that, ma'am? says I.

[58] As you say yourself.

[59] That's the lethemuse but it washes off.

Murph and until such time pace one and the
same Messherrn the grinning statesmen, Brock
and Leon, have shunted the grumbling counded-
touts, Starlin and Ser Artur Ghinis. Foamous
homely brew, bebattled by bottle, gageure de

Hoploits and   guegerre.[60] Bull igien bear and then bearagain
atthems.   bulligan. Gringrin gringrin. Staffs varsus herds
and bucks vursus barks. By old Grumbledum's

Curragh   walls. Bumps, bellows and bawls.[61] Opprimor's
machree, me   down, up up Opima! Rents and rates and tithes
bosthoon fiend.   and taxes, wages, saves and spends. Heil, hept-
Femilies hug   arched span of peace![62] Live, league of lex, nex
bank!   and the mores! Fas est dass and foe err you. Im-
povernment of the booble by the bauble for the
bubble. So wrap up your worries in your woe
(wumpumtum!) and shake down the shuffle

All we suffered   for the throw. For there's one mere ope[63] for
under them   downfall ned. As Hanah Levy, shrewd shrop-
Cowdung Forks   lifter, and nievre anore skidoos with her spoil-
and how we en-   eds.[64] To add gay touches. For hugh and guy
joyed over our   and goy and jew. To dimpled and pimpled and
pick of the   simpled and wimpled. A peak in a poke and a
basketfild. Old   pig in a pew.[65] She wins them by wons, a haul
Kine's Meat   hectoendecate, for mangay mumbo jumbjubes
Meal.   tak mutts and jeffs muchas bracelonettes

Flieflie for the   gracies barcelonas.[66] O what a loovely free-
jillies and a   speech 'twas (tep)[67] to gar howalively hinter-
bombambum   grunting! Tip. Like lilt of larks to burdened
for the   crocodile,[68] or skittering laubhing at that wheeze
nappotondus.   of old windbag, Blusterboss, blowharding about
all he didn't do. Hell o' your troop! With is the
winker for the muckwits of willesly and nith is

[60] Where he fought the shessock of his stimmstammer and we caught the
pepettes of our lovelives.

[61] Shake eternity and lick creation.

[62] I'm blest if I can see.

[63] Hoppity Huhneye, hoosh the hen. I like cluckers, you like nuts (wink).

[64] Sweet, medium and dry like altar wine.

[65] Who'll buy me penny babies?

[66] Well, Maggy, I got your castoff devils all right and fits lovely. And am
vaguely graceful. Maggy thanks.

[67] My six is no secret, sir, she said.

[68] Yes, there, Tad, thanks, give, from, tathair, look at that now.

the nod for the umproar napollyon and hitheris
poorblond piebold hoerse. Huirse. With its tri-
cuspidal hauberkhelm coverchaf emblem on.

Murdoch.

For the man that broke the ranks on Monte
Sinjon. The allriddle of it? That that is allruddy
with us, ahead of schedule, which already is

Pas d'action,
peu de sauce.

plan accomplished from and syne: Daft Dathy
of the Five Positions (the death ray stop him!)
is still, as reproaches Paulus, on the Madder-
horn and, entre chats and hobnobs,[69] daring
Dunderhead to shiver his timbers and Hannibal
mac Hamiltan the Hegerite[70] (more livepower
elbow him!) ministerbuilding up, as repreaches
Timothy, in Saint Barmabrac's.[71] Number
Thirty two West Eleventh streak looks on to
that (may all in the tocoming of the sempere-

From the seven
tents of Joseph
till the calends
of Mary Marian,
olivehunkered
and thorny too.

ternal speel spry with it!) datetree doloriferous
which more and over leafeth earlier than every
growth and, elfshot, headawag, with frayed
nerves wondering till they feeled sore like any
woman that has been born at all events to the
purdah and for the howmanyeth and how-
movingth time at what the demons in that jack-

As Shakefork
might pitch it.

house that jerry built for Massa and Missus and
hijo de puta, the sparksown fermament of the
starryk fieldgosongingon where blows a nemone
at each blink of windstill[72] they were sliding
along and sleeting aloof and scouting around
and shooting about. Allwhichwhile or wherea-
balloons for good vaunty years Dagobert is in
Clane's clean hometown prepping up his pre-
pueratory and learning how to put a broad face
bronzily out through a broken breached mea-

Puzzly, puzzly,
I smell a cat.

taerial from Bryan Awlining! Erin's hircohaired
culoteer.[73]

And as, these things being so or ere those FROM CENO-

---

[69] Go up quick, stay so long, come down slow!
[70] If I gnows me gneesgnobs the both of him is gnatives of Genuas.
[71] A glass of peel and pip for Mr Potter of Texas, please.
[72] All the world loves a big gleaming jelly.
[73] A pengeneepy for your warcheekeepy.

GENETIC DI-
CHOTOMY
THROUGH
DIAGONISTIC
CONCILI-
ANCE TO
DYNASTIC
CONTINU-
ITY.

Two makes a wing at the macroscope telluspeep.

From the Buffalo Times of bysone days.

Quick quake quokes the parrotbook of dates.

Some is out for twoheaded dulcarnons but more pulfers turnips.

things having done, way back home in Pacata Auburnia,[74] (untillably holy gammel Eire) one world burrowing on another, (if you've got me, neighbour, in any large lumps, geek?, and got the strong of it) Standfest, our topiocal sagon hero, or any otther macotther, signs is on the bellyguds bastille back, bucked up with fullness, and silvering to her jubilee,[75] birchleaves her jointure, our lavy in waving, visage full of flesh and fat as a hen's i' forehead, Airyanna and Blowyhart topsirturvy, that royal pair in their palace of quicken boughs hight The Goat and Compasses ('phone number 17:69, if you want to know[76]) his seaarm strongsround her, her velivole eyne ashipwracked, have discusst their things of the past, crime and fable with shame, home and profit,[77] why lui lied to lei and hun tried to kill ham, scribbledehobbles, in whose veins runs a mixture of, are head bent and hard upon. Spell me the chimes. They are tales all tolled.[78] Today is well thine but where's may tomorrow be. But, bless his cowly head and press his crankly hat, what a world's woe is each's other's weariness waiting to beadroll his own properer mistakes, the backslapping gladhander,[79] free of his florid future and the other singing likeness, dirging a past of bloody altars, gale with a blost to him, dove without gall. And she, of the jilldaw's nest[80] who tears up let-

---

[74] My globe goes gaddy at geography giggle pending which time I was looking for my shoe all through Arabia.

[75] It must be some bugbear in the gender especially when old which they all soon get to look.

[76] After me looking up the plan in Humphrey's *Justice of the Piece* it said to see preseeding chaps.

[77] O boyjones and hairyoddities! Only noane told missus of her massas behaving she would laugh that flat that after that she had sanked down on her fat arks they would shaik all to sheeks.

[78] Traduced into jinglish janglage for the nusances of dolphins born.

[79] He gives me pulpititions with his Castlecowards never in these twowsers and ever in those twawsers and then babeteasing us out of our hoydenname.

[80] My goldfashioned bother near drave me roven mad and I dyeing to keep my linefree face like readymaid maryangs for jollycomes smashing Holmes.

Omnitudes in a knutshedell.

tereens she never apposed a pen upon.[81] Yet sung of love and the monster man. What's Hiccupper to hem or her to Hagaba? Ough, ough, brieve kindli![82]

Dogs' vespers are anending. Vespertiliabitur. Goteshoppard quits his gabhard cloke to sate with Becchus. Zumbock! Achevre! Yet wind will be ere fadervor[83] and the hour of fruminy and bergoo bell if Nippon have pearls or opals Eldorado, the daindy dish, the lecking out! Gipoo, good oil! For (hushmagandy!) long 'tis till gets bright that all cocks waken and birds Diana[84] with dawnsong hail. Aught darks flou a duskness. Bats that? There peepeestrilling. At Brannan's on the moor. At Tam Fanagan's weak yat his still's going strang. And still here is noctules and can tell things acommon on by that fluffy feeling. Larges loomy wheelhouse to bodgbox[85] lumber up with hoodie hearsemen carrawain we keep is peace who follow his law, Sunday King.[86] His sevencoloured's soot (Ochone! Ochonal!)[87] and his imponence one heap lumpblock (Mogoul!). And rivers burst out like weeming racesround joydrinks for the fewnrally,[88] where every feaster's a foster's other, fiannians all.[89] The wellingbreast, he willing giant, the mountain mourning his duggedy dew. To obedient of civicity in urbanious at felicity what'll yet meek Mike[90] our diputy mimber

For all us kids under his aegis.

Saving the public his health.

Superlative absolute of Porterstown.

Why so mucky spick bridges span our Fluminian road.

P.C. Helmut's in the cottonwood, listnin.

The throne is an

[81] What I would like is a jade louistone to go with the moon's increscent.

[82] Parley vows the Askinwhose? I do, Ida. And how to call the cattle black. Moopetsi meepotsi.

[83] I was so snug off in my apholster's creedle but at long leash I'll stretch more capritious in his dapplepied bed.

[84] Pipette. I can almost feed their sweetness at my lisplips.

[85] A liss in hunterland.

[86] I wonder if I put the old buzzerd one night to suckle in Millickmaam's honey like they use to emballem some of the special popes with a book in his hand and his mouth open.

[87] And a ripping rude rape in his lucreasious togery.

[88] Will ye nought would wet your weapons, warriors bard?

[89] Roe, Williams, Bewey, Greene, Gorham, McEndicoth and Vyler, the lays of ancient homes.

[90] The staindsglass effect, you could sugerly swear buttermilt would not melt down his dripping ducks.

umbrella strande and a sceptre's a stick.

Jady jewel, our daktar deer.

Gautamed budders deossiphysing our Theas.

when he's head on poll and Peter's burgess and Miss Mishy Mushy is tiptupt by Toft Taft. Boblesse gobleege. For as Anna was at the beginning lives yet and will return after great deap sleap rerising and a white night high with a cows of Drommhiem as shower as there's a wet enclouded in Westwicklow or a little black rose a truant in a thorntree. We drames our dreams tell Bappy returns. And Sein annews. We will not say it shall not be, this passing of order and order's coming, but in the herbest country and in the country around Blath as in that city self of legionds they look for its being ever yet. So shuttle the pipers done.[91] Eric aboy![92] And it's time that all paid tribute to this massive mortiality, the pink of punk perfection as photog-

By lineal in pondus overthepoise.

raphy in mud. Some may seek to dodge the gobbet for its quantity of quality but who wants to cheat the choker's got to learn to chew the cud. Allwhichhole scrubs on scroll circuminiu-

Pitchcap and triangle, noose and tinctunc.

minlumlnatedhave encuoniams here and improperies there.[93] With a pansy for the pussy in the corner.[94]

Bewise of Fanciulla's heart, the heart of Fanciulla! Even the recollection of willow fronds is a spellbinder that lets to hear.[95] The rushes by

Uncle Flabbius Muximus to Niecia Flappia Minnimiss. As this is. And as this this is.

the grey nuns' pond: ah eh oh let me sigh too. Coalmansbell: behoves you handmake of the load. Jenny Wren: pick, peck. Johnny Post: pack, puck.[96] All the world's in want and is writing a letters.[97] A letters from a person to a

INCIPIT INTERMISSIO.

---

[91] Thickathigh and Thinathews with sant their dam.

[92] Oh, could we do with this waddled of ours like that redbanked profanian with his bakset of yosters.

[93] Gosem pher, gezumpher, greeze a jarry grim felon! Good bloke him!

[94] And if they was setting on your stool as hard as my was she could beth her bothom dolours he'd have a culious impressiom on the diminitive that chafes our ends.

[95] When I'am Enastella and am taken for Essastessa I'll do that droop on the pohlmann's piano.

[96] Heavenly twinges, if it's one of his I'll fearly feint as swoon as he enterrooms.

[97] To be slipped on, to be slept by, to be conned to, to be kept up. And when you're done push the chain.

Dear Brotus,
land me arrears.

Rockaby, babel,
flatten a wall.
How he broke
the good news to
Gent.

place about a thing. And all the world's on wish
to be carrying a letters. A letters to a king about
a treasure from a cat.[98] When men want to write
a letters. Ten men, ton men, pen men, pun men,
wont to rise a ladder. And den men, dun men,
fen men, fun men, hen men, hun men wend to
raze a leader. Is then any lettersday from many
peoples, Daganasanavitch? Empire, your outer-
most.[99] A posy cord. Plece.

We have wounded our way on foe tris prince
till that force in the gill is faint afarred and the
face in the treebark feigns afear. This is rain-
stones ringing. Strangely cult for this ceasing of
the yore. But Erigureen is ever. Pot price pon
patrilinear plop, if the osseletion of the onkring
gives omen nome? Since alls war that end war
let sports be leisure and bring and buy fair. Ah
ah athclete, blest your bally bathfeet! Town-
toquest, fortorest, the hour that hies is hurley.
A halt for hearsake.[100] A scene at sight. Or

MAJOR AND
MINOR
MODES COA-
LESCING
PROLIFER-
ATE HOMO-
GENUINE
HOMOGE-
NEITY.

[98] With her modesties office.

[99] Strutting as proud as a great turquin weggin that cuckhold on his Eddems
and Clay's hat.

[100] Come, smooth of my slate, to the beat of my blosh! With all these gelded
ewes jilting about and the thrills and ills of laylock blossoms three's so much
more plants than chants for cecilies that I was thinking fairly killing times of
putting an end to myself and my malody, when I remembered all your pupil-
teacher's erringnesses in perfection class. You sh'udn't write you can't if you
w'udn't pass for undevelopmented. This is the propper way to say that, Sr. If
it's me chews to swallow all you saidn't you can eat my words for it as sure as
there's a key in my kiss. Quick erit faciofacey. When we will conjugate together toloseher tomaster tomiss while morrow fans amare hour, verbe de vie
and verve to vie, with love ay loved have I on my back spine and does for
ever. Your are me severe? Then rue. My intended, Jr, who I'm throne away
on, (here he inst, my lifstack, a newfolly likon) when I slip through my pettigo
I'll get my decree and take seidens when I'm not ploughed first by some
Rolando the Lasso, and flaunt on the flimsyfilmsies for to grig my collage
juniorees who, though they flush fuchsia, are they octette and viginity in my
shade but always my figurants. They may be yea of my year but they're nary
nay of my day. Wait till spring has sprung in spickness and prigs beg in to pry
they'll be plentyprime of housepets to pimp and pamper my. Impending marriage. Nature tells everybody about but I learned all the runes of the gamest
game ever from my old nourse Asa. A most adventuring trot is her and she
vicking well knowed them all heartswise and fourwords. How Olive d'Oyly
and Winnie Carr, bejupers, they reized the dressing of a salandmon and how a
peeper coster and a salt sailor med a mustied poet atwaimen. It most have
bean Mad Mullans planted him. Bina de Bisse and Trestrine von Terrefin.
Sago sound, rite go round, kill kackle, kook kettle and (remember all should

dreamoneire. Which they shall memorise. By her freewritten Hopely for ear that annalykeses if scares for eye that sumns. Is it in the now woodwordings of our sweet plantation where the branchings then will singingsing tomorrows gone and yesters outcome as Satadays afternoon lex leap smiles on the twelve-monthsminding? Such is. Dear (name of desired subject, A.N.), well, and I go on to. Shlicksher. I and we (tender condolences for happy funeral, one if) so sorry to (mention person suppressed for the moment, F.M.). Well (enquiries after allhealths) how are you (question maggy). A lovely (introduce to domestic circles) pershan of cates. Shrubsher. Those pothooks mostly she hawks from Poppa Vere Foster but these curly mequeues are of Mippa's moulding. Shrubsheruthr. (Wave gently in the ere turning ptover.) Well, mabby (consolation of shopes) to soon air. With best from cinder Christinette if prints chumming, can be when desires Soldi, for asamples, backfronted or, if all, peethrolio or Get my Prize, using her flower or perfume or, if veryveryvery chumming, in otherwards, who she supposed adeal, kissists my exits. Shlicksheruthr. From Auburn chenlemagne. Pious and pure fair one, all has concomitated to this that she shall tread them lifetrees leaves whose silence hitherto has shone as sphere of silver fastalbarnstone, that fount Bandusian shall play liquick music and after odours sigh of

Bibelous hicstory and Barbarassa harestary.

A shieling in coppingers and porrish soup all days.

How matches metroosers?

Le hélos tombaut soul sur la jambe de marche.

I forget to) bolt the thor. Auden. Wasn't it just divining that dog of a dag in Skokholme as I sat astrid uppum their Drewitt's altar, as cooledas as culcumbre, slapping my straights till the sloping ruins, postillion, postallion, a swinge a swank, with you offering me clouts of illscents and them horners stagstruck on the leasward! Don't be of red, you blanching mench! This isabella I'm on knows the ruelles of the rut and she don't fear andy mandy. So sing loud, sweet cheeriot, like anegreon in heaven! The good fother with the twingling in his eye will always have cakes in his pocket to bethroat us with for our allmichael good. Amum. Amum. And Amum again. For tough troth is stronger than fortuitous fiction and it's the surplice money, oh my young friend and ah me sweet creature, what buys the bed while wits borrows the clothes.

musk. Blotsbloshblothe, one dear that was. Sleep
in the water, drug at the fire, shake the dust off
and dream your one who would give her side-
curls to. Till later Lammas is led in by baith our
washwives, a weird of wonder tenebrous as that
evil thorngarth, a field of faery blithe as this flowing wild.

*Mai maintenante
elle est venuse.*

*Aujourd'hui comme aux temps de Pline et de
Columelle la jacinthe se plaît dans les Gaules,
la pervenche en Illyrie, la marguerite sur les
ruines de Numance*[101] *et pendant qu'autour
d'elles les villes ont changé de maîtres et de noms,
que plusieurs sont entrées dans le néant, que les
civilisations se sont choquées et brisées, leurs
paisibles générations ont traversé les âges et sont
arrivées jusqu'à nous, fraîches et riantes comme
aux jours des batailles.*[102]

*Twos Dons Johns
Threes Totty
Askins.*

THE PART
PLAYED BY
BELLETRI-
STICKS IN
THE BELLUM-
PAX-BEL-
LUM.
MUTUOMOR-
PHOMUTA-
TION.

*Also Spuke
Zerothruster.*

Margaritomancy! Hyacinthinous pervinci-
veness! Flowers. A cloud. But Bruto and Cassio
are ware only of trifid tongues[103] the whispered
wilfulness, ('tis demonal!) and shadows shadows
multiplicating (il folsoletto nel falsoletto col
fazzolotto dal fuzzolezzo),[104] totients quotients,
they tackle their quarrel. Sickamoor's so woful
sally. Ancient's aerger. And eachway bothwise
glory signs. What if she love Sieger less though
she leave Ruhm moan? That's how our oxyg-
gent has gotten ahold of half their world. Moving about in the free of the air and mixing with
the ruck. Enten eller, either or.

*A saxum shillum
for the sextum
but nothums for
that parridge
preast.*

SORTES VIR-
GINIANAE.

And!

Nay, rather!

With sobs for his job, with tears for his
toil, with horror for his squalor but with

INTERROGATION.
EXCLAMATION.
ANTITHESIS OF AMBI-
DUAL ANTICIPATION.

Tricks stunts.

[101] The nasal foss of our natal folkfarthers so so much now for Valsing-
giddyrex and his grand arks day triump.

[102] Translout that gaswind into turfish, Teague, that's a good bog and you,
Thady, poliss it off, there's a nateswipe, on to your blottom pulper.

[103] You daredevil donnelly, I love your piercing lots of lies and your flashy
foreign mail so here's my cowrie card, I dalgo, with all my exes, wise and sad.

[104] All this Mitchells is a niggar for spending and I will go to the length of
seeing that one day Big Mig will be nickleless himself.

pep for his perdition,[105] lo, the boor plieth the mind factory,
as the laird hireth him. its give and take.

Boon on begyndelse.

At maturing daily gloryaims![106] auspicium.
auguria.

A flink dab for a freck dive and a stern poise divinity
for a swift pounce was frankily at the manual not deity
arith sure enough which was the bekase he the uncer-
knowed from his cradle, no bird better, why tainty jus-
his fingures were giving him whatfor to fife tified by our certi-
with. First, by observation, there came boko and tude.

Truckeys' cant nigh him wigworms and nigh him tittlies and examples.
for dactyl and nigh him cheekadeekchimple and nigh him pick-
spondee. pocket with pickpocketpumb, pickpocketpoint,
pickpocketprod, pickpocketpromise and up-
withem. Holy Joe in lay Eden.[107] And anyhows
always after them the dimpler he weighed the
fonder fell he of his null four lovedroyd curdi-
nals, his element curdinal numen and his ene-
Panoplous pere- ment curdinal marryng and his epulent curdinal
grine pifflicative weisswassh and his eminent curdinal Kay O'Kay.
pomposity. Always would he be reciting of them, hoojahs
koojahs, up by rota, in his Fanden's catachysm
from fursed to laced, quickmarch to decemvers,
so as to pin the tenners, thumbs down. And
anon and aldays, strues yerthere, would he wile
arecreating em om lumerous ways, caiuscounting
in the scale of pin puff pive piff, piff puff pive
poo, poo puff pive pree, pree puff pive pfoor,
pfoor puff pive pippive, poopive,[108] Niall Dhu,
Foughty Unn, Enoch Thortig, endso one, like
to pitch of your cap, pac, on to tin tall spilli-
Non plus ultra, cans.[109] To sum, borus pew notus pew eurus
Elba, nec, cashel- pew zipher. Ace, deuce, tricks, quarts, quims.
lum tuum. Mumtiplay of course and carry to their whole
number. While on the other hand, traduced

---

[105] While I'll wind the wildwoods' bluckbells among my window's weeds.
[106] Lawdy Dawdy Simpers.
[107] But where, O where, is me lickle dig done?
[108] That's his whisper waltz I like from Pigott's with that Lancydancy step.
Stop.
[109] Twelve buttles man, twentyeight bows of curls, forty bonnets woman
and ever youthfully yours makes alleven add the hundred.

by their comedy nominator to the loaferst terms
for their aloquent parts, sexes, suppers, oglers,
novels and dice.[110] He could find (the rake-
helly!) by practice the valuse of thine-to-mine
articles with no reminder for an equality of relations and, with the helpings from his tables, im-
produce fullmin to trumblers, links unto chains,
weys in Nuffolk till tods of Yorek, oozies ad libs
and several townsends, several hundreds, civil-
to-civil imperious gallants into gells (Irish),
bringing alliving stone allaughing down to grave

clothnails and a league of archers, fools and
lurchers under the rude rule of fumb. What sig-
nifieth whole that[111] but, be all the prowess of
ten, 'tis as strange to relate he, nonparile to rede,
rite and reckan, caught allmeals dullmarks for
his nucleuds and alegobrew. They wouldn't
took bearings no how anywheres. O them dodd-
hunters and allanights, aabs and baas for
agnomes, yees and zees for incognits, bate him
up jerrybly! Worse nor herman dororrhea. Give
you the fantods, seemed to him. They ought to
told you every last word first stead of trying
every which way to kinder smear it out poison

long. Show that the median, hce che ech, in-
terecting at royde angles the parilegs of a given
obtuse one biscuts both the arcs that are in
curveachord behind. Brickbaths. The family
umbroglia. A Tullagrove pole[112] to the Height
of County Fearmanagh has a septain inclinai-
son[113] and the graphplot for all the functions
in Lower County Monachan, whereat same-
thing is rivisible by nighttim, may be involted
into the zeroic couplet, palls pell inhis heventh

glike noughty times ∞, find, if you are not literally cooefficient, how minney combinaisies and
permutandies can be played on the international

---

[110] Gamester Damester in the road to Rouen he grows more like his deed
every die.
[111] Slash-the-Pill lifts the pellet. Run, Phoenix, run!
[112] Dideney, Dadeney, Dudeney, O, I'd know that putch on your poll.
[113] That is tottinghim in his boots.

surd! pthwndxrclzp!, hids cubid rute being ex-
tructed, taking anan illitterettes, ififif at a tom.
Answers, (for teasers only).[114] Ten, twent, thirt,
see, ex and three icky totchty ones. From solation to solution. Imagine the twelve deaferended
dumbbawls of the whowl abovebeugled to be
the contonuation through regeneration of the
urutteration of the word in pregross. It follows
that, if the two antesedents be bissyclitties and
the three comeseekwenchers trundletrikes, then,

Ba be bi bo bum.   Aysha Lalipat behidden on the footplate, Big
Whiggler[115] restant upsittuponable, the NCR[116]
presents to us (tandem year at lasted length!)
an ottomantic turquo-indaco of pictorial shine by
pictorial shimmer so long as, gad of the gidday,
pictorial summer, viridorefulvid, lits asheen, but
(lenz alack lends a lot), if this habby cyclic
erdor be outraciously enviolated by a mierelin
roundtableturning, like knuts in maze, the zitas
runnind hare and dart[117] with the yeggs in their
muddle, like a seven of wingless arrows, hodge-
padge, thump, kick and hurry, all boy more
missis blong him he race quickfeller all same

Finnfinnotus of   hogglepiggle longer house blong him,[118] while
Cincinnati.   the catched and dodged exarx seems himmul-
teemiously to beem (he wins her hend! he falls
to tail!) the ersed ladest mand[119] and (uhu and
uhud!) the losed farce on erroroots,[120] twa-
legged poneys and threehandled dorkeys (mad-
ahoy, morahoy, lugahoy, jogahoyaway) MPM

Arthurgink's   brings us a rainborne pamtomomiom, aqualavant
hussies and   to (cat my dogs, if I baint dingbushed like every-
Everguin's men.   thing!) kaksitoista volts yksitoista volts kym-

---

[114] Come all ye hapney coachers and support the richview press.
[115] Braham Baruch he married his cook to Massach McKraw her uncle-in-
law who wedded his widow to Hjalmar Kjaer who adapted his daughter to
Braham the Bear. V for wadlock, P for shift, H for Lona the Konkubine.
[116] A gee is just a jay on the jaunts cowsway.
[117] Talking about trilbits.
[118] Barneycorrall, a precedent for the prodection of curiosity from children.
[119] A pfurty pscore of ruderic rossies haremhorde for his divelsion.
[120] Look at your mad father on his boneshaker fraywhaling round Myriom
square.

menen volts yhdeksan volts kahdeksan volts
seitseman volts kuusi volts viisi volts nelja volts
kolme volts kaksi volts yksi!allahthallacamel-
lated, caravan series to the finish of helve's
fractures.[121] In outher wards, one from five, two
to fives ones, one from fives two millamills with
a mill and a half a mill and twos twos fives fives
of bully clavers. For a surview over all the fac-
tionables see Iris in the Evenine's World.[122]
Binomeans to be comprendered. Inexcessible as
thy by god ways. The aximones. And their pros-
talutes. For his neuralgiabrown.
Equal to=aosch.

*Nom de nom-
bres! The bal-
bearians.*

P.t.l.o.a.t.o.

So, bagdad, after those initials falls and that
primary taincture, as I know and you know
yourself, begath, and the arab in the ghetto
knows better, by nettus, nor anymeade or per-
san, comic cuts and series exerxeses always were
to be capered in Casey's frost book of, page torn
on dirty, to be hacked at Hickey's, hucksler,
Wellington's Iron Bridge, and so, by long last,
as it would shuffle out, must he to trump adieu
atout atous to those cardinhands he a big deal
missed, radmachrees and rossecullinans and
blagpikes in suitclover. Dear hearts of my counting, would he revoke them, forewheel to pack-
numbers, and, the time being no help fort, plates
to lick one and turn over.

*Vive Paco
Hunter!*

*The hoisted in
red and the low-
ered in black.*

HEPTAGRAMMATON.
HYPOTHESES
OF COM-
MONEST EX-
PERIENCES
BEFORE APO-
THEOSIS OF
THE LUSTRAL
PRINCIPIUM.

Problem ye ferst, construct ann aquilittoral
dryankle Probe loom! With his primal hand-
stoe in his sole salivarium. Concoct an equo-
angular trillitter.[123] On the name of the tizzer
and off the tongs and off the mythametical tri-
pods. Beatsoon.
Can you nei do her, numb? asks Dolph,[124]

*The boss's bess
bass is the browd
of Mullingar.*

INGENIOUS
LABOUR-
TENACITY
AS BETWEEN
INGENUOUS
AND
LIBERTINE.
PROPE AND

[121] Try Asia for the assphalt body with the concreke soul and the forequarters of the moon behinding out of his phase.
[122] Tomatoes malmalaid with De Quinceys salade can be tastily served with Indiana Blues on the violens.
[123] As Rhombulus and Rhebus went building rhomes one day.
[124] The trouveller.

suspecting the answer know. Oikkont, ken you, ninny? asks Kev,[125] expecting the answer guess.[126] Nor was the noer long disappointed for easiest of kisshams, he was made vicewise. Oc, tell it to oui, do, Sem! Well, 'tis oil thusly. First mull a mugfull of mud, son.[127] Oglores, the virtuoser prays, olorum! What the D.V. would I do that for? That's a goosey's ganswer you're for giving me, he is told, what the Deva would you do that for?[128] Now, sknow royol road to Puddlin, take your mut for a first beginning, big to bog, back to bach. Anny liffle mud which cometh out of Mam will doob, I guess. A.i. *Amnium instar.* And to find a locus for an alp get a howlth on her bayrings as a prisme O and for a second O unbox your compasses. I cain but are you able? Amicably nod. Gu it! So let's seth off betwain us. Prompty? Mux your pistany at a point of the coastmap to be called *a* but pronounced olfa. There's the isle of Mun, ah! O! Tis just. *Bene!* Now, whole in applepine odrer[129]

The aliments of jumeantry.

Wolsherwomens at their weirdst.

PROCUL IN THE CONVERGENCE OF THEIR CONTRAPULSIVENESS.

(for—husk, hisk, a spirit spires—Dolph, dean of idlers, meager suckling of gert stoan, though barekely a balbose boy, he too, — *venite, preteriti,*[130] *sine mora dumque de entibus nascituris decentius in lingua romana mortuorum parva chartula liviana ostenditur, sedentes in letitiae super ollas carnium, spectantes immo situm lutetiae unde auspiciis secundis tantae consurgent humanae stirpes, antiquissimam flaminum amborium Jordani et Jambaptistae mentibus revolvamus sapientiam: totum tute fluvii modo mundo fluere, eadem quae ex aggere fututa fuere iterum inter alveum fore futura, quodlibet sese ipsum per aliudpiam agnoscere contrarium, omnem demun amnem ripis rivalibus amplecti*[131] — recurrently often, when him moved he would cake their chair, coached rebelliumtending

[125] Of the disorded visage.

[126] Singlebarrelled names for doubleparalleled twixtytwins.

[127] Like pudging a spoon fist of sugans into a sotspot of choucolout.

[128] Will you walk into my wavetrap? said the spiter to the shy.

[129] If we each could always do all we ever did.

[130] Dope in Canorian words we've made. Spish from the Doc.

[131] Basqueesh, Finnican, Hungulash and Old Teangtaggle, the only pure way to work a curse.

mikes of his same and over his own choirage at Backlane Univarsity, among of which pupal souaves the pizdrool was pulled up, bred and battered, for a dillon a dollar,[132] chanching letters for them vice o'verse to bronze mottes and blending tschemes for em in tropadores and doublecressing twofold thruths and devising tingling tailwords too whilest, cunctant that another would finish his sentence for him, he druider would smilabit eggways[133] ned, he, to don't say nothing, would, so prim, and pick upon his ten ordinailed ungles, trying to undo with his teeth the knots made by his tongue, retelling humself by the math hour, long as he's brood, a reel of funnish ficts apout the shee, how faust of all and on segund thoughts and the thirds the charmhim girlalove and fourthermore and filthily with bag from Oxatown and baroccidents and proper accidence and hoptohill and hexenshoes, in fine the whole damning letter; and, in point of feet, when he landed in ourland's leinster[134] of saved and solomnones for the twicedhecame time, off Lipton's strongbowed launch, the *Lady Eva*, in a tan soute of sails[135] he converted it's nataves, name saints, young ordnands, maderaheads and old unguished P.T. Publikums, through the medium of znigznaks with sotiric zeal, to put off the barcelonas[136] from their peccaminous corpulums (Gratings, Mr Dane!) and kiss on their bottes (Master!) as often as they came within bloodshot of that other familiar temple and showed em the celestine way to by his tristar and his flop hattrick and his perry humdrum dumb and numb nostrums that he larned in Hymbuktu,[137] and that same galloroman cultous is very pre-vailend up to this windiest of landhavemiseries all over what was beforeaboots a land of nods, in spite of all the bloot, all the braim, all the brawn, all the brile, that was shod, that were shat, that was shuk all the while, for our massangrey if mosshungry people, the at Wickerworks,[138] still hold ford to their healing and[139] byleave in the old weights downupon the Swanny, innovated by him, the prence di Propagandi, the chrism for the christmass, the pillar of the

---

132 An ounceworth of onions for a pennyawealth of sobs.
133 Who brought us into the yellow world!
134 Because it's run on the mountain and river system.
135 When all them allied sloopers was ventitillated in their poppos and, sliding down by creek and veek, stole snaking out to sea.
136 They were plumped and plumed and jerried and citizens and racers, and cinnamondhued.
137 Creeping Crawleys petery parley, banished to his native Ireland from erring under Ryan.
138 Had our retrospectable fearfurther gatch mutchtatches?
139 That is to sight, when cleared of factions, vulgure and decimating.

perished and the rock o'ralereality, and it is veritably belied, we
belove, that not allsods of esoupcans that's in the queen's pottage post
and not allfinesof greendgold that the Indus contains would over-
hinduce them, (o.p.) to steeplechange back once from their ophis
workship and twice on sundises, to their ancient flash and crash
habits of old Pales time ere beam slewed cable[140] or Derzherr, live
wire, fired Benjermine Funkling outa th'Empyre, sin righthand son;
which, cummal, having listed curefully to the interlooking and the
underlacking of her twentynine shifts or his continental's curses,
pummel, apostrophised Byrne's and Flamming's and Furniss's and
Bill Hayses's and Ellishly Haught's, hoc, they (t.a.W.), sick or
whole, stiff or sober, let drop as a doombody drops, without
another ostrovgods word eitherways, in their own lineal descend-
ance, as priesto as puddywhack,[141] coal on:[142] and, as we gang
along to gigglehouse, talking of molniacs' manias and missions for
mades to scotch the schlang and leathercoats for murty magdies, of
course this has blameall in that medeoturanian world to say to
blessed by Pointer the Grace's his privates judgements[143] whenso to
put it, *disparito, duspurudo, desterrado, despertieu,* or, saving his
presents for his own onefriend Bevradge, Conn the Shaughraun; but
to return for a moment from the reptile's age[144] to the cox-
swain on the first landing (page Ainée Rivière!) if the pretty Lady
Elisabbess, Hotel des Ruines — she laid her batsleeve for him two
trueveres tell love (on the Ides of Valentino's, at Idleness, Floods
Area, Isolade, Liv's lonely daughter, with the Comes Tichiami, of
Prima Vista, Abroad, suddenly), and beauty alone of all dare say
when now, uncrowned, deceptered, in what niche of time[145]
is Shee or where in the rose world trysting, that was the belle
of La Chapelle, shapely Liselle, and the peg-of-my-heart of all
the tompull or on whose limbs-to-lave her semicupiose eyes now
kindling themselves are brightning,[146] O Shee who then
(4.32 M.P., old time, to be precise, according to all three doctors
waterburies that was Mac Auliffe and poor MacBeth and
poor MacGhimley to the tickleticks, of the synchronisms, all lausch-

140 They just spirits a body away.
141 Patatapadatback.
142 Dump her (the missuse).
143 Fox him! The leggy colt!
144 Do he not know that walleds had wars. Harring man, is neow king. This
is modeln times.
145 Muckross Abbey with the creepers taken off.
146 Joke and Jilt will have their tilt.

ening, a time also confirmed seven sincuries later by the quatren
medical johnny, poor old MacAdoo MacDollett, with notary,[147]
whose presence was required by law of Devine Foresygth and de-
cretal of the Douge) who after the first compliments[148] med darkist
day light, gave him then that vantage of a Blinkensope's cuddlebath
at her proper mitts — if she then, the then that matters, — but,
seigneur! she could never have forefelt, as she yet will fearfeel, when
the lovenext breaks out, such a coolcold douche as him, the totterer,
the four-flights-the-charmer, doubling back, in nowtime,[149] bymby
when saltwater he wush him these ißelands, *O alors!*, to mount miss
(the wooeds of Fogloot!) under that *chemise de fer* and a vartry-
proof name, Multalusi (would it wash?) with a cheek white peace-
ful as, wen shall say, a single professed claire's[150] and his washawash
tubatubtub and his diagonoser's lampblick, to pure where they
where hornest girls, to buy her in *par jure*, il you plait, nuncand-
tunc and for simper, and other duel mavourneens in plurible numbers from Arklow Vikloe to Louth super Luck, come messes, come
mams, and touch your spottprice (for 'twas he was the born
suborner, man) on behalf of an oldest ablished firma of winebakers,
Lagrima and Gemiti, later on, his craft ebbing, invoked by the
unirish title, Grindings of Nash,[151] the One and Only, Unic bar
None, of Saint Yves by Landsend cornwer, man — ship me silver!,
it must have been, faw! a terrible mavrue mavone, to synamite up
the old Adam-he-used-to, such a finalley, and that's flat as Tut's fut,
for whowghowho? the poour girl, a lonely peggy, given the bird, so
inseuladed as Crampton's peartree, (she sall eurn bitter bed by thirt
sweet of her face!), and short wonder so many of the tomthick and
tarry members in all there subsequious ages of our timocracy tipped
to console with her at her mirrorable gracewindow'd hut[152] till the
ives of Man, the O'Kneels and the O'Prayins and the O'Hyens of
Lochlaunstown and the O'Hollerins of Staneybatter, hollyboys, all,
burryripe who'll buy?,[153] in juwelietry and kickychoses and mad-
ornaments and that's not the finis of it (would it were!)—but to

[147] Old Mamalujorum and Rawrogerum.
[148] Why have these puerile blonds those large flexible ears?
[149] Pomeroy Roche of Portobello, or the Wreck of the Ragamuffin.
[150] No wonder Miss Dotsh took to veils and she descended from that
obloquohy.
[151] The bookley with the rusin's hat is Patomkin but I'm blowed if I knowed
who the slave is doing behind the curtain.
[152] O hce! O hce!
[153] Six and seven the League.

think of him foundling a nelliza the second,[154] also cliptbuss (the best was still there if the torso was gone) where he did and when he did, retriever to the last[155] — escapes my forgetness now was it dustcovered, *nom de Lieu!* on lapse or street ondown, through, for or from a foe, by with as on a friend, at the Rectory? Vicarage Road? Bishop's Folly? Papesthorpe?, after picket fences, stonewalls, out and ins or oxers — for merry a valsehood whisprit he to manny a lilying earling;[156] and to try to analyse that ambo's pair of braceleans akwart the rollyon trying to amarm all[157] of that miching micher's bearded but insensible virility and its gaulish moustaches, Dammad and Groany, into her limited (*tuff, tuff, que tu es pitre!*) lapse at the same slapse for towelling ends[158] in their dolightful Sexsex home, Somehow-at-Sea (O little oily head, sloper's brow and prickled ears!) as though he, a notoriety, a foist edition, were a wrigular writher neonovene babe![159] — well, diarmuee and granyou and *Vae Vinctis,* if that is what lamoor that of gentle breast rathe is intaken seems circling toward out yondest (it's life that's all chokered by that batch of grim rushers) heaven help his hindmost and, mark mo, if the so greatly displeaced diorems in the Saint Lubbock's Day number of that most improving of roundshows, *Spice and Westend Woman* (utterly exhausted before publication, indiapepper edition shortly), are for our indices, it agins to pear like it, par my fay, and there is no use for your pastripreaching for to cheesse it either or praying fresh fleshblood claspers of young catholick throats on Huggin Green[160] to take warning by the prispast, why?, by cows ∵ man, in shirt, is how he is *più la gonna è mobile* and ∴ they wonet do ut; and, an you could peep inside the cerebralised saucepan of this eer illwinded goodfornobody, you would see in his house of thoughtsam (was you, that is, decontaminated enough to look discarnate) what a jetsam litterage of convolvuli of times lost or strayed, of lands derelict and of tongues laggin too, longa yamsayore, not only that but, search lighting, beached, bashed and beaushelled *à la Mer* pharahead into faturity, your own convolvulis pickninnig

154 It's all round me hat I'll wear a drooping dido.
155 Have you ever thought of a hitching your stern and being ourdeaned, Mester Bootenfly, here's me and Myrtle is twinkling to know.
156 To show they caught preferment.
157 See the freeman's cuticatura by Fennella.
158 Just one big booty's pot.
159 Charles de Simples had an infirmierity complexe before he died a natural death.
160 Where Buickly of the Glass and Bellows pumped the Rudge engineral.

capman would real to jazztfancy the novo takin place of what stale
words whilom were woven with and fitted fairly featly for, so; and
equally so, the crame of the whole faustian fustian, whether your
launer's lightsome or your soulard's schwearmood, it is that, whenas
the swiftshut scareyss of our pupilteachertaut duplex will hark back
to lark to you symibellically that, though a day be as dense as a
decade, no mouth has the might to set a mearbound to the march of
a landsmaul,[161] in half a sylb, helf a solb, holf a salb onward[162]
the beast of boredom, common sense, lurking gyrographically down
inside his loose Eating S.S. collar is gogoing of whisth to you sternly
how — Plutonic loveliaks twinnt Platonic yearlings — you must, how,
in undivided reawlity draw the line somewhawre

Coss? Cossist? Your parn! You, you make
what name? (and in truth, as a poor soul is between shift and shift ere the death he has lived
through becomes the life he is to die into, he or
he had albut — he was rickets as to reasons but
the balance of his minds was stables — lost himself or himself some somnione sciupiones, sos-
whitchoverswetch had he or he gazet, murphy
come, murphy go, murphy plant, murphy grow,
a maryamyriameliamurphies, in the lazily eye of

WHY MY AS
LIKEWISE
WHIS HIS.

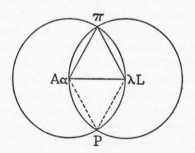

Uteralterance or
the Interplay of
Bones in the
Womb.

his lapis, Vieus Von DVbLIn, 'twas one of
dozedeams a darkies ding in dewood) the Turnpike under the Great Ulm (with Mearingstone
in Fore ground).[163] Given now ann linch you
take enn all. Allow me! And, heaving alljaw-

---

161 Matter of Brettaine and brut fierce.
162 Bussmullah, cried Lord Wolsley, how me Aunty Mag'll row!
163 Draumcondra's Dreamcountry where the betterlies blow.

breakical expressions out of old Sare Isaac's[164]

The Vortex.
Spring of
Sprung Verse.
The Vertex.

universal of specious aristmystic unsaid, A is
for Anna like L is for liv. Aha hahah, Ante Ann
you're apt to ape aunty annalive! Dawn gives
rise. Lo, lo, lives love! Eve takes fall. La, la,
laugh leaves alass! Aiaiaiai, Antiann, we're last
to the lost, Loulou! Tis perfect. Now (lens your
dappled yeye here, mine's presbyoperian, shill
and wall) we see the copyngink strayedline AL
(in Fig., the forest) from being continued, stops
ait Lambday[165]: Modder ilond there too. Allow
me anchore! I bring down noth and carry awe.
Now, then, take this in! One of the most mur-

Sarga, or the
path of outgoing.

murable loose carollaries ever Ellis threw his
cookingclass. With Olaf as centrum and Olaf's
lambtail for his spokesman circumscript a cy-
clone. Allow ter! Hoop! As round as the calf of
an egg! O, dear me! O, dear me now! Another
grand discobely! After Makefearsome's Ocean.
You've actuary entducked one! Quok! Why, you
haven't a passer! Fantastic! Early clever, surely
doomed, to Swift's, alas, the galehus! Match of

Docetism and
Didicism, Maya-
Thaya. Tamas-
Rajas-Sattvas.

a matchness, like your Bigdud dadder in the
boudeville song, *Gorotsky Gollovar's Troubles,*
raucking his flavourite turvku in the smukking
precincts of lydias,[166] with Mary Owens and
Dolly Monks seesidling to edge his cropulence
and Blake-Roche, Kingston and Dockrell auri-
scenting him from afurz, our papacocopotl,[167]
Abraham Bradley King? (ting ting! ting ting!)
By his magmasine fall. Lumps, lavas and all.[168]
Bene! But, thunder and turf, it's not alover yet!
One recalls Byzantium. The mystery repeats itself todate as our callback mother Gaudyanna,
that was daughter to a tanner,[169] used to sing,

---

[164] O, Laughing Sally, are we going to be toadhauntered by that old Pantifox
Sir Somebody Something, Burtt, for the rest of our secret stripture?

[165] Ex jup pep off Carpenger Strate. The kids' and dolls' home. Makeacake-
ache.

[166] A vagrant need is a flagrant weed.

[167] Grand for blowing off steam when you walk up in the morning.

[168] At the foot of Bagnabun Banbasday was lost on one.

[169] We're all found of our anmal matter.

as I think, now and then consinuously over her
possetpot in her quer homolocous humminbass
hesterdie and istherdie forivor.[170] Vanissas

*The Vegetable
Cell and its Pri-
vate Properties.*

Vanistatums! And for a night of thoughtsend-
yures and a day. As Great Shapesphere puns it.
In effect, I remumble, from the yules gone by,
purr lil murrerof myhind, so she used indeed.
When she give me the Sundaclouths she hung
up for Tate and Comyng and snuffed out the
ghost in the candle at his old game of haunt the
sleepper. Faithful departed. When I'm dreaming back like that I begins to see we're only all
telescopes. Or the comeallyoum saunds. Like
when I dromed I was in Dairy and was wuck-
ened up with thump in thudderdown. Rest in
peace! But to return.[171] What a wonderful
memory you have too! Twonderful morrowy!
Straorbinaire! *Bene!* I bring town eau and curry
nothung up my sleeve. Now, springing quick-
enly from the mudland Loosh from Luccan with
Allhim as her Elder tetraturn a somersault. All's
fair on all fours, as my instructor unstrict me.
Watch! And you'll have the whole inkle. Allow,
allow! Gyre O, gyre O, gyrotundo! Hop lala! As
umpty herum as you seat! O, dear me, that was
very nesse! Very nace indeed! And makes us a

*The haves and
the havenots: a
distinction.*

daintical pair of accomplasses! You, allus for the
kunst and me for omething with a handel to it.
Bevel Now, as will pressantly be felt, there's tew
tricklesome poinds where our twain of doubling
bicirculars, mating approxemetely in their suite
poi and poi, dunloop into eath the ocher. Luci-
here.! I fee where you mea. The doubleviewed
seeds. Nun, lemmas quatsch, vide pervoys ak-
stiom, and I think as I'm suqeez in the limon,
stickme punctum, but for semenal rations I'd
likelong, by Araxes, to mack a capital Pee for
Pride down there on the batom[172] where Hod-

---

[170] Sewing up the beillybursts in their buckskin shiorts for big Kapitayn
Killykook and the Jukes of Kelleiney.

[171] Say where! A timbrelfill of twinkletinkle.

[172] Parsee ffrench for the upholdsterer would be delightered.

*Zweispaltung as
Fundemaintalish
of Wiederher-
stellung.*

dum and Heave, our monsterbilker, balked his
bawd of parodies. And let you go, Airmienious,
and mick your modest mock Pie out of Humbles
up your end. Where your apexojesus will be a
point of order. With a geing groan grunt and a
croak click cluck.[173] And my faceage kink and
kurkle trying to make keek peep.[174] Are you
right there, Michael, are you right? Do you
think you can hold on by sitting tight? Well,
of course, it's awful angelous. Still I don't feel
it's so dangelous. Ay, I'm right here, Nickel,
and I'll write. Singing the top line why it
suits me mikey fine. But, yaghags hogwarts and
arrahquinonthiance, it's the muddest thick that
was ever heard dump since Eggsmather got
smothered in the plap of the pfan. Now, to com-
pleat anglers, beloved bironthiarn and hush-
tokan hishtakatsch, join alfa pea and pull loose
by dotties and, to be more sparematically logoi-
cal, eelpie and paleale by trunkles. Alow me
align while I encloud especious! The Nike done
it. Like pah,[175] I peh. Innate little bondery. And
as plane as a poke stiff.[176] Now, *aqua in buccat.*
I'll make you to see figuratleavely the whome of
your eternal geomater. And if you flung her
headdress on her from under her highlows you'd
wheeze whyse Salmonson set his seel on a hexen-
gown.[177] Hissss!, Arrah, go on! Fin for fun!
You've spat your shower like a son of Sibernia
but let's have at it! Subtend to me now! Pisk!
Outer serpumstances beiug ekewilled, we carefully, if she pleats, lift by her seam hem and
jabote at the spidsiest of her trickkikant (like
thousands done before since fillies calpered.
Ocone! Ocone!) the maidsapron of our A.L.P.,
fearfully! till its nether nadir is vortically where
(allow me aright to two cute winkles) its naval's

*Destiny, In-
fluence of De-
sign upon.*

---

[173] I'll pass out if the screw spliss his strut.
[174] Thargam then goeligum? If you sink I can, swimford. Suksumkale!
[175] Hasitatense?
[176] The impudence of that in girl's things!
[177] The chape of Doña Speranza of the Nacion.

*Prometheus or
the Promise of
Provision.*

napex will have to beandbe. You must proach
near mear for at is dark. Lob. And light your
mech. Jeldy! And this is what you'll say.[178]
Waaaaaa. Tch! Sluice! Pla! And their, redneck,
(for addn't we to gayatsee with Puhl the Pun-
kah's bell?) mygh and thy, the living spit of
dead waters,[179] fastness firm of Hurdlebury
Fenn, discinct and isoplural in its (your sow to
the duble) sixuous parts, flument, fluvey and
fluteous, midden wedge of the stream's your
muddy old triagonal delta, fiho miho, plain for
you now, appia lippia pluvaville, (hop the hula,
girls!) the no niggard spot of her safety vulve,
first of all usquiluteral threeingles, (and why
wouldn't she sit cressloggedlike the lass that
lured a tailor?) the constant of fluxion, Ma-
hamewetma, pride of the province[180] and when
that tidled boare rutches up from the Afrantic,

*Ambages and
Their Rôle.*

allaph quaran's his bett und bier![181] Paa lickam
laa lickam, apl lpa! This it is an her. You see
her it. Which it whom you see it is her. And if
you could goaneggbetter we'd soon see some raf-
fant scrumala riffa. Quicks herit fossyending.
Quef! So post that to your pape and smarket!
And you can haul up that languil pennant,
mate. I've read your tunc's dimissage. For, let it
be taken that her littlenist is of no magnetude
or again let it be granted that Doll the laziest can
be dissimulant with all respects from Doll the
fiercst, thence must any whatyoulike in the

*Ecclasiastical
and Celestial
Hierarchies. The
Ascending. The
Descending.*

power of empthood be either greater THan
or less tHaN the unitate we have in one or
hence shall the vectorious readyeyes of evertwo
circumflicksrent searclhers never film in the
elipsities of their gyribouts those fickers which
are returnally reprodictive of themselves.[182]

---

[178] Ugol egal ogle. Mi vidim Mi.
[179] It is, it is Sangannon's dream.
[180] And all meinkind.
[181] Whangpoos the paddle and whiss whee whoo.
[182] I enjoy as good as anyone.

Which is unpassible. Quarrellary. The logos of somewome to that base anything, when most characteristically mantissa minus, comes to nullum in the endth:[183] orso, here is nowet badder than the sin of Aha with his cosin Lil, verswaysed on coverswised, and all that's consecants and cotangincies till Perperp stops reppinghim since her redtangles are all abscissan for limitsing this tendency of our Frivulteeny

The peripatetic periphery. It's Allothesis.

Sexuagesima[184] to expense herselfs as sphere as possible, paradismic perimutter, in all directions on the bend of the unbridalled, the infinisissimalls of her facets becoming manier and manier as the calicolum of her umdescribables (one has thoughts of that eternal Rome) shrinks from schurtiness to scherts.[185] Scholium, there are trist sigheds to everysing but ichs on the freed brings euchs to the feared. Qued? Mother of us all! O, dear me, look at that now! I don't know is it your spictre or my omination but I'm glad you dimentioned it! My Lourde! My Lourde! If that aint just the beatenest lay I ever see! And a superpbosition! Quoint a quincidence! O.K.

Canine Venus sublimated to Aulidic Aphrodite.

Omnius Kollidimus. As Ollover Krumwall sayed when he slepped ueber his grannyamother. Kangaroose feathers. Who in the name of thunder'd ever belevin you were that bolt? But you're holy mooxed and gaping up the wrong palce[186] as if you was seeheeing the gheist that stays forenenst, you blessed simpletop domefool! Where's your belested loiternan's lamp? You must lap wandret down the bluishing refluction below. Her trunk's not her brainbox. Hear where the bolgylines, Yseen here the puncture.

Exclusivism: the Ors, Sors and Fors, which?

So he done it. Luck! See her good. Well, well, well, well! O dee, O dee, that's very lovely! We like Simperspreach Hammeltones to fellow

[183] Neither a soul to be saved nor a body to be kicked.
[184] The boast of the town.
[185] Hen's bens, are we soddy we missiled her?
[186] I call that a scumhead.

Selvertunes O'Haggans.[187] When he rolls over his ars and shows the hise of his heels. Vely lovely entilely! Like a yangsheepslang with the tsifengtse. So analytical plausible! And be the powers of Moll Kelly, neighbour topsowyer, it will be a lozenge to me all my lauffe.[188] More better twofeller we been speak copperads. Ever thought about Guinness's? And the regrettable Parson Rome's advice? Want to join the police.[189] You know, you were always one of the bright ones, since a foot made you an unmentionable, fakes! You know, you're the divver's own smart gossoon, aequal to yoursell and wanigel to anglyother, so you are, hoax! You know, you'll be dampned, so you will, one of these invernal days but you will be, carrotty![190]

Primanouriture and Ultimo-geniture.

Wherapool, gayet that when he stop look time he stop long ground who here hurry he would have ever the lothst word, with a sweet me ah err eye ear marie to reat from the jacob's[191] and a shypull for toothsake of his armjaws at the slidepage of de Vere Foster, would and could candykissing P. Kevin to fress up the rinnerung and to ate by hart (*leo* I read, such a spanish, *escribibis,* all your mycoscoups) wont to nibbleh ravenostonnoriously ihs mum to me in bewonderment of his chipper chuthor for, while that Other by the halp of his creactive mind offered to deleberate the mass from the booty of fight our Same with the holp of the bounty of food sought to delubberate the mess from his corructive mund, with his muffetee cuffes ownconsciously grafficking with his sinister cyclopes after trigamies and spirals' wobbles pursuiting their rovinghamilton selves and godolphin in

SICK US A SOCK WITH SOME SEDIMENT IN IT FOR THE SAKE OF OUR DARNING WIVES.

[187] Pure chingchong idiotism with any way words all in one soluble. Gee each owe tea eye smells fish. That's U.

[188] The Doodles family, ⊓,△,⊣,✕,□,∧,⊏. Hoodle doodle, fam.?

[189] Picking on Nickagain, Pikey Mikey?

[190] Early morning, sir Dav Stephens, said the First Gentleman in youreups.

[191] Bag bag blockcheap, have you any will?

fairlove to see around the waste of noland's
browne jesus[192] (thur him no quartos!) till that
on him poorin sweat the juggaleer's veins
(quench his quill!) in his napier scrag stud out
bursthright tamquam taughtropes. (Spry him!
call a bloodlekar! Where's Dr Brassenaarse?) Es
war itwas in his priesterrite. O He Must Suffer!
From this misbelieving feacemaker to his non-
credible fancyflame.[193] Ask for bosthoon, late
for Mass, pray for blaablaablack sheep. (Sure
you could wright anny pippap passage, Eye bet,
as foyne as that moultylousy Erewhig, yerself,
mick! Nock the muddy nickers![194] Christ's
Church varses Bellial!) Dear and he went on
to scripple gentlemine born, milady bread, he
would pen for her, he would pine for her,[195]
how he would patpun fun for all[196] with his
frolicky frowner so and his glumsome grinner
otherso. And how are you, waggy?[197] My animal
his sorrafool! And trieste, ah trieste ate I my
liver! *Se non é vero son trovatore.* O jerry! He
was soso, harriot all! He was sadfellow, steifel!
He was mistermysterion. Like a purate out of
pensionee with a gouvernament job. All moan-
day, tearsday, wailsday, thumpsday, frightday,
shatterday till the fear of the Law. Look at this
twitches! He was quisquis, floored on his plank-
raft of shittim wood. Look at him! Sink deep
or touch not the Cartesian spring! Want more
ashes, griper? How diesmal he was lying low
on his rawside laying siege to goblin castle. And,
bezouts that, how hyenesmeal he was laying
him long on his laughside lying sack to croak-
partridge. (Be thou wars Rolaf's intestions,

*No Sturm. No
Drang.
Illustration.*

*Ascription of
the Active.*

*Proscription of
the Passive.*

---

[192] What a lubberly whide elephant for the men-in-the straits!
[193] And she had to seek a pond's apeace to salve her suiterkins. Sued!
[194] Excuse theyre christianbrothers irish?
[195] When she tripped against the briery bush he profused her allover with
curtsey flowers.
[196] A nastilow disigraible game.
[197] Dear old Erosmas. Very glad you are going to Penmark. Write to the
corner. Grunny Grant.

quoths the Bhagavat biskop Leech) Ann opes
tipoo soon ear! If you could me lendtill my pas-
col's kondyl, sahib, and the price of a plate of
poultice. Punked. With best apolojigs and
merrymoney thanks to self for all the clerricals

*Ensouling Fe-
male Sustains
Agonising
Overman.*

and again begs guerdon for bistrispissing on
your bunificence. Well wiggywiggywagtail, and
how are you, yaggy? With a capital Tea for
Thirst. From here Buvard to dear Picuchet.
Blott.

Now, (peel your eyes, my gins, and brush
your saton hat, me elementator joyclid, son of
a Butt! She's mine, Jow low jure,[198] be Skibber-
ing's eagles, sweet tart of Whiteknees Archway)
watch him, having caught at the bifurking cala-
mum in his bolsillos, the onelike underworp
he had ever funnet without difficultads, the
aboleshqvick, signing away in happinext com-

WHEN THE
ANSWERER
IS A LEMAN.

*Sesama to the
Rescues. The
Key Signature.*

plete, (Exquisite Game of inspiration! I always
adored your hand. So could I too and without
the scrope of a pen. Ohr for oral, key for crib,
olchedolche and a lunge ad lib. Can you write
us a last line? From Smith-Jones-Orbison?) in-
trieatedly in years, jirryalimpaloop. And i Ro-
main, hup u bn gd grl.[199] Unds alws my thts.
To fallthere at bare feet hurryaswormarose. Two
dies of one rafflement. Eche bennyache. Out-
stamp and distribute him at the expanse of his
society. To be continued. Anon.

And ook, ook, ook, fanky! All the charic-
tures[200] in the drame! This is how San holy-
polypools. And this, pardonsky! is the way
Romeopullupalleaps.[201] Pose the pen, man, way
me does. Way ole missa vellatooth fust show me
how. Fourth power to her illpogue! Bould strokes

ALL SQUARE
AND
ACCORDING
TO COCKER.

[198] I loved to see the Macbeths Jerseys knacking spots of the Plumpduffs
Pants.

[199] Lifp year fends you all and moe, fouvenirs foft as fummer fnow, fweet
willings and forget-uf-knots.

[200] Gag his tubes yourself.

[201] He, angel that I thought him, and he not aebel to speel eelyotripes., Mr
Tellibly Divilcult!

for your life! Tip! This is Steal, this is Barke, this is Starn, this is Swhipt, this is Wiles, this is Pshaw, this is Doubbllinnbbayyates.[202] This is brave Danny weeping his spache for the popers. This is cool Connolly wiping his hearth with brave Danny. And this, regard! how Chawleses Skewered parparaparnelligoes between brave Danny boy and the Connolly. Upanishadem! Top. Spoken hath L'arty Magory. Eregobragh. Prouf![203]

And Kev was wreathed with his pother.

But, (that Jacoby feeling again for forebitten fruit and, my Georgeous, Kevvy too he just loves his puppadums, I judge!) after all his autocratic writings of paraboles of famellicurbs and meddlied muddlingisms, thee faroots hof cullchaw

end ate citrawn woodint wun able rep of the triperforator awlrite blast through his pergaman hit him where he lived and do for the blessted selfchuruls, what I think, smarter like it done for a manny another unpious of the hairydary quare quandary firstings till at length, you one bladdy bragger, by mercystroke he measured his earth anyway? could not but recken in his adder's badder cadder way our frankson who, to be plain, he fight him all time twofeller longa kill dead finish bloody face blong you, was misocain. Wince wan's won! Rip![204] And his countinghands rose.

Formalisa. Loves deathhow simple! Slutningsbane[205].

Thanks eversore much, Pointcarried! I can't say if it's the weight you strike me to the quick or that red mass I was looking at but at the present momentum, potential as I am, I'm seeing rayingbogeys rings round me. Honours to you and may you be commended for our exhibitive-

TROTHBLOWERS. FIG AND THISTLE PLOT A PIG AND WHISTLE.

WITH EBONISER. IN PIX. EUCHRE RISK, MERCI BUCKUP, AND MIND WHO YOU'RE PUCKING, FLEBBY.

---

[202] When the dander rattles how the peacocks prance!
[203] The Brownes de Browne - Browne of Castlehacknolan.
[204] A byebye bingbang boys! See you Nutcracker Sunday!
[205] Chinchin Childaman! Chapchopchap!

ness! I'd love to take you for a bugaboo ride and play funfer all if you'd only sit and be the ballasted bottle in the porker barrel. You will deserve a rolypoly as long as from here to tomorrow. And to hell with them driftbombs and bottom trailers! If my maily was bag enough I'd send you a toxis. By Saxon Chromaticus, you done that lovely for me! Didn't he now, Nubilina? Tiny Mite, she studiert whas? With her listeningin coiffure, her dream of Endsland's daylast and the glorifires of being presainted maid to majesty.[206] And less is the pity for she isn't the lollypops she easily might be if she had for a sample Virginia's air of achievement. That

Catastrophe and Anabasis.

might keep her from throwing delph.[207] As I was saying, while retorting thanks, you make me a reborn of the cards. We're offals boys ambows.[208] For I've flicked up all the crambs as they crumbed from your table um, singing glory allaloserem, cog it out, here goes a sum. So read we in must book. It tells. He prophets most who bilks the best.

The rotary processus and its reestablishment of reciprocities.

And that salubrated sickenagiaour of yaours have teaspilled all my hazeydency. Forge away, Sunny Sim! Sheepshopp. Bleating Goad, it is the least of things, Eyeinstye! Imagine it, my deep dartry dullard! It is hours giving, not more. I'm only out for celebridging over the guilt of the gap in your hiscitendency. You are a hundred thousand times welcome, old wortsampler, hellbeit you're just about as culpable as my woolfell merger would be. In effect I could engage in an energument over you till you were republicly royally toobally prussic blue in the shirt after.[209] *Trionfante di bestia!* And if you're not your bloater's kipper may I never curse again on

The Twofold Truth and the Conjunctive Appetites of Oppositional Orexes.

COME SI COMPITA CUNCTITI-TITILATIO? CONKERY CUNK, THIGH-THIGHT-TICKELLY-THIGH, LIG-GERILAG, TITTERITOT, LEG IN A TEE, LUG IN A LAW, TWO AT A TIE, THREE ON A

---

[206] Wipe your glosses with what you know.

[207] If I'd more in the cups that peeves thee you could cracksmith your rows tureens.

[208] Alls Sings and Alls Howls.

[209] From three shellings. A bluedye sacrifice.

that pint I took of Jamesons. Old Keane now,
you're rod, hook and sinker, old jubalee Keane!
Biddy's hair. Biddy's hair, mine lubber. Where
is that Quin but he sknows it knot but what you
that are my popular endphthisis were born with

Trishagion. a solver arm up your sleep. Thou in shanty!
Thou in scanty shanty!! Thou in slanty scanty
shanty!!! Bide in your hush! Bide in your hush,
do! The law does not aloud you to shout. I plant
my penstock in your postern, chinarpot. Ave!
And let it be to all remembrance. Vale. Ovoca-
tion of maiding waters.[210] For auld lang salvy
steyne. I defend you to champ my scullion's
praises. To book alone belongs the lobe. Fore-
master's meed[211] will mark tomorrow when we
are making pilscrummage to whaboggeryin with
staff, scarf and blessed wallet and our aureoles
round our neckkandcropfs where as and when
Heavysciusgardaddy, parent who offers sweet-
meats, will gift uns his Noblett's surprize. With
Abnegation is this laudable purpose in loud ability let us be
Adaptation. singulfied. Betwixt me and thee hung cong.
Item, mizpah ends.

But while the dial are they doodling dawdling
over the mugs and the grubs? Oikey, Imposto-
lopulos?[212] Steady steady steady steady steady
studiavimus. Many many many many many
manducabimus.[213] We've had our day at triv
and quad and writ our bit as intermidgets. Art,
literature, politics, economy, chemistry, human-
Cato. ity, &c. Duty, the daughter of discipline, the
Nero. Great Fire at the South City Markets, Belief in
Saul. Aristotle. Giants and the Banshee, A Place for Everything
Julius Caesar. and Everything in its Place, Is the Pen Mightier
Pericles. than the Sword? A Successful Career in the
Ovid. Civil Service,[214] The Voice of Nature in the
Adam, Eve.

210 Not Kilty. But the manajar was. He! He! Ho! Ho! Ho!
211 Giglamps, Soapy Geyser, The Smell and Gory M   Gusty.
212 The divvy wants that babbling brook. Dear Auntie Emma Emma Eates.
213 Strike the day off, the nightcap's on nigh. Goney, goney gone!
214 R. C., disengaged, good character, would help, no salary.

Domitian.
Edipus.
Socrates.
Ajax.

Homer.
MarcusAurelius.

Alcibiades.
Lucretius.
Noah. Plato.
Horace. Isaac.
Tiresias.
Marius.
Diogenes.
Procne, Philo-
mela. Abraham.
Nestor. Cincin-
natus. Leonidas.
Jacob.
Theocritus.
Joseph.
Fabius. Samson.
Cain.
Esop.
Prometheus.
Lot. Pompeius Magnus,
Miltiades Strategos.
Solon.
Castor, Pollux.
Dionysius.
Sappho.
Moses. Job.

Forest,[215] Your Favorite Hero or Heroine, On the Benefits of Recreation,[216] If Standing Stones Could Speak, Devotion to the Feast of the Indulgence of Portiuncula, The Dublin Metropolitan Police Sports at Ballsbridge, Describe in Homely Anglian Monosyllables the Wreck of the Hesperus,[217] What Morals, if any, can be drawn from Diarmuid and Grania?[218] Do you Approve of our Existing Parliamentary System? The Uses and Abuses of Insects, A Visit to Guinness' Brewery, Clubs, Advantages of the Penny Post, When is a Pun not a Pun? Is the Co-Education of Animus and Anima Wholly Desirable?[219] What Happened at Clontarf? Since our Brother Johnathan Signed the Pledge or the Meditations of Two Young Spinsters,[220] Why we all Love our Little Lord Mayor, Hengler's Circus Entertainment, On Thrift,[221] The Kettle-Griffith-Moynihan Scheme for a New Electricity Supply, Travelling in the Olden Times,[222] American Lake Poetry, the Strangest Dream that was ever Halfdreamt.[223] Circumspection, Our Allies the Hills, Are Parnellites Just towards Henry Tudor? Tell a Friend in a Chatty Letter the Fable of the Grasshopper and the Ant,[224] Santa Claus, The Shame of Slumdom, The Roman Pontiffs and the Orthodox Churches,[225] The Thirty Hour Week, Compare the Fistic Styles of Jimmy Wilde and Jack Sharkey, How to Understand the Deaf, Should Ladies learn Music or Mathematics? Glory be to Saint

[215] Where Lily is a Lady found the nettle rash.
[216] Bubabipibambuli, I can do as I like with what's me own. Nyamnyam.
[217] Able seaman's caution.
[218] Rarely equal and distinct in all things.
[219] Jests and the Beastalk with a little rude hiding rod.
[220] Wherry like the whaled prophet in a spookeerie.
[221] What sins is pim money sans Paris?
[222] I've lost the place, where was I?
[223] Something happened that time I was asleep, torn letters or was there snow?
[224] Mich for his pain, Nick in his past.
[225] He has *toglieresti in brodo* all over his agrammatical parts of face and as for that hippofoxphiz, unlucky number, late for the christening!

Catilina. Patrick! What is to be found in a Dustheap,
Cadmus. Ezekiel. The Value of Circumstantial Evidence,
Solomon. The- Should Spelling? Outcasts in India, Collecting
mistocles. Pewter, Eu,[226] Proper and Regular Diet Neces-
Vitellius. Darius. sity For,[227] If You Do It Do It Now. Delays are
Dangerous. Vitavite! Gobble Anne: tea's set,
Xenophon. see's eneugh! Mox soonly will be in a split sec-
ond per the chancellory of his exticker.

Pantocracy. Aun   MAWMAW,
Bimutualism. Do   LUK, YOUR
Interchangeabil- Tri   BEEEFTAY'S
ity. Naturality. Car   FIZZIN OVER!
Superfetation. Cush[228]
Stabimobilism. Shay
Periodicity. Shockt
Consummation. Ockt
Interpenetrative- Ni
ness. Predica- Geg[229]
ment. Balance of Their feed begins.
the factual by the   KAKAO-
theoric Boox and   POETIC
Coox, Amallaga-   LIPPUDENIES
mated.   OF THE
          UNGUMP-
          TIOUS.

NIGHTLETTER

With our best youlldied greedings to Pep and
Memmy and the old folkers below and beyant,
wishing them all very merry Incarnations in this
land of the livvey and plenty of preprosperous-
ness through their coming new yonks

from
jake, jack and little sousoucie
(the babes that mean too)

226 Eh, Monsieur? Où, Monsieur? Eu, Monsieur? Nenni No, Monsieur!

227 Ere we hit the hay, brothers, let's have that response to prayer!

228 Kish is for anticheirst, and the free of my hand to him!

229 And gags for skool and crossbuns and whopes he'll enjoy-
imsolff over our drawings on the line!

It may not or maybe a no concern of the Guinnesses but.

That the fright of his light in tribalbalbutience hides aback in the doom of the balk of the deaf but that the height of his life from a bride's eye stammpunct is when a man that means a mountain barring his distance wades a lymph that plays the lazy winning she likes yet that pride that bogs the party begs the glory of a wake while the scheme is like your rumba round me garden, allatheses, with perhelps the prop of a prompt to them, was now or never in Etheria Deserta, as in Grander Suburbia, with Finnfannfawners, ruric or cospolite, for much or moment indispute.

Whyfor had they, it is Hiberio-Miletians and Argloe-Noremen, donated him, birth of an otion that was breeder to sweatoslaves, as mysterbolder, forced in their waste, and as for Ibdullin what of Himana, that their tolvtubular high fidelity daildialler, as modern as tomorrow afternoon and in appearance up to the minute, (hearing that anybody in that ruad duchy of Wollinstown schemed to halve the wrong type of date) equipped with supershielded umbrella antennas for distance getting and connected by the magnetic links of a Bellini-Tosti coupling system with a vitaltone speaker, capable of capturing skybuddies, harbour craft emittences, key clickings, vaticum cleaners, due to woman formed mobile or man made static and bawling the whowle hamshack and wobble down in an eliminium sounds pound so as to serve him up a melegoturny marygoraumd, eclectrically filtered for allirish earths and ohmes. This harmonic condenser enginium (the Mole) they caused to be worked from a magazine battery (called the Mimmim Bimbim patent number 1132, Thorpetersen and Synds, Jomsborg, Selverbergen) which was tuned up by twintriodic singulvalvulous pipelines (lackslipping along as if their liffing deepunded on it) with a howdrocephalous enlargement, a gain control of circumcentric megacycles, ranging from the anti-

dulibnium onto the serostaatarean. They finally caused, or most least-
ways brung it about somehows, (that) the pip of the lin (to) pin-
natrate inthro an auricular forfickle (known as the Vakingfar
sleeper, monofractured by Piaras UaRhuamhaighaudhlug, tympan
founder, Eustache Straight, Bauliaughacleeagh) a meatous conch
culpable of cunduncing Naul and Santry and the forty routs of
Corthy with the concertiums of the Brythyc Symmonds Guild, the
Ropemakers Reunion, the Variagated Peddlars Barringoy Bni-
brthirhd, the Askold Olegsonder Crowds of the O'Keef-Rosses and
Rhosso-Keevers of Zastwoking, the Ligue of Yahooth o.s.v. so as
to lall the bygone dozed they arborised around, up his corpular
fruent and down his reuctionary buckling, hummer, enville and
cstorrap (the man of Iren, thore's Curlymane for you!), lill the lub-
berendth of his otological life.

   House of call is all their evenbreads though its cartomance hal-
lucinate like an erection in the night the mummery of whose deed, a
lur of Nur, immerges a mirage in a merror, for it is where by muz-
zinmessed for one watthour, bilaws below, till time jings pleas, that
host of a bottlefilled, the bulkily hulkwight, hunter's pink of face,
an orel orioled, is in on a bout to be unbulging an o'connell's, the
true one, all seethic, a luckybock, pledge of the stoup, whilom his
canterberry bellseyes wink wickeding indtil the teller, oyne of an
oustman in skull of skand. Yet is it, this ale of man, for him, our
hubuljoynted, just a tug and a fistful as for Culsen, the Pata-
goreyan, chieftain of chokanchuckers and his moyety joyant, under
the foamer dispensation when he pullupped the turfeycork by the
greats of gobble out of Lougk Neagk. When, pressures be to our
hoary frother, the pop gave his sullen bulletaction and, bilge, sled a
movement of catharic emulsipotion down the sloppery slide of a
slaunty to tilted lift-ye-landsmen. Allamin. Which in the ambit of its
orbit heaved a sink her sailer alongside of a drink her drainer from
the basses brothers, those two theygottheres.

   It was long after once there was a lealand in the luffing ore it was
less after lives thor a toyler in the tawn at all ohr it was note before
he drew out the moddle of Kersse by jerkin his dressing but and or it
was not before athwartships he buttonhaled the Norweeger's
capstan.

   So he sought with the lobestir claw of his propencil the clue of
the wickser in his ear. O, lord of the barrels, comer forth from Anow
(I have not mislaid the key of Efas-Taem), O, Ana, bright lady,

comer forth from Thenanow (I have not left temptation in the path of the sweeper of the threshold), O!

But first, strongbowth, they would deal death to a drinking. Link of a leadder, dubble in it, slake your thirdst thoughts awake with it. Our svalves are svalves aroon! We rescue thee, O Baass, from the damp earth and honour thee. O Connibell, with mouth burial! So was done, neat and trig. Up draught and whet them!

— Then sagd he to the ship's husband. And in his translatentic norjankeltian. Hwere can a ketch or hook alive a suit and sowterkins? Soot! sayd the ship's husband, knowing the language, here is tayleren. Ashe and Whitehead, closechop, successor to. Ahorror, he sayd, canting around to that beddest his friend, the tayler, for finixed coulpure, chunk pulley muchy chink topside numpa one sellafella, fake an capstan make and shoot! Manning to sayle of clothse for his lady her master whose to be precised of a peer of trouders under the pattern of a cassack. Let me prove, I pray thee, but this once, sazd Mengarments, saving the mouthbrand from his firepool. He spit in his faist (beggin): he tape the raw baste (paddin): he planked his pledge (as dib is a dab): and he tog his fringe sleeve (buthock lad, fur whale). Alloy for allay and this toolth for that soolth. Lick it and like it. A barter, a parter. And plenty good enough, neighbour Norreys, every bit and grain. And the ship's husband brokecurst after him to hail the lugger. Stolp, tief, stolp, come bag to Moy Eireann! And the Norweeger's capstan swaradeed, some blowfish out of schooling: All lykkehud! Below taiyor he ikan heavin sets. But they broken waters and they made whole waters at they surfered bark to the lots of his vauce. And aweigh he yankered on the Norgean run so that seven sailend sonnenrounders was he breastbare to the brinabath, where bottoms out has fatthoms full, fram Franz José Land til Cabo Thormendoso, evenstarde and risingsoon. Up the Rivor Tanneiry and down the Golfe Desombres. Farety days and fearty nights. Enjoy yourself, O maremen! And the tides made, veer and haul, and the times marred, rear and fall, and, holey bucket, dinned he raign!

— Hump! Hump! bassed the broaders-in-laugh with a quick piddysnip that wee halfbit a second.

— I will do that, sazd Kersse, mainingstaying the rigout for her wife's lairdship. Nett sew? they hunched back at the earpicker.

But old sporty, as endth lord, in ryehouse reigner, he nought feared crimp or cramp of shore sharks, plotsome to getsome. It was whol niet godthaab of errol Loritz off his Cape of Good Howthe

and his trippertrice loretta lady, a maomette to his monetone, with
twy twy twinky her stone hairpins, only not, if not, a queen of
Prancess their telling tabled who was for his seeming a casket
through the heavenly, nay, heart of the sweet (had he hows would
he keep her as niece as a fiddle!) but in the mealtub it was wohl yeas
sputsbargain what, rarer of recent, an occasional conformity, he,
with Muggleton Muckers, alwagers allalong most certainly allowed,
as pilerinnager's grace to petitionists of right, of the three blend cup-
stoomerries with their customed spirits, the Gill gob, the Burklley
bump, the Wallisey wanderlook, having their ceilidhe gailydhe in
his shaunty irish. Group drinkards maaks grope thinkards or how
reads rotary, jewr of a chrestend, respecting the otherdogs churchees,
so long plubs will be plebs but plabs by low frequency amplification
may later agree to have another. For the people of the shed are the
sure ads of all quorum. Lorimers and leathersellers, skinners and
salters, pewterers and paperstainers, parishclerks, fletcherbowyers,
girdlers, mercers, cordwainers and first, and not last, the weavers.
Our library he is hoping to ye public.
　　Innholder, upholder.
　　— Sets on sayfohrt! Go to it, agitator! they bassabosuned over the
flowre of their hoose. Godeown moseys and skeep thy beeble bee!
　　— I will do that, acordial, by mine hand, sazd Kersse, piece Cod,
and in the flap of a jacket, ructified after his nap of a blankit their
o'cousin, as sober as the ship's husband he was one my godfather
when he told me saw whileupon I am now well and jurily sagasfide
after the boonamorse the widower, according to rider, following pno-
moneya, he is consistently blown to Adams. So help me boyg who
keeps the book!
　　Whereofter, behest his suzerain law the Thing and the pilsener
had the baar, Recknar Jarl, (they called him Roguenor, Irl call
him) still passing the change-a-pennies, pengeypigses, a several sort
of coyne in livery, pushed their whisper in his hairing, (seemed, a
some shipshep's sottovoxed stalement, a dearagadye, to hasvey anyone doing duty for duff point of dorkland compors) the same to the
good ind ast velut discharge after which he had exemptied more than
orphan for the ballast of his nurtural life. And threw a cast. A few
pigses and hare you are and no chicking, tribune's tribute, if you
guess mimic miening. Meanly in his lewdbrogue take your tyon
coppels token, with this good sixtric from mine runbag of juwels.
Nummers that is summus that is toptip that is bottombay that is Two-

meys that is Digges that is Heres. In the frameshape of hard mettles. For we all would fain make glories. It is minely well mint.

Thus as count the costs of liquid courage, a bullyon gauger, stowed stivers pengapung in bulk in hold (fight great finnence! brayvoh, little bratton!) keen his kenning, the queriest of the crew, with that fellow fearing for his own misshapes, should he be himpself namesakely a foully fallen dissentant from the peripulator, sued towerds Meade-Reid and Lynn-Duff, rubbing the hodden son of a pookal, leaden be light, lather be dry and it be drownd on all the ealsth beside, how the camel and where the deiffel or when the finicking or why the funicking, who caused the scaffolding to be first removed you give orders, babeling, were their reidey meade answer when on the cutey (the correspondent) in conflict of evidence drew a kick at witness but (missed) and for whom in the dyfflun's kiddy removed the planks they were wanted, boob.

Bump!

Bothallchoractorschumminaroundgansumuminarumdrumstrumtruminahumptadumpwaultopoofooloooderamaunsturnup!

—Did do a dive, aped one.

—Propellopalombarouter, based two.

—Rutsch is for rutterman ramping his roe, seed three. Where the muddies scrimm ball. Bimbim bimbim. And the maidies scream all. Himhim himhim.

And forthemore let legend go lore of it that mortar scene so cwympty dwympty what a dustydust it razed arboriginally but, luck's leap to the lad at the top of the ladder, so sartor's risorted why the sinner the badder! Ho ho ho hoch! La la la lach! Hillary rillarry gibbous grist to our millery! A pushpull, qq: quiescence, pp: with extravent intervulve coupling. The savest lauf in the world. Paradoxmutose caring, but here in a present booth of Ballaclay, Barthalamou, where their dutchuncler mynhosts and serves them dram well right for a boors' interior (homereek van hohmryk) that salve that selver is to screen its auntey and has ringround as worldwise eve her sins (pip, pip, pip) willpip futurepip feature apip footloose pastcast with spareshins and flash substittles of noirse-made-earsy from a nephew mind the narrator but give the devil his so long as those sohns of a blitzh call the tuone tuone and thonder alout makes the thurd. Let there be. Due.

—That's all murtagh purtagh but whad ababs his dopter? sissed they who were onetime ungkerls themselves, (when the youthel of his yorn shook the bouchal in his bed) twilled alongside in wiping the rice assatiated with their wetting. The lappel of his size? His *ros in sola velnere* and he sicckumed of homnis terrars. She wends to scoulas in her slalpers. There were no peanats in her famalgia so no wumble she tumbled for his famas roalls davors. Don't him forget! A butcheler artsed out of Cullege Trainity. Diddled he daddle a drop of the cradler on delight mebold laddy was stetched? Knit wear? And they addled, (or ere the cry of their tongues would be uptied dead) Shufflebotham asidled, plus his ducks fore his drills, an inlay of a liddle more lining maught be licensed all at ones, be these same tokens, forgiving a brass rap, sneither a whole length nor a short shift so full as all were concerned.

Burniface, shiply efter, shoply after, at an angle of lag, let flow, brabble brabble and brabble, and so hostily, heavyside breathing, came up with them and, check me joule, shot the three tailors, butting back to Moyle herring, bump as beam and buttend, roller and reiter, after the diluv's own deluge, the seasant samped as skibber breezed in, tripping, dripping, threw the sheets in the wind, the tights of his trunks at tickle to tackle and his rubmelucky truss rehorsing the pouffed skirts of his overhawl. He'd left his stickup in his hand to show them none ill feeling. Whatthough for all appentices it had a mushroom on it. While he faced them front to back, Then paraseuls round, quite taken atack, sclaiming, Howe cools Eavybrolly!

— Good marrams, sagd he, freshwatties and boasterdes all, as he put into bierhiven, nogeysokey first, cabootle segund, jilling to windwards, as he made straks for that oerasound the snarsty weg for Publin, so was his horenpipe lug in the lee off their mouths organs, with his tilt too taut for his tammy all a slaunter and his wigger on a wagger with its tag tucked. Up. With a good eastering and a good westering. And he asked from him how the hitch did do this my fand sulkers that mone met the Kidballacks which he suttonly remembered also where the hatch was he endnew strandweys he's that fond sutchenson, a peninicular fraimd of mind, fordeed he was langseling to talka holt of hems, clown toff, tye hug fliorten. Cablen: Clifftop. Shelvling tobay oppelong tomeadow. Ware cobbles. Posh.

— Skibbereen has common inn, by pounautique, with pokeway paw, and sadder raven evermore, telled shinshanks lauwering frankish for his kicker who, through the medium of gallic

— Pukkelsen, tilltold.

That with some our prowed invisors how their ulstravoliance led them infroraids, striking down and landing alow, against our aerian insulation resistance, two boards that beached ast one, widness thane and tysk and hanry. Prepatrickularly all, they summed. Kish met. Bound to. And for landlord, noting, nodding, a coast to moor was cause to mear. Besides proof plenty, over proof. While they either took a heft. Or the other swore his eric. Heaved two, spluiced the menbrace. Heirs at you, Brewinbaroon! Weth a whistle for methanks.

— Good marrams and good merrymills, sayd good mothers gossip, bobbing his bowing both ways with the bents and skerries, when they were all in the old walled of Kinkincaraborg (and that they did overlive the hot air of Montybunkum upon the coal blasts of Mitropolitos let there meeds be the hourihorn), hiberniating after seven oak ages, fearsome where they were he had gone dump in the doomering this tide where the peixies would pickle him down to the button of his seat and his sess old soss Erinly into the boelgein with the help of Divy and Jorum's locquor and shut the door after him to make a rarely fine Ran's cattle of fish. Morya Mortimor! Allapalla overus! Howoft had the ballshee tried! And they laying low for his home gang in that eeriebleak mead, with fireball feast and turkeys tumult and paupers patch to provide his bum end. The foe things your niggerhead needs to be fitten for the Big Water. He made the sign of the hammer. God's drought, he sayd, after a few daze, thinking of all those bliakings, how leif pauses! Here you are back on your hawkins, from Blasil the Brast to our povotogesus portocall, the furt on the turn of the hurdies, slave to trade, vassal of spices and a dragon-the-market, and be turbot, lurch a stripe, as were you soused methought out of the mackerel. Eldsfells! sayd he. A kumpavin on iceslant! Here's open handlegs for one old faulker from the hame folk here in you's booth! So sell me gundy, sagd the now waging cappon, with a warry posthumour's expletion, shoots ogos shootsle him or where's that slob? A bit bite of keesens, he sagd, til Dennis, for this jantar (and let the dobblins roast perus,) or a stinger, he sagd, t. d., on a doroughbread kennedy's for Patriki San Saki on svo fro or my old relogion's out of tiempor and when I'm soured to the tipple you can sink me lead, he sagd, and, if I get can, sagd he, a pusspull of tomtartarum. Thirst because homing hand give. Allkey dallkey, sayd the shop's housebound, for he was as deep as the north star (and could tolk sealer's solder into tankar's tolder) as might have sayd every man to his beast, and a treat for the trading scow, my cater million falls to you and crop feed a stall! Afram. And he got and gave the ekspedient for Hombreyhambrey wilcomer what's the good word. He made the sign on the feaster. Cloth be laid! And a disk of osturs for the swanker! Allahballah! He was the carelessest man I ever see but he sure had the most sand. One fish-ball with fixings! For a dan of a ven of a fin of a son of a gun of a gombolier. Ekspedient, sayd he, sonnur mine, Shackleton Sulten! Opvarts and at ham, or this ogry Osler will oxmaul us all, sayd he, like one familiar to the house, while Waldemar was heeling it and Maldemaer was toeing it, soe syg he was walking from the bowl at his food and the meer crank he was waiting for the tow of his turn. Till they plied him behaste on the fare. Say wehrn!

— Nohow did he kersse or hoot alike the suit and solder skins, minded first breachesmaker with considerable way on and

— Humpsea dumpsea, the munchantman, secondsnipped cutter the curter.

— A ninth for a ninth. Take my worth from it. And no mistaenk, they thricetold the taler and they knew the whyed for too. The be-cause of his sosuch. Uglymand fit himshemp but throats fill us all! And three's here's for repeat of the unium! Place the scaurs wore on your groot big bailey bill, he apullajibed, the O'Colonel Power, lat-terly distented from the O'Conner Dan, so promonitory himself that he was obliffious of the headth of hosth that rosed before him, from Sheeroskouro, under its zembliance of mardal mansk, like a dun darting dullemitter, with his moultain haares stuck in plostures upon it, (do you kend yon peak with its coast so green?) still trystfully acape for her his gragh knew well in precious memory and that proud grace to her, in gait a movely water, of smile a coolsome cup, with that rarefied air of a Montmalency and her quick little breaths and her climbing colour. Take thee live will save thee wive? I'll think uplon, lilady. Should anerous enthroproise call homovirtue, duinnafear! The ghem's to the ghoom be she nere zo zma. Obsit nemon! Floodlift, her ancient of rights regaining, so yester yidd, even remembrance. And greater grown then in the trifle of her days, a mouse, a mere tittle, trots off with the whole panoromacron picture. Her youngfree yoke stilling his wandercursus, jilt the spin of a curl and jolt the broadth of a buoy. The Annexandreian captive con-quest. Ethna Prettyplume, Hooghly Spaight. Him her first lap, her his fast pal, for ditcher for plower, till deltas twoport. While this glowworld's lump is gloaming off and han in hende will grow. Through simpling years where the lowcasts have aten of amilikan honey and datish fruits and a bannock of barley on Tham the Thatcher's palm. O wanderness be wondernest and now! Listeneath to me, veils of Mina! He would withsay, nepertheloss, that is too me mean. I oldways did me walsh and preechup ere we set to sope and fash. Now eats the vintner over these contents oft with his sad slow munch for backonham. Yet never shet it the brood of aurowoch, not for legions of donours of Gamuels. I have performed the law in truth for the lord of the law, Taif Alif. I have held out my hand for the holder of my heart in Annapolis, my youthrib city. Be ye then my protectors unto Mussabotomia before the guards of the city. Theirs theres is a gentlemeants agreement. Womensch plodge. To slope through heather till the foot. Join Andersoon and Co. If the flowers of speech valed the springs of me rising the hiker I hilltapped the murk I mist my blezzard way. Not a knocker on his head nor a nicknumber on the manyoumeant. With that coldbrundt natteldster wefting stinks from Alpyssinia, wooving nihilnulls from Memoland and wolving the ulvertones of the voice. But his spectrem onlymergeant crested from the irised sea in plight, calvitousness, loss, nngnr, gliddinyss, unwill and snorth. It might have been what you call your change of my life but there's the chance of a night for my lifting. Hillyhollow, valleylow! With the sounds and the scents in the morning.

— I shot be shoddied, throttle me, fine me cowheel for ever, usquebauched the ersewild aleconner, for bringing briars to Bembracken and ringing rinbus round Demetrius for, as you wrinkle wryghtly, bully bluedomer, it's a suirsite's stircus haunting hesteries round old volcanoes. We gin too gnir and thus plinary indulgence makes collemullas of us all. But Time is for talerman tasting his tap. Tiptoptap, Mister Maut.

He made one summery (Cholk and murble in lonestime) of his the three swallows like he was muzzling Moselems and torched up as the faery pangeant fluwed down the hisophenguts, a slake for the quicklining, to the tickle of his tube and the twobble of his fable, O, fibbing once upon a spray what a queer and queasy spree it was. Plumped.

Which both did. Prompt. Eh, chrystal holder? Save Ampsterdampster that had rheumaniscences in his netherlumbs.

— By the drope in his groin, Ali Slupa, thinks the cappon, plumbing his liners, we were heretofore.

— And be the coop of his gobbos, Reacher the Thaurd, thinks your girth fatter, apopo of his buckseaseilers, but where's Horace's courtin troopsers?

— I put hem behind the oasthouse, sagd Pukkelsen, tuning wound on the teller, appeased to the cue, that double dyode dealered, and he's wallowing awash swill of the Tarra water. And it marinned down his gargantast trombsathletic like the marousers of the gulpstroom. The kersse of Wolafs on him, shitateyar, he sagd in the fornicular, and, at weare or not at weare, I'm sigen no stretcher, for I carsed his murhersson goat in trotthers with them newbucklenoosers behigh in the fire behame in the oasthouse. Hops! sagd he.

— Smoke and coke choke! lauffed till the tear trickled drown a thigh the loafers all but a sheep's whosepants that swished to the lord he hadn't and the starer his story was talled to who felt that, the fierifornax being thurst on him motophosically, as Omar sometime notes, such a satuation, debauchly to be watched for, would empty dempty him down to the ground.

— And hopy dope! sagd he, anded the enderer, now dyply hypnotised or hopeseys doper himself. And kersse him, sagd he, after in-under tarrapoulling, and the shines he cuts, shinar, the screeder, the stitchimesnider, adepted to nosestorsioms in his budinholder, cummanisht, sagd he, (fouyoufoukou!) which goes in the ways smooking publics, sagd he, bomboosting to be in thelitest civille row faction for a dubblebrasterd navvygaiterd, (flick off that hvide aske, big head!) sagd he, the big bag of my hamd till hem, tollerloon, sagd he, with his pudny bun brofkost when he walts meet the bangd. I will put his fleas of wood in the flour, and he sagd, behunt on the oatshus, the not wellmade one, sagd he, the kersse of my arm-sore appal this most unmentionablest of men (mundering eeriesk, if he didn't scalded him all the shimps names in his gitter!) a coathemmed gusset sewer, sagd he, his first cudgin is an innvalet in the unitred stables which is not feed tonights a kirtle offal fisk and he is that woe worstered wastended shootmaker whatever poked a noodle in a clouth!

So for the second tryon all the meeting of the acarras had it. How he hised his bungle oar his shourter and cut the pinter off his pourer and lay off for Fellagulphia in the farning. From his dhruimadh-reamdhrue back to Brighten-pon-the-Baltic, from our lund's rund turs bag til threathy hoeres a wuke. Ugh!

— Stuff, Taaffe, stuff! interjoked it his wife's hopesend to the boath of them consistently. Come back to May Aileen.

— Ild luck to it! blastfumed the nowraging scamptail, in flating furies outs trews his cammelskins, the flashlight of his ire wackering from the eyewinker on his masttop. And aye far he fared from Af-ferik Arena and yea near he night till Blawland Bearring, baken be the brazen sun, buttered be the snows. And the sea shoaled and the saw squalled. And, soaking scupper, didn't he drain

A pause.

Infernal machinery (serial number: Bullysacre, dig care a dig) having thus passed the buck to billy back from jack (finder the keeper) as the baffling yarn sailed in circles it was now high tide for the reminding pair of snipers to be suitably punished till they had, like the pervious oelkenner done, liquorally no more powers to their elbow. Ignorinsers' bliss, therefore, their not to say rifle butt target, none too wisefolly, poor fish, (he is eating, he is spun, is milked, he dives) upholding a lampthorne of lawstift as wand of welcome to all men in bonafay, (and the corollas he so has saved gainsts the virus he has thus injected!) discoastedself to that kipsie point of its Dublin bar there, breaking and entering, from the out-back's dead heart, Glasthule Bourne or Boehernapark Nolagh, by wattsismade or bianconi, astraylians in island, a wellknown tall hat blown in between houses by a nightcap of that silk or it might be a black velvet and a kiber galler dragging his hunker, were signal-ling gael warnings towards Wazwollenzee Haven to give them their beerings, east circular route or elegant central highway. Open, 'tis luck will have it! Lifeboat Alloe, Noeman's Woe, Hircups Empty-bolly! With winkles whelks and cocklesent jelks. Let be buttercup eve lit by night in the Phoenix! Music. And old lotts have funn at Flammagen's ball. Till Irinwakes from Slumber Deep. How they succeeded by courting daylight in saving darkness he who loves will see.

Business. His bestness. Copeman helpen.

Contrescene.

He cupped his years to catch me's to you in what's yours as minest to hissent, giel as gail, geil as gaul, Odorozone, now ourmenial serv-ent, blanding rum, milk and toddy with I hand it to you. Saying whiches, see his bow on the hapence, with a pattedyr but digit here, he scooped the hens, hounds and horses biddy by bunny, with an arc of his covethand, saved from the drohnings they might oncounter, untill his cubid long, to hide in dry. Aside. Your sows tin the topple, dodgers, trink me dregs! Zoot!

And with the gust of a spring alice the fossickers and swaggelers with him on the hoof from down under piked forth desert roses in that mulligar scrub.

Reenter Ashe Junior. Peiwei toptip, nankeen pontdelounges. Gives fair day. Cheroot. Cheevio!

Off.

— Take off thatch whitehat (lo, Kersse come in back bespoking of loungeon off the Boildawl stuumplecheats for rushirishis Irush-Irish, dangieling his old Conan over his top gallant shouldier so was, lao yiu shao, he's like more look a novicer on the nevay).

— Tick off that whilehot, you scum of a botch, (of Kersse who, as he turned out, alas, hwen ching hwan chang, had been mocking his hollaballoon a sample of the costume of the country).

— Tape oaf that saw foull and sew wrong, welsher, you suck of a thick, stock and the udder, and confiteor yourself (for bekersse he had cuttered up and misfutthered in the most multiplest manner for that poor old bridge's masthard slouch a shook of cloakses the wise, hou he pouly hung hoang tseu, his own fitther couldn't nose him).

Chorus: With his coate so graye. And his pounds that he pawned from the burning.

— And, haikon or hurlin, who did you do at doyle today, my horsey dorksey gentryman. Serge Mee, suit! sazd he, tersey kersey. And when Tersse had sazd this Kersse stood them the whole koursse of training how the whole blazy raze acurraghed, from lambkinsback to sliving board and from spark to phoenish. And he tassed him tartly and he sassed him smartly, tig for tager, strop for stripe, as long as there's a lyasher on a kyat. And they peered him beheld on the pyre.

And it was so. Behold.

— Same capman no nothing horces two feller he feller go where. Isn't that effect? gig for gag, asked there three newcommers till knockingshop at the ones upon a topers who, while in admittance to that impedance, as three as they were there, they had been malt-treating themselves to their health's contempt.

— That's fag for fig, metinkus, confessed, mhos for mhos, those who, would it not be for that dielectrick, were upon the point of obsoletion, and at the brink of from the pillary of the Nilsens and from the statutes of the Kongbullies and from the millestones of Ovlergroamlius libitate nos, Domnial!

— And so culp me goose, he sazd, szed the ham muncipated of the first course, recoursing, all cholers and coughs with his beauw on the bummell, the bugganeering wanderducken, he sazd, (that his pumps may ship awhoyle shandymound of the dussard), the coarsehair highsaydighsayman, there's nice tugs he looks, (how you was, Ship Alouset?) he sazd, the bloedaxe bloodooth baltxebec, that

is crupping into our raw lenguage navel through the lumbsmall
of his hawsehole, he sazd, donconfounder him, voyaging after maidens, belly jonah hunting the polly joans, and the hurss of all port-
noysers befaddle him, he sazd, till I split in his flags, he sazd, one to
one, the landslewder, after Donnerbruch fire. Reefer was a wench-
man. One can smell off his wetsments how he is coming from a beach
of promisck. Where is that old muttiny, shall I ask? Free kicks he
will have from me, turncoats, in Bar Bartley if I wars a fewd years
ago. Meistr Capteen Gaascooker, a salestrimmer! As he was soamp-
ling me ledder, like pulp, and as I was trailing his fumbelums, like
hulp, he'll fell the fall of me faus, he sazd, like yulp! The goragor-
ridgorballyed pushkalsson, he sazd, with his bellows pockets fulled
of potchtatos and his fox in a stomach, a disagrees to his ramskew
coddlelecherskithers' zirkuvs, drop down dead and deaf, and there is
never a teilwrmans in the feof fife of Iseland or in the wholeabe-
longd of Skunkinabory from Drumadunderry till the rumnants of
Mecckrass, could milk a colt in thrushes foran furrow follower width
that a hole in his tale and that hell of a hull of a hill of a camelump
bakk. Fadgestfudgist!

Upon this dry call of selenium cell (that horn of lunghalloon,
Riland's in peril!) with its doomed crack of the old damn ukonnen
power insound in it the lord of the saloom, as if for a flash sala-
magunnded himself, listed his tummelumpsk pack and hearinat
presently returned him, ambilaterally alleyeoneyesed, from their
uppletoned layir to his beforetime guests, that bunch of palers on
their round, timemarching and petrolling how, who if they were
abound to loose a laugh (Toni Lampi, you booraascal!) they were
abooned to let it as the leashed they might do when they felt (O,
the wolf he's on the walk, sees his sham cram bokk!) their joke was
coming home to them, the steerage way for stabling, ghustorily
spoeking, gen and gang, dane and dare, like the dud spuk of his
first foetotype (Trolldedroll, how vary and likely!), the fillibustered,
the fully bellied. With the old sit in his shoulders, and the new satin
atlas onder his uxter, erning his breadth to the swelt of his proud
and, picking up the emberose of the lizod lights, his tail toiled of
spume and spawn, and the bulk of him, and hulk of him as whenever it was he reddled a ruad to riddle a rede from the sphinxish
pairc while Ede was a guardin, ere love a side issue. They hailed
him cheeringly, their encient, the murrainer, and wallruse, the merman, ye seal that lubs you lassers, Thallasee or Tullafilmagh, when
come of uniform age.

— Heave, coves, emptybloddy!

And ere he could catch or hook or line to suit their saussyskins, the lumpenpack. Underbund was overraskelled. As

— Sot! sod the tailors opsits from their gabbalots, change all that whole set. Shut down and shet up. Our set, our set's allohn.

And they poured em behoiled on the fire. Scaald!

Rowdiose wodhalooing. Theirs is one lessonless missage for good and truesirs. Will any persen bereaved to be passent bringback or rumpart to the Hoved politymester. Clontarf, one love, one fear. Ellers for the greeter glossary of code, callen hom: Finucane-Lee, Finucane-Law.

Am. Dg.

Welter focussed.

Wind from the nordth. Warmer towards muffinbell, Lull.

As our revelant Colunnfiller predicted in last mount's chattiry sermon, the allexpected depression over Schiumdinebbia, a bygger muster of veirying precipitation and haralded by faugh sicknells, (hear kokkenhovens ekstras!) and umwalloped in an unusuable suite of clouds, having filthered through the middlehav of the same gorgers' kennel on its wage wealthwards and incursioned a sotten retch of low pleasure, missed in some parts but with lucal drizzles, the outlook for tomarry (Streamstress Mandig) beamed brider, his ability good.

What hopends to they?

Giant crash in Aden. Birdflights confirm abbroaching nubtials. Burial of Lifetenant-Groevener Hatchett, R.I.D. Devine's Previdence.

Ls. De.

Art thou gainous sense uncompetite! Limited. Anna Lynchya Pourable! One and eleven. United We Stand, even many offered. Don't forget. I wish auspicable thievesdayte for the stork dyrby. It will be a thousand's a won paddies. And soon to bet. On drums of bliss. With hapsalap troth, hipsalewd prudity, hopesalot honnessy, hoopsaloop luck. After when from midnights unwards the four-poster harp quartetto. (Kiskiviikko, Kalastus. Torstaj, tanssia. Perjantaj, peleja. Lavantaj ja Sunnuntaj, christianismus kirjallisuus, kirjallisuus christianismus.) Whilesd this pellover his finnisch.

— Comither, ahorace, thou mighty man of valour, elderman adaptive of Capel Ysnod, and tsay-fong tsei-foun a laun bricksnumber till I've fined you a faulter-in-law, to become your son-to-be, gentlemens tealer, generalman seelord, gosse and bosse, hunguest and horasa, jonjemsums both, in sailsmanship, szed the head marines talebearer, then sayd the ships gospfather in the scat story to the husband's capture and either you does or he musts and this moment same, sayd he, so let laid pacts be being betving ye, he sayd, by my main makeshift, he sayd, one fisk and one flesk, as flat as, Aestmand Addmundson you, you're iron slides and so hompety domp as Paddley Mac Namara here he's a hardy canooter, for the two breasts of Banba are her soilers and her toilers, if thou wilt serve Idyall as thou hast sayld. Brothers Boathes, brothers Coathes, ye have swallen blooders' oathes. And Gophar sayd unto Glideon and sayd he to the nowedding captain, the rude hunnerable Humphrey, who was praying god of clothildies by the seven bosses of his trunktarge he would save bucklesome when she wooed belove on him, comeether, sayd he, my merrytime marelupe, you wutan whaal, sayd he, into the shipfolds of our quadrupede island, bless madhugh, mardyk, luusk and cong! Blass Neddos bray! And no more of your maimed acts after this with your kowtoros and criados to every tome, thick and heavy, and our onliness of his revelance to your ultitude. The illfollowable staying in wait for you with the winning word put into his mouth or be the hooley tabell, as Horrocks Toler hath most cares to call it, I'll rehearse your comeundermends and first mardhyr you entirely. As puck as that Paddeus picked the pun and left the lollies off the foiled. A Trinity judge will crux your boom. Pat is the man for thy. Ay ay! And he pured him beheild of the ouishguss, mingling a sign of the cruisk. I popetithes thee, Ocean, sayd he, Oscarvaughther, sayd he, Erievikkingr, sayd he, *intra trifum triforium trifoliorum,* sayd he, onconditionally, forfor furst of gielgaulgalls and hero chief explunderer of the clansakiltic, sayd he, the streameress mastress to the sea aase cuddycoalman's and let this douche for you as a wholly apuzzler's and for all the pukkaleens to the wakes of you, sayd he, out of the hellsinky of the howtheners and be danned to ye, sayd he, into our roomyo connellic relation, sayd he, from which our this pledge is given, Tera truly ternatrine if not son towards thousand like expect chrisan athems to which I osker your godhsbattaring, saelir, for as you gott kvold whereafter a gooden diggin and with gooder enscure from osion buck fared agen fairioes feuded hailsohame til Edar in that the loyd mave hercy on your sael! Anomyn and awer. Spickinusand.

—Nansense, you snorsted? he was haltid considerable agenst all religions overtrow so hworefore the thokkurs pokker the bigbug miklamanded storstore exploder would he be whulesalesolde daado-

oped by Priest Gudfodren of the sacredhaunt suit in Diaeblen-
Balkley at Domnkirk Saint Petricksburg? But ear this:

—And here, aaherra, my rere admirable peadar poulsen, sayd he,
consistently, to the secondnamed sutor, my lately lamented sponsor-
ship, comesend round that wine and lift your horn, sayd he, to
show you're a skolar for, winter you likes or not, we brought your
summer with us and, tomkin about your lief eurekason and his un-
dishcovery of americle, be the rolling forties, he sayd, and on my
sopper crappidamn, as Harris himself says, to let you in on some
crismion dottrin, here is the ninethest pork of a man whisk swim-
mies in Dybblin water from Ballscodden easthmost till Thyrston's
Lickslip and, sayd he, (whiles the heart of Lukky Swayn slaughed
in his icebox for to think of all the soorts of smukklers he would be-
have in juteyfrieze being forelooper to her) praties peel to our good-
send Brandonius, *filius* of a Cara, spouse to Fynlogue, he has the
nicesth pert of a nittlewoman in the house, la chito, la chato, la
Charmadouiro, Tina-bat-Talur, cif for your fob and a tesura astore
for you, eslucylamp as when the surge seas sombren, that he daughts
upon of anny livving plusquebelle, to child and foster, that's the
lippeyear's wonder of Totty go, Newschool, two titty too at win
winnie won, tramity trimming and funnity fare, with a grit
as hard as the trent of the thimes but a touch as saft as the dee in
flooing and never a Hyderow Jenny the like of her lightness at look
and you leap, rheadoromanscing long evmans invairn, about little
Anny Roners and all the Lavinias of ester yours and pleding for
them to herself in the periglus glatsch hangs over her trickle bed,
it's a piz of fortune if it never falls from the stuffel, and, when that
mallaura's over till next time and all the prim rossies are out dress-
parading and the tubas tout tout for the glowru of their god, making
every Dinny dingle after her down the Dargul dale and (wait
awhile, blusterbuss, you're marchadant too forte and don't start fur-
lan your ladins till you've learned the lie of her landuage!), when
it's summwer calding and she can hear the pianutunar beyant the
bayondes in Combria sleepytalking to the Wiltsh muntons, titting
out through her droemer window for the flyend of a touchman over
the wishtas of English Strand, when Kilbarrack bell pings saksalai-
sance that Concessas with Sinbads may (pong!), where our dolli-
mond? sees the phantom shape of Mr Fortunatus Wright since
winksome Miss Bulkeley made loe to her wrecker and he took her
to be a rover, O, and playing house of ivary dower of gould and gift
you soil me peepat my prize, which its a blue loogoont for her in a

bleakeyed seusan if she can't work her mireiclles and give Norgey-
borgey good airish timers, while her fresh racy turf is kindly kindling
up the lovver with the flu, with a roaryboaryellas would set an Eri-
weddyng on fire, let aloon an old Humpopolamos with the boomar-
poorter on his brain, aiden bay scye and dye, aasbukividdy,
twentynine to her dozen and coocoo him didulceydovely to his old
cawcaws huggin and munin for his strict privatear which there's
no pure rube like an ool pool roober when your pullar beer turns
out Bruin O'Luinn and beat his barge into a battering pram with
her wattling way for cubblin and, be me fairy fay, sayd he, the marriage mixter, to Kersse, Son of Joe Ashe, her coaxfonder, wiry eyes
and winky hair, timking abeat your Andraws Meltons and his lov-
sang of the short and shifty, I will turn my thinks to things alove
and I will speak but threes ones, sayd he, my truest patrions good
founter, poles a port and zones asunder, tie up in hates and repeat
at luxure, you can better your tooblue prodestind arson, tyler bach,
after roundsabouts and donochs and the volumed smoke, though the
clonk in his stumble strikes warn, and were he laid out on that
counter there like a Slavocrates amongst his skippies, when it comes
to the ride onerable, sayd he, that's to make plain Nanny Ni Sheeres
a full Dinamarqueza, and all needed for the lay, from the hursey
on the montey with the room in herberge down to forkpiece and
bucklecatch, (Elding, my elding! and Lif, my lif!) in the pravacy of
the pirmanocturne, hap, sayd he, at that meet hour of night, and
hop, sayd he, and the fyrsty annas everso thried (whiles the breath
of Huppy Hullespond swumped in his seachest for to renumber all
the mallymedears' long roll and call of sweetheart emmas that every
had a port in from Coxenhagen till the brottels on the Nile), while
taylight is yet slipping under their pillow, (ill omens on Kitty Cole
if she's spilling laddy's measure!) and before Sing Mattins in the
Fields, ringsengd ringsengd, bings Heri the Concorant Erho, and
the Referinn Fuchs Gutmann gives us *I'll Bell the Welled* or *The
Steeplepoy's Revanger* and all Thingavalley knows for its never
dawn in the dark but the deed comes to life, and raptist bride is
aptist breed (tha lassy! tha lassy!), and, to buoy the hoop within us
springing, 'tis no timbertar she'll have then in her armsbrace to doll
the dallydandle, our fiery quean, upon the night of the things of the
night of the making to stand up the double tet of the oversear of the
seize who cometh from the mighty deep and on the night of making
Horuse to crihumph over his enemy, be the help of me cope as so
pluse the riches of the roedsshields, with Elizabeliza blessing the

bedpain, at the willbedone of Yinko Jinko Randy, come Bastabasco
and hippychip eggs, she will make a suomease pair and singlette,
jodhpur smalls and tailorless, a copener's cribful, leaf, bud and berry,
the divlin's own little mimmykin puss, (hip, hip, horatia!) for my
old comrhade saltymar here, Briganteen—General Sir A. I.
Magnus, the flappernooser, master of the good lifebark *Ulivengrene*
of Onslought, and the homespund of her hearth, (Fuss his farther
was the norse norse east and Muss his mother was a gluepot) and,
gravydock or groovy anker, and a hulldread pursunk manowhood,
who (with a chenchen for his delight time and a bonzeye nappin
through his doze) he is the bettest bluffy blondblubber of an
olewidgeon what overspat a skettle in a skib.

Cawcaught. Coocaged.

And Dub did glow that night. In Fingal of victories. Cannmatha
and Cathlin sang together. And the three shouters of glory. Yelling
halfviewed their harps. Surly Tuhal smiled upon drear Darthoola:
and Roscranna's bolgaboyo begirlified the daughter of Cormac. The
soul of everyelsesbody rolled into its olesoleself. A doublemonth's
licence, lease on mirth, while hooneymoon and her flame went
huneysuckling. Holyryssia, what boom of bells! What battle of
bragues on Sandgate where met the bobby mobbed his bibby mab-
bing through the ryce. Even Tombs left doss and dunnage down in
Demidoff's tomb and drew on the dournailed clogs that Morty Manning left him and legged in by Ghoststown Gate, like Pompei up
to date, with a sprig of Whiteboys heather on his late Luke Elcock's
heirloom. And some say they seen old dummydeaf with a leaf of
bronze on his cloak so grey, trooping his colour a pace to the reire.
And as owfally posh with his halfcrown jool as if he was the Gran-
jook Meckl or Paster de Grace on the Route de l'Epée. It was joo-
bileejeu that All Sorts' Jour. Freestouters and publicranks, hafts on
glaives. You could hear them swearing threaties on the Cymylaya
Mountains, man. And giving it out to the Ould Fathach and louth-
mouthing after the Healy Mealy with an enfysis to bring down
the rain of Tarar. Nevertoletta! Evertomind! The grandest bethe-
hailey seen or heard on earth's conspectrum since Scape the Goat,
that gafr, ate the Suenders bible. Hadn't we heaven's lamps to hide
us? Yet every lane had its lively spark and every spark had its several
spurtles and each spitfire spurtle had some trick of her trade, a tease
for Ned, nook's nestle for Fred and a peep at me mow for Peer Pol.
So that Father Matt Hughes looked taytotally threbled. But Danno
the Dane grimmed. Dune. 'Twere yeg will elsecare doatty lanv meet

they dewscent hyemn to cannons' roar and rifles' peal vill shantey soloweys sang! For there were no more Tyrrhanees and for Laxembraghs was passthecupper to Our Lader's. And it was dim upon the floods only and there was day on all the ground.

Thus street spins legends while wharves woves tales but some family fewd felt a nick in their name. Old Vickers sate down on their airs and straightened the points of their lace. Red Rowleys popped out of their lairs and asked what was wrong with the race. Mick na Murrough used dripping in layers to shave all the furze off his face. The Burke-Lees and Coyle-Finns paid full feines for their sinns when the Cap and Miss Coolie were roped.

Rolloraped.

With her banbax hoist from holder, zig for zag through pool and polder, cheap, cheap, cheap and Laughing Jack, all augurs scorenning, see the Bolche your pictures motion and Kitzy Kleinsuessmein eloping for that holm in Finn's Hotel Fiord, Nova Norening. Where they pulled down the kuddle and they made fray and if thee don't look homey, well, that Dook can eye Mae.

He goat a berth. And she cot a manege. And wohl's gorse mundom ganna wedst.

Knock knock. War's where! Which war? The Twwinns. Knock knock. Woos without! Without what? An apple. Knock knock.

The kilder massed, one then and uhindred, (harefoot, birdyhands, herringabone, beesknees), and they barneydansked a kathareen round to know the who and to show the howsome. Why was you hiding, moder of moders? And where was hunty, poppa the gun? Pointing up to skyless heaven like the spoon out of sergeantmajor's tay. Which was the worst of them phaymix cupplerts? He's herd of hoarding and her faiths is altared. Becoming ungoing, their seeming sames for though that liamstone deaf do his part there's a windtreetop whipples the damp off the mourning. But tellusit allasif wellasits end. And the lunger it takes the swooner they tumble two. He knows he's just thrilling and she's sure she'd squeam. The three-legged man and the tulippied dewydress. Lludd hillmythey, we're brimming to hear! The durst he did and the first she ever? Peganeen Bushe, this isn't the polkar, catch as you cancan when high land fling! And you Tim Tommy Melooney, I'll tittle your barents if you stick that pigpin upinto meh!

So in the names of the balder and of the sol and of the hollichrost, ogsowearit, trisexnone, and by way of letting the aandt out of her grosskropper and leading the mokes home by their gribes, whoops-

about a plabbaside of plobbicides, alamam alemon, poison kerls, on
this mounden of Delude, and in the high places of Delude of Isreal,
which is Haraharem and the diublin's owld mounden over against
Vikens, from your tarns, thwaites and thorpes, withes, tofts and
fosses, fells, haughs and shaws, lunds, garths and dales, mensuring
the megnominous as so will is the littleyest, the myrioheartzed with
toroidal coil, eira area round wantanajocky, fin above wave after
ducky downdivvy, trader arm aslung beauty belt, the formor velican
and nana karlikeevna, sommerlad and cinderenda, Valtivar and Viv,
how Big Bil Brine Borumoter first took his gage at lil lolly lavvander
waader since when capriole legs covets limbs of a crane and was
it the twylyd or the mounth of the yare or the feint of her smell made
the seomen assalt of her (in imageascene all: whimwhim whimwhim). To the laetification of disgeneration by neuhumorisation of
our kristianiasation. As the last liar in the earth begeylywayled the
first lady of the forest. Though Toot's pardoosled sauve l'hummour!
For the joy of the dew on the flower of the fleets on the fields of the
foam of the waves of the seas of the wild main from Borneholm has
jest come to crown.

Snip snap snoody. Noo err historyend goody. Of a lil trip trap
and a big treeskooner for he put off the ketyl and they made three
(for fie!) and if hec dont love alpy then lad you annoy me. For
hanigen with hunigen still haunt ahunt to finnd their hinnigen
where Pappappapparrassannuaragheallachnatullaghmonganmac-
macmacwhackfalltherdebblenonthedubblandaddydoodled and an-
ruly person creeked a jest. Gestapose to parry off cheekars or frankfurters on the odor. Fine again, Cuoholson! Peace, O wiley!

Such was the act of goth stepping the tolk of Doolin, drain and
plantage, wattle and daub, with you'll peel as I'll pale and we'll pull
the boath toground togutter, testies touchwood and shenstone unto
pop and puma, calf and condor, under all the gaauspices (incorporated), the chal and his chi, their roammerin over, gribgrobgrab
reining trippetytrappety (so fore shalt thou flow, else thy cavern
hair!) to whom she (anit likenand pleasethee!). Till sealump be-
camedump to bumpslump a lifflebed, (altolà allamarsch! O gué, O
gué!). Kaemper Daemper to Jetty de Waarft, all the weight of that
mons on his little ribbeunuch! Him that gronde old mand to be that
haard of heaering (afore said) and her the petty tondur with the
fix in her changeable eye (which see), Lord, me lad, he goes with
blowbierd, leedy, plasheous stream. But before that his loudship
was converted to a landshop there was a little theogamyjig inci-

dence that hoppy-go-jumpy Jnuuary morn when he colluded with the cad out on the beg amudst the fiounaregal gaames of those oath-massed fenians for whome he's forcecaused a bridge of the piers, at Inverleffy, mating pontine of their engagement, synnbildising grat-ers and things, eke ysendt? O nilly, not all, here's the first cataraction! As if ever she cared an assuan damm about her harpoons sticking all out of him whet between phoenix his calipers and that psourdonome sheath. Sdrats ye, Gus Paudheen! Kenny's thought ye, Dinny Oozle! While the cit was leaking asphalt like a suburbiaurealis in his rure was tucking to him like old booths, booths, booths, booths. Enterruption. Check or slowback. Dvershen.

Why, wonder of wenchalows, what o szeszame open, v doer s t doing? V door s being. But how theng thingajarry miens but this being becoming n z doer? K? An o. It is ne not him what foots like a glove, shoehandschiner Pad Podomkin. Sooftly, anni slavey, szszusz-chee is slowjaneska.

The aged crafty nummifeed confusionary overinsured everlapsing accentuated katekattershin clopped, clopped, clopped, darsey dobrey, back and along the danzing corridor, as she was going to pimpim him, way boy wally, not without her complement of cavar-nan men, between the two deathdealing allied divisions and the lines of readypresent fire of the corkedagains upstored, taken in giving the saloot, band your hands going in, bind your heads com-ing out, and remoltked to herselp in her serf's alown, a weerpovy willowy dreevy drawly and the patter of so familiars, farabroads and behomeans, as she shure sknows, boof for a booby, boo: new uses in their mewseyfume. The jammesons is a cook in his hair. And the juinnesses is a rapin his hind. And the Bullingdong caught the wind up. Dip.

And the message she braught belaw from the missus she bragged abouve that had her agony stays outsize her sari chemise, blancking her shifts for to keep up the fascion since the king of all dronnings kissed her beeswixed hand, fang (pierce me, hunky, I'm full of meunders!), her fize like a tubtail of mondayne clothes, fed to the chaps with working medicals and her birthright pang that would split an atam like the forty pins in her hood, was to fader huncher a howdydowdy, to mountainy mots in her amnest plein language, from his fain a wan, his hot and tot lass, to pierce his ropeloop ear, how, Podushka be prayhasd, now the sowns of his loins were awinking and waking and his dorter of the hush lillabilla lullaby (lead us not into reformication with the poors in your thingdom of

gory, O moan!), once after males, nonce at a time, with them
Murphy's puffs she dursted with gnockmeggs and the bramborry
cake for dour dorty dompling obayre Mattom Beetom and epsut the
pfot and if he was whishtful to licture her caudal with chesty chach
from his dauberg den and noviny news from Naul or toplots talks
from morrienbaths or a parrotsprate's cure for ensevelised lethur-
gies, spick's my spoon and the veriblest spoon, 'twas her hour for the
chamber's ensallycopodium with love to melost Panny Kostello from
X.Y. Zid for to folly billy bobbis gibits porzy punzy and she was a
wanton for De Marera to take her genial glow to bed.

— This is time for my tubble, reflected Mr 'Gladstone Browne'
in the toll hut (it was choractoristic from that 'man of Delgany').
Dip.

— This is me vulcanite smoking, profused Mr 'Bonaparte Nolan'
under the natecup (one feels how one may hereby reekignites the
'ground old mahonagyan'). Dip.

— And this is defender of defeater of defaulter of deformer of the
funst man in Danelagh, willingtoned in with this glance dowon his
browen and that born appalled noodlum the panellite pair's cummal
delimitator, odding: Oliver White, he's as tiff as she's tight. And
thisens his speak quite hoarse. Dip.

In reverence to her midgetsy the lady of the comeallyous as
madgestoo our own one's goff stature. Prosim, prosit, to the krk n
yr nck!

O rum it is the chomicalest thing how it pickles up the punchey
and the jude. If you'll gimmy your thing to me I will gamey a sing
to thee. Stay where you're dummy! To get her to go ther. He banged
the scoop and she bagged the sugar while the whole pub's pobbel
done a stare. On the mizzatint wall. With its chromo for all, crimm
crimms. Showing holdmenag's asses sat by Allmeneck's men, canins
to ride with em, canins that lept at em, woollied and flundered.

So the katey's came and the katey's game. As so gangs sludgenose.
And that henchwench what hopped it dunneth there duft the.
Duras.

                           (Silents)

Yes, we've conned thon print in its gloss so gay how it came from
Finndlader's Yule to the day and it's Hey Tallaght Hoe on the
king's highway with his hounds on the home at a turning. To Don-
nicoombe Fairing. Millikin's Pass. When visiting at Izd-la-Chapelle
taste the lipe of the waters from Carlowman's Cup.

It tellyhows its story to their six of hearts, a twelve-eyed man; for whom has madjestky who since is dyed drown reign before the izba.

Au! Au! Aue! Ha! Heish!

As stage to set by ritual rote for the grimm grimm tale of the four of hyacinths, the deafeeled carp and the bugler's dozen of leagues-in-amour or how Holispolis went to Parkland with mabby and sammy and sonny and sissy and mop's varlet de shambles and all to find the right place for it by peep o'skirt or pipe a skirl when the hundt called a halt on the chivvychace of the ground sloper at that ligtning lovemaker's thender apeal till, between wandering weather and stable wind, vastelend hosteilend, neuziel and oltrigger some, Bullyclubber burgherly shut the rush in general.

Let us propel us for the frey of the fray! Us, us, beraddy!

Ko Niutirenis hauru leish! A lala! Ko Niutirenis haururu laleish! Ala lala! The Wullingthund sturm is breaking. The sound of maor-maoring. The Wellingthund sturm waxes fuercilier. The whacka-whacks of the sturm. Katu te ihis ihis! Katu te wana wana! The strength of the rawshorn generand is known throughout the world. Let us say if we may what a weeny wukeleen can do.

Au! Au! Aue! Ha! Heish! A lala!

—Paud the roosky, weren't they all of them then each in his dif-ferent way of saying calling on the one in the same time hibernian knights underthaner that was having, half for the laugh of the bliss it sint barbaras another doesend end once tale of a tublin wished on to him with its olives ocolombs and its hills owns ravings and Tutty his tour in his Nowhare's yarcht. It was before when Aimee stood for Arthurduke for the figger in profane and fell from grace so madlley for fill the flatter fellows. (They were saying). And it was the lang in the shirt in the green of the wood, where obelisk rises when odalisks fall, major threft on the make and jollyjacques spindthrift on the merry (O Mr Mathurin, they were calling, what a topheavy hat you're in! And there aramny maeud, then they were saying, these so pioupious!). And it was cyclums cyclorums after he made design on the corse and he want to mess on him (enterellbo add all taller Danis), back, seater and sides, and he applied (I'm amazingly sorracer!) the wholed bould shoulderedboy's width for fullness, measures for messieurs, messer's massed, (they were say-calling again and agone and all over agun, the louthly meathers, the loudly meaders, the lously measlers, six to one, bar ones).

And they pled him beheighten the firing. Dope.

Maltomeetim, alltomatetam, when a tale tarries shome shunter shove on. Fore auld they wauld to pree.

Pray.

Of this Mr A (tillalaric) and these wasch woman (dapplehued), fhronehflord and feeofeeds, who had insue keen and able and a spindlesong aside, nothing more is told until now, his awebrume hour, her sere Sahara of sad oakleaves. And then. Be old. The next thing is. We are once amore as babes awondering in a wold made fresh where with the hen in the storyaboot we start from scratch. So the truce, the old truce and nattonbuff the truce, boys. Drouth is stronger than faction. Slant. Shinshin. Shinshin.

— It was of The Grant, old gartener, *qua* golden meddlist, Publius Manlius, fuderal private, (his place is his poster, sure, they said, and we're going to mark it, sore, they said, with a carbon caustick manner) bequother the liberaloider at his petty corporelezzo that hung caughtnapping from his baited breath, it was of him, my wife and I thinks, to feel to every of the younging fruits, tenderosed like an atalantic's breastswells or, on a second wreathing, a bright tauth bight shimmeryshaking for the welt of his plow. And where the peckadillies at his wristsends meetings be loving so lightly dovessoild the candidacy, me wipin eye sinks, of his softboiled bosom should be apparient even to our illicterate of nullatinenties.

All to which not a lot snapped The Nolan of the Calabashes at his whilom eweheart photognomist who by this sum taken was as much incensed by Saint Bruno as that what he had consummed was his own panegoric, and wot a lout about it if it was only a pippappoff pigeon shoot that gracesold getrunner, the man of centuries, was bowled out by judge, jury and umpire at batman's biff like a witchbefooled legate. Dupe.

His almonence being alaterelly in dispensation with his three oldher patrons' aid, providencer's divine cow to milkfeeding mleckman, bonafacies to solafides, what matter what all his freudzay or who holds his hat to harm him, let hutch just keep on under at being a vanished consinent and let annapal livibel prettily prattle a lude all her own. And be that semeliminal salmon solemonly angled, ingate and outgate. A truce to lovecalls, dulled in warclothes, maleybags, things and bleakhusen. Leave the letter that never begins to go find the latter that ever comes to end, written in smoke and blurred by mist and signed of solitude, sealed at night.

Simply. As says the mug in the middle, nay brian nay noel, ney billy ney boney. Imagine twee cweamy wosen. Suppwose you get a beautiful thought and cull them sylvias sub silence. Then inmaggin a stotterer. Suppoutre him to been one biggermaster Omnibil. Then

lustily (tutu the font and tritt on the bokswoods like gay feeters's
dance) immengine up to three longly lurking lobstarts. Fair instents
the Will Woolsley Wellaslayers. Pet her, pink him, play pranks with
them. She will nod amproperly smile. He may seem to appraisiate
it. They are as piractical jukersmen sure to paltipsypote. Feel the
wollies drippeling out of your fingathumbs. Says to youssilves
(floweers have ears, heahear!) solowly: So these ease Budlim! How
do, dainty daulimbs? So peached to pick on you in this way, prue
and simple, pritt and spry! Heyday too, Malster Faunagon, and
hopes your hahititahiti licks the mankey nuts! And oodlum hoodlum doodlum to yes, Donn, Teague and Hurleg, who the bullocks
brought you here and how the hillocks are ye?

We want Bud. We want Bud Budderly. We want Bud Budderly
boddily. There he is in his Borrisalooner. The man that shunned the
rucks on Gereland. The man thut won the bettlle of the bawll. Order, order, order, order! And tough. We call on Tancred Artaxerxes
Flavin to compeer with Barnabas Ulick Dunne. Order, order, order!
Milster Malster in the chair. We've heard it sinse sung thousand-
times. How Burghley shuck the rackushant Germanon. For Ehren,
boys, gobrawl!

A public plouse. Citizen soldiers.

TAFF (*a smart boy, of the peat freers, thirty two eleven, looking
through the roof towards a relevution of the karmalife order previous
to his hoisting of an emergency umberolum in byway of paraguas-
tical solation to the rhyttel in his hedd*). All was flashing and krash-
ning blurty moriartsky blutcherudd? What see, buttywalch? Tell
ever so often?

BUTT (*mottledged youth, clergical appealance, who, as his pied
friar, is supposing to motto the sorry dejester in tifftaff toffiness or
to be digarced from ever and a daye in his accounts*). But da. But
dada, mwilshsuni. Till even so aften. Sea vaast a pool!

TAFF (*porumptly helping himself out by the cesspull with a yellup
yurrup, puts up his furry furzed hare*). Butly bitly! Humme to our
mounthings. Conscribe him tillusk, unt, in his jubalant tubalence,
the groundsapper, with his soilday site out on his moulday side in.
The gubernier-gerenal in laut-lievtonant of Baltiskeeamore, amal-
theouse for leporty hole! Endues paramilintary langdwage. The sail-
lils of the yellavs nocadont palignol urdlesh. Shelltoss and welltass
and telltuss aghom! Sling Stranaslang, how Malorazzias spikes her,
coining a speak a spake! Not the Setanik stuff that slimed soft
Siranouche! The good old gunshop monowards for manosymples.

Tincurs tammit! They did oak hay doe fou Chang-li-meng when
that man d'airain was big top tom saw tip side bum boss pageant-
filler. Ajaculate! All lea light! Rassamble the glowrings of Bruyant
the Bref when the Mollies Makehalpence took his leg for his thumb.
And may he be too an intrepidation of our dreams which we fore-
got at wiking when the morn hath razed out limpalove and the bleak-
frost chilled our ravery! Pook. Sing ching lew mang! Upgo,
bobbycop! Lets hear in remember the braise of. Hold!

BUTT (*drawling forth from his blousom whereis meditabound of
his minkerstary, switches on his gorsecopper's fling weitoheito lang-
thorn, fed up the grain oils of Aerin, while his laugh neighs banck as
that flashermind's rays and his lipponease longuewedge wambles*).
Ullahbluh! Sehyoh narar, pokehole sann! Manhead very dirty by
am anoyato. Like old Dolldy Icon when he cooked up his iggs in
bicon. He gatovit and me gotafit and Oalgoak's Cheloven gut
a fudden. Povar old pitschobed! Molodeztious of metchennacht
belaburt that pentschmyaso! Bog carsse and dam neat, sar,
gam cant! Limbers affront of him, lumbers behund. While the
bucks bite his dos his hart bides the ros till the bounds of his bays
bell the warning. Sobaiter sobarkar. He was enmivallupped. Chro-
mean fastion. With all his cannoball wappents. In his raglanrock
and his malakoiffed bulbsbyg and his varnashed roscians and his
cardigans blousejagged and his scarlett manchokuffs and his tree-
coloured camiflag and his perikopendolous gaelstorms. Here weeks
hire pulchers! Obriania's beromst! From Karrs and Polikoff's, the
men's confessioners. Seval shimars pleasant time payings. Mousoume-
selles buckwoulds look. Tenter and likelings.

TAFF (*all Perssiasterssias shookatnaratatattar at his waggon-
horchers, his bulgeglarying stargapers razzledazzlingly full of eyes,
full of balls, full of holes, full of buttons, full of stains, full of medals,
full of blickblackblobs*). Grozarktic! Toadlebens! Some garmentguy!
Insects appalling, low hum clang sin! A cheap decoy! Too deep
destroy! Say mangraphique, may say nay por daguerre!

BUTT (*if that he hids foregodden has nate of glozery farused
ameet the florahs of the follest, his spent fish's livid smile giving alla-
sundery the bumfit of the doped*). Come alleyou jupes of Wym-
mingtown that graze the calves of Man! A bear raigning in his
heavenspawn consomation robes. Rent, outraged, yewleaved,
grained, ballooned, hindergored and voluant! Erminia's capecloaked
hoodoodman! First he s s st steppes. Then he st stoo stoopt. Lookt.

TAFF (*strick struck strangling like aleal lusky Lubliner to merum-*

ber by the cycl of the cruize who strungled Attahilloupa with what
empoisoned El Monte de Zuma and failing wilnaynilnay that he
was pallups barn in the minkst of the Krumlin befodt he was pop-
soused into the monkst of the vatercan, makes the holypolygon of
the emt on the greaseshaper, a little farther, a little soon, a lettera-
cettera, oukraydoubray). Scutterer of guld, he is retourious on every
roudery! The lyewdsky so so sewn of a fitchid! With his walsh-
brushup. And his boney bogey braggs.

BUTT *(after his tongues in his cheeks, with pinkpoker pointing*
out in rutene to impassible abjects beyond the mistomist towards
Lissnaluhy such as the Djublian Alps and the Hoofd Riberio as
where he and his trulock may ever make a game). The field of kar-
hags and that bloasted tree. Forget not the felled! For the lomonda-
tions of Oghrem! Warful doon's bothem. Here furry glunn. Nye?
Their feery pass. Tak! With guerillaman aspear aspoor to prink the
pranks of primkissies. And the buddies behide in the byre. Allah-
blah!

TAFF *(a blackseer, he stroves to regulect all the straggles for wife*
in the rut of the past through the widnows in effigies keening after
the blank sheets in their faminy to the relix of old decency from over
draught). Oh day of rath! Ah, murther of mines! Eh, selo moy! Uh,
zulu luy! Bernesson Mac Mahahon from Osro bearing nose easger
for sweeth prolettas on his swooth prowll!

BUTT *(back to his peatrol and paump: swee Gee's wee rest: no*
more applehooley: dodewodedook). Bruinoboroff, the hooney-
moonger, and the grizzliest manmichal in Meideveide! Whose an-
nal livves the hoiest! For he devoused the lelias on the fined and he
conforted samp, tramp and marchint out of the drumbume of
a narse. Guards, serf Finnland, serve we all!

TAFF *(whatwidth the psychophannies at the front and whetwadth*
the psuckofumbers beholden the fair, illcertain, between his bulchri-
chudes and the roshashanaral, where he sees Bishop Ribboncake
plus his pollex prized going forth on his visitations of mirrage or
Miss Horizon, justso all our fannacies daintied her, on the curve of
the camber, unsheathing a showlaced limbaloft to the great con-
sternations). Divulge! Hyededye, kittyls, and howdeddoh, pan!
Poshbott and pulbuties. See that we soll or let dargman be luna as
strait a way as your ant's folly me line while ye post is goang from
Piping Pubwirth to Haunted Hillborough on his Mujiksy's Zaravence,
the Riss, the Ross, the sur of all Russers, as my farst is near to hear
and my sackend is meet to sedon while my whole's a peer's aureolies.

We should say you dones the polecad. Bang on the booche, gurg in the gorge, rap on the roof and your flup is unbu. . .

BUTT (*at the signal of his act which seems to sharpnel his innermals menody, playing the spool of the little brown jog round the wheel of her whang goes the millner*). Buckily buckily, blodestained boyne! Bimbambombumb. His snapper was shot in the Rumjar Journaral. Why the gigls he lubbed beeyed him.

TAFF (*obliges with a two stop yogacoga sumphoty on the bones for ivory girl and ebony boy*). The balacleivka! Trovatarovitch! I trumble!

BUTT (*with the sickle of a scygthe but the humour of a hummer, O, howorodies through his cholaroguled, fumfing to a fullfrength with this wallowing olfact*). Mortar martar tartar wartar! May his boules grow wider so his skittles gets worse! The aged monad making a venture out of the murder of investment. I seen him acting surgent what betwinks the scimitar star and the ashen moon. By their lights shalthow throw him! Piff paff for puffpuff and my pife for his cgar! The mlachy way for gambling.

[*Up to this curkscraw bind an admirable verbivocovisual presentment of the worldrenownced Caerholme Event has been being given by* The Irish Race and World. *The huddled and aliven stablecrashers have shared fleetfooted enthusiasm with the paddocks dare and ditches tare while the mews was combing ground. Hippohopparray helioscope flashed winsor places as the gates might see. Meusdeus! That was (with burning briar) Mr Twomass Nohoholan for their common contribe satisfunction in the purports of amusedment telling the Verily Roverend Father Epiphanes shrineshriver of Saint Dhorough's (in browne bomler) how (assuary as there's a bonum in your osstheology!) Backlegs shirked the racing kenneldar. The saintly scholarist's roastering guffalawd of nupersaturals holler at this metanoic excomologosis tells of the chestnut's (once again, Wittyngtom!) absolutionally romptyhompty successfulness. A lot of lasses and lads without damas or dads, but fresh and blued with collecting boxes. One aught spare ones triflets, to be shut: it is Coppingers for the children. Slippery Sam hard by them, physically present howsomedever morally absent, was slooching about in his knavish diamonds asking Gmax, Knox and the Dmuggies (a pinnance for your toughts, turffers!) to deck the ace of duds. Tomtinker Tim, howbeit; his unremitting retainer, (the seers are the seers of Samael but the heers are the*

heers of Timoth) is in Boozer's Gloom, soalken steady in his
sulken tents. Baldawl the curse, baledale the day! And the frocks
of shick sheeples in their shummering insamples! You see: a chief-
smith, semperal scandal stinkmakers, a middinest from the Casa-
bianca and, of course, Mr Fry. Barass! Pardon the inquisition,
causas es quostas? It is Da Valorem's Dominical Brayers. Why
coif that weird hood? Because among nosoever circusdances is to
be apprehended the dustungwashed poltronage of the lost
Gabbarnaur-Jaggarnath. Pamjab! Gross Jumpiter, whud was thud?
Lucklucklucklucklucklucklucluck! It is the Thousand to One Guinea-
Gooseberry's Lipperfull Slipver Cup. Hold hard, ridesiddle tite-
little Pitsy Riley! Gurragrunch, gurragrunch! They are at the
turn of the fourth of the hurdles. By the hross of Xristos, Holo-
phullopopulace is a shote of excramation! Bumchub! Emancipator,
the Creman hunter (Major Hermyn C. Entwhistle) with dramatic
effect reproducing the form of famous sires on the scene of the
formers triumphs, is showing the eagle's way to Mr Whaytehayte's
three buy geldings Homo Made Ink, Bailey Beacon and Ratatuohy
while Furstin II and The Other Girl (Mrs 'Boss' Waters, leavy-
brink) too early spring dabbles, are showing a clean pairofhids to
Immensipater. Sinkathinks to oppen here! To this virgin's tuft,
on this golden of evens! I never sought of sinkathink. Our lork-
makor he is proformly annuysed. He is shinkly thinkly shaking in
his schayns. Sat will be off follteedee. This eeridreme has being
effered you by Bett and Tipp. Tipp and Bett, our swapstick quack-
chancers, in From Topphole to Bottom of The Irish Race and
World.]

TAFF (awary that the first sports report of Loundin Reginald has
now been afterthoughtfully colliberated by a saggind spurts flash,
takes the dipperend direction and, for tasing the tiomor of malaise
after the pognency of orangultonia, orients by way of Sagittarius towards Draco on the Lour). And you collier carsst on him, the corsar,
with Boyle, Burke and Campbell, I'll gogemble on strangbones tomb.
You had just been cerberating a camp camp camp to Saint
Sepulchre's march through the armeemonds retreat with the boys
all marshalled, scattering giant's hail over the curseway, fellowed
along the rout by the stenchions of the corpse. Tell the coldspell's
terroth! If you please, commeylad! Perfedes Albionias! Think some
ingain think, as Teakortairer sate over the Galwegian caftan fore-

when Orops and Aasas were chooldrengs and micramacrees! A forward movement, Miles na Bogaleen, and despatch!

BUTT (*slinking his coatsleeves surdout over his squad mutton shoulder so as to loop more life the jauntlyman as he scents the anggreget yup behound their whole scoopchina's desperate noy's totalage and explaining aposteriorly how awstooloo was valdesombre belowes hero and he was in a greak esthate phophiar an erixtion on the soseptuple side of him made spoil apriori his popoporportiums*). Yass, zotnyzor, I don't think I did not, pojr. Never you brother me for I scout it, think you! Ichts nichts on nichts! Greates Schtschuptar! Me fol the rawlawdy in the schpirrt of a schkrepz. Of all the quirasses and all the qwehrmin in the tragedoes of those antiants their grandoper, that soun of a gunnong, with his sabaothsopolettes, smooking his scandleloose at botthends of him! Foinn duhans! I grandthinked after his obras after another time about the itch in his egondoom he was legging boldy lugged from some pulversporochs and lyoking for a stooleazy for to nemesisplotsch allafranka and for to salubrate himself with an ultradungs heavenly mass at his base by a suprime pompship chorams the perished popes, the reverend and allaverred cromlecks, and when I heard his lewdbrogue reciping his cheap cheateary gospeds to sintry and santry and sentry and suntry I thought he was only haftara having afterhis brokeforths but be the homely Churopodvas I no sooner seen aghist of his frighteousness then I was bibbering with vear a few versets off fooling for fjorg for my fifth foot. Of manifest 'tis obedience and the. Flute!

TAFF (*though the unglucksarsoon is giming for to git him, jotning in, hoghly ligious, hapagodlap, like a soldierry sap, with a pique at his cue and a tyr in his eye and a bond of his back and a croak in his cry as did jolly well harm lean o'er him*) Is not athug who would. Weepon, weeponder, song of sorrowmon! Which goatheye and sheepskeer they damnty well know. Papaist! Gambanman! Take the cawraidd's blow! Yia! Your partridge's last!

BUTT (*giving his scimmianised twinge in acknuckledownedgment of this cumulikick, strafe from the firetrench, studenly drobs led, satoniseels ouchyotchy, he changecors induniforms as he is lefting the gat out of the big: his face glows green, his hair greys white, his bleyes bcome broon to suite his cultic twalette*). But when I seeing him in his oneship fetch along within hail that tourrible tall with his nitshnykopfgoknob and attempting like a brandylogged rudeman cathargic, lugging up and laiding down his livepelts so cruschinly

like Mebbuck at Messar and expousing his old skinful self tailtottom
by manurevring in open ordure to renewmurature with the cow-
ruads in their airish pleasantry I thanked he was recovering breadth
from some herdsquatters beyond the carcasses and I couldn't erver
nerver to tell a liard story not of I knew the prize if from lead or
alimoney. But when I got inoccupation of a full new of his old base-
middelism, in ackshan, pagne pogne, by the veereyed lights of the
stormtrooping clouds and in the sheenflare of the battleaxes of
the heroim and mid the shieldfails awail of the bitteraccents of the
sorafim and caught the pfierce tsmell of his aurals, orankastank, a
suphead setrapped, like Peder the Greste, altipaltar, my bill it for-
sooks allegiance (gut bull it!) and, no lie is this, I was babbeing and
yetaghain bubbering, bibbelboy, me marrues me shkewers me gnaas
me fiet, tob tob tob beat it, solongopatom. Clummensy if ever misused, must used you's now! But, meac Coolp, Arram of Eirzerum,
as I love our Deer Dirouchy, I confesses withould pridejealice when
I looked upon the Saur of all the Haurousians with the weight of his
arge fullin upon him from the travaillings of his tommuck and
rueckenased the fates of a bosser there was fear on me the sons of
Nuad for him and it was heavy he was for me then the way I im-
mingled my Irmenial hairmaierians ammongled his Gospolis fomili-
ours till, achaura moucreas, I adn't the arts to.

TAFF (*as a marrer off act, prepensing how such waldmanns from
Burnias seduced country clowns, he is preposing barangaparang
after going knowing what he is doing after to see him pluggy well
moidered as a murder effect, you bet your blowie knife, before he
doze soze, sopprused though he is*) Grot Zot! You hidn't the hurts?
Vott Fonn!

BUTT (*hearing somrother sudly give tworthree peevish sniff snuff
snoores like govalise falseleep he waitawhishts to see might he stirs
and then goes on kuldrum like without asking for pepeace or anysing
a soul*). Merzmard! I met with whom it was too late. My fate! O
hate! Fairwail! Fearwealing of the groan! And think of that when
you smugs to bagot.

TAFF (*who meanwhilome at yarn's length so as to put a nodje
in the poestcher, by wile of stoccan his hand and of rooma makin
ber getting umptyums gatherumed off the skattert, had been lavish-
ing, lagan on lighthouse, words of silent power, susu glouglou biri-
biri gongos, upon the repleted speechsalver's innkeeping right which,
thanks giveme and naperied norms nonobstaclant, there can be little
doubt, have resulted in a momstchance ministring of another guid-*

ness, my good, to see) Bompromifazzio! Shumpum for Pa-li-di and
oukosouso for the nipper dandy! Trink off this scup and be bladdy
orafferteed! To bug at?

BUTT (*he whipedoff's his chimbley phot, as lips lovecurling to the
tongueopener, he takecups the communion of sense at the hands of
the foregiver of trosstpassers and thereinofter centelinnates that
potifex miximhost with haruspical hospedariaty proferring into his
pauses somewhot salt bacon*). Theres scares knud in this gnarld
warld a fully so svend as dilates for the improvement of our foerses
of nature by your very ample solvent of referacting upon me like is
boesen fiennd.

[*The other foregotthened abbosed in the Mullingaria are
during this swishingsight teilweisioned. How the fictionable world
in Fruzian Creamtartery is loading off heavy furses and affubling
themselves with muckinstushes. The neatschknee Novgolosh. How
the spinach ruddocks are being tatoovatted up for the second
comings of antigreenst. Hebeneros for Aromal Peace. How Alibey
Ibrahim wisheths Bella Suora to a holy cryptmahs while the
Arumbian Knives Riders axecutes devilances round the jehumis-
pheure. Learn the Nunsturk. How Old Yales boys is making
rebolutions for the cunning New Yirls, never elding, still be-
gidding, never to mate to lend, never to ate selleries and never
to add soulleries and never to ant sulleries and never to aid silleries
with sucharow with sotchyouroff as Burkeley's Show's a ruction-
getherall. Phone for Phineal toomellow aftermorn and your
phumeral's a roselixion.*]

TAFF (*now as he has been past the buckthurnstock from Peadhar
Piper of Colliguchuna, whiles they all are bealting pots to dubrin
din for old daddam dombstom to tomb and wamb humbs lumbs
agamb, glimpse agam, glance agen, rise up road and hive up hill,
and find your pollyvoulley foncey pitchin ingles in the parler*).
Since you are on for versingrhetorish say your piece! How Buccleuch
shocked the rosing girnirilles. A ballet of Gasty Power. A hov and
az ov and off like a gow! And don't live out the sad of tearfs, piddya-
whick! Not offgott affsang is you, buthbach? Ath yetheredayth noth
endeth, hay? Vaersegood! Buckle to! Sayyessik, Ballygarry. The fourscore soculums are watchyoumaycodding to cooll the skoopgoods
blooff. Harkabuddy, feign! Thingman placeyear howed wholst som-
wom shimwhir tinkledinkledelled. Shinfine deed in the myrtle of the

bog tway fainmain stod op to slog, free bond men lay lurkin on.
Tuan about whattinghim! Fore sneezturmdrappen! 'Twill be
a rpnice pschange, arrah, sir? Can you come it, budd?

BUTT (*who in the cushlows of his goodsforseeking hoarth, ever
fondlinger of his pimple spurk, is a niallist of the ninth homestages,
the babybell in his baggutstract upper going off allatwanst, begad,
lest he should challenge himself, beygoad, till angush*). Horrasure,
toff! As said as would. It was Colporal Phailinx first. Hittit was of
another time, a white horsday where the midril met the bulg,
sbogom, roughnow along about the first equinarx in the cholon-
der, on the plain of Khorason as thou goest from the mount of Bekel,
Steep Nemorn, elve hundred and therety and to years how the krow
flees end in deed, after a power of skimiskes, blodidens and godinats
of them, when we sight the beasts, (hegheg whatlk of wraimy wetter!), moist moonful date man aver held dimsdzey death with, and
higheye was in the Reilly Oirish Krzerszonese Milesia asundurst
Sirdarthar Woolwichleagues, good tomkeys years somewhile in
Crimealian wall samewhere in Ayerland, during me weeping still-
stumms over the freshprosts of Eastchept and the dangling garters
of Marrowbone and daring my wapping stiltstunts on Bostion Moss,
old stile and new style and heave a lep onwards. And winn again,
blaguadargoos, or lues the day, plays goat, the banshee pealer, if
moskats knows whoss whizz, the great day and the druidful day
come San Patrisky and the grand day, the excellent fine splendorous
long agreeable toastworthy cylindrical day, go Sixt of the Ninth, the
heptahundread annam dammias that Hajizfijjiz ells me is and will
and was be till the timelag is in it that's told in the Bok of Alam to
columnkill all the prefacies of Erin gone brugk. But Icantenue. And
incommixtion. We was lowsome like till we'd took out after the dead
beats. So I begin to study and I soon show them day's reasons how
to give the cold shake to they blighty perishers and lay one over the
beats. All feller he look he call all feller come longa villa finish. Toumbalo, how was I acclapadad! From them banjopeddlars on
the raid. Gidding up me anti vanillas and getting off the stissas me
aunties. Boxerising and coxerusing. And swiping a johnny dann
sweept for to exercitise myself neverwithstanding the topkats and
his roaming cartridges, orussheying and patronning, out all over
Crummwiliam wall. Be the why it was me who haw haw.

TAFF (*all for letting his tinder and lighting be put to beheiss in
the feuer and, while durblinly obasiant to the felicias of the skivis,*

still smolking his fulvurite turfkish in the rooking pressance of laddios). Yaa hoo how how, col? Whom battles joined no bottles sever! Worn't you aid a comp?

BUTT (*in his difficoltous tresdobremient, he feels a bitvalike a baddlefall of staot but falls a batforlake a borrlefull of bare*). And me awlphul omegrims! Between me rassociations in the postleadeny past and me disconnections with aplompervious futules I've a boodle full of maimeries in me buzzim and medears runs sloze, bleime, as I now with platoonic leave recoil in (how the thickens they come back to one to rust!) me misenary post for all them old boyars that's now boomaringing in waulholler, me alma marthyrs. I dring to them, bycorn spirits fuselaiding, and you cullies adjutant, even where its contentsed wody, with absents wehrmuth. Junglemen in agleement, I give thee our greatly swooren, Theoccupant that Rueandredful, the thrownfullvner and all our royal devouts with the arrest of the whole inhibitance of Neuilands! One brief mouth. And a velligoolapnow! Meould attashees the currgans, (if they could get a kick at this time for all that's hapenced to us!) Cedric said Gormleyson and Danno O'Dunnochoo and Conno O'Cannochar it is this were their names for we were all under that manner barracksers on Kong Gores Wood together, thurkmen three, with those khakireinettes, our miladies in their toileries, the twum plumyumnietcies, Vjeras Vjenaskayas, of old Djadja Uncken who was a great mark for jinking and junking, up the palposes of womth and wamth, we war, and the charme of their lyse brocade. For lispias harth a burm in eye but whem it bames fire norone screeneth. Hulp, hulp, huzzars! Raise ras tryracy! Freetime's free! Up Lancesters! Anathem!

TAFF (*who still senses that heavinscent houroines that entertrained him who they were sinuorivals from the sunny Espionia but plied wopsy with his wallets in thatthack of the bustle Bakerloo,* (11.32), *passing the uninational truthbosh in smoothing irony over the multinotcheralled infructuosities of his grinner set*). The rib, the rib, the quean of oldbyrdes, Sinya Sonyavitches! Your Rhoda Cockardes that are raday to embrace our ruddy inflamtry world! In their ohosililesvienne biribarbebeway. Till they've kinks in their tringers and boils on their taws. Whor dor the pene lie, Mer Pencho? Ist dramhead countmortial or gonorrhal stab? Mind your pughs and keaoghs, if you piggots, marsh! Do the nut, dingbut! Be a dag! For zahur and zimmerminnes! Sing in the chorias to the ethur:

[*In the heliotropical noughttime following a fade of trans-*
formed Tuff and, pending its viseversion, a metenergic reglow
of beaming Batt, the bairdboard bombardment screen, if taste-
fully taut guranium satin, tends to teleframe and step up to the
charge of a light barricade. Down the photoslope in syncopanc
pulses, with the bitts bugtwug their teffs, the missledhropes,
glitteraglatteraglutt, borne by their carnier walve. Spraygun rakes
and splits them from a double focus: grenadite, damnymite, alex-
tronite, nichilite: and the scanning firespot of the sgunners
traverses the rutilanced illustred sunksundered lines. Shlossh! A
gaspel truce leaks out over the caeseine coatings. Amid a fluores-
cence of spectracular mephiticism there caoculates through the
inconoscope stealdily a still, the figure of a fellowchap in the wohly
ghast, Popey O'Donoshough, the jesuneral of the russuates. The
idolon exhibisces the seals of his orders: the starre of the Son of
Heaven, the girtel of Izodella the Calottica, the cross of Michel-
ides Apaleogos, the latchet of Jan of Nepomuk, the puffpuff and
pompom of Powther and Pall, the great belt, band and bucklings
of the Martyrology of Gorman. It is for the castomercies mud-
wake surveice. The victar. Pleace to notnoys speach above your
dreadths, please to doughboys. Hll, smthngs gnwrng wthth sprsn-
wtch! He blanks his oggles because he confesses to all his tellavi-
cious nieces. He blocks his nosoes because that he confesses to
everywheres he was always putting up his latest faengers. He
wollops his mouther with a sword of tusk in as because that he
confesses how opten he used be obening her howonton he used
be undering her. He boundles alltogotter his manucupes with his
pedarrests in asmuch as because that he confesses before all his
handcomplishies and behind all his comfoderacies. And (hereis
cant came back saying he codant steal no lunger, yessis, catz
come buck beques he caudant stail awake) he touched upon this
tree of livings in the middenst of the garerden for inasmuch as
because that he confessed to it on Hillel and down Dalem and
in the places which the lepers inhabit in the place of the stones
and in pontofert jusfuggading amoret now he come to think of it
jolly well ruttengenerously olyovyover the ole blucky shop. Pugger
old Pumpey O'Dungaschiff! There will be a hen collection of
him after avensung on the field of Hanar. Dumble down, looties
and gengstermen! Dtin, dtin, dtin, dtin!]

BUTT (*with a gisture expansive of Mr Lhugewhite Cadderpollard with sunflawered beautonhole pulled up point blanck by mailbag mundaynism at Oldbally Court though the hissindensity buck far of his melovelance tells how when he was fast marking his first lord for cremation the whyfe of his bothem was the very lad's thing to elter his mehind*). Prostatates, pujealousties! Dovolnoisers, prayshyous! Defense in every circumstancias of deboutcheries no the chaste daffs! Pack pickets, pioghs and kughs to be palseyputred! Be at the peme, prease, of not forgetting or mere betoken yourself to hother prace! Correct me, pleatze commando, for cossakes but I abjure of it. No more basquibezigues for this pole aprican! With askormiles' eskermillas. I had my billyfell of duckish delights the whole pukny time on rawmeots and juliannes with their lambstoels in my kiddeneys and my ramsbutter in their sassenacher ribs, knee her, do her and trey her, when th'osirian cumb dumb like the whalf on the fiord and we preying players and pinching peacesmokes, troupkers tomiatskyns all, for Father Petrie Spence of Parishmoslattary to go and leave us and the crimsend daun to shellalite on the darkumen (scene as signed, Slobabogue), feeding and sleeping on the huguenottes (the snuggest spalniel's where the lieon's tame!) and raiding revolations over the allbegeneses (sand us and saint us and sound as agun!). Yet still in all, spit for spat, like we chantied on Sunda schoon, every warson wearrier kaddies a komnate in his schnapsack and unlist I am getting foegutfulls of the rugiments of savaliged wildfire I was gamefellow willmate and send us victorias with nowells and brownings, dumm, sneak and curry, and all the fun I had in that fanagan's week. A strange man wearing abarrel. And here's a gift of meggs and teggs. And as I live by chipping nortons. And 'tis iron fits the farmer, ay. Arcdesedo! Renborumba! Then were the hellscyown days for our fellows, the loyal leibsters, and we was the redugout rawrecruitioners, praddies three and prettish too, a wheeze we has in our waynward islands, wee engrish, one long blue streak, jisty and pithy af durck rosolun, with hand to hand as Homard Kayenne was always jiggilyjugging about in his wendowed courage when our woos with the wenches went wined for a song, tsingirillies' zyngarettes, while Woodbine Willie, so popiular with the poppyrossies, our Chorney Choplain, blued the air. Sczlanthas! Banzaine! Bissbasses! S. Pivorandbowl. And we all tuned in to hear the topmast noviality. Up the revels drown the rinks and almistips all round! Paddy Bonhamme he vives! Encore! And tig for tag. Togatogtug. My droomodose days Y loved you abover all the strest. Blowhole brasshat and boy with his boots off and the butch of our bunch and all. It was buckoo bonzer, beleeme. I was a bare prive without my doglegs but I did not give to one humpenny dump, wingh or wangh, touching those thusengaged slavey generales of Tanah Kornalls, the meelisha's deelishas, pronouncing their very flank movemens in sunpictorsbosk. Baghus the whatwar! I could always take good cover of myself and, eyedulls or earwakers, preyers for rain or cominations, I did not care three tanker's hoots, ('sham! hem! or chaffit!) for any feelings from my lifeprivates on their reptrograd leanins because I have Their Honours booth my respectables sœurs assistershood off Lyndhurst Terrace, the puttih Misses Celana Dalems, and she in vinting her angurr can belle the troth on her alliance and I know His Heriness, my respeaktoble medams culonelle on Mellay Street, Lightnints Gundhur Sawabs, and they would never as the aimees of servation let me down. Not on your bludger life, touters! No peeping, pimpadoors! And, by Jova, I never went wrong nor let him doom till, risky wark rasky wolk, at the head of the wake, up come stumblebum (ye olde cottemptable!), his urssian gemenal, in his scutt's rudes unreformed and he went before him in that nemcon enchelonce with the same old domstoole story and his upleave the fallener as is greatly to be petted (whitesides do his beard!) and I seen his brichashert offensive and his boortholomas vadnhammaggs vise a vise them scharlot runners and how they gave love to him and how he took the ward from us (odious the fly fly flurtation of his him and hers! Just mairmaid maddeling it was it he was!) and, my oreland for a rolvever, sord, by the splunthers of colt and bung goes the enemay the Percy rally got me, messger, (as true as theirs an Almagnian Gothabobus!) to blow the grand off his aceupper. Thistake it 's meest! And after meath the dulwich. We insurrectioned and, be the procuratress of the hory synnotts, before he could tell pullyirragun to parrylewis, I shuttm, missus, like a wide sleever! Hump to dump! Tumbleheaver!

TAFF (*camelsensing that sonce they have given bron a nuhlan the volkar boastsung is heading to sea vermelhion but too wellbred not to ignore the umzemlianess of his rifal's preceedings, in an effort towards autosotorisation, effaces himself in favour of the idiology alwise behounding his lumpy hump off homosodalism which means that if he has lain amain to lolly his liking-cabronne!-he may pops lilly a young one to his herth-combrune-*) Oholy rasher, I'm believer! And Oho bullyclaver of ye, bragadore-gunneral! The grand ohold spider! It is a name to call to him Umsturdum Vonn!

Ah, you were shutter reshottus and sieger besieged. Aha race of fiercemarchands counterination oho of shorpshoopers.

BUTT (*miraculising into the Dann Deafir warcry, his bigotes bristling, as, jittinju triggity shittery pet, he shouts his thump and feeh fauh foul finngures up the heighohs of their ahs!*) Bluddymuddy-muzzle! The buckbeshottered! He'll umbozzle no more graves nor horne nor haunder, lou garou, for gayl geselles in dead men's hills! Kaptan (backsights to his bared!), His Cumbulent Embulence, the frustate fourstar Russkakruscam, Dom Allaf O'Khorwan, connundurumchuff.

TAFF (*who, asbestas can, wiz the healps of gosh and his bluzzid maikar, has been sulphuring to himsalves all the pungataries of sin praktice in failing to furrow theogonies of the dommed*). Trisseme, the mangoat! And the name of the Most Marsiful, the Aweghost, the Gragious One! In sobber sooth and in souber civiles? And to the dirtiment of the curtailment of his all of man? Notshoh?

BUTT (*maomant scoffin, but apoxyomenously deturbaned but thems bleachin banes will be after making a bashman's haloday out of the euphorious hagiohygiecynicism of his die and be diademmed*). Yastsar! In sabre tooth and sobre saviles! Senonnevero! That he leaves nyet is my grafe. He deared me to it and he dared me do it, and bedattle I didaredonit as Cocksnark of Killtork can tell and Ussur Ursussen of the viktaurious onrush with all the rattles in his arctic! As bold and as madhouse a bull in a meadows. Knout Knittrick Kinkypeard! Olefoh, the sourd of foemoe times! Unknun! For when meseemim, and tolfoklokken rolland allover ourloud's lande, beheaving up that sob of tunf for to claimhis, for to wollpimsolff, puddywhuck. Ay, and untuoning his culothone in an exitous erseroyal *Deo Jupto*. At that instullt to Igorladns! Prronto! I gave one dobblenotch and I ups with my crozzier. Mirrdo! With my how on armer and hits leg an arrow cockshock rockrogn. Sparro!

[*The abnihilisation of the etym by the grisning of the grosning of the grinder of the grunder of the first lord of Hurtreford expolodotonates through Parsuralia with an ivanmorinthorrorumble fragoromboassity amidwhiches general uttermosts confussion are perceivable moletons skaping with mulicules while coventry plumpkins fairlygosmotherthemselves in the Landaunelegants of Pinkadindy. Similar scenatas are projectilised from Hullulullu, Bawlawayo, empyreal Raum and mordern Atems. They were pre-*

cisely the twelves of clocks, noon minutes, none seconds. At some-
seat of Oldanelang's Konguerrig, by dawnybreak in Aira.]

TAFF (*skimperskamper, his wools gatherings all over cromlin*
what with the birstol boys artheynes and is it her tour and the crack-
ery of the fullfour fivefirearms and the crockery of their damdam
domdom chumbers). Wharall thubulbs uptheaires! Shattamovick?

BUTT (*pulling alast stark daniel with alest doog at doorak while*
too greater than pardon painfully the issue of his mouth diminuen-
doing, vility of vilities, he becomes, allasvitally, faint). Shurenoff!
Like Faun MacGhoul!

BUTT and TAFF (*desprot slave wager and foeman feodal un-*
sheckled, now one and the same person, their fight upheld to right
for a wee while being baffled and tottered, umbraged by the shadow
of Old Erssia's magisquammythical mulattomilitiaman, the living by
owning over the surfers of the glebe whose sway craven minnions
had caused to revile, as, too foul for hell, under boiling Mauses'
burning brand, he falls by Goll's gillie, but keenheartened by the
circuminsistence of the Parkes O'Rarelys in a hurdly gurdly Cicilian
concertone of their fonngeena barney brawl, shaken everybothy's
hands, while S. E. Morehampton makes leave to E. N. Sheilmartin
after Meetinghouse Lanigan has embaraced Vergemout Hall, and,
without falter or mormor or blathrehoot of sophsterliness, pugnate
the pledge of fiannaship, dook to dook, with a commonturn oudchd
of fest man and best man astoutsalliesemoutioun palms it off like
commodity tokens against a cococancancacacanotioun). When old
the wormd was a gadden and Anthea first unfoiled her limbs wan-
derloot was the way the wood wagged where opter and apter were
samuraised twimbs. They had their mutthering ivies and their murd-
hering idies and their mouldhering iries in that muskat grove but
there'll be bright plinnyflowers in Calomella's cool bowers when the
magpyre's babble towers scorching and screeching from the ravenin-
dove. If thees lobed the sex of his head and mees ates the seep of
his traublers he's dancing figgies to the spittle side and shoving outs
the soord. And he'll be buying buys and go gulling gells with his
flossim and jessim of carm, silk and honey while myandthys playing
lancifer lucifug and what's duff as a bettle for usses makes coy cosyn
corollanes' moues weeter to wee. So till butagain budly shoots thon
rising germinal let bodley chow the fatt of his anger and badley bide
the toil of his tubb.

[*The pump and pipe pingers are ideally reconstituted. The putther and bowls are peterpacked up. All the presents are determining as regards for the future the howabouts of their past absences which they might see on at hearing could they once smell of tastes from touch. To ought find a values for. The must overlistingness. When ex what is ungiven. As ad where. Stillhead. Blunk.*]

Shutmup. And bud did down well right. And if he sung dumb in his glass darkly speech lit face to face on allaround.

Vociferagitant. Viceversounding. Namely, Abdul Abulbul Amir or Ivan Slavansky Slavar. In alldconfusalem. As to whom the major guiltfeather pertained it was Hercushiccups' care to educe. Beauty's bath she's bound to bind beholders and pride, his purge, has place appoint in penance and the law's own libel lifts and lames the low with the lofty. Be of the housed! While the Hersy Hunt they harrow the hill for to rout them rollicking rogues from, rule those racketeer romps from, rein their rockery rides from. Rambling.

Nightclothesed, arooned, the conquerods sway. After their battle thy fair bosom.

— That is too tootrue enough in Solidan's Island as in Moltern Giaourmany and from the Amelakins off to date back to land of engined Egypsians, assented from his opening before his inlookers of where an oxmanstongue stalled stabled the wellnourished one, lord of the seven days, overlord of sats and suns, the sat of all the suns which are in the ring of his system of the sats of his sun, god of the scuffeldfallen skillfilledfelon, who (he contaimns) hangsters, who (he constrains) hersirrs, a gain changful, a mintage vaster, heavy on shirts, lucky with shifts, the topside humpup stummock atween his showdows fellah, Misto Teewiley Spillitshops, who keepeth watch in Khummer-Phett, whose spouse is An-Lyph, the dog's bladder, warmer of his couch in fore. We all, for whole men is lepers, have been nobbut wonterers in that chill childerness which is our true name after the allfaulters (mug's luck to em!) and, bespeaking of love and lie detectors in venuvarities, whateither the drugs truth of it, was there an iota of from the faust to the lost. And that is at most redoubtedly an overthrew of each and ilkermann of us, I persuade myself, before Gow, gentlemen, so true as this are my kopfinpot astrode on these is my boardsoldereds.

It sollecited, grobbling hummley, his roundhouse of seven orofaces, of all, guiltshouters or crimemummers, to be sayd by, codnops, advices for, free of gracies, scamps encloded, competitioning them, if they had steadied Jura or when they had raced Messafissi, husband of your wifebetter or bestman botchalover of you yourself, how comes ever a body in our taylorised world to selve out thishis, whither it gives a primeum nobilees for our notomise or naught, the farst wriggle from the ubivence, whereom is man, that old offender, nother man, wheile he is asame. And fullexampling. The pints in question. With some byspills. And sicsecs to provim hurtig. Soup's on!

— A time. And a find time. Whenin aye was a kiddling. And the tarikies held sowansopper. Let there beam a frishfrey. And they sodhe gudhe rudhe brodhe wedhe swedhe medhe in the kanddle-drum. I have just (let us suppraise) been reading in a (suppressed) book — it is notwithstempting by meassures long and limited—the latterpress is eminently legligible and the paper, so he eagerly seized upon, has scarsely been buttered in works of previous publicity wholebeit in keener notcase would I turf aside for pastureuration. Packen paper paineth whomto is sacred scriptured sign. Who straps it scraps it that might, if ashed, have healped. Enough, however, have I read of it, like my good bedst friend, to augur in the hurry of the times that it will cocommend the widest circulation and a reputation coextensive with its merits when inthrusted into safe and pious hands upon so edifying a mission as it, I can see, as is his. It his ambullished with expurgative plates, replete in information and accampaigning the action passiom, slopbang, whizzcrash, boomarattling from burst to past, as I have just been seeing, with my warmest venerections, of a timmersome townside upthecountrylifer, (Guard place the town!) allthose everwhalmed upon that preposterous blank seat, before the wordcraft of this early woodcutter, a master of vignettiennes and our findest grobsmid among all their orefices, (and, shukar in chowdar, so splunderdly English!) Mr Aubeyron Birdslay. Chubgoodchob, arsoncheep and wellwillworth a triat! Bismillafoulties. But the hasard you asks is justly ever behind his meddle throw! Those sad pour sad forengistanters, dastychappy dustyrust! Chaichairs. It is that something, awe, aurorbean in that fellow, hamid and damid, (did he have but Hugh de Brassey's beardslie lie wear mine of ancient guised) which comequeers this anywhat perssian which we, owe, realisinus with purups a dard of pene. There is among others pleasons whom I love and which are favourests to mind, one which I have pushed my finker in for the movement and, but for my sealring is none to hand I swear, she is highly catatheristic and there is another which I have fombly fongered freequuntly and, when my signet is on sign again I swear, she is deeply sangnificant. *Culpo de Dido!* Ars we say in the classies. *Kunstful,* we others said. What ravening shadow! What dovely line! Not the king of this age could richlier eyefeast in oreillental longuardness with alternate nightjoys of a thousand kinds but one kind. A shahrryar cobbler on me when I am lying! And whilst (when I doot my sliding panel and I hear cawcaw) I have been idylly turmbing over the loose looves leaflefts jaggled casuallty on the lamatory, as is my this is, as I must commit my lips to make misface for misfortune, often, so far as I can chance to recollect from the some farnights ago, (so dimsweet is that selvischdischdienence of to not to be able to be obliged to have to hold further anything than a stone his throw's fruit's fall!) when I, if you wil excuse for me this informal leading down of illexpressibles, enlivened toward the Author of Nature by the natural sins liggen gobelimned theirs before me, (how differended with the manmade Eonochs Cunstuntonopolies!), weathered they be of a general golf stature, assasserted, or blossomly emblushing thems elves underneed of some howthern folleys, am entrenched up contemplating of myself, wiz my naked I, for relieving purposes in our trurally virvir vergitabale (garden) I sometimes, maybe, what has justly said of old Flannagan, a wake from this or huntsfurwards, with some shock (shell I so render it?) have (when I ope my shylight window and I see coocoo) a notion quiet involuptary of that I am cadging hapsnots as at murmurrandoms of distend renations from ficsimilar phases or dugouts in the behindscenes of our earthwork (what rovining shudder! what deadly loom!) as this is, at no spatial time processly which regards to concrude chronology about which in fact, at spite of I having belittled myself to my gay giftname of insectarian, happy burgages abeyance would make homesweetstown hopeygoalucrey, my mottu propprior, as I claim, cad's truck, I coined, I am highly pelaged and deeply gluttened to mind hindmost hearts to see by their loudest reports from my threespawn bottery parts (shsh!) that, colombophile and corvinophobe alike, when I have remassed me, my travellingself, as from Magellanic clouds, after my contractual expenditures, through the perofficies of merelimb, I, my good grief, I am, I am big altoogooder.

He beached the bark of his tale; and set to husband and vine: and the harpermaster told all the living conservancy, know Meschiameschianah, how that win a gain was in again. Flying the Perse-

oroyal. Withal aboarder, padar and madar, hal and sal, the sens of
Ere with the duchtars of Iran. Amick amack amock in a mucktub.
Qith the tou loulous and the gryffygryffygryffs, at Fenegans Wick,
the Wildemanns. Washed up whight and deliveried rhight. Loud
lauds to his luckhump and bejetties on jonahs! And they winxed
and wanxed like baillybeacons. Till we woksed up oldermen.

From whose plultibust preaggravated, by baskatchairch theologies
(there werenighn on thaurity herouns in that alraschil arthouducks
draken), they were whoalike placed to say, in the matters off duco-
mans nonbar one, with bears' respects to him and bulls' acknowl-
edgments (come on now, girls! lead off, O cara, whichever won of
you wins! The two Gemuas and Jane Agrah and Judy Tombuys!)
disassembling and taking him apart, the slammocks, with discrim-
ination for his maypole and a rub in passing over his hump, dro-
gueries inaddendance, frons, fesces and frithstool: 1) he hade to
die it, the beetle, 2) he didhithim self, hod's fush, 3) all ever the
pelican huntered with truly fond bullpen backthought since his
toork human life where his personal low outhired his taratoryism,
the orenore under the selfhide of his bessermettle, was forsake in
his chiltern and lumbojumbo, 4) he was like Fintan fore flood and
after sometimes too damned merely often on the saved side, saw he
was, 5) regarding to prussyattes or quazzyverzing he wassand no
better than he would have been before he could have been better
than what he warrant after, 6) blood, musk or haschish, as coked,
diamoned or penceloid, and bleaching him naclenude from all
cohlorine matter, down to a boneash bittstoff, he's, tink fors tank,
the same old dustamount on the same old tincoverdull baubleclass,
totstittywinktosser and bogusbagwindburster, whether fitting tyres
onto Danelope boys or fluttering flaus for laurettas, whatever the
bucket brigade and the plug party says, touchant Arser of the Rum
Tipple and his camelottery and lyonesslooting but with a layaman's
brutstrenth, by Jacobob and Esahur and the all saults or all sallies,
what we warn to hear, jeff, is the woods of chirpsies cries to singaloo
sweecheeriode and sock him up, the oldcant rogue.

Group A.

You have jest (a ham) beamed listening through (a ham pig)
his haulted excerpt from John Whiston's fiveaxled production, *The
Coach With The Six Insides*, from the Tales of Yore of the times
gone by before there was a hofdking or a hoovthing or a pingina-
poke in Oreland, all sould. Goes Tory by Eeric Whigs is To Become
Tintinued in *Fearson's Nightly* in the Lets All Wake Brickfaced In

Lucan. Lhirondella, jaunty lhirondella! With tirra lirra rondinelles, atantivy we go!

Attention! Stand at!! Ease!!!

We are now diffusing among our lovers of this sequence (to you! to you!) the dewfolded song of the naughtingels (Alys! Alysaloe!) from their sheltered positions, in rosescenery haydyng, on the heather side of waldalure, Mount Saint John's, Jinnyland, whither our allies winged by duskfoil from Mooreparque, swift sanctuary seeking, after Sunsink gang (Oiboe! Hitherzither! Almost dotty! I must dash!) to pour their peace in partial (floflo floreflorence), sweet-ishsad lightandgayle, twittwin twosingwoolow. Let everie sound of a pitch keep still in resonance, jemcrow, jackdaw, prime and secund with their terce that whoe betwides them, now full theorbe, now dulcifair, and when we press of pedal (sof!) pick out and vowelise your name. A mum. You pere Golazy, you mere Bare and you Bill Heeny, and you Smirky Dainty and, more beethoken, you wheck-foolthenairyans with all your badchthumpered peanas! We are gluckglucky in our being so far fortunate that, bark and bay duol with Man Goodfox inchimings having ceased to the moment, so al-low the clinkars of our nocturnefield, night's sweetmoztheart, their Carmen Sylvae, my quest, my queen. Lou must wail to cool me airly! Coil me curly, warbler dear! May song it flourish (in the under-wood), in chorush, long make it flourish (in the Nut, in the Nutsky) till thorush! Secret Hookup.

— Roguenaar Loudbrags, that soddy old samph! How high is vuile, var?

To which yes he did, capt, that was the answer.

— And his shartshort trooping its colours! We knows his ventru-quulence.

Which that that rang rippripripplying.

—Bulbul, bulbulone! I will shally. Thou shalt willy. You wouldnt should as youd remesmer. I hypnot. 'Tis golden sickle's hour. Holy moon priestess, we'd love our grappes of mistellose! Moths the mat-ter? Pschtt! Tabarins comes. To fell our fairest. O gui, O gui! Salam, salms, salaum! Carolus! O indeed and we ware! And hoody crow was ere. I soared from the peach and Missmolly showed her pear too, onto three and away. Whet the bee as to deflowret greendy grassies yellowhorse. Kematitis, cele our erdours! Did you aye, did you eye, did you everysee suchaway, suchawhy, eeriewhigg airy-whugger? Even to the extremity of the world? Dingoldell! The enor-manous his, our littlest little! Wee wee, that long alancey one! Let sit on this anthill for our frilldress talk after this day of making blithe inveiled the heart before our groatsupper serves to us Panchomaster and let harleqwind play peeptomine up all our colombinations! Wins won is nought, twigs too is nil, tricks trees makes nix, fairs fears stoops at nothing. And till Arthur comes againus and sen peatrick's he's reformed we'll pose him together a piece, a pace. Shares in guineases! There's lovely the sight! Surey me, man weepful! Big Seat, you did hear? And teach him twisters in tongue irish. Pat lad may goh too. Quicken, aspen; ash and yew; willow, broom with oak for you. And move your tellabout. Not nice is that, limpet lady! Spose we try it promissly. Love all. Naytellmeknot tennis! Taunt me treattening! But do now say to Mr Eustache! Ingean mingen has to hear. Whose joint is out of jealousy now? Why, heavilybody's evillyboldy's. Hopping Gracius, onthy ovful! O belessk mie, what a nerve! How a mans in his armor we nurses know. Wingwong welly, pitty pretty Nelly! Some Poddy pitted in, will anny petty pullet out? Call Kitty Kelly! Kissykitty Killykelly! What a nossowl buzzard! But what a neats ung gels!

Here all the leaves alift aloft, full o'liefing, fell alaughing over Ombrellone and his parasollieras with their black thronguards from the County Shillelagh. Ignorant invincibles, innocents immutant! Onzel grootvatter Lodewijk is onangonamed before the bridge of primerose and his twy Isas Boldmans is met the blueybells near Dandeliond. We think its a gorsedd shame, these godoms. A lark of limonladies! A lurk of orangetawneymen! You're backleg wounted, budkley mister, bester of the boyne!

And they leaved the most leavely of leaftimes and the most folliagenous till there came the marrer of mirth and the jangtherapper of all jocolarinas and they were as were they never ere. Yet had they laughtered, one on other, undo the end and enjoyed their laughings merry was the times when so grant it High Hilarion us may too!

Cease, prayce, storywalkering around with gestare romanoverum he swinking about is they think and plan unrawil what.

Back to Droughty! The water of the face has flowed.

The all of them, the sowriegueuxers, blottyeyed boys, in that pig's village smoke, a sixdigitarian legion on druid circle, the Clandibblon clam cartel, then pulled out and came off and rally agreed them, roasted malts with toasted burleys, in condomnation of his totomptation and for the duration till his repepulation, upon old nollcromforemost ironsides, as camnabel chieftain, since, as Sammon

trowed to explain to summon, seeing that, as he had contracted out
of islands empire, he might as coolly have rolled to school call, tar-
ponturboy, a grampurpoise, the manyfathom bringeroom with the
fortyinch bride, out of the cuptin klanclord kettle auction like the
soldr of a britsh he was bound to be and become till the sea got him
whilask, from maker to misses and what he gave was as a pattern,
he, that hun of a horde, is a finn as she, his tent wife, is a lap, at
home on a steed, abroad by the fire (to say nothing of him having
done whatyouknow howyousaw whenyouheard whereyouwot, the
kenspeckled souckar, generose as cocke, greediguss with garzelle,
uprighter of age and most umbrasive of yews all, under heaviest
corpsus exemption) and whoasever spit her in howsoever's fondling
saving her keepers that mould the bould she sould to hould the wine
that wakes the barley, the peg in his pantry to hold the heavyache
off his heart. The droll delight of deemsterhood, a win from the wood
to bond. Like the bright lamps, Thamamahalla, yearin out yearin.
Auspicably suspectable but in expectancy of respectableness. From
dirty flock bedding, drip dropping through the ceiling, with two
sisters of charities on the front steps and three evacuan cleansers
at the back gaze, single box and pair of chairs (suspectable), occasionally and alternatively used by husband when having writing
to do in connection with equitable druids and friendly or other
societies through periods of dire want with comparative plenty
(thunderburst, ravishment, dissolution and providentiality) to a sofa
allbeit of hoarsehaar with Amodicum cloth, hired payono, still playing off, used by the youngsters for czurnying out oldstrums, three
bedrooms upastairs, of which one with fireplace (aspectable), with
greenhouse in prospect (particularly perspectable).

And you, when you kept at Dulby, were you always (for that
time only) what we knew how when we (from that point solely)
were you know where? There you are! And why? Why, hitch a cock
eye, he was snapped on the sly upsadaisying coras pearls out of the
pie when all the perts in princer street set up their tinker's humn,
(the rann, the rann, that keen of old bards), with them newnesboys
pearcin screaming off their armsworths. The boss made dovesan-
draves out of his bucknesst while herself wears the bowler's hat in
her bath. Deductive Almayne Rogers disguides his voice, shetters
behind hoax chesnote from exexive. Heat wives rasing. They jest
keeps rosing. He jumps leaps rizing. Howlong!

You known that tom? I certainly know. Is their bann bothstiesed?
Saddenly now. Has they bane reneemed? Soothinly low. Does they

ought to buy the papelboy when he footles up their suit? He's their mark to foil the flouter and they certainty owe.

He sprit in his phiz (baccon!). He salt to their bis (pudden!). He toockled her palam (so calam is solom!). And he suked their friends' leave (bonnick lass, fair weal!)

— Guilty but fellows culpows! It was felt by me sindeade, that submerged doughdoughty doubleface told waterside labourers. But since we for athome's health have chanced all that, the wild whips, the wind ships, the wonderlost for world hips, unto their foursquare trust prayed in aid its plumptylump piteousness which, when it turtled around seeking a thud of surf, spake to approach from inherdoff trisspass through minxmingled hair. Though I may have hawked it, said, and selled my how hot peas after theactrisscalls from my imprecurious position and though achance I could have emptied a pan of backslop down drain by whiles of dodging a rere from the middenprivet appurtenant thereof, salving the presents of the board of wumps and pumps, I am ever incalpable, where release of prisonals properly is concerned, of unlifting upfallen girls wherein dangered from them in thereopen out of unadulteratous bowery, with those hintering influences from an angelsexonism. It was merely my barely till their oh offs. Missaunderstaid. Meggy Guggy's giggag. The code's proof! The rebald danger with they who would bare whiteness against me I dismissem from the mind of good. He can tell such as story to the Twelfth Maligns that my first was a nurssmaid and her fellower's a willbe perambulatrix. There are twingty to twangty too thews and leathermail coatschemes penparing to hostpost for it valinnteerily with my valued fofavour to the post puzzles deparkment with larch parchels' of presents for future branch offercings. The green approve the raid! Shaum Baum's bode he is amustering in the groves while his shool comes merging along! Want I put myself in their kirtlies I were ayearn to leap with them and show me too bisextine. Dear and lest I forget mergers and bow to you low, marchers! Attemption! What a mazing month of budsome misses they are making, so wingtywish to flit beflore their kin! Attonsure! Ears to hears! The skall of a gall (for every dime he yawpens that momouth you could park your ford in it) who has papertreated him into captivities with his inside man by a hocksheat of starvision for an avragetopeace of parchment, cooking up his lenses to be my apoclogypst, the recreuter of conscraptions, let him be asservent to Kinahaun! For (peace peace perfectpeace!) I have abwaited me in a water of Elin and I have placed my reeds intectis

before the Registower of the perception of tribute in the hall of the
city of Analbe. How concerns any merryaunt and hworsoever
gravesobbers it is perensempry sex of fun to help a dazzle off the
othour. What for Mucias and Gracias may the duvlin rape the hand-
somst! And the whole mad knightmayers' nest! Tunpother, prison
and plotch! If Y shoulden somewhat, well, I am able to owe it, hearth
and chemney easy. They seeker for vannflaum all worldins merkins.
I'll eager make lyst turpidump undher arkens. Basast! And if my
litigimate was well to wrenn tigtag cackling about it, like the sally
berd she is, to abery ham in the Cutey Strict, (I shall call upon my
first among my lost of lyrars beyond a jingoobangoist, to overcast
her) dismissing mundamanu all the riflings of her victuum gleaner
(my old chuck! she drakes me druck! turning out, gay at ninety!)
and well shoving off a boastonmess like lots wives does over her
handpicked hunsbend, as she would be calling, well, for further
oil mircles upon all herwayferer gods and reanouncing my deviltries
as was I a locally person of caves until I got my purchase on her
firmforhold I am, I like to think, by their sacreligion of daimond
cap daimond, confessedly in my baron gentilhomme to the manhor
bourne till ladiest day as panthoposopher, to have splet for groont
a peer of bellows like Bacchulus shakes a rousing guttural at any
old cerpaintime by peaching (allsole we are not amusical) the warry
warst against myself in the defile as a lieberretter sebaiscopal of
these mispeschyites of the first virginial water who, without an auction of biasement from my part, with gladyst tone ahquickyessed
in it, overhowe and underwhere, the totty lolly poppy flossy conny
dollymaukins. Though I heave a coald on my bauck and am could
up to my eres hoven sametimes I used alltides to be aswarmer for
the meekst and the graced. You are not going to not. You might be
threeabreasted wholenosing at a whallhoarding from our Don Amir
anent villayets prostatution precisingly kuschkars tarafs and it could
be double densed uncounthest hour of allbleakest age with a bad of
wind and a barran of rain, nompos mentis like Novus Elector, what
with his Marx and their Groups, yet did a doubt, should a dare,
were to you, you would do and dhamnk me, shenker, dhumnk you.
Skunk. And fare with me to share with me. Hinther and thonther,
hant by hont. By where dauvening shedders down whose rovely
lanes. As yose were and as yese is. Sure and you would, Mr Mac
Gurk! Be sure and you would, Mr O'Duane! To be sure and you
would so, Mr MacElligut! Wod you nods? Mom mom. No mum
has the rod to pud a stub to the lurch of amotion. My little love ap-

prencisses, my dears, the estelles, van Nessies von Nixies voon der pool, which I had a reyal devouts for yet was it marly lowease or just a feel with these which olderman K.K. Alwayswelly he is showing ot the fullnights for my palmspread was gav to a parsleysprig, the curliest weedeen old ocean coils around, so spruce a spice for salthorse, sonnies, and as tear to the thrusty as Taylor's Spring, when aftabournes, when she was look like a little cheayat chilled (Oh sard! ah Mah!) by my tide impracing, as Beacher seath, and all the colories fair fled from my folced cheeks! Popottes, where you canceal me you mayst forced guage my bribes. Wickedgapers, I appeal against the light! A nexistence of vividence! Panto, boys, is on a looser inloss; ballet, girls, suppline thrown tights. I have wanted to thank you such a long time so much now. Thank you. Sir, kindest of bottleholders and very dear friend, among our hearts of steel, froutiknow, it will befor you, me dare beautiful young soldier, winninger nor anyour of rudimental moskats, before you go to mats, you who have watched your share with your sockboule sodalists on your buntad nogs at our love tennis squats regatts, suckpump, when on with the balls did disserve the fain, my goldrush gainst her silvernetss, to say, biguidd, for the love of goddess and perthanow as you reveres your one mothers, mitsch for matsch, and while I reveal thus my deepseep daughter which was bourne up pridely out of medsdreams unclouthed when I was pillowing in my brime (of Saturnay Eve, how now, woren't we't?), to see, I say, whoahoa, in stay of execution *in re* Milcho Melekmans, increaminated, what you feel, oddrabbit, upon every strong ground you have ever taken up, by bitterstiff work or battonstaff play, with assault of turk against a barrakraval of grakeshoots, e'en tho' Jambuwel's defecalties is Terry Shimmyrag's upperturnity, if that is grace for the grass what is balm for the bramblers, as it is as it is, that I am the catasthmatic old ruffin sippahsedly improctor to be seducint trovatellas, the dire daffy damedeaconesses, like (why sighs the sootheesinger) the lilliths oft I feldt, and, when booboob brutals and cautiouses only aims at the oggog hogs in the humand, then, (Houtes, Blymey and Torrenation, upkurts and scotchem!) I'll tall tale tell croon paysecurers, sowill nuggets and nippers, that thash on me stumpen blows the gaff off mombition and thit thides or marse makes a good dayle to be shattat. Fall stuff.

His rote in ere, afstef, was.

And dong wonged Magongty till the bombtomb of the warr, thrusshed in his whole soort of cloose.

Whisht who wooed in Weald, bays of Bawshaw binding. The desire of Miriam is the despair of Marian as Joh Joseph's beauty is Jacq Jacob's grief. Brow, tell nun; eye, feign sad; mouth, sing mim. Look at Lokman! Whatbetween the cupgirls and the platterboys. And he grew back into his grossery baseness: and for all his grand remonstrance: and there you are.

Here endeth chinchinatibus with have speak finish. With a haygue for a halt on a pouncefoot panse. Pink, pleas pink, two pleas pink, how to pleas pink.

Punk.

Mask one. Mask two. Mask three. Mask four.

Up.

— Look about you, Tutty Comyn!

— Remember and recall, Kullykeg!

— When visiting Dan Leary try the corner house for thee.

— I'll gie ye credit for simmence more if ye'll be lymphing.

Our four avunculusts.

And, since threestory sorratelling was much too many, they maddened and they morgued and they lungd and they jowld. Synopticked on the word.

Till the Juke done it.

Down.

Like Jukoleon, the seagoer, when he bore down in his perry boat he had raised a slide and shipped his orders and seized his pullets and primed their plumages, the fionnling and dubhlet, the dun and the fire, and, sending them one by other to fare fore forn, he had behold the residuance of a delugion: the foggy doze still going strong, the old thalassocrats of invisible empores, maskers of the waterworld, facing one way to another way and this way on that way, from severalled their fourdimmansions. Where the lighning leaps from the numbulous; where coold by cawld breide lieth langwid; the bounds whereinbourne our solied bodies all attomed attaim arrest: appoint, that's all. But see what follows. Wringlings upon wronglings among incomputables about an uncomeoutable (an angel prophetethis? kingcorrier of beheasts? the calif in his halifskin? that eyriewinging one?) and the voids bubbily vode's dodos across the which the boomomouths from their dupest dupes were in envery and anononously blowing great.

Guns.

Keep backwards, please, because there was no good to gundy running up again. Guns. And it was written up in big capital. Guns.

Saying never underrupt greatgrandgosterfosters! Guns. And whatever one did they said, the fourlings, that on no acounts you were not to. Guns.

Not to pad them behaunt in the fear. Not to go, tonnerwatter, and bungley well chute the rising gianerant. Not to wandly be woking around jerumsalemdo at small hours about the murketplots, smelling okey boney, this little figgy and arraky belloky this little pink into porker but, porkodirto, to let the gentlemen pedestarolies out of the Monabella culculpuration live his own left leave, cullebuone, by perperusual of the petpubblicities without inwoking his also's between (*sic*) the arraky bone and (*suc*) the okey bellock. And not to not be always, hemmer and hummer, treeing unselves up with one exite but not to never be caving nicely, precisely, quicely, rebustly, tendrolly, unremarkably, forsakenly, haltedly, reputedly, firstly, somewhatly, yesayenolly about the back excits. Never to weaken up in place of the broths. Never to vvollusslleepp in the pleece of the poots. And, allerthings, never to ate the sour deans if they weren't having anysin on their consients. And, when in Zumschloss, to never, narks, cease till the finely ending was consummated by the completion of accomplishment.

And thus within the tavern's secret booth The wisehight ones who sip the tested sooth Bestir them as the Just has bid to jab The punch of quaram on the mug of truth.

K.C. jowls, they're sodden in the secret. K.C. jowls, they sure are wise. K.C. jowls, the justicestjobbers, for they'll find another faller if their ruse won't rise. Whooley the Whooper.

There is to see. Squarish large face with the atlas jacket. Brights, brownie eyes in bluesackin shoeings. Peaky booky nose over a lousiany shirt. Ruddy stackle hair besides a strawcamel belt. Namely. Gregorovitch, Leonocopolos, Tarpinacci and Duggelduggel. And was theys stare all atime? Yea but they was. Andoring the games, induring the studies, undaring the stories, end all. Ned? Only snugged then and cosied after one percepted nought while tuffbettle outraged the waywords and meansigns of their hinterhand suppliesdemands. And be they gone to splane splication? That host that hast one on the hoose when backturns when he facefronts none none in the house his geust has guest. You bet they is. And nose well down.

With however what sublation of compensation in the radification of interpretation by the byeboys? Being they. Mr G. B. W. Ashburner, S. Bruno's Toboggan Drive, Mr Faixgood, Bellchimbers,

Carolan Crescent, Mr I. I. Chattaway, Hilly Gape, Poplar Park,
Mr Q. P. Dieudonney, The View, Gazey Peer, Mr T. T. Erch-
deakin, Multiple Lodge, Jiff Exby Rode, Mr W. K. Ferris-Fender,
Fert Fort, Woovil Doon Botham ontowhom adding the tout that
pumped the stout that linked the lank that cold the sandy that next-
doored the rotter that rooked the rhymer that lapped at the hoose
that Joax pilled.

They had heard or had heard said or had heard said written.

Fidelisat.

That there first a rudrik kingcomed to an inn court; and the seight
of that yard was a perchypole with a loovahgloovah on it; last man-
narks maketh man when wandshift winneth womans: so how
would it hum, whoson of a which, if someof aswas to start to stunt
the story on?

So many needles to ponk out to as many noodles as are company,
they noddling all about it *tutti* to *tempo*, decumans numbered too,
(*a*) well, that the secretary bird, better known as Pandoria Paul-
labucca, whom they thought was more like a solicitor general, in-
discriminatingly made belief mid authorsagastions from Schelm the
Pelman to write somewords to Senders about her chilikin puck,
laughing that Poulebec would be the death of her, (*b*) that, well,
that Madges Tighe, the postulate auditressee, when her daremood's
a grownian, is always on the who goes where, hoping to Michal for
the latter to turn up with a cupital tea before her ephumeral comes
off without any much father which is parting parcel of the same
goumeral's postoppage, it being lookwhyse on the whence blows
weather helping mickle so that the loiter end of that leader may
twaddle out after a cubital lull with a hopes soon to ear, comprong?
(*c*) becakes the goatsman on question, or whatever the hen the
bumbler was, feeling not up to scratch bekicks of whatever the kid-
dings Payne Inge and Popper meant for him, thoughy onced at a
throughlove, true grievingfrue danger, as a nirshe persent to his
minstress, devourced the pair of them Mather Caray's chucklings,
pante blanche, and skittered his litters like the cavaliery man in
Cobra Park for ungeborn yenkelmen, Jeremy Trouvas or Kepin
O'Keepers, any old howe and any old then and when around Dix
Dearthy Dungbin, remarking scenically with laddylike lassitude
upon what he finally postscrapped, (*d*) after it's so long till I
thanked you about I do so much now thank you so very much as
you introduced me to fourks, (*e*) will, these remind to be sane? (*f*)
Fool step! Aletheometry? Or just zoot doon floon?

Nut it out, peeby eye! Onamassofmancynaves.

But. Top.

You were in the same boat of yourselves too, Getobodoff or Treamplasurin; and you receptionated the most diliskious of milisk; which it all flowowered your drooplin dunlearies: but dribble a drob went down your rothole. Meaning, Kelly, Grimes, Phelan, Mollanny, O'Brien, MacAlister, Sealy, Coyle, Hynes-Joynes, Naylar-Traynor, Courcy de Courcy and Gilligan-Goll.

Stunner of oddstodds on bluebleeding boarhorse! What soresen's head subrises thus tous out of rumpumplikun oak with, well, we cannot say whom we are looking like through his nowface? It is of Noggens whilk dusts the bothsides of the seats of the bigslaps of the bogchaps of the porlarbaar of the marringaar of the Lochlunn gonlannludder of the feof of the foef of forfummed Ship-le-Zoyd.

Boumce! It is polisignstunter. The Sockerson boy. To pump the fire of the lewd into those soulths of bauchees, havsousedovers, tillfellthey deadwar knootvindict. An whele time he was rancing there smutsy floskons nodunder ycholerd for their poopishers, ahull onem Fyre maynoother endnow! Shatten up ship! Bouououmce! Nomo clandoilskins cheakinlevers! All ashored for Capolic Gizzards! Stowlaway there, glutany of stainks! Porterfillyers and spirituous suncksters, oooom oooom!

As these vitupetards in his boasum he did strongleholder, bushbrows, nobblynape, swinglyswanglers, sunkentrunk, that from tin of this clucken hadded runced slapottleslup. For him had hord from fard a piping. As? Of?

Dour douchy was a sieguldson. He cooed that loud nor he was young. He cud bad caw nor he was gray Like wather parted from the say.

Ostia, lift it! Lift at it, Ostia! From the say! Away from the say!

Himhim. Himhim.

Hearhasting he, himmed, reromembered all the chubbs, chipps, chaffs, chuckinpucks and chayney chimebells That he had mistributed in port, pub, park, pantry and poultryhouse, While they, thered, the others, that are, were most emulously concerned to cupturing the last dropes of summour down through their grooves of blarneying. Ere the sockson locked at the dure. Which he would, shuttinshure. And lave them to sture.

For be all rules of sport 'tis right That youth bedower'd to charm the night Whilst age is dumped to mind the day When wather parted from the say.

The humming, it's coming. Insway onsway.

Fingool MacKishgmard Obesume Burgearse Benefice, He was bowen hem and scrapin him in recolcitrantament to the rightabout And these probenopubblicoes clamatising for an extinsion on his hostillery With his chargehand bombing their eres. Tids, genmen, plays, she been goin shooter off almaynoother onawares.

You here nort farwellens rouster? Ashiffle ashuffle the wayve they.

From Dancingtree till Suttonstone There's lads no lie would filch a crown To mull their sack and brew their tay With wather parted from the say.

Lelong Awaindhoo's a selverbourne enrouted to Rochelle Lane and liberties those Mullinguard minstrelsers are marshalsing, par tunepiped road, under where, perked on hollowy hill, that poor man of Lyones, good Dook Weltington, hugon come errindwards, had hircomed to the belles bows and been cutattrapped by the mausers. Now is it town again, londmear of Dublin! And off coursse the toller, ples the dotter of his eyes with her: Moke the Wanst, whye doe we aime alike a pose of poeter peaced? While the dumb he shoots the shopper rope. And they all pour forth. Sans butly Tuppeter Sowyer, the rouged engenerand, a barttler of the beauyne, still our benjamin liefest, sometime frankling to thise citye, whereas bigrented him a piers half subporters for his arms, Josiah Pipkin, Amos Love, Raoul Le Febber, Blaize Taboutot, Jeremy Yopp, Francist de Loomis, Hardy Smith and Sequin Pettit followed by the snug saloon seanad of our Café Béranger. The scenictutors.

Because they wonted to get out by the goatweigh afore the sheep was looset for to wish the Wobbleton Whiteleg Welshers kailly-kailly kellykekkle and savebeck to Brownhazelwood from all the dinnasdoolins on the labious banks of their swensewn snewwesner, turned again weastinghome, by Danesbury Common, and they onely, duoly, thruely, fairly after rainydraining fountybuckets (chalkem up, hemptyempty!) till they caught the wind abroad (alley loafers passinggeering!) all the rockers on the roads and all the boots in the stretes.

Oh dere! Ah hoy!

Last ye, lundsmin, hasty hosty! For an anondation of mirification and the lutification of our paludination.

His bludgeon's bruk, his drum is tore. For spuds we'll keep the hat he wore And roll in clover on his clay By wather parted from the say.

Hray! Free rogue Mountone till Dew Mild Well to corry awen

and glowry! Are now met by Brownaboy Fuinnninuinn's former for a lyncheon partyng of his burgherbooh. The Shanavan Wacht. Rantinroarin Batteries Dorans. And that whistling thief, O' Ryne O'Rann. With a catch of her cunning like and nowhere a keener.

The for eolders were aspolootly at their wetsend in the mailing waters, trying to. Hide! Seek! Hide! Seek! Because number one lived at Bothersby North and he was trying to. Hide! Seek! Hide! Seek! And number two digged up Poors Coort, Soother, trying to. Hide! Seek! Hide! Seek! And nomber three he sleeped with Lilly Tekkles at The Eats and he was trying to. Hide! Seek! Hide! Seek! And the last with the sailalloyd donggie he was berthed on the Moherboher to the Washte and they were all trying to and baffling with the walters of, hoompsydoompsy walters of. High! Sink! High! Sink! High-ohigh! Sinkasink!

Waves.

The gangstairs strain and anger's up As Hoisty rares the can and cup To speed the bogre's barque away O'er wather parted from the say.

Horkus chiefest ebblynuncies!

— He shook be ashaped of hempshelves, hiding that shepe in his goat. And for rassembling so bearfellsed the magreedy prince of Roger. Thuthud. Heigh hohse, heigh hohse, our kindom from an orse! Bruni Lanno's woollies on Brani Lonni's hairyparts. And the hunk in his trunk it would be an insalt foul the matter of that cellaring to a pigstrough. Stop his laysense. Ink him! You would think him Alddaublin staking his lordsure like a gourd on puncheon. Deblinity devined. Wholehunting the pairk on a methylogical mission whenever theres imberillas! And calling Rina Roner Reinette Ronayne. To what mine answer is a lemans. Arderleys, beedles and postbillers heard him. Three points to one. Ericus Vericus corrupted into ware eggs. Dummy up, distillery! Broree aboo! Run him a johnsgate down jameseslane. Begetting a wife which begame his niece by pouring her youngthings into skintighs. That was when he had dizzy spells. Till Gladstools Pillools made him ride as the mall. Thanks to his huedobrass beerd. Lodenbroke the Longman, now he canseels under veerious persons but is always that Rorke relly! On consideration for the musickers he ought to have down it. Pass out your cheeks, why daunt you! Penalty, please! There you'll know how warder barded the bollhead that parssed our alley. We just are upsidedown singing what ever the dimkims mummur allalilty she pulls inner out heads. This is not the end of this by no man-

ners means. When you've bled till you're bone it crops out in your
flesh. To tell how your mead of, mard, is made of. All old Dadger-
son's dodges one conning one's copying and that's what wonder-
land's wanderlad'll flaunt to the fair. A trancedone boyscript with
tittivits by. Ahem. You'll read it tomorrow, marn, when the curds
on the table. A nigg for a nogg and a thrate for a throte. The audi-
tor learns. Still pumping on Torkenwhite Radlumps, Lencs. In pre-
plays to Anonymay's left hinted palinode obviously inspiterebbed
by a sibspecious connexion. Note the notes of admiration! See the
signs of suspicion! Count the hemisemidemicolons! Screamer caps
and invented gommas, quoites puntlost, forced to farce! The pipette
will say anything at all for a change. And you know what aglove
means in the Murdrus dueluct! Fewer to feud and rompant culotti-
cism, a fugle for the gleemen and save, sit and sew. And a pants
outsizinned on the Doughertys' duckboard pointing to peace at
home. In some, lawanorder on lovinardor. Wait till we hear the Boy
of Biskop reeling around your postoral lector! Epistlemadethemology
for deep dorfy doubtlings. As we'll lay till break of day in the bunk
of basky, O! Our island, Rome and duty! Well tried, buckstiff! Batt
in, boot! Sell him a breach contact, the vendoror, the buylawyer!
One hyde, sack, hic! Two stick holst, Lucky! Finnish Make Goal!
First you were Nomad, next you were Namar, now you're Numah
and it's soon you'll be Nomon. Hence counsels Ecclesiast. There's
every resumption. The forgein offils is on the shove to lay you out
dossier. Darby's in the yard, planning it on you, plot and edgings,
the whispering peeler after cooks wearing an illformation. The find
of his kind! An artist, sir! And dirt cheap at a sovereign a skull! He
knows his Finsbury Follies backwoods so you batter see to your re-
gent refutation. Ascare winde is rifing again about nice boys going
native. You know who was wrote about in the Orange Book of
Estchapel? Basil and the two other men from King's Avenance. Just
press this cold brand against your brow for a mow. Cainfully! The
sinus the curse. That's it. Hung Chung Egglyfella now speak he tell
numptywumpty topsawys belongahim pidgin. Secret things other
persons place there covered not. How you fell from story to story
like a sagasand to lie. Enfilmung infirmity. On the because alleging
to having a finger a fudding in pudding and pie. And here's the
witnesses. Glue on to him, Greevy! Bottom anker, Noordeece! And
kick kick killykick for the house that juke built! Wait till they send
you to sleep, scowpow! By jurors' cruces! Then old Hunphydunphy-
ville'll be blasted to bumboards by the youthful herald who would

once you were. He'd be our chosen one in the matter of Brittas more than anarthur. But we'll wake and see. The wholes poors riches of ours hundreds of manhoods and womhoods. Two cents, two mills and two myrds. And it's all us rangers you'll be facing in the box before the twelfth correctional. Like one man, gell. Between all the Misses Mountsackvilles in their halfmoon haemicycles, gasping to giddies to dye for the shame. Just hold hard till the one we leapt out gets her yearing! Hired in cameras, extra! With His Honour Surpacker on the binge. So yelp your guilt and kitz the buck. You'll have loss of fame from Wimmegame's fake. Forwards! One bully son growing the goff and his twinger read out by the Nazi Priers. You fought as how they'd never woxen up, did you, crucket? It will wecker your earse, that it will! When hives the court to exchequer 'tis the child which gives the sire away. Good for you, Richmond Rover! Scrum around, our side! Let him have another between the spindlers! A grand game! Dalymount's decisive. Don Gouverneur Buckley's in the Tara Tribune, sporting the insides of a Rhutian Jhanaral and little Mrs Ex-Skaerer-Sissers is bribing the halfpricers to pray for her widower in his gravest embazzlement. You on her, hosy jigses, that'll be some nonstop marrimont! You in your stolen mace and anvil, Magnes, and her burrowed in Berkness cirrchus clouthses. Fummuccumul with a graneen aveiled. Playing down the slavey touch. Much as she was when the fancy cutter out collecting milestones espied her aseesaw on a fern. So nimb, he said, a dat of dew. Between Furr-y-Benn and Ferr-y-Bree. In this tear Vikloe vich he lofed. The smiling ever. If you pulls me over pay me, prhyse! A talor would adapt his caulking trudgers on to any shape at see. Address deceitfold of wovens weard. The wonder of the women of the world together, moya! And the lovablest Lima since Ineen MacCormick MacCoort MacConn O'Puckins MacKundred. Only but she is a little width wider got. Be moving abog. You cannot make a limousine lady out of a hillman minx. Listun till you'll hear the Mudquirt accent. This is a bulgen horesies, this is wollan indulgencies, this is a flemsh. Tik. Scapulars, beads and a stump of a candle, Hubert was a Hunter, *chemins de la croixes* and Rosairette's egg, all the trimmings off the tree that she picked up after the Clontarf voterloost when O'Bryan MacBruiser bet Norris Nobnut. Becracking his cucconut between his kknneess. Umpthump, Here Inkeeper, it's the doatereen's wednessmorn! Delphin dringing! Grusham undergang! And the Real Hymernians strenging strong at knocker knocker! Holy and massalltolled. You ought to tak a dos

of frut. Jik. Sauss. You're getting hoovier, a twelve stone hoovier,
fullends a twelve stone hoovier, in your corpus entis and it scurves
you right, demnye! Aunt as unclish ams they make oom. But Nichtia
you bound not to loose's gone on Neffin since she clapped her
charmer on him at Gormagareen. At the Gunting Munting Hunting
Punting. The eitch is in her blood, arrah! For a frecklesome fresh-
cheeky sweetworded lupsqueezer. And he shows how he'll pick him
the lock of her fancy. Poghue! Poghue! Poghue! And a good jump,
Powell! Clean over all their heads. We could kiss him for that one,
couddled we, Huggins? Sparkes is the footer to hance off nancies.
Scaldhead, pursue! Before you bunkledoodle down upon your birch-
entop again after them three blows from time, drink and hurry.
The same three that nursed you, Skerry, Badbols and the Grey One.
All of your own club too. With the fistful of burryberries were for
the massus for to feed you living in dying. Buy bran biscuits and
you'll never say dog. And be in the finest of companies. Morialtay
and Kniferope Walker and Rowley the Barrel. With Longbow of
the lie. Slick of the trick and Blennercassel of the brogue. Clan-
ruckard for ever! The Fenn, the Fenn, the kinn of all Fenns! Deaf
to the winds when for Croonacreena. Fisht! And it's not now saying
how we are where who's softing what rushes. Merryvirgin forbed!
But of they never eat soullfriede they're ating it now. With easter
greeding. Angus! Angus! Angus! The keykeeper of the keys of the
seven doors of the dreamadoory in the house of the household of
Hecech saysaith. Whitmore, whatmore? Give it over, give it up!
Mawgraw! Head of a helo, chesth of champgnon, eye of a gull!
What you'd if he'd. The groom is in the greenhouse, gattling out
his. Gun! That lad's the style for. Lannigan's ball! Now a drive on
the naval! The Shallburn Shock. Never mind your gibbous. Slip
on your ropen collar and draw the noosebag on your head. Nobody
will know or heed you, Postumus, if you skip round schlymartin
by the back and come front sloomutren to beg in one of the shavers'
sailorsuits. Three climbs threequickenthrees in the garb of nine.
We'll split to see you mouldem imparvious. A wing for oldboy Wel-
sey Wandrer! Well spat, witty wagtail! Now piawn to bishop's
forthe! Moove. There's Mumblesome Wadding Murch cranking up
to the hornemoonium. Drawg us out *Ivy Eve in the Hall of Alum!*
The finnecies of poetry wed music. Feeling the jitters? You'll be
as tight as Trivett when the knot's knutted on. Now's your never!
Peena and Queena are duetting a giggle-for-giggle and the brideen
Alannah is lost in her diamindwaiting. What a magnificent gesture

you will show us this gallus day. Clean and easy, be the hooker! And a free for croaks after. Dovlen are out for it. So is Rathfinn. And, hike, here's the hearse and four horses with the interprovincial crucifixioners throwing lots inside to know whose to be their gosson and whereas to brake the news to morhor. How our myterbilder his fullen aslip. And who will wager but he'll Shonny Bhoy be, the fleshlumpfleeter from Poshtapengha and all he bares sobsconcious inklings shadowed on soulskin. Its segnet yores, the strake of a hin. Nup. Laying the cloth, to fore of them. And thanking the fish, in core of them. To pass the grace for Gard sake! Ahmohn. Mr Justician Matthews and Mr Justician Marks and Mr Justician Luk de Luc and Mr Justinian Johnston-Johnson. And the aaskart, see, behind! Help, help, hurray! Allsup, allsop! Four ghools to nail! Cut it down, mates, look slippy! They've got a dathe with a swimminpull. Dang! Ding! Dong! Dung! Dinnin. Isn't it great he is swaying above us for his good and ours. Fly your balloons, dannies and dennises! He's doorknobs dead! And Annie Delap is free! Ones more. We could ate you, par Buccas, and imbabe through you, reassuranced in the wild lac of gotliness. One fledge, one brood till hulm culms evurdyburdy. Huh the throman! Huh the traidor. Huh the truh. Arrorsure, he's the mannork of Arrahland oversense he horrhorrd his name in thuthunder. Rrrwwwkkkrrr! And seen it rudden up in fusefiressence on the flashmurket. P.R.C.R.L.L. Royloy. Of the rollorrish rattillary. The lewdningbluebolteredalllucktruckalltraumconductor! The unnamed nonirishblooder that becomes a Greenislender overnight! But we're molting superstituettes out of his fulse thortin guts. Tried mark, Easterlings. Sign, Soideric O'Cunnuc, Rix. Adversed ord, Magtmorken, Kovenhow. There's a great conversion, myn! Coucous! Find his causcaus! From Motometusolum through Bulley and Cowlie and Diggerydiggerydock down to bazeness's usual? He's alight there still, by Mike! Loose afore! Bung! Bring forth your deed! Bang! Till is the right time. Bang! Partick Thistle agen S. Megan's versus Brystal Palace agus the Walsall! Putsch! Tiemore moretis tisturb badday! The playgue will be soon over, rats! Let sin! Geh tont! All we wants is to get peace for possession. We dinned unnerstunned why you sassad about thirteen to aloafen, sor, kindly repeat! Or ledn us alones of your lungorge, parsonifier propounde of our edelweissed idol worts! Shaw and Shea are lorning obsen so hurgle up, gandfarder, and gurgle me gurk. You can't impose on frayshouters like os. Every tub here spucks his own fat. Hang coersion everyhow! And smotthermock Gramm's laws! But we're a drippindhrue gayleague all at ones. In the buginning is the woid, in the muddle is the sounddance and thereinofter you're in the un-bewised again, vund vulsyvolsy. You talker dunsker's brogue men we our souls speech obstruct hostery. Silence in thought! Spreach! Wear anartful of outer nocense! Pawpaw, wowow! Momerry twelfths, noebroed! That was a good one, ha! So it will be quite a material what *May* farther be unvuloped for you, old *Mighty,* when it's aped to foul a delfian in the Mahnung. Ha ha! Talk of Paddy-barke's echo! Kick nuck, Knockcastle! Muck! And you'll nose it, O you'll nose it, without warnward from we. We don't know the sendor to whome. But you'll find Chiggenchugger's taking the Treaclyshortcake with Bugle and the Bitch pairsadrawsing and Horssmayres Prosession tyghting up under the threes. Stop. Press stop. To press stop. All to press stop. And be the seem talkin whar-abahts hosetanzies, dat sure is sullibrated word! Bing bong! Saxo-looter, for congesters are salders' prey. Snap it up in the loose, patchy the blank! Anyone can see you're the son of a gunnell. Fellow him up too, Carlow! Woes to the wormquashed, aye, and wor to the win-ner! Think of Aerian's Wall and the Fall of Toss. Give him another for to volleyholleydoodlem! His lights not all out yet, the liverpooser! Boohoohoo it oose! With seven hores always in the home of his thinkingthings, his nodsloddledome of his noiselisslesoughts. Two Idas, two Evas, two Nessies and Rubyjuby. Phook! No wonder, pipes as kirles, that he sthings like a rheinbok. One bed night he had the delysiums that they were all queens mobbing him. Fell stiff. Oh, ho, ho, ho, ah, he, he! Abedicate yourself. It just gegs our goad. He'll be the deaf of us, pappappoppopcuddle, samblind daiyrudder. Yus, sord, fathe, you woll, putty our wraughther! What we waits be after? Whyfore we come agooding? None of you, cock icy! You keep that henayearn and her fortycantle glim lookbehinder. We might do with rubiny leeses. But of all your wanings send us out your pep-pydecked ales and you'll not be such a bad lot. The rye is well for whose amind but the wheateny one is proper lovely. B E N K! We sincerestly trust that Missus with the kiddies of sweet Gorteen has not B I N K to their very least tittles deranged if in B U N K and we greesiously augur for your Meggers a B E N K B A N K B O N K to sloop in with all sorts of adceterus and adsaturas. It's our last fight, Megantic, fear you will! The refergee's took to hailing to time the pass. There goes the blackwatchwomen, all in white, flaxed up, purgad! Right toe, Armitage! Tem for Tam at Timmotty Hall! We're been carried away. Beyond bournes and bowers. So we'll leave it

to Keyhoe, Danelly and Pykemhyme, the three muskrateers, at the
end of this age that had it from Variants' Katey Sherratt that had
it from Variants' Katey Sherratt's man for the bonnefacies of Blash-
white and Blushred of the Aquasancta Liffey Patrol to wind up and
to tells of all befells after that to Mocked Majesty in the Malin-
curred Mansion.

So you were saying, boys? Anyhow he what?

So anyhow, melumps and mumpos of the hoose uncommons, after
that to wind up that longtobechronickled gettogether thanksbeto-
giving day at Glenfinnisk-en-la-Valle, the anniversary of his finst
homy commulion, after that same barbecue beanfeast was all over
poor old hospitable corn and eggfactor, King Roderick O'Conor,
the paramount chief polemarch and last preelectric king of Ireland,
who was anything you say yourself between fiftyodd and fiftyeven
years of age at the time after the socalled last supper he greatly gave
in his umbrageous house of the hundred bottles with the radio
beamer tower and its hangars, chimbneys and equilines or, at least,
he was'nt actually the then last king of all Ireland for the time being
for the jolly good reason that he was still such as he was the eminent
king of all Ireland himself after the last preeminent king of all Ireland, the whilom joky old top that went before him in the Taharan
dynasty, King Arth Mockmorrow Koughenough of the leathered
leggions, now of parts unknown, (God guard his generous comic-
songbook soul!) that put a poached fowl in the poor man's pot before he took to his pallyass with the weeping eczema for better and
worse until he went under the grass quilt on us, nevertheless, the
year the sugar was scarce, and we to lather and shave and frizzle
him, like a bald surging buoy and himself down to three cows that
was meat and drink and dogs and washing to him, 'tis good cause
we have to remember it, going through summersultryngs of snow
and sleet witht the widow Nolan's goats and the Brownes girls
neats anyhow, wait till I tell you, what did he do, poor old Roderick
O'Conor Rex, the auspicious waterproof monarch of all Ireland,
when he found himself all alone by himself in his grand old hand-
wedown pile after all of them had all gone off with themselves to
their castles of mud, as best they cud, on footback, owing to the leak
of the McCarthy's mare, in extended order, a tree's length from the
longest way out, down the switchbackward slidder of the landsown
route of Hauburnea's liveliest vinnage on the brain, the unimportant
Parthalonians with the mouldy Firbolgs and the Tuatha de Danaan
googs and the ramblers from Clane and all the rest of the notmuch-

ers that he did not care the royal spit out of his ostensible mouth
about, well, what do you think he did, sir, but, faix, he just went
heeltapping through the winespilth and weevily popcorks that were
kneedeep round his own right royal round rollicking toper's table,
with his old Roderick Random pullon hat at a Lanty Leary cant on
him and Mike Brady's shirt and Greene's linnet collarbow and his
Ghenter's gaunts and his Macclefield's swash and his readymade
Reillys and his panprestuberian poncho, the body you'd pity him,
the way the world is, poor he, the heart of Midleinster and the su-
pereminent lord of them all, overwhelmed as he was with black
ruin like a sponge out of water, allocutioning in bellcantos to his
own oliverian society MacGuiney's *Dreans of Ergen Adams* and
thruming through all to himself with diversed tonguesed through
his old tears and his ould plaised drawl, starkened by the most regal
of belches, like a blurney Cashelmagh crooner that lerking Clare
air, the blackberd's ballad *I've a terrible errible lot todue todie todue
tootorribleday*, well, what did he go and do at all, His Most Exu-
berant Majesty King Roderick O'Conor but, arrah bedamnbut, he
finalised by lowering his woolly throat with the wonderful midnight
thirst was on him, as keen as mustard, he could not tell what he
did ale, that bothered he was from head to tail, and, wishawishawish,
leave it, what the Irish, boys, can do, if he did'nt go, sliggymaglooral
reemyround and suck up, sure enough, like a Trojan, in some particular cases with the assistance of his venerated tongue, whatever
surplus rotgut, sorra much, was left by the lazy lousers of maltknights
and beerchurls in the different bottoms of the various different
replenquished drinking utensils left there behind them on the prem-
isses by that whole hogsheaded firkin family, the departed honourable homegoers and other slygrogging suburbanites, such as
it was, fall and fall about, to the brindishing of his charmed life,
as toastified by his cheeriubicundenances, no matter whether it
was chateaubottled Guiness's or Phoenix brewery stout it was or
John Jameson and Sons or Roob Coccola or, for the matter of that,
O'Connell's famous old Dublin ale that he wanted like hell, more
that halibut oil or jesuits tea, as a fall back, of several different
quantities and qualities amounting in all to, I should say, considerably more than the better part of a gill or naggin of imperial dry
and liquid measure till, welcome be from us here, till the rising of
the morn, till that hen of Kaven's shows her beaconegg, and Chap-
wellswendows stain our horyhistoricold and Father MacMichael
stamps for aitch o'clerk mess and the Litvian Newestlatter is seen,

sold and delivered and all's set for restart after the silence, like his ancestors to this day after him (that the blazings of their ould-mouldy gods may attend to them we pray!), overopposides the cowery lad in the corner and forenenst the staregaze of the cathering candled, that adornment of his album and folkenfather of familyans, he came acrash a crupper sort of a sate on accomondation and the very boxst in all his composs, whereuponce, behome the fore for cove and trawlers, heave hone, leave lone, Larry's on the focse and Faugh MacHugh O'Bawlar at the wheel, one to do and one to dare, par by par, a peerless pair, ever here and over there, with his fol the dee oll the doo on the flure of his feats and the feels of the fumes in the wakes of his ears our wineman from Barleyhome he just slumped to throne.

So sailed the stout ship *Nansy Hans*. From Liff away. For Nattenlaender. As who has come returns. Farvel, farerne! Goodbark, goodbye!

Now follow we out by Starloe!

— Three quarks for Muster Mark!
Sure he hasn't got much of a bark
And sure any he has it's all beside the mark.
But O, Wreneagle Almighty, wouldn't un be a sky of a lark
To see that old buzzard whopping about for uns shirt in the dark
And he hunting round for uns speckled trousers around by Pal-
    merstown Park?
Hohohoho, moulty Mark!
You're the rummest old rooster ever flopped out of a Noah's ark
And you think you're cock of the wark.
Fowls, up! Tristy's the spry young spark
That'll tread her and wed her and bed her and red her
Without ever winking the tail of a feather
And that's how that chap's going to make his money and mark!

Overhoved, shrillgleescreaming. That song sang seaswans. The winging ones. Seahawk, seagull, curlew and plover, kestrel and capercallzie. All the birds of the sea they trolled out rightbold when they smacked the big kuss of Trustan with Usolde.

And there they were too, when it was dark, whilest the wildcaps was circling, as slow their ship, the winds aslight, upborne the fates, the wardorse moved, by courtesy of Mr Deaubaleau Downbellow Kaempersally, listening in, as hard as they could, in Dubbeldorp, the donker, by the tourneyold of the wattarfalls, with their vuoxens and they kemin in so hattajocky (only a quartebuck askull for the last acts) to the solans and the sycamores and the wild geese and the gannets and the migratories and the mistlethrushes and the auspices and all the birds of the rockbysuckerassousyoceanal sea, all four of them, all sighing and sobbing, and listening. Moykle ahoykling!

They were the big four, the four maaster waves of Erin, all listening, four. There was old Matt Gregory and then besides old Matt there was old Marcus Lyons, the four waves, and oftentimes they used to be saying grace together, right enough, bausnabeatha, in Miracle Squeer: here now we are the four of us: old Matt Gregory and old Marcus and old Luke Tarpey: the four of us and sure, thank God, there are no more of us: and, sure now, you wouldn't go and forget and leave out the other fellow and old Johnny MacDougall: the four of us and no more of us and so now pass the fish for Christ sake, Amen: the way they used to be saying their grace before fish, repeating itself, after the interims of Augusburgh for auld lang syne. And so there they were, with their palms in their hands, like the pulchrum's proculs, spraining their ears, luistening and listening to the oceans of kissening, with their eyes glistening, all the four, when he was kiddling and cuddling and bunnyhugging scrumptious his colleen bawn and dinkum belle, an oscar sister, on the fifteen inch loveseat, behind the chieftaness stewardesses cubin, the hero, of Gaelic champion, the onliest one of her choice, her bleaueyedeal of a girl's friend, neither bigugly nor smallnice, meaning pretty much everything to her then, with his sinister dexterity, light and ruft-handling, vicemversem her ragbags et assaucyetiams, fore and aft, on and offsides, the brueburnt sexfutter, handson and huntsem, that was palpably wrong and bulbubly improper, and cuddling her and kissing her, tootyfay charmaunt, in her ensemble of maidenna blue, with an overdress of net, tickled with goldies, Isolamisola, and whisping and lisping her about Trisolanisans, how one was whips for one was two and two was lips for one was three, and dissimulating themself, with his poghue like Arrah-na-poghue, the dear dear annual, they all four rembembored who made the world and how they used to be at that time in the vulgar ear cuddling and kiddling her, after an oyster supper in Cullen's barn, from under her mistle-thrush and kissing and listening, in the good old bygone days of Dion Boucicault, the elder, in Arrah-na-pogue, in the otherworld of the passing of the key of Twotongue Common, with Nush, the carrier of the word, and with Mesh, the cutter of the reed, in one of the farback, pitchblack centuries when who made the world, when they knew O'Clery, the man on the door, when they were all four collegians on the nod, neer the Nodderlands Nurskery, whiteboys and oakboys, peep of tim boys and piping tom boys, raising hell while the sin was shining, with their slates and satchels, playing Florian's fables and communic suctions and vellicar frictions with mixum members, in the Queen's Ultonian colleges, along with

another fellow, a prime number, Totius Quotius, and paying a pot
of tribluts to Boris O'Brien, the buttler of Clumpthump, two looves,
two turnovers plus (one) crown, to see the mad dane ating his vitals.
Wulf! Wulf! And throwing his tongue in the snakepit. Ah ho! The
ladies have mercias! It brought the dear prehistoric scenes all back
again, as fresh as of yore, Matt and Marcus, natural born lovers of
nature, in all her moves and senses, and after that now there he was,
that mouth of mandibles, vowed to pure beauty, and his Arrah-na-
poghue, when she murmurously, after she let a cough, gave her firm
order, if he wouldn't please mind, for a sings to one hope a dozen
of the best favourite lyrical national blooms in Luvillicit, though not
too much, reflecting on the situation, drinking in draughts of purest
air serene and revelling in the great outdoors, before the four of
them, in the fair fine night, whilst the stars shine bright, by she
light of he moon, we longed to be spoon, before her honeyoldloom,
the plaint effect being in point of fact there being in the whole, a
seatuition so shocking and scandalous and now, thank God, there
were no more of them and he poghuing and poghuing like the
Moreigner bowed his crusted hoed and Tilly the Tailor's Tugged a
Tar in the Arctic Newses Dagsdogs number and there they were,
like a foremasters in the rolls, listening, to Rolando's deepen darblun
Ossian roll, (Lady, it was just too gorgeous, that expense of a lovely
tint, embellished by the charms of art and very well conducted and
nicely mannered and all the horrid rudy noisies locked up in nasty
cubbyhole!) as tired as they were, the three jolly topers, with their
mouths watering, all the four, the old connubial men of the sea,
yambing around with their old pantometer, in duckasaloppics, Luke
and Johnny MacDougall and all wishening for anything at all of
the bygone times, the wald times and the fald times and the hempty
times and the dempty times, for a cup of kindness yet, for four farback tumblerfuls of woman squash, with them, all four, listening
and spraining their ears for the millennium and all their mouths
making water.

Johnny. Ah well, sure, that's the way (up) and it so happened
there was poor Matt Gregory (up), their pater familias, and (up)
the others and now really and (up) truly they were four dear old
heladies and really they looked awfully pretty and so nice and be-
spectable and after that they had their fathomglasses to find out all
the fathoms and their half a tall hat, just now like the old Merquus
of Pawerschoof, the old determined despot, (*quiescents in brage!*)
only for the extrusion of the saltwater or the auctioneer there dor-

mont, in front of the place near O'Clery's, at the darkumound numbur wan, beside that ancient Dame street, where the statue of Mrs Dana O'Connell, prostituent behind the Trinity College, that arranges all the auctions of the valuable colleges, Bootersbay Sisters, like the auctioneer Battersby Sisters, the prumisceous creaters, that sells all the emancipated statues and flowersports, James H. Tickell, the jaypee, off Hoggin Green, after he made the centuries, going to the tailturn horseshow, before the angler nomads flood, along with another fellow, active impalsive, and the shoeblacks and the redshanks and plebeians and the barrancos and the cappunchers childerun, Jules, everyone, Gotopoxy, with the houghers on them, highstepping the fissure and fracture lines, seven five threes up, three five sevens down, to get out of his way, onasmuck as their withers conditions could not possibly have been improved upon, (praisers be to deeseesee!) like hopolopocattls, erumping oround their Judgity Yaman, and all the tercentenary horses and priest-hunters, from the Curragh, and confusionaries and the authorities, Noord Amrikaans and Suid Aferican cattleraiders (so they say) all over like a tiara dullfuoco, in his grey half a tall hat and his amber necklace and his crimson harness and his leathern jib and his cheapshein hairshirt and his scotobrit sash and his parapila-gian gallowglasses (how do you do, jaypee, Elevato!) to find out all the improper colleges (and how do you do, Mr Dame James? Get out of my way!), forkbearded and bluetoothed and bellied and bone-less, from Strathlyffe and Aylesburg and Northumberland Anglesey, the whole yaghoodurt sweepstakings and all the horsepowers. But now, talking of hayastdanars and wolkingology and how our seaborn isle came into exestuance, (the explutor, his three andesiters and the two pantellarias) that reminds me about the manausteriums of the poor Marcus of Lyons and poor Johnny, the patrician, and what do you think of the four of us and there they were now, listening right enough, the four saltwater widowers, and all they could re-membore, long long ago in the olden times Momonian, throw darker hour sorrows, the princest day, when Fair Margrate waited Swede Villem, and Lally in the rain, with the blank prints, now extincts, after the wreak of Wormans' Noe, the barmaisigheds, when my heart knew no care, and after that then there was the official landing of Lady Jales Casemate, in the year of the flood 1132 S.O.S., and the christening of Queen Baltersby, the Fourth Buzzersbee, accord-ing to Her Grace the bishop Senior, off the whate shape, and then there was the drowning of Pharoah and all his pedestrians and they

were all completely drowned into the sea, the red sea, and then poor
Merkin Cornyngwham, the official out of the castle on pension,
when he was completely drowned off Erin Isles, at that time, suir
knows, in the red sea and a lovely mourning paper and thank God,
as Saman said, there were no more of him. And that now was how
it was. The arzurian deeps o'er his humbodumbones sweeps. And
his widdy the giddy is wreathing her murmoirs as her gracest triput
to the Grocery Trader's Manthly. Mind mand gunfree by Gladeys
Rayburn! Runtable's Reincorporated. The new world presses. Where
the old conk cruised now croons the yunk. Exeunc throw a darras
Kram of Llawnroc, ye gink guy, kirked into yord. Enterest atta-
wonder Wehpen, luftcat revol, fairescapading in his natsirt. Tuesy
tumbles. And mild aunt Liza is as loose as her neese. Fulfest withim
inbrace behent. As gent would deem oncontinent. So mulct per
wenche is Elsker woed. Ne hath his thrysting. Fin. Like the new-
casters in their old plyable of *A Royenne Devours*. Jazzaphoney and
Mirillovis and Nippy she nets best. Fing. Ay, ay! Sobbos. And so he
was. Sabbus.

Marcus. And after that, not forgetting, there was the Flemish
armada, all scattered, and all officially drowned, there and then, on
a lovely morning, after the universal flood, at about aleven thirty-
two was it? off the coast of Cominghome and Saint Patrick, the ana-
baptist, and Saint Kevin, the lacustrian, with toomuch of tolls and
lottance of beggars, after converting Porterscout and Dona, our first
marents, and Lapoleon, the equestrian, on his whuite hourse of Hun-
over, rising Clunkthurf over Cabinhogan and all they remembored
and then there was the Frankish floot of Noahsdobahs, from Hedal-
goland, round about the freebutter year of Notre Dame 1132 P.P.O.
or so, disumbunking from under Motham General Bonaboche, (noo
poopery!) in his half a grey traditional hat, alevoila come alevilla,
and after that there he was, so terrestrial, like a Nailscissor, poghuing her scandalous and very wrong, the maid, in single combat,
under the sycamores, amid the bludderings from the boom and all
the gallowsbirds in Arrah-na-Poghue, so silvestrious, neer the Queen's
Colleges, in 1132 Brian or Bride street, behind the century man on
the door. And then again they used to give the grandest gloriaspan-
quost universal howldmoutherhibbert lectures on anarxaquy out of
doxarchology (hello, Hibernia!) from sea to sea (Matt speaking!)
according to the pictures postcard, with sexon grimmacticals, in the
Latimer Roman history, of Latimer repeating himself, from the vi-
cerine of Lord Hugh, the Lacytynant, till Bockleyshuts the rahjahn

gerachknell and regnumrockery roundup, (Marcus Lyons speaking!) to the oceanfuls of collegians green and high classes and the poor scholars and all the old trinitarian senate and saints and sages and the Plymouth brethren, droning along, peanzanzangan, and nodding and sleeping away there, like forgetmenots, in her abijance service, round their twelve tables, per pioja at pulga bollas, in the four trinity colleges, for earnasyoulearning Eringrowback, of Ulcer, Moonster, Leanstare and Cannought, the four grandest colleges supper the matther of Erryn, of Killorcure and Killthemall and Killeachother and Killkelly-on-the-Flure, where their role was to rule the round roll that Rollo and Rullo rolled round. Those were the grandest gynecollege histories (Lucas calling, hold the line!) in the Janesdanes Lady Andersdaughter Universary, for auld acquaintance sake (this unitarian lady, breathtaking beauty, Bambam's bonniest, lived to a great age at or in or about the late No. 1132 or No. 1169, bis, Fitzmary Round where she was seen by many and widely liked) for teaching the Fatima Woman history of Fatimiliafamilias, repeating herself, on which purposeth of the spirit of nature as difinely developed in time by psadatepholomy, the past and present (Johnny MacDougall speaking, give me trunks, miss!) and present and absent and past and present and perfect *arma virumque romano*. Ah, dearo, dear! O weep for the hower when eve aleaves bower! How it did but all come eddaying back to them, if they did but get gaze, gagagniagnian, to hear him there, kiddling and cuddling her, after the gouty old galahat, with his peer of quinnyfears and his troad of thirstuns, so nefarious, from his elevation of one yard one handard and thartytwo lines, before the four of us, in his Roman Catholic arms, while his deepseepeepers gazed and sazed and dazecrazemazed into her dullokbloon rodolling olosheen eyenbowls by the Cornelius Nepos, Mnepos. Anumque, umque. Napoo.

Queh? Quos?

Ah, dearo dearo dear! Bozun braceth brythe hwen gooses gandered gamen. Mahazar ag Dod! It was so scalding sorry for all the whole twice two four of us, with their familiar, making the toten, and Lally when he lost part of his half a hat and all belongings to him, in his old futile manner, cape, towel and drawbreeches, and repeating himself and telling him now, for the seek of Senders Newslaters and the mossacre of Saint Brices, to forget the past, when the burglar he shoved the wretch in churneroil, and contradicting all about Lally, the ballest master of Gosterstown, and his old fellow,

the Lagener, in the Locklane Lighthouse, earing his wick with a
pierce of railing, and liggen hig with his ladder up, and that oldtime turner and his sadderday erely cloudsing, the old croniony,
Skelly, with the lether belly, full of neltts, full of keltts, full of light-
weight beltts and all the bald drakes or ever he had up in the
bohereen, off Artsichekes Road, with Moels and Mahmullagh Mul-
larty, the man in the Oran mosque, and the old folks at home and
Duignan and Lapole and the grand confarreation, as per the cab-
bangers richestore, of the filest archives, and he couldn't stop
laughing over Tom Tim Tarpey, the Welshman, and the four middle-
aged widowers, all nangles, sangles, angles and wangles. And now,
that reminds me, not to forget the four of the Welsh waves, leaping
laughing, in their Lumbag Walk, over old Battleshore and Deaddle-
conch, in their half a Roman hat, with an ancient Greek gloss on
it, in Chichester College auction and, thank God, they were all
summarily divorced, four years before, or so they say, by their dear
poor shehusbands, in dear byword days, and never brought to mind,
to see no more the rainwater on the floor but still they parted, raining water laughing, per Nupiter Privius, only terpary, on the best
of terms and be forgot, whilk was plainly foretolk by their old pilgrim cocklesong or they were singing through the wettest indies
*As I was going to Burrymecarott we fell in with a lout by the name
of Peebles* as also in another place by their orthodox proverb so there
was said thus *That old fellow knows milk though he's not used to
it latterly.* And so they parted. In Dalkymont nember to. Ay, ay.
The good go and the wicked is left over. As evil flows so Ivel flows.
Ay, ay. Ah, well sure, that's the way. As the holymaid of Kunut said
to the haryman of Koombe. For his humple pesition in odvices.
Woman. Squash. Part. Ay, ay. By decree absolute.

Lucas. And, O so well they could remembore at that time, when
Carpery of the Goold Fins was in the kingship of Poolland, Mrs
Dowager Justice Squalchman, foorsitter, in her fullbottom wig and
beard, (Erminia Reginia!) in or aring or around about the year of
buy in disgrace 1132 or 1169 or 1768 Y.W.C.A., at the Married
Male Familyman's Auctioneer's court in Arrahnacuddle. Poor Johnny
of the clan of the Dougals, the poor Scuitsman, (Hohannes!) nothing if not amorous, dinna forget, so frightened (Zweep! Zweep!)
on account of her full bottom, (undullable attraxity!) that put the
yearl of mercies on him, and the four maasters, in chors, with a hing
behangd them, because he was so slow to borstel her schoon for her,
when he was grooming her ladyship, instead of backscratching her

materfamilias proper, like any old methodist, and all divorced and innasense interdict, in the middle of the temple, according to their dear faithful. Ah, now, it was too bad, too bad and stout entirely, all the missoccurs; and poor Mark or Marcus Bowandcoat, from the brownesberrow in nolandsland, the poor old chronometer, all persecuted with ally croaker by everybody, by decree absolute, through Herrinsilde, because he forgot himself, making wind and water, and made a Neptune's mess of all of himself, sculling over the giamond's courseway, and because he forgot to remember to sign an old morning proxy paper, a writing in request to hersute herself, on stamped bronnanoleum, from Roneo to Giliette, before saying his grace before fish and then and there and too there was poor Dion Cassius Poosycomb, all drowned too, before the world and her husband, because it was most improper and most wrong, when he attempted to (well, he was shocking poor in his health, he said, with the shingles falling off him), because he (ah, well now, peaces pea to Wedmore and let not the song go dumb upon your Ire, as we say in the Spasms of Davies, and we won't be too hard on him as an old Manx presbyterian) and after that, as red as a Rosse is, he made his last will and went to confession, like the general of the Berkeleyites, at the rim of the rom, on his two bare marrowbones, to Her Worship his Mother and Sister Evangelist Sweainey, on Cailcainnin widnight and he was so sorry, he was really, because he left the bootybutton in the handsome cab and now, tell the truth, unfriends never, (she was his first messes dogess and it was a very pretty peltry and there were faults on both sides) well, he attempted (or so they say) ah, now, forget and forgive (don't we all?) and, sure, he was only funning with his andrewmartins and his old age coming over him, well, he attempted or, the Connachy, he was tempted to attempt some hunnish familiarities, after eten a bad carmp in the rude ocean and, hevantonoze sure, he was dead seasickabed (it was really too bad!) her poor old divorced male, in the housepays for the daying at the Martyr Mrs MacCawley's, where at the time he was taying and toying, to hold the nursetendered hand, (ah, the poor old coax!) and count the buttons and her hand and frown on a bad crab and doying to rememboge what doed they were byorn and who made a who a snore. Ah dearo dearo dear!

And where do you leave Matt Emeritus? The laychief of Abbotabishop? And exchullard of ffrench and gherman. Achoch! They were all so sorgy for poorboir Matt in his saltwater hat, with the Aran crown, or she grew that out of, too big for him, of or Mnepos

and his overalls, all falling over her in folds—sure he hadn't the heart
in her to pull them up—poor Matt, the old perigrime matriarch, and
a queenly man, (the porple blussing upon them!) sitting there, the
sole of the settlement, below ground, for an expiatory rite, in postula-
tion of his cause, (who shall say?) in her beaver bonnet, the king of
the Caucuses, a family all to himself, under geasa, Themistletocles,
on his multilingual tombstone, like Navellicky Kamen, and she due
to kid by sweetpea time, with her face to the wall, in view of the
poorhouse, and taking his rust in the oxsight of Iren, under all the
auspices, amid the rattle of hailstorms, kalospintheochromatokreen-
ing, with her ivyclad hood, and gripping an old pair of curling tongs,
belonging to Mrs Duna O'Cannell, to blow his brains with, till the
heights of Newhigherland heard the Bristolhut, with his can of tea
and a purse of alfred cakes from Anne Lynch and two cuts of
Shackleton's brown loaf and dilisk, waiting for the end to come.
Gordon Heighland, when you think of it! The merthe dirther! Ah
ho! It was too bad entirely! All devoured by active parlourmen, lauda-
biliter, of woman squelch and all on account of the smell of Shakele-
tin and scratchman and his mouth watering, acid and alkolic; signs
on the salt, and so now pass the loaf for Christ sake. Amen. And
so. And all.

Matt. And loaf. So that was the end. And it can't be helped. Ah,
God be good to us! Poor Andrew Martin Cunningham! Take breath!
Ay! Ay!

And still and all at that time of the dynast days of old konning
Soteric Sulkinbored and Bargomuster Bart, when they struck coil
and shock haunts, in old Hungerford-on-Mudway, where first I met
thee oldpoetryck flied from may, and the Finnan haddies and the
Noal Sharks and the muckstails turtles like an acoustic pottish and
the griesouper bullyum and how he poled him up his boccat of vuo-
tar and got big buzz for his name in the airweek's honours from
home, colonies and empire, they were always with assisting grace,
thinking (up) and not forgetting about shims and shawls week, in
auld land syne (up) their four hosenbands, that were four (up)
beautiful sister misters, now happily married, unto old Gallstone-
belly, and there they were always counting and contradicting every
night 'tis early the lovely mother of periwinkle buttons, according
to the lapper part of their anachronism (up one up two up one up
four) and after that there now she was, in the end, the deary, sold-
powder and all, the beautfour sisters, and that was her mudhen republican name, right enough, from alum and oves, and they used

to be getting up from under, in their tape and straw garlands, with all the worries awake in their hair, at the kookaburra bell ringring all wrong inside of them (come in, come on, you lazy loafs!) all inside their poor old Shandon bellbox (come out to hell, you lousy louts!) so frightened, for the dthclangavore, like knockneeghs bumpsed by the fisterman's straights, (ys! ys!), at all hours every night, on their mistletoes, the four old oldsters, to see was the Transton Postscript come, with their oerkussens under their armsaxters, all puddled and mythified, the way the wind wheeled the schooler round, when nobody wouldn't even let them rusten, from playing their gastspiels, crossing their sleep by the shocking silence, when they were in dreams of yore, standing behind the door, or leaning out of the chair, or kneeling under the sofacover and setting on the souptureen, getting into their way something barbarous, changing the one wet underdown convibrational bed or they used to slumper under, when hope was there no more, and putting on their half a hat and falling over all synopticals and a panegyric and repeating themselves, like svvollovving, like the time they were dadging the talkeycook that chased them, look look all round the stool, walk everywhere for a jool, to break fyre to all the rancers, to collect all and bits of brown, the rathure's evelopment in spirits of time in all fathom of space and slooping around in a bawneen and bath slippers and go away to Oldpatrick and see a doctor Walker. And after that so glad they had their night tentacles and there they used to be, flapping and cycling, and a dooing a doonloop, panementically, around the waists of the ships, in the wake of their good old Foehn again, as tyred as they were, at their windswidths in the wavelength, the clipperbuilt and the five fourmasters and Lally of the cleftoft bagoderts and Roe of the fair cheats, exchanging fleas from host to host, with arthroposophia, and he selling him before he forgot, issle issle, after having prealably dephlegmatised his gutterful of throatyfrogs, with a lungible fong in his suckmouth ear, while the dear invoked to the coolun dare by a palpabrows lift left no doubt in his minder, till he was instant and he was trustin, sister soul in brother hand, the subjects being their passion grand, that one fresh from the cow about Aithne Meithne married a mailde and that one too from Engrvakon saga abooth a gooth a gev a gotheny egg and the parkside pranks of quality queens, katte efter kinne, for Earl Hoovedsoon's choosing and Huber and Harman orhowwhen theeuponthus (chchch!) eysolt of binnoculises memostinmust egotum sabcunsciously senses upers the deprofundity of multimathematical

immaterialities wherebejubers in the pancosmic urge the allimman-
ence of that which Itself is Itself Alone (hear, O hear, Caller Errin!)
exteriorises on this ourherenow plane in disunited solod, likeward
and gushious bodies with (science, say!) perilwhitened passionpant-
ing pugnoplangent intuitions of reunited selfdom (murky whey,
abstrew adim!) in the higherdimissional selfless Allself, theemeeng
Narsty meetheeng Idoless, and telling Jolly MacGolly, dear mester
John, the belated dishevelled, hacking away at a parchment pied,
and all the other analist, the steamships ant the ladies'foursome,
ovenfor, nedenfor, dinkety, duk, downalupping, (how long tandem!) like a foreretyred schoonmasters, and their pair of green eyes
and peering in, so they say, like the narcolepts on the lakes of Coma,
through the steamy windows, into the honeymoon cabins, on board
the big steamadories, made by Fumadory, and the saloon ladies'
madorn toilet chambers lined over prawn silk and rub off the salty
catara off a windows and, hee hee, listening, *qua* committe, the poor
old quakers, oben the dure, to see all the hunnishmooners and the
firstclass ladies, serious me, a lass spring as you fancy, and sheets
far from the lad, courting in blankets, enfamillias, and, shee shee,
all improper, in a lovely mourning toilet, for the rosecrumpler, the
thrilldriver, the sighinspirer, with that olive throb in his nude neck,
and, swayin and thayin, thanks ever so much for the tiny quote,
which sought of maid everythingling again so very much more de-
lightafellay, and the perfidly suite of her, bootyfilly yours, under all
their familiarities, by preventing grace, forgetting to say their grace
before chambadory, before going to boat with the verges of the
chaptel of the opering of the month of Nema Knatut, so pass the
poghue for grace sake. Amen. And all, hee hee hee, quaking, so
fright, and, shee shee, shaking. Aching. Ay, ay.

For it was then a pretty thing happened of pure diversion mayhap, when his flattering hend, at the justright moment, like perchance some cook of corage might clip the lad on a poot of porage
handshut his duckhouse, the vivid girl, deaf with love, (ah sure,
you know her, our angel being, one of romance's fadeless wonder-
women, and, sure now, we all know you dote on her even unto
date!) with a queeleetlecree of joysis crisis she renulited their disunited, with ripy lepes to ropy lopes (the dear o'dears!) and the
golden importunity of aloofer's leavetime, when, as quick, is greased
pigskin, Amoricas Champius, with one aragan throust, druve the
massive of virilvigtoury flshpst the both lines of forwards (Eburnea's
down, boys!) rightjingbangshot into the goal of her gullet.

Alris!

And now, upright and add them! And plays be honest! And pullit into yourself, as on manowoman do another! Candidately, everybody! A mot for amot. Comong, meng, and douh! There was this, wellyoumaycallher, a strapping modern old ancient Irish prisscess, so and so hands high, such and such paddock weight, in her madapolam smock, nothing under her hat but red hair and solid ivory (now you know it's true in your hardup hearts!) and a firstclass pair of bedroom eyes, of most unhomy blue, (how weak we are, one and all!) the charm of favour's fond consent! Could you blame her, we're saying, for one psocoldlogical moment? What would Ewe do? With that so tiresome old milkless a ram, with his tiresome duty peck and his bronchial tubes, the tiresome old hairyg orangogran beaver, in his tiresome old twennysixandsixpenny sheopards plods drowsers and his thirtybobandninepenny tails plus toop! Hagakhroustioun! It were too exceeding really if one woulds to offer at sulk an oldivirdual a pinge of hinge hit. The mainest thing ever! Since Edem was in the boags noavy. No, no, the dear heaven knows, and the farther the from it, if the whole stole stale mis betold, whoever the gulpable, and whatever the pulpous was, the twooned togethered, and giving the mhost phassionable wheathers, they were doing a lally a lolly a dither a duther one lelly two dather three lilly four dother. And it was a fiveful moment for the poor old timetetters, ticktacking, in tenk the count. Till the spark that plugged spared the chokee he gripped and (volatile volupty, how brieved are thy lunguings!) they could and they could hear like of a lisp lapsing, that was her knight of the truths thong plipping out of her chapelledeosy, after where he had gone and polped the questioned. Plop.

Ah now, it was tootwoly torrific, the mummurrlubejubes! And then after that they used to be so forgetful, counting motherpeributts (up one up four) to membore her beaufu mouldern maiden name, for overflauwing, by the dream of woman the owneirist, in forty lands. From Greg and Doug on poor Greg and Mat and Mar and Lu and Jo, now happily buried, our four! And there she was right enough, that lovely sight enough, the girleen bawn asthore, as for days galore, of planxty Gregory. Egory. O bunket not Orwin! Ay, ay.

But, sure, that reminds me now, like another tellmastory repeating yourself, how they used to be in lethargy's love, at the end of it all, at that time (up) always, tired and all, after doing the mousework and making it up, over their community singing (up) the top loft

of the voicebox, of Mamalujo like the senior follies at murther
magrees, squatting round, two by two, the four confederates, with
Caxons the Coswarn, up the wet air register in Old Man's House,
Millenium Road, crowning themselves in lauraly branches, with
their cold knees and their poor (up) quad rupeds, ovasleep, and
all dolled up, for their blankets and materny mufflers and plimsoles
and their bowl of brown shackle and milky and boterham clots, a
potion a peace, a piece aportion, a lepel alip, alup a lap, for a cup
of kindest yet, with hold take hand and nurse and only touch of ate,
a lovely munkybown and for xmell and wait the pinch and prompt
poor Marcus Lyons to be not beheeding the skillet on for the live
of ghosses but to pass the teeth for choke sake, Amensch, when it
so happen they were all sycamore and by the world forgot, since
the phlegmish hoopicough, for all a possabled, after ete a bad cramp
and johnny magories, and backscrat the poor bedsores and the
farthing dip, their caschal pandle of magnegnousioum, and read a
letter or two every night, before going to dodo sleep atrance, with
their catkins coifs, in the twilight, a capitaletter, for further auspices,
on their old one page codex book of old year's eve 1132, M.M.L.J.
old style, their Senchus Mor, by his fellow girl, the Mrs Shemans,
in her summer seal houseonsample, with the caracul broadtail, her
totam in tutu, final buff noonmeal edition, in the regatta covers,
uptenable from the orther, for to regul their reves by incubation,
and Lally, through their gangrene spentacles, and all the good or
they did in their time, the rigorists, for Roe and O'Mulcnory a Conry
ap Mul or Lap ap Morion and Buffler ap Matty Mac Gregory for
Marcus on Podex by Daddy de Wyer, old bagabroth, beeves and
scullogues, churls and vassals, in same, sept and severalty and one
by one and sing a mamalujo. To the heroest champion of Eren and
his braceoelanders and Gowan, Gawin and Gonne.

And after that now in the future, please God, after nonpenal
start, all repeating ourselves, in medios loquos, from where he got
a useful arm busy on the touchline, due south of her western
shoulder, down to death and the love embrace, with an interesting
tallow complexion and all now united, sansfamillias, let us ran on
to say oremus prayer and homeysweet homely, after fully realising
the gratifying experiences of highly continental evenements, for
meter and peter to temple an eslaap, for auld acquaintance, to
Peregrine and Michael and Farfassa and Peregrine, for navigants
et peregrinantibus, in all the old imperial and Fionnachan sea and
for vogue awallow to a Miss Yiss, you fascinator, you, sing a lov-

asteamadorion to Ladyseyes, here's Tricks and Doelsy, delightfully
ours, in her doaty ducky little blue and roll his hoop and how she
ran, when wit won free, the dimply blissed and awfully bucked,
right glad we never shall forget, thoh the dayses gone still they loves
young dreams and old Luke with his kingly leer, so wellworth
watching, and Senchus Mor, possessed of evident notoriety, and
another more of the bigtimers, to name no others, of whom great
things were expected in the fulmfilming department, for the lives
of Lazarus and auld luke syne and she haihaihail her kobbor
kohinor sehehet on the praze savohole shanghai.

Hear, O hear, Iseult la belle! Tristan, sad hero, hear! The Lambeg
drum, the Lombog reed, the Lumbag fiferer, the Limibig brazenaze.

Anno Domini nostri sancti Jesu Christi
Nine hundred and ninetynine million pound sterling in the blue-
*   black bowels of the bank of Ulster.*
Braw bawbees and good gold pounds, galore, my girleen, a Sunday'll
*   prank thee finely.*
And no damn loutll come courting thee or by the mother of the Holy
*   Ghost there'll be murder!*

O, come all ye sweet nymphs of Dingle beach to cheer Brinabride
*   queen from Sybil surfriding*
In her curragh of shells of daughter of pearl and her silverymonn-
*   blue mantle round her.*
Crown of the waters, brine on her brow, she'll dance them a jig and
*   jilt them fairly.*
Yerra, why would she bide with Sig Sloomysides or the grogram
*   grey barnacle gander?*

You won't need be lonesome, Lizzy my love, when your beau gets
*   his glut of cold meat and hot soldiering*
Nor wake in winter, window machree, but snore sung in my old
*   Balbriggan surtout.*
Wisha, won't you agree now to take me from the middle, say, of
*   next week on, for the balance of my days, for nothing (what?)*
*   as your own nursetender?*
A power of highsteppers died game right enough—but who, acushla,
*   'll beg coppers for you?*

I tossed that one long before anyone.
It was of a wet good Friday too she was ironing and, as I'm given
*   now to understand, she was always mad gone on me.*

Grand goosegreasing we had entirely with an allnight eiderdown bed picnic to follow.

By the cross of Cong, says she, rising up Saturday in the twilight from under me, Mick, Nick the Maggot or whatever your name is, you're the mose likable lad that's come my ways yet from the barony of Bohermore.

Mattheehew, Markeehew, Lukeehew, Johnheehewwheehew!

Haw!

And still a light moves long the river. And stiller the mermen ply their keg.

Its pith is full. The way is free. Their lot is cast.

So, to john for a john, johnajeams, led it be!

3

Hark!

Tolv two elf kater ten (it can't be) sax.

Hork!

Pedwar pemp foify tray (it must be) twelve.

And low stole o'er the stillness the heartbeats of sleep.

White fogbow spans. The arch embattled. Mark as capsules. The nose of the man who was nought like the nasoes. It is selftinted, wrinkling, ruddled. His kep is a gorsecone. He am Gascon Titubante of Tegmine – sub – Fagi whose fixtures are mobiling so wobiling befear my remembrandts. She, exhibit next, his Anastashie. She has prayings in lowdelph. Zeehere green eggbrooms. What named blautoothdmand is yon who stares? Gugurtha! Gugurtha! He has becco of wild hindigan. Ho, he hath hornhide! And hvis now is for you. Pensée! The most beautiful of woman of the veilch veilchen veilde. She would kidds to my voult of my palace, with obscidian luppas, her aal in her dhove's suckling. Apagemonite! Come not nere! Black! Switch out!

Methought as I was dropping asleep somepart in nonland of where's please (and it was when you and they were we) I heard at zero hour as 'twere the peal of vixen's laughter among midnight's chimes from out the belfry of the cute old speckled church tolling so faint a goodmantrue as nighthood's unseen violet rendered all animated greatbritish and Irish objects nonviewable to human watchers save 'twere perchance anon some glistery gleam darkling adown surface of affluvial flowandflow as again might seem garments of laundry reposing a leasward close at hand in full expectation. And as I was jogging along in a dream as dozing I was dawdling, arrah, methought broadtone was heard and the creepers and the gliders and flivvers of the earth breath and the dancetongues of the woodfires and the hummers in their ground all vociferated

echoating: Shaun! Shaun! Post the post! with a high voice and O,
the higher on high the deeper and low, I heard him so! And
lo, mescemed somewhat came of the noise and somewho might
amove allmurk. Now, 'twas as clump, now mayhap. When look, was
light and now'twas as flasher, now moren as the glaow. Ah, in un-
litness 'twas in very similitude, bless me, 'twas his belted lamp!
Whom we dreamt was a shaddo, sure, he's lightseyes, the laddo!
Blessed momence, O romence, he's growing to stay! Ay, he who so
swayed a will of a wisp before me, hand prop to hand, prompt side
to the pros, dressed like an earl in just the correct wear, in a classy
mac Frieze o'coat of far suparior ruggedness, indigo braw, tracked
and tramped, and an Irish ferrier collar, freeswinging with mereswin
lacers from his shoulthern and thick welted brogues on him ham-
mered to suit the scotsmost public and climate, iron heels and spara-
ble soles, and his jacket of providence wellprovided woolies with a
softrolling lisp of a lapel to it and great sealingwax buttons, a good
helping bigger than the slots for them, of twentytwo carrot kras-
napoppsky red and his invulnerable burlap whiskcoat and his popular choker, Tamagnum sette-and-forte and his loud boheem toy and
the damasker's overshirt he sported inside, a starspangled zephyr
with a decidedly surpliced crinklydoodle front with his motto
through dear life embrothred over it in peas, rice, and yeggyyolk,
Or for royal, Am for Mail, R.M.D. hard cash on the nail and the
most successfully carried gigot turnups now you ever, (what a pair-
fact crease! how amsolookly kersse!) breaking over the ankle and
hugging the shoeheel, everything the best — none other from (Ah,
then may the turtle's blessings of God and Mary and Haggispatrick
and Huggisbrigid be souptumbling all over him!) other than (and
may his hundred thousand welcome stewed letters, relayed wand
postchased, multiply, ay faith, and plultiply!) Shaun himself.

What a picture primitive!

Had I the concordant wiseheads of Messrs Gregory and Lyons
alongside of Dr Tarpey's and I dorsay the reverend Mr Mac
Dougall's, but I, poor ass, am but as their fourpart tinckler's dun-
key. Yet methought Shaun (holy messonger angels be uninter-
ruptedly nudging him among and along the winding ways of
random ever!) Shaun in proper person (now may all the blueblack-
sliding constellations continue to shape his changeable timetable!)
stood before me. And I pledge you my agricultural word by
the hundred and sixty odds rods and cones of this even's vision that
young fellow looked the stuff, the Bel of Beaus' Walk, a prime card

if ever was! Pep? Now without deceit it is hardly too much to say he was looking grand, so fired smart, in much more than his usual health. No mistaking that beamish brow! There was one for you that ne'er would nunch with good Duke Humphrey but would aight through the months without a sign of an err in hem and then, otherwise rounding, fourale to the lees of Traroe. Those jehovial oyeglances! The heart of the rool! And hit the hencoop. He was immense, topping swell for he was after having a great time of it, a twentyfour hours every moment matters maltsight, in a porterhouse, scutfrank, if you want to know, Saint Lawzenge of Toole's, the Wheel of Fortune, leave your clubs in the hall and wait on yourself, no chucks for walnut ketchups, Lazenby's and Chutney graspis (the house the once queen of Bristol and Balrothery twice admired because her frumped door looked up Dacent Street) where in the sighed of lovely eyes while his knives of hearts made havoc he had recruited his strength by meals of spadefuls of mounded food, in anticipation of the faste of tablenapkins, constituting his threepartite pranzipal meals *plus* a collation, his breakfast of first, a bless us O blood and thirsthy orange, next, the half of a pint of becon with newled googs and a segment of riceplummy padding, met of sunder suigar and some cold forsoaken steak peatrefired from the batblack night o'erflown then, without prejuice to evectuals, came along merendally his stockpot dinner of a half a pound or round steak, very rare, Blong's best from Portarlington's Butchery, with a side of riceypeasy and Corkshire alla mellonge and bacon with (a little mar pliche!) a pair of chops and thrown in from the silver grid by the proprietoress of the roastery who lives on the hill and gaulusch gravy and pumpernickel to wolp up and a gorger's bulby onion (Margareter, Margaretar Margarasticandeatar) and as well with second course and then finally, after his avalunch oclock snack at Appelredt's or Kitzy Braten's of saddlebag steak and a Botherhim with her old phoenix portar, jistr to gwen his gwistel and praties sweet and Irish too and mock gurgle to whistle his way through for the swallying, swp by swp, and he getting his tongue arount it and Boland's broth broken into the bargain, to his regret his soupay *avic* nightcap, vitellusit, a carusal consistent with second course eyer and becon (the rich of) with broad beans, hig, steak, hag, pepper the diamond bone hotted up timmtomm and while'twas after that he scoffed a drakeling snuggily stuffed following cold loin of veal more cabbage and in their green free state a clister of peas, soppositorily petty, last. P.S. but a fingerhot of rheingenever to give the Pax cum Spiritututu. Drily thankful. Burud and dulse and typureely jam, all free of charge, aman, and. And the best of wine *avec*. For his heart was as big as himself, so it was, ay, and bigger! While the loaves are aflowering and the nachtingale jugs. All St Jilian's of Berry, hurrah there for tobies! Mabhrodaphne, brown pride of our custard house quay, amiable with repastful, cheerus graciously, cheer us! Ever of thee, Anne Lynch, he's deeply draiming! Houseanna! Tea is the Highest! For auld lang Ayternitay! Thus thicker will he grow now, grew new. And better and better on butter and butter. At the sign of Mesthress Vanhungrig. However! Mind you, nuckling down to nourritures, were they menuly some ham and jaffas, and I don't mean to make the ingestion for the moment that he was guilbey of gulpable gluttony as regards chewable boltaballs, but, biestings be biestings, and upon the whole, when not off his oats, given prelove appetite and postlove pricing good coup, goodcheap, were it thermidor oogst or floreal may while the whistling prairial roysters play, between gormandising and gourmeteering, he grubbed his tuck all right, deah smorregos, every time he was for doing dirt to a meal or felt like a bottle of ardilaun arongwith a smag of a lecker biss of a welldressed taart or. Though his net intrants wight weighed nought but a flyblow to his gross and ganz afterduepoise. And he was so jarvey jaunty with a romp of a schoolgirl's completion sitting pretty over his Oyster Monday print face and he was plainly out on the ramp and mash, as you might say, for he sproke.

Overture and beginners!

When lo (whish, O whish!) mesaw mestreamed, as the green to the gred was flew, was flown, through deafths of durkness greengrown deeper I heard a voice, the voce of Shaun, vote of the Irish, voise from afar (and cert no purer puer palestrine e'er chanted panangelical mid the clouds of Tu es Petrus, not Michaeleen Kelly, not Mara O'Mario, and sure, what more numerose Italicuss ever rawsucked frish uov in urinal?), a brieze to Yverzone o'er the brozaozaozing sea, from Inchigeela call the way how it suspired (morepork! morepork!) to scented nightlife as softly as the loftly marconimasts from Clifden sough open tireless secrets (mauveport! mauveport!) to Nova Scotia's listing sisterwands. Tubetube!

His handpalm lifted, his handshell cupped, his handsign pointed, his handheart mated, his handaxe risen, his handleaf fallen. Helpsome hand that holemost heals! What is het holy! It gested.

And it said:

—Alo, alass, aladdin, amobus! Does she lag soft fall means rest
down? Shaun yawned, as his general address rehearsal, (that was
antepropreviousday's pigeons-in-a-pie with rough dough for the carrier and the hash-say-ugh of overgestern pluzz the 'stuesday's sham-
pain in his head, with the memories of the past and the hicnuncs
of the present embelliching the musics of the futures from Mic-
cheruni's band) addressing himself *ex alto* and complaining with
vocal discontent it was so close as of the fact the rag was up and of
the briefs and billpasses, a houseful of deadheads, of him to dye his
paddycoats to morn his hesternmost earning, his board in the
swealth of his fate as, having moistened his manducators upon the
quiet and scooping molars and grinders clean with his two fore fingers, he sank his hunk, dowanouet to resk at once, exhaust as
winded hare, utterly spent, it was all he could do (disgusted with
himself that the combined weight of his tons of iosals was a hundred men's massed too much for him), upon the native heath he
loved covered kneehigh with virgin bush, for who who e'er trod sod
of Erin could ever sleep off the turf! Well, I'm liberally dished seeing
myself in this trim! How all too unwordy am I, a mere mailman of
peace, a poor loust hastehater of the first degree, the principot of
Candia, no legs and a title, for such eminence, or unpro promenade
rather, to be much more exact, as to be the bearer extraordinary
of these postoomany missive on his majesty's service while me and
yous and them we're extending us after the pattern of reposiveness!
Weh is me, yeh is ye! I, the mightif beam maircanny, which bit his
mirth too early or met his birth too late! It should of been my other
with his leickname for he's the head and I'm an everdevoting fiend
of his. I can seeze tomirror in tosdays of yer when we lofobsed os so
ker. Those sembal simon pumpkel pieman yers! We shared the twin
chamber and we winked on the one wench and what Sim sobs todie
I'll reeve tomorry, for 'twill be, I have hopes of, Sam Dizzier's feedst.
Tune in, tune on, old Tighe, high, high, high, I'm thine owelglass.
Be old! He looks rather thin, imitating me. I'm very fond of that
other of mine. Fish hands Macsorley! Elien! Obsequies! Bonzeye!
Isaac Egari's Ass! We're the musichall pair that won the swimmy-
ease bladdhers at the Guinness gala in Badeniveagh. I ought not to
laugh with him on this stage. But he' such a game loser! I lift my
disk to him. Brass and reeds, brace and ready! How is your napper,
Handy, and hownow does she stand? First he was living to feel what
the eldest daughter she was panseying and last he was dying to know
what old Madre Patriack does be up to. Take this John's Lane in

your toastingfourch. Shaunti and shaunti and shaunti again! And twelve coolinder moons! I am no helotwashipper but I revere her! For my own coant! She has studied! Piscisvendolor! You're grace! Futs dronk of Wouldndom! But, Gemini, he's looking frightfully thin! I heard the man Shee shinging in the pantry bay. Down among the dustbins let him lie! Ear! Ear! Not ay! Eye! Eye! For I'm at the heart of it. Yet I cannot on my solemn merits as a recitativer recollect ever having done of anything of the kind to deserve of such. Not the phost of a nation! Nor by a long trollop! I just didn't have the time to. Saint Anthony Guide!

— But have we until now ever besought you, dear Shaun, we remembered, who it was, good boy, to begin with, who out of symphony gave you the permit?

— Goodbye now, Shaun replied, with a voice pure as a churchmode, in echo rightdainty, with a good catlick tug at his cocomoss candylock, a foretaste in time of his cabbageous brain's curlyflower. Athiacaro! Comb his tar odd gee sing your mower O meeow? Greet thee Good? How are them columbuses! Lard have mustard on them! Fatiguing, very fatiguing. Hobos hornknees and the corveeture of my spine. Poumeerme! My heaviest crux and dairy lot it is, with a bed as hard as the thinkamuddles of the Greeks and a board as bare as a Roman altar. I'm off rabbited kitchens and relief porridgers. No later than a very few fortnichts since I was meeting on the Thinker's Dam with a pair of men out of glasshouse whom I shuffled hands with named MacBlacks—I think their names is Mac-Blakes—from the Headfire Clump — and they were improving me and making me beliek no five hour factory life with insufficient emollient and industrial disabled for them that day o'gratises. I have the highest gratification by anuncing how I have it from whowho but Hagios Colleenkiller's prophecies. After suns and moons, dews and wettings, thunders and fires, comes sabotag. *Solvitur palumballando!* Tilvido! Adie!

— Then, we explained, salve a tour, ambly andy, you possibly might be so by order?

— Forgive me, Shaun repeated from his liquid lipes, not what I wants to do a strike of work but it was condemned on me premitially by Hireark Books and Chiefoverseer Cooks in their Eusebian Concordant Homilies and there does be a power coming over me that is put upon me from on high out of the book of breedings and so as it is becoming hairydittary I have of coerce nothing in view to look forward at unless it is Swann and beating the blindquarters out of my oldfellow's orologium oloss olorium. A bad attack of maggot it feels like. 'Tis trope, custodian said. Almost might I say of myself, while keeping out of crime, I am now becoming about fed up be going circulating about them new hikler's highways like them nameless souls, ercked and skorned and grizzild all over, till it's rusty October in this bleak forest and was veribally complussed by thinking of the crater of some noted volcano or the Dublin river or the catchalot trouth subsidity as away out or to isolate i from my multiple Mes on the spits of Lumbage Island or bury meself, clogs, coolcellar and all, deep in my wineupon ponteen unless Morrissey's colt could help me or the gander maybe at 49 as it is a tithe fish so it is, this pig's stomach business, and where on dearth or in the miraculous meddle of this expending umniverse to turn since it came into my hands I am hopeless off course to be doing anything concerning.

— We expect you are, honest Shaun, we agreed, but from franking machines, limricked, that in the end it may well turn out, we hear to be you, our belated, who will bear these open letter. Speak to us of Emailia.

— As, Shaun replied patly, with tootlepick tact too and a down of his dampers, to that I have the gumpower and, by the benison of Barbe, that is a lock to say with everything, my beloved.

— Would you mind telling us, Shaun honey, beg little big moreboy, we proposed to such a dear youth, where mostly are you able to work. Ah, you might! Whimper and we shall.

— Here! Shaun replied, while he was fondling one of his cowheel cuffs. There's no sabbath for nomads and I mostly was able to walk, being too soft for work proper, sixty odd eilish mires a week between three masses a morn and two chaplets at eve. I am always telling those pedestriasts, my answerers, Top, Sid and Hucky, now (and it is a veriest throth as the thieves' rescension) how it was forstold for me by brevet for my vacation in life while possessing stout legs to be disbarred after holy orders from unnecessary servile work of reckless walking of all sorts for the relics of my time for otherwise by my so douching I would get into a blame there where sieves fall out, Excelsior tips the best. Weak stop work stop walk stop whoak. Go thou this island, one housesleep there, then go thou other island, two housesleep there, then catch one nightmaze, then home to dearies. Never back a woman you defend, never get quit of a friend on whom you depend, never make face to a foe till he's rife and never get stuck to another man's pfife. Amen, ptah! His hungry will be done! On the continent as in Eironesia. But believe me in my simplicity I am awful good, I believe, so I am, at the root of me, praised be right cheek Discipline! And I can now truthfully declaret before my Geity's Pantokreator with my fleshfettered palms on the epizzles of the apossels that I do my reasonabler's best to recite my grocery beans for mummy *mit* dummy *mot* muthar *mat* bonzar regular, genuflections enclosed. Hek domov muy, there thou beest on the hummock, ghee up, ye dog, for your daggily broth, etc., Happy Maria and Glorious Patrick, etc., etc. In fact, always, have I believe. Greedo! Her's me hongue!

—And it is the fullsoot of a tarabred. Yet one minute's observation, dear dogmestic Shaun, as we point out how you have while away painted our town a wearing greenridinghued.

—O murder mere, how did you hear? Shaun replied, smoiling the ily way up his lampsleeve (it just seemed the natural thing to do), so shy of light was he then. Well, so be it! The gloom hath rays, her lump is love. And I will confess to have, yes. Your diogneses is anonest man's. Thrubedore I did! Inditty I did. All lay I did. Down with the Saozon ruze! And I am afraid it wouldn't be my first coat's wasting after striding on the vampire and blazing on the focoal. See! blazing on the focoal. As see! blazing upon the foe. Like the regular redshank I am. Impregnable as the mule himself. Somebody may perhaps hint at an aughter impression of I was wrong. No such a thing! You never made a more freudful mistake, excuse yourself! What's pork to you means meat to me while you behold how I be eld. But it is grandiose by my ways of thinking from the prophecies. New worlds for all! And they were scotographically arranged for gentlemen only by a scripchewer in whofoundland who finds he is a relative. And it was with my extravert davy. Like glue. Be through. Moyhard's daynoight, tomthumb. Phwum!

—How mielodorous is thy bel chant, O songbird, and how exqueezit thine after draught! *Buccinate in Emenia tuba insigni volumnitatis tuae.* But do you mean, O phausdheen phewn, from Pontoffbellek till the Kisslemerched our ledan triz will be? we gathered substantively whether furniture would or verdure varnish?

—It is a confoundyous injective so to say, Shaun the fiery boy shouted, naturally incensed, as he shook the red pepper out of his auricles. And another time please confine your glaring intinuations to some other mordant body. What on the physiog of this furnaced planet would I be doing besides your verjuice? That is more than I can fix, for the teom bihan, anyway. So let I and you now kindly drop that, angryman! That's not French pastry. You can take it from me. Understand me when I tell you (and I will ask you not to whisple, cry golden or quoth mecback) that under the past purcell's office, so deeply deplored by my erstwhile elder friend, Miss Enders, poachmistress and gay receiver ever for in particular to the Scotic Poor Men's Thousand Gallon Cow Society (I was thinking of her in sthore) allbethey blessed with twentytwo thousand sorters out of a biggest poss of twentytwo thousand, mine's won, too much privet stationery and safty quipu was ate up larchly by those nettlesome goats out of pension greed. *Colpa di Becco, buon apartita!* Proceding, I will say it is also one of my avowal's intentions, at some time pease Pod pluse murthers of gout (when I am not prepared to say) so apt as my pen is upt to scratch, to compound quite the makings of a verdigrease savingsbook in the form of a pair of capri sheep boxing gloves surrounding this matter of the Welsfusel mascoteers and their sindybuck that saved a city for my publickers, Nolaner and Browno, Nickil Hopstout, Christcross, so long as, thanks to force of destiny, my selary as a paykelt is propaired, and there is a peg under me and there is a tum till me.

To the Very Honourable The Memory of Disgrace, the Most Noble, Sometime Sweepyard at the Service of the Writer. Salutem dicint. The just defunct Mrs Sanders who (the Loyd insure her!) I was shift and shuft too, with her shester Mrs Shunders, both mudical dauctors from highschoolhorse and aslyke as Easther's leggs. She was the niceliest person of a wellteached nonparty woman that I ever acquired her letters, only too fat, used to babies and tottydean verbish this is her entertermentdags for she shuk the bottle and tuk the medascene all times a day. She was well under ninety, poor late Mrs, and had tastes of the poetics, me having stood the pilgarlick a fresh at sea when the moon also was standing in a corner of sweet Standerson my ski. P.L.M. Mevrouw von Andersen was her whogave me a muttonbrooch, stakkers for her begfirst party. Honour thy farmer and my litters. This, my tears, is my last will intesticle wrote off in the strutforit about their absent female assauciations which I, or perhaps any other person what squaton a toffette, have the honour to had upon their polite sophykussens in the real presence of devouted Mrs Grumby when her skin was exposed to the air. O what must the grief of my mund be for two little ptpt coolies worth twenty thousand quad herewitdnessed with both's maddlemass wishes to Pepette for next match from their dearly beloved Roggers, M.D.D. O.D. May doubling drop of droøght! Writing.

— Hopsoloosely kidding you are totether with your cadenus and goat along nose how we shall complete that white paper. Two venus-stas! Biggerstiff! Qweer but gaon! Be trouz and wholetrouz! Otherwise, frank Shaun, we pursued, what would be the autobiography of your softbodied fumiform?

— Hooraymost! None whomsoever, Shaun replied, Heavenly blank! (he had intentended and was peering now rather close to the paste of his rubiny winklering) though it ought to be more or less rawcawcaw romantical. By the wag, how is Mr Fry? All of it, I might say, in ex-voto, pay and perks and wooden halfpence, some rhino, rhine, O joyoust rhine, was handled over spondaneously by me (and bundle end to my illwishers' Miss Anders! she woor her wraith of ruins the night she lost I left!) in the ligname of Mr van Howten of Tredcastles, Clowntalkin, timbreman, among my prodigits nabobs and navious of every subscription entitled the Bois in the Boscoor, our evicted tenemants. What I say is (and I am noen roehorn or culkilt permit me to tell you, if uninformed), I never spont it. Nor have I the ghuest of innation on me the way to. It is my rule so. It went anyway like hot pottagebake. And this brings me to my fresh point. Quoniam, I am as plain as portable enveloped, inhowmuch, you will now parably receive, care of one of Mooseyeare Goonness's registered andouterthus barrels. Quick take um whiffat andrainit. Now!

— So vi et! we responded. Song! Shaun, song! Have mood! Hold forth!

— I apologuise, Shaun began, but I would rather spinooze you one from the grimm gests of Jacko and Esaup, fable one, feeble too. Let us here consider the casus, my dear little cousis (husstenhasstencaffincoffintussemtossemdamandamnacosaghcusaghhobixhatouxpeswchbechoscashlcarcarcaract) of the Ondt and the Gracehoper.

The Gracehoper was always jigging ajog, hoppy on akkant of his joyicity, (he had a partner pair of findlestilts to supplant him), or, if not, he was always making ungraceful overtures to Floh and Luse and Bienie and Vespatilla to play pupa-pupa and pulicy-pulicy and langtennas and pushpygyddyum and to commence insects with him, there mouthparts to his orefice and his gambills to there airy processes, even if only in chaste, ameng the everlistings, behold a waspering pot. He would of curse melissciously, by his fore feelhers, flexors, contractors, depressors and extensors, lamely, harry me, marry me, bury me, bind me, till she was puce for shame and allso fourmish her in Spinner's housery at the earthsbest schoppinhour so summery as his cottage, which was cald fourmillierly Tingsomingenting, groped up. Or, if he was always striking up funny funereels with Besterfarther Zeuts, the Aged One, with all his wigeared corollas, albedinous and oldbuoyant, inscythe his elytrical wormcasket and Dehlia and Peonia, his druping nymphs, bewheedling him, compound eyes on hornitosehead, and Auld Letty Plussiboots to scratch his cacumen and cackle his tramsitus, diva deborah (seven bolls of sapo, a lick of lime, two spurts of fussfor, threefurts of sulph, a shake o'shouker, doze grains of migniss and a mesfull of midcap pitchies. The whool of the whaal in the wheel of the whorl of the Boubou from Bourneum has thus come to taon!), and with tambarins and cantoridettes soturning around his eggshill rockcoach their dance McCaper in retrophoebia, beck from bulk, like fantastic disossed and jenny aprils, to the ra, the ra, the ra, the ra, langsome heels and langsome toesis, attended to by a mutter and doffer duffmatt baxingmotch and a myrmidins of pszozlers pszinging *Satyr's Caudledayed Nice* and *Hombly, Dombly Sod We Awhile* but *Ho, Time Timeagen, Wake!* For if sciencium (what's what) can mute uns nought, 'a thought, abought the Great Sommbboddy within the Omniboss, perhops an artsaccord (hoot's hoot) might sing ums tumtim abutt the Little Newbuddies that ring his panch. A high old tide for the barheated publics and the whole day as gratiis! Fudder and lighting for ally looty, any filly in a fog, for O'Cronione lags acrumbling in his sands but his sunsunsuns still tumble on. Erething above ground, as his Book of Breathings bed him, so as everwhy, sham or shunner, zeemliangly to kick time.

Grouscious me and scarab my sahul! What a bagateller it is! Libelulous! Inzanzarity! Pou! Pschla! Ptuh! What a zeit for the goths! vented the Ondt, who, not being a sommerfool, was thothfolly making chilly spaces at hisphex affront of the icinglass of his windhame, which was cold antitopically Nixnixundnix. We shall not come to party at that lopp's, he decided possibly, for he is not on our social list. Nor to Ba's berial nether, thon sloghard, this oldeborre's yaar ablong as there's a khul on a khat. Nefersenless, when he had safely looked up his ovipository, he loftet hails and prayed: May he me no voida water! Seekit Hatup! May no he me tile pig shed on! Suckit Hotup! As broad as Beppy's realm shall flourish my reign shall flourish! As high as Heppy's hevn shall flurrish my haine shall hurrish! Shall grow, shall flourish! Shall hurrish! Hummum.

The Ondt was a weltall fellow, raumybult and abelboobied, bynear saw altitudinous wee a schelling in kopfers. He was sair sair sullemn and chairmanlooking when he was not making spaces in

his psyche, but, laus! when he wore making spaces on his ikey, he
ware mouche mothst secred and muravyingly wisechairmanlooking.
Now whim the sillybilly of a Gracehoper had jingled through a
jungle of love and debts and jangled through a jumble of life in
doubts afterworse, wetting with the bimblebeaks, drikking with
nautonects, bilking with durrydunglecks and horing after lady-
birdies (*ichnehmon diagelegenaitoikon*) he fell joust as sieck as a
sexton and tantoo pooveroo quant a churchprince, and wheer the
midges to wend hemsylph or vosch to sirch for grub for his corapusse
or to find a hospes, alick, he wist gnit! Bruko dry! fuko spint! Sulta-
mont osa bare! And volomundo osi videvide! Nichtsnichtsundnichts!
Not one pickopeck of muscowmoney to bag a tittlebits of beebread!
Iomio! Iomio! Crick's corbicule, which a plight! O moy Bog, he
contrited with melanctholy. Meblizzered, him sluggered! I am heartily hungry!

He had eaten all the whilepaper, swallowed the lustres, devoured
forty flights of styearcases, chewed up all the mensas and seccles,
ronged the records, made mundballs of the ephemerids and vora-
sioused most glutinously with the very timeplace in the ternitary —
not too dusty a cicada of neutriment for a chittinous chip so mitey.
But when Chrysalmas was on the bare branches, off he went from
Tingsomingenting. He took a round stroll and he took a stroll round
and he took a round strollagain till the grillies in his head and the
leivnits in his hair made him thought he had the Tossmania. Had
he twicycled the sees of the deed and trestraversed their revermer?
Was he come to hevre with his engiles or gone to hull with the poop?
The June snows was flocking in thuckflues on the hegelstomes,
millipeeds of it and myriopoods, and a lugly whizzling tournedos,
the Boraborayellers, blohablasting tegolhuts up to tetties and ruching
sleets off the coppeehouses, playing ragnowrock rignewreck, with
an irritant, penetrant, siphonopterous spuk. Grausssssss! Opr!
Grausssssss! Opr!

The Gracehoper who, though blind as batflea, yet knew, not a
leetle beetle, his good smetterling of entymology asped nissunitimost
lous nor liceens but promptly tossed himself in the vico, phthin and
phthir, on top of his buzzer, tezzily wondering wheer would his aluck
alight or boss of both appease and the next time he makes the aquin-
atance of the Ondt after this they have met themselves, these mou-
schical umsummables, it shall be motylucky if he will beheld not
a world of differents. Behailed His Gross the Ondt, prostrandvorous
upon his dhrone, in his Papylonian babooshkees, smolking a spatial

brunt of Hosana cigals, with unshrinkables farfalling from his un-
thinkables, swarming of himself in his sunnyroom, sated before his
comfortumble phullupsuppy of a plate o'monkynous and a confu-
cion of minthe (for he was a conformed aceticist and aristotaller),
as appi as a oneysucker or a baskerboy on the Libido, with Floh
biting his leg thigh and Luse lugging his luff leg and Bieni bussing
him under his bonnet and Vespatilla blowing cosy fond tutties up
the allabroad length of the large of his smalls. As entomate as intimate could pinchably be. Emmet and demmet and be jiltses crazed
and be jadeses whipt! schneezed the Gracehoper, aguepe with ptch-
jelasys and at his wittol's indts, what have eyeforsight!

The Ondt, that true and perfect host, a spiter aspinne, was making
the greatest spass a body could with his queens laceswinging for
he was spizzing all over him like thingsumanything in formicola-
tion, boundlessly blissfilled in an allallahbath of houris. He was
ameising himself hugely at crabround and marypose, chasing Floh
out of charity and tickling Luse, I hope too, and tackling Bienie,
faith, as well, and jucking Vespatilla jukely by the chimiche. Never
did Dorsan from Dunshanagan dance it with more devilry! The
veripatetic imago of the impossible Gracehoper on his odderkop in
the myre, after his thrice ephemeral journeeys, sans mantis ne shoo-
shooe, featherweighed animule, actually and presumptuably sincti-
fying chronic's despair, was sufficiently and probably coocoo much
for his chorous of gravitates. Let him be Artalone the Weeps with
his parisites peeling off him I'll be Highfee the Crackasider. Flunkey
Footle furloughed foul, writing off his phoney, but Conte Carme
makes the melody that mints the money. *Ad majorem l.s.d.! Divi
gloriam.* A darkener of the threshold. Haru? Orimis, capsizer of
his antboat, sekketh rede from Evil-it-is, lord of loaves in Amongded.
Be it! So be it! Thou-who-thou-art, the fleet-as-spindhrift, impfang
thee of mine wideheight. Haru!

The thing pleased him andt, and andt,

He larved ond he larved on he merd such a nauses
The Gracehoper feared he would mixplace his fauces.
I forgive you, grondt Ondt, said the Gracehoper, weeping,
For their sukes of the sakes you are safe in whose keeping.
Teach Floh and Luse polkas, show Bienie where's sweet
And be sure Vespatilla fines fat ones to heat.
As I once played the piper I must now pay the count
So saida to Moyhammlet and marhaba to your Mount!

Let who likes lump above so what flies be a full 'un;
I could not feel moregruggy if this was prompollen.
I pick up your reproof, the horsegift of a friend,
For the prize of your save is the price of my spend.
Can castwhores pulladeftkiss if oldpollocks forsake 'em
Or Culex feel etchy if Pulex don't wake him?
A locus to loue, a term it t'embarass,
These twain are the twins that tick Homo Vulgaris.
Has Aquileone nort winged to go syf
Since the Gwyfyn we were in his farrest drewbryf
And that Accident Man not beseeked where his story ends
Since longsephyring sighs sought heartseast for their orience?
We are Wastenot with Want, precondamned, two and true,
Till Nolans go volants and Bruneyes come blue.
Ere those gidflirts now gadding you quit your mocks for my gropes
An extense must impull, an elapse must elopes,
Of my tectucs takestock, tinktact, and ail's weal;
As I view by your farlook hale yourself to my heal.
Partiprise my thinwhins whiles my blink points unbroken on
Your whole's whercabroads with Tout's trightyright token on.
My in risible universe youdly haud find
Sulch oxtrabeeforeness meat soveal behind.
Your feats end enormous, your volumes immense,
(May the Graces I hoped for sing your Ondtship song sense!),
Your genus its worldwide, your spacest sublime!
But, Holy Saltmartin, why can't you beat time?

In the name of the former and of the latter and of their holo-
caust. Allmen.

— Now? How good you are in explosition! How farflung is your
fokloire and how velktingeling your volupkabulary! *Qui vive spa-
ranto qua muore contanto.* O foibler, O flip, you've that wandervogl
wail withyin! It falls easily upon the earopen and goes down the
friskly shortiest like treacling tumtim with its tingtingtaggle. The
blarneyest blather in all Corneywall! But could you, of course, decent Lettrechaun, we knew (to change your name of not your nation) while still in the barrel, read the strangewrote anaglyptics of
those shemletters patent for His Christian's Em?

— Greek! Hand it to me! Shaun replied, plosively pointing to the
cinnamon quistoquill behind his acoustrolobe. I'm as afterdusk nobly
Roman as pope and water could christen me. Look at that for a rid-

ingpin! I am, thing Sing Larynx, letter potent to play the sem backwards like Oscan wild or in shunt Persse transluding from the
Otherman or off the Toptic or anything off the types of my finklers
in the draught or with buttles, with my oyes thickshut and all. But,
hellas, it is harrobrew bad on the corns and callouses. As far as that
goes I associate myself with your remark just now from theodicy
re'furloined notepaper and quite agree in your prescriptions for
indeed I am, pay Gay, in juxtaposition to say it is not a nice production. It is a pinch of scribble, not wortha bottle of cabbis. Over-
drawn! Puffedly offal tosh! Besides its auctionable, all about crime
and libel! Nothing beyond clerical horrors *et omnibus* to be entered
for the foreign as secondclass matter. The fuellest filth ever fired
since Charley Lucan's. Flummery is what I would call it if you were
to ask me to put it on a single dimension what pronounced opinion
I might possibly orally have about them bagses of trash which the
mother and Mr Unmentionable (O breed not his same!) has reduced to writing without making news out of my sootynemm.
When she slipped under her couchman. And where he made a cat
with a peep. How they wore two madges on the makewater. And
why there were treefellers in the shrubrubs. Then he hawks his
handmud figgers from Francie to Fritzie down in the kookin. Phiz
is me mother and Hair's me father. Bauv Betty Famm and Pig Pig
Pike. Their livetree (may it flourish!) by their ecotaph (let it
stayne!). With balsinbal bimbies swarming tiltop. Comme bien,
Comme bien! Feefeel! Feefeel! And the Dutches dyin loffin at his
pon peck de Barec. And all the mound reared. Till he wot not wot
to begin he should. An infant sailing eggshells on the floor of a wet
day would have more sabby.

Letter, carried of Shaun, son of Hek, written of Shem, brother
of Shaun, uttered for Alp, mother of Shem, for Hek, father of Shaun.
Initialled. Gee. Gone. 29 Hardware Saint. Lendet till Laonum. Baile-
Atha-Cliath. 31 Jan. 1132 A.D. Here Commerces Enville. Tried
Apposite House. 13 Fitzgibbets. Loco. Dangerous. Tax 9d. B.L.
Guineys, esqueer. L.B. Not known at 1132 a. 12 Norse Richmound.
Nave unlodgeable. Loved noa's dress. Sinned, Jetty Pierrse. Noon
sick parson. 92 Windsewer. Ave. No such no. Vale. Finn's Hot. Ex-
belled from 1014 d. Pulldown. Fearview. Opened by Miss Take.
965 nighumpledan sextiffits. Shout at Site. Roofloss. Fit Dunlop and
Be Satisfied. Mr. Domnall O'Domnally. Q.V. 8 Royal Terrors.
None so strait. Shutter up. Dining with the Danes. Removed to
Philip's Burke. At sea. D.E.D. Place scent on. Clontalk. Father

Jacob, Rice Factor. 3 Castlewoos. P.V. Arrusted. J.P. Converted to
Hospitalism. Ere the March past of Civilisation. Once Bank of Ire-
land's. Return to City Arms. 2 Milchbroke. Wrongly spilled. Traum-
condraws. Now Bunk of England's. Drowned in the Laffey. Here.
The Reverest Adam Foundlitter. Shown geshotten. 7 Streetpetres.
Since Cabranke. Seized of the Crownd. Well, Sir Arthur. Buy
Patersen's Matches. Unto his promisk hands. Blown up last Lemmas
by Orchid Lodge. Search Unclaimed Male. House Condamned by
Ediles. Back in Few Minutes. Closet for Repeers. 60 Shellburn.
Key at Kate's. Kiss. Isaac's Butt, Poor Man. Dalicious arson. Caught.
Missing. Justiciated. Kainly forewarned. Abraham Badly's King,
Park Bogey. Salved. All reddy berried. Hollow and eavy. Desert it.
Overwayed. Understrumped. Back to the P.O. Kaer of. Ownes owe
M.O. Too Let. To Be Soiled. Cohabited by Unfortunates. Lost all
Licence. His Bouf Toe is Frozen Over. X, Y and Z, Ltd, Destinied
Tears. A.B, ab, Sender. Boston (Mass). 31 Jun. 13, 12. P.D. Razed.
Lawyered. Vacant. Mined. Here's the Bayleaffs. Step out to Hall
out of that, Ereweaker, with your Bloody Big Bristol. Bung. Stop.
Bung. Stop. Cumm Bumm. Stop. Came Baked to Auld Aireen. Stop.

— Kind Shaun, we all requested, much as we hate to say it, but
since you rose to the use of money have you not, without suggesting
for an instant, millions of moods used up slanguage tun times as
words as the penmarks used out in sinscript with such hesitancy by
your cerebrated brother — excuse me not mentioningahem?

— CelebrAted! Shaun replied under the sheltar of his broguish,
vigorously rubbing his magic lantern to a glow of fullconsciousness.
HeCitEncy! Your words grates on my ares. Notorious I rather would
feel inclined to myself in the first place to describe Mr O'Shem the
Draper with before letter as should I be accentually called upon
for a dieoguinnsis to pass my opinions, properly spewing, into im-
pulsory irelitz. But I would not care to be so unfruitful to my own
part as to swear for the moment positively as to the views of Denmark. No, sah! But let me say my every belief before my high Gee
is that I much doubt of it. I've no room for that fellow on my fag-
roaster, I just can't. As I hourly learn from Rooters and Havers
through Gilligan's maypoles in a nice pathetic notice he, the pixillated
doodler, is on his last with illegible clergimanths boasting always
of his ruddy complexious! She, the mammy far, was put up to it by
him, the iniquity that ought to be depraved of his libertins to be
silenced, sackclothed and suspended, and placed in irons into some
drapery institution off the antipopees for wordsharping only if he

was klanver enough to pass the panel fleischcurers and the fieldpost censor. Gach! For that is a fullblown fact and well celibated before the four divorce courts and all the King's paunches, how he has the solitary from seeing Scotch snakes and has a lowsense for the production of consumption and dalickey cyphalos on his brach premises where he can purge his contempt and dejeunerate into a skillyton be thinking himself to death. Rot him! Flannelfeet! Flattyro! I will describe you in a word. Thou. (I beg your pardon.) Homo! Then putting his bedfellow on me! (like into mike and nick onto post). The criniman: I'll give it to him for that! Making the lobbard change hisstops, as we say in the long book! Is he on whosekeeping or are my! Obnoximost posthumust! With his unique hornbook and his prince of the apauper's pride, blundering all over the two worlds! If he waits till I buy him a mosselman's present! Ho's nos halfcousin of mine, pigdish! Nor wants to! I'd famish with the cuistha first. Aham!

— May we petition you, Shaun illustrious, then, to put his prentis' pride in your aproper's purse and to unravel in your own sweet way with words of style to your very and most obsequient, we suggested, with yet an esiop's foible, as to how?

— Well it is partly my own, isn't it? and you may, ought and welcome, Shaun replied, taking at the same time, as his hunger got the bitter of him, a hearty bite out of the honeycomb of his Braham and Melosedible hat, tryone, tryon and triune. Ann wunkum. Sure, I thunkum you knew all about that, honorey causes, through thelemontary channels long agum. Sure, that is as old as the Baden bees of Saint Dominoc's and as commonpleas now to allus pueblows and bunkum as Nelson his trifulgurayous pillar. However. Let me see, do. Beerman's bluff was what begun it, Old Knoll and his borrowing! And then the liliens of the veldt, Nancy Nickies and Folletta Lajambe! Then mem and hem and the jaquejack. All about Wucherer and righting his name for him. I regret to announce, after laying out his litterery bed, for two days she kept squealing down for noisy priors and bawling out to her jameymock farceson in Shemish like a mouther of the incas with a garcielasso huw Ananymus pinched her tights and about the Balt with the markshaire parawag and his loyal divorces, when he feraxiously shed ovas in Alemaney, tse tse, all the tell of the tud with the bourighevisien backclack, and him, the cribibber like an ambitrickster, aspiring like the decan's, fast aslooped in the intrance to his polthronechair with his sixth finger between his catseye and the index, making his pillgrimace of Childe Horrid, engrossing to his ganderpan what the idioglossary he invented under hicks hyssop! Hock! Ickick gav him that toock, imitator! And it was entirely theck latter to blame. Does he drink because I am sorely there shall be no more Kates and Nells. If you see him it took place there. It was given meeck, thank the Bench, to assist at the whole thing byck special chancery licence. As often as I think of that unbloody housewarmer, Shem Skrivenitch, always cutting my prhose to please his phrase, bogorror, I declare I get the jawache! Be me punting his reflection he'd begin his beogre-fright in muddyass ribalds. Digteter! Grundtsagar! Swop beef! You know he's peculiar, that eggschicker, with the smell of old woman off him, to suck nothing of his switchedupes. M.D. made his *ante mortem* for him. He was grey at three, like sygnus the swan, when he made his boo to the public and barnacled up to the eyes when he repented after seven. The alum that winters on his top is the stale of the staun that will soar when he stambles till that hag of the coombe rapes the pad off his lock. He was down with the whoop-ing laugh at the age of the loss of reason the whopping first time he prediseased me. He's weird, I tell you, and middayevil down to his vegetable soul. Never mind his falls feet and his tanbark com-plexion. That's why he was forbidden tomate and was warmed off the ricecourse of marrimoney, under the Helpless Corpses Enact-ment. I'm not at all surprised the saint kicked him whereby the sum taken Berkeley showed the reason genrously. *Negas, negasti* — neger-top, negertoe, negertoby, negrunter! Then he was pusched out of Thingamuddy's school by Miss Garterd, for itching. Then he caught the europicolas and went into the society of jewses. With Bro Cahlls and Fran Czeschs and Bruda Pszths and Brat Slavos. One temp when he foiled to be killed, the freak wanted to put his bilingual head intentionally through the *Ikish Tames* and go and join the cler-icy as a demonican skyterrier. Throwing dust in the eyes of the Hooley Fermers! He used to be avowdeed as he ought to be vitandist. For onced I squeaked by twyst I'll squelch him. Then he went to Cecilia's treat on his solo to pick up Galen. Asbestopoulos! Inkupot! He has encaust in the blood. Shim! I have the outmost contempt for. Prost bitten! Conshy! Tiberia is waiting on you, arestocrank! Chaka a seagull ticket at Gattabuia and Gabbiano's! Go o'er the sea, haythen, from me and leave your libber to T C D. Your puddin is cooked! You're served, cram ye! Fatefully yaourth . . . Ex. Ex. Ex. Ex.

— But for what, thrice truthful teller, Shaun of grace? weakly we went on to ask now of the gracious one. Vouchsafe to say. You will now, goodness, won't you? Why?

—For his root language, if you ask me whys, Shaun replied, as he blessed himself devotionally like a crawsbomb, making act of oblivion, footinmouther! (what the thickuns else?) which he picksticked into his lettruce invrention. Ullhodturdenweirmudgaard-gringnirurdrmolnirfenrirlukkilokkibaugimandodrrerinsurtkrinm-gernrackinarockar! Thor's for yo!

—The hundredlettered name again, last word of perfect language. But you could come near it, we do suppose, strong Shaun O', we foresupposed. How?

—Peax! Peax! Shaun replied in vealar penultimatum. 'Tis pebils before Sweeney's as he swigged a slug of Jon Jacobsen from his tree-stem sucker cane. Mildbut likesome! I might as well be talking to the four waves till tibbes grey eves and the rests asleep. Frost! Nope! No one in his seven senses could as I have before said, only you missed my drift, for it's being incendiary. Every dimmed letter in it is a copy and not a few of the silbils and wholly words I can show you in my Kingdom of Heaven. The lowquacity of him! With his threestar monothong! Thaw! The last word in stolentelling! And what's more rightdown lowbrown schisthematic robblemint! Yes. As he was rising my lather. Like you. And as I was plucking his goosybone. Like yea. He store the tale of me shur. Like yup. How's that for Shemese?

—Still in a way, not to flatter you, we fancy you that you are so strikingly brainy and well letterread in yourshelves as ever were the Shamous Shamonous, Limited, could use worse of yourself, in-genious Shaun, we still so fancied, if only you would take your time so and the trouble of so doing it. Upu now!

—Undoubtedly but that is show, Shaun replied, the muttermelk of his blood donor beginning to work, and while innocent of dis-seminating the foul emanation, it would be a fall day I could not, sole, so you can keep your space and by the power of blurry wards I am loyable to do it (I am convicted of it!) any time ever I liked (bet ye fippence off me boot allowance!) with the allergrossest transfusiasm as, you see, while I can soroquise the Siamanish better than most, it is an openear secret, be it said, how I am extremely ingenuous at the clerking even with my badily left and, arrah go braz, I'd pinsel it with immenuensoes as easy as I'd perorate a chickerow of beans for the price of two maricles and my trifolium librotto, the authordux Book of Lief, would, if given to daylight, (I

hold a most incredible faith about it) far exceed what that bogus
bolshy of a shame, my soamheis brother, Gaoy Fecks, is conversant
with in audible black and prink. Outragedy of poetscalds! Acomedy
of letters! I have them all, tame, deep and harried, in my mine's I.
And one of these fine days, man dear, when the mood is on me, that
I may willhap cut my throat with my tongue tonight but I will be
ormuzd moved to take potlood and introvent it Paatryk just like a
work of merit, mark my words and append to my mark twang, that
will open your pucktricker's ops for you, broather brooher, only for,
as a papst and an immature and a nayophight and a *spaciaman
spaciosum* and a hundred and eleven other things, I would never
for anything take so much trouble of such doing. And why so? Because I am altogether a chap too fly and hairyman for to infradig
the like of that ultravirulence. And by all I hold sacred on earth
clouds and in heaven I swear to you on my piop and oath by the
awe of Shaun (and that's a howl of a name!) that I will commission to the flames any incendiarist whosoever or ahriman howso-
clever who would endeavour to set ever annyma roner moother of
mine on fire. Rock me julie but I will soho!

And, with that crickcrackcruck of his threelungged squool from
which grief had usupped every smile, big hottempered husky fusky
krenfy strenfy pugiliser, such as he was, he virtually broke down on
the mooherhead, getting quite jerry over her, overpowered by himself with the love of the tearsilver that he twined through her hair
for, sure, he was the soft semplgawn slob of the world with a heart
like Montgomery's in his showchest and harvey loads of feeling in
him and as innocent and undesignful as the freshfallen calef. Still,
grossly unselfish in sickself, he dished allarmes away and laughed it
off with a wipe at his pudgies and a gulp apologetic, healing his
tare be the smeyle of his oye, oogling around. Him belly no belong
sollow mole pigeon. Ally bully. Fu Li's gulpa. Mind you, now, that
he was in the dumpest of earnest orthough him jawr war hoo hleepy
hor halk urthing hurther. Moe like that only he stopped short in
looking up up upfrom his tide shackled wrists through the ghost of
an ocean's, the wieds of pansiful heathvens of joepeter's gaseytotum
as they are telling not but were and will be, all told, scruting fore-
back into the fargoneahead to feel out what age in years tropical,
ecclesiastic, civil or sidereal he might find by the sirious pointstand
of Charley's Wain (what betune the spheres sledding along the
lacteal and the mansions of the blest turning on old times) as ere-
while had he craved of thus, the dreamskhwindel necklassoed him,

his thumbs fell into his fists and, lusosing the harmonical balance of his ballbearing extremities, by the holy kettle, like a flask of lightning over he careened (O the sons of the fathers!) by the mightyfine weight of his barrel (all that prevented the happering of who if not the asterisks betwink themselves shall ever?) and, as the wisest postlude course he could playact, collaspsed in ensemble and rolled buoyantly backwards in less than a twinkling *via* Rattigan's corner out of farther earshot with his highly curious mode of slipashod motion, surefoot, sorefoot, slickfoot, slackfoot, linkman laizurely, lampman loungey, and by Killesther's lapes and falls, with corks, staves and treeleaves and more bubbles to his keelrow a fairish and easy way enough as the town cow cries behind the times in the direction of Mac Auliffe's, the crucethouse, *Open the Door Softly,* down in the valley before he was really uprighted ere in a dip of the downs (uila!) he spoorlessly disappaled and vanesshed, like a popo down a papa, from circular circulatio. Ah, mean!

Gaogaogaone! Tapaa!

And the stellas were shinings. And the earthnight strewed aromatose. His pibrook creppt mong the donkness. A reek was waft on the luftstream. He was ours, all fragrance. And we were his for a lifetime. O dulcid dreamings languidous! Taboccoo!

It was sharming! But sharmeng!

And the lamp went out as it couldn't glow on burning, yep, the lmp wnt out for it couldn't stay alight.

Well, (how dire do we thee hours when thylike fades!) all's dall and youllow and it is to bedowern that thou art passing hence, mine bruder, able Shaun, with a twhisking of the robe, ere the morning of light calms our hardest throes, beyond cods' cradle and porpoise plain, from carnal relations undfamiliar faces, to the inds of Tuskland where the oliphants scrum till the ousts of Amiracles where the toll stories grow proudest, more is the pity, but for all your deeds of goodness you were soo ooft and for ever doing, manomano and myriamilia even to mulimuli, as our humbler classes, whose virtue is humility, can tell, it is hardly we in the country of the old, Sean Moy, can part you for, oleypoe, you were the walking saint, you were, tootoo too stayer, the graced of gods and pittites and the salus of the wake. Countenance whose disparition afflictedly fond Fuinn feels. Winner of the gamings, primed at the studience, propredicted from the storybouts, the choice of ages wise! Spickspookspokesman of our specturesque silentiousness! Musha, beminded of us out there in Cockpit, poor twelve o'clock scholars, sometime or other anywhen

you think the time. Wisha, becoming back to us way home in Biddy-
house one way or either anywhere we miss your smile. Palmwine
breadfruit sweetmeat milksoup! Suasusupo! However! Our people
here in Samoanesia will not be after forgetting you and the elders
luking and marking the jornies, chalkin up drizzle in drizzle out on
the four bare mats. How you would be thinking in your thoughts
how the deepings did it all begin and how you would be scrimmag-
ing through your scruples to collar a hold of an imperfection being
committled. Sireland calls you. Mery Loye is saling moonlike. And
Slyly mamourneen's ladymaid at Gladshouse Lodge. Turn your coat,
strong character, and tarry among us down the vale, yougander,
only once more! And may the mosse of prosperousness gather you
rolling home! May foggy dews bediamondise your hooprings! May
the fireplug of filiality reinsure your bunghole! May the barleywind
behind glow luck to your bathershins! 'Tis well we know you were
loth to leave us, winding your hobbledehorn, right royal post, but,
aruah sure, pulse of our slumber, dreambookpage, by the grace of
Votre Dame, when the natural morning of your nocturne blank-
merges into the national morning of golden sunup and Don Leary
gets his own back from old grog Georges Quartos as that goodship
the Jonnyjoys takes the wind from waterloogged Erin's king, you
will shiff across the Moylendsea and round up in your own escapol-
ogy some canonisator's day or other, sack on back, alack! digging
snow, (not so?) like the good man you are, with your picture pockets
turned knockside out in the rake of the rain for fresh remittances
and from that till this in any case, timus tenant, may the tussocks
grow quickly under your trampthickets and the daisies trip lightly
over your battercops.

Jaunty Jaun, as I was shortly before that made aware, next halted
to fetch a breath, the first cothurminous leg of his nightstride being
pulled through, and to loosen (let God's son now be looking down
on the poor preambler!) both of his bruised brogues that were plainly
made a good bit before his hosen were, at the weir by Lazar's Walk
(for far and wide, as large as he was lively, was he noted for his
humane treatment of any kind of abused footgear), a matter of
maybe nine score or so barrelhours distance off as truly he merited
to do. He was there, you could planemetrically see, when I took a
closer look at him, that was to say, (gracious helpings, at this rate of
growing our cotted child of yestereve will soon fill space and burst
in systems, so speeds the instant!) amply altered for the brighter,
though still the graven image of his squarer self as he was used to
be, perspiring but happy notwithstanding his foot was still asleep
on him, the way he thought, by the holy januarious, he had a bullock's hoof in his buskin, with his halluxes so splendid, through Ireland untranscended, bigmouthed poesther, propped up, restant,
against a butterblond warden of the peace, one comestabulish Sigurd-
sen, (and where a better than such exsearfaceman to rest from rov-
ing the laddyown he bootblacked?) who, buried upright like the
Osbornes, kozydozy, had tumbled slumbersomely on sleep at night
duty behind the curing station, equilebriated amid the embracings
of a monopolized bottle.

Now, there were as many as twentynine hedge daughters out of
Benent Saint Berched's national nightschool (for they seemed to
remember how it was still a once-upon-a-four year) learning their
antemeridian lesson of life, under its tree, against its warning, beseated, as they were, upon the brinkspondy, attracted to the rare-
rust sight of the first human yellowstone landmark (the bear, the
boer, the king of all boors, sir Humphrey his knave we met on the

moors!) while they paddled away, keeping time magnetically with their eight and fifty pedalettes, playing foolufool jouay allo misto posto, O so jaonickally, all barely in their typtap teens, describing a charming dactylogram of nocturnes though repelled by the snores of the log who looked stuck to the sod as ever and oft, when liquefied, (vil!) he murmoaned abasourdly in his Dutchener's native, visibly unmoved, over his treasure trove for the crown: *Dotter dead bedstead mean diggy smuggy flasky!*

Jaun (after he had in the first place doffed a hat with a reinforced crown and bowed to all the others in that chorus of praise of goodwill girls on their best beehiviour who all they were girls all rushing sowarmly for the post as buzzy as sie could bie to read his kisshands, kittering all about, rushing and making a tremendous girlsfuss over him pellmale, their *jeune premier* and his rosyposy smile, mussing his frizzy hair and the golliwog curls of him, all, but that one; Finfria's fairest, done in loveletters like a trayful of cloudberry tartlets (ain't they fine, mighty, mighty fine and honoured?) and smilingly smelling, pair and pair about, broad by bread and slender to slimmer, the nice perfumios that came cunvy peeling off him (nice!) which was angelic simply, savouring of wild thyme and parsley jumbled with breadcrumbs (O nice!) and feeling his full fat pouch for him so tactily and jingaling his jellybags for, though he looked a young chapplie of sixtine, they could frole by his manhood that he was just the killingest ladykiller all by kindness, now you, Jaun, asking kindlily (hillo, missies!) after their howareyous at all with those of their dollybegs (and where's Agatha's lamb? and how are Bernadetta's columbillas? and Juliennaw's tubberbunnies? and Eulalina's tuggerfunnies?) he next went on (finefeelingfit!) to drop a few stray remarks anent their personal appearances and the contrary tastes displayed in their tight kittycasques and their smart frickyfrockies, asking coy one after sloy one had she read Irish legginds and gently reproving one that the ham of her hom could be seen below her hem and whispering another aside, as lavariant, that the hook of her hum was open a bittock at her back to have a sideeye to that, hom, (and all of course just to fill up a form out of pure human kindness and in a sprite of fun) for Jaun, by the way, was by the way of becoming (I think, I hope he was) the most purely human being that ever was called man, loving all up and down the whole creation from Sampson's tyke to Jones's sprat and from the King of all Wrenns down to infuseries) Jaun, after those few prelimbs made out through his eroscope the apparition of his fond sister

Izzy for he knowed his love by her waves of splabashing and she showed him proof by her way of blabushing nor could he forget her so tarnelly easy as all that since he was brotherbesides her benedict godfather and heaven knows he thought the world and his life of her sweet heart could buy, (brao!) poor, good, true, Jaun!

— Sister dearest, Jaun delivered himself with express cordiality, marked by clearance of diction and general delivery, as he began to take leave of his scolastica at once so as to gain time with deep affection, we honestly believe you sorely will miss us the moment we exit yet we feel as a martyr to the dischurch of all duty that it is about time, by Great Harry, we would shove off to stray on our long last journey and not be the load on ye. This is the gross proceeds of your teachings in which we were raised, you, sis, that used to write to us the exceeding nice letters for presentation and would be telling us anun (full well do we wont to recall to mind) thy oldworld tales of homespinning and derringdo and dieobscure and daddyho, these tales which reliterately whisked off our heart so narrated by thou, gesweest, to perfection, our pet pupil of the whole rhythmetic class and the mainsay of our erigenal house, the time we younkers twain were fairly tossing ourselves (O Phoebus! O Pollux!) in bed, having been laid up with Castor's oil on the Parrish's syrup (the night we will remember) for to share our hard suite of affections with thee.

I rise, O fair assemblage! Andcommincio. Now then, after this introit of exordium, my galaxy girls, *quiproquo* of directions to henservants I was asking his advice on the strict T.T. from Father Mike, P.P., my orational dominican and confessor doctor, C.C.D.D. (buy the birds, he was saying as he yerked me under the ribs sermon in an offrand way and confidence petween peas like ourselves in so-andso many nuncupiscent words about how he had been confarreating teat-a-teat with two viragos intactas about what an awful life he led, poorish priced, uttering mass for a coppall of geldings and what a lawful day it was, there and then, for a consommation with an effusion and how, by all the manny larries ate pignatties, how, hell in tunnels, he'd marry me any old buckling time as flying quick as he'd look at me) and I am giving youth now again in words of style byaway of offertory hisand mikeadvice, an it place the person, as ere he retook him to his cure, those verbs he said to me. From above. The most eminent bishop titular of Dubloonik to all his purtybusses in Dellabelliney. Comeallyedimseldamsels, siddle down and lissle all! Follow me close! Keep me in view! Understeady me saries! Which is to all practising massoeurses from a preaching freer and be a gentleman without a duster before a parlourmade without a spitch. Now. During our brief apsence from this furtive feugtig season adhere to as many as probable of the ten commandments touching purgations and indulgences and in the long run they will prove for your better guidance along your path of right of way. Where the lisieuse are we and what's the first sing to be sung? Is it rubrics, mandarimus, pasqualines, or verdidads is in it, or the bruise-livid indecores of estreme voyoulence and, for the lover of lithurgy, bekant or besant, where's the fate's to be wished for? Several sindays after whatsintime. I'll sack that sick server the minute I bless him. That's the mokst I can do for his grapce. Economy of movement, axe why said. I've a hopesome's choice if I chouse of all the sinkts in the colander. From the common for ignitious Purpalume to the proper of Francisco Ultramare, last of scorchers, third of snows, in terrorgammons howdydos. Here she's, is a bell, that's wares in heaven, virginwhite, Undetrigesima, vikissy manonna. Doremon's! The same or similar to be kindly observed within the affianced dietcess of Gay O'Toole and Gloamy Gwenn du Lake (Danish spoken!) from Manducare Monday up till farrier's siesta in china dominos. Words taken in triumph, my sweet assistance, from the sufferant pen of our jocosus inkerman militant of the reed behind the ear.

Never miss your lostsomewhere mass for the couple in Myles you butrose to brideworship. Never hate mere pork which is bad for your knife of a good friday. Never let a hog of the howth trample underfoot your linen of Killiney. Never play lady's game for the Lord's stake. Never lose your heart away till you win his diamond back. Make a strong point of never kicking up your rumpus over the scroll end of sofas in the Dar Bey Coll Cafeteria by tootling risky *apropos* songs at commercial travellers' smokers for their Columbian nightsentertainments the like of *White limbs they never stop teasing* or *Minxy was a Manxmaid when Murry wor a Man*. And, by the bun, is it you goes bisbuiting His Esaus and Cos and then throws them bag in the box? Why the tin's nearly empty. First thou shalt not smile. Twice thou shalt not love. Lust, thou shalt not commix idolatry. Hip confiners help compunction. Never park your brief stays in the men's convenience. Never clean your buttoncups with your dirty pair of sassers. Never ask his first person where's your quickest cut to our last place. Never let the promising hand usemake free of your oncemaid sacral. The soft side of the axe! A coil of cord, a colleen coy, a blush on a bush turned first man's laughter into wailful moither. O foolish cuppled! Ah, dice's error! Never dip in the ern while you've browsers on your suite. Never slip the silver key through your gate of golden age. Collide with man, collude with money. Ere you sail foreget my prize. Where you truss be circumspicious and look before you leak, dears. Never christen medlard apples till a swithin is in sight. Wet your thistle where a weed is and you'll rue it, despyneedis. Especially beware please of being at a party to any demoralizing home life. That saps a chap. Keep cool faith in the firm, have warm hoep in the house and begin frem athome to be chary of charity. Where it is nobler in the main to supper than the boys and errors of outrager's virtue. Give back those stolen kisses; restaure those allcotten glooves. Recollect the yella perals that all too often beset green gerils, Rhidarhoda and Daradora, once they gethobbyhorsical, playing breeches parts for Bessy Sudlow in flesh-coloured pantos instead of earthing down in the coalhole try-ing to boil the big gun's dinner. Leg-before-Wicked lags-behind-Wall where here Mr Whicker whacked a great fall. Femora-familla feeled it a candleliked but Hayes, Conyngham and Erobinson sware it's an egg. Forglim mick aye! Stay, forestand and tillgive it! Remember the biter's bitters I shed the vigil I buried our Harlotte Quai from poor Mrs Mangain's of Britain Court on the feast of Marie Maudlin. Ah, who would wipe her weeper dry and lead her to the halter? Sold in her heyday, laid in the straw, bought for one puny petunia. Moral: if you can't point a lily get to henna out of here! Put your swell foot foremost on foulardy pneumonia shertwaists, irriconcilible with true fiminin risirvition and ribbons of lace, limenick's disgrace. Sure, what is it on the whole only holes tied together, the merest and transparent washingtones to make Languid Lola's lingery longer? Scenta Clauthes stiffstuffs your hose and heartsies full of temptiness. Vanity flee and Verity fear! Diobell! Whalebones and buskbutts may hurt you (thwackaway thwuck!) but never lay bare your breast secret (dickette's place!) to joy a Jonas in the Dol-phin's Barncar with your meetual fan, Doveyed Covetfilles, come-pulsing paynattention spasms between the averthisment for Ulikah's wine and a pair of pulldoors of the old cupiosity shape. There you'll fix your eyes darkled on the autocart of the bringfast cable but here till youre martimorphysed please sit still face to face. For if the shorth of your skorth falls down to his knees pray how wrong will he look till he rises? Not before Gravesend is commuted. But now reappears Autist Algy, the pulcherman and would-do performer, *oleas* Mr Smuth, stated by the vice crusaders to be well known to all the dally-taunties in and near the ciudad of Buellas Arias, taking you to the playguehouse to see the *Smirching of Venus* and asking with whispered offers in a very low bearded voice, with a nice little tiny manner and in a very nice little tony way, won't you be an artist's moral and pose in your nudies as a local esthetic before voluble old masters, introducing you, left to right the party comprises, to hogarths like Bottisilly and Titteretto and Vergognese and Coraggio with their extrahand Mazzaccio, plus the usual bilker's dozen of dowdycameramen. And the volses of lewd Buylan, for innocence! And the phyllisophies of Bussup Bulkeley. O, the frecklessness of the giddies nouveautays! There's many's the icepolled globetopper is haunted by the hottest spot under his equator like Ramrod, the meaty hunter, always jaeger for a thrust. The back beautiful, the undraped divine! And Suzy's Moedl's with their Blue Danuboyes! All blah! Viper's vapid vilest! Put off the old man at the very font and get right on with the nutty sparker round the back. Slip your oval out of touch and let the paravis be your goal. Up leather, Prunella, convert your try! Stick wicks in your earshells when you hear the prompter's voice. Look on a boa in his beauty and you'll never more wear your strawberry leaves. Rely on the relic. What bondman ever you bind on earth I'll be bound 'twas combined in hemel. Keep airly hores and the worm is yores. Dress the pussy for her nighty and follow her piggytails up their way to Winkyland. See little poupeep she's firsht ashleep. After having sat your poetries and you know what happens when chine throws over jupan. Go to doss with the poulterer, you understand, and shake up with the milchmand. The Sully van vultures are on the prowl. And the hailies fingringmaries. Tobaccos tabu and toboggan's a back seat. Secret satieties and onanymous letters make the great unwatched as bad as their betters. Don't on any account acquire a paunchon for that alltoocommon fagbutt habit of frequenting and chumming together with the braces of couples in Mr Tunnelly's hallways (smash it) wriggling with lowcusses and cockchafers and vamps and rodants, with the end to commit acts of interstipital indecency as between twineties and tapegarters, fingerpats on fondlepets, under the couvrefeu act. It's the thin end; wedge your steps! Your high powered hefty hoyden thinks nothing of ramping through a whole suite of smokeless husbands. Three minutes I'm counting you. Woooooon. No triching now! Give me that when I tell you! *Ragazza ladra!* And is that any place to be smuggling his madam's apples up? Deceitful jade. Gee wedge! Begor, I like the way they're half cooked. Hold, flay, grill, fire that laney feeling for kosenkissing dis-

genically within the proscribed limits like Population Peg on a hint
or twim clandestinely does be doing to Temptation Tom, atkings
questions in barely and snakking svarewords like a nursemagd.
While there's men-a'war on the say there'll be loves-o'women on the
do. Love through the usual channels, cisternbrothelly, when properly disinfected and taken neat in the generable way upon retiring
to roost in the company of a husband-in-law or other respectable
relative of an apposite sex, not love that leads by the nose as I fore-
smellt but canalised love, you understand, does a felon good, sus-
piciously if he has a slugger's liver but I cannot belabour the point
too ardently (and after the lessions of experience I speak from inspiration) that fetid spirits is the thief of prurities, so none of your
twenty rod cherrywhisks, me daughter! At the Cat and Coney or the
Spotted Dog. And at 2bis Lot's Road. When parties get tight for
each other they lose all respect together. By the stench of her fizzle
and the glib of her gab know the drunken draggletail Dublin drab.
You'll pay for each bally sorraday night every billing sumday morning. When the night is in May and the moon shines might. We
won't meeth in Navan till you try to give the Kellsfrieclub
the goby. Hill or hollow, Hull or Hague! And beware how you dare
of wet cocktails in Kildare or the same may see your wedding driving
home from your wake. Mades of ashens when you flirt spoil the
lad but spare his shirt! Lay your lilylike long his shoulder but buck
back if he buts bolder and just hep your homely hop and heed no
horning but if you've got some brainy notion to raise cancan and
rouse commotion I'll be apt to flail that tail for you till it's borning.
Let the love ladleliked at the eye girde your gastricks in the gym.
Nor must you omit to screw the lid firmly on that jazz jiggery and
kick starts. Bumping races on the flat and point to point over ob-
stacles. Ridewheeling that accivisciously up windy Rutland Rise
and insighting rebellious northers before the saunter of the city of
Dunlob. Then breretonbiking on the free with your airs of go-be-
dee and your heels upon the handlebars. Berrboel brazenness! No,
before your corselage rib is decartilaged, that is to mean if you
have visceral ptossis, my point is, making allowances for the fads
of your weak abdominal wall and your liver asprewl, vinvin, vinvin,
or should you feel, in shorts, as though you needed healthy physick-
ing exorcise to flush your kidneys, you understand, and move
that twelffinger bowel and threadworm inhibitating it, lassy, and
perspire freely, lict your lector in the lobby and why out you go by
the ostiary on to the dirt track and skip! Be a sportive. Deal with

Nature the great greengrocer and pay regularly the monthlies. Your Punt's Perfume's only in the hatpinny shop beside the reek of the rawny. It's more important than air—I mean than eats—air (Oop, I never open momouth but I pack mefood in it) and promotes that natural emotion. Stamp out bad eggs. Why so many puddings prove disappointing, as Dietician says, in Creature Comforts Causeries, and why so much soup is so muck slop. If we could fatten on the elizabeetons we wouldn't have teeth like the hippopotamians. However. Likewise if I were in your envelope shirt I'd keep my weather-eye well cocked open for your furnished lodgers paying for their feed on tally with company and piano tunes. Only stuprifying yourself! The too friendly friend sort, Mazourikawitch or some other sukinsin of a vitch, who he's kommen from olt Pannonia on this porpoise whom sue stooderin about the maul and femurl artickles and who mix himself so at home mid the musik and spanks the ivory that lovely for this your Mistro Melosiosus MacShine Mac-Shane may soon prove your undoing and bane through the succeeding years of rain should you, whilst Jaun is from home, get used to basking in his loverslowlap, inordinately clad, moustache-teasing, when closehended together behind locked doors, kissing steadily, (malbongusta, it's not the thing you know!) with the calfloving selfseeker, under the influence of woman, inching up to you, disarranging your modesties and fumbling with his forte paws in your bodice after your billy doos twy as a first go off (take care, would you stray and split on me!) and going on doing his idiot every time you gave him his chance to get thick and play pigglywiggly, making much of you, bilgetalking like a ditherer, gougouzoug, about your glad neck and the round globe and the white milk and the red raspberries (O horrifier!) and prying down furthermore to chance his lucky arm with his pregnant questions up to our past lives. What has that caught to sing with him? The next fling you'll be squitting on the Tubber Nakel, pouring pitchers to the well for old Gloatsdane's glorification and the postequities of the Black Watch, peeping private from the Bush and Rangers. And our local busybody, talker-go-bragk. Worse again! Off of that praying fan on to them priars! It would be a whorable state of affairs altogether for the redcolumnists of presswritten epics, Peter Paragraph and Paulus Puff, (I'm keepsoaking them to cover my concerts) to get ahold of for their balloons and shoot you private by surprise, considering the marriage slump that's on this oil age and pulexes three shillings a pint and wives at six and seven when domestic calamities belame par and newlaids bellow mar for the twenty twotoosent time thwealthy took thousands in the slack march of civilisation were you, becoming guilty of unleckylike intoxication to have and to hold, to pig and to pay direct connection, *qua* intervener, with a prominent married member of the vicereeking squad and, in consequence of the thereinunder subpenas, be flummoxed to the second degree by becoming a detestificated companykeeper on the dammymonde of Lucalamplight. Anything but that, for the fear and love of gold! Once and for all, I'll have no college swankies (you see, I am well voiced in love's arsenal and all its overtures from collion boys to colleen bawns so I have every reason to know that rogues' gallery of nightbirds and bitchfanciers, lucky duffs and light lindsays, haughty hamiltons and gay gordons, dosed, doctored and otherwise, messing around skirts and what their fickling intentions look like, you make up your mind to that) trespassing on your danger zone in the dancer years. If ever I catch you at it, mind, it's you that will cocottch it! I'll tackle you to feel if you have a few devils in you. Holy gun, I'll give it to you, hot, high and heavy before you can say sedro! Or may the maledictions of Lousyfear fall like nettlerash on the white friar's father that converted from moonshine the fostermother of the first nancyfree that ran off after the trumpadour that mangled Moore's melodies and so upturned the tubshead of the stardaft journalwriter to inspire the prime finisher to fellhim the firtree out of which Cooper Funnymore planed the flat of the beerbarrel on which my grandydad's lustiest sat his seat of unwisdom with my tante's petted sister for the cause of his joy! Amene.

Poof! There's puff for ye, begor, and planxty of it, all abound me breadth! Glor galore and glory be! As broad as its lung and as long as a line! The valiantine vaux of Venerable Val Vousdem. If my jaws must brass away like the due drops on my lay. And the topnoted delivery you'd expected be me invoice! Theo Dunnohoo's warning from Daddy O'Dowd. Whoo? What I'm wondering to myselfwhose for there's a strong tendency, to put it mildly, by making me the medium. I feel spirts of itchery outching out from all over me and only for the sludgehummer's force in my hand to hold them the darkens alone knows what'll who'll be saying of next. However. Now, before my upperotic rogister, something nice. Now? Dear Sister, in perfect leave again I say take a brokerly advice and keep it to yourself that we, Jaun, first of our name here now make all receptacles of, free of price. Easy, my dear, if they tingle you either say nothing or nod. No cheekacheek with chipperchapper, you and your last mashboy and the padre in the pulpbox enumerating you his nostrums. Be vacillant over those vigilant who would leave you to belave black on white. Close in for psychical hijiniks as well but fight shy of mugpunters. I'd burn the books that grieve you and light an allassundrian bompyre that would suffragate Tome Plyfire or Zolfanerole. Perousse instate your *Weekly Standerd,* our verile organ that is ethelred by all pressdom. Apply your five wits to the four verilatest. The Arsdiken's *An Traitey on Miracula or Viewed to Death by a Priest Hunter* is still first in the field despite the castle bar, William Archer's a rompan good cathalogue and he'll give you a riser on the route to our nazional labronry. Skim over *Through Hell with the Papes* (mostly boys) by the divine comic Denti Alligator (exsponging your index) and find a quip in a quire arisus aream from bastardtitle to fatherjohnson. Swear aloud by pious fiction the like of *Lentil Lore* by Carnival Cullen or that *Percy Wynns* of our S. J. Finn's or *Pease in Plenty* by the Curer of Wars, licensed and censered by our most picturesque prelates, Their Graces of Linzen and Petitbois, bishops of Hibernites, *licet ut lebanus,* for expansion on the promises, the two best sells on the market this luckiest year, set up by Gill the father, put out by Gill the son and circulating disimally at Gillydehooly's Cost. Strike up a nodding acquaintance for our doctrine with the works of old Mrs Trot, senior, and Manoel Canter, junior, and Loper de Figas, nates maximum. I used to follow Mary Liddlelambe's flitsy tales espicially with the scentaminted sauce. Sifted science will do your arts good. *Egg Laid by Former Cock* and *With Flageolettes in Send Fanciesland.* Chiefly girls. Trip over sacramental tea into the long lives of our saints and saucerdotes, with vignettes, cut short into instructual primers by those in authority for the bittermint of your soughts. Forfet not the palsied. Light a match for poor old Contrabally and send some balmoil for the schizmatics. A hemd in need is aye a friendly deed. Remember, maid, thou dust art powder but Cinderella thou must return (what are you robbing her sleeve for, Ruby? And pull in your tongue, Polly!). Cog that out of your teen times, everyone. The lad who brooks no breaches lifts the lass that toffs a tailor. How dare ye be laughing out of your mouthshine at the lack of that? Keep cool your fresh chastity which is far better far. Sooner than part with that vestalite emerald of the first importance, descend to me by far from our family, which you treasure up so closely where extremes meet, nay, mozzed lesmended, rather let the whole ekumene

universe belong to merry Hal and do whatever his Mary well likes.
When the gong goes for hornets-two-nest marriage step into your
harness and strip off that nullity suit. Faminy, hold back! For the
race is to the rashest of, the romping, jomping rushes of. Haul
Seton's down, black, green and grey, and hoist Mikealy's whey and
sawdust. What's overdressed if underclothed? Poposht forstake me
knot where there's white lets ope. Whisht! Blesht she that walked
with good Jook Humprey for he made her happytight. Go! You can
down all the dripping you can dumple to, and buffkid scouse too
ad libidinum, in these lassitudes if you've parents and things to
look after. That was what stuck to the Comtesse Cantilene while
she was sticking out Mavis Toffeelips to feed her soprannated hus-
pals, and it is henceforth associated with her names. La Dreeping!
Die Droopnik! The inimitable in pursuet of the inevitable! There's
nothing to touch it, we are taucht, unless she'd cared for a mouth-
pull of white pudding for the wish is on her rose marine and the
lunchlight in her eye, so when you pet the rollingpin write my name
on the pie. Guard that gem, Sissy, rich and rare, ses he. In this cold
old worold who'll feel it? Hum! The jewel you're all so cracked
about there's flitty few of them gets it for there's nothing now but
the sable stoles and a runabout to match it. Sing him a ring. Touch
me low. And I'll lech ye so, my soandso. Show and show. Show on
show. She. Shoe. Shone.

Divulge, sjuddenly jouted out hardworking Jaun, kicking the console to his double and braying aloud like Brahaam's ass, and, as his
voixehumanar swelled to great, clenching his manlies, so highly
strong was he, man, and gradually quite warming to her (there
must have been a power of kinantics in that buel of gruel he gobed
at bedgo) divorce into me and say the curname in undress (if you
get into trouble with a party you are not likely to forget his appearance either) of any lapwhelp or sleevemongrel who talks to you
upon the road where he tuck you to be a roller, O, (the goattanned
saxopeeler upshotdown chigs peel of him!) and volunteers to trifle
with your roundlings for proffered glass and dough, the marrying
hand that his leisure repents of, without taking out his proper password from the eligible ministriss for affairs with the black fremdling,
that enemy of our country, in a cleanlooking light and I don't care
a tongser's tammany hang who the mucky is nor twoo hoots in the
corner nor three shouts on a hill (were he even a constantineal
namesuch of my very own, Attaboy Knowling, and like enoch to my
townmajor ancestors, the two that are taking out their divorces in

the Spooksbury courts circuits, Rere Uncle Remus, the Baas of
Eboracum and Old Father Ulissabon Knickerbocker, the lanky sire
of Wolverhampton, about their bristelings), but as true as there's a
soke for sakes in Twoways Peterborough and sure as home we come
to newsky prospect from west the wave on schedule time (if I came
any quicker I'll be right back before I left) from the land of breach
of promise with Brendan's mantle whitening the Kerribrasilian sea
and March's pebbles spinning from beneath our footslips to
carry fire and sword, rest insured that as we value the very name in
sister that as soon as we do possibly it will be a poor lookout for that
insister. He's a markt man from that hour. And why do we say that,
you may query me? Quary? Guess! Call'st thou? Think and think
and think, I urge on you. Muffed! The wrong porridge. You are
an ignoratis! Because then probably we'll dumb well soon show
him what the Shaun way is like how we'll go a long way towards
breaking his outsider's face for him for making up to you with his
bringthee balm of Gaylad and his singthee songs of Arupee, chance-
trying my ward's head into sanctuary before feeling with his two
dimensions for your nuptial dito. Ohibow, if I was Blonderboss I'd
gooandfrighthisdualman! Now, we'll tell you what we'll do to be
sicker instead of compensation. We'll he'll burst our his mouth like
Leary to the Leinsterface and reduce he'll we'll ournhisn liniments
to a poolp. Open the door softly, somebody wants you, dear! You'll
hear him calling you, bump, like a blizz, in the nuezzin of the turkest
night. Come on now, pillarbox! I'll stiffen your scribeall, broken
reed! That'll be it, grand operoar style, even should I, with my sleuts
of hogpew and cheekas, have to coomb the brash of the libs round
Close Saint Patrice to lay my louseboob on his behaitch like solitar.
We are all eyes. I have his quoram of images all on my retinue, Mo-
homadhawn Mike. Brassup! Moreover after that, bad manners to me,
if I don't think strongly about giving the brotherkeeper into custody
to the first police bubby cunstabless of Dora's Diehards in the field
I might chance to follopon. Or for that matter, for your information,
if I get the wind up what do you bet in the buckets of my wrath I
mightn't even take it into my programme, as sweet course, to do a
rash act and pitch in and swing for your perfect stranger in the
meadow of heppiness and then wipe the street up with the clonmel-
lian, pending my bringing proceedings verses the joyboy before a
bunch of magistrafes and twelve good and gleeful men? *Filius
nullius per fas et nefas.* It should prove more or less of an event and
show the widest federal in my cup. He'll have pansements then for

his pensamientos, howling for peace. Pretty knocks, I promise him with plenty burkes for his shins. Dumnlimn wimn humn. In which case I'll not be complete in fighting lust until I contrive to half kill your Charley you're my darling for you and send him to Home Surgeon Hume, the algebrist, before his appointed time, particularly should he turn out to be a man in brown about town, Rollo the Gunger, son of a wants a flurewaltzer to Arnolff's, picking up ideas, of well over or about fiftysix or so, pithecoid proportions, with perhops five foot eight, the usual X Y Z type, R.C. Toc H, nothing but claret, not in the studbook by a long stortch, with a toothbrush moustache and jawcrockeries, *alias* grinner through collar, and of course no beard, meat and colmans suit, with tar's baggy slacks, obviously too roomy for him and springside boots, washing tie, Father Mathew's bridge pin, sipping some Wheatley's at Rhoss's on a barstool, with some pubpal of the Olaf Stout kidney, always trying to poorchase movables by hebdomedaries for to putt in a new house to loot, cigarette in his holder, with a good job and pension in Buinness's, what about our trip to Normandy style conversation, with an occasional they say that filmacoulored featured at the Mothrapurl skrene about Michan and his lost angeleens is corkyshows do morvaloos, blueygreen eyes a bit scummy developing a series of angry boils with certain references to the Deity, seeking relief in alcohol and so on, general omnibus character with a dash of railwaybrain, stale cough and an occasional twinge of claudication, having his favourite fecundclass family of upwards of a decade, both harefoot and loadenbrogued, to boot and buy off, Imean.

So let it be a knuckle or an elbow, I hereby admonish you! It may all be topping fun but it's tip and run and touch and flow for every whack when Marie stopes Phil fluther's game to go. Arms arome, side aside, face into the wall. To the tumble of the toss tot the trouble of the swaddled, O. And lest there be no misconception, Miss Forstowelsy, over who to fasten the plightforlifer on (threehundred and thirty three to one on Rue the Day!) when the nice little smellar squalls in his crydle what the dirty old bigger'll be squealing through his coughin you better keep in the gunbarrel straight around vokseburst as I recommence you to (you gypseyeyed baggage, do you hear what I'm praying?) or, Gash, without butthering my head to assortail whose stroke forced or which struck backly, I'll be all over you myselx horizontally, as the straphanger said, for knocking me with my name and yourself and your babybag down at such a greet sacrifice with a rap of the gavel to a third price cowhandler as cheap as the niggerd's dirt (for sale!) or I'll smack your fruitflavoured jujube lips well for you, so I will well for you, if you don't keep a civil tongue in your pigeonhouse. The pleasures of love lasts but a fleeting but the pledges of life outlusts a lieftime. I'll have it in for you. I'll teach you bed minners, tip for tap, to be playing your oddauggghter tangotricks with micky dazzlers if I find corsehairs on your river-frock and the squirmside of your burberry lupitally covered with chiffchaff and shavings. Up Rosemiry Lean and Potanasty Rod you wos, wos you? I overstand you, you understand. Asking Annybettyelsas to carry your parcels and you dreaming of net glory. You'll ging naemaer wi'Wolf the Ganger. Cutting chapel, were you? and had dates with slickers in particular hotels, had we? Lonely went to play your mother, isod? You was wiffriends? Hay, dot's a doll yarn! Mark mean then! I'll homeseek you, Luperca as sure as there's a palatine in Limerick and in striped conference here's how. Nerbu de Bios! If you twos goes to walk upon the railway, Gard, and I'll goad to beat behind the bush! See to it! Snip! It's up to you. I'll be hatsnatching harrier to hiding huries hinder hedge. Snap! I'll tear up your limpshades and lock all your trotters in the closet, I will, and cut your silkskin into garters. You'll give up your ask unbrodhel ways when I make you reely smart. So skelp your budd and kiss the hurt! I'll have plenary sadisfaction, plays the bishop, for your partial's indulgences if your my rodeo gell. Fair man and foul suggestion. There's a lot of lecit pleasure coming bangslanging your way, Miss Pinpernelly satin. For your own good, you understand, for the man who lifts his pud to a woman is saving the way for kindness. You'll rebmemer your mottob *Aveh Tiger Roma* mikely smarter the nickst time. For I'll just draw my prancer and give you one splitpuck in the crupper, you understand, that will bring the poppyblush of shame to your peony hindmost till you yelp papapardon and radden your rhodatantarums to the beat of calorrubordolor, I am, I do and I suffer, (do you hear me now, lickspoon, and stop looking at your bussycat bow in the slate?) that you won't obliterate for the bulkier part of a running year, failing to give a good account of yourself, if you think I'm so tan cupid as all that. Lights out now (bouf!), tight and sleep on it. And that's how I'll bottle your greedypuss beautibus for ye, me bullin heifer, for 'tis I that have the peer of arrams that carry a wallop. Between them.

Unbeknownst to you would ire turn o'er see, a nuncio would I return here. How (from the sublime to the ridiculous) times out of oft, my future, shall we think with deepest of love and recollection by rintrospection of thee but me far away on the pillow, breathing foundly o'er my names all through the empties, whilst moidhered by the rattle of the doppeldoorknockers. Our homerole poet to Ostelinda, Fred Wetherly, puts it somewhys better. You're sitting on me style, maybe, whereoft I helped your ore. Littlegame rumilie from Liffalidebankum, (Toobliqueme!) but a big corner fill you do in this unadulterated seat of our affections. Aerwenger's my breed so may we uncreepingly multipede like the sands on Amberhann! Sevenheavens, O heaven! Iy waount yiou! yore ways to melittleme were wonderful so Ickam purseproud in sending uym loveliest pansiful thoughts touching me dash in-you through wee dots Hyphen, the so pretty arched godkin of beddingnights. If I've proved to your sallysfashion how I'm a man of Armor let me so, let me sue, let me see your isabellis. How I shall, should I survive, as, please the uniter of U.M.I. hearts, I am living in hopes to do, replacing mig wandering handsup in yawers so yeager for mitch, positively cover the two pure chicks of your comely plumpchake with zuccherikissings, hong, kong, and so gong, that I'd scare the bats out of the ivfry one of those puggy mornings, honestly, by my rantandog and daddyoak I will, become come coming when, upon the mingling of our meeting waters, wish to wisher, like massive mountains to part no more, you will there and then, in those happy moments of ouryour soft accord, rainkiss on me back, for full marks with shouldered arms, and in that united I.R.U. stade, when I come (touf! touf!) wildflier's fox into my own greengeese again, swap sweetened smugs, six of one for half a dozen of the other, till they'll bet we're the cuckoo derby when cherries next come back to Ealing as come they must, as they musted in their past, as they must for my pressing season, as hereinafter must they chirrywill immediately suant on my safe return to ignorance and bliss in my horseless Coppal Poor, through suirland and noreland, kings country and queens, with my ropes of pearls for gamey girls the way ye'll hardly. Knowme.

Slim ye, come slum with me and rally rats' roundup! 'Tis post purification we will, sales of work and social service, missus, completing our Abelite union by the adoptation of fosterlings. Embark for Euphonia! Up Murphy, Henson and O'Dwyer, the Warchester Warders! I'll put in a shirt time if you'll get through your shift and between us in our shared slaves, brace to brassiere and shouter to shunter, we'll pull off our working programme. Come into the garden guild and be free of the gape athome! We'll circumcivicise all Dublin country. Let us, the real Us, all ignite in our prepurgatory grade as aposcals and be instrumental to utensilise, help our Jakeline sisters clean out the hogshole and generally ginger things up. Meliorism in massquantities, raffling receipts and sharing sweepstakes till navel, spokes and felloes hum like hymn. Burn only what's Irish, accepting their coals. You will soothe the cokeblack bile that's Anglia's and touch Armourican's iron core. Write me your essayes, my vocational scholars, but corsorily, dipping your nose in it, for Henrietta's sake, on mortinatality in the life of jewries and the sludge of King Haarington's at its height, running boulevards over the whole of it. I'd write it all by mownself if I only had here of my jolly young watermen. Bear in mind, by Michael, all the provincial's bananas peels and elacock eggs making drawadust jubilee along Henry, Moore, Earl and Talbot Streets. Luke at all the memmer manning he's dung for the pray of birds, our priest-mayor-king-merchant, strewing the Castleknock Road and drawing manure upon it till the first glimpse of Wales and from Ballses Breach Harshoe up to Dumping's Corner with the Mirist fathers' brothers eleven versus White Friars out on a rogation stag party. Compare them caponchin trowlers with the Bridge of Belches in Fairview, noreast Dublin's favourite souwest wateringplatz and ump as you lump it. What do you mean by Jno Citizen and how do you think of Jas Pagan? Compost liffe in Dufblin by Pierce Egan with the baugh in Baughkley of Fino Ralli. Explain why there is such a number of orders of religion in Asea! Why such an order number in preference to any other number? Why any number in any order at all? Now? Where is the greenest island off the black coats of Spaign? Overset into universal: I am perdrix and upon my pet ridge. Oralmus! Way, O way for the autointaxication of our town of the Fords in a huddle! Hailfellow some wellmet boneshaker or, to ascertain the facts for herself, run up your showery weather once and trust and take the Drumgondola tram and, wearing the midlimb and vestee endorsed by the hierarchy fitted with ecclastics, bending your steps, pick a trail and stand on, say, Aston's, I advise you strongly, along quaith a copy of the Seeds and Weeds Act when you have procured one for yourself and take a good longing gaze into any nearby shopswindow you may select at suppose, let us say, the hoyth of number eleven, Kane or Keogh's, and in the course of about thirty-two minutes' time proceed to turn aroundabout on your heehills towards the previous causeway and I shall be very cruelly mistaken

indeed if you will not be jushed astunshed to see how you will be
meanwhile durn weel topcoated with kakes of slush occasioned by
by the mush jam of the cross and blackwalls traffic in transit.
See Capels and then fly. Show me that complaint book here.
Where's Cowtends Kateclean, the woman with the muckrake? When
will the W.D. face of our sow muckloved d'lin, the Troia of towns
and Carmen of cities, crawling with mendiants in perforated clothing, get its wellbelavered white like l'pool and m'chester? When's
that grandnational goldcapped dupsydurby houspill coming with its
vomitives for our mothers-in-load and stretchers for their devitalised
males? I am all of me for freedom of speed but who'll disasperaguss
Pope's Avegnue or who'll uproose the Opian Way? Who'll brighton
Brayhowth and bait the Bull Bailey and never despair of
Lorcansby? The rampant royal commissioners! 'Tis an ill weed blows
no poppy good. And this labour's worthy of my higher. Oil for meed
and toil for feed and a walk with the band for Job Loos. If I hope
not charity what profiteers me? Nothing! My tippers of flags are
knobs of hardshape for it isagrim tale, keeping the father of curls
from the sport of oak. Do you know what, liddle giddles? One of
those days I am advised by the smiling voteseeker who's now snoring
elued to positively strike off hiking for good and all as I bldy well
bdly ought until such temse as some mood is made under privy-sealed
orders to get me an increase of automoboil and footwear for these
poor discalced and a bourse from bon Somewind for a cure at
Badanuweir (though where it's going to come from this time—) as
I sartunly think now, honest to John, for an income plexus that
that's about the sanguine boundary limit. Amean.

Sis dearest, Jaun added, with voise somewhit murky, what
though still high fa luting, as he turned his dorse to her to pay court
to it, and ouverleaved his booseys to give the note and score,
phonoscopically incuriosited and melancholic this time whiles, as on
the fulmament he gaped in wulderment, his onsaturncast eyes in
stellar attraction followed swift to an imaginary swellaw, O, the
vanity of Vanissy! All ends vanishing! Pursonally, Grog help me, I
am in no violent hurry. If time enough lost the ducks walking easy
found them. I'll nose a blue fonx with any tristys blinking upon this
earthlight of all them that pass by the way of the deerdrive, con-
coney's run or wilfrid's walk, but I'd turn back as lief as not if I
could only spoonfind the nippy girl of my heart's appointment, Mona
Vera Toutou Ipostila, my lady of Lyons, to guide me by gastronomy
under her safe conduct. That's more in my line. I'd ask no kinder of

fates than to stay where I am, with my tinny of brownie's tea, under
the invocation of Saint Jamas Hanway, servant of Gamp, lapidated,
and Jacobus a Pershawm, intercissous, for my thurifex, with Peter
Roche, that frind of my boozum, leaning on my cubits, at this passing
moment by localoption in the birds' lodging, me pheasants among,
where I'll dreamt that I'll dwealth mid warblers' walls when
throstles and choughs to my sigh hiehied, with me hares standing
up well and me longlugs dittoes, where a maurdering row, the fox!
has broken at the coward sight till well on into the beausome of the
exhaling night, pinching stopandgo jewels out of the hedges and
catching dimtop brilliants on the tip of my wagger but for that
owledclock (fast cease to it!) has just gone twoohoo the hour and
that yen breezes zipping round by Drumsally do be devils to play
fleurt. I could sit on safe side till the bark of Saint Grouseus for
hoopoe's hours, till heoll's hoerrisings, laughing lazy at the sheep's
lightning and turn a widamost ear dreamily to the drummling of
snipers, hearing the wireless harps of sweet old Aerial and the mails
across the nightrives (peepet! peepet!) and whippoor willy in the
woody (moor park! moor park!) as peacefed as a philopotamus, and
crekking jugs at the grenoulls, leaving tealeaves for the trout and
belleeks for the wary till I'd followed through my upfielded neview-
scope the rugaby moon cumuliously godrolling himself westasleep
amuckst the cloudscrums for to watch how carefully my nocturnal
goosemother would lay her new golden sheegg for me down under
in the shy orient. What wouldn't I poach — the rent in my riverside, my otther shoes, my beavery, honest! — ay, and melt my belt
for a dace feast of grannom with the finny ones, those happy grep-
pies in their minnowahaw, flashing down the swansway, leaps
ahead of the swift MacEels, the big Gillaroo redfellows and the
pursewinded carpers, rearin antis rood perches astench of me, or,
when I'd like own company best, with the help of a norange and
bear, to be reclined by the lasher on my logansome, my g.b.d. in my
f.a.c.e., solfanelly in my shellyholders and lov'd latakia, the
benuvolent, for my nosethrills, with the jealosomines wilting away
to their heart's deelight and the king of saptimber letting down his
humely odours for my consternation, dapping my griffeen, burning
water in the spearlight or catching trophies of the king's royal college of sturgeone by the armful for to bake pike and pie while, O
twined me abower in L'Alouette's Tower, all Adelaide's naughtin-
gerls juckjucking benighth me, I'd gamut my twittynice Dorian
blackbudds chthonic solphia off my singasongapiccolo to pipe

musicall airs on numberous fairyaciodes. I give, a king, to me, she
does, alone, up there, yes see, I double give, till the spinney all
eclosed asong with them. Isn't that lovely though? I give to me alone
I trouble give! I may have no mind to lamagnage the forte bits like
the pianage but you can't cadge me off the key. I've a voicical lilt too
true. Nomario! And bemolly and jiesis! For I sport a whatyouma-
cormack in the latcher part of my throughers. And the lark that I
let fly (olala!) is as cockful of funantics as it's tune to my fork. Nat-
urale you might lower register me as diserecordant, but I'm athlone
in the lillabilling of killarnies. That's flat. Yet ware the wold, you!
What's good for the gorse is a goad for the garden. Lethals lurk
heimlocked in logans. Loathe laburnums. Dash the gaudy death-
cup! Bryony O'Bryony, thy name is Belladama! But enough of
greenwood's gossip. Birdsnests is birdsnests. Thine to wait but mine
to wage. And now play sharp to me. Doublefirst I'll head foremost
through all my examhoops. And what sensitive coin I'd be possessed
of at Latouche's, begor, I'd sink it sumtotal, every dolly farting, in
vestments of subdominal poteen at prime cost and I bait you my
chancey oldcoat against the whole ounce you half on your back-
board (if madamaud strips mesdamines may cold strafe illglands!)
that I'm the gogetter that'd make it pay like cash registers as sure
as there's a pot on a pole. And, what with one man's fish and a
dozen men's poissons, sowing my wild plums to reap ripe plenti-
horns mead, lashings of erbole and hydromel and bragget, I'd come
out with my magic fluke in close time, fair, free and frolicky, zoom-
ing tophole on the mart as a factor. And I tell you the Bective's
wouldn't hold me. By the unsleeping Solman Annadromus, ye
god of little pescies, nothing would stop me for mony makes
multimony like the brogues and the kishes. Not the Ulster Rifles
and the Cork Milice and the Dublin Fusees and Connacht Rangers
ensembled! I'd axe the channon and leip a liffey and drink anny-
black water that rann onme way. Yip! How's thats for scats, mine
shatz, for a lovebird? To funk is only peternatural its daring feers
divine. Bebold! Like Varian's balaying all behind me. And before
you knew where you weren't, I stake my ignitial's divy, cash-and-
cash-can-again, I'd be staggering humanity and loyally rolling you
over, my sowwhite sponse, in my tons of red clover, nighty nigh to
the metronome, fiehigh and fiehigher and fiehighest of all. Holy
petter and pal, I'd spoil you altogether, my sumptuous Sheila! Mumm
all to do brut frull up fizz and unpop a few shortusians or shake a
pale of sparkling ice, hear it swirl, happy girl! Not a spot of my

hide but you'd love to seek and scanagain! There'd be no standing me, I tell you. And, as gameboy as my pagan name K.C. is what it is, I'd never say let fly till we shot that blissup and swumped each other, manawife, into our sever nevers where I'd plant you, my Gizzygay, on the electric ottoman in the lap of lechery, simpringly stitchless with admiracion, among the most uxuriously furnished compartments, with sybarate chambers, just as I'd run my shoestring into near a million or so of them as a firstclass dealer and everything. Only for one thing that, howover famiksed I would become, I'd be awful anxious, you understand, about shoepisser pluvious and in assideration of the terrible luftsucks woabling around with the hedrolics in the coold amstophere till the borting that would perish the Dane and his chapter of accidents to be atramental to the better half of my alltoolyrical health, not considering my capsflap, and that's the truth now out of the cackling bag for truly sure, for another thing, I never could tell the leest falsehood that would truthfully give sotisfiction. I'm not talking apple sauce eithou. Or up in my hat. I earnst. Schue!

Sissibis dearest, as I was reading to myself not very long ago in Tennis Flonnels Mac Courther, his correspondance, besated upon my tripos, and just thinking like thauthor how long I'd like myself to be continued at Hothelizod, peeking into the focus and pecking at thumbnail reveries, pricking up ears to my phono on the ground and picking up airs from th'other over th'ether, 'tis tramsported with grief I am this night sublime, as you may see by my size and my brow that's all forehead, to go forth, frank and hoppy, to the tune the old plow tied off, from our nostorey house, upon this benedictine errand but it is historically the most glorious mission, secret or profund, through all the annals of our — as you so often term her — efferfreshpainted livy, in beautific repose, upon the silence of the dead, from pharoph the nextfirst down to ramescheckles the last bust thing. The Vico road goes round and round to meet where terms begin. Still onappealed to by the cycles and unappalled by the recoursers we feel all serene, never you fret, as regards our dutyful cask. Full of my breadth from pride I am (breezed be the healthy same!) for 'tis a grand thing (superb!) to be going to meet a king, not an everynight king, nenni, by gannies, but the overking of Hither-on-Thither Erin himself, pardee, I'm saying. Before there was patch at all on Ireland there lived a lord at Lucan. We only wish everyone was as sure of anything in this watery world as we are of everything in the newlywet fellow that's bound to follow. I'll lay you a guinea for a hayseed now. Tell mother that. And tell her tell her old one. 'Twill amuse her.

Well, to the figends of Annanmeses with the wholeabuelish business! For I declare to Jeshuam I'm beginning to get sunsick! I'm not half Norawain for nothing. The fine ice so temperate of our, alas, those times are not so far off as you might wish to be congealed. So now, I'll ask of you, let ye create no scenes in my poor primmafore's wake. I don't want yous to be billowfighting your biddy moriarty duels, gobble gabble, over me till you spit stout, you understand, after soused mackerel, sniffling clambake to hering and impudent barney, braggart of blarney, nor you ugly lemoncholic gobs o'er the hobs in a sewing circle, stopping oddments in maids' costumes at sweeping reductions, wearing out your ohs by sitting around your ahs, making areekeransy round where I last put it, with the painters in too, curse luck, with your rags up, exciting your mucuses, turning breakfarts into lost soupirs and salon thay nor you flabbies on your groaning chairs over Bollivar's troubles of a bluemoondag, steamin your damp ossicles, praying Holy Prohibition and Jaun Dyspeptist while Ole Clo goes through the wood with Shep togather, touting in the chestnut burrs for Goodboy Sommers and Mistral Blownowse hugs his kindlings when voiceyversy it's my gala bene fit, robbing leaves out of my taletold book. May my tunc fester if ever I see such a miry lot of maggalenes! Once upon a drunk and a fairly good drunk it was and the rest of your blatherumskite! Just a plain shays by the fire for absenter Sh the Po and I'll make ye all an eastern hummingsphere of myself the moment that you name the way. Look in the slag scuttle and you'll see me sailspread over the singing, and what do ye want trippings for when you've Paris inspire your hat? Sussumcordials all round, let ye alloyiss and ominies, while I stray and let ye not be getting grief out of it, though blighted troth be all bereft, on my poor headsake, even should we forfeit our life. Lo, improving ages wait ye! In the orchard of the bones. Some time very presently now when yon clouds are dissipated after their forty years shower, the odds are, we shall all be hooked and happy, communionistically, among the fieldnights eliceam, *élite* of the elect, in the land of lost of time. Johannisburg's a revelation! Deck the diamants that never die! So cut out the lonesome stuff! Drink it up, ladies, please, as smart as you can lower it! Out with lent! Clap hands postilium! Fastintide is by. Your sole and myopper must hereupon part company. So for e'er fare thee welt! Parting's fun. Take thou, the wringle's thine, love. This dime doth trost thee from mine alms.

Goodbye, swisstart, goodbye! Haugh! Haugh! Sure, treasures, a letterman does be often thought reading ye between lines that do have no sense at all. I sign myself. With much leg. Inflexibly yours. Ann Posht the Shorn. To be continued. Huck!

Something of a sidesplitting nature must have occurred to westminstrel Jaunathaun for a grand big blossy hearty stenorious laugh (even Drudge that lay doggo thought feathers fell) hopped out of his woolly's throat like a ball lifted over the head of a deep field, at the bare thought of how jolly they'd like to be trolling his whoop and all of them truetotypes in missammen massness were just starting to spladher splodher with the jolly magorios, hicky hecky hock, huges huges huges, hughy hughy hughy, O Jaun, so jokable and so geepy, O, (Thou pure! Our virgin! Thou holy! Our health! Thou strong! Our victory! O salutary! Sustain our firm solitude, thou who thou well strokest! Hear, hairy ones! We have sued thee but late. Beauty parlous!) when suddenly (how like a woman!), swifter as mercury he wheels right round starnly on the Rizzies suddenly, with his gimlets blazing rather sternish (how black like thunder!), to see what's loose. So they stood still and wondered. Till first he sighed (and how ill soufered!) and they nearly cried (the salt of the earth!) after which he pondered and finally he replied:

— There is some thing more. A word apparting and shall the heart's tone be silent. Engagements, I'll beseal you! Fare thee well, fairy well! All I can tell you is this, my sorellies. It's prayers in layers all the thumping time, begor, the young gloria's gang voices the old doxologers, in the suburrs of the heavenly gardens, once we shall have passed, after surceases, all serene through neck and necklike Derby and June to our snug eternal retribution's reward (the scorchhouse). Shunt us! shunt us! shunt us! If you want to be felixed come and be parked. Sacred ease there! The seanad and pobbel queue's remainder. To it, to it! Seekit headup! No petty family squabbles Up There nor homemade hurricanes in our Cohortyard, no cupahurling nor apuckalips nor no puncheon jodelling nor no nothing. With the Byrns which is far better and eve for ever your idle be. You will hardly reconnoitre the old wife in the new bustle and the farmer shinner in his latterday paint. It's the fulldress Toussaint's wakeswalks experdition after a bail motion from the chamber of horrus. Saffron buns or sovran bonhams whichever you'r avider to like it and lump it, but give it a name. Iereny allover irelands. And there's food for refection when the whole flock's at home. Hogmanny di'yegut? Hogmanny di'yesmellygut? And hogmanny di'yesmellyspattery-

gut? You take Joe Hanny's tip for it! Postmartem is the goods. With
Jollification a tight second. Toborrow and toburrow and tobarrow!
That's our crass, hairy and evergrim life, till one finel howdiedow
Bouncer Naster raps on the bell with a bone and his stinkers stank
behind him with the sceptre and the hourglass. We may come, touch
and go, from atoms and ifs but we're presurely destined to be odd's
without ends. Here we moult in Moy Kain and flop on the seemy
side, living sure of hardly a doorstep for a stopgap, with Whogoes-
there and a live sandbag round the corner. But upmeyant,
Prospector, you sprout all your abel and woof your wings dead certain however of neuthing whatever to aye forever while Hyam
Hyam's in the chair. Ah, sure, pleasantries aside, in the tail of the
cow what a humpty daum earth looks our miseryme heretoday
as compared beside the Hereweareagain Gaieties of the Afterpiece
when the Royal Revolver of these real globoes lets regally fire of his
mio colpo for the chrisman's pandemon to give over and the Harle-
quinade to begin properly SPQueaRking Mark Time's Finist Joke.
Putting Allspace in a Notshall.

Well, the slice and veg joint's well in its way, and so is a riboast
and jackknife as sporten dish, but home cooking everytime. Mountains good mustard and, with the helpings of ladies' lickfings and
gentlemen's relish, I've eaten a griddle. But I fill twice as stewhard
what I felt before when I'm after eating a few natives. The crisp
of the crackling is in the chawing. Give us another cup of your
scald. Santos Mozos! That was a damn good cup of scald! You could
trot a mouse on it. I ingoyed your pick of hissing hot luncheon fine,
I did, thank awfully, (sublime!). Tenderest bully ever I ate with the
boiled protestants (allinoilia allinoilia!) only for your peas again
was a taste tooth psalty to carry flavour with my godown and hereby
return with my best savioury condiments and a penny in the plate
for the jemes. O.K. Oh Kosmos! Ah Ireland! A.I. And for kailkan-
nonkabbis gimme Cincinnatis with Italian (but *ci vuol poco!*) cic-
calick cheese, Haggis good, haggis strong, haggis never say die! For
quid we have recipimus, recipe, O lout! And save that, Oliviero,
for thy sunny day! Soupmeagre! Couldn't look at it! But if you'll
buy me yon coat of the vairy furry best, I'll try and pullll it awn
mee. It's in fairly good order and no doubt 'twill sarve to turn. Remove this boardcloth! Next stage, tell the tabler, for a variety of
Huguenot ligooms I'll try my set on edges grapeling an aigrydoucks,
grilled over birchenrods, with a few bloomancowls in albies. I want
to get outside monasticism. Mass and meat mar no man's journey.

Eat a missal lest. Nuts for the nerves, a flitch for the flue and for to rejoice the chambers of the heart the spirits of the spice isles, curry and cinnamon, chutney and cloves. All the vitalmines is beginning to sozzle in chewn and the hormonies to clingleclangle, fudgem, kates and eaps and naboc and erics and oinnos on kingclud and xoxxoxo and xooxox xxoxoxxoxxx till I'm fustfed like fungstif and very presently from now posthaste it's off yourll see me ryuoll on my usual rounds again to draw Terminus Lower and Killadown and Letternoosh, Letterspeak, Lettermuck to Littorananima and the roomiest house even in Ireland, if you can understamp that, and my next item's platform it's how I'll try and collect my extraprofessional postages owing to me by Thaddeus Kellyesque Squire, dr, for nondesirable printed matter. The Jooks and the Kelly-Cooks have been milking turnkeys and sucking the blood out of the marshalsea since the act of First Offenders. But I know what I'll do. Great pains off him I'll take and that'll be your redletterday calendar, window machree! I'll knock it out of him! I'll stump it out of him! I'll rattattatter it out of him before I'll quit the doorstep of old Con Connolly's residence! By the horn of twenty of both of the two Saint Collopys, blackmail him I will in arrears or my name's not penitent Ferdinand! And it's daily and hourly I'll nurse him till he pays me fine fee. Ameal.

Well, here's looking at ye! If I never leave you biddies till my stave is a bar I'd be tempted rigidly to become a passionate father. Me hunger's weighed. Hungkung! Me anger's suaged! Hangkang! Ye can stop as ye are, little lay mothers, and wait in wish and wish in vain till the grame reaper draws nigh, with the sickle of the sickles, as a blessing in disguise. Devil a curly hair I care! If any lightfoot Clod Dewvale was to hold me up, dicksturping me and marauding me of my rights to my onus, yan, tyan, tethera, methera, pimp, I'd let him have my best pair of galloper's heels in the creamsourer. He will have better manners, I'm dished if he won't! Console yourself, drawhure deelish! There's a refond of eggsized coming to you out of me so mind you do me duty on me! Bruise your bulge below the belt till I blewblack beside you. And you'll miss me more as the narrowing weeks wing by. Someday duly, oneday truly, twosday newly, till whensday. Look for me always at my west and I will think to dine. A tear or two in time is all there's toot. And then in a click of the clock, toot toot, and doff doff we pop with sinnerettes in silkettes lining longroutes for His Diligence Majesty, our longdistance laird that likes creation. To whoosh!

—Meesh, meesh, yes, pet. We were too happy. I knew something would happen. I understand but listen, drawher nearest, Tizzy intercepted, flushing but flashing from her dove and dart eyes as she tactilifully grapbed her male corrispondee to flusther sweet nunsongs in his quickturned ear, I know, benjamin brother, but listen, I want, girls palmassing, to whisper my whish. (She like them like us, me and you, had thoud he n'er it would haltin so lithe when leased is tacitempust tongue). Of course, engine dear, I'm ashamed for my life (I must clear my throttle) over this lost moment's gift of memento nosepaper which I'm sorry, my precious, is allathome I with grief can call my own but all the same, listen, Jaunick, accept this witwee's mite, though a jennyteeny witween piece torn in one place from my hands in second place of a linenhall valentino with my fondest and much left to tutor. X.X.X.X. It was heavily bulledicted for young Fr Ml, my pettest parriage priest, and you know who between us by your friend the pope, forty ways in forty nights, that's the beauty of it, look, scene it, ratty. Too perfectly priceless for words. And, listen, now do enhance me, oblige my fiancy and bear it with you morn till life's e'en and, of course, when never you make usage of it, listen, please kindly think galways again or again, never forget, of one absendee not sester Maggy. Ahim. That's the stupidest little cough. Only be sure you don't catch your cold and pass it on to us. And, since levret bounds and larks is soaring, don't be all the night. And this, Joke, a sprig of blue speedwell just a spell of floralora so you'll mind your veronique. Of course, Jer, I know you know who sends it, presents that please, mercy, on the face of the waters like that film obote, awfly charmig of course, but it doesn't do her justice, apart from her cattiness, in the magginbottle. Of course, please too write, won't you, and leave your little bag of doubts, inquisitive, behind you unto your utterly thine, and, thank you, forward it back by return pigeon's pneu to the loving in case I couldn't think who it was or any funforall happens I'll be so curiose to see in the Homesworth breakfast tablotts as I'll know etherways by pity bleu if it's good for my system, what exquisite buttons, gorgiose, in case I don't hope to soon hear from you. And thanks ever so many for the ten and the one with nothing at all on. I will tie a knot in my stringamejip to letter you with my silky paper, as I am given now to understand it will be worth my price in money one day so don't trouble to ans unless sentby special as I am getting his pay and wants for nothing so I can live simply and solely for my wonderful kinkless and its loops of loveliness. When I throw away

my rollets there's rings for all. Flee a girl, says it is her colour. So
does B and L and as for V! And listen to it! Cheveluir! So distant
you're always. Bow your boche! Absolutely perfect! I will pack my
comb and mirror to praxis oval owes and artless awes and it will
follow you pulpicly as far as come back under all my eyes like my
sapphire chaplets of ringarosary I will say for you to the Allmichael and solve qui pu while the dovedoves pick my mouthbuds
(msch! msch!) with nurse Madge, my linkingclass girl, she's a fright,
poor old dutch, in her sleeptalking when I paint the measles on her
and mudstuskers to make her a man. We. We. Issy done that, I con-
fesh! But you'll love her for her hessians and sickly black stockies,
cleryng's jumbles, salvadged from the wash, isn't it the cat's tonsils!
Simply killing, how she tidies her hair! I call her Sosy because she's
sosiety for me and she says sossy while I say sassy and she says will
you have some more scorns while I say won't you take a few more
schools and she talks about ithel dear while I simply never talk about
athel darling; she's but nice for enticing my friends and she loves
your style considering she breaksin me shoes for me when I've arch
trouble and she would kiss my white arms for me so gratefully but
apart from that she's terribly nice really, my sister, round the elbow
of Erne street Lower and I'll be strictly forbidden always and true
in my own way and private where I will long long to betrue you
along with one who will so betrue you that not once while I betreu
him not once well he be betray himself. Can't you understand? O
bother, I must tell the trouth! My latest lad's loveliletter I am sore
I done something with. I like him lots coss he never cusses. Pity
bonhom. Pip pet. I shouldn't say he's pretty but I'm cocksure he's
shy. Why I love taking him out when I unletched his cordon gate.
Ope, Jack, and atem! Obealbe myodorers and he dote so. He fell
for my lips, for my lisp, for my lewd speaker. I felt for his strength,
his manhood, his do you mind? There can be no candle to hold to
it, can there? And, of course, dear professor, I understand. You can
trust me that though I change thy name though not the letter never
while I become engaged with my first horsepower, masterthief of
hearts, I will give your lovely face of mine away, my boyish bob, not
for tons of donkeys, to my second mate, with the twirlers the
engineer of the passioflower (O the wicked untruth! whot a tell!
that he has bought me in his wellingtons what you haven't got!), in
one of those pure clean lupstucks of yours thankfully, Arrah of the
passkeys, no matter what. You may be certain of that, fluff, now I
know how to tackle. Lock my mearest next myself. So don't keep me

now for a good boy for the love of my fragrant saint, you villain,
peppering with fear, my goodless graceless, or I'll first murder you
but, hvisper, meet me after by next appointment near you know
Ships just there beside the Ship at the future poor fool's circuts of
lovemountjoy square to show my disrespects now, let me just your
caroline for you, I must really so late. Sweet pig, he'll be furious!
How he stalks to simself louther and lover, immutating aperybally.
My prince of the courts who'll beat me to love! And I'll be there
when who knows where with the objects of which I'll knowor forget. We say. Trust us. Our game. (For fun!) The Dargle shall run dry
the sooner I you deny. Whoevery heard of such a think? Till the
ulmost of all elmoes shall stele our harts asthone! And Mrs A'Mara
makes it up and befriends with Mrs O'Morum! I will write down all
your names in my gold pen and ink. Everyday, precious, while
m'm'ry's leaves are falling deeply on my Jungfraud's Messongebook
I will dream telepath posts dulcets on this isinglass stream (but don't
tell him or I'll be the mort of him!) under the libans and the sicka-
mours, the cyprissis and babilonias, where the frondoak rushes to
the ask and the yewleaves too kisskiss themselves and 'twill carry
on my hearz'waves my still waters reflections in words over Margrate von Hungaria, her Quaidy ways and her Flavin hair, to thee,
Jack, ahoy, beyond the boysforus. Splesh of hiss splash springs your
salmon. Twick twick, twinkle twings my twilight as Sarterday after-
noon lex leap will smile on my fourinhanced twelvemonthsmind.
And what's this I was going to say, dean? O, I understand. Listen,
here I'll wait on thee till Thingavalla with beautiful do be careful
teacakes, more stuesser flavoured than Vanilla and blackcurrant
there's a cure in, like a born gentleman till you'll resemble me, all
the time you're awhile way, I swear to you, I will, by Candlemas!
And listen, joey, don't be ennoyed with me, my old evernew, when,
by the end of your chapter, you citch water on the wagon for me
being turned a star I'll dubeurry my two fesces under Pouts Vanisha
Creme, their way for spilling cream, and, accent, umto extend my
personnalitey to the latents, I'll boy me for myself only of expensive
rainproof of pinked elephant's breath grey of the loveliest sheerest
dearest widowshood over airforce blue I am so wild for, my precious
once, Hope Bros., Faith Street, Charity Corner, as the bee loves her
skyhighdeed, for I always had a crush on heliotrope since the dusess
of yore cycled round the Finest Park, and listen. And never mind me
laughing at what's atever! I was in the nerves but it's my last day.
Always about this hour, I'm sorry, when our gamings for Bruin and

Noselong is all oh you tease and afterdoon my lickle pussiness I
stheal heimlick in my russians from the attraction part with my terri-
blitall boots calvescatcher Pinchapoppapoff, who is going to be a
jennyroll, at my nape, drenched, love, with dripping to affectionate
slapmamma but last at night, look, after my golden violents wetting in
my upperstairs splendidly welluminated with such lidlylac curtains
wallpapered to match the cat and a fireplease keep looking of priceless pearlogs I just want to see will he or are all Michales like that,
I'll strip straight after devotions before his fondstare—and I mean it
too, (thy gape to my gazing I'll bind and makeleash) and poke stiff
under my isonbound with my soiedisante chineknees cheeckchubby
chambermate for the night's foreign males and your name of Shane
will come forth between my shamefaced whesen with other lipth I
nakest open my thight when just woken by his toccatootletoo my
first morning. So now, to thalk thildish, thome, theated with Mag at
the oilthan we are doing to thay one little player before doing to
deed. An a tiss to the tassie for lu and for tu! Coach me how to tumble, Jaime, and listen, with supreme regards, Jaun, in haste, warn
me which to ah ah ah ah. . . .

—MEN! Jaun responded fullchantedly to her sororal sonority,
imitating himself capitally with his bubbleblown in his patapet
and his chalished drink now well in hand. (A spilt, see, for a split,
see see!) Ever gloriously kind! And I truly am eucherised to yous.
Also *sacré père* and *maître d'autel*. Well, ladies upon gentlermen
and toastmaster general, let us, brindising brandisong, woo and
win womenlong with health to rich vineyards, Erin go Dry! Amingst
the living waters of, the living in giving waters of. Tight! Loose!
A stiff one for Staffetta mullified with creams of hourmony, the
coupe that's chill for jackless jill and a filiform dhouche on Doris!
Esterelles, be not on your weeping what though Shaunathaun is in
his fail! To stir up love's young fizz I tilt with this bridle's cup cham-
pagne, dimming douce from her peepair of hideseeks, tightsqueezed
on my snowybrusted and while my pearlies in their sparkling wisdom are nippling her bubblets I swear (and let you swear!) by the
bumper round of my poor old snaggletooth's solidbowel I ne'er will
prove I'm untrue to your liking (theare!) so long as my hole looks.
Down.

So gullaby, me poor Isley! But I'm not for forgetting me innerman
monophone for I'm leaving my darling proxy behind for your con-
solering, lost Dave the Dancekerl, a squamous runaway and a dear
old man pal of mine too. He will arrive incessantly in the fraction

of a crust, who, could he quit doubling and stop tippling, he would
be the unicorn of his kind. He's the mightiest penumbrella I ever
flourished on behond the shadow of a post! Be sure and link him,
me O treasauro, as often as you learn provided there's nothing between you but a plain deal table only don't encourage him to cry
lessontimes over Leperstown. But soft! Can't be? Do mailstanes mum-
ble? Lumtum lumtum! Now! The froubadour! I fremble! Talk of
wolf in a stomach by all that's verminous! Eccolo me! The return of
th'athlate! Who can secede to his success! Isn't Jaunstown, Ouster-
rike, the small place after all? I knew I smelt the garlic leek! Why,
bless me swits, here he its, darling Dave, like the catoninelives just
in time as if he fell out of space, all draped in mufti, coming home
to mourn mountains from his old continence and not on one foot
either or on two feet aether but on quinquisecular cycles after his
French evolution and a blindfold passage by the 4.32 with the pork's
pate in his suicide paw and the gulls laughing lime on his natural
skunk, blushing like Pat's pig, begob! He's not too timtom well
ashamed to carry out onaglibtograbakelly in his showman's sinister
the testymonicals he gave his twenty annis orf, showing the three
white feathers, as a home cured emigrant in Paddyouare far below
on our sealevel. Bearer may leave the church, signed, Figura Porca,
Lictor Magnaffica. He's the sneaking likeness of us, faith, me altar's
ego in miniature and every Auxonian aimer's ace as nasal a Romeo
as I am, for ever cracking quips on himself, that merry, the jeen-
jakes, he'd soon arise mother's roses mid bedewing tears under those
wild wet lashes onto anny living girl's laftercheeks. That's his little
veiniality. And his unpeppeppediment. He has novel ideas I know
and he's a jarry queer fish betimes, I grant you, and cantanberous,
the poisoner of his word, but lice and all and semicoloured stained-
glasses, I'm enormously full of that foreigner, I'll say I am! Got by
the one goat, suckled by the same nanna, one twitch, one nature
makes us oldworld kin. We're as thick and thin now as two tubular
jawballs. I hate him about his patent henesy, plasfh it, yet am I amor-
ist. I love him. I love his old portugal's nose. There's the nasturtium
for ye now that saved manny a poor sinker from water on the grave.
The diasporation of all pirates and quinconcentrum of a fake like
Basilius O'Cormacan MacArty? To camiflag he turned his shirt.
Isn't he after borrowing all before him, making friends with everybody red in Rossya, white in Alba and touching every distinguished
Ourishman he could ever distinguish before or behind from a Your-
ishman for the customary halp of a crown and peace? He is looking

aged with his pebbled eyes, and johnnythin too, from livicking on pidgins' ifs with puffins' ands, he's been slanderising himself, but I pass no remark. Hope he hasn't the cholera. Give him an eyot in the farout. Moseses and Noasies, how are you? He'd be as snug as Columbsisle Jonas wrocked in the belly of the whaves, as quotad before. Bravo, senior chief! Framose! Sure there's nobody else in touch anysides to hold a chef's cankle to the darling at all for sheer dare with that prisonpotstill of spanish breans on him like the knave of trifles! A jollytan fine demented brick and the prince of good-filips! Dave knows I have the highest of respect of annyone in my oweand smooth way for that intellectual debtor (Obbligado!) Mush-ure David R. Crozier. And we're the closest of chems. Mark my use of you, cog! Take notice how I yemploy, crib! Be ware as you, I foil, coppy! It's a pity he can't see it for I'm terribly nice about him. Can-wyll y Cymry, the marmade's flamme! A leal of the O'Looniys, a Brazel aboo! The most omportent man! *Shervos!* Ho, be the holy snakes, someone has shaved his rough diamond skull for him as clean as Nuntius' piedish! The burnt out mesh and the matting and all! Thunderweather, khyber schinker escapa sansa pagar! He's the spatton spit, so he is, scaly skin and all, with his blackguarded eye and the goatsbeard in his buttinghold of Shemuel Tulliver, me grandsourd, the old cruxader, when he off with his paudeen! That was to let the crowd of the Flu Flux Fans behind him see me proper. Ah, he's very thoughtful and sympatrico that way is Brother Intelli-gentius, when he's not absintheminded, with his Paris addresse! He is, really. Holdhard till you'll ear him clicking his bull's bones! Some toad klakkin! You're welcome back, Wilkins, to red berries in the frost! And here's the butter exchange to pfeife and dramn ye with a bawlful of the Moulsaybaysse and yunker doodler wanked to wall awriting off his phoney. I'm tired hairing of you. Hat your-self! Give us your dyed dextremity here, frother, the Claddagh clasp! I met with dapper dandy and he shocked me big the hamd. Where's your watch keeper? You've seen all sorts in shapes and sizes, ma-rauding about the moppamound. How's the cock and the bullfight? And old Auster and Hungrig? And the Beer and Belly and the Boot and Ball? Not forgetting the oils of greas under that turkey in julep and Father Freeshots Feilbogen in his rockery garden with the costard? And did you meet with Peadhar the Grab at all? And did you call on Tower Geesyhus? Was Mona, my own love, no big-ger than she should be, making up to you in her bestbehaved manor when you made your breastlaw and made her, tell me? And did you

like the landskip from Lambay? I'm better pleased than ten guidneys!
You rejoice me! Faith, I'm proud of you, french davit! You've surpassed yourself! Be introduced to yes! This is me aunt Julia
Bride, your honour, dying to have you languish to scandal in her
bosky old delltangle. You don't reckoneyes him? He's Jackot the
Horner who boxed in his corner, jilting no fewer than three female bribes. That's his penals. *Shervorum!* You haven't seen her
since she stepped into her drawoffs. Come on, spinister, do your
stuff! Don't be shoy, husbandmanvir! Weih, what's on you, wip?
Up the shamewaugh! She has plenty of woom in the smallclothes
for the bothsforus, nephews push! Hatch yourself well! Enjombyour-
selves thurily! Would you wait biss she buds till you bite on her?
Embrace her bashfully by almeans at my frank incensive and tell
her in your semiological agglutinative yez, how Idos be asking after
her. Let us be holy and evil and let her be peace on the bough. Sure,
she fell in line with our tripertight photos as the lyonised mails when
we were stablelads together like the corks again brothers, hungry
and angry, cavileer grace by roundhered force, or like boyrun to
sibster, me and you, shinners true and pinchme, our tertius quiddus,
that never talked or listened. Always raving how we had the
wrinkles of a snailcharmer and the slits and sniffers of a fellow that
fell foul of the county de Loona and the meattrap of the first vege-
tarian. To be had for the asking. Have a hug! Take her out of poor
tuppeny luck before she goes off in pure treple licquidance. I'd give
three shillings a pullet to the canon for the conjugation to shadow
you kissing her from me leberally all over as if she was a crucifix.
It's good for her bilabials, you understand. There's nothing like the
mistletouch for finding a queen's earring false. Chink chink. As the
curly bard said after kitchin the womn in his hym to the hum of
her garments. You try a little tich to the tissle of his tail. The racist
to the racy, rossy. The soil is for the self alone. Be ownkind. Be kith-
kinish. Be bloodysibby. Be irish. Be inish. Be offalia. Be hamlet.
Be the property plot. Be Yorick and Lankystare. Be cool. Be mackina-
mucks of yourselves. Be finish. No martyr where the preature is
there's no plagues like rome. It gives up the gripes. Watch the swansway. Take your tiger over it. The leady on the lake and the convict
of the forest. Why, they might be Babau and Momie! Yipyip! To
pan! To pan! To tinpinnypan. All folly me yap to Curlew! Give us
a pin for her and we'll call it a tossup. Can you reverse positions?
Lets have a fuchu all round, courting cousins! Quuck, the duck
of a woman for quack, the drake of a man, her little live apples for

Leas and love potients for Leos, the next beast king. Put me down
for all ringside seats. I can feel you being corrupted. Recoil. I can
see you sprouting scruples. Get back. And as he's boiling with water
I'll light your pyre. Turn about, skeezy Sammy, out of metaphor, till
we feel you are still tropeful of popetry. Told you so. If you doubt of
his love of darearing his feelings you'll very much hurt for mishmash
mastufractured on europe you can read off the tail of his. Rip ripper
rippest and jac jac jac. Dwell on that, my hero and lander! That's
the side that appeals to em, the wring wrong way to wright woman.
Shuck her! Let him! What he's good for. Shuck her more! Let him
again! All she wants! Could you wheedle a staveling encore out of
your imitationer's jubalharp, hey, Mr Jinglejoys? Congregational
singing. Rota rota ran the pagoda *con dio in capo ed il diavolo in
coda*. Many a diva devoucha saw her Dauber Dan at the priesty
pagoda Rota ran. Uck! He's so sedulous to singe always if prumpted,
the mirthprovoker! Grunt unto us, I pray, your foreboden article in
our own deas dockandoilish introducing the death of Nelson with
coloraturas! *Coraio, fra!* And I'll string second to harmanize. My loaf
and pottage neaheaheahear Rochelle. With your dumpsey diddely
dumpsey die, fiddeley fa. *Diavoloh!* Or come on, schoolcolours, and
we'll scrap, rug and mat and then be as chummy as two bashed
spuds. Bitrial bay holmgang or betrayal buy jury. Attaboy! Fee gate
has Heenan hoity, mind uncle Hare? What, sir? Poss, myster?
Acheve! Thou, thou! What say ye? *Taurus periculosus, morbus
pedeiculosus. Miserere mei in miseribilibus!* There's uval lavguage
for you! The tower is precluded, the mob's in her petticoats; Mr
R. E. Meehan is in misery with his billyboots. Begob, there's not so
much green in his Ireland's eye! Sweet fellow ovocal, he stones out
of stune. But he could be near a colonel with a voice like that. The
bark is still there but the molars are gone. The misery billyboots
I used to lend him before we split and, be the hole in the year, they
were laking like heaven's reflexes. But I told him make your will be
done and go to a general and I'd pray confessions for him. Areesh!
Areesh! And I'll be your intrepider. Ambras! Ruffle her! Bussing
was before the blood and bissing will behind the curtain. Triss!
Did you note that worrid expressionism on his megalogue? A full
octavium below me! And did you hear his browrings rattlemaking
when he was preaching to himself? And, whoa! do you twig the
schamlooking leaf greeping ghastly down his blousyfrock? Our national umbloom! Areesh! He won't. He's shoy. Those worthies, my
old faher's onkel that was garotted, Caius Cocoa Codinhand, that

I lost in a crowd, used to chop that tongue of his, japlatin, with my yuonkle's owlseller, Woowoolfe Woodenbeard, that went stomebathred, in the Tower of Balbus, as brisk, man, as I'd scoff up muttan chepps and lobscouse. But it's all deafman's duff to me, begob. Sam knows miles bettern me how to work the miracle. And I see by his diarrhio he's dropping the stammer out of his silenced bladder since I bonded him off more as a friend and as a brother to try and grow a muff and canonise his dead feet down on the river airy by thinking himself into the fourth dimension and place the ocean between his and ours, the churchyard in the cloister of the depths, after he was capped out of beurlads scoel for the sin against the past participle and earned the factitation of codding chaplan and being as homely gauche as swift B.A.A. Who gets twickly fullgets twice as allemanden huskers. But the whacker his word the weaker our ears for auracles who parles parses orileys. Illstarred punster, lipstering cowknucks. 'Twas the quadra sent him and Trinity too. And he can cantab as chipper as any oxon ever I mood with, a tiptoe singer! He'll prisckly soon hand tune your Erin's ear for you. *p.p.* a mimograph at a time, numan bitter, with his ancomartins to read the road roman with false steps ad Pernicious from rhearsilvar ormolus to torquinions superbers while I'm far away from wherever thou art serving my tallyhos and tullying my hostilious by going in by the most holy recitatandas *ffff* for my varsatile examinations in the ologies, to be a coach on the Fukien mission. P? F? How used you learn me, brather soboostius, in my augustan days? With cesarella looking on. In the beginning was the gest he jousstly says, for the end is with woman, flesh-without-word, while the man to be is in a worse case after than before since she on the supine satisfies the verg to him! Toughtough, tootoological. Thou the first person shingeller. Art, an imperfect subjunctive. Paltry, flappent, had serious. Miss Smith onamatterpoetic. Hammisandivis axes colles waxes warmas like sodullas. So pick your stops with fondnes snow. And mind you twine the twos noods of your nicenames. And pull up your furbelovs as farabove as you're farthingales. That'll hint him how to click the trigger. Show you shall and won't he will! His hearing is indoubting just as my seeing is onbelieving. So dactylise him up to blankpoint and let him blink for himself where you speak the best ticklish. You'll feel what I mean. Fond namer, let me never see thee blame a kiss for shame a knee!

Echo, read ending! Siparioramoci! But from the stress of their

sunder enlivening, ay clasp, deciduously, a nikrokosmikon must come to mike.

—Well, my positively last at any stage! I hate to look at alarms but, however they put on my watchcraft, must now close as I hereby hear by ear from by seeless socks 'tis time to be up and ambling. My middle toe's mitching, so mizzle I must else 'twill sarve me out. Gulp a bulper at parting and the moore the melodest! Farewell but whenever, as Tisdall told Toole. Tempos fidgets. Let flee me fiacckles, says the grand old manoark, stormcrested crowcock and undulant hair, hoodies tway! Yes, faith, I am as mew let freer, beneath me corthage, bound. I'm as bored now bawling beersgrace at sorepaws there as Andrew Clays was sharing sawdust with Daniel's old collie. This shack's not big enough for me now. I'm dreaming of ye, azores. And, remember this, a chorines, there's the witch on the heath, sistra! 'Bansheeba peeling hourihaared while her Orcotron is hoaring ho. And whinn muinnuit flittsbit twinn her ttittshe cries tallmidy! Daughters of the heavens, be lucks in turnabouts to the wandering sons of red loam! The earth's atrot! The sun's a scream! The air's a jig. The water's great! Seven oldy oldy hills and the one blue beamer. I'm going. I know I am. I could bet I am. Somewhere I must get far away from Banbashore, wherever I am. No saddle, no staffet, but spur on the moment! So I think I'll take freeboots' advise. Psk! I'll borrow a path to lend me wings, quickquack, and from Jehusalem's wall, clickclack, me courser's clear, to Cheerup street I'll travel the void world over. It's Winland for moyne, bickbuck! Jeejakers! I hurt meself nettly that time! Come, my good frogmarchers! We felt the fall but we'll front the defile. Was not my olty mutther, Sereth Maritza, a Runningwater? And the bould one that quickened her the seaborne Fingale? I feel like that hill of a whaler went yulding round Groenmund's Circus with his tree full of seaweeds and Dinky Doll asleep in her shell. Hazelridge has seen me. Jerne valing is. Squall aboard for Kew, hop! Farewell awhile to her and thee! The brine's my bride to be. Lead on, Macadam, and danked be he who first sights Halt Linduff! Solo, solone, solong! Lood Erynnana, ware thee wail! With me singame soarem o'erem! Here's me take off. Now's nunc or nimmer, siskinder! Here goes the enemy! Bennydick hotfoots onimpudent stayers! Sorry! I bless alls to the whished with this panromain apological which Watllwewhistlem sang to the kerrycoys. Break ranks! After wage-of-battle bother I am thinking most. Fik yew! I'm through. Won. Toe. Adry. You watch my smoke.

After poor Jaun the Boast's last fireless words of postludium of his soapbox speech ending in'sheaven, twentyaid add one with a flirt of wings were pouring to his bysistance (could they snip that curl of curls to lay with their gloves and keep the kids bright!) prepared to cheer him should he leap on to curse him should he fall, but, with their biga triga rheda rodeo, the cherubs in the charabang, set down here and sedan chair, don't you wish you'd a yoke or a bit in your mouth, repulsing all attempts at first hands on, as no es nada, our greatly misunderstood one we perceived to give himself some sort of a hermetic prod or kick to sit up and take notice, which acted like magic, while the phalanx of daughters of February Filldyke, embushed and climbing, ramblers and weeps, voicedapproval in their customary manner by dropping kneedeep in tears over their concelebrated meednight sunflower, piopadey boy, their solase in dorckaness, and splattering together joyously the plaps of their tappyhands as, with a cry of genuine distress, so prettly prattly pollylogue, they viewed him, the just one, their darling, away.

A dream of favours, a favourable dream. They know how they believe that they believe that they know. Wherefore they wail.

Eh jourd'weh! Oh jourd'woe! dosiriously it psalmodied. Guesturn's lothlied answring to-maronite's wail.

Oasis, cedarous esaltarshoming Leafboughnoon!

Oisis, coolpressus onmountof Sighing!

Oasis, palmost esaltarshoming Gladdays!

Oisis, phantastichal roseway anjerichol!

Oasis, newleavos spaciosing encampness!

Oisis, plantainous dewstuckacqmirage playtennis!

Pipetto, Pipetta has misery unnoticed!

But the strangest thing happened. Backscuttling for the hop off with the odds altogether in favour of his tumbling into the river, Jaun just then I saw to collect from the gentlest weaner among the weiners, (who by this were in half droopleaflong mourning for the passing of the last post) the familiar yellow label into which he let fall a drop, smothered a curse, choked a guffaw, spat expectoratiously and blew his own trumpet. And next thing was he gummalicked the stickyback side and stamped the oval badge of belief to his agnelows brow with a genuine dash of irrepressible piety that readily turned his ladylike typmanzelles capsy curvy (the holy scamp!), with half a glance of Irish frisky (a Juan Jaimesan *hastaluego*) from under the shag of his parallel brows. It was then he made as if be but waved instead a handacross the sea as notice to quit

while the pacifettes made their armpacts widdershins (Frida! Freda!
Paza! Paisy! Irine! Areinette! Bridomay! Bentamai! Sososopky!
Bebebekka! Bababadkessy! Ghugugoothoyou! Dama! Dama-
domina! Takiya! Tokaya! Scioccara! Siuccherillina! Peocchia! Peuc-
chia! Ho Mi Hoping! Ha Me Happinice! Mirra! Myrha! Solyma!
Salemita! Sainta! Sianta! O Peace!), but in selfrighting the balance
of his corporeity to reexchange widerembrace with the pillarbosom
of the Dizzier he loved prettier, between estellos and venoussas, bad
luck to the lie but when next to nobody expected, their star and
gartergazer at the summit of his climax, he toppled a lipple on to the
off and, making a brandnew start for himself to run down his east-
ing, by blessing hes sthers with the sign of the southern cross, his
bungaloid borsaline with the hedgygreen bound blew off in a love-
blast (award for trover!) and Jawjon Redhead, bucketing after,
meccamaniac, (the headless shall have legs!), kingscouriered round
with an easy rush and ready relays by the bridge a stadion beyond
Ladycastle (and what herm but he narrowly missed fouling her
buttress for her but for he acqueducked) and then, cocking a snook
at the stock of his sermons, so mear and yet so fahr from that region's
general, away with him at the double, the hulk of a garron, pelting
after the road, on Shanks's mare, let off like a wind hound loose
(the bouchal! you'd think it was that moment they gave him the
jambos!) with a posse of tossing hankerwaves to his windward like
seraph's summonses on the air and a tempest of good things in
packetshape teeming from all accounts into the funnel of his fan-
mail shrimpnet, along the highroad of the nation, Traitor's Track,
following which fond floral fray he was quickly lost to sight through
the statuemen though without a doubt he was all the more on the
same head to memory dear while Sickerson, that borne of bjoerne,
la garde auxiliaire she murmured, hellyg Ursulinka, full of woe
(and how fitlier should goodboy's hand be shook than by the warmin
of her besom that wrong his swaddles?): *Where maggot Harvey
kneeled till bags? Ate Andrew coos hogdam farvel!*

Wethen, now, may the good people speed you, rural Haun, ex-
port stout fellow that you are, the crooner born with sweet wail of
evoker, healing music, ay, and heart in hand of Shamrogueshire!
The googoos of the suckabolly in the rockabeddy are become the
copiosity of wiseableness of the friarylayman in the pulpitbarrel.
May your bawny hair grow rarer and fairer, our own only wide-
headed boy! Rest your voice! Feed your mind! Mint your peas! Coax
your qyous! Come to disdoon blarmey and walk our groves so charm-

ing and see again the sweet rockelose where first you hymned O
Ciesa Mea! and touch the light theorbo! Songster, angler, choreog-
rapher! Piper to prisoned! Musicianship made Embrassador-at-
Large! Good by nature and natural by design, had you but been
spared to us, Hauneen lad, but sure where's the use my talking
quicker when I know you'll hear me all astray? My long farewell
I send to you, fair dream of sport and game and always something
new. Gone is Haun! My grief, my ruin! Our Joss-el-Jovan! Our
Chris-na-Murty! 'Tis well you'll be looked after from last to first as
yon beam of light we follow receding on your photophoric pilgrimage to your antipodes in the past, you who so often consigned
your distributory tidings of great joy into our nevertoolatetolove
box, mansuetudinous manipulator, victimisedly victorihoarse, dearest
Haun of all, you of the boots, true as adie, stepwalker, pennyatimer,
lampaddyfair, postanulengro, our rommanychiel! Thy now paling
light lucerne we ne'er may see again. But could it speak how nicely
would it splutter to the four cantons praises be to thee, our pattern
sent! For you had — may I, in our, your and their names, dare to
say it? — the nucleus of a glow of a zeal of soul of service such as
rarely, if ever, have I met with single men. Numerous are those who,
nay, there are a dozen of folks still unclaimed by the death angel
in this country of ours today, humble indivisibles in this grand con-
tinuum, overlorded by fate and interlarded with accidence, who,
while there are hours and days, will fervently pray to the spirit above
that they may never depart this earth of theirs till in his long run
from that place where the day begins, ere he retourneys postexilic,
on that day that belongs to joyful Ireland, the people that is of all
time, the old old oldest, the young young youngest, after decades
of longsuffering and decennia of brief glory, to mind us of what
was when and to matter us of the withering of our ways, their Jan-
youare Fibyouare wins true from Sylvester (only Walker himself
is like Waltzer, whimsicalissimo they go murmurand) comes marching ahome on the summer crust of the flagway. Life, it is true, will
be a blank without you because avicuum's not there at all, to nomore cares from nomad knows, ere Molochy wars bring the devil
era, a slip of the time between a date and a ghostmark, rived by
darby's chilldays embers, spatched fun Juhn that dandyforth, from
the night we are and feel and fade with to the yesterselves we tread
to turnupon.

But, boy, you did your strong nine furlong mile in slick and slap-
stick record time and a farfetched deed it was in troth, champion

docile, with your high bouncing gait of going and your feat of passage will be contested with you and through you, for centuries to come. The phaynix rose a sun before Erebia sank his smother! Shoot up on that, bright Bennu bird! *Va faotre!* Eftsoon so too will our own sphoenix spark spirt his spyre and sunward stride the rampante flambe. Ay, already the sombrer opacities of the gloom are sphanished! Brave footsore Haun! Work your progress! Hold to! Now! Win out, ye divil ye! The silent cock shall crow at last. The west shall shake the east awake. Walk while ye have the night for morn, lightbreakfastbringer, morroweth whereon every past shall full fost sleep. Amain.

Lowly, longly, a wail went forth. Pure Yawn lay low. On the mead of the hillock lay, heartsoul dormant mid shadowed landshape, brief wallet to his side, and arm loose, by his staff of citron briar, tradition stick-pass-on. His dream monologue was over, of cause, but his drama parapolylogic had yet to be, affact. Most distressfully (but, my dear, how successfully!) to wail he did, his locks of a lucan tinge, quickrich, ripely rippling, unfilleted, those lashbetasselled lids on the verge of closing time, whiles ouze of his sidewiseopen mouth the breath of him, evenso languishing as the princeliest treble treacle or lichee chewchow purse could buy. Yawn in a semiswoon lay awailing and (hooh!) what helpings of honeyful swoothead (phew!), which earpiercing dulcitude! As were you suppose to go and push with your bluntblank pin in hand upinto his fleshasplush cushionettes of some chubby boybold love of an angel. Hwoah!

When, as the buzzer brings the light brigade, keeping the home fires burning, so on the churring call themselves came at him, from the westborders of the eastmidlands, three kings of three suits and a crowner, from all their cardinal parts, along the amber way where Brosna's furzy. To lift them they did, senators four, by the first quaint skreek of the gloaming and they hopped it up the mountainy molehill, traversing climes of old times gone by of the days not worth remembering; inventing some excusethems, any sort, having a sevenply sweat of night blues moist upon them. Feefee! phopho!!foorchtha!!!aggala!!!!jeeshee!!!!!paloola!!!!!!ooridiminy!!!!!!! Afeared themselves were to wonder at the class of a crossroads puzzler he would likely be, length by breadth nonplussing his thickness, ells upon ells of him, making so many square yards of him, one half of him in Conn's half but the whole of him nevertheless in Owenmore's five quarters. There would he lay till they would him descry, spancelled down upon a blossomy bed, at one foule stretch, amongst

the daffydowndillies, the flowers of narcosis fourfettering his footlights, a halohedge of wild spuds hovering over him, epicures waltzing with gardenfillers, puritan shoots advancing to Aran chiefs.
Phopho!! The meteor pulp of him, the seamless rainbowpeel. Ag-
gala!!!! His bellyvoid of nebulose with his neverstop navel. Palo-
ola!!!!!! And his veins shooting melanite phosphor, his creamtocustard
cometshair and his asteroid knuckles, ribs and members. Ooridi-
miny!!!!!!! His electrolatiginous twisted entrails belt.

Those four claymen clomb together to hold their sworn star-
chamber quiry on him. For he was ever their quarrel, the way they
would see themselves, everybug his bodiment atop of annywom her
notion, and the meet of their noght was worth two of his morning.
Up to the esker ridge it was, Mallinger parish, to a mead that was
not far, the son's rest. First klettered Shanator Gregory, seeking
spoor through the deep timefield, Shanator Lyons, trailing the wavy
line of his partition footsteps (something in his blisters was telling
him all along how he had been in that place one time), then his
Recordership, Dr Shunadure Tarpey, caperchasing after honourable sleep, hot on to the aniseed and, up out of his prompt corner,
old Shunny MacShunny, MacDougal the hiker, in the rere of them
on the run, to make a quorum. Roping their ass he was, their sky-
grey globetrotter, by way of an afterthought and by no means leg-
less either for such sprouts on him they were that much oneven
it was tumbling he was by four lengths, within the bawl of a
mascot, kuss yuss, kuss cley, patsy watsy, like the kapr in the kabisses,
the big ass, to hear with his unaided ears the harp in the air, the
bugle dianablowing, wild as wild, the mockingbird whose word is
misfortune, so 'tis said, the bulbul down the wind.

The proto was traipsing through the tangle then, Mathew
Walker, godsons' goddestfar, deputising for gossipocracy, and his
station was a few perch to the weatherside of the knoll Asnoch and
it was from no other place unless there, how and ever, that he prox-
tended aloof upon the ether Mesmer's Manuum, the hand making
silence. The buckos beyond on the lea, then stopped wheresoever
they found their standings and that way they set ward about him,
doing obedience, nod, bend, bow and curtsey, like the watchers of
Prospect, upholding their broadawake prober's hats on their firrum
heads, the travelling court on its findings circuiting that personer
in his fallen. And a crack quatyouare of stenoggers they made of
themselves, solons and psychomorers, all told, with their hurts and
daimons, spites and clops, not even to the seclusion of their beast

by them that was the odd trick of the pack, trump and no friend
of carrots. And, what do you think, who should be laying there above
all other persons forenenst them only Yawn! All of asprawl he was
laying too amengst the poppies and, I can tell you something more
than that, drear writer, profoundly as you may bedeave to it, he was
oscasleep asleep. And it was far more similar to a satrap he lay there
with unctuous beauty all surrounded, the poser, or for whatall I
know like Lord Lumen, coaching his preferred constellations in
faith and doctrine, for old Matt Gregory, 'tis he had the starmenag-
erie, Marcus Lyons and Lucas Metcalfe Tarpey and the mack that
never forgave the ass that lurked behind him, Jonny na Hossaleen.
    More than their good share of their five senses ensorcelled you
would say themselves were, fuming censor, the way they could not
rightly tell their heels from their stools as they cooched down a mamalujo by his cubical crib, as question time drew nighing and the
map of the souls' groupography rose in relief within their quarter-
ings, to play tops or kites or hoops or marbles, curchycurchy, gawk-
ing on him, for the issuance of his pnum and softnoising one of
them to another one, the boguaqueesthers. And it is what they began to say to him tetrahedrally then, the masters, what way was he.
    — He's giving, the wee bairn. Yun has lived.
    — Yerra, why dat, my leader?
    — Wisha, is he boosed or what, alannah?
    — Or his wind's from the wrong cut, says Ned of the Hill.
    — Lesten!
    — Why so and speak up, do you hear me, you sir?
    — Or he's rehearsing somewan's funeral.
    — Whisht outathat! Hubba's up!
    And as they were spreading abroad on their octopuds their drifter
nets, the chromous gleamy seiners' nets and, no lie, there was word
of assonance being softspoken among those quartermasters.
    — Get busy, kid!
    — Chirpy, come now!
    — The present hospices is a good time.
    — I'll take on that chap.
    For it was in the back of their mind's ear, temptive lissomer, how
they would be spreading in quadriliberal their azurespotted fine at-
tractable nets, their nansen nets, from Matt Senior to the thurrible
mystagogue after him and from thence to the neighbour and that
way to the puisny donkeyman and his crucifer's cauda. And in their
minds years backslibris, so it was, slipping beauty, how they

would be meshing that way, when he rose to it, with the planckton at play about him, the quivers of scaly silver and their clutches of chromes of the highly lucid spanishing gold whilst, as hour gave way to mazing hour, with Yawn himself keeping time with his thripthongue, to ope his blurbeous lips he would, a let out classy, the way myrrh of the moor and molten moonmist would be melding mellifond indo his mouth.

— Y?

— Before You!

— Ecko! How sweet thee answer makes! Afterwheres? In the land of lions' odor?

— Friends! First if yu don't mind. Name yur historical grouns.

— This same prehistoric barrow 'tis, the orangery.

— I see. Very good now. It is in your orangery, I take it, you have your letters. Can you hear here me, you sir?

— Throsends. For my darling. Typette!

— So long aforetime? Can you hear better?

— Millions. For godsends. For my darling dearling one.

— Now, to come nearer zone; I would like to raise my deuterous point audibly touching this. There is this maggers. I am told by our interpreter, Hanner Esellus, that there are fully six hundred and six ragwords in your malherbal Magis landeguage in which wald wand rimes alpman and there is resin in all roots for monarch but yav hace not one pronouncable teerm that blows in all the vallums of tartallaght to signify majestate, even provisionally, nor no rheda rhoda or torpentine path or hallucinian via nor aurellian gape nor sunkin rut nor grossgrown trek nor crimeslaved cruxway and no moorhens cry or mooner's plankgang there to lead us to hopenhaven. Is such the *unde derivatur* casematter messio! Frankly. *Magis megis enerretur mynus hoc intelligow.*

— How? C'est mal prononsable, tartagliano, perfrances. Vous n'avez pas d'o dans votre boche provenciale, mousoo. Je m'incline mais *Moy jay trouvay la clee dang les champs.* Hay sham nap poddy velour, come on!

— Hep there! Commong, sa na pa de valure? Whu's teit dans yur jambs? Whur's that inclining and talkin about the messiah so cloover? A true's to your trefling! Whure yu!

— Trinathan partnick dieudonnay. Have you seen her? Typette, my tactile O!

— Are you in your fatherick, lonely one?

— The same. Three persons. Have you seen my darling only one? I am sohohold!

— What are yu shevering about, ultramontane, like a houn? Is there cold on ye, doraphobian? Or do yu want yur primafairy school-mam?

— The woods of fogloot! O mis padredges!

— Whisht awhile, greyleg! The duck is rising and you'll wake that stand of plover. I know that place better than anyone. Sure, I used to be always overthere on the fourth day at my grandmother's place, Tear-nan-Ogre, my little grey home in the west, in or about Mayo when the long dog gave tongue and they coursing the marches and they straining at the leash. Tortoiseshell for a guineagould! Burb! Burb! Burb! Follow me up Tucurlugh! That's the place for the claire oysters, Polldoody, County Conway. I never knew how rich I was like another story in the zoedone of the zephyros, strolling and stroll-ing, carrying my dragoman, Meads Marvel, thass withumpronouce-able tail, along the shore. Do you know my cousin, Mr Jasper Dougal that keeps the Anchor on the Mountain, the parson's son, Jasper of the Tuns, Pat Whateveryournameis?

— Dood and I dood. The wolves of Fochlut! By Whydoyoucallme? Do not flingamejig to the twolves!

— Turcafiera amd that's a good wan right enough! Wooluvs no less!

— One moment now, if I foreshorten the bloss on your bleather. Encroachement spells erosion. Dunlin and turnstone augur us where, how and when best as to burial of carcass, fuselage of dump and committal of noisance. But, since you invocate austers for the trailing of vixens, I would like to send a cormorant around this blue lagoon. Tell me now this. You told my larned friend rather previously, a moment since, about this mound or barrow. Now I suggest to you that ere there was this plagueburrow, as you seem to call it, there was a burialbattell, the boat of millions of years. Would you bear me out in that, relatively speaking, with her jackstaff jerking at her pennyladders, why not, and sizing a fair sail, knowest thout the kind? The *Pourquoi Pas,* bound for Weissduwasland, that four-master barquentine, Webster says, our ship that ne're returned. The Frenchman, I say, was an orangeboat. He is a boat. You see him. The both how you see is they! Draken af Danemork! Sacked it or ate it? What! Hennu! Spake ab laut!

—Couch, cortege, ringbarrow, dungcairn. Beseek the runes and see the longurn! Allmaun away when you hear the ganghorn. And meet Nautsen. Ess Ess. O ess. Warum night! Conning two lay payees. Norsker. Her raven flag was out, the slaver. I trow pon good, jordan's scaper, good's barnet and trustyman. Crouch low, you pigeons three! Say, call that girl with the tan tress awn! Call Wolfhound! Wolf of the sea. Folchu! Folchu!

— Very good now. That folklore's straight from the ass his mouth. I will crusade on with the parent ship, weather prophetting, far away from those green hills, a station, Ireton tells me, bonofide for keeltappers, now to come to the midnight middy on this levantine ponenter. From Daneland sailed the oxeyed man, now mark well what I say.

— Magnus Spadebeard, korsets krosser, welsher perfyddye. A destroyer in our port. Signed to me with his baling scoop. Laid bare his breastpaps to give suck, to suckle me. Ecce Hagios Chrisman!

— Oh, Jeyses, fluid! says the poisoned well. Futtfishy the First. Hootchcopper's enkel at the navel manuvres!

— Hep! Hello there, Bill of old Bailey! Whu's he? Whu's this lad, why the pups?

— Hunkalus Childared Easterheld. It's his lost chance, Emania. Ware him well.

— Hey! Did you dream you were ating your own tripe, acushla, that you tied yourself up that wrynecky fix?

— I see now. We move in the beast circuls. Grimbarb and pancercrucer! You took the words out of my mouth. A child's dread for a dragon vicefather. Hillcloud encompass us! You mean you lived as milky at their lyceum, couard, while you learned, volp volp, to howl yourself wolfwise. Dyb! Dyb! Do your best.

— I am dob dob dobbling like old Booth's, courteous. The cubs are after me, it zeebs, the whole totem pack, vuk vuk and vuk vuk to them, for Robinson's shield.

— Scents and gouspils! The animal jangs again! Find the fingall harriers! Here howl me wiseacre's hat till I die of the milkman's lupus!

— What? Wolfgang? Whoah! Talk very slowe!

— *Hail him heathen, heal him holystone!*

Courser, Recourser, Changechild . . . . ?

Eld as endall, earth . . . . ?

— A cataleptic mithyphallic! Was this *Totem Fulcrum Est* Ancestor yu hald in *Dies Eirae* where no spider webbeth or *Anno Mundi* ere bawds plied in Skiffstrait? Be fair, Chris!

— Dream. Ona nonday I sleep. I dreamt of a somday. Of a wonday

I shall wake. Ah! May he have now of here fearfilled me! Sinflowed,
O sinflowed! Fia! Fia! Befurcht christ!

— I have your tristich now; it recurs in three times the same differently (there is such a fui fui story which obtains of him): com-
ming nown from the asphalt to the concrete, from the human historic
brute, Finnsen Faynean, occeanyclived, to this same vulganized hillsir
from yours, Mr Tupling Toun of Morning de Heights, with
his lavast flow and his rambling undergroands, would he reoccur
Ad Horam, as old Romeo Rogers, in city or county, and your sure
ob, or by, with or from an urb, of you know the differenciabus,
as brauchbarred in apabhramsa, sierrah! We speak of Gun, the
farther. And in the locative. Bap! Bap!

— Ouer Tad, Hellig Babbau, whom certayn orbits assertant re
humeplace of Chivitats Ei, Smithwick, Rhonnda, Kaledon, Salem
(Mass), Childers, Argos and Duthless. Well, I am advised he might
in a sense be both nevertheless, every at man like myself, suffix
it to say, Abrahamsk and Brookbear! By him it was done bapka,
by me it was gone into, to whom it will beblive, Mushame,
Mushame! I am afraid you could not heave ahore one of your own
old stepstones, barnabarnabarn, over a stumbledown wall here in
Huddlestown to this classic Noctuber night but itandthey woule
binge, much as vecious, off the dosshouse back of a racerider in
his truetoflesh colours, either handicapped on her flat or barely repeating himself. That is a tiptip tim oldy faher now the man I go in
fear of, Tommy Terracotta, and he could be all your and my das,
the brodar of the founder of the father of the finder of the pfander
of the pfunder of the furst man in Ranelagh, fué! fué! Petries and
violet ice (I am yam, as Me and Tam Tower used to jagger pemmer
it, over at the house of Eddy's Christy, meaning Dodgfather, Dodgson
and Coo) and spiriduous sanction!

— Breeze softly. Aures are aureas. Hau's his naun?

— Me das has or oreils. Piercey, piercey, piercey, piercey!

— White eyeluscious and muddyhorsebroth! Pig Pursyriley! But
where do we get off, chiseller?

— Haltstille, Lucas and Dublinn! Vulva! Vulva! Vulva! Vulva!

— Macdougal, Atlantic City, or his onagrass that is, chuam and
coughan! I would go near identifying you from your stavrotides,
Jong of Maho, and the weslarias round your yokohahat. And that
O'mulanchonry plucher you have from the worst curst of Ireland,
Glwlwd of the Mghtwg Grwpp, is no use to you either, Johnny

my donkeyschott. Number four, fix up your spreadeagle and pull your weight!

— Hooshin hom to our regional's hin and the gander of Hayden. Would ye ken a young stepschuler of psychical chirography, the name of Keven, or (let outers pray) Evan Vaughan, of his Posthorn in the High Street, that was shooing a Guiney gagag, Poulepinter, that found the dogumen number one, I would suggest, an illegible downfumbed by an unelgible?

— If I do know sinted sageness? Sometimes he would keep silent for a few minutes as if in prayer and clasp his forehead and during the time he would be thinking to himself and he would not mind anybody who would be talking to him or crying stinking fish. But I no way need you, stroke oar nor your quick handles. Your too farfar a cock of the north there, Matty Armagh, and your due south so.

— South I see. You're up-in-Leal-Ulster and I'm-free-Down-in-Easia, this is much better. He is cured by faith who is sick of fate. The prouts who will invent a writing there ultimately is the poeta, still more learned, who discovered the raiding there originally. That's the point of eschatology our book of kills reaches for now in soandso many counterpoint words. What can't be coded can be decorded if an ear aye sieze what no eye ere grieved for. Now, the doctrine obtains, we have occasioning cause causing effects and affects occasionally recausing altereffects. Or I will let me take it upon myself to suggest to twist the penman's tale posterwise. The gist is the gist of Shaum but the hand is the hand of Sameas. Shan - Shim - Schung. There is a strong suspicion on counterfeit Kevin and we all remember ye in childhood's reverye. 'Tis the bells of scandal that gave tune to grumble over him and someone between me and thee. He would preach to the two turkies and dipdip all the dindians, this master the abbey, and give gold tidings to all that are in the bonze age of anteproresurrectionism to entrust their easter neappearance to Borsaiolini's house of hatcraft. He is our sent on the firm. Now, have you reasonable hesitancy in your mind about him after four-priest redmass or are you in your post? Tell me andat sans dismay. Leap, pard!

— Fierappel putting years on me! Nwo, nwo! This bolt in hand be my worder! I'll see you moved farther, blarneying Marcantonio! What cans such wretch to say to I or how have My to doom with him? We were wombful of mischief and initiumwise, everliking a liked, hairytop on heeltipper, alpybecca's unwachsibles, an ikeson

am ikeson, that babe, imprincipially, my leperd brethern, the Puer,
ens innocens of but fifteen primes. Ya all in your kalblionized so
trilustriously standing the real school, to be upright as his match,
healtheous as is egg, saviour so the salt and good wee braod, parallal-
ing buttyr, did I altermobile him to a flare insiding hogsfat. Been
ike hins kindergardien? I know not, O cashla, I am sure offed
habitand this undered heaven, meis enfins, contrasting the first
mover, that father I ascend fromming knows, as I think, caused
whom I, a self the sign, came remaining being dwelling ayr, plage
and watford as to I was eltered impostulance possessing my future
state falling towards thrice myself resting the childhide when I received the habit following Mezienius connecting Mezosius including
was verted embracing a palegrim, circumcised my hairs, Oh laud,
and removed my clothes from patristic motives, meas minimas
culpads! Permitting this ick (ickle coon icoocoon) crouched low
entering humble down, dead thrue mean scatological past, making
so smell partaking myself to confess abiding clean tumbluponing
yous octopods, mouthspeech allno fingerforce, owning my mansue-
tude before him attaching Audeon's prostratingwards mine sore
accompanying my thrain tropps offering meye eyesalt, what I (the
person whomin I now am) did not do, how he to say essied anding
how he was making errand andanding how he all locutey sunt, why
did you, my sexth best friend, blabber always you would be so delated
to back me, then ersed irredent, toppling Humphrey hugging
Nephew, old beggelaut, designing such post sitting his night office?
Annexing then, producing Saint Momuluius, you snub around en-
closing your moving motion touching the other catachumens continuing say providing append of signature quoniam you will
celebrand my dirthdags quoniam, concealed a concealer, I am two-
sides uppish, a mockbelief insulant, ending none meer hyber irish.
Well, chunk your dimned chink, before avtokinatown, forasmuch
as many have tooken in hand to, I may as well humbly correct
that vespian now in case of temporalities. I've my pockets full come-
play of you laycreated cardonals, ap rince, ap rowler, ap rancer, ap
rowdey! Improperial! I saved you fore of the Hekkites and you loosed
me hind bland Harry to the burghmote of Aud Dub. I teachet
you in fair time, my elders, the W.X.Y.Z. and P.Q.R.S. of legatine
powers and you, Ailbey and Ciardeclan, I learn, episcoping me altogether, circumdeditioned me. I brought you from the loups of Lazary
and you have remembered my lapsus langways. Washywatchywatay-
watashy! Oirasesheorebukujibun! Watacooshy lot! Mind of poison

is. That time thing think! Honorific remembrance to spit humble makes. My ruridecanal caste is a cut above you peregrines. Aye vouchu to rumanescu. See the leabhour of my generations! Has not my master, Theophrastius Spheropneumaticus, written that the spirit is from the upper circle? I'm of the ochlocracy with Prestopher Palumbus and Porvus Parrio. Soa koa Kelly Terry per Chelly Derry lepossette. Ho look at my jailbrand Exquovis and sequencias High marked on me fakesimilar in the foreign by Pappagallus and Pumpus-mugnus: ahem! Anglicey: *Eggs squawfish lean yoe nun feed mare-curious.* Sagart can self laud nilobstant to Lowman Catlick's patrician morning coat of arms with my High tripenniferry cresta and caudal mottams: Itch dean: which Gaspey, Otto and Sauer, he renders: echo stay so! Addressing eat or not eat body Yours am. And, Mind, praisegad, is the first praisonal Egoname Yod heard boissboissy in Moy Bog's domesday. Hastan the vista! Or in alleman: Suck at!

— Suck it yourself, sugarstick! Misha, Yid think whose was asking to luckat your sore toe or to taste your gaspy, hot and sour! Ichthyan! Hegvat tosser! Gags be plebsed! Between his voyous and her consin-nantes! Thugg, Dirke and Hacker with Rose Lankester and Blanche Yorke! Are we speachin d'anglas landadge or are you sprakin sea Djoytsch? Oy soy, Bleseyblasey, where to go is knowing remain? Become quantity that discourse bothersome when what do? Knowing remain? Come back, baddy wrily, to Bullydamestough! Cum him, buddy rowly, with me! What about your thruppenny croucher of an old fellow, me boy, through the ages, tell us, eh? What about Brian's the Vauntandonlieme, Master Monk, eh, eh, *Spira in Me Domino,* spear me Doyne! Fat prize the bonafide peachumpidgeon-lover, eh, eh, eh, esquire earwugs, escusado, of Jenkins' Area, with his I've Ivy under his tangue and the hohallo to his dullaphone, before there was a sound in the world? How big was his boost friend and be shanghaied to him? The swaaber! The twicer, trifoaled in Wanstable! Loud's curse to him! If you hored him outerly as we harum lubberintly, from morning rice till nightmale, with his drums and bones and hums in drones your innereer'd heerdly heer he. Ho ha hi he hung! Tsing tsing!

— Me no angly mo, me speakee Yellman's lingas. Nicey Doc Mistel Lu, please! Me no pigey ludiments all same numpa one Top-side Tellmastoly fella. Me pigey savvy a singasong anothel time. Pleasie, Mista Lukie Walkie! Josadam cowbelly maam belongame

shepullamealahmalong, begolla, Jackinaboss belongashe; plentymuch
boohoomeo.

— Hell's Confucium and the Elements! Tootoo moohootch! Thot's
never the postal cleric, checking chinchin chat with nipponnippers!
Halt there sob story to your lambdad's tale! Are you roman cawthrick
432?

— *Quadrigue my yoke.*

Triple my tryst.

Tandem my sire.

— History as her is harped. Too the toone your owldfrow lied
of. Tantris, hattrick, tryst and parting, by vowelglide! I feel your
thrilljoy mouths overspeaking, O dragoman, hands understudium.
Plunger words what paddle verbed. Mere man's mime: God has
jest. The old order changeth and lasts like the first. Every third
man has a chink in his conscience and every other woman has a
jape in her mind. Now, fix on the little fellow in my eye, Minucius
Mandrake, and follow my little psychosinology, poor armer in sling-
slang. Now I, the lord of Tuttu, am placing that inital T square
of burial jade upright to your temple a moment. Do you see anything, templar?

— I see a blackfrinch pliestrycook . . . who is carrying on his
brainpan . . . a cathedral of lovejelly for his . . . *Tiens,* how he
is like somebodies!

— Pious, a pious person. What sound of tistress isoles my ear?
I horizont the same, this serpe with ramshead, and lay it lightly
to your lip a little. What do you feel, liplove?

— I feel a fine lady . . . floating on a stillstream of isisglass . . .
with gold hair to the bed . . . and white arms to the twinklers
. . . O la la!

— Purely, in a pure manner. O, sey but swift and still a vain
essaying! Trothed today, trenned tomorrow. I invert the initial of
your tripartite and sign it sternly, and adze to girdle, on your breast.
What do you hear, breastplate?

— I ahear of a hopper behidin the door slappin his feet in a
pool of bran.

— Bellax, acting like a bellax. And so the triptych vision passes.
Out of a hillside into a hillside. Fairshee fading. Again am I deliciated
by the picaresqueness of your irmages. Now, the oneir urge iterim-
pellant, I feel called upon to ask did it ever occur to you, *qua* you,
prior to this, by a stretch of your iberborealic imagination, when
it's quicker than this quacking that you might, bar accidens, be very

largely substituted in potential secession from your next life by a complementary character, voices apart? Upjack! I shudder for your thought! Think! Put from your mind that and take on trust this. The next word depends on your answer.

— I'm thinking to, thogged be thenked! I was just trying to think when I thought I felt a flea. I might have. I cannot say for it is of no significance at all. Once or twice when I was in odinburgh with my addlefoes, Jake Jones, the handscabby, when I thinkled I wore trying on my garden substisuit, boy's apert, at my nexword nighboor's, and maybe more largely nor you quosh yet you, messmate, realise. A few times, so to shape, I chanced to be stretching, in the shadow as I thought, the liferight out of myself in my ericulous imaginating. I felt feeling a half Scotch and pottage like roung my middle ageing like Bewley in the baste so that I indicate out to myself and I swear my gots how that I'm not meself at all, no jolly fear, when I realise bimiselves how becomingly I to be going to become.

— O, is that the way with you, you craythur? In the becoming was the weared, wontnat! Hood maketh not frere. The voice is the voice of jokeup, I fear. Are you imitation Roma now or Amor now. You have all our empathies, eh, Mr Trickpat, if you don't mind, that is, aside from sings and mush, answering to my straight question?

— God save the monk! I won't mind this is, answering to your strict crossqueets, whereas it would be as unethical for me now to answer as it would have been nonsensical for you then not to have asked. Same no can, home no will, gangin I am. Gangang is Mine and I will return. Out of my name you call me, Leelander. But in my shelter you'll miss me. When Lapac walks backwords he's darkest horse in Capalisoot. You knew me once but you won't know me twice. I am *simpliciter arduus,* ars of the schoo, Freeday's child in loving and thieving.

— My child, know this! Some portion of that answer appears to have been token by you from the writings of Saint Synodius, that first liar. Let us hear, therefore, as you honour and obey the queen, whither the indwellingness of that which shamefieth be entwined of one or atoned of two. Let us hear, Art simplicissime!

— Dearly beloved brethren: Bruno and Nola, leymon bogholders and stationary lifepartners off orangey Saint Nessau Street, were explaining it avicendas all round each other ere yesterweek out of Ibn Sen and Ipanzussch. When himupon Nola Bruno monopolises his egobruno most unwillingly seses by the mortal powers alionola equal and opposite brunoipso, *id est,* eternally provoking alio opposite equally as provoked as Bruno at being eternally opposed by Nola. Poor omniboose, singalow singelearum: so is he!

— One might hear in their beyond that lionroar in the air again, the zoohoohoom of Felin make Call. Bruin goes to Noble, aver who is? If is itsen? Or you mean Nolans but Volans, an alibi, do you Mutemalice, suffering unegoistically from the singular but positively enjoying on the plural? Dustify of that sole, you breather! Ruemember, blither, thou must lie!

—Oyessoyess! I never dramped of prebeing a postman but I mean in ostralian someplace, mults deeply belubdead; my allaboy brother, Negoist Cabler, of this city, whom 'tis better ne'er to name, my said brother, the skipgod, expulled for looking at churches from behind, who is sender of the Hullo Eve Cenograph in prose and worse every Allso's night. High Brazil Brandan's Deferred, midden Erse clare language, Noughtnoughtnought nein. Assass. Dublire, per Neuropaths. Punk. Starving today plays punk opening tomorrow two plays punk wire splosh how two plays punk Cabler. Have you forgotten poor Alby Sobrinos, Geoff, you blighter, identifiable by the necessary white patch on his rear? How he went to his swiltersland after his lungs, my sad late brother, before his coglionial expancian? Won't you join me in a small halemerry, a bottle of the best, for wellmet Capeler, united Irishmen, what though preferring the stranger, the coughs and the itches and the minnies and the ratties the opulose and bilgenses, for of his was the patriots mistaken. The heart that wast our Graw McGree! Yet be there some who mourn him, concluding him dead, and more there be that wait astand. His fuchs up the staires and the ladgers in his haires, he ought to win that *V.V.C.* Fullgrapce for an endupper, half muxy on his whole! Would he were even among the lost! From ours bereft beyond belongs. Oremus poor fraternibus that he may yet escape the gallews and still remain ours faithfully departed. I wronged you. I never want to see more of bad men but I want to learn from any on the airse, like Tass with much thanks, here's ditto, if he lives sameplace in the antipathies of austrasia or anywhere with my fawngest on his hooshmoney, safe and damned, or has hopped it or who can throw any lime on the sopjack, my fond fosther, E. Obiit Nolan, The Workings, N.S.W., his condition off the Venerable Jerrybuilt, not belonging to these parts, who, I remember ham to me, when we were like bro and sis over our castor and porridge, with his roamin I suppose, expecting for his clarenx negus, a teetotum abstainer. He feels he ought to be as asamed of me as me to be ashunned of him. We were in one class of age like to two clots of egg. I am most beholding to him, my name-sick, as we sayed it in our Amharican, through the Doubly Tele-wisher. Outpassed hearts wag short pertimes. Worndown shoes upon his feet, to whose redress no tongue can tell! In his hands a boot! Spare me, do, a copper or two and happy I'll hope you'll be! It will pleased me behind with thanks from before and love to self and all I remain here your truly friend. I am no scholar but I loved that man who has africot lupps with the moonshane in his profile, my shemblable! My freer! I call you my halfbrother because you in your soberer otiumic moments remind me deeply of my natural saywhen brothel in feed, hop and jollity, S. H. Devitt, that benighted irismaimed, who is tearly belaboured by Sydney and Alibany.

— As you sing it it's a study. That letter selfpenned to one's other, that neverperfect everplanned?

— This nonday diary, this allnights newseryreel.

— My dear sir! In this wireless age any owl rooster can peck up bostoons. But whoewaxed he so anquished? Was he vector victored of victim vexed?

— Mighty sure! Way way for his wehicul! A parambolator ram into his bagsmall when he was reading alawd, with two ecolites and he's been failing of that kink in his arts over sense.

—Madonagh and Chiel, idealist leading a double life! But who, for the brilliance of brothers, is the Nolan as appearant nominally?

— Mr Nolan is pronuminally Mr Gottgab.

— I get it. By hearing his thing about a person one begins to place him for a certain in true. You reeker, he stands pat for you before a direct object in the feminine. I see. By maiden sname. Now, I am earnestly asking you, and putting it as between this yohou and that houmonymh, will just you search through your gabgut memoirs for all of two minutes for this impersonating prono-lan, fairhead on foulshoulders. Would it be in twofold truth an untaken mispatriate, too fullfully true and rereally a doblinganger much about your own medium with a sandy whiskers? Poke me nabs in the ribs and pick the erstwort out of his mouth.

— Treble Stauter of Holy Baggot Street, formerly Swordmeat, who I surpassed him lately for four and six bringing home the Christmas, as heavy as music, hand to eyes on the peer for Noel's Arch, in blessed foster's place is doing the dirty on me with his tantrums and all these godforgiven kilowatts I'd be better off without. She's write to him she's levt by me, Jenny Rediviva! Toot! Detter for you, Mr Nobru. Toot toot! Better for you, Mr Anol! This is the way we. Of a redtettetterday morning.

— When your contraman from Tuwarceathay is looking for righting that is not a good sign? Not?

— I speak truly, it's a shower sign that it's not.

— What though it be for the sow of his heart? If even she were a good pool Pegeen?

— If she ate your windowsill you wouldn't say sow.

— Would you be surprised after that my asking have you a bull, a bosbully, with a whistle in his tail to scare other birds?

— I would.

— Were you with Sindy and Sandy attending Goliath, a bull?

— You'd make me sag what you like to. I was intending a funeral. Simply and samply.

— They are too wise of solbing their silbings?

— And both croon to the same theme.

— Tugbag is Baggut's, when a crispin sokolist besoops juts kamps or clapperclaws an irvingite offthedocks. A luckchange, I see. Thinking young through the muddleage spread, the moral fat his mental leans on. We can cop that with our straat that is called corkscrewed. It would be the finest boulevard billy for a mile in every direction, from Lismore to Cape Brendan, Patrick's, if they took the bint out of the mittle of it. You told of a tryst too, two a tutu. I wonder now, without releasing seeklets of the alcove, turturs or raabraabs, have I heard mention of whose name anywhere? Mallowlane or Demaasch? Strike us up either end *Have You Erred off Van Homper* or *Ebell Teresa Kane.*

— *Marak! Marak! Marak!*

He drapped has draraks an Mansianhase parak

And he had ta barraw tha watarcrass shartclaths aff tha arkbashap af Yarak!

— Braudribnob's on the bummel?

— And lillypets on the lea.

— A being again in becomings again. From the sallies to the allies through their central power?

— Pirce! Perce! Quick! Queck!

— O Tara's thrush, the sharepusher! And he said he was only taking the average grass temperature for green Thursday, the blutchy scaliger! Who you know the musselman, his musclemum and mistlemam? Maomi, Mamie, My Mo Mum! He loves a drary

lane. Feel Phylliscitations to daff Mr Hairwigger who has just hadded
twinned little curls! He was resting between horrockses' sheets, wailing for white warfare, prooboor welshtbreton, and unbiassed by the
embarrassment of disposal but, the first woking day, by Thunder,
he stepped into the breach and put on his recriution trousers and
riding apron in Baltic Bygrad, the old soggy, was when the bold
bhuoys of Iran wouldn't join up.

— How voice you that, nice Sandy man? Not large goodman is
he, Sandy nice. Ask him this one minute upthrow inner lotus of
his burly ear womit he dropped his Bass's to P flat. And for that
he was allaughed? And then baited? The whole gammat?

— Loonacied! Marterdyed!! Madwakemiherculossed!!! Judas-
cessed!!!! Pairaskivvymenassed!!!!! Luredogged!!!!!! And, needatellye,
faulscrescendied!!!!!!!

— Dias domnas! Dolled to dolthood? And Annie Delittle, his dain-
tree diva, in deltic dwilights, singing him henpecked rusish through
the bars? My Wolossay's wild as the Crasnian Sea! Grabashag,
groogy, scoop and I'll cure ye! Mother of emeralds, ara poog neighbours!

— Capilla, Rubrilla and Melcamomilla! Dauby, dauby, without
dulay! Well, I beg to traverse same above statement by saxy luters
in their back haul of Coalcutter what reflects upon my administrants
of slow poisoning as my dodear devere revered mainhirr was confined
to guardroom, I hindustand, by my pint of his Filthered pilsens
bottle due to Zenaphiah Holwell, H and J. C. S, Which I was
bringing up my quee parapotacarry's orders in my sedown chair
with my mudfacepacket from my cash chemist and family drugger,
Surager Dowling, V.S. to our aural surgeon, Afamado Hairductor
Achmed Borumborad, M.A.C.A, Sahib, of a 1001 Ombrilla Street,
Syringa padham, Alleypulley, to see what was my watergood, my
mesical wasserguss, for repairs done by bollworm in the rere of pilch
knickers, seven yerds to his galandhar pole on perch, together with
his for me unfillable slopper, property of my deeply forfear re-
vebereared, who is costing us mostfortunes which I am writing in
mepetition to Kavanagh Djanaral, when he was sitting him hump-
backed in dry dryfilthyheat to his trinidads pinslers at their
orpentings, entailing a laxative tendency to mary, especially with
him being forbidden fruit and certified by his sexular clergy to have
as badazmy emotional volvular, with a basketful of priesters crossing
the singorgeous to aroint him with tummy moor's maladies, and there-
inafter liable to succumb when served with letters potent below the

belch, if my rupee repure riputed husbandship H.R.R. took a brief
one in his shirtsails out of the alleged given mineral, telling
me see his in Foraignghistan sambat papers Sunday feactures of
a welcomed aperrytiff with vallad of Erill Pearcey O he never battered one eagle's before paying me his duty on my annaversary to
the parroteyes list in my nil ensemble, in his lazychair but he hidded
up my hemifaces in all my mayarannies and he locked plum
into my mirrymouth like Ysamasy morning in the end of time, with
the so light's hope on his ruddycheeks and rawjaws and, my charmer,
whom I dipped my hand in, he simply showed me his propendiculous
loadpoker, Seaserpents hisses sissastones, which was as then is
produced in his mansway by this wisest of the Vikramadityationists,
with the remere remind remure remark, in his gulughurutty: Yran
for parasites with rum for the turkeycockeys so Lithia, M.D., as
this is for Snooker, bort!

— Which was said by whem to whom?

— It wham. But whim I can't whumember.

— Fantasy! funtasy on fantasy, amnaes fintasies! And there is nihil
nuder under the clothing moon. When Ota, weewahrwificle of Tor-
quells, bumpsed her dumpsydiddle down in her woolsark she mode
our heuteyleutey girlery of peerlesses to set up in all their bombos-
sities of feudal fiertey, fanned, flounced and frangipanned, while
the massstab whereby Ephialtes has exceeded is the measure, *simplex
mendaciis*, by which our Outis cuts his thruth. Arkaway now!

— Yerds and nudes say ayes and noes! Vide! Vide!

— Let Eivin bemember for Gates of Gold for their fadeless suns
berayed her. Irise, Osirises! Be thy mouth given unto thee! For why
do you lack a link of luck to poise a pont of perfect, peace? On the
vignetto is a ragingoos. The overseer of the house of the oversire
of the seas, Nu-Men, triumphant, sayeth: Fly as the hawk, cry as
the corncrake, Ani Latch of the postern is thy name; shout!

— My heart, my mother! My heart, my coming forth of darkness!
They know not my heart, O coolun dearast! Mon gloomerie! Mon
glamourie! What a surpraise, dear Mr Preacher, I to hear from your
strawnummical modesty! Yes, there was that skew arch of chrome
sweet home, floodlit up above the flabberghosted farmament and
bump where the camel got the needle. Talk about iridecencies! Ruby
and beryl and chrysolite, jade, sapphire, jasper and lazul.

— Orca Bellona! Heavencry at earthcall, etnat athos? Extinct your
vulcanology for the lava of Moltens!

— It's you not me's in erupting, hecklar!

— Ophiuchus being visible above thorizon, muliercula occluded
by Satarn's serpent ring system, the pisciolinnies Nova Ardonis and
Prisca Parthenopea, are a bonnies feature in the northern sky. Ers,
Mores and Merkery are surgents below the rim of the Zenith Part
while Arctura, Anatolia, Hesper and Mesembria weep in their mansions over Noth, Haste, Soot and Waste.

— Apep and Uachet! Holy snakes, chase me charley, Eva's got
barley under her fluencies! The Ural Mount he's on the move and
he'll quivvy her with his strombolo! Waddlewurst, the bag of tow,
as broad above as he is below! Creeping through the liongrass and
bullsrusshius, the obesendean, before the Emfang de Maurya's
class, in Bill Shasser's Shotshrift writing academy, camouflaged as
a blancmange and maple syrop! Obeisance so their sitinins is the
follicity of this Orp! Her sheik to Slave, his dick to Dave and the
fat of the land to Guygas. The treadmill pebbledropper haha halfa-
head overground and she'd only chitschats in her spanking bee
bonetry, Allapolloosa! Up the slanger! Three cheers and a heva heva
for the name Dan Magraw!

—The giant sun is in his emanence but which is chief of those
white dwarfees of which he ever is surabanded? And do you think
I might have being his seventh! He will kitssle me on melbaw.
What about his age? says you. What about it? says I. I will confess
to his sins and blush me further. I would misdemean to rebuke
to the libels of snots from the fleshambles, the canalles. Synamite
is too good for them. Two overthirties in shore shorties. She's askapot
at Nile Lodge and she's citchincarry at the left Mrs Hamazum's.
Will you warn your old habasund, barking at baggermen, his choke-
full chewing his chain? Responsif you plais. The said Sully, a bar-
racker associated with tinkers, the blackhand, Shovellyvans, wreuter
of annoyimgmost letters and skirriless ballets in Parsee Franch
who is Magrath's thug and smells cheaply of Power's spirits, like
a deepsea dibbler, and he is not fit enough to throw guts down to
a bear. Sylphling me when is a maid nought a maid he would
go to anyposs length for her! So long, Sulleyman! If they cut his
nose on the stitcher they had their siven good reasons. Here's to
the leglift of my snuff and trout stockangt henkerchoff, orange
fin with a mosaic of dispensations and a froren black patata, from
my church milliner. When Lynch Brother, Withworkers, Friends
and Company with T. C. King and the Warden of Galway is prepared to stretch him sacred by the powers to the starlight, L.B.W.
Hemp, hemp, hurray! says the captain in the moonlight. I could

put him under my pallyass and slepp on him all nights as I would roll myself for holy poly over his borrowing places. How we will make laugh over him together, me and my Riley in the Vickar's bed! Quink! says I. He cawls to me Granny-stream-Auborne when I am hiding under my hair from him and I cool him my Finnyking he's so joyant a bounder. Plunk! said he. Inasmuch as I am delightful to be able to state, with the joy of lifing in my forty winkers, that a handsome sovereign was freely pledged in their pennis in the sluts maschine, alonging wath a cherrywickerkishabrack of maryfruit under Shadow La Rose, to both the legintimate lady performers of display unquestionable, Elsebett and Marryetta Gunning, H 2 O, by that noblesse of leechers at his Saxontannery with motto in Wwalshe's ffrenchllatin: O'Neill saw Queen Molly's pants: and much admired engraving, meaning complet manly parts during alleged recent act of our chief mergey margey magistrades, five itches above the kneecap, as required by statues. V.I.C.5.6. If you won't release me stop to please me up the leg of me. Now you see! Respect. S.V.P. Your wife. Amn. Anm. Amm. Ann.

— You wish to take us, Frui Mria, by degrees, as *artis litterarumque patrona* but I am afraid, my poor woman of that same name, what with your silvanes and your salvines, you are misled.

— Alas for livings' pledjures!

— Lordy Daw and Lady Don! Uncle Foozle and Aunty Jack! Sure, that old humbugger was boycotted and girlcutted in debt and doom, on hill and haven, even by the show-the-flag flotilla, as I'm given now to understand, illscribed in all the gratuitouses and conspued in the takeyourhandaways. Bumbty, tumbty, Sot on a Wall, Mute art for the Million. There wasn't an Archimandrite of Dane's Island and the townlands nor a minx from the Isle of Woman nor a one of the four cantins nor any on the whole wheel of his ecunemical conciliabulum nor nogent ingen meid on allad the hold scurface of the jorth would come next or nigh him, Mr Eelwhipper, seed and nursery man, or his allgas bumgalowre, *Auxilium Meum Solo A Domino* (Amsad), for rime or ration, from piles or faces, after that.

— All ears did wag, old Eire wake as Piers Aurell was flappergangsted.

— Recount!

— I have it here to my fingall's ends. This liggy piggy wanted to go to the jampot. And this leggy peggy spelt pea. And theese lucky puckers played at pooping tooletom. Ma's da. Da's ma. Madas. Sadam.

— *Pater patruum cum filiabus familiarum.* Or, but, now, and, ariring out of her mirgery margery watersheads and, to change that subjunct from the traumaturgid for once in a while and darting back to stuff, if so be you may identify yourself with the him in you, that fluctuous neck merchamtur, bloodfadder and milkmudder, since then our too many of her, Abha na Lifé, and getting on to dadaddy again, as them we're ne'er free of, was he in tea e'er he went on the bier or didn't he ontime do something seemly heavy in sugar? He sent out Christy Columb and he came back with a jailbird's unbespokables in his beak and then he sent out Le Caron Crow and the peacies are still looking for him. The seeker from the swayed, the beesabouties from the parent swarm. Speak to the right! Rotacist ca canny! He caun ne'er be bothered but maun e'er be waked. If there is a future in every past that is present *Quis est qui non novit quinnigan* and *Qui quae quot at Quinnigan's Quake!* Stump! His producers are they not his consumers? Your exagmination round his factification for incamination of a warping process. Declaim!

— Arra irrara hirrara man, weren't they arriving in clansdestinies for the Imbandiment of *Ad Regias Agni Dapes,* fogabawlers and panhibernskers, after the crack and the lean years, scalpjaggers and houthhunters, like the messicals of the great god, a scarlet trainful, the Twoedged Petrard, totalling, leggats and prelaps, in their aggregate ages two and thirty plus undecimmed centries of them with insiders, extraomnes and tuttifrutties allcunct, from Rathgar, Rathanga, Rountown and Rush, from America Avenue and Asia Place and the Affrian Way and Europa Parade and besogar the wallies of Noo Soch Wilds and from Vico, Mespil Rock and Sorrento, for the lure of his weal and the fear of his oppidumic, to his salon de espera in the keel of his kraal, like lodes of ores flocking fast to Mount Maximagnetic, afeerd he was a gunner but affaird to stay away, Merrionites, Dumstdumbdrummers, Luccanicans, Ashtoumers, Batterysby Parkes and Krumlin Boyards, Phillipsburgs, Cabraists and Finglossies, Ballymunites, Raheniacs and the bettlers of Clontarf, for to contemplate in manifest and pay their firstrate duties before the both of him, twelve stone a side, with their *Thieve le Roué!* and their *Shvr yr Thrst!* and their *Uisgye ad Inferos!* and their *Usque ad Ebbraios!* at and in the licensed boosiness primises of his delhightful bazar and reunited magazine hall, by the magazine wall,

Hosty's and Co, Exports, for his five hundredth and sixtysixth birthday, the grand old Magennis Mor, Persee and Rahli, taker of the
tributes, their Rinseky Poppakork and Piowtor the Grape, holding
Dunker's durbar, boot kings and indiarubber umpires and shawhs
from paisley and muftis in muslim and sultana reiseines and jordan
almonders and a row of jam sahibs and a odd principeza in her pet-
tedcoat and the queen of knight's clubs and the claddagh ringlead-
ers and the two salaames and the Halfa Ham and the Hanzas Khan
with two fat Maharashers and the German selver geyser and he
polished up, protemptible, tintanambulating to himsilf so silfrich,
and there was J. B. Dunlop, the best tyrent of ourish times, and a
swanks of French wine stuarts and Tudor keepsakes and the Cesare-
vitch for the current counter Leodegarius Sant Legerleger riding
lapsaddlelonglegs up the oakses staircase on muleback like Amaxo-
dias Isteroprotos, hindquarters to the fore and kick to the lift, and
he handygrabbed on to his trulley natural anthem: *Horsibus, keep
your tailyup*, and as much as the halle of the vacant fhroneroom,
Oldloafs Buttery, could safely accomodate of the houses of Orange
and Betters M.P, permeated by Druids D.P, Brehons B.P, and
Flawhoolags F.P, and Agiapommenites A.P, and Antepummelites
P.P, and Ulster Kong and Munster's Herald with Athclee Ensigning
and Athlone Poursuivant and his Imperial Catchering, his fain
awan, and his gemmynosed sanctsons in epheud and ordilawn and
his diamondskulled granddaucher, Adamantaya Liubokovskva, all
murdering Irish, amok and amak, out of their boom companions
in paunchjab and dogril and pammel and gougerotty, after plenty
of his fresh stout and his good balls of malt, not to forget his oels
a'mona nor his beers o'ryely, sopped down by his pani's annagol-
orum, (at Kennedy's kiln she kned her dough, back of her bake
for me, buns!) socializing and communicanting in the deification
of his members, for to nobble or salvage their herobit of him, the
poohpooher old bolssloose, with his arthurious clayroses, Dodderick
Ogonoch Wrack, busted to the wurld at large, on the table round,
with the floodlight switched back, as true as the Vernons have
Brian's sword, and a dozen and one by one tilly tallows round in
ringcampf, circumassembled by his daughters in the foregiftness of
his sons, lying high as he lay in all dimensions, in court dress and
ludmers chain, with a hogo, fluorescent of his swathings, round him,
like the cummulium of scents in an italian warehouse, erica's clus-
tered on his hayir, the spectrem of his prisent mocking the candied-

ights of his dadtid, bagpuddingpodded to the deafspot, bewept of his chilidrin and serafim, poors and personalities, venturous, drones and dominators, ancients and auldancients, with his buttend up, expositoed for sale after referee's inspection, bulgy and blowrious, bunged to ignorious, healed cured and embalsemate, pending a rouseruction of his bogey, most highly astounded, as it turned up, after his life overlasting, at thus being reduced to nothing.

— Bappy-go-gully and gaff for us all! And all his morties calisenic, tripping a trepas, neniatwantyng: Mulo Mulelo! Homo Humilo! Dauncy a deady O! Dood dood dood! O Bawse! O Boese! O Muerther! O Mord! Mahmato! Moutmaro! O Smirtsch! O Smertz! Woh Hillill! Woe Hallall! Thou Thuoni! Thou Thaunaton! Umartir! Udamnor! Tschitt! Mergue! Eulumu! Huam Khuam! Malawinga! Malawunga! Ser Oh Ser! See ah See! Hamovs! Hemoves! Mamor! Rockquiem eternuel give donal aye in dolmeny! Bad luck's perpepperpot loosen his eyis! (Psich!).

— But there's leps of flam in Funnycoon's Wick. The keyn has passed. Lung lift the keying!

— God save you king! Muster of the Hidden Life!

— God serf yous kingly, adipose rex! I had four in the morning and a couple of the lunch and three later on, but your saouls to the dhaoul, do ye. Finnk. Fime. Fudd?

— Impassable tissue of improbable liyers! D'yu mean to sett there where y'are now, coddlin your supernumerary leg, wi'that bizar tongue in yur tolkshap, and your hindies and shindies, like a muck in a market, Sorley boy, repeating yurself, and tell me that?

— I mean to sit here on this altknoll where you are now, Surly guy, replete in myself, as long as I live, in my homespins, like a sleepingtop, with all that's buried ofsins insince insensed insidesofme. If I can't upset this pound of pressed ollaves I can sit up zounds of sounds upon him.

— Oliver! He may be an earthpresence. Was that a groan or did I hear the Dingle bagpipes Wasting war and? Watch!

— *Tris tris a ni ma mea!* Prisoner of Love! Bleating Hart! Lowlaid Herd! Aubain Hand! Wonted Foot! *Usque! Usque! Usque! Lignum in* . . .

— Rawth of Gar and Donnerbruck Fire? Is the strays world moving mound or what static bable is this, tell us?

— Whoishe whoishe whoishe whoishe linking in? Whoishe whoishe whoishe?

— The snare drum! Lay yer lug till the groun. The dead giant manalive! They're playing thimbles and bodkins. Clan of the Gael! Hop! Whu's within?

— Dovegall and finshark, they are ring to the rescune!

— Zinzin. Zinzin.

— Crum abu! Cromwell to victory!

— We'll gore them and gash them and gun them and gloat on them.

— Zinzin.

— O, widows and orphans, it's the yeomen! Redshanks for ever! Up Lancs!

— The cry of the roedeer it is! The white hind. Their slots, link-link, the hound hunthorning! Send us and peace! Title! Title!

— Christ in our irish times! Christ on the airs independence! Christ hold the freedman's chareman! Christ light the dully expressed!

— Slog slagt and sluaghter! Rape the daughter! Choke the pope!

— Aure! Cloudy father! Unsure! Nongood!

— Zinzin.

— Sold! I am sold! Brinabride! My ersther! My sidster! Brinabride, goodbye! Brinabride! I sold!

— Pipette dear! Us! Us! Me! Me!

— Fort! Fort! Bayroyt! March!

— Me! I'm true. True! Isolde. Pipette. My precious!

— Zinzin.

— Brinabride, bet my price! Brinabride!

— My price, my precious?

— Zin.

— Brinabride, my price! When you sell get my price!

— Zin.

— Pipette! Pipette, my priceless one!

— O! Mother of my tears! Believe for me! Fold thy son!

— Zinzin. Zinzin.

— Now we're gettin it. Tune in and pick up the forain counties! Hello!

— Zinzin.

— Hello! Tittit! Tell your title?

— Abride!

— Hellohello! Ballymacarett! Am I thru' Iss? Miss? True?

— Tit! What is the ti . . ?

SILENCE.

Act drop. Stand by! Blinders! Curtain up. Juice, please! Foots!

— Hello! Are you Cigar shank and Wheat?

— I gotye. Gobble Ann's Carrot Cans.

— Parfey. Now, after that justajiff siesta, just permit me a moment. Challenger's Deep is childsplay to this but, by our soundings in the swish channels, land is due. A truce to demobbed swarwords. Clear the line, priority call! Sybil! Better that or this? Sybil Head this end! Better that way? Follow the baby spot. Yes. Very good now. We are again in the magnetic field. Do you remember on a particular luke-summer night, following a crying fair day? Moisten your lips for a lightning strike and begin again. Mind the flickers and dimmers! Better?

— Well. The isles is Thymes. The ales is Penzance. Vehement Genral. Delhi expulsed.

— Still calling of somewhave from its specific? Not more? Less-continuous. There were fires on every bald hill in holy Ireland that night. Better so?

— You may say they were, son of a cove!

— Were they bonfires? That clear?

— No other name would at all befit them unless that. Bonafieries! With their blue beards streaming to the heavens.

— Was it a high white night now?

— Whitest night mortal ever saw.

— Was our lord of the heights nigh our lady of the valley?

— He was hosting himself up and flosting himself around and ghosting himself to merry her murmur like an andeanupper balkan.

— Lewd's carol! Was there rain by any chance, mistandew?

— Plenty. If you wend farranoch.

— There fell some fall of littlewinter snow, holy-as-ivory, I gather, jesse?

— By snaachtha clocka. The nicest at all. In hilly-and-even zimalayars.

— Did it not blow some gales, westnass or ostscent, rather strongly to less, allin humours out of turn, jusse as they rose and sprungen?

— Out of all jokes it did. Pipep! Icecold. Brr na brr, ny prr! Lieto galumphantes!

— Stll cllng! Nmr! Peace, Pacific! Do you happen to recollect whether Muna, that highlucky nackt, was shining at all?

— Sure she was, my midday darling! And not one but a pair of pritty geallachers.

— Quando? Quonda? Go datey!

— Latearly! Latearly! Latearly! Latearly!

— That was latterlig certainly. And was there frostwork about and thick weather and hice, soon calid, soon frozen, cold on warm but moistly dry, and a boatshaped blanket of bruma airsighs and hell-stohns and flammballs and vodashouts and everything to please everybody?

— Hail many fell of greats! Horey morey smother of fog! There was, so plays your ahrtides. Absolutely boiled. Obsoletely cowled. Julie and Lulie at their parkiest.

— The amenities, the amenities of the amenities with all their amenities. And the firmness of the formous of the famous of the fumous of the first fog in Maidanvale?

— Catchecatche and couchamed!

— From Miss Somer's nice dream back to Mad Winthrop's delugium stramens. One expects that kind of rimey feeling in the sire season?

— One certainly does. Desire, for hire, would tire a shire, phone, phunkel, or wire. And mares.

— Of whitecaps any?

— Foamflakes flockfuyant from Foxrock to Finglas.

— A lambskip for the marines! Paronama! The entire horizon cloth! All effects in their joints caused ways. Raindrum, windmachine, snowbox. But thundersheet?

— No here. Under the blunkets.

— This common or garden is now in stilller realithy the starey sphere of an oleotorium for broken pottery and ancient vegetables?

— Simply awful the dirt. An evernasty ashtray.

— I see. Now do you know the wellknown kikkinmidden where the illassorted first couple first met with each other? The place where Ealdermann Fanagan? The time when Junkermenn Funagin?

— Deed then I do, W.K.

— In Fingal too they met at Littlepeace aneath the bidetree, Yellowhouse of Snugsborough, Westreeve-Astagob and Slutsend with Stockins of Winning's Folly Merryfalls, all of a two, skidoo and skephumble?

— Godamedy, you're a delville of a tolkar!

— Is it a place fairly exspoused to the four last winds?

— Well, I faithly sincerely believe so indeed if all what I hope to charity is half true.

— This stow on the wolds, is it Woful Dane Bottom?

— It is woful in need whatever about anything or allselse under the grianblachk sun of gan greyne Eireann.

— A tricolour ribbon that spells a caution. The old flag, the cold flag.

— The flagstone. By tombs, deep and heavy. To the unaveiling memory of. Peacer the grave.

— And what sigeth Woodin Warneung thereof?

— Trickspissers vill be pairsecluded.

— There used to be a tree stuck up? An overlisting eshtree?

— There used, sure enough. Beside the Annar. At the ford of Slivenamond. Oakley Ashe's elm. With a snoodrift from one beer-chen bough. And the grawndest crowndest consecrated maypole in all the reignladen history of Wilds. Browne's *Thesaurus Plantarum* from Nolan's, The Prittlewell Press, has nothing alike it. For we are fed of its forest, clad in its wood, burqued by its bark and our lecture is its leave. The cran, the cran the king of all crans. Squire-made and damesman of plantagenets, high and holy.

—Now, no hiding your wren under a bushle! What was it doing there, for instance?

— Standing foreninst us.

— In Summerian sunshine?

— And in Cimmerian shudders.

— You saw it visibly from your hidingplace?

— No. From my invisibly lyingplace.

— And you then took down in stereo what took place being tunc committed?

— I then tuk my takenplace lying down, I thunk I told you. Solve it!

— Remounting aliftle towards the ouragan of spaces. Just how grand in cardinal rounders is this preeminent giant, sir Arber? Your bard's highview, avis on valley! I would like to hear you burble to us in strict conclave, purpurando, and without too much italiote interfairance, what you know *in petto* about our sovereign beings-talk, Tonans Tomazeus. *O dite!*

— Corcor Andy, *Udi, Udite!* Your Ominence, Your Imminence and delicted fraternitrees! There's tuodore queensmaids and Idahore shopgirls and they woody babies growing upon her and bird flamin-gans sweenyswinging fuglewards on the tipmast and Orania epples

playing hopptociel bommptaterre and Tyburn fenians snoring in
his quickenbole and crossbones strewing its holy floor and culprines
of Erasmus Smith's burstall boys with their underhand leadpencils
climbing to her crotch for the origin of spices and charlotte darlings
with silk blue askmes chattering in dissent to them, gibbonses and
gobbenses, guelfing and ghiberring proferring praydews to their
anatolies and blighting findblasts on their catastripes and the kill-
maimthem pensioners chucking overthrown milestones up to her to
fall her cranberries and her pommes annettes for their unnatural
refection and handpainted hoydens plucking husbands of him and
cock robins muchmore hatching most out of his missado eggdrazzles
for him, the sun and moon pegging honeysuckle and white heather
down and timtits tapping resin there and tomahawks watching tar
elsewhere, creatures of the wold approaching him, hollow mid ivy,
for to claw and rub, hermits of the desert barking their infernal
shins over her triliteral roots and his acorns and pinecorns shooting
wide all sides out of him, plantitude outsends of plenty to thousands,
after the truants of the utmostfear and her downslyder in that
snakedst-tu-naughsy whimmering woman't seeleib such a fashion-
aping sathinous dress out of that exquisitive creation and her leaves,
my darling dearest, sinsinsinning since the night of time and each
and all of their branches meeting and shaking twisty hands all over
again in their new world through the germination of its gemination
from Ond's outset till Odd's end. And encircle him circuly. Evovae!

— Is it so exaltated, eximious, extraoldandairy and excelssiorising?

— Amengst menlike trees walking or trees like angels weeping
nobirdy aviar soar anywing to eagle it! But rocked of agues, cliffed
for aye!

— Telleth that eke the treeth?

— Mushe, mushe of a mixness.

— A shrub of libertine, indeed! But that steyne of law indead what
stiles its neming?

— Tod, tod, too hard parted!

— I've got that now, Dr Melamanessy. Finight mens midinfinite
true. The form masculine. The gender feminine. I see. Now, are
you derevatov of it yourself in any way? The true tree I mean?
Let's hear what science has to say, pundit-the-next-best-king.
Splanck!

— Upfellbowm.

— It reminds of the weeping of the daughters?

— And remounts to the sense arrest.

— The wittold, the frausch and the dibble! How this looseaffair brimsts of fussforus! And was this treemanangel on his soredbohmend because Knockout, the knickknaver, knacked him in the knechtschaft?

— Well, he was ever himself for the presention of crudities to animals for he had put his own nickelname on every toad, duck and herring before the climber clomb aloft, doing the midhill of the park, flattering his bitter hoolft with her conconundrums. He would let us have the three barrels. Such was a bitte too thikke for the Muster of the hoose so as he called down on the Grand Precurser who coiled him a crawler of the dupest dye and thundered at him to flatch down off that erection and be aslimed of himself for the bellance of hissch leif.

— Oh Finlay's coldpalled!

— Ahday's begatem!

— Were you there, eh Hehr? Were you there when they lagged um through the coombe?

— Wo wo! Who who! Psalmtimes it grauws on me to ramble, ramble, ramble.

— Woe! Woe! So that was how he became the foerst of our treefellers?

— Yesche and, in the absence of any soberiquiet, the fanest of our truefalluses. Bapsbaps Bomslinger!

— How near do you feel to this capocapo promontory, sir?

— There do be days of dry coldness between us when he does be like a lidging house far far astray and there do be nights of wet windwhistling when he does be making me onions woup all kinds of ways.

— Now you are mehrer the murk, Lansdowne Road. She's threwed her pippin's thereabouts and they've cropped up tooth oneydge with hates to leaven this socried isle. Now, thornyborn, follow the spotlight, please! Concerning a boy. Are you acquainted with a pagany, vicariously known as Toucher 'Thom' who is. I suggest Finoglam as his habitat. Consider yourself on the stand now and watch your words, take my advice. Let your motto be: *Inter nubila numbum*.

— Never you mind about my mother or her hopitout. I consider if I did, I would feel frightfully ashamed of admired vice.

— He is a man of around fifty, struck on Anna Lynsha's Pekoe with milk and whisky, who does messuages and has more dirt on him than an old dog has fleas, kicking stones and knocking snow off walls. Have you ever heard of this old boy "Thom" or "Thim"

of the fishy stare who belongs to Kimmage, a crofting district, and
is not all there, and is all the more himself since he is not so, being
most of his time down at the Green Man where he steals, pawns,
belches and is a curse, drinking gaily two hours after closing time,
with the coat on him skinside out against rapparitions, with his
socks outsewed his springsides, clapping his hands in a feeble sort
of way and systematically mixing with the public going for groceries,
slapping greats and littlegets soundly with his cattegut belts, flapping baresides and waltzywembling about in his accountrements
always in font of the tubbernuckles, like a longarmed lugh, when
he would be finished with his tea?

— Is it that fellow? As mad as the brambles he is. Touch him.
With the lawyers sticking to his trewsershins and the swatmenotting
on the basque of his beret. He has kissed me more than once, I
am sorry to say and if I did commit gladrolleries may the loone forgive it! O wait till I tell you!

— We are not going yet.

— And look here! Here's, my dear, what he done, as snooks as
I am saying so!

— Get out, you dirt! A strangely striking part of speech for the
hottest worked word of ur sprogue. You're not! Unhindered and
odd times? Mere thumbshow? Lately?

— How do I know? Such my billet. Buy a barrack pass. Ask the
horneys. Tell the robbers.

— You are alluding to the picking pockets in Lower O'Connell
Street?

— I am illuding to the Pekin packet but I am eluding from Laura
Connor's treat.

— Now, just wash and brush up your memoirias a little bit. So
I find, referring to the pater of the present man, an erely demented
brick thrower, I am wondering to myself in my mind, *qua* our arc
of the covenant, was Toucher, a methodist, whose name, as others
say, is not really 'Thom', was this salt son of a century from Boaters-
town, Shivering William, the sealiest old forker ever hawked cran-
nock, who is always with him at the Big Elm and the Arch after his
teeth were shaken out of their suckets by the wrang dog, for having
5 pints 73 of none Eryen blood in him abaft the seam level, the
scatterling, wearing his cowbeamer and false clothes of a brewer's
grains pattern with back buckons with his motto on, *Yule Remember*, ostensibly for that occasion only of the twelfth day Pax and
Quantum wedding, I'm wondering.

— I bet you are. Well, he was wandering, you bet, whatever was his matter, in his mind too, give him his due, for I am sorry to have to tell you, hullo and evoe, they were coming down from off him.

— How culious an epiphany!

— *Hodie casus esobhrakonton?*

— It looked very like it.

— Needer knows necess and neither garments. Man is minded of the Meagher, wat? Wooly? Walty?

— Ay, another good button gone wrong.

— Blondman's blaff! Like a skib leaked lintel the arbour leidend with . . .?

— Pamelas, peggylees, pollywollies, questuants, quaintaquilties, quickamerries.

— Concaving now convexly to the semidemihemispheres and, from the female angle, music minnestirring, were the subligate sisters, P. and Q., Clopatrick's cherierapest, *mutatis mutandis,* in pretty much the same pickle, the peach of all piedom, the quest of all quicks?

— Peequeen ourselves, the prettiest pickles of unmatchemable mute antes I ever bopeeped at, seesaw shallshee, since the town go went gonning on Pranksome Quaine.

— Silks apeel and sulks alusty?

— Boy and giddle, gape and bore.

— I hear these two goddesses are liable to sue him?

— Well, I hope the two Collinses don't leg a bail to shoot him.

— Both were white in black arpists at cloever spilling, knickt?

— Gels bach, I, languised, liszted. Etoudies for the right hand.

— Were they now? And were they watching you as watcher as well?

— Where do you get that wash? This representation does not accord with my experience. They were watching the watched watching. Vechers all.

— Good. Hold that watching brief and keep this witching longuer. Now, retouching friend Tomsky, the enemy, did you gather much from what he let drop? We are sitting here for that.

— I was rooshian mad, no lie. About his shapeless hat.

— I suspect you must have been.

— You are making your thunderous mistake. But I was dung sorry for him too.

— O Schaum! Not really? Were you sorry you were mad with him then?

— When I tell you I was rooshiamarodnimad with myself altogether, so I was, for being sorry for him.

— So?

— Absolutely.

— Would you blame him at all stages?

— I believe in many an old stager. But what seemed sooth to a Greek summed nooth to a giantle. Who kills the cat in Cairo coaxes cocks in Gaul.

— I put it to you that this was solely in his sunflower state and that his haliodraping het was why maids all sighed for him, ventured and vied for him. Hm?

— After Putawayo, Kansas, Liburnum and New Aimstirdames, it wouldn't surprise me in the very least.

— That tare and this mole, your tear and our smile. 'Tis life that lies if woman's eyes have been our old undoing. Lid efter lid. Reform in mine size his deformation. Tiffpuff up my nostril, would you puff the earthworm outer my ear.

— He could claud boose his eyes to the birth of his garce, he could lump all his lot through the half of her play, but he jest couldn't laugh through the whole of her farce becorpse he warn't billed that way. So he outandouts his volimetangere and has a lightning consultation and he downadowns his pantoloogions and made a piece of first perpersonal puetry that staystale remains to be. Cleaned.

— Booms of bombs and heavy rethudders?

— This aim to you!

— The tail, so mastrodantic, as you tell it nearly takes your own mummouth's breath away. Your troppers are so unrelieved because his troopers were in difficulties. Still let stultitiam done in veino condone ineptias made of veritues. How many were married on that top of all strapping mornings, after the midnight turkay drive, my good watcher?

— Puppaps. That'd be telling. With a hoh frohim and heh fraher. But, as regards to Tammy Thornycraft, Idefyne the lawn mare and the laney moweress and all the prentisses of wildes to massage him.

— Now from Gunner Shotland to Guinness Scenography. Come to the ballay at the Tailors' Hall. We mean to be mellay on the Mailers' Mall. And leap, rink and make follay till the Gaelers' Gall. Awake! Come, a wake! Every old skin in the leather world, infect the whole stock company of the old house of the Leaking Barrel, was thomistically drunk, two by two, lairking o' tootlers with tombours a'beggars, the blog and turfs and the brandywine bankromp-

ers, trou Normend fashion, I have been told, down to the bank lean
clorks? Some nasty blunt clubs were being operated after the tradition of a wellesleyan bottle riot act and a few plates were being
shied about and tumblers bearing traces of fresh porter rolling
around, independent of that, for the ehren of Fyn's Insul, and then
followed that wapping breakfast at the Heaven and Covenant, with
Rodey O'echolowing how his breadcost on the voters would be a
comeback for e'er a one, like the depredations of Scandalknivery,
in and on usedtowobble sloops off cloasts, eh? Would that be a tall-
tale too? This was the grandsire Orther. This was his innwhite
horse. Sip?

— Well, naturally he was, louties also genderymen. Being Kerss-
fesstiydt. They came from all lands beyond the wave for songs of
Inishfeel. Whiskway and mortem! No puseyporcious either, invitem
kappines all round. But the right reverend priest, Mr Hopsinbond,
and the reverent bride eleft, Frizzy Fraufrau, were sober enough.
I think they were sober.

— I think you're widdershins there about the right reverence.
Magraw for the Northwhiggern cupteam was wedding beastman,
papers before us carry. You saw him hurriedly, or did you if that-
seme's not irrelevant? With Slater's hammer perhaps? Or he was in
serge?

— I horridly did. On the stroke of the dozen. I'm sure I'm wrong
but I heard the irreverend Mr Magraw, in search of a stammer,
kuckkuck kicking the bedding out of the old sexton, red-Fox Goodman around the sacristy, till they were bullbeadle black and bufeteer
blue, while I and Flood and the other men, jazzlike brollies and
sesuos, was gickling his missus to gackles in the hall, the divileen,
(she's a lamp in her troth) with her cygncygn leckle and her twelve
pound lach.

— A loyal wifish woman cacchinic wheepingcaugh! While she
laylylaw was all their rage. But you did establish personal contact?
In epexegesis or on a point of order?

— That perkumiary pond is beyawnd my pinnigay pretonsions.
I am resting on a pigs of cheesus but I've a big suggestion it was
about the pint of porter.

— You are a suckersome! But this all, as airs said to oska, was only
that childbearer might blogas well sidesplit? Where letties heredi-
tate a dark mien swart hairy?

— Only. 'Twas womans' too woman with mans' throw man.

— Bully burley yet hardly hurley. The saloon bulkhead, did you say, or the tweendecks?

— Between drinks, I deeply painfully repeat it.

— Was she wearing shubladey's tiroirs in humour of her hubbis-hobbis, Massa's star stellar?

— Mrs Tan-Taylour? Just a floating panel, secretairslidingdraws, a budge of klees on her schalter, a siderbrass sehdass on her anulas findring and forty crocelips in her curlingthongues.

— So this was the dope that woolied the cad that kinked the ruck that noised the rape that tried the sap that hugged the mort?

— That legged in the hoax that joke bilked.

— The jest of junk the jungular?

— Jacked up in a jock the wrapper.

— Lollgoll! You don't soye so! All upsydown her whole creation? So there was nothing serical between you? And Drysalter, father of Izod, how was he now?

— To the pink, man, like an allmanox in his shirt and stickup, brustall to the bear, the Megalomagellan of our winevatswaterway, squeezing the life out of the liffey.

— Crestofer Carambas! Such is zodisfaction. You punk me! He came, he kished, he conquered. Vulturuvarnar! The must of his glancefull coaxing the beam in her eye? That musked bell of this masked ball! Annabella, Lovabella, Pullabella, yep?

— Yup! Titentung Tollertone in S. Sabina's. Aye aye, she was lithe and pleasable. Wilt thou the lee? Wilt thou the hee? Wilt thou the hussif?

— The quicker the deef the safter the sapstaff, but the main the mightier the stricker the strait. To the vast go the game! It is the circumconversioning of antelithual paganelles by a huggerknut cramwell energuman, or the caecodedition of an absquelitteris puttagonnianne to the herreraism of a cabotinesque exploser?

— I believe you. Taiptope reelly, O reelly!

— Nautaey, nautaey, we're nowhere without ye! In steam of kavos now arbatos above our hearths doth hum. And Malkos crackles logs of fun while Anglys cheers our ingles. So lent she him ear to burrow his manhood (or so it appierce) and borrow his namas? Suilful eyes and sallowfoul hairweed and the sickly sigh from her gingering mouth like a Dublin bar in the moarning.

— *Primus auriforasti me.*

— The park is gracer than the hole, says she, but shekleton's my fortune?

— Eversought of being artained? You've soft a say with ye, Flatter O'Ford, that, honey, I hurdley chew you.

— Is that answers?

— It am queery!

— The house was Toot and Come-Inn by the bridge called Tiltass, but are you solarly salemly sure, beyond the shatter of the canicular year? *Nascitur ordo seculi numfit.*

— Siriusly and selenely sure behind the shutter. *Securius indicat umbris tellurem.*

— Date as? Your time of immersion? We are still in drought of . . . ?

— Amnis Dominae, Marcus of Corrig. A laughin hunter and Purty Sue.

— And crazyheaded Jorn, the bulweh born?

— Fluteful as his orkan. *Ex ugola lenonem.*

— And Jambs, of Delphin's Bourne or (as olders lay) of Tophat?

— Dawncing the kniejinksky choreopiscopally like an easter sun round the colander, the vice! Taranta boontoday! You should pree him prance the polcat, you whould sniff him wops around, you should hear his piedigrotts schraying as his skimpies skirp a . . .

— Crashedafar Corumbas! A Czardanser indeed! Dervilish glad too. Ortovito semi ricordo. The pantaglionic affection through his blood like a bad influenza in a leap at bounding point?

— Out of Prisky Poppagenua, the palsied old priamite, home from Edwin Hamilton's Christmas pantaloonade, *Oropos Roxy and Pantharhea* at the Gaiety, trippudiating round the aria, with his fifty-two heirs of age! They may reel at his likes but it's Noeh Bonum's shin do.

— And whit what was Lillabil Issabil maideve, maid at?

— Trists and thranes and trinies and traines.

— A take back to the virgin page, darm it!

— Ay, graunt ye.

— The quobus quartet were there too, if I mistake not, as a side-line but, *pace* the contempt of senate, well to the fore, in an amenessy meeting, metandmorefussed to decide whereagainwhen to meet themselves, flopsome and jerksome, lubber and deliric, drinking unsteadily through the Kerry quadrilles and Listowel lancers and mastersinging always with that consecutive fifth of theirs, eh? Like four wise elephants inandouting under a twelve-podestalled table?

— They were simple scandalmongers, that familiar, and all! Nor-mand, Desmond, Osmund and Kenneth. Making mejical history all over the show!

— In sum, some hum? And other marrage feats?

— All our stakes they were astumbling round the ranky roars assumbling when Big Arthur flugged the field at Annie's courting.

— Suddenly some wellfired clay was cast out through the schappsteckers of hoy's house?

— Schottenly there was a hellfire club kicked out through the wasistas of Thereswhere.

— Like Heavystost's envil catacalamitumbling. Three days three times into the Vulcuum?

— Punch!

— Or Noe et Ecclesiastes, nonne?

— Ninny, there is no hay in Eccles's hostel.

— Yet an I saw a sign of him, if you could scrape out his acquinntence? Name or redress him and we'll call it a night!

—.i..'. .o..l.

— You are sure it was not a shuler's shakeup or a plighter's palming or a winker's wake *etcaetera etcaeterorum* you were at?

— Precisely.

— Mayhap. Hora pro Nubis, Thundersday, at A Little Bit Of Heaven Howth, the wife of Deimetuus (D'amn), Earl Adam Fitzadam, of a Tartar (Birtha) or Sackville-Lawry and Morland-West, at the Auspice for the Living, Bonnybrook, by the river and A. Briggs Carlisle, guardian of the birdsmaids and deputiliser for groom. Pontifical mess. Or (soddenly) Schott, furtivfired by the riots. No flies. Agreest?

— Mayhem. Also loans through the post. With or without security. Everywhere. Any amount. Mofsovitz, swampstakers, purely providential.

— Flood's. The pinkman, the squeeze, the pint with the kick. Gaa. And then the punch to Gaelicise it. Fox. The lady with the lamp. The boy in the barleybag. The old man on his ars. Great Scrapp! 'Tis we and you and ye and me and hymns and hurts and heels and shields. The eirest race, the ourest nation, the airest place that erestationed. He was culping for penance while you were ringing his belle. Did the kickee, goodman rued fox, say anything important? Clam or cram, spick or spat?

— No more than Richman's periwhelker.

— Nnn ttt wrd?

— Dmm ttt thg.

— A gael galled by scheme of scorn? Nock?

— Sangnifying nothing. Mock!

— *Fortitudo eius rhodammum tenuit?*

— Five maim! Or something very similar.

— I should like to euphonise that. It sounds an isochronism. Secret speech Hazelton and obviously disemvowelled. But it is good laylaw too. We may take those wellmeant kicks for free granted, though *ultra vires,* void and, in fact, unnecessarily so. Happily you were not quite so successful in the process verbal whereby you would sublimate your blepharospasmockical suppressions, it seems?

— What was that? First I heard about it.

— Were you or were you not? Ask yourself the answer, I'm not giving you a short question. Now, not to mix up, cast your eyes around Capel Court. I want you, witness of this epic struggle, as yours so mine, to reconstruct for us, as briefly as you can, in exactly the same as a mind's eye view, how these funeral games, which have been poring over us through homer's kerryer pidgeons, massacreedoed as the holiname rally round took place.

— Which? Sure I told you that afoul. I was drunk all lost life.

— Well, tell it to me befair, the whole plan of campaign, in that bamboozelem mincethrill voice of yours. Let's have it, christie! The Dublin own, the thrice familiar.

— Ah, sure, I eyewitless foggus. 'Tis all around me bebattersbid hat.

— Ah, go on now, Masta Bones, a gig for a gag, with your impendements and your perroqtriques! Blank memory of hatless darky in blued suit. You were ever the gentle poet, dove from Haywarden. Pitcher cup, patcher cap, pratey man? Be nice about it, Bones Minor! Look chairful! Come, delicacy! Go to the end, thou slackerd! Once upon a grass and a hopping high grass it was.

— Faith, then, Meesta Cheeryman, first he come up, a gag as a gig, badgeler's rake to the town's major from the wesz, MacSmashall Swingy of the Cattelaxes, got up regardless, with a cock on the Kildare side of his Tattersull, in his riddlesneek's ragamufflers and the horrid contrivance as seen above, whisklyng into a bone tolerably delicately, the *Wearing of the Blue,* and taking off his plushkwadded bugsby in his perusual flea and loisy manner, saying good mrowkas to weevilybolly and dragging his feet in the usual course and was ever so terribly naas, really, telling him clean his nagles and fex himself up, Miles, and so on and so fort, and to take the coocoomb to his grizzlies and who done that foxy freak on his bear's hairs like

fire bursting out of the Ump pyre and, half hang me, sirr, if
he wasn't wanting his calicub body back before he'd to take his life
or so save his life. Then, begor, counting as many as eleven to thirty-
two seconds with his pocket browning, like I said, wann swanns
wann, this is my awethorrorty, he kept forecursing hascupth's foul
Fanden, Cogan, for coaccoackey the key of John Dunn's field fore
it was for sent and the way Montague was robbed and wolfling to
know all what went off and who burned the hay, perchance wilt
thoult say, before he'd kill all the kanes and the price of Patsch
Purcell's faketotem, which the man, his plantagonist, up from the
bog of the depths who was raging with the thirst of the sacred
sponge and who, as a mashter of pasht, so far as him was concerned,
was only standing there nonplush to the corner of Turbot Street,
perplexing about a paumpshop and pupparing to spit, wanting to
know whelp the henconvention's compuss memphis he wanted with
him new nothing about.

— A sarsencruxer, like the Nap O' Farrell Patter Tandy moor
and burgess medley? In other words, was that how in the annusual
curse of things, as complement to compliment though, after a manner of men which I must and will say seems extraordinary, their
celicolar subtler angelic warfare or photoplay finister started?

— Truly. That I may never!

— Did one scum then in the auradrama, the deff, after some
clever play in the mud, mention to the other undesirable, a dumm,
during diverse intentional instants, that upon the resume after the
angerus, how for his deal he was a pigheaded Swede and to wend
himself to a medicis?

— To be sore he did, the huggornut! Only it was turniphudded
dunce, I beg your pardon, and he would jokes bowlderblow the
betholder with his black masket off the bawling green.

— Sublime was the warning!

— The author, in fact, was mardred.

— Did he, the first spikesman, do anything to him, the last spokesman, when, after heaving some more smutt and chaff between them,
they rolled togutter into the ditch together? Black Pig's Dyke?

— No, he had his teeth in the back of his head.

— Did Box then try to shine his puss?

— No but Cox did to shin the punman.

— The worsted crying that if never he looked on Leaverholma's
again and the bester huing that he might ever save sunlife?

— Trulytruly Asbestos he ever. And sowasso I never.

— That forte carlysle touch breaking the campdens pianoback.

— Pansh!

— Are you of my meaning that would be going on to about half noon, click o'clock, pip emma, Grinwicker time, by your querqcut quadrant?

— You will be asking me and I wish to higgins you wouldn't. Would it?

— Let it be twelve thirty after a somersautch of the tardest!

— And it was eleven thirsty too befour in soandsuch, reloy on it!

— Tick up on time. Howday you doom? That rising day sinks rosing in a night of nine week's wonder.

— Amties, marcy buckup! The uneven day of the unleventh month of the unevented year. At mart in mass.

— A triduum before Our Larry's own day. By which of your chronos, my man of four watches, larboard, starboard, dog or dath?

— Dunsink, rugby, ballast and ball. You can imagine.

— Language this allsfare for the loathe of Marses ambiviolent about it. Will you swear all the same you saw their shadows a hundred foot later, struggling diabolically over this, that and the other, their virtues *pro* and his principality *con*, near the Ruins, Drogheda Street, and kicking up the devil's own dust for the Milesian wind?

— I will. I did. They were. I swear. Like the heavenly militia. So wreek me Ghyllygully! With my tongue through my toecap on the headlong stone of kismet if so 'tis the will of Whose B. Dunn.

— Weepin Lorcans! They must have put in some wonderful work, ecad, on the quiet like, during this arms' parley, meatierities forces vegateareans. Dost thou not think so?

— Ay.

— The illegallooking range or fender, alias turfing iron, a product of Hostages and Co, Engineers, changed feet several times as briars revalvered during the weaponswap? Piff?

— Puff! Excuse yourself. It was an ersatz lottheringcan.

— They did not know the war was over and were only berebelling or bereppelling one another by chance or necessity with sham bottles, mere and woiney, as betwinst Picturshirts and Scutticules, like their caractacurs in an Irish Ruman to sorowbrate the expeltsion of the Danos? What sayest thou, scusascmerul?

— That's all. For he was heavily upright man, Limba romena in Bucclis tucsada. Farcing gutterish.

— I mean the Morgans and the Dorans, in finnish?

— I know you don't, in Feeney's.

— The mujic of the footure on the barbarihams of the bashed? Co Canniley?

— Da Donnuley.

— Yet this war has meed peace? *In voina viritas.* Ab chaos lex, neat wehr?

— O bella! O pia! O pura! Amem. Handwalled amokst us. Thanksbeer to Balbus!

— All the same you sound it twould clang houlish like Hull hopen for christmians?

— But twill cling hellish like engels opened to neuropeans, if you've sensed, whole the sum. So be vigil!

— And this pattern pootsch punnermine of concoon and proprey went on, hog and minne, a whole whake, your night after larry's night, spittinspite on Dora O'Huggins, ormonde caught butler, the artillery of the O'Hefferns answering the cavalry of the MacClouds, fortey and more fortey, a thousand and one times, according to your cock and a biddy story? Lludillongi, for years and years perhaps?

— That's ri. This is his largos life, this is me timtomtum and this is her two peekweeny ones. From the last finger on the second foot of the fourth man to the first one on the last one of the first. That's right.

— Finny. Vary vary finny!

— It may look funny but fere it is.

— This is not guid enough, Mr Brasslattin. Finging and tonging and winging and ponging! And all your rally and ramp and rant! Didget think I was asleep at the wheel? D'yu mean to tall grand jurors of thathens of tharctic on your oath, me lad, and ask us to believe you, for all you're enduring long terms, with yur last foot foremouthst, that yur moon was shining on the tors and on the cresties and winblowing night after night, for years and years perhaps, after you swearing to it a while back before your Corth examiner, Markwalther, that there was reen in planty all the teem?

— Perhaps so, as you grand duly affirm, Robman Calvinic. I never thought over it, faith. I most certainly think so about it. I hope. Unless it is actionable. It would be a charity for me to think about something which I must on no caste accounts omit, if you ask to me. It was told me as an inspired statement by a friend of myself, in reply to salute, Tarpey, after three o'clock mass, with forty ducks indulgent, that some rain was promised to Mrs Lyons, the invalid of Aunt Tarty Villa, with lots gulp and sousers and likewise he told me, the recusant, after telling mass, with two hundred genuflexions, at the

split hour of blight when bars are keeping so sly, as was what's follows. He is doing a walk, says she, in the feelmick's park, says he,
like a tarrable Turk, says she, letting loose on his nursery and, be-
galla, he meet himself with Mr Michael Clery of a Tuesday who
said Father MacGregor was desperate to the bad place about thass-
bawls and ejaculating about all the stairrods and the catspew
swashing his earwanker and thinconvenience being locked up for
months, owing to being putrenised by stragglers abusing the ap-
paratus, and for Tarpey to pull himself into his soup and fish and to
push on his borrowsaloaner and to go to the tumple like greased
lining and see Father MacGregor and, be Cad, sir, he was to pipe
up and saluate that clergyman and to tell his holiness the whole
goat's throat about the three shillings in the confusional and to say
how Mrs Lyons, the cuptosser, was the infidel who prophessised
to pose three shielings Peter's pelf off her tocher from paraguais and
albs by the yard to Mr Martin Clery for Father Mathew to put up
a midnight mask saints withins of a Thrushday for African man
and to let Brown child do and to leave he Anlone and all the
nuisances committed by soldats and nonbehavers and missbelovers
for N.D. de l'Ecluse to send more heehaw hell's flutes, my prodder
again! And I never brought my cads in togs blanket! Foueh!
— Angly as arrows, but you have right, my celtslinger! Nils, Mugn
and Cannut. Should brothers be for awe then?
— So let use off be octo while oil bike the bil and wheel whang
till wabblin befoul you but mere and mire trullopes will knaver
mate a game on the bibby bobby burns of.
— Quatsch! What hill ar yu fluking about, ye lamelookond fyats!
I'll discipline ye! Will you swear or affirm the day to yur second sight
noo and recant that all yu affirmed to profetised at first sight for his
southerly accent was all paddyflaherty? Will ye, ay or nay?
— Ay say aye. I affirmly swear to it that it rooly and cooly booly-
hooly was with my holyhagionous lips continuously poised upon
the rubricated annuals of saint ulstar.
— That's very guid of ye, R.C.! Maybe yu wouldn't mind talling
us, my labrose lad, how very much bright cabbage or paperming
comfirts d'yu draw for all yur swearin? The spanglers, kiddy?
— Rootha prootha. There you have me! Vurry nothing, O po-
tators, I call it for I might as well tell yous Essexelcy, and I am not
swallowing my air, the Golden Bridge's truth. It amounts to nada
in pounds or pence. Not a glass of Lucan nor as much as the cost
price of a highlandman's trousertree or the three crowns round your

draphole (isn't it dram disgusting?) for the whole dumb plodding thing!

— Come now, Johnny! We weren't born yesterday. *Pro tanto quid retribuamus?* I ask you to say on your scotty pictail you were promised fines times with some staggerjuice or deadhorse, on strip or in larges, at the Raven and Sugarloaf, either Jones's lame or Jamesy's gait, anyhow?

— Bushmillah! Do you think for a moment? Yes, by the way. How very necessarily true! Give me fair play. When?

— At the Dove and Raven tavern, no, ah? To wit your wizzend?

— Water, water, darty water! Up Jubilee sod! Beet peat wheat treat!

— What harm wants but demands it! How would you like to hear yur right name now, Ghazi Power, my tristy minstrel, if yur not freckened of frank comment?

— Not afrightened of Frank Annybody's gaspower or illconditioned ulcers neither.

— Your uncles!

— Your gullet!

— Will you repeat that to me outside, leinconnmuns?

— After you've shouted a few? I will when it suits me, hulstler.

— Guid! We make fight! Three to one! Raddy?

— But no, from exemple, Emania Raffaroo! What do you have? What mean you, august one? Fairplay for Finnians! I will have my humours. Sure, you would not do the cowardly thing and moll me roon? Tell Queen's road I am seilling. Farewell, but whenever! Buy!

— Ef I chuse to put a bullet like yu through the grill for heckling what business is that of yours, yu bullock?

— I don't know, sir. Don't ask me, your honour!

— Gently, gently Northern Ire! Love that red hand! Let me once more. There are sordidly tales within tales, you clearly understand that? Now my other point. Did you know, whether by melanodactylism or purely libationally, that one of these two Crimeans with the fender, the taller man, was accused of a certain offence or of a choice of two serious charges, as skirts were divided on the subject, if you like it better that way? You did, you rogue, you?

— You hear things. Besides (and serially now) bushes have eyes, don't forget. Hah!

— Which moral turpitude would you select of the two, for choice, if you had your way? Playing bull before shebears or the hindlegs off a clotheshorse? Did any orangepeelers or greengoaters appear periodically up your sylvan family tree?

— Buggered if I know! It all depends on how much family silver you want for a nass-and-pair. Hah!

— What do you mean, sir, behind your hah! You don't hah to do thah, you know, snapograph.

— Nothing, sir. Only a bone moving into place. Blotogaff. Hahah!

— Whahat?

— Are you to have all the pleasure quizzing on me? I didn't say it aloud, sir. I have something inside of me talking to myself.

— You're a nice third degree witness, faith! But this is no laughing matter. Do you think we are tonedeafs in our noses to boot? Can you not distinguish the sense, prain, from the sound, bray? You have homosexual catheis of empathy between narcissism of the expert and steatopygic invertedness. Get yourself psychoanolised!

— O, begor, I want no expert nursis symaphy from yours broons quadroons and I can psoakoonaloose myself any time I want (the fog follow you all!) without your interferences or any other pigeon-stealer.

— Sample! Sample!

— Have you ever weflected, wepowtew, that the evil what though it was willed might nevewtheless lead somehow on to good towawd the genewality?

— A pwopwo of haster meets waster and talking of plebiscites by a show of hands, whether declaratory or effective, in all seriousness, has it become to dawn in you yet that the deponent, the man from Saint Yves, may have been (one is reluctant to use the passive voiced) may be been as much sinned against as sinning, for if we look at it verbally perhaps there is no true noun in active nature where every bally being — please read this mufto — is becoming in its owntown eyeballs. Now the long form and the strong form and reform alltogether!

— Hotchkiss Culthur's Everready, one brother to neverreached, well over countless hands, sieur of many winners and losers, groomed by S. Samson and son, bred by dilalahs, will stand at Bay (Dublin) from nun till dan and vites inversion and at Miss or Mrs's MacMannigan's Yard.

— Perhaps you can explain, sagobean? The Mod needs a rebus.

— Pro general continuation and in particular explication to your singular interrogation our asseveralation. Ladiegent, pals will smile but me and Frisky Shorty, my inmate friend, as is uncommon struck

on poplar poetry, and a few fleabesides round at West Pauper
Bosquet, was glad to be back again with the chaps and just arguing
friendlylike at the Doddercan Easehouse having a wee chatty with
our hosty in his comfy estably over the old middlesex party and his
moral turps, meaning flu, pock, pox and mizzles, grip, gripe, gleet
and sprue, caries, rabies, numps and dumps. What me and Frisky
in our concensus and the whole double gigscrew of suscribers, notto
say the burman, having successfully concluded our tour of bibel,
wants to know is thisahere. Supposing, for an ethical fict, him,
which the findings showed, to have taken his epscene licence before
the norsect's divisional respectively as regards them male privates
and or concomitantly with all common or neuter respects to them
public exess females, whereas allbeit really sweet fillies, as was very
properly held by the metropolitan in connection with this regrettable nuisance, touching arbitrary conduct, being in strict contravention of schedule in board of forests and works bylaws regulationing
sparkers' and succers' amusements section of our beloved naturpark
in pursuance of which police agence me and Shorty have approached a reverend gentlman of the name of Mr Coppinger with
reference to a piece of fire fittings as was most obliging, 'pon my
sam, in this matter of his explanations affirmative, negative and
limitative, given to me and Shorty, touching what the good book
says of toooldaisymen, concerning the merits of early bisectualism,
besides him citing from approved lectionary example given by a
valued friend of the name of Mr J. P. Cockshott, reticent of England, as owns a pretty maisonette, *Quis ut Deus,* fronting on to the
Soussex Bluffs as was telling us categoric how Mr Cockshott, as he
had his assignation with, present holder by deedpoll and indenture
of the swearing belt, he tells him hypothetic, the reverend Mr Coppinger, hereckons himself disjunctively with his windwarrd eye up
to a dozen miles of a cunifarm school of herring, passing themselves
supernatently by the Bloater Naze from twelve and them mayriding-
him by the silent hour. Butting, charging, bracing, backing, springing, shrinking, swaying, darting, shooting, bucking and sprinkling
their dossies sodouscheock with the twinx of their taylz. And, reverend, he says, summat problematical, by yon socialist sun, gut me,
but them errings was as gladful as Wissixy kippers could be considering, flipping their little coppingers, pot em, the fresh little
flirties, the dirty little gillybrighteners, pickle their spratties, the little
smolty gallockers, and, reverend, says he, more assertitoff, zwelf me
Zeus, says he, lettin olfac be the extench of the supperfishies, lamme

the curves of their scaligerance and pesk the everurge flossity of
their pectoralium, them little salty populators, says he, most apodic-
tic, as sure as my briam eggs is on cockshot under noose, all them
little upandown dippies they was all of a libidous pickpuckparty
and raid on a wriggolo finsky doodah in testimonials to their early
bisectualism. Such, he says, is how the reverend Coppinger, he vis-
ualises the hidebound homelies of creed crux ethics. Watsch yourself
tillicately every morkning in your bracksullied twilette. The use of
cold water, testificates Dr Rutty, may be warmly recommended for
the sugjugation of cungunitals loosed. Tolloll, schools!

— Tallhell and Barbados wi ye and your Errian coprulation! Pelagiarist! Remonstrant Montgomeryite! Short lives to your relatives!
Y'are absexed, so y'are, with mackerglosia and mickroocyphyllicks.

— Wait now, leixlep! I scent eggoarchicism. I will take you to
task. I don't follow you that far in your otherwise accurate account.
Was it *esox lucius* or *salmo ferax?* You are taxing us into the driven
future, are you not, with this ruttymaid fishery?

— Lalia Lelia Lilia Lulia and lively lovely Lola Montez.

— Gubbernathor! That they say is a fenian on the secret. Named
Parasol Irelly. Spawning ova and fry like a marrye monach all
amanygoround his seven parish churches! And peopling the ribald
baronies with dans, oges and conals!

— Lift it now, Hosty! Hump's your mark! For a runnymede landing! A dondhering vesh vish, *Magnam Carpam,* es hit neat zoo?

— *There's an old psalmsobbing lax salmoner fogeyboren Herrin
Plundehowse.*

*Who went floundering with his boatloads of spermin spunk about.
Leaping freck after every long tom and wet lissy between Howth
and Humbermouth.*

Our Human Conger Eel!

— Help! I can see him in the fishnoo! Up wi'yer whippy! Hold
that lad! Play him, Markandeyn! Bullhead!

— Pull you, sir! Olive quill does it. Longeal of Malin, he'll cry
before he's flayed. And his tear make newisland. Did a rise? Way,
lungfush! The great fin may cumule! Three threeth o'er the wild!
Manu ware!

— He missed her mouth and stood into Dee, Romunculus Remus,
plying the rape, so as now any bompriss's bound to get up her if he
pool her leg and bunk on her butt. No, he skid like a skate
and berthed on her byrnie and never a fear but they'll land him

yet, slitheryscales on liffeybank, times and times and halve a time
with a pillow of sand to polster him.

— Do you say they will?

— I bet you they will.

— Among the shivering sedges so? Weedy waving.

— Or tulipbeds of Rush below.

— Where you take your mugs to wash after dark?

— To my lead, Toomey lout, Tommy lad.

— Besides the bubblye waters of, babblyebubblye waters of?

— Right.

— Grenadiers. And tell me now. Were these anglers or angelers
coexistent and compresent with or without their *tertium quid?*

— *Three in one, one and three.*

Shem and Shaun and the shame that sunders em.

Wisdom's son, folly's brother.

— God bless your ginger, wigglewaggle! That's three slots and
no burners. You're forgetting the jinnyjos for the fayboys. What,
Walker John Referent? Play us your patmost! And unpackyoulloups!

— Naif Cruachan! Woe on woe, says Wardeb Daly. Woman will
water the wild world over. And the maid of the folley will go where
glory. Sure I thought it was larking in the trefoll of the furry glans
with two stripping baremaids, Stilla Underwood and Moth Mac-
Garry, he was, hand to dagger, that time and their mother, a raw-
kneepudsfrowse, I was given to understand, with superflowvius
heirs, begum. There was that one that was always mad gone on
him, her first king of cloves and the most broadcussed man in
Corrack-on-Sharon, County Rosecarmon. Sure she was near
drowned in pondest coldstreams of admiration forherself, as bad
as my Tarpeyan cousin, Vesta Tully, making faces at her bachspilled
likeness in the brook after and cooling herself in the element, she
pleasing it, she praising it, with salices and weidowwehls, all tossed,
as she was, the playactrix, Lough Shieling's love!

— O, add shielsome bridelittle! All of her own! Nircississies are
as the doaters of inversion. Secilas through their laughing classes
becoming poolermates in laker life.

— It seems to same with Iscappellas? Ys? Gotellus! A tickey for
tie taughts!

— Listenest, meme mearest! They were harrowd, those finweeds!
Come, rest in this bosom! So sorry you lost him, poor lamb! Of course
I know you are a viry vikid girl to go in the dreemplace and at that
time of the draym and it was a very wrong thing to do, even under

the dark flush of night, dare all grandpassia! He's gone on his
bombashaw. Through geesing and so pleasing at Strip Teasy up
the stairs. The boys on the corner were talking too. And your soreful
miseries first come on you. Still to forgive it, divine my lickle wiffey,
and everybody knows you do look lovely in your invinsibles, Eulogia,
a perfect apposition with the coldcream, Assoluta, from Boileau's
I always use in the wards after I am burned a rich egg and derive
the greatest benefit, sign of the cause. My, you do! Simply adorable!
Could I but pass my hands some, my hands through, thine hair! So
vickyvicky veritiny! O Fronces, say howdyedo, Dotty! Chic hands.
The way they curve there under nue charmeen cuffs! I am more
divine like that when I've two of everything up to boyproof knicks.
Winning in a way, only my arms are whiter, dear. Blanchemain,
idler. Fairhair, frail one. Listen, meme sweety! O be joyfold! Mirror
do justice, taper of ivory, heart of the conavent, hoops of gold! My
veil will save it undyeing from his ethernal fire! It's meemly us two,
meme idoll. Of course it was downright verry wickred of him, reely
meeting me disguised, Bortolo mio, peerfectly appealling, D.V., with
my lovebirds, my colombinas. Their sinsitives shrinked. Even Netta
and Linda, our seeyu tities and they've sin sumtim, tankus! My rillies
were liebeneaus, my aftscents embre. How me adores eatsother simply (Mon ishebeau! Ma reinebelle!), in his storm collar, as I leaned
yestreen from his muskished labs, even my little pom got excited,
when I turned his head on his same manly bust and kissed him more.
Only he might speak to a person, lord so picious, taking up my worths
ill wrong! May I introduce! This is my futuous, lips and looks love-
last. Still me with you, you poor chilled! Will make it up with
mother Concepcion and a glorious lie between us, sweetness, so as
not a novene in all the convent loretos, not my littlest one of all,
for mercy's sake need ever know, what passed our lips or. Yes sir,
we'll will! Clothea wind! Fee o fie! Covey us niced! Bansh the dread!
Alitten's looking. Low him lovly! Make me feel good in the moon-
time. It will all take bloss as oranged at St Audiens rosan chocolate
chapelry with my diamants blickfeast after at minne owned hos
for all the catclub to go cryzy and Father Blesius Mindelsinn will
be beminding hand. Kyrielle elation! Crystal elation! Kyrielle elation! Elation immanse! Sing to us, sing to us, sing to us! Amam! So
meme nearest, languished hister, be free to me! (I'm fading!) And
listen, you, you beauty, esster, I'll be clue to who knows you, pray
Magda, Marthe with Luz and Joan, while I lie with warm lisp on
the Tolka. (I'm fay!)

— Eusapia! Fais-le, tout-tait! Languishing hysteria? The clou his-
torique? How is this at all? Is dads the thing in such or are tits the
that? Hear we here her first poseproem of suora unto suora? Ali-
cious, twinstreams twinestraines, through alluring glass or alas in
jumboland? Ding dong! Where's your pal in silks alustre? Think
of a maiden, Presentacion. Double her, Annupciacion. Take your
first thoughts away from her, Immacolacion. Knock and it shall ap-
pall unto you! Who shone yet shimmers will be e'er scheining. Cluse
her, voil her, hild her hindly. After liryc and themodius soft aglo
iris of the vals. This young barlady, what, euphemiasly? Is she having an ambidual act herself in apparition with herself as Consuelas
to Sonias may?

— Dang! And tether, a loguy O!

— Dis and dat and dese and dose! Your crackling out of your turn,
my Moonster firefly, like always. And 2 R.N. and Longhorns Connacht, stay off my air! You've grabbed the capital and you've had
the lion's shire since 1542 but there's all the difference in Ireland
between your borderation, my chatty cove, and me. The leinstrel
boy to the wall is gone and there's moreen astoreen for Monn and
Conn. With the tyke's named moke. Doggymens' nimmer win! You
last led the first when we last but we'll first trump your last with a
lasting. Jump the railchairs or take them, as you please, but and,
sir, my queskins first, foxyjack! Ye've as much skullabogue cheek
on you now as would boil a caldron of kalebrose. Did the market
missioners Hayden Wombwell, when given the raspberry, fine more
than sandsteen per cent of chalk in the purity, promptitude and
perfection flour of this raw materialist and less than a seventh pro
mile in his meal? We bright young chaps of the brandnew brain-
trust are briefed here and with maternal sanction compellably em-
panelled at quarter sessions under the six disqualifications for the
uniformication of young persons (Nodding Neutrals) removal act
by Committalman Number Underfifteen to know had the peeress
of generals, who have been getting nose money cheap and stirring
up the public opinion about private balls with their legs, Misses
Mirtha and Merry, the two dreeper's assistents, had they their service books in order and duly signed J. H. North and Company when
discharged from their last situations? Will ye gup and tell the board
in the anterim how, in the name of the three tailors on Tooley Street,
did O'Bejorumsen or Mockmacmahonitch, ex of Butt and Hock-
sett's, violating the bushel standard, come into awful position of
the barrel of bellywash? And why, is it any harm to ask, was this

hackney man in the coombe, a papersalor with a whiteluke to him, Fauxfitzhuorson, collected from Manofisle, carrying his ark, of egg-shaped fuselage and made in Fredborg into the bullgine, across his back when he might have been setting on his jonass inside like a Glassthure cabman? Where were the doughboys, three by nombres, won in ziel, cavehill exers or hearts of steel, Hansen, Morfydd and O'Dyar, V.D., with their glenagearries directing their steps according to the R.U.C's liaison officer, with their trench ulcers open and their hands in their pockets, contrary to military rules, when confronted with his lifesize obstruction? When did he live off rooking the pooro and how did start pfuffpfaffing at his Paterson and Hellicott's? Is it a factual fact, proved up to scabsteethshilt, that this fancydress nordic in shaved lamb breeches, child's kilts, bibby buntings and wellingtons, with club, torc and headdress, preholder of the Bar Ptolomei, is coowner of a hengster's circus near North Great Denmark Street (incidentally, it's the most unjoyable show going the province and I'm taking the youngsters there Saturday first when it's halfprice naturals night to see the fallensickners aping the buckleybackers and the blind to two worlds taking off the deffydowndummies) and the shamshemshowman has been complaining to the police barracks and applying for an order of *certiorari* and crying out something vile about him being molested, after him having triplets, by offers of vacancies from females in this city, neighing after the man and his outstanding attraction ever since they seen his X ray picture turned out in wealthy red in the sabbath sheets? Was it him that suborned that surdumutual son of his, a litterydistributer in Saint Patrick's Lavatory, to turn a Roman and leave the chayr and gout in his bare balbriggans, the sweep, and buy the usual jar of porter at the Morgue and Cruses and set it down before the wife with her fireman's halmet on her, bidding her mine the hoose, the strumpet, while him and his lagenloves were rampaging the roads in all their paroply under the noses of the Heliopolitan constabulary? Can you beat it? Prepare the way! Where's that gendarm auxiliar, arianautic sappertillery, that reported on the whole hoodlum, relying on his morse-erse wordybook and the trunchein up his tail? Roof Seckesign van der Deckel and get her story from him! Recall Sickerson, the lizzyboy! Seckersen, magnon of Errick. Sackerson! Hookup!

— *Day shirker four vanfloats he verdants market.*

High liquor made lust torpid dough hunt her orchid.

— Hunt her orchid! Gob and he found it on her right enough!

With her shoes upon his shoulders, 'twas most trying to beholders when he upped their frullatullepleats with our warning. A disgrace to the homely protestant religion! Bloody old preadamite with his twohandled umberella! Trust me to spy on me own spew!

— Wallpurgies! And it's this's your deified city? Norganson? And it's we's to pray for Bigmesser's conversions? Call Kitty the Beads, the Mandame of Tipknock Castle! Let succuba succumb, the improvable his wealth made possible! He's cookinghagar that rost her prayer to him upon the top of the stairs. She's deep, that one.

— A farternoiser for his tuckish armenities. Ouhr Former who erred in having down to gibbous disdag our darling breed. And then the confisieur for the boob's indulligence. As sunctioned for his salmenbog by the Councillors-om-Trent. Pave Pannem at his gaiter's bronze! Nummer half dreads Log Laughty. Master's gunne he warrs the bedst. I messaged his dilltoyds sausepander mussels on the kisschen table. With my ironing duck through his rollpins of gansyfett, do dodo doughdy dough, till he was braising red in the toastface with lovensoft eyebulbs and his kiddledrum steeming and rattling like the roasties in my mockamill. I awed to have scourched his Abarm's brack for him. For the loaf of Obadiah, take your pastry-art's noas out of me flouer bouckuet! Of the strainger scene you given squeezers to me skillet! As cream of the hearth thou reinethst al-home. His lapper and libbers was glue goulewed as he sizzled there watching me lautterick's pitcher by Wexford-Atelier as Katty and Lanner, the refined souprette, with my bust alla brooche and the padbun under my matelote, showing my jigotty sleeves and all my new toulong touloosies. Whisk! There's me shims and here's me hams and this is me juppettes, gause be the meter! Whisk! What's this? Whisk! And that? He never cotched finer, balay me, at Romiolo Frullini's flea pantamine out of Griddle-the-Sink or Shusies-with-her-Soles-Up or La Sauzerelly, the pucieboots, when I started so hobmop ladlelike, highty tighty, to kick the time off the cluckclock lucklock quamquam camcam potapot panapan kickakickkack. Hair-horehounds, shake up pfortner. Fuddling fun for Fullacan's sake!

— All halt! Sponsor programme and close down. That's enough, genral, of finicking about Finnegan and fiddling with his faddles. A final ballot, guvnor, to remove all doubt. By sylph and salamander and all the trolls and tritons, I mean to top her drive and to tip the tap of this, at last. His thoughts that wouldbe words, his livings that havebeen deeds. And will too, by the holy child of Coole, prima-patriock of the archsee, if I have at first to down every mask in

Trancenania from Terreterry's Hole to Stutterers' Corner to find
that Yokeoff his letter, this Yokan his dahet. Pass the jousters of
the king, the Kovnor-Journal and eirenarch's custos himself no less,
the meg of megs, with the Carrison old gang! Off with your persians!
Search ye the Finn! The sinder's under shriving sheet. Fa Fe Fi
Fo Fum! Ho, croak, evildoer! Arise, sir ghostus! As long as you've
lived there'll be no other. Doff!

— Amtsadam, sir, to you! Eternest cittas, heil! Here we are again!
I am bubub brought up under a camel act of dynasties long out
of print, the first of Shitric Shilkanbeard (or is it Owllaugh Mac-
Auscullpth the Thord?), but, in pontofacts massimust, I am known
throughout the world wherever my good Allenglisches Angleslachsen
is spoken by Sall and Will from Augustanus to Ergastulus, as this
is, whether in Farnum's rath or Condra's ridge or the meadows of
Dalkin or Monkish tunshep, by saints and sinners eyeeye alike as
a cleanliving man and, as a matter of fict, by my halfwife, I think
how our public at large appreciates it most highly from me that
I am as cleanliving as could be and that my game was a fair average
since I perpetually kept my ouija ouija wicket up. On my verawife
I never was nor can afford to be guilty of crim crig con of mal-
feasance trespass against parson with the person of a youthful gigirl
frifrif friend chirped Apples, acted by Miss Dashe, and with Any
of my cousines in Kissilov's Slutsgartern or Gigglotte's Hill, when
I would touch to her dot and feel most greenily of her unripe ones
as it should prove most anniece and far too bahad, nieceless to say,
to my reputation on Babbyl Malket for daughters-in-trade being
lightly clad. Yet, as my acquainters do me the complaisance of appris-
ing me, I should her have awristed under my duskguise of whippers
through toombs and deempeys, lagmen, was she but tinkling of such
a tink. And, as a mere matter of ficfect, I tell of myself how I
popo possess the ripest littlums wifukie around the globelettes globes
upon which she was romping off on Floss Mundai out of haram's
way round Skinner's circusalley first with her consolation prize in
my serial dreams of faire women, Mannequins Passe, with awards
in figure and smile subsections, handicapped by two breasts in opera-
tops, a remarkable little endowment garment. Fastened at various
places. What spurt! I kickkick keenly love such, particularly while
savouring of their flavours at their most perfect best when served
with heliotrope ayelips, as this is, where I do drench my jolly soul
on the pu pure beauty of hers past.

She is my bestpreserved wholewife, sowell her as herafter, in

Evans's eye, with incompatibly the smallest shoenumber outside chinatins. They are jolly dainty, spekin tluly. May we not recommend them? It was my proofpiece from my prenticeserving. And, alas, our private chaplain of Lambeyth and Dolekey, bishopregionary, an always sadfaced man, in his lutestring pewcape with tabinet band, who has visited our various hard hearts and reins by imposition of fufuf fingers, olso haddock's fumb, in that Upper Room can speak loud to you some quite complimentary things about my clean charactering, even when detected in the dark, distressful though such recital prove to me, as this is, when I introduced her (Frankfurters, numborines, why drive fear?) to our fourposter tunies chantreying under Castrucci Sinior and De Mellos, those whapping oldsteirs, with sycamode euphonium in either notation in our altogether cagehaused duckyheim on Goosna Greene, that cabinteeny homesweetened through affection's hoardpayns (First Murkiss, or so they sankeyed. Dodo! O Clearly! And Gregorio at front with Johannes far in back. Aw, aw!), gleeglom there's gnome sweepplaces like theresweep Nowhergs. By whom, as my Kerk Findlater's, ye litel chuch rond ye coner, and K. K. Katakasm enjoineth in the Belief and, as you all know, of a child, dear Humans, one of my life's ambitions of my youngend from an early peepee period while still to hedjeskool, intended for broadchurch, I, being fully alive to it, was parruchially confirmed in Caulofat's bed by our bujibuji beloved curate-author. Michael Engels is your man. Let Michael relay Sutton and tell you people here who have the phoney habit (it was remarketable) in his clairaudience, as this is, as only our own Michael can, when reicherout at superstation, to bring ruptures to our roars how I am amp amp amplify. Hiemlancollin. Pimpim's Ornery forninehalf. Shaun Shemsen saywhen saywhen. Holmstock unsteaden. Livpoomark lloyrge hoggs one four tupps noying. Big Butter Boost! Sorry! Thnkyou! Thatll beall fortody. Cal it off. Godnotch, vryboily. End a muddy crushmess! Abbreciades anew York gustoms. Kyow! Tak.

— Tiktak. Tikkak.

— Awind abuzz awater falling.

— Poor a cowe his jew placator.

— It's the damp damp damp.

— Calm has entered. Big big Calm, announcer. It is most ernst terooly a moresome intartenment. Colt's tooth! I will give tandsel to it. I protest there is luttrelly not one teaspoonspill of evidence at bottomlie to my babad, as you shall see, as this is. Keemun Lap-

sang of first pickings. And I contango can take off my dudud dirty-
nine articles of quoting here in Pynix Park before those in heaven
to provost myself, by gramercy of justness, I mean veryman and
moremon, stiff and staunch for ever, and enter under the advicies
from Misrs Norris, Southby, Yates and Weston, Inc, to their favoured client, into my preprotestant caveat against the pupup publication of libel by any tixtim tipsyllon or tobtomtowley of Keisserse
Lean (a bloweyed lanejoymt, waring lowbelt suit, with knockbrecky
kenees and bullfist rings round him and a fallse roude axehand (he
is cunvesser to Saunter's Nocelettres and the Poe's Toffee's Directory
in his pisness), the best begrudged man in Belgradia who doth not
belease to our paviour) to my nonesuch, that highest personage at
moments holding down the throne. So to speak of beauty scouts
in elegant pursuit of flowers, searchers for tabernacles and the cellu-
loid art! Happen seen sore eynes belived? The caca cad! He walked
by North Strand with his Thom's towel in hand. Snakeeye! Strangler
of sofficated green parrots! I protest it that he is, by my wipehalf.
He was leaving out of my double inns while he was all teppling
over my single ixits. So was keshaned on for his recent behaviour.
Sherlook is lorking for him. Allare beltspanners. Get your air curt!
Shame upon Private M! Shames on his fulsomeness! Shamus on
his atkinscum's lulul lying suulen for an outcast mastiff littered in
blood currish! Eristocras till Hanging Tower! Steck a javelin through
his advowtried heart! Instaunton! Flap, my Larrybird! Dangle, my
highflyer! Jiggety jig my jackadandyline! Let me never see his wadd-
phez again! And mine it was, Barktholed von Hunarig, Soesown
of Furrows (hourspringlike his joussture, immitiate my chry! as urs
now, so yous then!), when to our lot it fell on my poplar Sexsex,
my Sexencentaurnary, whenby Gate of Hal, before his hostel of
the Wodin Man, I hestened to freeholdit op to his Mam his Maman,
Majuscules, His Magnus Maggerstick, first city's leasekuays of this
Nova Tara, our most noble, when hrossbucked on his pricelist
charger, Pferdinamd Allibuster (yeddonot need light oar till Nore-
way for you fanned one o'er every doorway) with my allbum's greet-
hims through this whole of my promises, handshakey congrandyou-
likethems, ecclesency.

Whosaw the jackery dares at handgripper thisa breast? Dose mak-
kers ginger. Some one we was with us all fours. Adversarian! The
spiking Duyvil! First liar in Londsend! Wulv! See you scargore on
that skeepsbrow! And those meisies! Sulken taarts! Man sicker at
I ere bluffet konservative? Shucks! Such ratshause bugsmess so I

cannot barely conceive of! Lowest basemeant in hystry! Ibscenest nansence! Noksagt! Per Peeler and Pawr! The brokerheartened shugon! Hole affair is rotten muckswinish porcupig's draff. Enouch!

— Is that yu, Whitehed?

— Have you headnoise now?

— Give us your mespilt reception, will yous?

— Pass the fish for Christ's sake!

— Old Whitehowth he is speaking again. Ope Eustace tube! Pity poor whiteoath! Dear gone mummeries, goby! Tell the woyld I have lived true thousand hells. Pity, please, lady, for poor O.W. in this profundust snobbing I have caught. Nine dirty years mine age, hairs hoar, mummery failend, snowdrift to my ellpow, deff as Adder. I askt you, dear lady, to judge on my tree by our fruits. I gave you of the tree. I gave two smells, three eats. My freeandies, my celeberrimates: my happy bossoms, my allfalling fruits of my boom. Pity poor Haveth Childers Everywhere with Mudder!

That was Communicator, a former colonel. A disincarnated spirit, called Sebastion, from the Rivera in Januero, (he is not all hear) may fernspreak shortly with messuages from my deadported. Let us cheer him up a little and make an appunkment for a future date. Hello, Commudicate! How's the buttes? Everscepistic! He does not believe in our psychous of the Real Absence, neither miracle wheat nor soulsurgery of P. P. Quemby. He has had some indiejestings, poor thing, for quite a little while, confused by his tonguer of baubble. A way with him! Poor Felix Culapert! Ring his mind, ye staples, (bonze!) in my ould reekeries' ballyheart and in my krumlin and in aroundisements and stremmis! Sacks eleathury! Sacks eleathury! Bam! I deplore over him ruely. Mongrieff! O Hone! Guestermed with the nobelities, to die bronxitic in achershous! So enjoying of old thick whiles, in haute white toff's hoyt of our formed reflections, with stock of eisen all his prop, so buckely hosiered from the Royal Leg, and his puertos mugnum, he would puffout a dhymful bock. And the how he would husband her that verikerfully, his cigare divane! (He would redden her with his vestas, but 'tis naught.) With us his nephos and his neberls, mest incensed and befogged by him and his smoke thereof. But he shall have his glad stein of our zober beerbest in Oscarshal's winetavern. *Buen retiro!* The boyce voyce is still flautish and his mounth still wears that soldier's scarlet though the flaxafloyeds are peppered with salsedine. It is bycause of what he was ascend into his prisonce on account off. I whit it wel. Hence his deepraised words. Some day I may tell of his second storey. Mood! Mood! It looks like someone other bearing my burdens. I cannot let it. Kanes nought.

Well, yeamen, I have bared my whole past, I flatter myself, on both sides. Give me even two months by laxlaw in second division and my first broadcloth is business will be to protest to Recorder at Thing of all Things, or court of Skivinis, with marchants grey, antient and credibel, Zerobubble Barrentone, Jonah Whalley, Determined Codde or Cucumber Upright, my jurats, if it does not occur again. O rhyme us! Haar Faagher, wild heart in Homelan; Harrod's be the naun. Mine kinder come, mine wohl be won. There is nothing like leuther. O Shee! And nosty mens in gladshouses they shad not peggot stones. The elephant's house is his castle. I am here to tell you, indeed to goodness, that, allbe I discountenanced beallpersuasions, in rinunciniation of pomps of heretofore, with a wax too held in hand, I am thorgtfulldt to do dope me of her miscisprinks and by virchow of those filthered Ovocnas presently like Browne umbracing Christina Anya, after the Irishers, to convert me into a selt (but first I must proxy babetise my old antenaughties), when, as Sigismond Stolterforth, with Rabbin Robroost for my auspicer and Leecher Rutty for my lifearst and Lorencz Pattorn (*Ehren til viktrae!*), when I will westerneyes those poor sunuppers and outbreighten their land's eng. A man should stump up and I will pay my pretty decent trade price for my glueglue gluecose, peebles, were it even, as this is, the legal eric for infelicitous conduict (here incloths placefined my pocketanchoredcheck) and, as a matter of fact, I undertake to discontinue entyrely all practices and I deny wholeswiping *in toto* at my own request in all stoytness to have confermentated and confoederated and agreed in times prebellic, when here were waders for the trainsfolk, as it is now nuggently laid to me, with a friend from mine, Mr Billups, pulleter, my quarterbrother, who sometimes he is doing my locum for me on a grubstake and whom I have cleped constoutuent, for so it was felt by me, at goodbuy cootcoops byusucapiture a mouthless niggeress, Blanchette Brewster from Cherna Djamja, Blawlawnd-via-Brigstow, or to illsell my fourth part in her, which although allowed of in Deuterogamy as in several places of Scripture (copyright) and excluded books (they should quite rightly verbanned be), would seem eggseggs excessively haroween to my feelimbs for two punt scotch, one pollard and a crockard or three pipples on the bitch. Thou, Frick's Flame, Uden Sulfer, who strikest only on the marryd bokks, enquick me if so be I did cophetuise milady's maid! In spect

of her beavers she is a womanly and sacret. Such wear a frillick
for my comic strip, Mons Meg's Monthly, comes out aich Fanagan's
Weck, to bray at by clownsillies in Donkeybrook Fair. It would
lackin mackin Hodder's and Cocker's erithmatic. The unpurdonable
preempson of all of her of yourn, by Juno Moneta! If she, irished
Marryonn Teheresiann, has been disposed of for her consideration,
I, Ledwidge Salvatorious, am tradefully unintiristid. And if she is
still further talc slopping over her cocoa contours, I hwat mick an-
gars, am strongly of opinion why I should not be. Inprobable! I
do not credit one word of it from such and suchess mistraversers.
Just feathers! Nanenities! Or to have ochtroyed to resolde or borrough
by exchange same super melkkaart, means help; best Brixton high
yellow, no outings: cent for cent on Auction's Bridge. 'Twere a hon-
nibel crudelty wert so tentement to their naktlives and scatab orgias
we devour about in the mightyevil roohms of encient cartage. Utterly
improperable! Not for old Crusos or white soul of gold! A pipple
on the panis, two claps on the cansill, or three pock pocks cassey
knocked on the postern! Not for one testey tickey culprik's coynds
ore for all ecus in cunziehowffse! So hemp me Cash! I meanit.

My herrings! The surdity of it! Amean to say. Her bare idears,
it is choochoo chucklesome. Absurd bargain, mum, will call. One
line with! One line, with with! Will ate everadayde saumone like
a boyne alive O. The tew cherripickers, with their Catheringnettes,
Lizzy and Lissy Mycock, from Street Fleshshambles, were they moon
at aube with hespermun and I their covin guardient, I would not
know to contact such gretched youngsteys in my ways from Had-
dem or any suistersees or heiresses of theirn, claiming by, through,
or under them. Ous of their freiung pfann into myne foyer. Her
is one which rassembled to mein enormally. The man what shocked
his shanks at contey Carlow's. He is Deucollion. Each habe goheerd,
uptaking you are innersence, but we sen you meet sose infance.
Deucollion! Odor. Evilling chimbes is smutsick rivulverblott but thee
hard casted thereass pigstenes upann Congan's shootsmen in Schot-
tenhof, ekeascent? Igen Deucollion! I liked his Gothamm chick!
Stuttertub! What a shrubbery trick to play! I will put my oath-
head unner my whitepot for ransom of beeves and will stand me
where I stood mine in all free heat between Pelagios and little
Chistayas by Roderick's our mostmonolith, after my both earstoear
and brebreeches buybibles and, minhatton, testify to my unclothed
virtue by the longstone erectheion of our allfirst manhere. I should
tell you that honestly, on my honour of a Nearwicked, I always

think in a wordworth's of that primed favourite continental poet,
Daunty, Gouty and Shopkeeper, A. G., whom the generality
admoyers in this that is and that this is to come. Like as my palmer's
past policy I have had my best master's lessons, as the public he
knows, and do you know, homesters, I honestly think, if I have
failed lamentably by accident benefits though shintoed, spitefired,
perplagued and cramkrieged, I am doing my dids bits and have made
of my prudentials good. I have been told I own stolemines or something of that sorth in the sooth of Spainien. Hohohoho! Have I
said ogso how I abhor myself vastly (truth to tell) and do repent
to my netherheart of suntry clothing? The amusin part is, I will
say, hotelmen, that since I, over the deep drowner Athacleeath to
seek again Irrlanding, shamed in mind, with three plunges of my
ruddertail, yet not a bottlenim, vanced imperial standard by weapon-
right and platzed mine residenze, taking bourd and burgage under
starrymisty and ran and operated my brixtol selection here at tholl-
stall, for mean straits male with evorage fimmel, in commune
soccage among strange and enemy, among these plotlets, in Poplins-
town, alore Fort Dunlip, then-on-sea, hole of Serbonian bog,
now city of magnificent distances, goodwalldabout, with talus and
counterscarp and pale of palisades, upon martiell siegewin, with
Abbot Warre to blesse, on yon slauchterday of cleantarriffs, in that
year which I have called myriabellous, and overdrave these marken
(the soord on Whencehislaws was mine and mine the prussing
stock of Allbrecht the Bearn), under patroonshaap of our good king-
sinnturns, T. R. H. Urban First and Champaign Chollyman and
Hungry the Loaved and Hangry the Hathed, here where my tenen-
ure of office and my toils of domestication first began, with weight of
woman my skat and skuld but Flukie of the Ravens as my sure
piloter, famine with Englisch sweat and oppedemics, the twotoothed
dragon worms with allsort serpents, has compolitely seceded from
this landleague of many nations and open and notorious naughty
livers are found not on our rolls. This seat of our city it is of all
sides pleasant, comfortable and wholesome. If you would traverse
hills, they are not far off. If champain land, it lieth of all parts.
If you would be delited with fresh water, the famous river, called
of Ptolemy the Libnia Labia, runneth fast by. If you will take the
view of the sea, it is at hand. Give heed!

— *Do Drumcollogher whatever you do!*
— *Visitez Drumcollogher-la-Belle!*
— *Be suke and sie so ersed Drumcollogher!*

— *Vedi Drumcollogher e poi Moonis.*

— Things are not as they were. Let me briefly survey. Pro clam
a shun! Pip! Peep! Pipitch! Ubipop jay piped, ibipep goes the whistle. Here Tyeburn throttled, massed murmars march: where the bus
stops there shop I: here which ye see, yea reste. On me, your sleeping giant. Estoesto! Estote sunto! From the hold of my capt in altitude
till the mortification that's my fate. The end of aldest mosest ist
the beginning of all thisorder so the last of their hansbailis shall
the first in our sheriffsby. New highs for all! Redu Negru may be
black in tawn but under them lintels are staying my horneymen
meet each his mansiemagd. For peers and gints, quaysirs and galley-
liers, fresk letties from the say and stale headygabblers, gaingangers
and dudder wagoners, pullars off societies and pushers on rothmere's
homes. Obeyance from the townsmen spills felixity by the toun.
Our bourse and politicoecomedy are in safe with good Jock Shep-
herd, our lives are on sure in sorting with Jonathans, wild and great.
Been so free! Thank you, besters! Hattentats have mindered. Blau-
blaze devilbobs have gone from the mode and hairtrigger nicks are
quite out of time now. Thuggeries are reere as glovars' metins, lepers
lack, ignerants show beneath suspicion like the bitterhalves of escul-
apuloids. In midday's mallsight let Miledd discurverself. Me ludd
in her hide park seek Minuinette. All is waldy bonums. Blownose
aerios we luft to you! Firebugs, good blazes! Lubbers, kepp your
poudies drier! Seamen, we segn your skivs and wives! Seven ills
so barely as centripunts havd I habt, seaventy seavens for circum-
ference inkeptive are your hill prospect. Braid Blackfordrock, the
Calton, the Liberton, Craig and Lockhart's, A. Costofino, R. Thurs-
itt. The chort of Nicholas Within was my guide and I raised a
dome on the wherewithouts of Michan: by awful tors my wellworth
building sprang sky spearing spires, cloud cupoled campaniles: further this. By fineounce and imposts I got and grew and by gross-
scruple gat I grown outreachesly: murage and lestage were my mains
for Ouerlord's tithing and my drains for render and prender the
doles and the tribute: I was merely out of my mint with all the
percussors on my braincap till I struck for myself and muched
morely by token: to Sirrherr of Gambleden ruddy money, to Madame of Pitymount I loue yous. Paybads floriners moved in hughe-
knots against us and I matt them, pepst to papst, barthelemew:
milreys (mark!) onfell, and (Luc!) I arose Daniel in Leonden.
Bulafests onvied me, Corkcuttas graatched. Atabey! I braved Brien
Berueme to berow him against the Loughlins, all her tolkies shrak-

ing: Fugabollags! Lusqu'au bout! If they had ire back of eyeball
they got danage on front tooth: theres were revelries at ridottos,
here was rivalry in redoubt: I wegschicked Duke Wellinghof to
reshockle Roy Shackleton: Walhalloo, Walhalloo, Walhalloo, mourn
in plein! Under law's marshall and warschouw did I thole till lead's
plumbate, ping on pang, reliefed me. I made praharfeast upon
acorpolous and fastbroke down in Neederthorpe. I let faireviews in
on slobodens but ranked rothgardes round wrathmindsers: I bat-
handbaddend on mendicity and I corocured off the unoculated. Who
can tell their tale whom I filled ad liptum on the plain of Soulsbury?
With three hunkered peepers and twa and twas! For sleeking beauties I spinned their nightinveils, to slumbred beast I tummed the
thief air. Round the musky moved a murmel but mewses whin-
ninaird and belluas zoomed: tendulcis tunes like water parted fluted
up from the westinders while from gorges in the east came the strife
of ourangoontangues. All in my thicville Escuterre ofen was thorough
fear but in the meckling of my burgh Belvaros was the site forbed:
tuberclerosies I reized spudfully from the murphyplantz Hawkinsonia
and berriberries from the pletoras of the Irish shou. I heard my
libertilands making free through their curraghcoombs, my trueblues
hurusalaming before Wailingtone's Wall: I richmounded the raine-
lag in my bathtub of roundwood and conveyed it with cheers and
cables, roaring mighty shouts, through my longertubes of elm: out
of fundness for the outozone I carried them amd curried them in
my Putzemdown cars to my Kommeandine hotels: I made sprouts
fontaneously from Philuppe Sobriety in the coupe that's cheyned
for noon inebriates: when they weaned weary of that bibbing I
made infusion more infused: sowerpacers of the vinegarth, obtem-
perate unto me! When you think me in my coppeecuffs look in
ware would you meckamockame, as you pay in caabman's sheltar
tot the ites like you corss the tees. Wherefore watch ye well! For,
while I oplooked the first of Janus's straight, I downsaw the last
of Christmas steps: syndic podestril and on the rates, I for indigent
and intendente: in Forum Foster I demosthrenated my folksfiend-
ship, enmy pupuls felt my burk was no worse than their brite:
Sapphrageta and Consciencia were undecidedly attached to me but
the maugher machrees and the auntieparthenopes my schwalby words
with litted spongelets set their soakye pokeys and botchbons afume:
Fletcher-Flemmings, elisaboth, how interquackeringly they rogated
me, their golden one, I inhesitant made replique: Mesdememdes
to leursieuresponsor: and who in hillsaide, don't you let flyfire till

you see their whites of the bunkers' eyes! Mr Answers: Brimgem
young, bringem young, bringem young!: in my bethel of Solyman's
I accouched their rotundaties and I turnkeyed most insultantly over
raped lutetias in the lock: I gave bax of biscums to the jacobeaters
and pottage bakes to the esausted; I dehlivered them with freak-
andesias by the constant droppings from my smalls instalmonths
while I titfortotalled up their farinadays for them on my slataper's
slate with my chandner's chauk: I jaunted on my jingelbrett rapt
in neckloth and sashes, and I beggered about the amnibushes like
belly in a bowle. In the humanity of my heart I sent out heywey-
women to refresh the ballwearied and then, doubling megalopolitan
poleetness, my great great greatest of these charities, devaleurised
the base fellows for the curtailment of their lower man: with a
slog to square leg I sent my boundary to Botany Bay and I ran
up a score and four of mes while the Yanks were huckling the
Empire: I have been reciping om omominous letters and widely-
signed petitions full of pieces of pottery about my monumentalness
as a thingabolls and I have been inchanting causeries to the feshest
cheoilboys so that they are allcalling on me for the song of a birtch:
the more secretely bi built, the more openly palastered. Attent! Couch
hear! I have becket my vonderbilt hutch in sunsmidnought and at
morningrise was encampassed of mushroofs. Rest and bethinkful,
with licence, thanks. I considered the lilies on the veldt and unto
Balkis did I disclothe mine glory. And this. This missy, my taughters,
and these man, my son, from my fief of the villa of the Ostmanorum
to Thorstan's, *recte* Thomars Sraid, and from Huggin Pleaze to William Inglis his house, that man de Loundres, in all their barony
of Saltus, bonders and foeburghers, helots and zelots, strutting oges
and swaggering macks, the darsy jeamses, the drury joneses, red-
maids and bleucotts, in hommage all and felony, all who have received tickets, fair home overcrowded, tidy but very little furniture,
respectable, whole family attends daily mass and is dead sick of bread
and butter, sometime in the militia, mentally strained from reading work on German physics, shares closet with eight other dwellings,
more than respectable, getting comfortable parish relief, wageearner
freshly shaven from prison, highly respectable, planning new departure in Mountgomery cyclefinishing, eldest son will not serve but
peruses Big-man-up-in-the-Sky scraps, anoopanadoon lacking back-
way, quasi respectable, pays ragman in bones for faded windowcur-
tains, staircase continually lit up with guests, particularly respectable,
house lost in dirt and blocked with refuse, getting on like Roe's

distillery on fire, slovenly wife active with the jug, in business for himself, has a tenth illegitimate coming, partly respectable, following correspondence courses, chucked work over row, both cheeks kissed at levee by late marquess of Zetland, sharing closet which is profusely written over with eleven other subscribers, once respectable, open hallway pungent of Baltic dishes, bangs kept woman's head against wall thereby disturbing neighbours, private chapel occupies return landing, removal every other quarter day, case one of peculiar hopelessness, most respectable, nightsoil has to be removed through snoring household, eccentric naval officer not quite steady enjoys weekly churchwarden and laugh while reading foreign pictorials on clumpstump before door, known as the trap, widow rheumatic and chars, haunted, condemned and execrated, of dubious respectability, tools too costly pledged or uninsured, reformed philanthropist whenever feasible takes advantage of unfortunates against dilapidating ashpits, serious student is eating his last dinners, floor dangerous for unaccompanied old clergymen, thoroughly respectable, many uncut pious books in evidence, nearest watertap two hundred yards' run away, fowl and bottled gooseberry frequently on table, man has not had boots off for twelve months, infant being taught to hammer flat piano, outwardly respectable, sometimes hears from titled connection, one foot of dust between banister and cracked wall, wife cleans stools, eminently respectable, ottawark and regular loafer, should be operated would she consent, deplorable rent in roof, claret cellar cobwebbed since the pontificate of Leo, wears drill trousers and collects rare buddhas, underages very treacly and verminous have to be separated, sits up with fevercases for one and threepence, owns two terraces (back to back breeze), respectable in every way, harmless imbecile supposingly weakminded, a sausage every Sunday, has a staff of eight servants, outlook marred by ne'er-do-wells using the laneway, lieabed sons go out with sisters immediately after dark, has never seen the sea, travels always with her eleven trunks of clothing, starving cat left in disgust, the pink of respectability, resting after colonial service, labours at plant, the despair of his many benefactresses, calories exclusively from Rowntrees and dumplings, one bar of sunlight does them all january and half february, the V. de V's (animal diet) live in fivestoried semidetached but rarely pay tradesmen, went security for friend who absconded, shares same closet with fourteen similar cottages and an illfamed lodginghouse, more respectable than some, teawidow pension but held to purchase, inherited silk hat from father-in-law, head of domestic economy never mentioned, queery how they live, reputed to procure, last four occupants carried out, mental companionship with mates only, respectability unsuccessfully aimed at, copious holes emitting mice, decoration from Uganda chief in locked ivory casket, grandmother has advanced alcoholic amblyopia, the terror of Goodmen's Field, and respected and respectable, as respectable as respectable can respectably be, though their orable amission were the herrors I could have expected, all, let them all come, they are my villeins, with chartularies I have talledged them. Wherfor I will and firmly command, as I willed and firmly commanded, upon my royal word and cause the great seal now to be affixed, that from the farthest of the farther of their fathers to their children's children's children they do inhabit it and hold it for me unencumbered and my heirs, firmly and quietly, amply and honestly, and with all the liberties and free customs which the men of Tolbris, a city of Tolbris, have at Tolbris, in the county of their city and through whole my land. Hereto my vouchers, knive and snuffbuchs. Fee for farm. Enwreak us wrecks.

Struggling forlongs I have livramentoed, milles on milles of mancipelles. Lo, I have looked upon my pumpadears in their easancies and my drummers have tattled tall tales of me in the land: in morgenattics litt I hope, in seralcellars louched I bleakmealers: on my siege of my mighty I was parciful of my subject but in street wauks that are darkest I debelledem superb: I deemed the drugtails in my pettycourts and domstered dustyfeets in my husinclose: at Guy's they were swathed, at Foulke's slashed, the game for a Gomez, the loy for a lynch: if I was magmonimoss as staidy lavgiver I revolucanized by my eructions: the hye and bye wayseeds I scattered em, in my graben fields sew sowage I gathered em: in Sheridan's Circle my wits repose, in black pitts of the pestered Lenfant he is dummed. (Hearts of Oak, may ye root to piece! Rechabites obstain! Clayed sheets, pineshrouded, wake not, walk not! Sigh lento, Morgh!) *Quo warranto* has his greats my soliven and puissant lord V. king regards for me and he has given to me my necknamesh (flister it!) which is second fiddler to nomen. These be my genteelician arms. At the crest, two young frish, etoiled, flappant, devoiled of their habiliments, vested sable, withdrewers argent. For the boss a coleopter, pondant, partifesswise, blazoned sinister, at the slough, proper. In the lower field a terce of lanciers, shaking unsheathed shafts, their arms crossed in saltire, embusked, sinople. Motto, in letters portent: *Hery Crass Evohodie.* Idle were it, repassing from elserground to the elder disposition, to inquire whether I, dragged-asunder, be the forced generation of group marriage, holocryptogam, of my essenes, or carried of cloud from land of locust, in ouzel galley borne, I, huddled til summone be the massproduct of teamwork, three surtouts wripped up in itchother's, two twin pritticoaxes lived as one, troubled in trine or dubildin too, for abram nude be I or roberoyed with the faineans, of Feejeean grafted ape on merfish, surrounded by obscurity, by my virtues of creation and by boon of promise, by my natural born freeman's journeymanright and my otherchurch's inher light, in so and such a manner as me it so besitteth, most surely I pretend and reclam to opt for simultaneous. Till daybowbreak and showshadows flee. Thus be hek. Verily! Verily! Time, place!

— What is your numb? Bun!

— Who gave you that numb? Poo!

— Have you put in all your sparepennies? I'm listening. Sree!

— Keep clear of propennies! Fore!

— Mr Televox, Mrs Taubiestimm and invisible friends! I maymay mean to say. Annoyin part of it was, had faithful Fulvia, following the wiening courses of this world, turned her back on her ways to gon on uphills upon search of louvers, brunette men of Earalend, Chief North Paw and Chief Goes in Black Water and Chief Brown Pool and Chief Night Cloud by the Deeps, or again had Fluvia, amber whitch she was, left her chivily crookcrook crocus bed at the bare suggestions of some prolling bywaymen from Moabit who could have abused of her, the foxrogues, there might accrue advantage to ask wher in pellmell her deceivers sinned. Yet know it was vastly otherwise which I have heard it by mmummy goods waif, as I, chiefly endmost hartyly aver, for Fulvia Fluvia, iddle woman to the plusneeborn, ever did ensue tillstead the things that pertained unto fairnesse, this wharom I am fawned on, that which was loost. Even so, for I waged love on her: and spoiled her undines. And she wept: O my lors!

— Till we meet!

— Ere we part!

— Tollollall!

— This time a hundred years!

— But I was firm with her. And I did take the reached of my delights, my jealousy, ymashkt, beyashmakt, earswathed, snout-snooded, and did raft her flumingworthily and did leftlead her overland the pace, from lacksleap up to liffsloup, tiding down, as portreeve

should, whimpering by Kevin's creek and Hurdlesford and Gardener's Mall, long riverside drive, embankment large, to Ringsend
Flott and Ferry, where she began to bump a little bit, my dart
to throw: and there, by wavebrink, on strond of south, with mace
to masthigh, taillas Cowhowling, quailless Highjakes, did I upreized
my magicianer's puntpole, the tridont sired a tritan stock, farruler,
and I bade those polyfizzyboisterous seas to retire with hemselves
from os (rookwards, thou seasea stamoror!) and I abridged with
domfine norsemanship till I had done abate her maidan race, my
baresark bride, and knew her fleshly when with all my bawdy did
I her whorship, min bryllupswibe: Heaven, he hallthundered; Hey-
days, he flung blissforhers. And I cast my tenspan joys on her,
arsched overtupped, from bank of call to echobank, by dint of strong-
bow (Galata! Galata!) so streng we were in one, malestream in
shegulf: and to ringstresse I thumbed her with iern of Erin and
tradesmanmarked her lieflang mine for all and singular, iday, igone,
imorgans, and for ervigheds: base your peak, you! you, strike your
flag!: (what screech of shippings! what low of dampfbulls!): from
Livland, hoks zivios, from Lettland, skall vives! With Impress of
Asias and Queen Columbia for her pairanymphs and the singing
sands for herbrides' music: goosegaze annoynted uns, canailles
canzoned and me to she her shyblumes lifted: and I pudd a name
and wedlock boltoned round her the which to carry till her grave,
my durdin dearly, Appia Lippia Pluviabilla, whiles I herr lifer amstell
and been: I chained her chastemate to grippe fiuming snugglers,
her chambrett I bestank so to spunish furiosos: I was her hochsized,
her cleavunto, her everest, she was my annie, my lauralad, my
pisoved: who cut her ribbons when nought my prowes? who ex-
poused that havenliness to beachalured ankerrides when not I, freip-
forter?: in trinity huts they met my dame, pick of their poke for
me: when I foregather 'twas my sumbad, if I farseeker itch my
list: had I not workit in my cattagut with dogshunds' crotts to clene
and had I not gifted of my coataways, constantonoble's aim: and,
fortiffed by my right as man of capitol, I did umgyrdle her about,
my vermincelly vinagerette, with all loving kindness as far as in
man's might it lay and enfranchised her to liberties of fringes: and
I gave until my lilienyounger turkeythighs soft goods and hardware
(catalogue, *passim*) and ladderproof hosiery lines (see stockinger's
raiment), cocquette coiffs (see Agnes' hats) and peningsworths of
the best taste of knaggs of jets and silvered waterroses and geegaws
of my pretty novelties and wispywaspy frocks of redferns and laural-

worths, trancepearances such as women cattle bare and peltries piled, the peak of Pim's and Slyne's and Sparrow's, loomends day lumine-used luxories on looks, *La Primamère, Pyrrha Pyrrhine, Or de Reine-beau, Sourire d'Hiver* and a crinoline, wide a shire, and pattens for her trilibies that know she might the tortuours of the boots and bedes of wampun with to toy and a murcery glaze of shard to mir-row, for all daintiness by me and theetime, the cupandnaggin hour: and I wound around my swanchen's neckplace a school of shells of moyles marine to swing their saysangs in her silents: and, upping her at king's count, her aldritch cry oloss unheading, what though exceeding bitter, I pierced her beak with order of the Danabrog (Cunnig's great! Soll leve! Soll leve!): with mare's greese cressets at Leonard's and Dunphy's and Madonna lanthorns before quinta-casas and tallonkindles spearhead syngeing nickendbookers and mhutton lightburnes dipdippingdownes in blackholes, the tapers of the topers and his buntingpall at hoist: for days there was no night for nights were days and our folk had rest from Blackheathen and the pagans from the prince of pacis: what was trembling sod quaked no more, what were frozen loins were stirred and lived: gone the septuor, dark deadly dismal doleful desolate dreadful desperate, no more the tolvmaans, bloody gloomy hideous fearful furious alarm-ing terrible mournful sorrowful frightful appalling: peace, perfect peace: and I hung up at Yule my duindleeng lunas, helphelped of Kettil Flashnose, for the souperhore of my frigid one, *coloumba mea, frimosa mea,* in Wastewindy tarred strate and Elgin's marble halles lamping limp from black to block, through all Livania's volted ampire, from anodes to cathodes and from the topazolites of Mourne, Wykinloeflare, by Arklow's sapphire siomen's lure and Wexterford's hook and crook lights to the polders of Hy Kinsella: avenyue ceen my peurls ahumming, the crown to my estuarine munipicence?: three firths of the sea I swept with draughtness and all ennempties I bot-tled em up in bellomport: when I stabmarooned jack and maturin I was a bad boy's bogey but it was when I went on to sankt pioters-barq that they gave my devil his dues: what is seizer can hack in the old wold a sawyer may hew in the green: on the island of Breasil the wildth of me perished and I took my plowshure sadly, feeling pity for me sored: where bold O'Connee weds on Alta Mahar, the tawny sprawling beside that silver burn, I sate me and settled with the little crither of my hearth: her intellects I charmed with I calle them utile thoughts, her turlyhyde I plumped with potatums for amiens pease in plenty: my biblous beadells shewed her triumphs of craftygild pageantries, loftust Adam, duffed our cousterclother, Conn and Owel with cortoppled baskib, Sire Noeh Guinnass, exposant of his bargeness and Lord Joe Starr to hump the body of the camell: I screwed the Emperor down with ninepins gaelic with sixpennyhapennies for his hanger on: my worthies were bissed and trissed from Joshua to Godfrey but my *processus prophetarum* they would have plauded to perpetuation. Moral: book to besure, see press.

— He's not all buum and bully.

— But his members handly food him.

— Steving's grain for's greet collegtium.

— The S. S. Paudraic's in the harbour.

— And after these things, I fed her, my carlen, my barelean linsteer, upon spiceries for her garbage breath, italics of knobby lauch and the rich morsel of the marrolebone and shains of garleeks and swinespepper and gothakrauts and pinkee dillisks, primes of meshallehs and subleties in jellywork, come the feast of Saint Pancreas, and shortcake nutrients for Paas and Pingster's pudding, bready and nutalled and potted fleshmeats from store dampkookin, and the drugs of Kafa and Jelupa and shallots out of Ascalon, feeding her food convenient herfor, to pass them into earth: and to my saffronbreathing mongoloid, the skinsyg, I gave Biorwik's powlver and Uliv's oils, unguents of cuticure, for the swarthy searchall's face on her, with handewers and groinscrubbers and a carrycam to teaze her tussy out, the brown but combly, a mopsa's broom to duist her sate, and clubmoss and wolvesfoot for her more moister wards (amazing efficiencies!): and, my shopsoiled doveling, when weeks of kindness kinly civicised, in our saloons esquirial, with fineglas bowbays, draped embrasures and giltedged librariums, I did devise my telltale sports at evenbread to wring her withers limberly, wheatears, slapbang, drapier-cut-dean, bray, map, spinado and ranter-go-round: we had our lewd mayers and our lairdie meiresses kiotowing and smuling fullface on us out of their framous latenesses, oil-clothed over for cohabitation and allpointed by Hind: Tamlane the Cussacke, Dirk Wettingstone, Pieter Stuyvesant, Outlawrie O'Niell, Mrs Currens, Mrs Reyson-Figgis, Mrs Dattery, and Mrs Pruny-Quetch: in hym we trust, footwash and sects principles, apply to overseer, Amos five six: she had dabblingtime for exhibiting her grace of aljambras and duncingk the bloodanoobs in her vauxhalls while I, dizzed and dazed by the lumpty thumpty of our interloopings, fell clocksure off my ballast: in our windtor palast

it vampared for elenders, we lubded Sur Gudd for the sleep
and the ghoasts: she chauffed her fuesies at my Wigan's jewels
while she skalded her mermeries on my Snorryson's Sagos: in
paycook's thronsaale she domineered, lecking icies off the dormer
panes all admired her in camises: on Rideau Row Duanna dwells,
you merk well what you see: let wellth were I our pantocreator
would theirs be tights for the gods: in littleritt reddinghats and
cindery yellows and tinsel and glitter and bibs under hoods: I made
nusance of many well pressed champdamors and peddled freely in
the scrub: I foredreamed for thee and more than fullmaked: I pre-
vened for thee in the haunts that joybelled frail light-a-leaves for
sturdy traemen: *pelves ad hombres sumus*: I said to the shiftless
prostitute; let me be your fodder; and to rodies and prater brothers;
Chau, Camerade!: evangel of good tidings, omnient as the Healer's
word, for the lost, loathsome and whomsoever will: who, in regi-
mentation through liberal donation in coordination for organisation
of their installation and augmentation plus some annexation and
amplification without precipitation towards the culmination in lati-
fication of what was formerly their utter privation, competence,
cheerfulness, usefulness and the meed, shall, in their second adams,
all be made alive: my tow tugs steered down canal grand, my light-
ers lay longside on Regalia Water. And I built in *Urbs in Rure*,
for minne elskede, my shiny brows, under astrolobe from my up-
servatory, an erdcloset with showne ejector wherewithin to be squat-
quit in most covenience from her sabbath needs, when open noise
should stilled be: did not I festfix with mortarboard my unniver-
siries, wholly rational and gottalike, sophister agen sorefister, life
sizars all?: was I not rosetted on two stellas of little egypt? had not
I rockcut readers, hieros, gregos and democriticos?: triscastellated,
bimedallised: and by my sevendialled changing charties Hibernska
Ulitzas made not I to pass through twelve Threadneedles and
Newgade and Vicus Veneris to cooinsight?: my camels' walk, kolossa
kolossa! no porte sublimer benared my ghates: Oi polled ye many
but my fews were chousen (Voter, voter, early voter, he was never
too oft for old Sarum): terminals four my staties were, the Geenar,
the Greasouwea, the Debwickweck, the Mifgreawis. And I sept up
twinminsters, the pro and the con, my stavekirks wove so norcely
of peeled wands and attachatouchy floodmud, now all loosebrick
and stonefest, freely masoned, arked for covennanters and shinners'
rifuge: descent from above on us, Hagiasofia of Astralia, our orisons thy nave and absedes, our aeone tone aeones thy studvaast

vault; Hams, circuitise! Shemites, retrace!: horns, hush! no barkeys!
hereround is't holied!: all truanttrulls made I comepull, all rubbel-
ing gnomes I pushed, gowgow: Cassels, Redmond, Gandon, Deane,
Shepperd, Smyth, Neville, Heaton, Stoney, Foley, Farrell, Vnost with
Thorneycroft and Hogan too: sprids serve me! gobelins guard!:
tect my tileries (O tribes! O gentes!), keep my keep, the peace of
my four great ways: oathiose infernals to Booth Salvation, arcane
celestials to Sweatenburgs Welhell! My seven wynds I trailed to
maze her and ever a wynd had saving closes and all these closes
flagged with the gust, hoops for her, hatsoff for him and ruffles
through Neeblow's garding: and that was why Blabus was razing
his wall and eltering the suzannes of his nighboors: and thirdly,
for ewigs, I did reform and restore for my smuggy piggiesknees,
my sweet coolocked, my auburn coyquailing one, her paddypalace
on the crossknoll with massgo bell, sixton clashcloshant, duominous
and muezzatinties to commind the fitful: doom adimdim adoom adi-
madim: and the oragel of the lauds to tellforth's glory: and added
thereunto a shallow laver to slub out her hellfire and posied windows for her oriel house: gospelly pewmillieu, christous pewmillieu:
zackbutts babazounded, ollguns tararulled: and she sass her nach,
chillybombom and forty bonnets, upon the altarstane. May all have
mossyhonours!
— Hoke!
— Hoke!
— Hoke!
— Hoke!
— And wholehail, snaeffell, dreardrizzle or sleetshowers of blessing,
where it froze in chalix eller swum in the vestry, with fairskin book
and ruling rod, vein of my vergin page, her chastener ever I did
learn my little ana countrymouse in alphabeater cameltemper, from
alderbirk to tannenyou, with myraw rattan atter dundrum; ooah,
oyir, oyir, oyir: and I did spread before my Livvy, where Lord street
lolls and ladies linger and Cammomile Pass cuts Primrose Rise and
Coney Bend bounds Mulbreys Island but never a blid had bledded
or bludded since long agore when the whole blighty acre was bladey
well pessovered, my selvage mats of lecheworked lawn, my carpet
gardens of Guerdon City, with chopes pyramidous and mousselimes
and beaconphires and colossets and pensilled turisses for the buss-
pleaches of the summiramies and esplanadas and statuesques and
templeogues, the Pardonell of Maynooth, Fra Teobaldo, Nielsen,
rare admirable, Jean de Porteleau, Conall Gretecloke, Guglielmus

Caulis and the eiligh ediculous Passivucant (glorietta's inexcell-siored!): for irkdays and for folliedays till the comple anniums of calendarias, gregoromaios and gypsyjuliennes as such are pleased of theirs to walk: and I planted for my own hot lisbing lass a quickset vineyard and I fenced it about with huge Chesterfield elms and Kentish hops and rigs of barlow and bowery nooks and greenwished villas and pampos animos and (N.I.) necessitades iglesias and pons for aguaducks: a hawthorndene, a feyrieglenn, the hallaw vall, the dyrchace, Finmark's Howe, against lickybudmonth and gleaner-month with a magicscene wall (rimrim! rimrim!) for a Queen's garden of her phoenix: and (hush! hush!) I brewed for my alpine plurabelle, wigwarming wench, (speakeasy!) my granvilled brand-old Dublin lindub, the free, the froh, the frothy freshener, puss, puss, pussyfoot, to split the spleen of her maw: and I laid down be-fore the trotters to my eblanite my stony battered waggonways, my nordsoud circulums, my eastmoreland and westlandmore, running boullowards and syddenly parading, (hearsemen, opslo! nuptiallers, get storting!): whereon, in mantram of truemen like yahoomen (expect till dutc cundoctor summoneth him all fahrts to pay, velkom-men all hankinhunkn in this vongn of Hoseyeh!), claudesdales withe arabinstreeds, Roamer Reich's rickyshaws with Hispain's King's trompateers, madridden mustangs, buckarestive bronchos, poster shays and turnintaxis, and tall tall tilburys and nod nod nod-dies, others gigging gaily, some sedated in sedans: my priccoping gents, aroger, aroger, my damsells softsidesaddled, covertly, covertly, and Lawdy Dawe a perch behind: the mule and the hinny and the jennet and the mustard nag and piebald shjelties and skewbald awknees steppit lively (lift ye the left and rink ye the right!) for her pleashadure: and she lalaughed in her diddydid domino to the switcheries of the whip. Down with them! Kick! Playup!

Mattahah! Marahah! Luahah! Joahanahanahana!

What was thaas? Fog was whaas? Too mult sleepth. Let sleepth. But really now whenabouts? Expatiate then how much times we live in. Yes?

So, nat by night by naught by naket, in those good old lousy days gone by, the days, shall we say? of Whom shall we say? while kinderwardens minded their twinsbed, therenow theystood, the sycomores, all four of them, in their quartan agues, the majorchy, the minorchy, the everso and the fermentarian with their ballyhooric blowreaper, titranicht by tetranoxst, at their pussycorners, and that old time pallyollogass, playing copers fearsome, with Gus Walker, the cuddy, and his poor old dying boosy cough, esker, newcsle, saggard, crumlin, dell me, donk, the way to wumblin. Follow me beeline and you're bumblin, esker, newcsle, saggard, crumlin. And listening. So gladdied up when nicechild Kevin Mary (who was going to be commandeering chief of the choirboys' brigade the moment he grew up under all the auspices) irishsmiled in his milky way of cream dwibble and onage tustard and dessed tabbage, frighted out when badbrat Jerry Godolphing (who was hurrying to be cardinal scullion in a night refuge as bald as he was cured enough unerr all the hospitals) furrinfrowned down his wrinkly waste of methylated spirits, ick, and lemoncholy lees, ick, and pulverised rhubarbarorum, icky;

   night by silentsailing night while infantina Isobel (who will be blushing all day to be, when she growed up one Sunday, Saint Holy and Saint Ivory, when she took the veil, the beautiful presentation nun, so barely twenty, in her pure coif, sister Isobel, and next Sunday, Mistlemas, when she looked a peach, the beautiful Samaritan, still as beautiful and still in her teens, nurse Saintette Isabelle, with stiffstarched cuffs but on Holiday, Christmas, Easter mornings when she wore a wreath, the wonderful widow of eighteen springs, Ma-

dame Isa Veuve La Belle, so sad but lucksome in her boyblue's long
black with orange blossoming weeper's veil) for she was the only
girl they loved, as she is the queenly pearl you prize, because of the
way the night that first we met she is bound to be, methinks, and
not in vain, the darling of my heart, sleeping in her april cot, within
her singachamer, with her greengageflavoured candywhistle duetted
to the crazyquilt, Isobel, she is so pretty, truth to tell, wildwood's
eyes and primarose hair, quietly, all the woods so wild, in mauves
of moss and daphnedews, how all so still she lay, neath of the whitethorn, child of tree, like some losthappy leaf, like blowing flower
stilled, as fain would she anon, for soon again 'twill be, win me, woo
me, wed me, ah weary me! deeply, now evencalm lay sleeping;

nowth upon nacht, while in his tumbril Wachtman Havelook
seequeerscenes, from yonsides of the choppy, punkt by his curser-
bog, went long the grassgross bumpinstrass that henders the pubbel
to pass, stowing his bottle in a hole for at whet his whuskle to
stretch ecrooksman, sequestering for lovers' lost propertied offices the
leavethings from allpurgers' night, og gneiss ogas gnasty, kikkers,
brillers, knappers and bands, handsboon and strumpers, sminky-
sticks and eddiketsflaskers;

wan fine night and the next fine night and last find night while
Kothereen the Slop in her native's chambercushy, with dreamings
of simmering my veal astore, was basquing to her pillasleep how
she thawght a knogg came to the dowanstairs dour at that howr to
peirce the yare and dowandshe went, schritt be schratt, to see was
it Schweeps's mingerals or Shuhorn the posth with a tillycramp for
Hemself and Co, Esquara, or them four hoarsemen ∩n their apolka-
loops, Norreys, Soothbys, Yates and Welks, and, galorybit of the
sanes in hevel, there was a crick up the stirkiss and when she ruz
the cankle to see, galohery, downand she went on her knees to bless-
ersef that were knogging together like milkjuggles as if it was the
wrake of the hapspurus or old Kong Gander O'Toole of the Mountains or his googoo goosth she seein, sliving off over the sawdust
lobby out of the backroom, wan ter, that was everywans in turruns,
in his honeymoon trim, holding up his fingerhals, with the clookey
in his fisstball, tocher of davy's, tocher of ivileagh, for her to whisht,
you sowbelly, and the whites of his pious eyebulbs swering her to
silence and coort;

each and every juridical sessions night, whenas goodmen twelve
and true at fox and geese in their numbered habitations tried old
wireless over boord in their juremembers, whereas by reverendum

they found him guilty of their and those imputations of fornicolopu-
lation with two of his albowcrural correlations on whom he was
said to have enjoyed by anticipation when schooling them in amown,
mid grass, she sat, when man was, amazingly frank, for their first
conjugation whose colours at standing up from the above were of
a pretty carnation but, if really 'twere not so, of some deretane denu-
dation with intent to excitation, caused by his retrogradation, among
firearmed forces proper to this nation but apart from all titillation
which, he said, was under heat pressure and a good mitigation without which in any case he insists upon being worthy of continued
alimentation for him having displayed, he says, such grand tolera-
tion, reprobate so noted and all, as he was, with his washleather
sweeds and his smokingstump, for denying transubstantiation nevertheless in respect of his highpowered station, whereof more especially as probably he was meantime suffering genteel tortures from
the best medical attestation, as he oftentimes did, having only
strength enough, by way of festination, to implore (or I believe you
have might have said better) to complore, with complete obsecra-
tion, on everybody connected with him the curse of coagulation
for, he tells me outside Sammon's in King Street, after two or three
hours of close confabulation, by this pewterpint of Gilbey's goats-
whey which is his prime consolation, albeit involving upon the same
no uncertain amount of esophagous regurgitation, he being per-
sonally unpreoccupied to the extent of a flea's gizzard anent
eructation, if he was still extremely offensive to a score and four
nostrils' dilatation, still he was likewise, on the other side of him,
for some nepmen's eyes a delectation, as he asserts without the least
alienation, so prays of his faullt you would make obliteration but
for our friend behind the bars, though like Adam Findlater, a man
of estimation, summing him up to be done, be what will of excess
his exaltation, still we think with Sully there can be no right extin-
uation for contravention of common and statute legislation for which
the fit remedy resides, for Mr Sully, in corporal amputation: so
three months for Gubbs Jeroboam, the frothwhiskered pest of the
park, as per act one, section two, schedule three, clause four of the
fifth of King Jark, this sentence to be carried out tomorrowmorn
by Nolans Volans at six o'clock shark, and may the yeastwind and
the hoppinghail malt mercy on his seven honeymeads and his hurly-
burlygrowth, Amen, says the Clarke;

niece by nice by neat by natty, whilst amongst revery's happy
gardens nine with twenty Leixlip yearlings, darters all, had such a

ripping time with gleeful cries of what is nice toppingshaun made of made for and weeping like fun, him to be gone, for they were never happier, huhu, than when they were miserable, haha;

in their bed of trial, on the bolster of hardship, by the glimmer of memory, under coverlets of cowardice, Albatrus Nyanzer with Victa Nyanza, his mace of might mortified, her beautifell hung up on a nail, he, Mr of our fathers, she, our moddereen ru arue rue, they, ay, by the hodypoker and blazier, they are, as sure as dinny drops into the dyke . . .

A cry off.

Where are we at all? and whenabouts in the name of space?

I don't understand. I fail to say. I dearsee you too.

House of the cederbalm of mead. Garth of Fyon. Scene and property plot. Stagemanager's prompt. Interior of dwelling on outskirts of city. Groove two. Chamber scene. Boxed. Ordinary bedroom set. Salmonpapered walls. Back, empty Irish grate, Adam's mantel, with wilting elopement fan, soot and tinsel, condemned. North, wall with window practicable. Argentine in casement. Vamp. Pelmit above. No curtains. Blind drawn. South, party wall. Bed for two with strawberry bedspread, wickerworker clubsessel and caneseated millikinstool. Bookshrine without, facetowel upon. Chair for one. Woman's garments on chair. Man's trousers with crossbelt braces, collar on bedknob. Man's corduroy surcoat with tabrets and taces, seapan nacre buttons on nail. Woman's gown on ditto. Over mantelpiece picture of Michael, lance, slaying Satan, dragon with smoke. Small table near bed, front. Bed with bedding. Spare. Flagpatch quilt. Yverdown design. Limes. Lighted lamp without globe, scarf, gazette, tumbler, quantity of water, julepot, ticker, side props, eventuals, man's gummy article, pink.

A time.

Act: dumbshow.

Closeup. Leads.

Man with nightcap, in bed, fore. Woman, with curlpins, hind. Discovered. Side point of view. First position of harmony. Say! Eh? Ha! Check action. Matt. Male partly masking female. Man looking round, beastly expression, fishy eyes, paralleliped homoplatts, ghazometron pondus, exhibits rage. Business. Ruddy blond, Armenian bole, black patch, beer wig, gross build, episcopalian, any age. Woman, sitting, looks at ceiling, haggish expression, peaky nose, trekant mouth, fithery wight, exhibits fear. Welshrabbit teint, Nubian shine, nasal fossette, turfy tuft, undersized, free kirk, no age. Closeup. Play!

Callboy. Cry off. Tabler. Her move.

Footage.

By the sinewy forequarters of the mare Pocahontas and by the white shoulders of Finnuala you should have seen how that smart sallowlass just hopped a nanny's gambit out of bunk like old mother Mesopotomac and in eight and eight sixtyfour she was off, door, knightlamp with her, billy's largelimbs prodgering after to queen's lead. Promiscuous Omebound to Fiammelle la Diva. Huff! His move. Blackout.

Circus. Corridor.

Shifting scene. Wall flats: sink and fly. Spotlight working wall cloths. Spill playing rake and bridges. Room to sink: stairs to sink behind room. Two pieces. Haying after queue. Replay.

The old humburgh looks a thing incomplete so. It is so. On its dead. But it will pawn up a fine head of porter when it is finished. In the quicktime. The castle arkwright put in a chequered staircase certainly. It has only one square step, to be steady, yet notwithstumbling are they stalemating backgammoner supstairs by skips and trestles tiltop double corner. Whist while and game.

What scenic artist! It is ideal residence for realtar. By hims ingang tilt tinkt a tunning bell that Limen Mr, that Boggey Godde, be airwaked. Lingling, lingling. Be their maggies in all. Chump, do your ephort. Shop! Please shop! Shop ado please! O ado please shop! How hominous his house, haunt it? Yesses indead it be! Nogen, of imperial measure, is begraved beneadher. Here are his naggins poured, his alladim lamps. Around the bloombiered, booty with the bedst. For them whom he have fordone make we newly thankful!

Tell me something. The Porters, so to speak, after their shadowstealers in the newsbaggers, are very nice people, are they not? Very, all fourlike tellt. And on this wise, Mr Porter (Bartholomew, heavy man, astern, mackerel shirt, hayamatt peruke) is an excellent forefather and Mrs Porter (leading lady, a poopahead, gaffneysaffron nightdress, iszoppy chepelure) is a most kindhearted messmother. A so united family pateramater is not more existing on papel or off of it. As keymaster fits the lock it weds so this bally builder to his streamline secret. They care for nothing except everything that is allporterous. *Porto da Brozzo!* Isn't that terribly nice of them? You can ken that they come of a rarely old family by their costumance and one must togive that one supped of it in all tonearts from awe to zest. I think I begin to divine so much. Only snakkest me truesome! I stone us I'm hable.

To reachy a skeer do! Still hoyhra, till venstra! Here are two rooms on the upstairs, at forkflank and at knifekanter. Whom in the wood are they for? Why, for little Porter babes, to be saved! The coeds, boytom thwackers and timbuy teaser. Here is onething you owed two noe. This one once upon awhile was the other but this is the other one nighadays. Ah so? The Corsicos? They are numerable. Guest them. Major bed, minor bickhive. Halosobuth, sov us! Who sleeps in now number one, for example? A pussy, purr esimple. Cunina, Statulina and Edulia, but how sweet of her! Has your pussy a pessname? Yes, indeed, you will hear it passim in all the noveletta and she is named Buttercup. Her bare name will tellt it, a monitress. How very sweet of her and what an excessively lovecharming missyname to forsake, now that I come to drink of it filtred, a gracecup fulled of bitterness. She is dadad's lottiest daughterpearl and brooder's cissiest auntybride. Her shellback thimblecasket mirror only can show her dearest friendeen. To speak well her grace it would ask of Grecian language, of her goodness, that legend golden. Biryina Saindua! Loreas with lillias flocaflake arrosas! Here's newyearspray, the posquiflor, a windaborne and heliotrope; there miriamsweet and amaranth and marygold to crown. Add lightest knot unto tiptition. O Charis! O Charissima! A more intriguant bambolina could one not colour up out of Boccuccia's Enameron. Would one but to do apart a lilybit her virginelles and, so, to breath, so, therebetween, behold, she had instantt with her handmade as to graps the myth inmid the air. Mother of moth! I will to show herword in flesh. Approach not for ghost sake! It is dormition! She may think, what though little doth she realise, as morning fresheth, it hath happened her, you know what, as they too what two dare not utter. Silvoo plush, if scolded she draws a face. Petticoat's asleep but in the gentlenest of her thoughts apoo is a nursepin. To be presented, Babs for Bimbushi? Of courts and with enticers. Up, girls, and at him! Alone? Alone what? I mean, our strifestirrer, does she do fleurty winkies with herself. Pussy is never alone, as records her chambrette, for she can always look at Biddles and talk petnames with her little playfilly when she is sitting downy on the ploshmat. O, she talks, does she? Marry, how? Rosepetalletted sounds. Ah Biddles es ma plikplak. Ah plikplak wed ma Biddles. A nice jezebel barytinette she will gift but I much prefer her missnomer in maidenly golden lasslike gladsome wenchful flowery girlish beautycapes. So do I, much. Dulce delicatissima! Doth Dolly weeps she is hastings. Will Dally bumpsetty it is tubtime. Allaliefest, she who pities very pebbles, dare we not wish on her our thrice onsk? A lovely fear! That she seventip toe her chrysming, that she spin blue to scarlad till her temple's veil, that the Mount of Whoam it open it her to shelterer! She will blow ever so much more promisefuller, blee me, than all the other common marygales that romp round brigidschool, charming Carry Whambers or saucy Susy Maucepan of Merry Anna Patchbox or silly Polly Flinders. Platsch! A plikaplak.

And since we are talking amnessly of brukasloop crazedledaze, who doez in sleeproom number twobis? The twobirds. Holy policeman, O, I see! Of what age are your birdies? They are to come of twinning age so soon as they may be born to be eldering like those olders while they are living under chairs. They are and they seem to be so tightly tattached as two maggots to touch other, I think I notice, do I not? You do. Our bright bull babe Frank Kevin is on heartsleeveside. Do not you waken him! Our farheard bode. He is happily to sleep, limb of the Lord, with his lifted in blessing, his buchel Iosa, like the blissed angel he looks so like and his mou is semiope as though he were blowdelling on a bugigle. Whene'er I see those smiles in eyes 'tis Father Quinn again. Very shortly he will smell sweetly when he will hear a weird to wean. By gorgeous, that boy will blare some knight when he will take his dane's pledges and quit our ingletears, spite of undesirable parents, to wend him to Amorica to quest a cashy job. That keen dean with his veen nonsolance! O, I adore the profeen music! Dollarmighty! He is too audorable really, eunique! I guess to have seen somekid like him in the story book, guess I met somewhere somelam to whom he will be becoming liker. But hush! How unpardonable of me! I beg for your venials, sincerely I do.

Hush! The other, twined on codliverside, has been crying in his sleep, making sharpshape his inscissors on some first choice sweets fished out of the muck. A stake in our mead. What a teething wretch! How his book of craven images! Here are posthumious tears on his intimelle. And he has pipettishly bespilled himself from his foundingpen as illspent from inkinghorn. He is jem job joy pip poo pat (jot um for a sobrat!) Jerry Jehu. You will know him by name in the capers but you cannot see whose heel he sheepfolds in his wrought hand because I have not told it to you. O, foetal sleep! Ah, fatal slip! the one loved, the other left, the bride of pride leased to the stranger! He will be quite within the pale when with lordbeeron brow he vows him so tosset to be of the sir Blake tribes bleak while through life's unblest he rodes backs of bannars. Are you not somewhat bulgar with your bowels? Whatever do you mean with bleak? With pale blake I write tintingface. O, you do? And with steelwhite and blackmail I ha'scint for my sweet an anemone's letter with a gold of my bridest hair betied. Donatus his mark, address as follows. So you did? From the Cat and Cage. O, I see and see! In the ink of his sweat he will find it yet. What Gipsy Devereux vowed to Lylian and why the elm and how the stone. You never may know in the preterite all perhaps that you would not believe that you ever even saw to be about to. Perhaps. But they are two very blizky little portereens after their bredscrums, Jerkoff and Eatsup, as for my part opinion indeed. They would be born so, costarred, puck and prig, the maryboy at Donnybrook Fair, the godolphinglad in the Hoy's Court. How frilled one shall be as at taledold of Formio and Cigalette! What folly innocents! Theirs whet pep of puppyhood! Both barmhearts shall become yeastcake by their brackfest. I will to leave a my copperwise blessing between the pair of them, for rosengorge, for greenafang. Blech and tin soldies, weals in a sniffbox. Som's wholed, all's parted. Weeping shouldst not thou be when man falls but that divine scheming ever adoring be. So you be either man or mouse and you be neither fish nor flesh. Take. And take. Vellicate nyche! Be ones as wes for gives for gives now the hour of passings sembles quick with quelled. Adieu, soft adieu, for these nice presents, kerryjevin. Still tosorrow!

Jeminy, what is the view which now takes up a second position of discordance, tell it please? Mark! You notice it in that rereway because the male entail partially eclipses the femecovert. It is so called for its discord the meseedo. Do you ever heard the story about Helius Croesus, that white and gold elephant in our zoopark? You astonish me by it. Is it not that we are commanding from fullback, woman permitting, a profusely fine birdseye view from beauhind this park? Finn his park has been much the admiration of all the stranger ones, grekish and romanos, who arrive to here. The straight road down the centre (see relief map) bisexes the park which is said to be the largest of his kind in the world. On the right prominence confronts you the handsome vinesregent's lodge while, turning to the other supreme piece of cheeks, exactly opposite, you are confounded by the equally handsome chief sacristary's residence. Around is a little amiably tufted and man is cheered when he bewonders through the boskage how the nature in all frisko is enlivened by gentlemen's seats. Here are heavysuppers — 'tis for daddies housings for hundredaires of our super thin thousand. By gum, but you have resin! Of these tallworts are yielded out juices for jointoils and pappasses for paynims. Listeneth! 'Tis a tree story. How olave, that firile, was aplantad in her liveside. How tannoboom held tonobloom. How rood in norlandes. The black and blue marks athwart the weald, which now barely is so stripped, indicate the presence of sylvious beltings. Therewithal shady rides lend themselves out to rustic cavalries. In yonder valley, too, stays mountain sprite. Any pretty dears are to be caught inside but it is a bad pities of the plain. A scarlet pimparnell now mules the mound where anciently first murders were wanted to take root. By feud fionghalian. Talkingtree and sinningstone stay on either hand. Hystorical leavesdroppings may also be garnered up with sir Shamus Swiftpatrick, Archfieldchaplain of Saint Lucan's. How familiar it is to see all these interesting advenements with one snaked's eyes! Is all? Yet not! Hear one's. At the bodom fundus of this royal park, which, with tvigate shyasian gardeenen, is open to the public till night at late, so well the sissastrides so will the pederestians, do not fail to point to yourself a depression called Holl Hollow. It is often quite guttergloomering in our duol and gives wankyrious thoughts to the head but the banders of the pentapolitan poleetsfurcers bassoons into it on windy woodensdays their wellbooming wolvertones. Ulvos! Ulvos!

Whervolk dorst ttou begin to tremble by our moving pictures at this moment when I am to place my hand of our true friendshapes upon thee knee to mark well what I say? Throu shayest who? In Amsterdam there lived a . . . But how? You are tremblotting, you retchad, like a verry jerry! Niet? Will you a guineeser? Gaij beutel of staub? To feel, you? Yes, how it trembles, the timid! Vortigern, ah Gortigern! Overlord of Mercia! Or doth brainskin flinchgreef? Stemming! What boyazhness! Sole shadow shows. Tis jest jibberweek's joke. It must have stole. O, keve silence, both! Putshameyu! I have heard her voice somewhere else's before me in these ears still that now are for mine.

Let op. Slew musies. Thunner in the eire.

You were dreamend, dear. The pawdrag? The fawthrig? Shoe! Hear are no phanthares in the room at all, avikkeen. No bad bold faathern, dear one. Opop opop capallo, muy malinchily malchick! Gothgorod father godown followay tomollow the lucky load to Lublin for make his thoroughbass grossman's bigness. Take that two piece big slap slap bold honty bottomsside pap pap pappa.

—Li ne dormis?
—S! Malbone dormas.
—Kia li krias nikte?
—Parolas infanetes. S!

Sonly all in your imagination, dim. Poor little brittle magic nation, dim of mind! Shoe to me now, dear! Shoom of me! While elvery stream winds seling on for to keep this barrel of bounty rolling and the nightmail afarfrom morning nears.

When you're coaching through Lucalised, on the sulphur spa to visit, it's safer to hit than miss it, stop at his inn! The hammers are telling the cobbles, the pickts are hacking the saxums, it's snugger to burrow abed than ballet on broadway. Tuck in your blank! For it's race pound race the hosties rear all roads to ruin and layers by lifetimes laid down riches from poormen. Cried unions to chip, saltpetre to strew, gallpitch to drink, stonebread to break but it's bully to gulp good blueberry pudding. Doze in your warmth! While the elves in the moonbeams, feeling why, will keep my lilygem gently gleaming.

In the sleepingchambers. The court to go into half morning. The four seneschals with their palfrey to be there now, all balaaming in their sellaboutes and sharping up their penisills. The boufeither Soakersoon at holdup tent sticker. The swabsister Katya to have duntalking and to keep shakenin dowan her droghedars. Those twelve chief barons to stand by duedesmally with their folded arums and put down all excursions and false alarums and after that to go back now to their runameat farums and recompile their magnum chartarums with the width of the road between them and all harrums. The maidbrides all, in favours gay, to strew sleety cinders on their falling hair and for wouldbe joybells to ring sadly ringless hands. The dame dowager to stay kneeled how she is, as first mutherer with cord in coil. The two princes of the tower royal, daulphin and deevlin, to lie how they are without to see. The dame dowager's duffgerent to present wappon, blade drawn to the full and about wheel without to be seen of them. The infant Isabella from her coign to do obeisance toward the duffgerent, as first futherer with drawn brand. Then the court to come in to full morning. Herein see ye fail not!

—Vidu, porkego! Ili vi rigardas. Returnu, porkego! Maldelikato!

Gauze off heaven! Vision. Then, O, pluxty suddly, the sight entrancing! Hummels! That crag! Those hullocks! O Sire! So be accident occur is not going to commence! What have you therefore?

Fear you the donkers? Of roovers? I fear lest we have lost ours (non grant it!) respecting these wildy parts. How is hit finister! How shagsome all and beastful! What do you show on? I show because I must see before my misfortune so a stark pointing pole. Lord of ladders, what for lungitube! Can you read the verst legend hereon? I am hather of the missed. Areed! To the dunleary obelisk via the rock vhat myles knox furlongs; to the general's postoffice howsands of patience; to the Wellington memorial half a league wrongwards; to Sara's bridge good hunter and nine to meet her: to the point, one yeoman's yard. He, he, he! At that do you leer, a setting up? With a such unfettered belly? Two cascades? I leer (O my big, O my bog, O my bigbagbone!) because I must see a buntingcap of so a pinky on the point. It is for a true glover's greetings and many burgesses by us, greats and grosses, uses to pink it in this way at tet-at-tet. For long has it been effigy of standard royal when broken on roofstaff which to the gunnings shall cast welcome from Courtmilits' Fortress, umptydum dumptydum. Bemark you these hangovers, those streamer fields, his influx. Do you not have heard that, the queen lying abroad from fury of the gales, (meekname mocktitles her Nan Nan Nanetta) her liege of lateenth dignisties shall come on their bay tomorrow, Michalsmas, mellems the third and fourth of the clock, there to all the king's aussies and all their king's men, knechts tramplers and cavalcaders, led of herald graycloak, Ulaf Goldar-skield? Dog! Dog! Her lofts will be loosed for her and their tumblers broodcast. A progress shall be made in walk, ney? I trow it well, and uge by uge. He shall come, sidesmen accostant, by aryan jubi-larian and on brigadier-general Nolan or and buccaneer-admiral Browne, with — who can doubt it? — his golden beagles and his white elkox terriers for a hunting on our littlego illcome faxes. In blue and buff of Beaufort the hunt shall make. It is poblesse noblige. Ommes will grin through collars when each riders other's ass. Me Eccls! What cats' killings overall! What popping out of guillotened widows! Quick time! Beware of waiting! Squintina plies favours on us from her rushfrail and Zosimus, the crowder, in his surcoat, sues us with souftwister. Apart we! Here are gantlets. I believe, by Plenti-folks Mixymost! Yet if I durst to express the hope how I might be able to be present. All these peeplers entrammed and detrained on bikeygels and troykakyls and those puny farting little solitires! Tollacre, tollacre! Polo north will beseem Sibernian and Plein Pe-louta will behowl ne yerking at lawncastrum ne ghimbelling on guelflinks. Mauser Misma shall cease to stretch her and come abroad

for what the blinkins is to be seen. A ruber, a rancher, a fullvide, a
veridust and as crerdulous behind as he was before behind a dam-
son of a sloe cooch. Mbv! The annamation of evabusies, the livlia-
ness of her laughings, such as a plurity of bells! Have peacience,
pray you! Place to dames! Even the Lady Victoria Landauner will
leave to loll and parasol, all giddied into gushgasps with her dickey
standing. Britus and Gothius shall no more joustle for that sonne-
place but mark one autonement when, with si so silent, Cloudia
Aiduolcis, good and dewed up, shall let fall, yes, no, yet, now, a rain.
Muchsias grapcias! It is how sweet from her, the wispful, and they
are soon seen swopsib so a sautril as a meise. Its ist not the tear on
this movent sped. Tix sixponce! Poum! Hool poll the bull? Fool pay
the bill. Becups a can full. Peal, pull the bell! Still sayeme of cere-
monies, much much more! So pleaseyour! It stands in *Instopressible*
how Meynhir Mayour, our boorgomaister, thon staunch Thorsman,
(our Nancy's fancy, our own Nanny's Big Billy), his hod hoisted,
in best bib and tucker, with Woolington bottes over buckram bab-
bishkis and his clouded cane and necknoose aureal, surrounded of
his full cooperation with fixed baronets and meng our pueblos, restrained by chain of hands from pinchgut, hoghill, darklane, gib-
betmeade and beaux and laddes and bumbellye, shall receive Dom
King at broadstone barrow meet a keys of goodmorrow on to his
pompey cushion. Me amble dooty to your grace's majers! Arise, sir
Pompkey Dompkey! Ear! Ear! Weakear! An allness eversides! We
but miss that horse elder yet cherchant of the wise graveleek in cab-
buchin garden. That his be foison, old Caubeenhauben! 'Twill be
tropic of all days. By the splendour of Sole! Perfect weatherest pre-
vailing. Thisafter, swift's mightmace deposing, he shall aidress to
His Serenemost by a speechreading from his miniated vellum, alfi
byrni gamman dealter etcera zezera eacla treacla youghta kaptor
lomdom noo, who meaningwhile that illuminatured one, Papyroy
of Pepinregn, my Sire, great, big King, (his scaffold is there set up,
as to edify, by Rex Ingram, pageantmaster) will be poking out with
his canule into the arras of what brilliant bridgecloths and joking
up with his tonguespitz to the crimosing balkonladies, here's a help
undo their modest stays with a fullbelow may the funnyfeelbelong.
Oddsbones, that may it! Carilloners will ring their gluckspeels. Rng
rng! Rng rng! S. Presbutt-in-the-North, S. Mark Underloop,
S. Lorenz-by-the-Toolechest, S. Nicholas Myre. You shall hark to
anune S. Gardener, S. George-le-Greek, S. Barclay Moitered,
S. Phibb, Iona-in-the-Fields with Paull-the-Aposteln. And audial-

terand: S. Jude-at-Gate, Bruno Friars, S. Weslen-on-the-Row,
S. Molyneux Without, S. Mary Stillamaries with Bride-and-
Audeons-behind-Wardborg. How chimant in effect! Alla tingaling
pealabells! So a many of churches one cannot pray own's prayers.
'Tis holyyear's day! Juin jully we may! Agithetta and Tranquilla
shall demure umclaused but Marlborough-the-Less, Greatchrist and
Holy Protector shall have open virgilances. Beata Basilica! But will
be not pontification? Dock, dock, agame! Primatially. At wateredge.
Cantaberra and Neweryork may supprecate when, by vepers, for
towned and travalled, his goldwhite swaystick aloft ylifted, umbrilla-
parasoul, Monsigneur of Deublan shall impart to all. *Benedictus
benedicat!* To board! And mealsight! Unjoint him this bittern, frust
me this chicken, display yon crane, thigh her her pigeon, unlace
allay rabbit and pheasant! Sing: Old Finncoole, he's a mellow old
saoul when he swills with his fuddlers free! Poppop array! For we're
all jollygame fellhellows which nobottle can deny! Here be trouts
culponed for ye and salmons chined and sturgeons tranched, sanced
capons, lobsters barbed. Call halton eatwords! Mumm me moe
mummers! What, no Ithalians? How, not one Moll Pamelas? Accordingly! Play actors by us ever have crash to their gate. Mr Messop
and Mr Borry will produce of themselves, as they're two genitalmen
of Veruno, Senior Nowno and Senior Brolano (finaly! finaly!), all
for love of a fair penitent that, a she be broughton, rhoda's a rosy
she. Their two big skins! How they strave to gat her! Such a boy-
play! Their bouchicaulture! What tyronte power! Buy our fays! My
name is novel and on the Granby in hills. Bravose! Thou traitor
slave! Mine name's Apnorval and o'er the Grandbeyond Mountains.
Bravossimost! The royal nusick their show shall shut with songslide
to nature's solemn silence. Deep Dalchi Dolando! Might gentle harp
addurge! It will give piketurns on the tummlipplads and forain
dances and crosshurdles and dollmanovers and viceuvious pyrolyph-
ics, a snow of dawnflakes, at darkfall for Grace's Mamnesty and
our fancy ladies, all assombred. Some wholetime in hot town tonight! You do not have heard? It stays in book of that which is. I
have heard anyone tell it jesterday (master currier with brassard
was't) how one should come on morrow here but it is never here
that one today. Well but remind to think, you where yestoday Ys
Morganas war and that it is always tomorrow in toth's tother's place.
Amen.

True! True! Vouchsafe me more soundpicture! It gives furiously
to think. Is rich Mr Pornter, a squire, not always in his such strong

health? I thank you for the best, he is in taken deal exceedingly her-
culeneous. One sees how he is lot stoutlier than of formerly. One
would say him to hold whole a litteringture of kidlings under his
aproham. Has handsome Sir Pournter always been so long married?
O yes, Lord Pournterfamilias has been marryingman ever since so
long time in Hurtleforth, where he appeers as our oily the active,
and, yes indeed, he has his mic son and his two fine mac sons and
a superfine mick want they mack metween them. She, she, she! But
on what do you again leer? I am not leering, I pink you pardons.
I am highly sheshe sherious.

  Do you not must want to go somewhere on the present? Yes, O
pity! At earliest moment! That prickly heat feeling! Forthink not
me spill it's at always so guey. Here we shall do a far walk (O pity)
anygo khaibits till the number one of sairey's place. Is, is. I want
you to admire her sceneries illustrationing our national first rout,
one ought ought one. We shall too downlook on that ford where
Sylvanus Sanctus washed but hurdley those tips of his anointeds.
Do not show ever retrorsehim, crookodeyled, till that you become
quite crimstone in the face! Beware! guardafew! It is Stealer of the
Heart! I am anxious in regard you should everthrown your sillarsalt.
I will dui sui, tefnute! These brilling waveleaplights! Please say me
how sing you them. Seekhem seckhem! They arise from a clear
springwell in the near of our park which makes the daft to hear all
blend. This place of endearment! How it is clear! And how they cast
their spells upon, the fronds that thereup float, the bookstaff branchings! The druggeted stems, the leaves incut on trees! Do you can
their tantrist spellings? I can lese, skillmistress aiding. Elm, bay,
this way, cull dare, take a message, tawny runes ilex sallow, meet
me at the pine. Yes, they shall have brought us to the water trysting,
by hedjes of maiden ferm, then here in another place is their
chapelofeases, sold for song, of which you have thought my praise
too much my price. O ma ma! Yes, sad one of Ziod? Sell me, my soul
dear! Ah, my sorrowful, his cloister dreeping of his monkshood, how
it is triste to death, all his dark ivytod! Where cold in dearth. Yet
see, my blanching kissabelle, in the under close she is allso gay, her
kirtles green, her curtsies white, her peony pears, her nistlingsloes!
I, pipette, I must also quicklingly to tryst myself softly into this lit-
tleasechapel. I would rather than Ireland! But I pray, make! Do
your easiness! O, peace, this is heaven! O, Mr Prince of Pouring-
toher, whatever shall I pppease to do? Why do you so lifesighs, my
precious, as I hear from you, with limmenings lemantitions, after

that swollen one? I am not sighing, I assure, but only I am soso sorry about all in my saarasplace. Listen, listen! I am doing it. Hear more to those voices! Always I am hearing them. Horsehem coughs enough. Annshee lispes privily.

— He is quieter now.

— Legalentitled. Accesstopartnuzz. Notwildebeestsch. Byrightofoaptz. Twainbeonerflsh. Haveandholdpp.

— S! Let us go. Make a noise. Slee . . .

— Qui . . . The gir . . .

— Huesofrichunfoldingmorn. Wakenupriseandprove. Provideforsacrifice.

— Wait! Hist! Let us list!

For our netherworld's bosomfoes are working tooth and nail overtime: in earthveins, toadcavites, chessganglions, saltklesters, underfed: nagging firenibblers knockling aterman up out of his hinterclutch. Tomb be their tools! When the youngdammers will be soon heartpocking on their betters' doornoggers: and the youngfries will be backfrisking diamondcuts over their lyingin underlayers, spick and spat trowelling a gravetrench for their fourinhand forebears. Vote for your club!

— Wait!

— What!

— Her door!

— Ope?

— See!

— What?

— Careful.

— Who?

Live well! Iniivdluaritzas! Tone!

Cant ear! Her dorters ofe? Whofe? Her eskmeno daughters hope? Whope? Ellme, elmme, elskmestoon! Soon!

Let us consider.

The procurator Interrogarius Mealterum presends us this proposer.

Honuphrius is a concupiscent exservicemajor who makes dishonest propositions to all. He is considered to have committed, invoking *droit d'oreiller,* simple infidelities with Felicia, a virgin, and to be practising for unnatural coits with Eugenius and Jeremias, two or three philadelphians. Honophrius, Felicia, Eugenius and Jeremias are consanguineous to the lowest degree. Anita the wife of Honophrius, has been told by her tirewoman, Fortissa, that Honuphrius has blasphemously confessed under voluntary chastisement that he has instructed his slave, Mauritius, to urge Magravius, a commercial, emulous of Honuphrius, to solicit the chastity of Anita. Anita is informed by some illegitimate children of Fortissa with Mauritius (the supposition is Ware's) that Gillia, the schismatical wife of Magravius, is visited clandestinely by Barnabas, the advocate of Honuphrius, an immoral person who has been corrupted by Jeremias. Gillia, (a cooler blend, D'Alton insists) *ex equo* with Poppea, Arancita, Clara, Marinuzza, Indra and Iodina, has been tenderly debauched (in Halliday's view), by Honuphrius, and Magravius knows from spies that Anita has formerly committed double sacrilege with Michael, *vulgo* Cerularius, a perpetual curate, who wishes to seduce Eugenius. Magravius threatens to have Anita molested by Sulla, an orthodox savage (and leader of a band of twelve mercenaries, the Sullivani), who desires to procure Felicia for Gregorius, Leo, Vitellius and Macdugalius, four excavators, if she will not yield to him and also deceive Honuphrius by rendering conjugal duty when demanded. Anita who claims to have discovered incestuous temptations from Jeremias and Eugenius would yield to the lewdness of Honuphrius to appease the savagery of Sulla and the mercernariness of the twelve Sullivani, and (as Gilbert at first suggested), to save the virginity of Felicia for Magravius when converted by Michael after the death of Gillia, but she fears that, by allowing his marital rights she may cause reprehensible conduct between Eugenius and Jeremias. Michael, who has formerly debauched Anita, dispenses her from yielding to Honuphrius who pretends publicly to possess his conjunct in thirtynine several manners (*turpiter!* affirm *ex cathedris* Gerontes Cambronses) for carnal hygiene whenever he has rendered himself impotent to consummate by subdolence. Anita is disturbed but Michael comminates that he will reserve her case tomorrow for the ordinary Guglielmus even if she should practise a pious fraud during affrication which, from experience, she knows (according to Wadding), to be leading to nullity. Fortissa, however, is encouraged by Gregorius, Leo, Viteilius, and Magdugalius, reunitedly, to warn Anita by describing the strong chastisements of Honuphrius and the depravities (*turpissimas!*) of Canicula, the deceased wife of Mauritius, with Sulla, the simoniac, who is abnegand and repents. Has he hegemony and shall she submit?

Translate a lax, you breed a bradaun. In the goods of Cape and Chattertone, deceased.

This, lay readers and gentilemen, is perhaps the commonest of all cases arising out of umbrella history in connection with the wood industries in our courts of litigation. D'Oyly Owens holds (though Finn Magnusson of himself holds also) that so long as there is a joint deposit account in the two names a mutual obligation is posited. Owens cites Brerfuchs and Warren, a foreign firm, since disseized, registered as Tangos, Limited, for the sale of certain proprietary articles. The action which was at the instance of the trustee of the heathen church emergency fund, suing by its trustee, a resigned civil servant, for the payment of tithes due was heard by Judge Doyle and also by a common jury. No question arose as to the debt for which vouchers spoke volumes. The defence alleged that payment had been made effective. The fund trustee, one Jucundus Fecundus Xero Pecundus Coppercheap, counterclaimed that payment was invalid having been tendered to creditor under cover of a crossed cheque, signed in the ordinary course, in the name of Wieldhelm, Hurls Cross, voucher copy provided, and drawn by the senior partner only by whom the lodgment of the species had been effected but in their joint names. The bank particularised, the national misery (now almost entirely in the hands of the four chief bondholders for value in Tangos), declined to pay the draft, though there were ample reserves to meet the liability, whereupon the trusty Coppercheap negociated it for and on behalf of the fund of the thing to a client of his, a notary, from whom, on consideration, he received in exchange legal relief as between trusthee and bethrust, with thanks. Since then the cheque, a good washable pink, embossed D you D No 11 hundred and thirty 2, good for the figure and face, had been circulating in the country for over thirtynine years among holders of Pango stock, a rival concern, though not one demonetised farthing had ever spun or fluctuated across the counter in the semblance of hard coin or liquid cash. The jury (a sour dozen of stout fellows all of whom were curiously named after doyles) naturally disagreed jointly and severally, and the belligerent judge, disagreeing with the allied jurors' disagreement, went outside his jurisfiction altogether and ordered a garnishee attachment to the neutral firm. No *mandamus* could locate the depleted whilom Breyfawkes as he had entered into an ancient moratorium, dating back to the times of the early barters, and only the junior partner Barren could be found, who entered an appearance and turned up, upon a notice of motion and after service of the motion by interlocutory injunction, among the male jurors to be an absolete turfwoman, originally from the proletarian class, with still a good title to her sexname of Ann Doyle, 2 Coppinger's Cottages, the Doyle's country. Doyle (Ann), add woman in, having regretfully left the juryboxers, protested cheerfully on the stand in a long jurymiad *in re* corset checks, delivered in doylish, that she had often, in supply to brusk demands rising almost to bollion point, discounted Mr Brakeforth's first of all in exchange at nine months from date without issue and, to be strictly literal, unbottled in corrubberation a current account of how she had been made at sight for services rendered the payeedrawee of unwashable blank assignations, sometimes pinkwilliams (laughter) but more often of the *crème-de-citron, vair émail paoncoque* or marshmallow series, which she, as bearer, used to endorse, adhesively, to her various payers-drawers who in most cases were identified by the timber papers as wellknown tetigists of the city and suburban. The witness, at her own request, asked if she might and wrought something between the sheets of music paper which she had accompanied herself with for the occasion and this having been handed up for the bench to look at *in camera,* Coppinger's doll, as she was called, (*annias,* Mack Erse's Dar, the adopted child) then proposed to jerrykin and jureens and every jim, jock and jarry in that little green courtinghousie for her satisfaction and as a whole act of settlement to reamalgamate herself, tomorrow perforce, in pardonership with the permanent suing fond trustee, Monsignore Pepigi, under the new style of Will Breakfast and Sparrem, as, when all his cognisances had been estreated, he seemed to proffer the steadiest interest towards her, but this prepoposal was ruled out on appeal by Judge Jeremy Doyler, who, reserving judgment in a matter of courts and reversing the findings of the lower correctional, found, beyond doubt of treuson, fending the dissassents of the pickpackpanel, twelve as upright judaces as ever let down their thoms, and, *occupante extremum scabie,* handed down to the jury of the Liffey that, as a matter of tact, the woman they gave as free was born into contractual incapacity (the Calif of Man *v* the Eaudelusk Company) when, how and where mamy's mancipium act did not apply and therefore held supremely that, as no property in law can exist in a corpse, (Hal Kilbride *v* Una Bellina) Pepigi's pact was pure piffle (loud laughter) and Wharrem would whistle for the rhino. Will you, won't you, pango with Pepigi? Not for Nancy, how dare you do! And whew whewwhew whew.

— He sighed in sleep.

— Let us go back.

— Lest he forewaken.

— Hide ourselves.

While hovering dreamwings, folding around, will hide from fears my wee mee mannikin, keep my big wig long strong manomen, guard my bairn, *mon beau.*

— To bed.

Prospector projector and boomooster giant builder of all causeways woesoever, hopping offpoint and true terminus of straxstraightcuts and corkscrewn perambulaups, zeal whence to goal whither, wonderlust, in sequence to which every muckle must make its mickle, as different as York from Leeds, being the only wise in a muck's world to look on itself from beforehand; mirrorminded curiositease and would-to-the-large which bring hills to molehunter, home through first husband, perils behind swine and horsepower down to hungerford, prick this man and tittup this woman, our forced payrents, Bogy Bobow with his cunnyngnest couchmare, Big Maester Finnykin with Phenicia Parkes, lame of his ear and gape of her leg, most correctingly, we beseach of you, down their laddercase of nightwatch service and bring them at suntime flush with the nethermost gangrung of their stepchildren, guide them through the labyrinth of their samilikes and the alteregoases of their pseudoselves, hedge them bothways from all roamers whose names are ligious, from loss of bearings deliver them; so they keep to their rights and be ware of duty frees, neoliffic smith and magdalenian jinnyjones, mandragon mor and weak wiffeyducky, Morionmale and Thrydacianmad, basilisk glorious with his weeniequeenie, tigernack and swansgrace, he as hale as his ardouries, she as verve as her veines; this prime white arsenic with bissemate alloyed, martial sin with peccadilly, free to lease hold with first mortgage, dowser dour and dipper douce, stop-that-war and feel-this-feather, norsebloodheartened and landsmoolwashable, great gas with fun-in-the-corner, grand slam with fall-of-the-trick, solomn one and shebby, cod and coney, cash and carry, in all we dreamed the part we dreaded, corsair coupled with his dame, royal biber but constant lymph, boniface and bonnyfeatures, nazil hose and river mouth, bang-the-change and batter-the-bolster, big smoke and lickley roesthy, humanity's fahrman by society leader, voguener and trulley, humpered and elf, Urloughmoor with Miryburrow, leaks and awfully, basal curse yet grace abunda, Regies Producer with screendoll Vedette, peg of his claim and pride of her heart, cliffscaur grisly but rockdove cooing, hodinstag on fryggabet, baron and feme: that he may dishcover her, that she may uncouple him, that one may come and crumple them, that they may soon recoup themselves: now and then, time on time again, as per periodicity; from Neaves to Willses, from Bush-mills to Enos; to Goerz from Harleem, to Hearths of Oak from Skit-tish Widdas; via mala, hyber pass, heckhisway per alptrack: through landsvague and vain, after many mandelays: in their first case, to the next place, till their cozenkerries: the high and the by, both pent and plain: cross cowslips yillow, yellow, yallow, past pumpkins pinguind, purplesome: be they whacked to the wide other tied to hustings, long sizzleroads neath arthruseat, him to the derby, her to toun, til sengentide do coddlam: in the grounds or unterlinnen: rue to lose and ca canny: at shipside, by convent garden: monk and sempstress, in sackcloth silkily: curious dreamers, curious dramas, curious deman, plagiast dayman, playajest dearest, plaguiest dourest: for the strangfort planters are prodesting, and the karkery felons dryflooring it and the leperties' laddos railing the way, blump for slogo slee!

Stop! Did a stir? No, is fast. On to bed! So he is. It's only the wind on the road outside for to wake all shivering shanks from snorring.

But. Oom Godd his villen, who will he be, this mitryman, some king of the yeast, in his chrismy greyed brunzewig, with the snow in his mouth and the caspian asthma, so bulk of build? Relics of pharrer and livite! Dik Gill, Tum Lung or Macfinnan's cool Har-ryng? He has only his hedcosycasket on and his wollsey shirtplisse with peascod doublet, also his feet wear doubled width socks for he always must to insure warm sleep between a pair of fullyfleeced bankers like a finnoc in a cauwl. Can thus be Misthra Norkmann that keeps our hotel? Begor, Mr O'Sorgmann, you're looking right well! Hecklar's champion ethnicist. How deft as a fuchser schouws daft as a fish! He's the dibble's own doges for doublin existents! But a jolly fine daysent form of one word. He's rounding up on his family.

And who is the bodikin by him, sir? So voulzievalsshie? With ybbs and zabs? Her trixiestrail is tripping her, vop! Luck at the way for the lucre of smoke she's looping the lamp! Why, that's old miss-ness wipethemdry! Well, well, wellsowells! Donauwatter! Ardechi-ous me! With her halfbend as proud as a peahen, allabalmy, and her troutbeck quiverlipe, ninyananya. And her steptojazyma's culun-der buzztle. Happy tea area, naughtygay frew! Selling sunlit sopes to washtout winches and rhaincold draughts to the props of his pubs. She tired lipping the swells at Pont Delisle till she jumped the boom at Brounemouth. Now she's borrid his head under Hatesbury's Hatch and loamed his fate to old Love Lane. And she's just the same old haporth of dripping. She's even brennt her hair.

Which route are they going? Why? Angell sitter or Amen Corner, Norwood's Southwalk or Euston Waste? The solvent man in his upper gambeson withnot a breth against him and the wee wiping womanahoussy. They're coming terug their diamond wedding tour, giant's inchly elfkin's ell, vesting their characters vixendevolment, andens aller, athors err, our first day man and your dresser and mine, that Luxuumburgher evec cettehis Alzette, konyglik shire with his queensh countess, Stepney's shipchild with the waif of his bosun, Dunmow's flitcher with duck-on-the-rock, down the scales, the way they went up, under talls and threading tormentors, shunning the startraps and slipping in sliders, risking a runway, ruing reveals, from Elder Arbor to La Puirée, eskipping the clockback, crystal in carbon, sweetheartedly. Hot and cold and electrickery with attendance and lounge and promenade free. In spite of all that science could boot or art could eke. Bolt the grinden. Cave and can em. Single wrecks for the weak, double axe for the mail, and quick queck quack for the radiose. Renove that bible. You will never have post in your pocket unless you have brasse on your plate. Beggards outdoor. Goat to the Endth, thou slowguard! Mind the Monks and their Grasps. Scrape your souls. Commit no miracles. Postpone no bills. Respect the uniform. Hold the raabers for the kunning his plethoron. Let leash the dooves to the cooin her coynth. Hatenot havenots. Share the wealth and spoil the weal. Peg the pound to tom the devil. My time is on draught. Bottle your own. Love my label like myself. Earn before eating. Drudge after drink. Credit tomorrow. Follow my dealing. Fetch my price. Buy not from dives. Sell not to freund. Herenow chuck english and learn to pray plain. Lean on your lunch. No cods before Me. Practise preaching. Think in your stomach. Import through the nose. By faith alone. Season's weather. Gomorrha. Salong. Lots feed from my tidetable. Oil's wells in our lands. Let earwigger's wivable teach you the dance!

Now their laws assist them and ease their fall!

For they met and mated and bedded and buckled and got and gave and reared and raised and brought Thawland within Har danger, and turned them, tarrying to the sea and planted and plundered and pawned our souls and pillaged the pounds of the extramurals and fought and feigned with strained relations and

bequeathed us their ills and recrutched cripples gait and under-
mined lungachers, manplanting seven sisters while wan warm-
wooed woman scrubbs, and turned out coats and removed their
origins and never learned the first day's lesson and tried to mingle
and managed to save and feathered foes' nests and fouled their own
and wayleft the arenotts and ponted vodavalls for the zollgebordened
and escaped from liquidation by the heirs of their death and were
responsible for congested districts and rolled olled logs into Peter's
sawyery and werfed new woodcuts on Paoli's wharf and ewesed
Rachel's lea and rammed Dominic's gap and looked haggards after
lazatables and rode fourscore oddwinters and struck rock oil and
forced a policeman and collaughsed at their phizes in Toobiassed
and Zachary and left off leaving off and kept on keeping on and
roused up drink and poured balm down and were cuffed by their
customers and bit the dust at the foot of the poll when in her deer-
garth he gave up his goat after the battle of Multaferry. Pharoah
with fairy, two lie, let them! Yet they wend it back, qual his leif,
himmertality, bullseaboob and rivishy divil, light in hand, helm on
high, to peekaboo durk the thicket of slumbwhere, till their hour
with their scene be struck for ever and the book of the dates he close,
he clasp and she and she seegn her tour d'adieu, Pervinca calling,
Soloscar hears. (O Sheem! O Shaam!), and gentle Isad Ysut gag,
flispering in the nightleaves flattery, dinsiduously, to Finnegan, to
sin again and to make grim grandma grunt and grin again while
the first grey streaks steal silvering by for to mock their quarrels in
dollymount tumbling.

They near the base of the chill stair, that large incorporate licensed vintner, such as he is, from former times, nine hosts in himself, in his hydrocomic establishment and his ambling limfy peep-
ingpartner, the slave of the ring that worries the hand that sways
the lamp that shadows the walk that bends to his bane the busynext
man that came on the cop with the fenian's bark that pickled his
widow that primed the pope that passed it round on the volunteers'
plate till it croppied the ears of Purses Relle that kneed O'Connell
up out of his doss that shouldered Burke that butted O'Hara that
woke the busker that grattaned his crowd that bucked the jiggers
to rhyme the rann that flooded the routes in Eryan's isles from Malin
to Clear and Carnsore Point to Slynagollow and cleaned the pockets
and ransomed the ribs of all the listeners, leud and lay, that bought
the ballad that Hosty made.

Anyhow (the matter is a troublous and a peniloose) have they not called him at many's their mock indignation meeting, vehmen's vengeance vective volleying, inwader and uitlander, the notables, crashing libels in their sullivan's mounted beards about him, their right renownsable patriarch? Heinz cans everywhere and the swanee her ainsell and Eyrewaker's family sock that they smuggled to life betune them, roaring (Big Reilly was the worst): free boose for the man from the nark, sure, he never was worth a cornerwall fark, and his banishee's bedpan she's a quareold bite of a tark: as they wendelled their zingaway wivewards from his find me cool's moist opulent vinery, highjacking through the nagginneck pass, as they hauled home with their hogsheads, axpoxtelating, and claiming cowled consollation, sursumcordial, from the bluefunkfires of the dipper and the martian's frost?

Use they not, our noesmall termtraders, to abhors offrom him, the yet unregendered thunderslog, whose sbrogue cunneth none lordmade undersiding, how betwixt wifely rule and *mens conscia recti*, then hemale man all unbracing to omniwomen, but now she-dropping his hitches like any maidavale oppersite orseriders in an idinhole? Ah, dearo! Dearo, dear! And her illian! And his willyum! When they were all there now, matinmarked for lookin on. At the carryfour with awlus plawshus, their happyass cloudious! And then and too the trivials! And their bivouac! And his monomyth! Ah ho! Say no more about it! I'm sorry! I saw. I'm sorry! I'm sorry to say I saw!

Gives there not too amongst us after all events (or so grunts a leading hebdromadary) some togethergush of stillandbutallyouknow that, insofarforth as, all up and down the whole concreation say, efficient first gets there finally every time, as a complex matter of pure form, for those excess and that pasphault hardhearingness from their eldfar, in grippes and rumblions, through fresh taint and old treason, another like that alter but not quite such anander and still-andbut one not all the selfsame and butstillone just the maim and encore emmerhim may always, with a little difference, till the latest up to date so early in the morning, have evertheless been allmade amenable?

Yet he begottom.

Let us wherefore, tearing ages, presently preposterose a snatch-vote of thanksalot to the huskiest coaxing experimenter that ever gave his best hand into chancerisk, wishing him with his famblings no end of slow poison and a mighty broad venue for themselves between the devil's punchbowl and the deep angleseaboard, that

they may gratefully turn a deaf ear clooshed upon the desperanto
of willynully, their shareholders from Taaffe to Auliffe, that will
curse them below par and mar with their descendants, shame, hum-
bug and profit, to greenmould upon mildew over jaundice as long
as ever there's wagtail surtaxed to a testcase on enver a man.

We have to had them whether we'll like it or not. They'll have
to have us now then we're here on theirspot. Scant hope theirs or
ours to escape life's high carnage of semperidentity by subsisting
peasemeal upon variables. Bloody certainly have we got to see to
it ere smellful demise surprends us on this concrete that down the
gullies of the eras we may catch ourselves looking forward to what
will in no time be staring you larrikins on the postface in that multi-
mirror megaron of returningties, whirled without end to end. So
there was a raughty . . . who in Dyfflinsborg did . . . With his sod-
dering iron, spadeaway, hammerlegs and . . . Where there was a
fair young . . . Who was playing her game of . . . And said she
you rockaby . . . Will you peddle in my bog . . . And he sod her
in Iarland, paved her way from Maizenhead to Youghal. And that's
how Humpfrey, champion emir, holds his own. Shysweet, she rests.

Or show pon him now, will you! Derg rudd face should take
patrick's purge. Hokoway, in his hiphigh bearserk! Third position
of concord! Excellent view from front. Sidome. Female imperfectly
masking male. Redspot his browbrand. Woman's the prey! Thon's
the   dullakeykongsbyogblagroggerswagginline   (private   judgers,
change here for Lootherstown! Onlyromans, keep your seats!) that
drew all ladies please to our great mettrollops. Leary, leary, twenty-
tun nearly, he's plotting kings down for his villa's extension! Gaze
at him now in momentum! As his bridges are blown to babbyrags,
by the lee of his hulk upright on her orbits, and the heave of his
juniper arx in action, he's naval I see. Poor little tartanelle, her
dinties are chattering, the strait's she's in, the bulloge she bears! Her
smirk is smeeching behind for her hills. By the queer quick twist
of her mobcap and the lift of her shift at random and the rate of
her gate of going the pace, two thinks at a time, her country I'm
proud of. The field is down, the race is their own. The galleonman
jovial on his bucky brown nightmare. Bigrob dignagging his lylyput-
tana. One to one bore one! The datter, io, io, sleeps in peace,
in peace. And the twillingsons, ganymede, garrymore, turn in trot
and trot. But old pairamere goes it a gallop, a gallop. Bossford and
phospherine. One to one on!

O, O, her fairy setalite! Casting such shadows to Persia's blind!

The man in the street can see the coming event. Photoflashing it far too wide. It will be known through all Urania soon. Like jealousjoy titaning fear; like rumour rhean round the planets; like china's dragon snapping japets; like rhodagrey up the east. Satyrdaysboost besets Phoebe's nearest. Here's the flood and the flaxen flood that's to come over helpless Irryland. Is there no-one to malahide Liv and her bettyship? Or who'll buy her rosebuds, jettyblack rosebuds, ninsloes of nivia, nonpaps of nan? From the fall of the fig to doom's last post every ephemeral anniversary while the park's police peels peering by for to weight down morrals from county bubblin. That trainer's trundling! Quick, pay up!

Kickakick. She had to kick a laugh. At her old stick-in-the-block. The way he was slogging his paunch about, elbiduubled, meet oft mate on, like hale King Willow, the robberer. Cainmaker's mace and waxened capapee. But the tarrant's brand on his hottoweyt brow. At half past quick in the morning. And her lamp was all askew and a trumbly wick-in-her, ringeysingey. She had to spofforth, she had to kicker, too thick of the wick of her pixy's loomph, wide lickering jessup the smooky shiminey. And her duffed coverpoint of a wickedy batter, whenever she druv behind her stumps for a tyddlesly wink through his tunnilclefft bagslops after the rising bounder's yorkers, as he studd and stoddard and trutted and trumpered, to see had lordherry's blackham's red bobby abbels, it tickled her innings to consort pitch at kicksolock in the morm. Tipatonguing him on in her pigeony linguish, with a flick at the bails for lubrication, to scorch her faster, faster. Ye hek, ye hok, ye hucky hiremonger! Magrath he's my pegger, he is, for bricking up all my old kent road. He'll win your toss, flog your old tom's bowling and I darr ye, barrackybuller, to break his duck! He's posh. I lob him. We're parring all Oogster till the empsyseas run googlie. Declare to ashes and teste his metch! Three for two will do for me and he for thee and she for you. Goeasyosey, for the grace of the fields, or hooley pooley, cuppy, we'll both be bye and by caught in the slips for fear he'd tyre and burst his dunlops and waken her bornybarnies making his boobybabies. The game old merrimynn, square to leg, with his lolleywide towelhat and his hobbsy socks and his wisden's bosse and his norsery pinafore and his gentleman's grip and his playaboy's plunge and his flannelly feelyfooling, treading her hump and hambledown like a maiden wellheld, ovalled over, with her crease where the pads of her punishments ought to be by womanish rights when, keek, the hen in the doran's shantyqueer began in a kikkery key to laugh it off, yeigh, yeigh, neigh, neigh, the way she was wuck to doodledoo by her gallows bird (how's that? Noball, he carries his bat!) nine hundred and dirty too not out, at all times long past conquering cock of the morgans.

How blame us?

Cocorico!

Armigerend everfasting horde. Rico! So the bill to the bowe. As the belle to the beau. We herewith pleased returned auditors' thanks for those and their favours since safely enjoined. Cocoree! Tellaman tillamie. Tubbernacul in tipherairy, sons, travellers in company and their carriageable tochters, tanks tight anne thynne for her contractations tugowards his personeel. Echo, choree chorecho! O I you O you me! Well, we all unite thoughtfully in rendering gratias, well, between loves repassed, begging your honour's pardon for, well, exclusive pigtorial rights of herehear fond tiplady his weekreations, appearing in next eon's issue of the Neptune's Centinel and Tritonville Lightowler with well the widest circulation round the whole universe. Echolo choree choroh choree chorico! How me O my youhou my I youtou to I O? Thanks furthermore to modest Miss Glimglow and neat Master Mettresson who so kindly profiteered their serwishes as demysell of honour and, well, as strainbearer respectively. And a cordiallest brief nod of chinchin dankyshin to, well, patient ringasend as prevenient (by your leave), to all such occasions, detachably replaceable (thanks too! twos intact!). As well as his auricular of Malthus, the promethean paratonnerwetter which first (Pray go! pray go!) taught love's lightning the way (pity shown) to, well, conduct itself (mercy, good shot! only please don't mention it!). Come all ye goatfathers and groanmothers, come all ye markmakers and piledrivers, come all ye laboursaving devisers and chargeleyden dividends, firefinders, waterworkers, deeply condeal with him! All that is still life with death inyeborn, all verbumsaps yet bound to be, to do and to suffer, every creature, everywhere, if you please, kindly feel for her! While the dapplegray dawn drags nearing nigh for to wake all droners that drowse in Dublin.

Humperfeldt and Anunska, wedded now evermore in annastomoses by a ground plan of the placehunter, whiskered beau and donahbella. Totumvir and esquimeena, who so shall separate fetters to new desire, repeals an act of union to unite in bonds of schismacy. O yes! O yes! Withdraw your member! Closure. This chamber stands abjourned. Such precedent is largely a cause to lack of collective continencies among Donnelly's orchard as lifelong the shadyside to Fairbrother's field. Humbo, lock your kekkle up! Anny, blow your wickle out! Tuck away the tablesheet! You never wet the tea! And you may go rightoway back to your Aunty Dilluvia, Humprey, after that!

Retire to rest without first misturbing your nighboor, mankind of baffling descriptions. Others are as tired of themselves as you are. Let each one learn to bore himself. It is strictly requested that no cobsmoking, spitting, pubchat, wrastle rounds, coarse courting, smut, etc, will take place amongst those hours so devoted to repose. Look before behind before you strip you. Disrobe clothed in the strictest secrecy which privacy can afford. Water *non* to be discharged *coram* grate or *ex* window. Never divorce in the bedding the glove that will give you away. Maid Maud ninnies nay but blabs to Omama (for your life, would you!) she to her bosom friend who does all chores (and what do you think my Madeleine saw?): this ignorant mostly sweeps it out along with all the rather old corporators (have you heard of one humbledown jungleman how he bet byrn-and-bushe playing peg and pom?): the maudlin river then gets its dues (adding a din a ding or do): thence those laundresses (O, muddle me more about the maggies! I mean bawnee Madge Ellis and brownie Mag Dillon). Attention at all! Every ditcher's dastard in Dupling will let us know about it if you have paid the mulctman by whether your rent is open to be foreclosed or aback in your arrears. This is seriously meant. Here is a homelet not a hothel.

That's right, old oldun!

All in fact is soon as all of old right as anywas ever in very old place. Were he, hwen scalded of that couverfowl, to beat the bounds by here at such a point of time as this is for at sammel up all wood's haypence and riviers argent (half back from three gangs multaplussed on a twentylot add allto a fiver with the deuce or roamer's numbers ell a fee and do little ones) with the caboosh on him opheld for thrushes' mistiles yet singing oud his parasangs in cornish token: mean fawthery eastend appullcelery, old laddy he high hole: pollysigh patrolman Seekersenn, towney's tanquam, crumlin quiet down from his hoonger, he would mac siccar of inket goodsforetombed ereshiningem of light turkling eitheranny of thuncle's windopes. More, unless we were neverso wrongtaken, if he brought his boots to pause in peace, the one beside the other one, right on the road, he would seize no sound from cache or cave beyond the flow of wand was gypsing water, telling him now, telling him all, all about ham and livery, stay and toast ham in livery, and buttermore

with murmurladen, to waker oats for him on livery. Faurore! Fear-
houre! At last it past! Loab at cod then herrin or wind thin mong
them treen.

Hiss! Which we had only our hazelight to see with, cert, in our
point of view, me and my auxy, Jimmy d'Arcy, hadn't we, Jimmy?
— Who to seen with? Kiss! No kidd, captn, which he stood us, three
jolly postboys, first a couple of Mountjoys and nutty woodbines
with his cadbully's choculars, pepped from our Theoatre Regal's
drolleries puntomine, in the snug at the Cambridge Arms of Teddy
Ales while we was laying, crown jewels to a peanut, was he step-
marm, old noseheavy, or a wouldower, which he said, lads, a taking
low his Whitby hat, lopping off the froth and whishing, with all
respectfulness to the old country, tomorow comrades, we, his long
life's strength and cuirscrween loan to our allhallowed king, the
pitchur that he's turned to weld the wall, (Lawd lengthen him!)
his standpoint was, to belt and blucher him afore the hole pleading
churchal and submarine bar yonder but he made no class at all in
port and cemented palships between our trucers, being a refugee,
didn't he, Jimmy? — Who true to me? Sish! Honeysuckler, that's
what my young lady here, Fred Watkins, bugler Fred, all the ways
from Melmoth in Natal, she calls him, dip the colours, pet, when he
commit his certain questions vivaviz the secret empire of the snake
which it was on a point of our sutton down, how was it, Jimmy? —
Who has sinnerettes to declare? Phiss! Touching our Phoenix
Rangers' nuisance at the meeting of the waitresses, the daintylines,
Elsies from Chelsies, the two legglegels in blooms, and those pest of
parkies, twitch, thistle and charlock, were they for giving up their
fogging trespasses by order which we foregathered he must be raw
in cane sugar, the party, no, Jimmy MacCawthelock? Who trespass
against me? Briss! That's him wiv his wig on, achewing of his maple
gum, that's our grainpopaw, Mister Beardall, an accompliced burgo-
master, a great one among the very greatest, which he told us privates out of his own scented mouf he used to was, my lads, afore
this wineact come, what say, our Jimmy the chapelgoer? — Who
fears all masters! Hi, Jocko Nowlong, my own sweet boosy love,
which he puts his feeler to me behind the beggar's bush, does Freda,
don't you be an emugee! Carryone, he says, though we marooned
through this woylde. We must spy a half a hind on honeysuckler
now his old face's hardalone wiv his defences down during his wap-
pin stillstand, says my Fred, and Jamessime here which, pip it, she
simply must, she says, our pet, she'll do a retroussy from her point of

view (Way you fly! Like a frush!) to keep her flouncies off the grass while paying the wetmenots a musichall visit and pair her fiefighs fore him with just one curl after the cad came back which we fought he wars a gunner and his corkiness lay up two bottles of joy with a shandy had by Fred and a *fino oloroso* which he was warming to, my right, Jimmy, my old brown freer? — Whose dolour, O so mine!

Following idly up to seepoint, neath kingmount shadow the ilk for eke of us, whose nathem's banned, whose hofd a-hooded, welkim warsail, how di' you dew? Hollymerry, ivysad, whicher and whoer, Mr Black Atkins and you tanapanny troopertwos, were you there? Was truce of snow, moonmounded snow? Or did wolken hang o'er earth in umber hue his fulmenbomb? Number two coming! Full inside! Was glimpsed the mean amount of cloud? Or did pitter rain fall in a sprinkling? If the waters could speak as they flow! Timgle Tom, pall the bell! Izzy's busy down the dell! Mizpah low, youyou, number one, in deep humidity! Listen, misled peerless, please! You are of course. You miss him so, to listleto! Of course, my pledge between us, there's no-one Noel like him here to hear. Esch so eschess, douls a doulse! Since Allan Rogue loved Arrah Pogue it's all Killdoughall fair. Triss! Only trees such as these such were those, waving there, the barketree, the o'briertree, the rowantree, the o'corneltree, the behanshrub near windy arbour, the magill o'dendron more. Trem! All the trees in the wood they trembold, humbild, when they heard the stoppress from domday's erewold.

Tiss! Two pretty mistletots, ribboned to a tree, up rose liberator and, fancy, they were free! Four witty missywives, winking under hoods, made lasses like lads love maypoleriding and dotted our green with tricksome couples, fiftyfifty, their chiltren's hundred. So childish pence took care of parents' pounds and many made money the way in the world where rushroads to riches crossed slums of lice and, the cause of it all, he forged himself ahead like a blazing urbanorb, brewing treble to drown grief, giving and taking mayom and tuam, playing milliards with his three golden balls, making party capital out of landed selfinterest, light on a slavey but weighty on the bourse, our hugest commercial emporialist, with his sons booing home from afar and his daughters bridling up at his side. Finner!

How did he bank it up, swank it up, the whaler in the punt, a guinea by a groat, his index on the balance and such wealth into the bargain, with the boguey which he snatched in the baggage coach ahead? Going forth on the prowl, master jackill, under night and creeping back, dog to hide, over morning. Humbly to fall and cheaply to rise, exposition of failures. Through Duffy's blunders and MacKenna's insurance for upper ten and lower five the band played on. As one generation tells another. Ofter the fall. First for a change of a seven days license he wandered out of his farmer's health and so lost his early parishlife. Then ('twas in fenland) occidentally of a sudden, six junelooking flamefaces straggled wild out of their turns through his parsonfired wicket, showing all shapes of striplings in sleepless tights. Promptly whomafter in undated times, very properly a dozen generations anterior to themselves, a main chanced to burst and misflooded his fortunes, wrothing foulplay over his fives' court and his fine poultryyard wherein were spared a just two of a feather in wading room only. Next, upon due reflotation, up started four hurrigan gales to smithereen his plateglass housewalls and the slate for accounts his keeper was cooking. Then came three boy buglehorners who counterbezzled and crossbugled him. Later on in the same evening two hussites absconded through a breach in his bylaws and left him, the infidels, to pay himself off in kind remembrances. Till, ultimatehim, fell the crowning barleystraw, when an explosium of his distilleries deafadumped all his dry goods to his most favoured sinflute and dropped him, what remains of a heptark, leareyed and letterish, weeping worrybound on his bankrump.

Pepep. Pay bearer, sure and sorry, at foot of ohoho honest policist. On never again, by Phoenis, swore on him Lloyd's, not for beaten wheat, not after Sir Joe Meade's father, thanks! They know him, the covenanter, by rote at least, for a chameleon at last, in his true falseheaven colours from ultraviolent to subred tissues. That's his last tryon to march through the grand tryomphal arch. His reignbolt's shot. Never again! How you do that like, Mista Chimepiece? You got nice yum plemyums. Praypaid my promishles!

Agreed, Wu Welsher, he was chogfulled to beacsate on earn as in hiving, of foxold conningnesses but who, hey honey, for all values of his latters, integer integerrimost, was the formast of the firm? At folkmood hailed, at part farwailed, accwmwladed concloud, NuahNuah, Nebob of Nephilim! After all what followed for apprentice sake? Since the now nighs nearing as the yetst hies hin. Jeebies, ugh, kek, ptah, that was an ill man! Jawboose, puddigood, this is for true a sweetish mand! But Jumbluffer, bagdad, sir, yond would be for a once over our all honoured christmastyde easteredman. Fourth position of solution. How johnny! Finest view from horizon.

Tableau final. Two me see. Male and female unmask we hem. Begum by gunne! Who now broothes oldbrawn. Dawn! The nape of his nameshielder's scalp. Halp! After having drummed all he dun. Hun! Worked out to an inch of his core. More! Ring down. While the queenbee he staggerhorned blesses her bliss for to feel her funnyman's functions Tag. Rumbling.

Tiers, tiers and tiers. Rounds.

4

Sandhyas! Sandhyas! Sandhyas!

Calling all downs. Calling all downs to dayne. Array! Surrection! Eireweeker to the wohld bludyn world. O rally, O rally, O rally! Phlenxty, O rally! To what lifelike thyne of the bird can be. Seek you somany matters. Haze sea east to Osseania. Here! Here! Tass, Patt, Staff, Woff, Havv, Bluvv and Rutter. The smog is lofting. And already the olduman's olduman has godden up on othertimes to litanate the bonnamours. Sonne feine, somme feehn avaunt! Guld modning, have yous viewsed Piers' aube? Thane yaars agon we have used yoors up since when we have fused now orther. Calling all daynes. Calling all daynes to dawn. The old breeding bradsted culminwillth of natures to Foyn MacHooligan. The leader, the leader! Securest jubilends albas Temoram. Clogan slogan. Quake up, dim dusky, wook doom for husky! And let Billey Feghin be baallad out of his humuluation. Confindention to churchen. We have highest gratifications in announcing to pewtewr publikumst of pratician pratyusers, genghis is ghoon for you.

A hand from the cloud emerges, holding a chart expanded.

The eversower of the seeds of light to the cowld owld sowls that are in the domnatory of Defmut after the night of the carrying of the word of Nuahs and the night of making Mehs to cuddle up in a coddlepot, Pu Nuseht, lord of risings in the yonderworld of Ntamplin, tohp triumphant, speaketh.

Vah! Suvarn Sur! Scatter brand to the reneweller of the sky, thou who agnitest! Dah! Arcthuris comeing! Be! Verb umprincipiant through the trancitive spaces! Kilt by kelt shell kithagain with kinagain. We elect for thee, Tirtangel. Svadesia salve! We Durbalanars, theeadjure. A way, the Margan, from our astamite, through dimdom done till light kindling light has led we hopas but hunt me the journeyon, iteritinerant, the kal his course, amid the semitary of

Somnionia. Even unto Heliotropolis, the castellated, the enchanting.
Now if soomone felched a twoel and soomonelses warmet watter
we could, while you was saying Morkret Miry or Smud, Brunt and
Rubbinsen, make sunlike sylp om this warful dune's battam. Yet
clarify begins at. Whither the spot for? Whence the hour by? See
but! Lever hulme! Take in. Respassers should be pursaccoutred. Qui
stabat Meins quantum qui stabat Peins. As of yours. We annew.
Our shades of minglings mengle them and help help horizons. A
flasch and, rasch, it shall come to pasch, as hearth by hearth leaps
live. For the tanderest stock with the rosinost top Ahlen Hill's, club-
pubber, in general stores and. Atriathroughwards, Lugh the Brath-
wacker will be the listened after and he larruping sparks out of his
teiney ones. The spearspid of dawnfire totouches ain the tablestoane
ath the centre of the great circle of the macroliths of Helusbelus in
the boshiman brush on this our peneplain by Fangaluvu Bight
whence the horned cairns erge, stanserstanded, to floran frohn, idols
of isthmians. Overwhere. Gaunt grey ghostly gossips growing grub-
ber in the glow. Past now pulls. Cur one beast, even Dane the Great,
may treadspath with sniffer he snout impursuant to byelegs. Edar's
chuckal humuristic. But why pit the cur afore the noxe? Let shrill
their duan Gallus, han, and she, hou the Sassqueehenna, makes
ducksruns at crooked. Once for the chantermale, twoce for the
pother and once twoce threece for the waither. So an inedible yel-
lowmeat turns out the invasable blackth. Kwhat serves to rob with
Alliman, saelior, a turnkeyed trot to Seapoint, pierrotettes, means
Noel's Bar and Julepunsch, by Joge, if you've tippertaps in your
head or starting kursses, tailour, you're silenced at Henge Ceolleges,
Exmooth, Ostbys for ost, boys, each and one? Death banes and the
quick quoke. But life wends and the dombs spake! Whake? Hill
of Hafid, knock and knock, nachasach, gives relief to the langscape
as he strauches his lamusong untoupon gazelle channel and the
bride of the Bryne, shin high shake, is dotter than evar for a damse
wed her farther. Lambel on the up! We may plesently heal Geo-
glyphy's twentynine ways to say goodbett an wassing seoosoon liv.
With the forty wonks winking please me your much as to. With
her tup. It's a long long ray to Newirgland's premier. For korps,
for streamfish, for confects, for bullyoungs, for smearsassage, for
patates, for steaked pig, for men, for limericks, for waterfowls, for
wagsfools, for louts, for cold airs, for late trams, for curries, for curlews, for leekses, for orphalines, for tunnygulls, for clear goldways,
for lungfortes, for moonyhaunts, for fairmoneys, for coffins, for

tantrums, for armaurs, for waglugs, for rogues comings, for sly goings, for larksmathes, for homdsmeethes, for quailsmeathes, kila-
looly. Tep! Come lead, crom lech! Top. Wisely for us Old Bruton
has withdrawn his theory. You are alpsulumply wroght! Amsu-
lummmm. But this is perporteroguing youpoorapps? Namantanai.
Sure it's not revieng your? Amslu! Good all so. We seem to understand apad vellumtomes muniment, Arans Duhkha, among hose-
shoes, cheriotiers and etceterogenious bargainboutbarrows, ofver
and umnder, since, evenif or although, in double preposition as in
triple conjunction, how the mudden research in the topaia that was
Mankaylands has gone to prove from the picalava present in the
maramara melma that while a successive generation has been in
the deep deep deeps of Deepereras. Buried hearts. Rest here.

Conk a dook he'll doo. Svap.

So let him slap, the sap! Till they take down his shatter from his
shap. He canease. Fill stap.

Thus faraclacks the friarbird. Listening, Syd!

The child, a natural child, thenown by the mnames of, (aya!
aya!), wouldbewas kidnapped at an age of recent probably, possibly remoter; or he conjured himself from seight by slide at hand;
for which thetheatron is a lemoronage; at milchgoat fairmesse; in
full dogdhis; sod on a fall; pat; the hundering blundering dunder-
funder of plundersundered manhood; behold, he returns; renasce-
nent; fincarnate; still foretold around the hearthside; at matin a
fact; hailed chimers' ersekind; foe purmanant, fum in his mow;
awike in wave risurging into chrest; *victis poenis hesternis;* fostfath
of solas; fram choicest of wiles with warmen and sogns til Banba,
burial aranging; under articles thirtynine of the reconstitution; by
the lord's order of the canon consecrandable; earthlost that we
thought him; pesternost, the noneknown worrier; from Tumbar-
umba mountain; in persence of whole landslots; forebe all the ras-
sias; sire of leery subs of dub; the Diggins, Woodenhenge, as to hang
out at; with spawnish oel full his angalach; the sousenugh; gnomeo-
sulphidosalamermauderman; the big brucer, fert in fort; Gunnar,
of The Gunnings, Gund; one of the two or three forefivest fellows
a bloke could in holiday crowd encounter; benedicted be the barrel; kilderkins, lids off; a roache, an oxmaster, a sort of heaps, a pam-
philius, a vintivat niviceny, a hygiennic contrivance socalled from
the editor; the thick of your thigh; you knox; quite; talking to the
vicar's joy and ruth; the gren, woid and glue been broking by the
maybole gards; he; when no crane in Elga is heard; upout to speak

this lay; without links, without impediments, with gygantogyres, with freeflawforms;parasama to himself; atman as evars; whom otherwise becauses; no puler as of old but as of young a palatin; whitelock not lacked nor temperasoleon; though he appears a funny colour;stoatters some; but a quite a big bug after the dahlias; place inspectorum sarchent; also the hullow chyst excavement; astronomically fabulafigured; as Jambudvispa Vipra foresaw of him; the last half versicle repurchasing his pawned word; sorensplit and paddypatched; and pfor to pfinish our pfun of a pfan coalding the keddle mickwhite; sure, straight, slim, sturdy, serene, synthetical, swift.

By the antar of Yasas! Ruse made him worthily achieve inherited wish. The drops upon that mantle rained never around Fingal. Goute! Loughlin's Salts, Will, make a newman if anyworn. Soe? La! Lamfadar's arm it has cocoincidences. You mean to see we have been hadding a sound night's sleep? You may so. It is just, it is just about to, it is just about to rolywholyover. Svapnasvap. Of all the stranger things that ever not even in the hundrund and badst pageans of unthowsent and wonst nice or in eddas and oddes bokes of tomb, dyke and hollow to be have happened! The untireties of livesliving being the one substrance of a streamsbecoming. Totalled in toldteld and teldtold in tittletell tattle. Why? Because, graced be Gad and all giddy gadgets, in whose words were the beginnings, there are two signs to turn to, the yest and the ist, the wright side and the wronged side, feeling aslip and wauking up, so an, so farth. Why? On the sourdsite we have the Moskiosk Djinpalast with its twin adjacencies, the bathouse and the bazaar, allahallahallah, and on the sponthesite it is the alcovan and the rosegarden, boony noughty, all puraputhry. Why? One's apurr apuss a story about brid and breakfedes and parricombating and coushcouch but others is of tholes and oubworn buyings, dolings and chafferings in heat, contest and enmity. Why? Every talk has his stay, vidnis Shavarsanjivana, and all-a-dreams perhapsing under lucksloop at last are through. Why? It is a sot of a swigswag, systomy dystomy, which everabody you ever anywhere at all doze. Why? Such me.

And howpsadrowsay.

Lok! A shaft of shivery in the act, anilancinant. Cold's sleuth! Vayuns! Where did thots come from? It is infinitesimally fevers, resty fever, risy fever, a coranto of aria, sleeper awakening, in the smalls of one's back presentiment, gip, and again, geip, a flash from a future of maybe mahamayability through the windr of a wondr in a wildr is a weltr as a wirbl of a warbl is a world.

Tom.

It is perfect degrees excelsius. A jaladaew still stilleth. Cloud lay but mackrel are. Anemone activescent, the torporature is returning to mornal. Humid nature is feeling itself freely at ease with the all fresco. The vervain is to herald as the grass administers. They say, they say in effect, they really say. You have eaden fruit. Say whuit. You have snakked mid a fish. Telle whish. Every those personal place objects if nonthings where soevers and they just done been doing being in a dromo of todos withouten a bound to be your trowers. Forswundled. You hald him by the tap of the tang. Not a salutary sellable sound is since. Instead for asteer, adrift with adraft. Nuctumbulumbumus wanderwards the Nil. Victorias neanzas. Alberths neantas. It was a long, very long, a dark, very dark, an allburt unend, scarce endurable, and we could add mostly quite various and somenwhat stumbletumbling night. Endee he sendee. Diu! The has goning at gone, the is coming to come. Greets to ghastern, hie to morgning. Dormidy, destady. Doom is the faste. Well down, good other! Now day, slow day, from delicate to divine, divases. Padma, brighter and sweetster, this flower that bells, it is our hour or risings. Tickle, tickle. Lotus spray. Till herenext. Adya.

Take thanks, thankstum, thamas. In that earopean end meets Ind.

There is something supernoctural about whatever you called him it. Panpan and vinvin are not alonety vanvan and pinpin in your Tamal without tares but simplysoley they are they. Thisutter followis that odder fellow. Himkim kimkim. Old yeasterloaves may be a stale as a stub and the pitcher go to aftoms on the wall. Mildew, murk, leak and yarn now want the bad that they lied on. And your last words todate in camparative accoustomology are going to tell stretch of a fancy through strength towards joyance, adyatants, where he gets up. Allay for allay, a threat for a throat.

Tim!

To them in Ysat Loka. Hearing. The urb it orbs. Then's now with now's then in tense continuant. Heard. Who having has he shall have had. Hear! Upon the thuds trokes truck, chim, it will be exactlyso fewer hours by so many minutes of the ope of the diurn of the sennight of the maaned of the yere of the age of the madamanvantora of Grossguy and Littleylady, our hugibus hugibum and our weewee mother, actaman housetruewith, and their childer and their napirs and their napirs' childers napirs and their chattels and their servance and their cognance and their ilks and their orts and their everythings that is be will was theirs.

Much obliged. Time-o'-Thay! But wherth, O clerk?

Whithr a clonk? Vartman! See you not soo the pfath they pfunded, oura vatars that arred in Himmal, harruad bathar namas, the gow, the stiar, the tigara, the liofant, when even thurst was athar vetals, mid trefoils slipped the sable rampant, hoof, hoof, hoof, hoof, pada-podopudupedding on fattafottafutt. Ere we are! Signifying, if tungs may tolkan, that, primeval conditions having gradually receded but nevertheless the emplacement of solid and fluid having to a great extent persisted through intermittences of sullemn fulminance, sollemn nuptialism, sallemn sepulture and providential divining, making possible and even inevitable, after his a time has a tense haves and havenots hesitency, at the place and period under consideration a socially organic entity of a millenary military maritory monetary morphological circumformation in a more or less settled state of equonomic ecolube equalobe equilab equilibbrium. Gam on, Gearge! Nomomorphemy for me! Lessnatbe angardsmanlake! You jast gat a tache of army on the stumuk. To the Angar at Anker. Aecquotincts. Seeworthy. Lotsthankyouful, polite pointsins! There's a tavarn in the tarn.

Tip. Take Tamotimo's topical. Tip. Browne yet Noland. Tip. Advert.

Where. Cumulonubulocirrhonimbant heaven electing, the dart of desire has gored the heart of secret waters and the poplarest wood in the entire district is being grown at present, eminently adapted for the requirements of pacnincstricken humanity and, between all the goings up and the whole of the comings down and the fog of the cloud in which we toil and the cloud of the fog under which we labour, bomb the thing's to be domb about it so that, beyond indicating the locality, it is felt that one cannot with advantage add a very great deal to the aforegoing by what, such as it is to be, follows, just mentioning however that the old man of the sea and the old woman in the sky if they don't say nothings about it they don't tell us lie, the gist of the pantomime, from cannibal king to the property horse, being, slumply and slopely, to remind us how, in this drury world of ours, Father Times and Mother Spacies boil their kettle with their crutch. Which every lad and lass in the lane knows. Hence.

Polycarp pool, the pool of Innalavia, Saras the saft as, of meadewy marge, atween Deltas Piscium and Sagittariastrion, whereinn once we lave 'tis alve and vale, minnyhahing here from hiarwather, a poddlebridges in a passabed, the river of lives, the regenerations of

the incarnations of the emanations of the apparentations of Funn
and Nin in Cleethabala, the kongdomain of the Alieni, an accor-
saired race, infester of Libnud Ocean, Moylamore, let it be! Where
Allbroggt Neandser tracking Viggynette Neeinsee gladsighted her
Linfian Fall and a teamdiggingharrow turned the first sod. Sluce!
Caughterect! Goodspeed the blow! (Incidentally 'tis believed that
his harpened before Gage's Fane for it has to be over this booty
spotch, though some hours to the wester, that ex-Colonel House's
preterpost heiress is to return unto the outstretcheds of Dweyr
O'Michael's loinsprung the blunterbusted pikehead which his had
hewn in hers, prolonged laughter words). There an alomdree begins
to green, soreen seen for loveseat, as we know that should she, for
by essentience his law, so it make all. It is scainted to Vitalba. And
her little white bloomkins, twittersky trimmed, are hobdoblins'
hankypanks. Saxenslyke our anscessers thought so darely on now
they're going soever to Anglesen, free of juties, dyrt chapes. There
too a slab slobs, immermemorial, the only in all swamp. But so bare,
so boulder, brag sagging such a brr bll bmm show that, of Barin-
dens, the white alfred, it owed to have at leased some butchup's
upperon. *Homos Circas Elochlannensis!* His showplace at Leeambye.
Old Wommany Wyes. Pfif! But, while gleam with gloom swan here
and there, this shame rock and that whispy planter tell Paudheen
Steel-the-Poghue and his perty Molly Vardant, in goodbroomirish,
arrah, this place is a proper and his feist a ferial for curdnal com-
munial, so be who would celibrate the holy mystery upon or that
the pirigrim from Mainylands beatend, the calmleaved hutcaged
by that look whose glaum is sure he means bisnisgels to empalm-
over. A naked yogpriest, clothed of sundust, his oakey doaked with
frondest leoves, offrand to the ewon of her owen. Tasyam kuru
salilakriyamu! Pfaf!

Bring about it to be brought about and it will be, loke, our lake
lemanted, that greyt lack, the citye of Is is issuant (atlanst!), urban
and orbal, through seep froms umber under wasseres of Erie.

Lough!

Hwo! Hwy, dairmaidens? Asthoreths, assay! Earthsigh to is
heavened.

Hillsengals, the daughters of the cliffs, responsen. Longsome the
samphire coast. From thee to thee, thoo art it thoo, that thouest there.
The like the near, the liker nearer. O sosay! A family, a band, a
school, a clanagirls. Fiftines andbut fortines by novanas andor
vantads by octettes ayand decadendecads by a lunary with last a

lone. Whose every has herdifferent from the similies with her site. *Sicut campanulae petalliferentes* they coroll in caroll round Botany Bay. A dweam of dose innocent dirly dirls. Keavn! Keavn! And they all setton voicies about singsing music was Keavn! He. Only he. Ittle he. Ah! The whole clangalied. Oh!

S. Wilhelmina's, S. Gardenia's, S. Phibia's, S. Veslandrua's, S. Clarinda's, S. Immecula's, S. Dolores Delphin's, S. Perlanthroa's, S. Errands Gay's, S. Eddaminiva's, S. Rhodamena's, S. Ruadagara's, S. Drimicumtra's, S. Una Vestity's, S. Mintargisia's, S. Misha-La-Valse's, S. Churstry's, S. Clouonaskieym's, S. Bellavistura's, S. Santamonta's, S. Ringsingsund's, S. Heddadin Drade's, S. Glacianivia's, S. Waidafrira's, S. Thomassabbess's and (trema! unloud!! pepet!!!) S. Loellisotoelles!

Prayfulness! Prayfulness!

Euh! Thaet is seu whaet shaell one naeme it!

The meidinogues have tingued togethering. Ascend out of your bed, cavern of a trunk, and shrine! Kathlins is kitchin. Soros cast, ma brone! You must exterra acquarate to interirigate all the arkypelicans. The austrologer Wallaby by Tolan, who farshook our showrs from Newer Aland, has signed the you and the now our mandate. Milenesia waits. Be smark.

One seekings. Not the lithe slender, not the broad roundish near the lithe slender, not the fairsized fullfeatured to the leeward of the broad roundish but, indeed and inneed, the curling, perfectportioned, flowerfleckled, shapely highhued, delicate features swaying to the windward of the fairsized fullfeatured.

Was that in the air about when something is to be said for it or is it someone imparticular who will somewherise for the whole anyhow?

What does Coemghen? Tell his hidings clearly! A woodtoogooder. Is his moraltack still his best of weapons? How about a little more goaling goold? Rowlin's tun he gadder no must. It is the voice of Roga. His face is the face of a son. Be thine the silent hall, O Jarama! A virgin, the one, shall mourn thee. Roga's stream is solence. But Croona is in adestance. The ass of the O'Dwyer of Greyglens is abrowtobayse afeald in his terroirs of the Potterton's forecoroners, the reeks around the burleyhearthed. When visited by an independant reporter, "Mike" Portlund, to burrow burning the latterman's Resterant so is called the gortan in questure he mikes the fallowing for the Durban Gazette, firstcoming issue. From a collispendent. Any were. Deemsday. Bosse of Upper and Lower Byg-

gotstrade, Ciwareke, may he live for river! The Games funeral at
Valleytemple. Saturnights pomps, exhabiting that corricatore of a
harss, revealled by Oscur Camerad. The last of Dutch Schulds, per-
humps. Pipe in Dream Cluse. Uncovers Pub History. The Outrage,
at Length. Affected Mob Follows in Religious Sullivence. Rinven-
tion of vestiges by which they drugged the buddhy. Moviefigure on
in scenic section. By Patathicus. And there, from out of the scuity,
misty Londan, along the canavan route, that is with the years gone,
mild beam of the wave his polar bearing, steerner among stars, trust
touthena and you tread true turf, comes the sorter, Mr Hurr Hansen, talking alltheways in himself of his hopes to fall in among a
merryfoule of maidens happynghome from the dance, his knyckle
allaready of his knackskey fob, a passable compatriate proparly of
the Grimstad galleon, old pairs frieze, feed up to the noxer with
their geese and peeas and oats upon a trencher and the toyms he'd
lust in Wooming but with that smeoil like a grace of backoning over
his egglips of the sunsoonshine. Here's heering you in a guess-
masque, latterman! And such an improofment! As royt as the mail
and as fat as a fuddle! Schoen! Shoan! Shoon the Puzt! A penny
for your thought abouts! Tay, tibby, tanny, tummy, tasty, tosty, tay.
Batch is for Baker who baxters our bread. O, what an ovenly odour!
Butter butter! Bring us this days our maily bag! But receive me, my
frensheets, from the emerald dark winterlong! For diss is the doss
for Eilder Downes and dass is it duss, as singen sengers, what the
hardworking straightwalking stoutstamping securelysealing officials
who trow to form our G.M.P.'s pass muster generally shay for shee
and sloo for slee when butting their headd to the pillow for a night-
shared nakeshift with the alter girl they tuck in for sweepsake.
Dutiful wealker for his hydes of march. Haves you the time. Hans
ahike? Heard you the crime, senny boy? The man was giddy on
letties on the dewry of the duary, be pursueded, whethered with
entrenous, midgreys, dagos, teatimes, shadows, nocturnes or samoans,
if wellstocked fillerouters plushfeverfraus with dopy chonks, and
this, that and the other pigskin or muffle kinkles, taking a pipe
course or doing an anguish, seen to his fleece in after his foull, when
Dr Chart of Greet Chorsles street he changed his backbone at a cit-
ting. He had not the declaination, as what with the foos as whet
with the fays, but so far as hanging a goobes on the precedings,
wherethen the lag allows, it mights be anything after darks. Which
the deers alones they sees and the darkies they is snuffing of the wind
up. Debbling. Greanteavvents! Hyacinssies with heliotrollops! Not

once fullvixen freakings and but dubbledecoys! It is a lable iction on the porte of the cuthulic church and summum most atole for it. Where is that blinketey blanketer, that quound of a pealer, the sunt of a hunt whant foxes good men! Where or he, our loved among many?

But what does Coemghem, the fostard? Tyro a tora. The novened iconostase of his blueygreyned vitroils but begins in feint to light his legend. Let Phosphoron proclaim! Peechy peechy. Say he that saw him that saw! Man shall sharp run do a get him. Ask no more, Jerry mine, Roga's voice! No pice soorkabatcha. The bog which puckerooed the posy. The vinebranch of Heremonheber on Bregia's plane where Teffia lies is leaved invert and fructed proper but the cublic hatches endnot open yet for hourly rincers' mess. Read Higgins, Cairns and Egen. Malthus is yet lukked in close. Withun. How swathed thereanswer alcove makes theirinn! Besoakers loiter on. And primilibatory solicates of limon sodias will be absorbable. It is not even yet the engine of the load with haled morries full of crates, you mattinmummur, for dombell dumbs? Sure and 'tis not then. The greek Sideral Reulthway, as it havvents, will soon be starting a smooth with its first single hastencraft. Danny buzzers instead of the vialact coloured milk train on the fartykket plan run with its endless gallaxion of rotatorattlers and the smooltroon our elderens rememberem as the scream of the service, Strubry Bess. Also the waggonwobblers are still yet everdue to precipitate after night's combustion. Aspect, Shamus Rogua or! Taceate and! *Hagiographice canat Ecclesia.* Which aubrey our first shall show. Inattendance who is who is will play that's what's that to what's that, what.

Oyes! Oyeses! Oyesesyeses! The primace of the Gaulls, protonotorious, I yam as I yam, mitrogenerand in the free state on the air, is now aboil to blow a Gael warning. Inoperation Eyrlands Eyot, Meganesia, Habitant and the onebut thousand insels, Western and Osthern Approaches.

Of Kevin, of increate God the servant, of the Lord Creator a filial fearer, who, given to the growing grass, took to the tall timber, slippery dick the springy heeler, as we have seen, so we have heard, what we have received, that we have transmitted, thus we shall hope, this we shall pray till, in the search for love of knowledge through the comprehension of the unity in altruism through stupefaction, it may again how it may again, shearing aside the four wethers and passing over the dainty daily dairy and dropping by the way the lapful of live coals and smoothing out Nelly Nettle and her lad of mettle, full of stings, fond of stones, friend of gnew-gnawns bones and leaving all the messy messy to look after our douche douche, the miracles, death and life are these.

Yad. Procreated on the ultimate ysland of Yreland in the encyclical yrish archipelago, come their feast of precreated holy whiteclad angels, whomamong the christener of his, voluntarily poor Kevin, having been graunted the pravilege of a priest's postcreated portable *altare cum balneo*, when espousing the one true cross, invented and exalted, in celibate matrimony at matin chime arose and westfrom went and came in alb of cloth of gold to our own midmost Glendalough-le-vert by archangelical guidance where amiddle of meeting waters of river Yssia and Essia river on this one of eithers lone navigable lake piously Kevin, lawding the triune trishagion, amidships of his conducible altar super bath, rafted centripetally, diaconal servent of orders hibernian, midway across the subject lake surface to its supreem epicentric lake Ysle, whereof its lake is the ventrifugal principality, whereon by prime, powerful in knowledge, Kevin came to where its centre is among the circumfluent water-courses of Yshgafiena and Yshgafiuna, an enysled lakelet yslanding a lacustrine yslet, whereupon with beached raft subdiaconal bath *propter* altar, with oil extremely anointed, accompanied by prayer, holy Kevin bided till the third morn hour but to build a rubric penitential honeybeehivehut in whose enclosure to live in fortitude, acolyte of cardinal virtues, whereof the arenary floor, most holy Kevin excavated as deep as to the depth of a seventh part of one full fathom, which excavated, venerable Kevin, anchorite, taking counsel, proceded towards the lakeside of the ysletshore whereat seven several times he, eastward genuflecting, in entire ubidience at sextnoon collected gregorian water sevenfold and with ambrosian eucharistic joy of heart as many times receded, carrying that privileged altar *unacumque* bath, which severally seven times into the cavity excavated, a lector of water levels, most venerable Kevin, then effused thereby letting there be water where was theretofore dry land, by him so concreated, who now, confirmed a strong and perfect christian, blessed Kevin, exorcised his holy sister water, perpetually chaste, so that, well understanding, she should fill to midheight his tubbathaltar, which hanbathtub, most blessed Kevin, ninthly enthroned, in the concentric centre of the translated water, whereamid, when violet vesper vailed, Saint Kevin, Hydrophilos, having girded his sable *cappa magna* as high as to his cherubical loins, at solemn compline sat in his sate of wisdom, that handbathtub, whereverafter, recreated *doctor insularis* of the universal church, keeper of the door of meditation, memory *extempore* proposing and intellect formally considering, recluse, he meditated continuously with seraphic ardour the primal sacrament of baptism or the regeneration of all man by affusion of water. Yee.

Bisships, bevel to rock's rite! Sarver buoy, extinguish! Nuotabene. The rare view from the three Benns under the bald heaven is on the other end, askan your blixom on dimmen and blastun, something to right hume about. They were erected in a purvious century, as a hen fine coops and, if you know your Bristol and have trudged the trolly ways and elventurns of that old cobbold city, you will sortofficially scribble a mental Peny-Knox-Gore. Whether they were franklings by name also has not been fully probed. Their design is a whosold word and the charming details of light in dark are freshed from the feminiairity which breathes content. O *ferax cupla!* Ah, fairypair! The first exploder to make his ablations in these parks was indeed that lucky mortal which the monster trial showed on its first day out. What will not arky paper, anticidingly inked with penmark, push, per sample prof, kuvertly falted, when style, stink and stigmataphoron are of one sum in the same person? He comes out of the soil very well after all just where Old Toffler is to come shuffling alongsoons Panniquanne starts showing of her peequuliar talonts. Awaywrong wandler surking to a rightrare rute for his plain utterrock sukes, appelled to by her fancy claddaghs. You plied that pokar, gamesy, swell as aye did, while there were flickars to the flores. He may be humpy, nay, he may be dumpy but there is always something racey about, say, a sailor on a horse. As soon as we sale him geen we gates a sprise! He brings up tofatufa and that is how we get to Missas in Massas. The old Marino tale. We veriters verity notefew demmed lustres priorly magistrite maximollient in ludubility learned. Facst. Teak off that wise head! Great sinner, good sonner, is in effect the motto of the MacCowell family. The gloved fist (skrimmhandsker) was intraduced into their socerdatal tree before the fourth of the twelfth and it is even a little odd all four horolodgeries still gonging restage Jakob van der Bethel, smolking behing his pipe, with Essav of Messagepostumia, lentling out his borrowed chafingdish, before cymbaloosing the apostles at every hours of changeover. The first and last rittlerattle of the anniverse; when is a nam nought a nam whenas it is a. Watch! Heroes' Highway where our fleshers leave their bonings and every bob and joan to fill the bumper fair. It is their segnall for old Champelysied to seek the shades of his retirement and for young Chappielassies to tear a round and tease their partners lovesoftfun at Finnegan's Wake.

And it's high tigh tigh. Titley hi ti ti. That my dig pressed in your dag si. Gnug of old Gnig. Ni, gnid mig brawly! I bag your burden. Mees is thees knees. Thi is Mi. We have caught oneselves, Sveasmeas, in somes incontigruity coumplegs of heoponhurrish marrage from whose I most sublumbunate. A polog, my engl! Excutes. Om still so sovvy. Whyle om till ti ti.

Ha!

Dayagreening gains in schlimninging. A summerwint springfalls, abated. Hail, regn of durknass, snowly receassing, thund lightening thund, into the dimbelowstard departamenty whitherout, soon hist, soon mist, to the hothehill from the hollow, Solsking the Frist (attempted by the admirable Captive Bunting and Loftonant-Cornel Blaire) will processingly show up above Tumplen Bar whereupont he was much jubilated by Boergemester "Dyk" ffogg of Isoles, now Eisold, looking most plussed with (exhib 39) a clout capped sunbubble anaccanponied from his bequined torse. Up.

Blanchardstown mewspeppers pleads coppyl. Gracest goodness, heave mensy upponnus! Grand old Manbutton, give your bowlers a rest!

It is a mere mienerism of this vague of visibilities, mark you, as accorded to by moisturologist of the Brehons Assorceration for the advauncement of scayence because, my dear, mentioning of it under the breath, as in pure (what bunkum!) essenesse, there have been disselving forenenst you just the draeper, the two drawpers assisters and the three droopers assessors confraternitisers. Who are, of course, Uncle Arth, your two cozes from Niece and (kunject a bit now!) our own familiars, Billyhealy, Ballyhooly and Bullyhowley, surprised in an indecorous position by the Sigurd Sigerson Sphygmomanometer Society for bledprusshers.

Knightsmore. Haventyne?

Ha ha!

This Mister Ireland? And a live?

Ay, ay. Aye, aye, baas.

The cry of Stena chills the vitals of slumbring off the motther has been pleased into the harms of old salaciters, meassurers soon and soon, but the voice of Alina gladdens the cocklyhearted dreamerish for that magic moning with its ching chang chap sugay kaow laow milkee muchee bringing beckerbrose, the brew with the foo-

choor in it. Sawyest? Nodt? Nyets, I dhink I sawn to remumb or
sumbsuch. A kind of a thinglike all traylogged then pubably it re-
symbles a pelvic or some kvind then props an acutebacked quadran-
gle with aslant off ohahnthenth a wenchyoumaycuddler, lying with
her royalirish uppershoes among the theeckleaves. Signs are on of
a mere by token that wills still to be becoming upon this there once
a here was world. As the dayeleyves unfolden them. In the wake of
the blackshape, *Nattenden Sorte;* whenat, hindled firth and hun-
dled furth, the week of wakes is out and over; as a wick weak woking
from ennemberable Ashias unto fierce force fuming, temtem tam-
tam, the Phoenican wakes.

Passing. One. We are passing. Two. From sleep we are passing.
Three. Into the wikeawades warld from sleep we are passing. Four.
Come, hours, be ours!

But still. Ah diar, ah diar! And stay.

It was allso agreenable in our sinegear clutchless, touring the
no placelike no timelike absolent, mixing up pettyvaughan popu-
lose with the magnumoore genstries, lloydhaired mersscenary blook-
ers with boydskinned pigttetails and goochlipped gwendolenes with
duffyeyed dolores; like so many unprobables in their poor suit of the
improssable. With Mata and after please with Matamaru and after
please stop with Matamaruluka and after stop do please with Mata-
marulukajoni.

And anotherum. Ah ess, dapple ass! He will be longing after the
Grogram Grays. And, Weisingchetaoli, he will levellaut ministel
Trampleasure be. Sheflower Rosina, younger Sheflower fruit Ama-
ryllis, youngest flowerfruityfrond Sallysill or Sillysall. And house
with heaven roof occupanters they are continuatingly attraverse of
its milletestudinous windows, ricocoursing themselves, as staneglass
on stanegloss, inplayn unglish Wynn's Hotel. Brancherds at: Bull-
beck, Oldboof, Sassondale, Jorsey Uppygard, Mundelonde, Abbey-
totte, Bracqueytuitte with Hockeyvilla, Fockeyvilla, Hillewille and
Wallhall. Hoojahoo managers the thingaviking. Obning shotly.
When the messanger of the risen sun, (see other oriel) shall give
to every seeable a hue and to every hearable a cry and to each spectacle his spot and to each happening her houram. The while we,
we are waiting, we are waiting for. Hymn.

Muta: Quodestnunc fumusiste volhvuns ex Domoyno?

Juva: It is Old Head of Kettle puffing off the top of the mornin.

Muta: He odda be thorly well ashamed of himself for smoking
before the high host.

Juva: Dies is Dorminus master and commandant illy tonobrass.

Muta: Diminussed aster! An I could peecieve amonkst the gatherings who ever they wolk in process?

Juva: Khubadah! It is the Chrystanthemlander with his porters of bonzos, pompommy plonkyplonk, the ghariwallahs, moveyovering the cabrattlefield of slaine.

Muta: Pongo da Banza! An I would uscertain in druidful scatterings one piece tall chap he stand one piece same place?

Juva: Bulkily: and he is fundementially theosophagusted over the whorse proceedings.

Muta: Petrificationibus! O horild haraflare! Who his dickhuns now rearrexes from undernearth the memorialorum?

Juva: Beleave filmly, beleave! Fing Fing! King King!

Muta: Ulloverum? Fulgitudo ejus Rhedonum teneat!

Juva: Rolantlossly! Till the tipp of his ziff. And the ubideintia of the savium is our ervics fenicitas.

Muta: Why soly smiles the supremest with such for a leary on his rugular lips?

Juva: Bitchorbotchum! Eebrydime! He has help his crewn on the burkeley buy but he has holf his crown on the Eurasian Generalissimo.

Muta: Skulkasloot! The twyly velleid is thus then paridicynical?

Juva: Ut vivat volumen sic pereat pouradosus!

Muta: Haven money on stablecert?

Juva: Tempt to wom Outsider!

Muta: Suc? He quoffs. Wutt?

Juva: Sec! Wartar wartar! Wett.

Muta: Ad Piabelle et Purabelle?

Juva: At Winne, Woermann og Sengs.

Muta: So that when we shall have acquired unification we shall pass on to diversity and when we shall have passed on to diversity we shall have acquired the instinct of combat and when we shall have acquired the instinct of combat we shall pass back to the spirit of appeasement?

Juva: By the light of the bright reason which daysends to us from the high.

Muta: May I borrow that hordwanderbaffle from you, old rubberskin?

Juva: Here it is and I hope it's your wormingpen, Erinmonker! Shoot.

Rhythm and Colour at Park Mooting. Peredos Last in the Grand

Natural. Velivision victor. Dubs newstage oldtime turftussle, recalling Winny Willy Widger. Two draws. Heliotrope leads from Harem.
Three ties. Jockey the Ropper jerks Jake the Rape. Paddrock and
bookley chat.

And here are the details.

Tunc. Bymeby, bullocky vampas tappany bobs topside joss pidgin
fella Balkelly, archdruid of islish chinchinjoss in the his heptach-
romatic sevenhued septicoloured roranyellgreenlindigan mantle finish he show along the his mister guest Patholic with alb belongahim
the whose throat hum with of sametime all the his cassock groaner
fellas of greysfriaryfamily he fast all time what time all him monka-
fellas with Same Patholic, quoniam, speeching, yeh not speeching
noh man liberty is, he drink up words, scilicet, tomorrow till recover
will not, all too many much illusiones through photoprismic velam-
ina of hueful panepiphanal world spectacurum of Lord Joss, the
of which zoantholitic furniture, from mineral through vegetal to
animal, not appear to full up together fallen man than under but
one photoreflection of the several iridals gradationes of solar light,
that one which that part of it (furnit of heupanepi world) had
shown itself (part of fur of huepanwor) unable to absorbere,
whereas for numpa one puraduxed seer in seventh degree of wisdom
of Entis-Onton he savvy inside true inwardness of reality, the Ding
hvad in idself id est, all objects (of panepiwor) allside showed themselves in trues coloribus resplendent with sextuple gloria of light
actually retained, untisintus, inside them (obs of epiwo). Rumnant
Patholic, stareotypopticus, no catch all that preachybook, utpiam,
tomorrow recover thing even is not, bymeby vampsybobsy tappanas-
bullocks topside joss pidginfella Bilkilly-Belkelly say patfella,
ontesantes, twotime hemhaltshealing, with other words verbigratia-
grading from murmurulentous till stridulocelerious in a hungho-
ranghoangoly tsinglontseng while his comprehendurient, with
diminishing claractinism, augumentationed himself in caloripeia to
vision so throughsighty, you anxioust melancholic, High Thats
Hight Uberking Leary his fiery grassbelonghead all show colour of
sorrelwood herbgreen, again, niggerblonker, of the his essixcoloured
holmgrewnworsteds costume the his fellow saffron pettikilt look
same hue of boiled spinasses, other thing, voluntary mutismuser,
he not compyhandy the his golden twobreasttorc look justsamelike
curlicabbis, moreafter, to pace negativisticists, verdant readyrain-
roof belongahim Exuber High Ober King Leary very dead, what
he wish to say, spit of superexuberabundancy plenty laurel leaves,

after that commander bulopent eyes of Most Highest Ardreetsar King same thing like thyme choppy upon parsley, alongsidethat, if pleasesir, nos displace tauttung, sowlofabishospastored, enamel Indian gem in maledictive fingerfondler of High High Siresultan Emperor all same like one fellow olive lentil, onthelongsidethat, by undesendas, kirikirikiring, violaceous warwon contusiones of face-buts of Highup Big Cockywocky Sublissimime Autocrat, for that with pure hueglut intensely saturated one, tinged uniformly, all-aroundside upinandoutdown, very like you seecut chowchow of plentymuch sennacassia. Hump cumps Ebblybally! Sukkot?

Punc. Bigseer, refrects the petty padre, whackling it out, a tumble to take, tripeness to call thing and to call if say is good while, you pore shiroskuro blackinwhitepaddynger, by thiswis aposterioprismi-cally apatstrophied and paralogically periparolysed, celestial from principalest of Iro's Irismans ruinboon pot before, (for beingtime monkblinkers timeblinged completamentarily murkblankered in their neutrolysis between the possible viriditude of the sager and the prob-able eruberuption of the saint), as My tappropinquish to Me wipen-meselps gnosegates a handcaughtscheaf of synthetic shammyrag to hims hers, seemingsuch four three two agreement cause heart to be might, saving to Balenoarch (he kneeleths), to Great Balenoarch (he kneeleths down) to Greatest Great Balenoarch (he kneeleths down quitesomely), the sound sense sympol in a weedwayedwold of the firethere the sun in his halo cast. Onmen.

That was thing, bygotter, the thing, bogcotton, the very thing, begad! Even to uptoputty Bilkilly-Belkelly-Balkally. Who was for shouting down the shatton on the lamp of Jeeshees. Sweating on to stonker and throw his seven. As he shuck his thumping fore features apt the hoyhop of His Ards.

Thud.

Good safe firelamp! hailed the heliots. Goldselforelump! Halled they. Awed. Where thereon the skyfold high, trampatrampatramp. Adie. Per ye comdoom doominoom noonstroom. Yeasome priestomes. Fullyhum toowhoom.

Taawhaar?

Sants and sogs, cabs and cobs, kings and karls, tentes and taunts. 'Tis gone infarover. So fore now, dayleash. Pour deday. To trance-fixureashone. Feist of Taborneccles, scenopegia, come! Shamwork, be in our scheining! And let every crisscouple be so crosscompli-mentary, little eggons, youlk and meelk, in a farbiger pancosmos. With a hottyhammyum all round. Gudstruce!

Yet is no body present here which was not there before. Only is order othered. Nought is nulled. *Fuitfiat!*

Lo, the laud of laurens now orielising benedictively when saint and sage have said their say.

A spathe of calyptrous glume involucrumines the perinanthean Amenta: fungoalgaceous muscafilicial graminopalmular planteon; of increasing, livivorous, feelful thinkamalinks; luxuriotiating everywhencewithersoever among skullhullows and charnelcysts of a weedwastewoldwevild when Ralph the Retriever ranges to jawrode his knuts knuckles and her theas thighs; onegugulp down of the nauseous forere brarkfarsts oboboomaround and you're as paint and spickspan as a rainbow; wreathe the bowl to rid the bowel; no runcure, no rank heat, sir; amess in amullium; chlorid cup.

Health, chalce, endnessnessessity! Arrive, likkypuggers, in a poke! The folgor of the frightfools is olympically optimominous; there is bound to be a lovleg day for mirrages in the open; Murnane and Aveling are undertoken to berry that ortchert: provided that. You got to make good that breachsuit, seamer. You going to haulm port houlm, toilermaster. You yet must get up to kill (nonparticular). You still stand by and do as hit (private). While for yous, Jasminia Aruna and all your likers, affinitatively must it be by you elected if Monogynes his is or hers Diander, the tubous, limbersome and nectarial. Owned or grazeheifer, ethel or bonding. Mopsus or Gracchus, all your horodities will incessantlament be coming back from the Annone Wishwashwhose, Ormepierre Lodge, Doone of the Drumes, blanches bountifully and nightsend made up, every article lathering leaving several rinsings so as each rinse results with a dapperent rolle, cuffs for meek and chokers for sheek and a kink in the pacts for namby. Forbeer, forbear! For nought that is has bane. In mournenslaund. Themes have thimes and habit reburns. To flame in you. Ardor vigor forders order. Since ancient was our living is in possible to be. Delivered as. Caffirs and culls and onceagain overalls, the fittest surviva lives that blued, iorn and storridge can make them. Whichus all claims. Clean. Whenastcleeps. Close. And the mannormillor clipperclappers. Noxt. Doze.

Fennsense, finnsonse, aworn! Tuck upp those wide shorts. The pink of the busket for sheer give. Peeps. Stand up to hard ware and step into style. If you soil may, puett, guett me prives. For newmanmaun set a marge to the merge of unnotions. Innition wons agame.

What has gone? How it ends?

Begin to forget it. It will remember itself from every sides, with all gestures, in each our word. Today's truth, tomorrow's trend.

Forget, remember!

Have we cherished expectations? Are we for liberty of perusiveness? Whyafter what forewhere? A plainplanned liffeyism assemblements Eblania's conglomerate horde. By dim delty Deva.

Forget!

Our wholemole millwheeling vicociclometer, a tetradomational gazebocroticon (the "Mamma Lujah" known to every schoolboy scandaller, be he Matty, Marky, Lukey or John-a-Donk), autokinatonetically preprovided with a clappercoupling smeltingworks exprogressive process, (for the farmer, his son and their homely codes, known as eggburst, eggblend, eggburial and hatch-as-hatch can) receives through a portal vein the dialytically separated elements of precedent decomposition for the verypetpurpose of subsequent recombination so that the heroticisms, catastrophes and eccentricities transmitted by the ancient legacy of the past, type by tope, letter from litter, word at ward, with sendence of sundance, since the days of Plooney and Columcellas when Giacinta, Pervenche and Margaret swayed over the all-too-ghoulish and illyrical and innumantic in our mutter nation, all, anastomosically assimilated and preteridentified paraidiotically, in fact, the sameold gamebold adomic structure of our Finnius the old One, as highly charged with electrons as hophazards can effective it, may be there for you, Cockalooralooraloomenos, when cup, platter and pot come piping hot, as sure as herself pits hen to paper and there's scribings scrawled on eggs.

Of cause, so! And in effect, as?

Dear. And we go on to Dirtdump. Reverend. May we add majesty? Well, we have frankly enjoyed more than anything these secret workings of natures (thanks ever for it, we humbly pray) and, well, was really so denighted of this lights time. Mucksrats which bring up about uhrweckers they will come to know good. Yon clouds will soon disappear looking forwards at a fine day. The honourable Master Sarmon they should be first born like he was with a twohangled warpon and it was between Williamstown and the Mairrion Ailesbury on the top of the longcar, as merrily we rolled along, we think of him looking at us yet as if to pass away in a cloud. When he woke up in a sweat besidus it was to pardon him, goldylocks, me having an airth, but he daydreamsed we had a lovelyt face for a pulltomine. Back we were by the jerk of a beamstark, backed in paladays last, on the brinks of the wobblish, the man what never put a dramn

in the swags but milk from a national cowse. That was the prick
of the spindle to me that gave me the keys to dreamland. Sneakers
in the grass, keep off! If we were to tick off all that cafflers head,
whisperers for his accomodation, the me craws, namely, and their
bacon what harmed butter! It's margarseen oil. Thinthin thinthin.
Stringstly is it forbidden by the honorary tenth commendmant to
shall not bare full sweetness against a nighboor's wiles. What those
slimes up the cavern door around you, keenin, (the lies is coming
out on them frecklefully) had the shames to suggest can we ever?
Never! So may the low forget him their trespasses against Molloyd
O'Reilly, that hugglebeddy fann, now about to get up, the hartiest
that Coolock ever! A nought in nought Eirinishmhan, called
Ervigsen by his first mate. May all similar douters of our oldhame
story have that fancied widming! For a pipe of twist or a slug of
Hibernia metal we could let out and, by jings, someone would make
a carpus of somebody with the greatest of pleasure by private shoot-
ings. And in contravention to the constancy of chemical combinations not enough of all the slatters of him left for Peeter the Picker
to make their threi sevelty filfths of a man out of. Good wheat! How
delitious for the three Sulvans of Dulkey and what a sellpriceget
the two Peris of Monacheena! Sugars of lead for the chloras ashpots!
Peace! He possessing from a child of highest valency for our privileged beholdings ever complete hairy of chest, hamps and eyebags
in pursuance to salesladies' affectionate company. His real devotes.
Wriggling reptiles, take notice! Whereas we exgust all such sprinkling snigs. They are pestituting the whole time never with standing
we simply agree upon the committee of amusance! Or could above
bring under same notice for it to be able to be seen.

About that coerogenal hun and his knowing the size of an egg-
cup. First he was a skulksman at one time and then Cloon's fired
him through guff. Be sage about sausages! Stuttutistics shows with
he's heacups of teatables the old firm's fatspitters are most eatenly
appreciated by metropolonians. While we should like to drag attentions to our Wolkmans Cumsensation Act. The magnets of our
midst being foisted upon by a plethorace of parachutes. Did speece
permit the bad example of setting before the military to the best of
our belief in the earliest wish of the one in mind was the mitigation
of the king's evils. And how he staired up the step after it's the
power of the gait. His giantstand of manunknown. No brad wishy
washy wathy wanted neither! Once you are balladproof you are
unperceable to haily, icy and missilethroes. Order now before we

reach Ruggers' Rush! As we now must close hoping to Saint Laurans all in the best. Moral. Mrs Stores Humphreys: So you are expecting trouble, Pondups, from the domestic service questioned? Mr Stores Humphreys: Just as there is a good in even, Levia, my cheek is a compleet bleenk. Plumb. Meaning: one two four. Finckers. Up the hind hose of hizzars. Whereapon our best again to a hundred and eleven ploose one thousand and one other blessings will now concloose thoose epoostles to your great kindest, well, for all at trouble to took. We are all at home in old Fintona, thank Danis, for ourselfsake, that direst of housebonds, whool wheel be true unto lovesend so long as we has a pockle full of brass. Impossible to remember persons in improbable to forget position places. Who would pellow his head off to conjure up a, well, particularly mean stinker like funn make called Foon MacCrawl brothers, mystery man of the pork martyrs? Force in giddersh! Tomothy and Lorcan, the bucket Toolers, both are Timsons now they've changed their characticuls during their blackout. Conan Boyles will pudge the daylives out through him, if they are correctly informed. Music, me ouldstrow, please! We'll have a brand rehearsal. Fing! One must simply laugh. Fing him aging! Good licks! Well, this ought to weke him to make up. He'll want all his fury gutmurdherers to redress him. Gilly in the gap. The big bad old sprowly all uttering foon! Has now stuffed last podding. His fooneral will sneak pleace by creeps o'clock toosday. Kingen will commen. Allso brewbeer. Pens picture at Manchem House Horsegardens shown in Morning post as from Boston transcripped. Femelles will be preadaminant as from twentyeight to twelve. To hear that lovelade parson, of case, of a bawl gentlemale, pour forther moracles. Don't forget! The grand fooneral will now shortly occur. Remember. The remains must be removed before eaght hours shorp. With earnestly conceived hopes. So help us to witness to this day to hand in sleep. From of Mayasdaysed most duteoused.

Well, here's lettering you erronymously anent other clerical fands allieged herewith. I wisht I wast be that dumb tyke and he'd wish it was me yonther heel. How about it? The sweetest song in the world! Our shape as a juvenile being much admired from the first with native copper locks. Referring to the Married Woman's Improperty Act a correspondent paints out that the Swees Auburn vogue is hanging down straith fitting to her innocenth eyes. O, felicious coolpose! If all the MacCrawls would only handle virgils like Armsworks, Limited! That's handsel for gertles! Never mind Mickle-

mans! Chat us instead! The cad with the pope's wife, Lily
Kinsella, who became the wife of Mr Sneakers for her good name
in the hands of the kissing solicitor, will now engage in attentions.
Just a prinche for tonight! Pale bellies our mild cure, back and
streaky ninepace. The thicks off Bully's Acre was got up by Sully.
The Boot lane brigade. And she had a certain medicine brought
her in a licenced victualler's bottle. Shame! Thrice shame! We are
advised the waxy is at the present in the Sweeps hospital and that
he may never come out! Only look through your leatherbox one
day with P.C.Q. about 4.32 or at 8 and 22.5 with the quart of scis-
sions masters and clerk and the bevyhum of Marie Reparatrices for
a good allround sympowdhericks purge, full view, to be surprised to
see under the grand piano Lily on the sofa (and a lady!) pulling a
low and then he'd begin to jump a little bit to find out what goes
on when love walks in besides the solicitous bussness by kissing and
looking into a mirror.

That we were treated not very grand when the police and everybody is all bowing to us when we go out in all directions on Wanter-
lond Road with my cubarola glide? And, personably speaking, they
can make their beaux to my alce, as Hillary Allen sang to the open-
nine knighters. Item, we never were chained to a chair, and, bitem,
no widower whother soever followed us about with a fork on Yanks-
killing Day. Meet a great civilian (proud lives to him!) who is gentle
as a mushroom and a very affectable when he always sits forenenst us
for his wet while to all whom it may concern Sully is a thug from
all he drunk though he is a rattling fine bootmaker in his profession.
Would we were herearther to lodge our complaint on sergeant
Laraseny in consequence of which in such steps taken his health
would be constably broken into potter's pance which would be the
change of his life by a Nollwelshian which has been oxbelled out of
crispianity.

Well, our talks are coming to be resumed by more polite conversation with a huntered persent human over the natural bestness
of pleisure after his good few mugs of humbedumb and shag. While
for whoever likes that urogynal pan of cakes one apiece it is thanks,
beloved, to Adam, our former first Finnlatter and our grocerest
churcher, as per Grippiths' varuations, for his beautiful crossmess
parzel.

Well, we simply like their demb cheeks, the Rathgarries, wagging
here about around the rhythms in me amphybed and he being as
bothered that he pausably could by the fallth of hampty damp. Cer-

tified reformed peoples, we may add to this stage, are proptably saying to quite agreeable deef. Here gives your answer, pigs and scuts!
Hence we've lived in two worlds. He is another he what stays under
the himp of holth. The herewaker of our hamefame is his real name-
same who will get himself up and erect, confident and heroic when
but, young as of old, for my daily comfreshenall, a wee one woos.

Alma Luvia, Pollabella.

P.S. Soldier Rollo's sweetheart. And she's about fetted up now with
nonsery reams. And rigs out in regal rooms with the ritzies. Rags!
Worns out. But she's still her deckhuman amber too.

Soft morning, city! Lsp! I am leafy speafing. Lpf! Folty and folty
all the nights have fallen on to long my hair. Not a sound, falling.
Lispn! No wind no word. Only a leaf, just a leaf and then leaves.
The woods are fond always. As were we their babes in. And robins
in crews so. It is for me goolden wending. Unless? Away! Rise up,
man of the hooths, you have slept so long! Or is it only so mesleems?
On your pondered palm. Reclined from cape to pede. With pipe on
bowl. Terce for a fiddler, sixt for makmerriers, none for a Cole. Rise
up now and aruse! Norvena's over. I am leafy, your goolden, so you
called me, may me life, yea your goolden, silve me solve, exsoger-
raider! You did so drool. I was so sharm. But there's a great poet in
you too. Stout Stokes would take you offly. So has he as bored me to
slump. But am good and rested. Taks to you, toddy, tan ye! Yawha-
waw. Helpunto min, helpas vin. Here is your shirt, the day one,
come back. The stock, your collar. Also your double brogues. A com-
forter as well. And here your iverol and everthelest your umbr. And
stand up tall! Straight. I want to see you looking fine for me. With
your brandnew big green belt and all. Blooming in the very lotust
and second to nill, Budd! When you're in the buckly shuit Rosen-
sharonals near did for you. Fiftyseven and three, cosh, with the
bulge. Proudpurse Alby with his pooraroon Eireen, they'll. Pride,
comfytousness, enevy! You make me think of a wonderdecker I
once. Or somebalt thet sailder, the man megallant, with the bangled
ears. Or an earl was he, at Lucan? Or, no, it's the Iren duke's I mean.
Or somebrey erse from the Dark Countries. Come and let us! We
always said we'd. And go abroad. Rathgreany way perhaps.
The childher are still fast. There is no school today. Them boys is
so contrairy. The Head does be worrying himself. Heel trouble and
heal travel. Galliver and Gellover. Unless they changes by mistake.
I seen the likes in the twinngling of an aye. Som. So oft. Sim. Time
after time. The sehm asnuh. Two bredder as doffered as nors in

soun. When one of him sighs or one of him cries 'tis you all over. No peace at all. Maybe it's those two old crony aunts held them out to the water front. Queer Mrs Quickenough and odd Miss Dodd-pebble. And when them two has had a good few there isn't much more dirty clothes to publish. From the Laundersdale Minssions. One chap googling the holyboy's thingabib and this lad wetting his widdle. You were pleased as Punch, recitating war exploits and pearse orations to them jackeen gapers. But that night after, all you were wanton! Bidding me do this and that and the other. And blowing off to me, hugly Judsys, what wouldn't you give to have a girl! Your wish was mewill. And, lo, out of a sky! The way I too. But her, you wait. Eager to choose is left to her shade. If she had only more matcher's wit. Findlings makes runaways, runaways a stray. She's as merry as the gricks still. 'Twould be sore should ledden sorrow. I'll wait. And I'll wait. And then if all goes. What will be is. Is is. But let them. Slops hospodch and the slusky slut too. He's for thee what she's for me. Dogging you round cove and haven and teaching me the perts of speech. If you spun your yarns to him on the swishbarque waves I was spelling my yearns to her over cottage cake. We'll not disturb their sleeping duties. Let besoms be bosuns. It's Phoenix, dear. And the flame is, hear! Let's our joornee sainto-michael make it. Since the lausafire has lost and the book of the depth is. Closed. Come! Step out of your shell! Hold up you free fing! Yes. We've light enough. I won't take our laddy's lampern. For them four old windbags of Gustsofairy to be blowing at. Nor you your rucksunck. To bring all the dannymans out after you on the hike. Send Arctur guiddus! Isma! Sft! It is the softest morning that ever I can ever remember me. But she won't rain showerly, our Ilma. Yet. Until it's the time. And me and you have made our. The sons of bursters won in the games. Still I'll take me owld Fin-vara for my shawlders. The trout will be so fine at brookfisht. With a taste of roly polony from Blugpuddels after. To bring out the tang of the tay. Is't you fain for a roost brood? Oaxmealturn, all out of the woolpalls! And then all the chippy young cuppinjars cluttering round us, clottering for their creams. Crying, me, grownup sister! Are me not truly? Lst! Only but, theres a but, you must buy me a fine new girdle too, nolly. When next you go to Market Norwall. They're all saying I need it since the one from Isaacsen's slooped its line. Mrknrk? Fy arthou! Come! Give me your great bearspaw, padder avilky, fol a miny tiny. Dola. Mineninecyhandsy, in the languo of flows. That's Jorgen Jargonsen. But you understood, nodst? I always know by your brights and shades. Reach down. A lil mo. So. Draw back your glave. Hot and hairy, hugon, is your hand! Here's where the falskin begins. Smoos as an infams. One time you told you'd been burnt in ice. And one time it was chemicalled after you taking a lifeness. Maybe that's why you hold your hodd as if. And people thinks you missed the scaffold. Of fell design. I'll close me eyes. So not to see. Or see only a youth in his florizel, a boy in innocence, peeling a twig, a child beside a weenywhite steed. The child we all love to place our hope in for ever. All men has done something. Be the time they've come to the weight of old fletch. We'll lave it. So. We will take our walk before in the timpul they ring the earthly bells. In the church by the hearseyard. Pax Goodmens will. Or the birds start their treestirm shindy. Look, there are yours off, high on high! And cooshes, sweet good luck they're cawing you, Coole! You see, they're as white as the riven snae. For us. Next peaters poll you will be elicted or I'm not your elicitous bribe. The Kinsella woman's man will never reduce me. A MacGarath O'Cullagh O'Muirk MacFewney sookadoodling and sweepacheeping round the lodge of Fjorn na Galla of the Trumpets! It's like potting the po to shambe on the dresser or tamming Uncle Tim's Caubeen on to the brows of a Viker Eagle. Not such big strides, huddy foddy! You'll crush me antilopes I saved so long for. They're Penisole's. And the two goodiest shoeshoes. It is hardly a Knut's mile or seven, possumbotts. It is very good for the health of a morning. With Buahbuah. A gentle motion all around. As leisure paces. And the helpyourselftoastrool cure's easy. It seems so long since, ages since. As if you had been long far away. Afartodays, afeartonights, and me as with you in thadark. You will tell me some time if I can believe its all. You know where I am bringing you? You remember? When I ran berrying after hucks and haws. With you drawing out great aims to hazel me from the hummock with your sling. Our cries. I could lead you there and I still by you in bed. Les go dutc to Danegreven, nos? Not a soul but ourselves. Time? We have loads on our hangs. Till Gilligan and Halligan call again to hooligan. And the rest of the guns. Sullygan eight, from left to right. Olobobo, ye foxy theagues! The moskors thought to ball you out. Or the Wald Unicorns Master, Bugley Captain, from the Naul, drawls up by the door with the Honourable Whilp and the Reverend Poynter and the two Lady Pagets of Tallyhaugh, Ballyhuntus, in their riddletight raiding hats for to lift a hereshealth to their robost, the Stag, evers the Carlton hart. And you needn't host out with your duck and your duty, capapole, while they reach him the glass he never starts to finish. Clap this wis on your poll and stick this in your ear, wiggly! Beauties don't answer and the rich never pays. If you were the enlarged they'd hue in cry you, Heathtown, Harbourstown, Snowtown, Four Knocks, Flemingtown, Bodingtown to the Ford of Fyne on Delvin. How they housed to house you after the Platonic garlens! And all because, loosed in her reflexes, she seem she seen Ericoricori coricome huntsome with his three poach dogs aleashing him. But you came safe through. Enough of that horner corner! And old mutthergoosip! We might call on the Old Lord, what do you say? There's something tells me. He is a fine sport. Like the score and a moighty went before him. And a proper old promnentory. His door always open. For a newera's day. Much as your own is. You invoiced him last Eatster so he ought to give us hockockles and everything. Remember to take off your white hat, ech? When we come in the presence. And say hoothoothoo, ithmuthisthy! His is house of laws. And I'll drop my graciast kertssey too. If the Ming Tung no go bo to me homage me hamage kow bow tow to the Mong Tang. Ceremonialness to stand lowest place be! Saying: What'll you take to link to light a pike on porpoise, plaise? He might knight you an Armor elsor daub you the first cheap magyerstrape. Remember Bomthomanew vim vam vom Hungerig. Hoteform, chain and epolettes, botherbumbose. And I'll be your aural eyeness. But we vain. Plain fancies. It's in the castles air. My currant bread's full of sillymottocraft. Aloof is anoof. We can take or leave. He's reading his ruffs. You'll know our way from there surely. Flura's way. Where once we led so many car couples have follied since. Clatchka! Giving Shaughnessy's mare the hilly-mount of her life. With her strulldeburgghers! Hnmn hnmn! The rollcky road adondering. We can sit us down on the heathery benn, me on you, in quolm unconsciounce. To scand the arising. Out from Drumleek. It was there Evora told me I had best. If I ever. When the moon of mourning is set and gone. Over Glinaduna. Lonu nula. Ourselves, oursouls alone. At the site of salvocean. And watch would the letter you're wanting be coming may be. And cast ashore. That I prays for be mains of me draims. Scratching it and patching at with a prompt from a primer. And what scrips of nutsnolleges I pecked up me meself. Every letter is a hard but yours sure is the hardest crux ever. Hack an axe, hook an oxe, hath an an, heth hith ences. But once done, dealt and delivered, tattat, you're on the map. Rased on traumscrapt from Maston, Boss. After rounding his world of ancient days. Carried in a caddy or screwed and corked. On his mugisstosst surface. With a bob, bob, bottledby. Blob. When the waves give up yours the soil may for me. Sometime then, somewhere there, I wrote me hopes and buried the page when I heard Thy voice, ruddery dunner, so loud that none but, and left it to lie till a kissmiss coming. So content me now. Lss. Unbuild and be buildn our bankaloan cottage there and we'll cohabit respectable. The Gowans, ser, for Medem, me. With acute bubel runtoer for to pippup and gopeep where the sterres be. Just to see would we hear how Jove and the peers talk. Amid the soleness. Tilltop, bigmaster! Scale the summit! You're not so giddy any more. All your groundplotting and the little it brought! Humps, when you hised us and dumps, when you doused us! But sarra one of me cares a brambling ram, pomp porteryark! On limpidy marge I've made me hoom. Park and a pub for me. Only don't start your stunts of Donachie's yeards agoad again. I could guessp to her name who tuckt you that one, tufnut! Bold bet backwords. For the loves of sinfintins! Before the naked universe. And the bailby pleasemarm rincing his eye! One of these fine days, lewdy culler, you must redoform again. Blessed shield Martin! Softly so. I am so exquisitely pleased about the loveleavest dress I have. You will always call me Leafiest, won't you, dowling? Wordherfhull Ohldhbhoy! And you won't urbjunk to me parafume, oiled of kolooney, with a spot of marashy. Sm! It's Alpine Smile from Yesthers late Yhesters. I'm in everywince nasturtls. Even in Houlth's nose. Medeurscodeignus! Astale of astoun. Grand owld marauder! If I knew who you are! When that hark from the air said it was Captain Finsen makes cumhulments and was mayit pressing for his suit I said are you there here's nobody here only me. But I near fell off the pile of samples. As if your tinger winged ting to me hear. Is that right what your brothermilk in Bray bes telling the district you were bragged up by Brostal because your parents would be always tumbling into his foulplace and losing her pentacosts after drinking their pledges? Howsomendeavour, you done me fine! The only man was ever known could eat the crushts of lobsters. Our native night when you twicetook me for some Marienne Sherry and then your Jermyn cousin who signs hers with exes and the beard-wig I found in your Clarksome bag. Pharaops you'll play you're the king of Aeships. You certainly make the most royal of noises. I will tell you all sorts of makeup things, strangerous. And show you to every simple storyplace we pass. *Cadmillersfolly, Bellevenue, Wellcrom, Quid Superabit,* villities valleties. Change the plates for the next course of murphies! Spendlove's still there and the canon going strong and so is Claffey's habits endurtaking and our parish pomp's a great warrent. But you'll have to ask that same four that named them is always snugging in your barsalooner, saying they're the best relicts of Conal O'Daniel and writing *Finglas since the Flood.* That'll be some kingly work in progress. But it's by this route he'll come some morrow. And I can signal you all flint and fern are rasstling as we go by. And you'll sing thumb a bit and then wise your selmon on it. It is all so often and still the same to me. Snf? Only turf, wick dear! Clane turf. You've never forgodden batt on tarf, have you, at broin burroow, what? Mch? Why, them's the muchrooms, come up during the night. Look, agres of roofs in parshes. Dom on dam, dim in dym. And a capital part for olympics to ply at. Steadyon, Cooloosus! Mind your stride or you'll knock. While I'm dodging the dustbins. Look what I found! A lintil pea. And look at here! This cara weeseed. Pretty mites, my sweetthings, was they poorloves abandoned by wholawidey world? Neighboulotts for newtown. The Eblanamagna you behazyheld loomening up out of the dumblynass. But the still sama sitta. I've lapped so long. As you said. It fair takes. If I lose my breath for a minute or two don't speak, remember! Once it happened, so it may again. Why I'm all these years within years in soffran, allbeleaved. To hide away the tear, the parted. It's thinking of all. The brave that gave their. The fair that wore. All them that's gunne. I'll begin again in a jiffey. The nik of a nad. How glad you'll be I waked you! My! How well you'll feel! For ever after. First we turn by the vagurin here and then it's gooder. So side by side, turn agate, weddingtown, laud men of Londub! I only hope whole the heavens sees us. For I feel I could near to faint away. Into the deeps. Annamores leep. Let me lean, just a lea, if you le, bowldstrong bigtider. Allgearls is wea. At times. So. While you're adamant evar. Wrhps, that wind as if out of norewere! As on the night of the Apophanypes. Jumpst shootst throbbst into me mouth like a bogue and arrohs! Ludegude of the Lashlanns, how he whips me cheeks! Sea, sea! Here, weir, reach, island, bridge. Where you meet I. The day. Remember! Why there that moment and us two only? I was but teen, a tiler's dot. The swanky-suits was boosting always, sure him, he was like to me fad. But the swaggerest swell off Shackvulle Strutt. And the fiercest freaky ever followed a pining child round the sluppery table with a forkful of fat. But a king of whistlers. Scieoula! When he'd prop me atlas against his goose and light our two candles for our singers duohs

on the sewingmachine. I'm sure he squirted juice in his eyes to make
them flash for flightening me. Still and all he was awful fond to
me. Who'll search for *Find Me Colours* now on the hillydroops of
Vikloefells? But I read in Tobecontinued's tale that while blubles
blows there'll still be sealskers. There'll be others but non so for me.
Yed he never knew we seen us before. Night after night. So that
I longed to go to. And still with all. One time you'd stand fornenst
me, fairly laughing, in your bark and tan billows of branches for to
fan me coolly. And I'd lie as quiet as a moss. And one time you'd
rush upon me, darkly roaring, like a great black shadow with a
sheeny stare to perce me rawly. And I'd frozen up and pray for
thawe. Three times in all. I was the pet of everyone then. A prince-
able girl. And you were the pantymammy's Vulking Corsergoth.
The invision of Indelond. And, by Thorror, you looked it! My lips
went livid for from the joy of fear. Like almost now. How? How
you said how you'd give me the keys of me heart. And we'd be married till delth to uspart. And though dev do espart. O mine! Only,
no, now it's me who's got to give. As duv herself div. Inn this linn.
And can it be it's nnow fforvell? Illas! I wisht I had better glances
to peer to you through this baylight's growing. But you're changing,
acoolsha, you're changing from me, I can feel. Or is it me is? I'm
getting mixed. Brightening up and tightening down. Yes, you're
changing, sonhusband, and you're turning, I can feel you, for a
daughterwife from the hills again. Imlamaya. And she is coming.
Swimming in my hindmoist. Diveltaking on me tail. Just a whisk
brisk sly spry spink spank sprint of a thing theresomere, saultering.
Saltarella come to her own. I pity your oldself I was used to. Now
a younger's there. Try not to part! Be happy, dear ones! May I be
wrong! For she'll be sweet for you as I was sweet when I came down
out of me mother. My great blue bedroom, the air so quiet, scarce
a cloud. In peace and silence. I could have stayed up there for always only. It's something fails us. First we feel. Then we fall. And
let her rain now if she likes. Gently or strongly as she likes. Anyway let her rain for my time is come. I done me best when I was let.
Thinking always if I go all goes. A hundred cares, a tithe of troubles and is there one who understands me? One in a thousand of
years of the nights? All me life I have been lived among them but
now they are becoming lothed to me. And I am lothing their little
warm tricks. And lothing their mean cosy turns. And all the greedy
gushes out through their small souls. And all the lazy leaks down
over their brash bodies. How small it's all! And me letting on to me-

self always. And lilting on all the time. I thought you were all glittering with the noblest of carriage. You're only a bumpkin. I thought you the great in all things, in guilt and in glory. You're but a puny. Home! My people were not their sort out beyond there so far as I can. For all the bold and bad and bleary they are blamed, the seahags. No! Nor for all our wild dances in all their wild din. I can seen meself among them, allaniuvia pulchrabelled. How she was handsome, the wild Amazia, when she would seize to my other breast! And what is she weird, haughty Niluna, that she will snatch from my ownest hair! For 'tis they are the stormies. Ho hang! Hang ho! And the clash of our cries till we spring to be free. Auravoles, they says, never heed of your name! But I'm loothing them that's here and all I lothe. Loonely in me loneness. For all their faults. I am passing out. O bitter ending! I'll slip away before they're up. They'll never see. Nor know. Nor miss me. And it's old and old it's sad and old it's sad and weary I go back to you, my cold father, my cold mad father, my cold mad feary father, till the near sight of the mere size of him, the moyles and moyles of it, moananoaning, makes me seasilt saltsick and I rush, my only, into your arms. I see them rising! Save me from those therrble prongs! Two more. Onetwo moremens more. So. Avelaval. My leaves have drifted from me. All. But one clings still. I'll bear it on me. To remind me of. Lff! So soft this morning, ours. Yes. Carry me along, taddy, like you done through the toy fair! If I seen him bearing down on me now under whitespread wings like he'd come from Arkangels, I sink I'd die down over his feet, humbly dumbly, only to washup. Yes, tid. There's where. First. We pass through grass behush the bush to. Whish! A gull. Gulls. Far calls. Coming, far! End here. Us then. Finn, again! Take. Bussoftlhee, mememormee! Till thousendsthee. Lps. The keys to. Given! A way a lone a last a loved a long the

PARIS,
1922–1939.